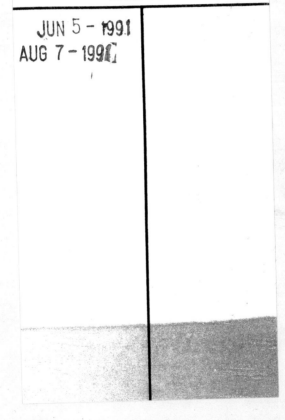

WINDY CITY

By SAM ROSS

WINDY CITY
by
Sam Ross

G. P. Putnam's Sons
New York

c.1

Library of Congress Cataloging in Publication Data

Ross, Sam, date.
  Windy city.

  I. Title.
PZ3.R7365Wi 1979   [PS3535.07493]   813'.5'4   78-27087
ISBN 0-399-12335-0

BL

SEP 1 3 '79

IN MEMORY
Of my mother
and grandmother

BOOK 1

Jake, an intercollegiate backstroke
champion who wins every prize he tries
for, moves from adoring college girls
to sophisticated divorcees, from Chicago's brawling Westside to the glittering Gold Coast.

In 1929, when he was about to graduate high school, Jake
Davidson sometimes went downtown on a Saturday morning,
and he'd roam through Marshall Field's and Carson's and the
Hub, yearning for what the well-dressed collegian was wearing
that year. He'd try on tweeds and flannels and corduroys and
cashmere sweaters. He'd look at the expensive plaid and Oxford
shirts and imported lisle socks and heavy wing-tipped shoes, and
he'd try on rakish caps and elegant hats. He'd look at himself in
the three-way mirrors, and he would think: Not bad. One thing
about Jake, he liked himself. Liked himself an awful lot. So he
looked terrific in everything. He was of medium height, broad-
shouldered, narrow-hipped, with a bull-like neck, and he looked
as if he were always ready to take off in a dive. His face, after a
long winter, was dry and pale from too much indoor swimming
and indoor living. He had high cheekbones, a solid bony nose,
full, sensual lips, sandy-colored hair, and clear, deepset blue
eyes. He could pass as a *goy.*

After glutting himself on clothes, he'd go to a movie at the
Oriental or the Chicago and see Paul Ash and even Paul
Whiteman with Bix Beiderbecke on stage; then he'd get a

hamburger smothered in onions at Pixley and Ehler's or chili and crackers in Hutchinson's; then he'd stand on the corner of State and Madison and watch the crowds of people hustle by, and he'd bet he knew where they were from by their smells, their clothes, and their accents. He's a Bohunk from the stockyards, he would think. She's strictly from Bucktown. A hooker from the Levee. Elegant, Gold Coast. Black meat from the black belt. That's Albany Park. A West Side hood. A cowboy from Texas. High-class from Hyde Park.

Chicago in those days was a city of neighborhoods, where trees lined the streets of private homes standing next to two- and three-story apartment buildings, where each neighborhood had a park with a lagoon and an outdoor pool and statues of famous people in history. The emerald of the city, of course, was the lake, miles and miles of unbroken horizons going all the way up to Wisconsin and Michigan. That's where the sun rose and poured more gold each day on the Gold Coast and Belmont Harbor, the North Shore and the South Shore.

Sometimes he'd walk up Michigan Avenue, past the iron lions at the Art Institute, the huge Public Library facing Grant Park, past the new skyscrapers with the pure white Wrigley Building and the Tribune Tower standing like big whipped-cream cakes over the bridge at Wacker Drive. Farther up, he could see the Water Tower like a medieval fortress dwarfed by the modern Palmolive Building with its Lindbergh Beacon, and Jake would choke up from the enormousness, splendor, and power of the avenue. But it didn't take much to distract him. A pair of well-shaped legs in silk stockings, when legs were sexier than tits, would have him following like a dog. He'd wonder what she looked like, but he wouldn't dare go past and glance back; he might be disappointed; it was enough just to stay a few steps behind and enjoy. Ah, that Michigan Avenue with all the classy people from Evanston and Oak Park and the Gold Coast.

But when Jake stood at the corner of State and Madison with the huge clock at Marshall Field's ticking the time away, he felt as if he were at the crossroads of the universe. He could feel a sense of the frontier in the trains and freight cars thundering in from the cattle ranges, the mines, the rich farms, the western forests, into the depots, the stockyards, the big manufacturing plants, the boats and tugs creeping up the river, the drawbridges opening up and stopping traffic to let them in. You could start out on the iron and asphalt streets where he was standing and go anywhere in the world. That's the kind of town it was.

In the fall the winds began to blow. Scattered the leaves from the trees and the smoke from the factories. The wind picked up velocity until it roared in off the lake in the winter, raw, whistling, shrieking, biting through your clothes. You could hardly breathe, you could hardly move, when the northeasters blew. Especially on Michigan Avenue, where winds of hurricane force could slam you into the stone buildings. Even the winds, blasting across the flat prairies all the way from the Rockies, could send icy shivers through you.

Oh, that WINDY CITY! That big, raw, slangy, toddlin' town!

But in the spring, ah, the spring, with the howling winds dying down and the gray, bleak days giving way to warmth and sunshine and rain, making the buds pop out on trees and shrubs, everything started coming alive. Lake boats began their cruises. People strolled the beaches and parks. Cars jammed the streets. Picnics were planned. Lovers huddled in the various lanes. The rich in splendid riding habits hit the bridle paths. The Cubs and Sox went into their long season. And Jake Davidson was worrying about his future.

Right after Jake Davidson won the national high school backstroke championship at the Illinois Athletic Club (IAC), Wally Blake, a former Olympic star from Stanford, said, "Kid, how'd you like to go to Stanford?"

"You listen to him," said the great Johnny Weissmuller, who was with Wally.

"I'm listening, I'm listening," Jake said. "Where's Stanford?"

"Palo Alto, California," Wally said.

Palo Alto, California. Only the South Seas was farther away. To a Jewish boy raised on the West Side of Chicago, nourished on *latkes,* gefilte fish, Tom Mix, Buck Jones, and the Cisco Kid, you have no idea how romantic the Far West sounded.

"It's in the beautiful Santa Clara Valley," Wally said. "Close to San Francisco. Not too far from Hollywood."

"You go there, you'll come down to Hollywood, and I'll fix you up with some great cunt," Weissmuller said.

They were killing Jake. Make way, Cisco. Open the doors

wide, Norma Shearer. Here comes Jake Davidson, the next intercollegiate backstroke champ. But he had to be practical, too.

"What's the school known for?"

"Herbert Hoover," Wally said.

"No shit."

"Best engineering school in the country."

They wanted him all over. This Jewish kid, a refugee from the Russian synagogue and the Arbeiterring Shul, they all wanted him, circumcision and all, because he had qualified for the final Olympic trials the year before, he was one of the ranking swimmers in the world, he was a star.

"So what'll they give me?" he asked Wally Blake.

"Tuition. A job for your expenses. Room rent."

"They got fraternities?" he asked, because without a fraternity a college was not a college, he wouldn't go.

"The best in the country."

At home, sitting around the kitchen table, where the family usually socialized, he said, "I can go to Stanford, to Rutgers, to Chicago, or Michigan, you name it."

"Fly, *boychik*, fly," his father said.

"What's the matter with the University of Chicago?" his mother said. "They say it's the finest college in the world. Nobel prizewinners they got."

"I wouldn't be caught dead there."

"Do they want you there?" his father asked.

"Yes, they want me. The coach there spoke to me. He said they got silver platters waiting for me."

"Tell me, Jake. What are you going to college for? To swim or to be a scholar?"

"Swimming will make me a scholar."

"Jake," his father concluded, "it's your America."

Yep, in those days, America belonged to the kids. They could shape it, make it, break it, hang it on the wall like a pennant.

Still, Jake had the problem of choosing the right college. He discussed it with his swimming pals at the Jewish People's Institute, called the JPI. Most of them were going to Illinois when they graduated. A state college, no class, it had to accept you. They stood naked in the hot showers and in the airless, dank, wall-sweaty pool, kicking Jake's future around.

"Stanford!" they said. "Where the hell is that?"

"Palo Alto, California," Jake informed them. "It's where Herbie Hoover went to school. Big engineering school."

"That what you want to be?"

"Why not?"

"You good in math? Physics?"

"I'll learn."

"Oh, what a dumb dildock."

He could get no help from them.

There was nobody, really, he could talk to. He turned to his coach, Sean H. Fitzgerald.

A word about Fitzgerald. He had gone to Notre Dame for two years, tried out for the football team, but couldn't make it, then dropped out because he couldn't find enough work to take him through. He got a degree in physical education at the YMCA College in Chicago, going nights for five years. When the job of swimming instructor opened up at the JPI, he applied.

The director of the institution and the head of the athletic department had a difficult time deciding on him: He was a *goy*, a Catholic on top of that; how would he fit in with a world of Jews? But he was handsome, personable, blue-eyed, clean-cut; he spoke well and knew athletics; it was decided to give him a chance. They didn't make a mistake. He was a good teacher and a great coach. Kids would swim oceans and tear their hearts out for him. He was also awe-inspiring.

In the world of the steamy showers and the noisy pool there was also a world of *shlangs,* the Jewish word for penises. It was a world of comparisons, of how you measured up on this island, this sanctuary off the rough-tough streets. In this world, Sean H. Fitzgerald never wore trunks or a bathing suit. He had the thick thighs and calves of a Roman gladiator, the broad chest of a Goliath, and he flaunted his uncut colossal cock and heavy balls like weapons. He could have taken them to Barnum & Bailey and opened a sideshow. Men wanted to take pictures of him and send them to girls with inscriptions like:"Yours for the asking"; "Let me be good to you"; "The bigger they come, the harder they fall." The sight of him brought immediate openmouthed wonder and intimidation. You could never keep your eyes off him. This was Jake's mentor.

At thirteen, after Jake had won the grammar school 20-yard

championship for kids under eighty-five pounds, Fitzgerald came to him and said, "Son, how would you like to be an Olympic man?"

This from a man who had led the JPI swimming team to six AAF championships. Jake almost died.

"You do what I tell you, and you'll make it."

Jake hadn't made the Olympic team in 1928, but he'd come close. Sixth. That was when he was only sixteen. In 1932 he knew he was going to be first, representing not the JPI but some college. Which one?

"Notre Dame," said Fitzgerald, because he was still loyal to the Irish.

"But I'm a Jewboy."

"They'll make an exception for you."

"But they haven't got a swimming team."

"You'll be the swimming team."

"But I never thought of Notre Dame."

"Think about it. Wrap your mind around it. If you'd like, I'll talk to Monsignor O'Brien about you."

Jake's bowels suddenly became loose, and he ran off to the toilet. One Jew among all those Catholics. He spit three times, a thing he watched his mother do when nuns or a priest passed by; it was a protection from their demons.

After wrestling with himself for weeks, he decided on Stanford. They wanted him to start the summer semester.

Each day he rummaged through the house, looking for things he'd need at college: socks, handkerchiefs, shirts, sweaters. Each day his mother looked sadder and sadder, and his cardboard suitcase looked shabbier and shabbier, and the clothes he threw into it looked as if they'd come out of a rag pile.

"I need a whole new wardrobe," he announced.

"You're not going away to become a clotheshorse," his mother said. "You're going away to study. In the old country the *yeshiva bochers* sat in threadbare clothes and studied all day. They never worried about clothes."

"All right, all right. I know where you stand. You want me to go like a slob. But look at that suitcase."

The cardboard was nicked and dented; one of the clasps didn't work; he'd need rope to tie it up; he'd look like an immigrant.

"How could I be seen with that?" he said.

"It holds clothes. It'll do the job."

"Mom, Stanford's a rich school. It costs a fortune to go there. Kids there'll have the best."

"It's a *goyish* school."

"What isn't a *goyish* school?"

"The yeshiva, the JPI."

"Mom, for God's sake, we're talking about my future."

"Let the millionaire *goyim* buy you a suitcase."

"Guys have trunks, whole trunks full of clothes."

"What would you put in a trunk, if you had one?"

There was no talking to her. "Tuxedoes. Okay?"

His little brother, Harry, dark-eyed, black-haired like their mother, who woke up every morning with something new he wanted to buy, spoke up. "You get him a trunk, I want a water pistol."

His mother, with her stout, full-breasted body and deepset gray eyes, turned to Jake's sister, Miriam, who was a junior in highaf17school: "And what would you like, princess?"

Miriam, blue-eyed, radiant, with soft, even features and usually quiet in the house, said, "Peace and quiet. Ever since Jake's been ready to graduate the house has been in an uproar."

"You don't want me to go to college," Jake said. "That's it. That's the story. I get the opportunity of a lifetime, and you piss all over it, all of you. You want my whole career to go down the drain."

"What career?" his father said. He'd been counting pennies from his newsstand, and he finally looked up.

"My swimming career. What else?"

"Did Weissmuller go to college?"

"You're talking about the world's champion. Whipped cream and halvah. He sits around the IAC like an Egyptian king. He's turned pro. He's going to Hollywood. He doesn't have to go to college."

"Aren't you going to be the world's champ?" Miriam asked.

"Not like Weissmuller. He's like Red Grange and Jack

Dempsey, only one of a kind. I need a little hedge, some protection, just in case."

"Confidence," his father said. "Confidence."

"Where'd you hear that?"

"Your new friend Herbert Hoover."

"You'd like to see me rot, wouldn't you?"

"Go," his father said. "Go."

"You won't even be here when your grandma and your uncle Nachum come from Russia," his mother said.

"Ma, I'm not going to the moon. I'll be back. I'll meet them another time."

"No respect."

"Stanford is only twenty-five hundred miles away. It's not on another planet."

His mother began to cry. "Twenty-five hundred miles. So far, so far. You'll never come back."

"Talk to her, will you, Pa?"

"What should I tell her? Not to worry? Not to care?"

"You don't want me to go either."

He left the house. He wasn't getting any help from anybody.

He walked aimlessly down the treelined street, past wooden and brick apartment houses. It was late spring. Smells from lingering suppers of cabbage soup and brisket of beef and gefilte fish were in the air. The streets were dusty, with old newspapers in the gutters, and there was a feeling of decaying flesh and rotting bones in the old buildings. Slowly, the neighborhood was becoming a slum. The rich Jews were moving away from Douglas and Independence boulevards farther west to Oak Park and River Forest, to the lakefront in Rogers Park and Belmont Harbor, to the South Shore, leaving the huge gray-stone synagogues to build newer, more impressive ones in other neighborhoods. Like Temple Sholom on Lake Shore Drive. In the migrations of the Jews from one neighborhood to another was the miniature story of their Diaspora, but instead of running from droughts, pestilence, famine, and persecution, they were moving up to their affluence, reaching for more room and a better environment for their children. It reminded Jake of a story his father told of the Jew who had a truss shop on the East Side of New York. The sign on the window read: "Your Rupture Is

My Living." The Jew made a lot of money. Moved up to Park Avenue. The new sign on his window read: "Your Rupture Is My Rapture."

He smiled briefly; then he thought: Here I am, a champion, headlines in the sports pages, a celebrity, with access to the richest athletic clubs in the world, wooed by the most famous colleges in the country, a guy who will one day write his own ticket, nobody on the street knows me, everybody passes by like I'm a total stranger. I am alone, I am absolutely alone, and I am scared shitless. Maybe I ought to go to Illinois with all the guys. I won't be alone. But there'd be no distinction in going there. Just a state school. Maybe I ought to be like Weissmuller and Arne Borg and Stubby Kruger. They never went to college. They lived off the fat of the land. But I'm not a world's champ yet, I'm not in their league, all I've got is the potential, and if I've got the brain, I should make it cash in for me. Fitzgerald said, "They're all bums. What are they going to do when they're no longer champions? Nobody's going to give them their seven-dollars-a-day amateur expense money. Do you want to settle for seven dollars a day for the rest of your life?"

"No!" he said with terror.

Fitzgerald made much less, only $30 a week, but nobody questioned Fitzgerald's pronouncements; to the kids he was God.

"Look at Stubby Kruger. He made it in the *Black Pirate* with Douglas Fairbanks. Sliding down the sails and ropes. Doing all that underwater stuff. What was he? A clown. What did he become? A bit actor, a stunt man. He made it big, didn't he? Real big!"

Fitzgerald was not only a maker of champions but a builder of character, a man who cemented the glue of ambition, the paste of success into the fiber of a boy. He stood there like a naked emperor, six feet tall, 200 pounds, scratching his huge balls, his enormous cock rising slightly from the sensation, and lectured: "You want to become a clown, a stunt man? You want to settle for a broken back, a tin cup, and pencils like some stumblebum fighter? You want that?"

"No."

"You're at the most crucial crossroad of your life. Picking your college is like selecting your career. You can't afford mistakes. College is not only education, it's contacts. So pick the right school."

"How do you know what's right?"

"You've got to feel it in your gut. When it's in there hard, then you know it's right."

Jake had no real gut feeling about Stanford. Oh, if only his old man had been an alumnus of some great college. All he had to offer was his alumnus standing from the Russian *cheder*.

"You're going to college, son. I'll lose you. Another coach will achieve fame through you, will cash in on the architecture of my work, but I won't mind. All I want is for you to put in the same drive and energy and dedication in your career, whatever you choose, as you did in the pool, and I'll be well rewarded."

"What career, coach?"

"Whatever you decide."

That was the trouble: decision. Lawyer, doctor, engineer, CPA, businessman, what? Swimming had been so easy. He had once been thrown into the deep end of a pool, and he had swum out of it. Once he learned, he got his parents to let him join the Y. There, at an exhibition, after the 1924 Olympics, he saw three Olympic champions perform. They were so graceful, they moved so effortlessly, his throat got hard from the beauty of it. Then the great Johnny Weissmuller plunged in. Oh, Christ, that was it; he almost stopped breathing. He couldn't keep away from the pools, even on the coldest winter days: practicing, practicing, getting stronger. He was a natural at it all because he loved it, felt buoyant and powerful, as strong as Samson in water. That all came so easy. Would his career be that easy? What career? Engineering? Herbert Hoover's footsteps? President of the United States?

Hey, help me, somebody. Throw me into a pile of books; let me find my way; let me swim out of it. How about it? He looked up at the darkening sky, and the few stars blistering through. You, up there, how about it? Give me a word. You talked to Abraham and Isaac and Jacob, my namesake, to Moses and Christ knows who else, why not me? Why all that silence all these years? The world too tricky for you? There too many people around now? The world so screwed up you got dumb? Or are there too many *shnooks* like me pestering you? How about it, Old Sport, give me a word.

Nyet, as his father would say. God talks only to lunatics.

He decided to drop in on Ida Braverman, the girl he was going with, not steady, but now and then, here and there. She'd talk to him, pay some attention.

The smell of the delicatessen her parents owned was overwhelming. The store was on 16th and Kedzie, which was certainly not the fashionable part of the West Side. Flies were already out, and the first place they found was Braverman's Delicatessen; they were thick on the sticky paper that hung from the ceiling.

Mrs. Braverman, a short, stocky woman with a greasy face and a down of hair on her chin, was serving corned beef sandwiches and tea to a couple of customers. Mr. Braverman, thin, emaciated, a chain smoker with a hacking tubercular cough, was shaping a mound of liver with the care and diligence of a Michelangelo.

"Is Ida in?"

With cigarette dangling from his mouth, ashes perilously about to drop from it, Mr. Braverman said, "In the back."

This was a ma-and-pa store, where you worked in the front and lived in the back. Jake walked to the back of the store, past the barrels of marinated herring and sour pickles and burlap bags of potatoes and cartons of groceries. He knocked, and Ida opened the door. Her face was as smooth and creamy as a baby's ass. She had dimples in her cheeks and in her chin; she had full, hot lips and dark, passionate eyes and soft, black, bobbed hair. She was a little *zoftig* from all the corned beef and pastrami and briskets but firm to touch and exciting.

"Why didn't you call first?" she said, offended at his taking her for granted.

"I was passing by. I thought I'd take a chance."

"You think all I do is wait for you? What if I was out?"

"I live dangerously. I take chances."

"You think I'm always in?"

"No. You got a million things to do." That's the way it always was. The fucking pride these cunts have. "I'll go out and call you. Okay."

"Well, you're here, so you're here."

"No kidding. I'll find a phone somewhere and call you."

Then she smiled, got soft and pretty and dimply, and said, "You're cute."

He didn't like sitting around the back of her store, which consisted of a couple of bedrooms and a kitchen. The sink was always piled with dirty dishes, the stove always had something cooking, and the table usually had containers of coleslaw and chopped herring and red beets and lox and whatever was left over and had to be refrigerated. What a love nest!

"Let's do something," he said.

"Like what?"

"Take a walk or something, or maybe go to a movie."

"What's playing?"

"There's a cowboy picture at the Central Park."

She made a face and said, "Wait a minute."

She went into the store, then came back and said, "The folks said I could use the car tonight."

"Great."

They got into a black Hupmobile with mohair seats and a motor you didn't have to crank and drove east toward the lake. The lake not only provided drinking water and recreation but had the substance of dreams. Everybody wanted to live near it. Success was generally measured by how close you lived to the Gold Coast. They drove along 12th Street, which later was renamed Roosevelt Road, past smoke-pocked houses and small stores, past neighborhoods where most of the houses were of wood, built quickly after the great fire, where Jake lived when his father first brought him and his mother to America. The flats were lit by gas jets. You cooked and warmed the places with coal-burning stoves, and you had to heat kettles of water for a bath in a galvanized tub. Jake remembered toilets in the hallway and outhouses in the backyards and going, terrified, down rickety wooden stairs during bitterly cold nights; sometimes he became constipated for days for fear of going. Then his mother would give him castor oil, which made him vomit, and, if that didn't work, an enema, which made him scream with pain.

Passing Little Italy, they could smell the bootleg booze being made in every other Italian flat for Capone and the Genna gang.

They almost got drunk from the heady odors. Soon they were in the factory district and the Wells Street freight depot with hundreds of boxcars and Pullmans on the sidings being shunted from one track to another; it was like a sea of puffing, chugging whales floundering to find some room. She turned on to Michigan Avenue to go south through the old Levee district, where saloons, gambling, and prostitution flourished, where Capone ruled his Chicago empire from the Lexington and Metropole hotels and where hundreds of his whores turned $2 and $3 tricks around the clock. It was still a wild shoot-'em-up western town. Only the names had changed. Instead of Jesse James, it was Al Capone. Machine Gun Jack McGurn took the place of Billy the Kid. Charles Fischetti roamed the asphalt range instead of Wild Bill Hickok. She turned east over the Illinois Central tracks to the Outer Drive. Soldier Field loomed darkly behind them, the lighted skyline of the Loop receded, as they rode farther south.

Then the lake. Oh, the lake. The vastness, the mystery, the beauty of it. The lights of the Municipal Pier were like big yellow beads stretching a mile out into the dark waters. The stars suddenly popped out in distant clusters. The Palmolive beacon swept its great blue light over the city and lake, whirling ceaselessly about, probing the dark sky.

They parked along the breakwater at 35th Street among many cars: a lover's lane on wheels and cushioned seats. Jake put his arm around Ida, and they looked out dreamily and silently at the ghosts of granite rocks above the water. Then Jake drew her close, the preliminary to getting into the back seat and doing some hot and heavy loving, French kissing until their mouths became dry; then she'd get her hand inside his pants, and he'd blow into his underwear or he'd dry-fuck her. This time she pulled away from him.

"Are you really going to Stanford, Jake?"

Though he was packing to go, he still didn't know how he was going to get there. His father had not offered railroad or bus fare, nor had Wally Blake or the university. There were still a hundred details to discuss, like where he was going to live, how he was going to live until he got settled with a job, what fraternity would ask him to pledge, who would meet him in Palo

Alto, who would get him oriented. He was going alone. All alone. The first time in his life. And so far. But the question only solidified his decision.

"Yep, that's where yours truly is going."

Suddenly Ida burst into tears.

"Hey, what the hell is that for? What'd I do?"

"I'll never see you again."

"Sure you will. I'll be back. Vacation time."

"No, you won't. You'll get so collegiate and sophisticated you'll never come back. And some rich, beautiful coed will fall in love with you."

He wanted to say aw-shucks and kick the manure around like Tom Mix or Gary Cooper. But she could be so right; it was all part of his fantasies.

"Then you'll go to Hollywood. You'll become a college champ, and you'll go to Hollywood and go to all those wild parties with Barbara Stanwyck and Joan Crawford and Clara Bow."

"Hollywood is five hundred miles away from Stanford." But he, too, dreamed of Hollywood and Barbara Stanwyck and Joan Crawford and Clara Bow.

She flung her arms around him and wept uncontrollably. Awkwardly he tried to comfort her, patted her back, nuzzled his cheek against her tear-wet face, said, his heart lumped up, "Don't, don't."

She sniffed and held him tight, and he felt limp and uncomfortable in her arms. Christ, all he wanted was a dry fuck or a hand job, not a parting as if he were going off to war. After all, he wasn't in love with the girl.

"Maybe we better go back home," he said.

"No, no." She sat up, wiped her tears. She turned on the light and made up her face. By the time she finished she looked bright again, soft, her rouged lips sparkling. "Jake, what if I went all the way with you?"

"Huh?"

"Yesterday was my birthday. I'm eighteen. I'm of age. Since I was fourteen, I said when I'm eighteen I'm going to go all the way. I want to go with you, Jake. Because I love you and because the past year I've been out of my skin wanting you."

She took a container, round as a compact, out of her purse, opened it, and pulled out a round brown rubber thing with a flexible rim.

"My birthday present," she said. "I got it for myself yesterday."

"What the hell is it?"

"A diaphragm."

"A diaphragm! It looks more like a rubber yarmulke."

"It's a ladies' condom, dummy. With this, we can do it bare, the way it should be."

Whatever passion he had for her slowly dissipated. First the tears. Now this.

She started the car.

"Where we going?"

"You'll see."

He looked out at the dark, mysterious lake. What next? he asked.

Next, they were in the Loop, across the street from the Hotel Morrison.

"Go in and register, Jake. Mr. and Mrs. Jones. How about that? Then I'll come in."

He swallowed hard. The skyscrapers turned into mausoleums, burying him. "I don't have any money."

She handed him $5.

"You're kidding."

"Jake, for God's sake, I've got to go through with it, the right way. I didn't take lessons at the Margaret Sanger clinic and have that diaphragm fitted for nothing. I'm not going to waste it."

"We don't have any luggage. They'll know. What if we're caught?"

"Please, Jake."

He was in a sweat. "I can't, Ida."

"You're scared."

"We're not married. If we're caught, they can throw us in jail. There goes my whole career."

"That's all you can think about."

She started the car again, slammed the gear into first, and took off. The ride, over boulevards and car tracks, was long, tedious, silent, tooth- and fist-clenched. The wind blew the smell of the stockyards into their noses. They squirmed and grimaced. All of a sudden the whole world stank.

When they reached her house, the lights were out in the delicatessen. Only dim yellow pools of light came from the lampposts.

"When are you leaving?" she asked.

"In a week."

Silence. Then . . .

"I wanted to give you a going-away present. Something to really remember me by."

He didn't know what to say. He had behaved like a first-class *shmuck*. He could have had it all, the big bareback ride. Now, in familiar territory, he felt a tension in his stomach, his penis, without conscience, hardening; he moved closer to her.

"There isn't much time left," she said.

"No." He felt her thigh against his, felt the heat of her plump body. "Will you do it with somebody else?"

"I don't know. I wanted to do it with you."

There it went, like a wild stallion. He lost all control. He threw his arms around her and crushed her to himself and drove his tongue into her mouth. She opened it wide, as if all of her was opening to him, and he could taste her spit. He felt her big, firm breasts, her nipples growing hard.

"Let's go in the back seat," she said.

They flopped over onto the back seat. His hand was up her thigh, through her silky step-ins, and his fingers moved inside her moist vagina. She began to move and writhe against him, moaning and sucking his tongue, and suddenly she clutched him hard, tightening all over, she began quivering and gasping, oh, she was so hot and ready, with her hands frantically unbuttoning his pants, and there it was . . . out . . . bare . . . never before out of his pants with her, free and hard and probing and moving against her wet bush, and then she lurched away from him and swooped down on him and put her whole mouth around it until he thought he'd yell and scream from the shock and the exquisite delight, and he couldn't help himself, he blew right into her mouth, and she kept on sucking and sucking at him, she couldn't stop, until he had to pull away from her.

She was breathing hard, holding her hands over her mouth, looking away from him; then she said, "I don't know what happened. I got so carried away. I never felt like that before. Maybe it was your going away and my never seeing you again and all I went through with that diaphragm. Oh, Jesus, Jake, I don't know what I'm going to do, it was so awful and so wonderful."

She reached for him and kissed him, and he felt squeamish about it, feeling as if he were tasting his own jism. When she released him, he started buttoning his pants.

"Next time we'll go all the way, Jake."

"Sure."

"Don't leave town, Jake."

"I've got to."

"I'll give you all the loving you want if you don't go."

Right now he didn't want any more; he wanted to be far, far away.

"I read up on Stanford. Very few girls there. Only five hundred. All dogs and geniuses. Whores are all you'll get. You'll miss me. You'll see."

Right now he felt as if he could live in a monastery.

"Don't go, Jake."

She flung her arms around him and held him tight, and once again he could feel her quivering against him.

Walking home later, he was filled with the strange thing that had happened. Thinking about it, how she had got so carried away, he began to feel warm toward her again. Strangely, as she'd predicted, he was only a few minutes away from her and he was beginning to miss her. Goddamn the tricks these women had. Everybody was conspiring to keep him from going away. His father wasn't giving him his blessing, his mother was weeping, his pals were of no help, and now this girl gave him a going-away present he'd never forget, even if it was a perverted, degenerate thing.

In less than a week now Jake was going away. He was as nervous as the days before a swimming meet. He found himself constantly running to the bathroom. He hardly slept. His throat felt clogged; he was always clearing it. He began sucking his teeth like a baby. His skin itched. Especially his athlete's foot and the head of his penis. He scratched his feet until sores developed; they got so raw he could hardly walk. He scratched his penis until he thought he'd jump out of his skin. It didn't take long for it to get hard. He found himself masturbating all hours of the day and night. And a sore developed along the glans; it looked suspiciously like the pictures of syphillis that were hung around the JPI locker room, and he shuddered at the thought of spirochetes shooting through his veins, then eating away at his body. He wore a cloth IAC jockstrap in the pool. But that was one place you couldn't hide a secret.

"Hey, what the hell's the jockstrap for?" said Fasso Sardell. His rubber lips spread wide, and he let out his nigger laugh and jellyrolled his belly.

Nobody could fool the weisenheimers, not these smart heebie-jeebies from the West Side. So he took the jockstrap off.

"Hey, you got the syph." That was his best pal, Benny Gordon, who wasn't going off to college like the others, who was facing a future of hard work and no fun.

"How could I have the syph?" he wanted to say. "I'm not getting any." Which he would not admit. Or could you get it from being sucked off?

Instead, he said, "Ah, you guys are full of shit."

"Who you been getting it from?" said Joey Gans, whose hatchet face looked lobster red from the sun. He was going to be a doctor. A big chancre mechanic, the boys said.

In the past Joey'd been getting it from Lila Shulman, who was known to put out for only two parties: the Democrats and the Republicans. They were referring to her.

"That's herpes progenitalis," said Bo Linsky, who could have been a freestyle champ if he hadn't spent half his time driving a booze truck for the syndicate or in jail.

Bo's pal Lala Bloomberg, who hobbled about on a broken ankle and a crutch after an arson job, laughed and said, "That's chancre progenitalis."

"Just like in the locker room," said Joey.

"Come on, you guys." Jake was plenty worried already. They didn't have to rub it in. How he wished he had a foreskin, one like Sean H. Fitzgerald's. It was as big as a circus tent; it could hide a thousand chancres.

"Let's find out," said Joey.

They dragged Jake down to the health club where Fingers Feinberg, the massage artist, presided. Dapper, slick-mustached, hairy-chested, with powerful arms, Fingers had three businessmen under the sun lamp, four men in the steam room, and one under his pounding hands on the rubbing table.

"Hey, Fingers, you got a septic pencil?" Joey asked.

"In the medicine chest."

"Cut it out, you guys," said Jake.

"Don't you want to find out if you've got the herpes progenitalis?" said Bo.

"What the hell is the herpes?" said Jake, feeling barnacles of spirochetes festering in his body.

"Third-stage syph."

"Where the hell would I get it?"

"It can be passed on by the hand." Joey tittered, waving the septic pencil he'd found. Then with authority, he said, "Third stage is incurable. It's in the bloodstream. Locomotor ataxia. Let's find out."

Worried, Jake let Joey rub the white pencil over the sore on his glans penis. Waited for the burning to start. Gritted his teeth. Everybody else waited. Maybe Jake didn't have it.

"Nothing," Jake said.

"Nothing? You sure?"

"Not a goddamn thing."

"Then you got it from the hand," Lala said, wobbling on his crutch. "Strictly from the hand."

And everybody laughed and slapped Jake's back, and they rushed up into the pool and spent their wild energy playing sock water polo, where you tried to knock a guy's head off with the hard ball.

That night, in bed, he scratched his toes until they oozed and became raw; he almost went out of his mind, the sensation was so great. Then in the middle of the night he thought he'd really blow his mind from the itch on his penis. He tried to stop himself from scratching it and finally gave up. He thought he'd lose his brains.

All the next day he walked on raw, itchy feet, and as he moved about, his bruised penis hurt and became itchier rubbing against his underpants. At lunchtime in school Lila Shulman sat down next to him. She was the one who had copped his cherry two years before. She wore her skirts brazenly high at the kneecap; her dyed blond hair was bobbed in a shingle; she even smoked. She was the siren of Harrison High, her husky voice full of sexual innuendos. She was one bold, outrageous step ahead of the latest fashion.

"You going to the prom tonight?"

"No," he said. He'd already asked Ida.

"You're a fucking liar," she said. Lila had the biggest, fastest, dirtiest mouth in the Midwest. "I know for a fact you're going."

"So I'm going. So why'd you ask?"

"Just to be sociable. Let me be more sociable. I hear you're going to Stanford."

"The word gets around."

"Don't go, Jake."

Nobody wanted him to go. Not even Lila, whom he hadn't laid in months. Not since he'd heard she had the clap. But even if he weren't afraid of getting clap, he hadn't been able to get it up for her the last couple of times anyhow. He always had the feeling that Lila, during the sex act, was a hawk scrutinizing him.

"What are you doing?" he asked her once.

"Go ahead." As if he were under a microscope. "Don't stop."

Then she'd say, "You like that? Yummy-yummy?"

"Oh, yes."

"How about that?"

"Oh, Jesus."

She tried everything.

"That sends you, huh?"

"Christ."

"What about this?"

"You're like a whore, you know."

She'd laugh huskily. "But first-class. And high-class."

Afterward he felt like carrion, as if he'd been picked to pieces. To her, everybody was a *shmuck*. She had no respect. Only contempt for the world.

"I can do you a lot of good here if you don't go away," she said.

"Like what?"

"Next week I start doing publicity for the Hotel Sherman and the College Inn."

"You're kidding."

"Assisting the head of publicity there. I'll have contacts galore. A suite at the hotel. Money-money-money." There was a cash-register gleam in her shining teeth. "I'll let you ride on my cushions. Silk and satin." Her dark eyes danced. Her dyed blond hair was like a medieval helmet on her head. Then she laughed and bounced her breasts obscenely with her hands. "Jake, I could make you a Persian prince." She stood up and laughed louder. Her parting word was: "What a *shmuck* you are."

Prom night was a breathtaking night for some, a sad night for others. It was a scary night, too. It marked the end of one kind of life, the beginning of another. Most of the boys and girls were going to start work or were going to look for work. Most of them didn't know what they wanted to do, except the girls; they wanted to get married, and their problems, they thought, would be solved. The only thing the boys knew they wanted was money and a job that didn't drain them. College was a luxury, but most of those who were going to college also didn't know what they wanted to do.

But there was great optimism that spring of 1929. The big bull stock market had reached dizzying heights. Fortunes had been made in radio, electric, auto, steel, grains, and other stocks. Prosperity had reached peaks beyond dreams. There were real, oversized heroes in those days: Jack Dempsey, Red Grange, Johnny Weissmuller, Lucky Lindy Lindbergh, even Al Capone. But the market made the biggest news. Somebody said, "As the market goes, so do women's skirts. If it goes any higher, skirts will go up to the navel." The bulls were raging and running. Margin was the key. Horizons were as bright as any Hollywood ending in the sunset. The class of '29 had a boundless future. That was the word—from Bernard Baruch to Herbert Hoover.

"What school you going into?" Jake asked the future collegians.

"Liberal arts."

"What's that?"

"Well, everybody starts there, and then you find your way, and you decide where you want to specialize."

"Me, I'm going to be an engineer," Jake said.

"That's tough. That takes brains."

Jake was full of confidence. He graduated in the first quarter of his class, making him a fairly bright student on paper, but he'd seldom studied, seldom read anything but the sports pages and the swimming record books. Everything seemed to come easily for him. His pal Benny Gordon said of him, "He walks through life like a balloon. He never had a hard day. Peaches and cream. Milk and honey. Handouts from Moses. That's Jake." At that time in his life Jake felt there was nothing he couldn't do. He was invincible. He'd win the intercollegiates, and he was sure he'd be invited to the White House and shake Hoover's hand.

That night he wore white duck pants and a dark jacket from his Passover suit of the year before. His light hair was greasy with Stacomb. His blue eyes shone like gems. His face, though bony and dried out from hours in water, was clean-cut and vigorous-looking. He had a thick, muscular size sixteen neck. The padded shoulders and wide, peaked lapels of his jacket made him look like a football player. His waist narrowed down to twenty-eight inches. And he had no ass. He was solid bone and muscle, big-chested, flat-bellied, in the peak of condition, a confident young man on the threshold of becoming a champion, which would lead him into anything he wanted. With a college degree you could really write your name on the moon.

But he was sad with the sad young men who were going out the next day to slug it out in the world and confident with those who were going to grab the world by the balls. He was looking forward to the great collegiate times of fraternities and home-coming bonfires and football games and the razzle-dazzle of campus life with those who were going off to Illinois and Chicago and Wisconsin and other schools. Everybody knew Jake was going to make it. Stanford. Scholarships. Imagine that, it won't cost him a dime, a *gelt*-edged future, the lucky bastard. Hollywood, watch out, here comes Jake Davidson.

Ida was so proud of him, clinging to him, loving him more than ever, all aglow, not minding his awkward toddle and waltzes, moving dreamily and lightly along while he stumbled on the floor and sweated as if he were in a steambath. Afterward, over barbecue ribs in The Pit on Rush Street, Ida became somber.

"Tomorrow I'm going to start looking for a job," she said.

"What doing?"

"Secretary, I guess. What else can I do?"

"Why don't you relax awhile?"

"I've got to get out of my house. It's no good living there. I'll find a job and move out. I'll have my own place, but what good will it do me?" Her lower lip trembled. "I'll be all alone."

"Where are you going to move?"

"The Near North Side, I hope."

"Where all the action is, huh?"

"If I get a job. I hear I'll not only have to be fast on the typewriter but also faster on my feet." She smiled to control her lip.

"Wolf-wolf."

"First thing they ask, I hear, is: "Can you work nights?""

"You're strictly a day worker, tell them."

"A lot you care. You're going away."

"Not forever. Nine months I'll be back."

"Nine months. You can have a baby in that time."

"Eat your ribs. They're great."

"I'm not hungry."

He finished her ribs.

"The whole world revolves around your belly," she said.

"The most direct way to a man's heart."

"What about his you-know-what?"

"Now you're talking."

"Jake, you're a bastard."

"Don't spoil it, Ida. We're still a couple of punks. Who knows what the future will bring?"

"My mother was married at sixteen."

"That was the old country. Matchmakers and all that. You're talking like I owe you, like we should get hooked."

"I'm talking like I love you."

"What the hell do you love? A guy just getting out of high school, a guy without a pot to piss in, a guy with no future if he doesn't go to college, a guy who'll sink and drown if he has to drop his career to support a wife. It's not desperation time, Ida. You're a beautiful girl. Let's see what happens. Okay?"

"You could go to college here."

"I know I could go here, but I want to go there."

She swallowed hard. Her lower lip began to tremble again.

"I'm sorry. I've been practicing hard to be eighteen, and all of a sudden I don't know what I've been practicing for."

What a sad night, he thought. As if they were at the end of everything instead of at the beginning. All the way home, through the dimly lit streets, it was glum, glum, glum.

Instead of stopping in front of her delicatessen and letting Jake walk home, she parked in front of his gray-stone apartment building. The bay windows were dark on the first floor, where he lived. The streets looked grim. He was glad he was going away. Sunny California. Oranges, mountains, the vast Pacific. Oh, boy.

"I had a great time, Ida."

"So did I. Thanks for everything."

He reached over and kissed her. She quivered in his arms. She clutched him with desperation, as if she would lose not only him but her whole past if she let go. She felt like a little bird.

When she let go, she said brightly and bravely, "Jake, remember that going-away present I was going to give you?"

"Yah."

"What about your house?"

"We'll wake everybody up."

"What about the back porch?"

"The boards are creaky."

"Let's go in the back seat then."

He flipped over onto the back seat.

"I'll be there in a jiffy," she said.

He watched her pull out her diaphragm; then she squatted on the seat and put her hand under her skirt.

"What are you doing?"

"Trying to get it in."

"Hurry."

"I'm trying." She grunted and groaned. "They fitted me, but I can't get it through." She gave up. "Oh, shit." She was in tears. He'd never heard her swear before; she was always delicate, ladylike, and proper. "You got anything?"

"No."

"To hell with it."

She climbed into the back seat with him, lifted her skirt, and lay back. She had no step-ins. She was really prepared to go all the way.

"You think we should? Bare?"

"Jake, I'll kill you if you don't."

He pulled his pants down and felt the cool air on his buttocks and penis. He got terribly excited when his cock moved along her silk flesh-colored stockings. He got more excited when he began to probe her curly pubic area and her moist vagina.

"I'm ready, Jake." She squirmed against him.

"Jesus, you're tight."

"That's why I couldn't get that thing in. Push harder."

"Christ, I'm trying."

"I'll help you."

Her hand on his penis, directing him, almost made him *plotz*. He groveled, writhed, poked, battered against her. Her membrane was like a steel wall.

"Harder."

"I can't get through."

"Deeper."

The sore from all his rubbing and scratching began to hurt. He went limp.

"You didn't, did you, Jake?"

"No."

"What happened?"

"I don't know. I just got bushed."

"I hurt you."

"No."

"Yes, I did. I'm a total bust." She sat up. She was shaking. She put her soft, smooth, hot hand on his penis. "I'll make up for it."

He felt her quivering as she fondled his penis, then began to stroke it. The pain went away.

"Oh, God," she said, and she swooped down on him, taking his whole cock into her mouth, her full, delicate lips and hot tongue sucking away, her body tightening and moving as if he were completely in her, and then he felt as if a cannonball had exploded through him. It was the best, most exciting present he'd ever had. She was really making it hard for him to leave.

The following afternoon, with nothing to do, Jake took a long slow ride to Clarendon Beach. Albie Karlin, the intercollegiate swimming champ from Northwestern, had called that morning while he was buying some groceries for his mother.

"What'd he want?"

"I don't know," his mother said. "He didn't say. 'Just tell him Albie called.' That's all he said."

Albie had never called him before. He wondered all through lunch what he wanted. He decided to go to Clarendon Beach, where the city lifeguard school was being held. Everybody'd be there.

To avoid the Loop, he took a Crawford Avenue streetcar to Lawrence Avenue, then another streetcar to Sheridan Road. He was jolted and lurched about for more than an hour with nothing to interest his eyes but small stores, brick buildings of all shapes and sizes, factories, and empty lots full of late-spring sunflowers and ragweed. New construction was going on, without any harmony, any plan. Chicago, already the hog butcher and railroad center of the world, was busting at the seams, sprawling to the outskirts of town. One of his English teachers, Homer Lovelace, an effete man who had traveled a lot in Europe, once said, "All the architects in Chicago must have come from Munich, where everything looks like bologna and wurst. Their *wurst* is our best." Very few students got the pun, but Mr. Lovelace went on. "There's no character, no grace, no style, no distinction, no heart, no soul, ergo, no love in our buildings. Why couldn't we have had a few Italians, a few Frenchmen, even a Christopher Wren?"

Anyhow, Sheridan Road was a classy street. Big apartment buildings, where the rich lived. And there was the lake, clear, fresh, a gem, with the sun sparkling over the sailboats and motorboats, with nothing to stop your eye to the horizon. Did Europe have a lake like Lake Michigan? Did anybody?

And there were the guys at lifeguard school. Some were in rowboats, learning how to patrol the beaches. Others were taking instruction in artificial respiration from a doctor. Others were learning first aid.

"Look who's here!" That was Moish Bender, short, squat, barrel-chested with squinty eyes, who'd been on the 1928 Olympic water polo team. He was captain of the guards at Clarendon.

Albie Karlin, the iconoclast, who had won the 50, 100, and 220 freestyle at the national intercollegiates in the spring, stepped over and looked down at Jake from his six-foot broad-shouldered height. He was going to head the lifeguards at Lincoln Park.

"I called this morning," he said. Albie always said as little as possible. His performances talked for him. So every word he uttered seemed to have great weight.

"My mom told me."

"I hear you're all packed to go to Stanford."

"Yah." Jake always found it difficult to talk to Albie.

"Why didn't you talk to me about it?"

"I don't know. You were up at Northwestern. You never talked to me."

"Poor kid," Moish said. "Nobody ever talks to him. He comes here because he's lonely."

"I came here to say good-bye," Jake said. "I didn't want to leave without that."

"Good-bye," growled Moish.

"Good-bye," Jake said, suddenly sad.

"You're not going anywhere," said Albie.

"Huh?" Jake was stunned.

"You're going to stay right here."

Jake didn't get it. He stared at them. If a stranger had been watching, he'd have thought Jake was going to be beaten to a pulp.

"You're going to Northwestern, punk," said Albie.

Jake's mouth opened. He didn't know what to say. Albie had been like a god to him when he first started to swim. He'd watch his graceful style and imitate him. Albie coached him from time to time. Later he'd introduced him to Weissmuller and his coach, Bachrach, at the Illinois Athletic Club. They said he could come there, and both Weissmuller and Bachrach gave him pointers. Sometimes he'd pace Albie and Weissmuller when they were working out, and he'd feel as big and powerful as they, and he'd float all the way home, as on a cloud, after drying himself with five towels and slicking his hair down with their pomade and pouring shaving lotions and powder all over himself. Though Jake was getting up in their league, he was still in awe of Albie,

especially after Albie had won three intercollegiate championships in one night and broke two records, the first contestant ever
to accomplish this; now that Weissmuller was turning pro, Albie
was the number one ranked swimmer in the world.

"Where did you say you were going, punk?" Moish said,
looking as if he were ready to break Jake's leg.

Jake was no longer sure. "Stanford?"

"You're shit going to Stanford," said Moish. "You know how
far away it is?"

"I know, I know."

"Who do you know out there?" Moish growled.

"Halvorsen. I met him at the nationals last year."

"He's a diving coach, strictly with the fancy divers," said
Moish. "You want to wind up doing one and a half gainers and
full twists?"

A fate worse than death.

"He'll have you diving into a damp rag," said Moish. "He'll
make you dry yourself afterward with that rag."

Jake looked to Albie for protection, but Albie wasn't saying a
word. Then he said, "What about Wally Blake? He was the
national freestyle champ. He made the Olympics."

"He was made before he got to Stanford," said Moish.

"I'm made, too," said Jake. "What more do I need? I'm all
there. I know how to train. I've got the strokes. Fitzgerald gave it
all to me."

"You don't know what training is." Albie finally spoke. He
sounded like an oracle. "You won't have any competition. You
won't have me and Weissmuller and Bachrach to sharpen you
up. You won't have the IAC and guys coming from all over the
world around there. You'll go down the drain."

Everything in Jake began to sink. Weakly he said, "But I'm all
set there."

"With what?" Albie said.

"Tuition."

"You'll get tuition at Northwestern." Now Albie was pitching.

"A job."

"You'll get a job there, too."

"My room'll be taken care of."

"You won't have to worry about that. But I'll tell you what

you will have to worry about. You won't have any friends there. The whole school, wall-to-wall *goyim*. You'll be a total stranger. You won't have anybody looking out for you, nobody to talk to, and if you don't make it, kid, you're stranded three thousand miles away."

"I'll join a frat. The Phi Eps, like you."

"What frat? What Phi Eps? There are no Jewish frats out there. And the *goyish* frats won't have you. You'll live in a dorm, like army barracks."

"No Jewish frats?" Jake's heart dropped twenty stories down a swift elevator.

"No."

What the hell was college without fraternities? Without ukuleles and raccoon coats and razzmatazz and homecomings and breezing along in roadsters with coeds? Army barracks yet. Wall-to-wall *goyim*.

"We'll pledge you at the Phi Eps," Albie said. He was talking ten times more than he ever had before. "We've got a job for you there for your meals. You'll sell programs at the football games. That's seven bucks every Saturday. The coach has a job at the pool for you. Seventy-five cents an hour, ten hours a week. You'll be doing better than the football players. Tuition you'll get. You won't get a better deal in the country."

"Believe me, you won't," Moish said.

"Tomorrow you're going to get a call from Milton B. Morgenstern, President of the Alumni 'N' Men's Association. Any problems, financial or otherwise, he'll take care of them. He'll arrange to pay your room rent at the fraternity. You'll room with me. Okay?"

Jake stared at Albie. Now he really didn't know what to say.

"Listen to him," Moish said. "You'll be taken care of. You'll have friends. You'll get help. You'll make contacts. It's the contacts you make in school who'll help make you when you graduate. Milton B. will take care of that. He knows everybody. So listen to Albie."

Jake's bastions of resistance were caving in on all sides.

"So what's Northwestern good for?" he said. "I mean what do I specialize in there?"

"We've got the best business school in the country west of

Harvard," Albie said. "The best journalism school outside of Columbia. The finest medical, law, dental, and engineering schools. You name it, we've got the best for you. A Northwestern graduate commands a lot of respect."

"Make up your mind," Moish said.

"I told all my friends already, my folks," said Jake.

"You've got a right to change your mind," said Albie. "You just tell them you got a better offer."

"Why didn't you let me know about this before?"

"I had to get the whole thing laid out for you," Albie said. "You don't take it, we'll give it to somebody else. Okay?"

Jake was all mixed up now. He said, "I'll think about it."

"Don't think about it," said Albie. "Be a stubborn jerk. Go to Stanford."

"He's stupid," Moish said. "Fuck him."

They started to walk away. He stood there in the sand and felt it suddenly turn into quicksand, and he was being sucked down, down.

"Okay!" he called after them. "I'm taking it! Okay!"

Afterward, after the most crucial decision of his life, Jake plunged into the lake. He felt as if he'd thrown off a huge bear he'd been wrestling with for months. The water was fresh and cold and deep blue in the sun, and he was stronger and more buoyant than ever. He was going to swim to the three-mile water-purifying crib out there and back. But it'd be way after dark if he went the full distance. The whole lifeguard force would be out dragging for him. So he turned back after a strenuous mile and came out of the water, his chest broad and tight and heaving, his tanned body smooth and rippling.

The swim was tiring enough to tone down his excitement. The sun hurt his eyes as it was going down during the long streetcar ride home. Then with darkness, exhausted, he fell asleep and was lurched awake a dozen times until he got off. He came home in time to have supper with his father. His kid brother was playing on the linoleum with a windup locomotive he'd wheedled out of his mother. His sister was reading a book and listening to the Victrola his father had built. The music was "One Alone" from *The Desert Song*.

"It tears your heart out," his mother said. "Like mine is torn to shreds all day with your going so far away next week."

Before Jake could tell them his latest decision, she left the kitchen and came back with a plaid flannel shirt.

"Here," she said. "For college. The saleslady said it's the latest collegiate style. What everybody is wearing."

"I'm not going."

"It's not collegiate enough for you?"

"You're not listening, Ma. I'm not going to Stanford. I'm going to Northwestern in Evanston. I'm going to stay right here."

Excited, his mother said, "What is he talking about? Aaron, tell me, what is he saying?"

"He's saying," his father said, "he's not going away, he's staying here."

His mother, overwhelmed, kissed him, hugged him. "Ay, Yonkel, Yonkel, you're such a good boy." Whenever she was emotional, she called him by his Jewish name. "You'll stay here. You'll live here. You'll never regret it. Every day strudel and sweet cream. You'll see."

"But I won't live here," Jake said. "I'll live there, in a fraternity."

"Why there? What's the matter with here?"

"Here he's a boy," his father said. "There he's a man."

"To me, he's a *pisher* no matter where he is." She hugged Jake again. "But here, there, so long as he's close."

"So," his father said, "what has Northwestern got to offer?"

"It won't cost you a dime, Pa. My muscle will earn my keep."

"But will it give you a brain?"

"That's what college is for, isn't it?"

"I hope so. You still going to study to be an engineer?"

"I changed my mind. Business. Rothschild, make way."

His father laughed. His mother was delighted. His kid brother said, "So what's in it for me? What am I going to get?"

His sister, who was happy Jake was staying, mostly because it'd keep her mother from becoming a nervous wreck, said, "Yonkel, the banker."

"You ever hear of Harvard?" Jake asked.

His father nodded. He was a well-informed man, a reader of all the American newspapers and the *Jewish Daily Forward* and the *Freiheit* occasionally. "What's Harvard got to do with your new decision?"

"Next to Harvard, Northwestern has the best business school in the world."

"You're always taking the best anybody has to offer," his sister said.

"Why not?"

"They're offering, he's taking," his father said.

"Wow!" Jake jumped up and hugged himself, unable to contain himself.

"Calm down, *boychik*," his father said. "Help me count my money. Rothschild can wait."

His mother and sister cleared the table. His father poured a bag full of change on the oilcloth table and began, with Jake, to count his day's take and wrapping them for the bank.

Aaron Davidson had a newsstand on the corner of 22nd and Crawford on the Far West Side of Chicago. Cicero, Capone's town, was just a mile away. Between Capone's headquarters and the newsstand was the big Western Electric plant, which employed more than 50,000 workers. When they left the works at six o'clock, they charged off the streetcars like stampeding cattle to make their transfers to other cars, tearing papers off the stand and out of Aaron's hands and throwing pennies at him at bewildering speeds. In their wake, they littered the sidewalk with hundreds of pennies, which Aaron had to pick up when the crowds subsided. Jake used to work the stand when he was younger, freeze in the winters and sweat bullets in the hot, windy summers. He used to feel like forty octopuses whirling with newspapers. Afterward, when he wasn't training, he'd help his father count the money. They'd sit in the kitchen, spread the money out on the clean oilcloth, count and wrap, and get both the tablecloth and their hands dirty.

"This proves," his father would say, "that no matter how clean your hands are, money is dirty."

"Especially the horse money."

"Now that is a strange phenomenon," his father would say. "The money you freeze for, the money you sweat for, the money you honestly earn makes your hands filthy dirty. But the money you play with, the money you gamble with, the money that is corrupt is always paper, and your hands, no matter how much you handle the money, come out clean. Someday I will pose this problem to the rabbi. It is a Talmudic proposition."

Picture if you will . . . Aaron Davidson, an unobtrusive, composed man, who had lived quietly, as if under a rug, most of his life, a short, slender man, so skinny his ribs showed, with buck false teeth and sunken cheeks. His face was weather-beaten and tanned, except for his white, clear forehead, which was covered by a cap outdoors. He was a socialist and a Talmudist, a student of the Mishna and the Midrash and the *Jewish Daily Forward,* which he read religiously for the truthful interpretation of the news after reading the American papers, which he never trusted except for the race results. He was a man steeped in *shul* protocol and ritual, in tradition that went back 4,000 years, but like most of his kind, he had learned to bend the Hebraic law but never to break it. He was a victim of Russian pogroms who had had all his teeth pulled so that he wouldn't have to serve in the Czar's army. He was the son of a *sofer,* a man who inscribed the Torah and the mezuzah, a man who had to be as pure as rainwater, as clean as the heavens, before he could touch the holy scrolls. Once, on one of his journeys to do his work, he took Aaron along. That was a year before Aaron's bar mitzvah. It was in the dead of a Russian winter, ten below zero, and the water supply in the town of Katsivya had frozen. No *mikvahs.* Nothing but the river, where a hole a foot thick had been chopped in the ice. The Jewish men of the town chopped enough ice out to form a small pool for the ritual bath.

"Come, we will go to the river."

"It's bitter cold, Papa."

"You will help me. We must be clean. Come."

They wore all the woolen clothes they possessed to the river.

"Quick. Undress. Go in."

Aaron watched his father undress, but after he got his coat and sweater off, he shivered so hard he couldn't move.

"Hurry."

"I can't."

His father, a stern, no-nonsense man, tore off the rest of Aaron's clothes, took him in his arms, and plunged into the icy water. The shock took Aaron's breath away. It was as if a knife had cut off his wind. He turned purple-blue as if his blood had been drained. Everything in him shriveled up. His testicles disappeared into their sockets, and his small penis seemed to have gone inside his body. Terrified, he yelled, *"Tahteh! Tahteh!"*

When his father saw what had happened, he, too, became alarmed. In a panic he wrapped his great overcoat around Aaron and ran naked with him to the nearest house, yelling, "For you, Lord, he has purified himself. You cannot take his manhood away. You must bring it back. You must, dear Lord. He must be able to enter your congregation."

In the house, where the *shamus* of the *shul* lived, a hovel with chickens squawking and running about, Aaron was put to bed and wrapped in a feather quilt that was a foot thick. Aaron doubled up, shivered and shivered. His father jumped about naked to keep warm until the *shamus* brought him his clothes.

"He won't be bar mitzvah," his father cried. "My son, my oldest, how can you take away his manhood, Lord?"

Women came in with black shawls over their heads. They uncovered Aaron to look at him, and they, too, saw the terrible catastrophe. One of the women rubbed his private parts, pulled at them. Nothing. Aaron was paralyzed with cold. The women wrapped him up again. They threw garlands of garlic and elder leaves around his neck. They came in with a brew of salt, oil, pepper, and garlic and forced it through his chattering mouth. They lit candles and prayed over him. His father called for kiddush wine and prayed over him, too. Then Leah, the sorceress, came in. She began to recite incantations. She invoked the angels, the patriarchs, the matriarchs, the heavens, the scrolls of the Torah, to bring back the boy's manhood.

Gradually, as Aaron thawed out, his shivering subsided. Color returned to him. His manhood slowly began to come out. Relief flooded through everybody. They began to sing and dance. But Aaron decided then he'd never follow his father's trade. He couldn't be forced, for his father never left that town alive. He developed pneumonia before he finished his work and died. Aaron was brought home on a sled with his dead father. His mother, who had been left speechless and deaf from scarlet fever when she was young, could only cry and make her unformed sounds. All she could weep was: *"Tahteh, tahteh."*

Later Aaron was apprenticed to a carpenter in Kiev and there, during the 1905 revolution, he came under the influence of the trade unionists and socialists, and he felt that it was the only way of life for a workingman. He still observed the teachings of the Talmud; he still believed in God, in an existential way. He believed that God was God, a Supreme Being who made order out of the world but that the human being was accountable for all his actions. And as long as he exploited no one, made a living by his own efforts, lived by the Mosaic code, he was on the side of the angels, both Jehovah's and the socialistic ones.

In America he was unemployed as a carpenter as much as he was employed. Hard times were nothing new to him. And he was afraid, being as thin as he was, that he'd get consumption from being indoors with the sawdust and the bad air. When he heard about newsstands, he went to his *landsman's verein* and borrowed money at heavy interest rates and bought a newsstand. He saved and scrimped to pay off his debt, and now, for the first time in his life, he was able to provide for his family without too much worry.

So, imagine a man like this, a *yeshiva bocher,* a scholar, who could have become a *sofer,* even a rabbi . . . now a newsstand owner and a bookie. Yes, a bookie. Not full time. Only part time. Known among his relatives—warmly, with a gentle smile, mind you—as an American *goniff.* In America you could be a *goniff,* a thief, if you didn't hurt anybody or really steal, and still live under a benevolent heaven.

It began so simply. It happened so deceptively it had to be the work of the devil. But oh, what a devil.

One hundred yards away from the newsstand, on Ogden Avenue, were the streetcar barns. Hundreds of motormen and conductors and repairmen came in and out of there. Many of them bought newspapers at Aaron's newsstand, and many of them were horseplayers. The place became a hangout for horseplayers, who bought newspapers and studied the entries and handicappers and talked nothing but horses. Even cops on the beat and in squad cars coming by for free papers participated. All the talk was foreign as Babel to Aaron.

"Hey, Aaron, you like Eany-Meany in the sixth at Belmont?"
"Hah?" Aaron would answer.
"How about going halves with me? Goose 'Em High in the eighth at Pimlico?"
"Hah?"
All Babel.

The reason Aaron got all this action was very simple. Around the corner was Johnson's, a Capone handbook run by Bill Johnson, who operated a number of gambling joints around the city for Capone. The front was a cigar store. The back room, which you entered after going through a secret passageway and being carefully frisked by a flat-nosed muscular giant named Big Frank, was a bookie joint. At night, after the torn betting tickets were cleaned up and the racing charts were taken down, the place was turned into an elegant gambling casino with all the free drinks and free food you could handle.

Soon after Aaron took over the newsstand, two of Johnson's boys stopped by and told him to order twenty-five racing forms and fifteen scratch sheets each day and to bring them in. That was more than $3 profit a day, a gold mine. Then the boys said one day, "Hey, Pop, the streetcar boys and cops can't come in the joint. Take their bets. We'll give you five percent."

Aaron began to get slips of paper and money from uniformed motormen, conductors, cops, even a few priests and ministers. At first he'd bring their slips of paper and money, along with the day's forms and scratch sheets, into Johnson's, and he'd get paid for the papers and his 5 percent commission. Sometimes he'd make as much as $10-a-day commission. Another gold mine. And when these people won, Johnson's would give him the money to pay them off.

Later he'd listen to the horseplayers, and Babel began to make sense when he turned to the form and sports sections of the newspapers. He began to read the handicappers' selections, the performances of jockeys and horses, what stables they came from, who sired whom, until he became an encyclopedia of horses. They became another family to him. Following the horses was like following the steps of his own children. He'd be permissive when they failed, proud when they won. Emotion would sometimes grip his throat when one of his favorites died. "Hah?" turned into professional opinions.

"Who do you like in the fifth at Hawthorne?"

"Black Hamlet," Aaron would say with authority.

Then he began to look at the slips of papers with the names of horses. "A dog," he'd say, and he'd put the money in his pocket. "Also ran," he'd say, and keep the money. He started to get less commission from Johnson's but brought home more money by keeping the whole bet. Sometimes he was hit hard, but that was horse racing.

"What I'm taking Capone won't miss," he'd say.

He was a small dreamer. Never in terms of fur coats and diamonds and fancy motorcars. Never power-hungry. He was a satisfied man who asked little. A man who loved and supported his family. A gentle man. A $2 bet was his limit. That was Jake's father. Small-time, part-time bookie. Full-time newspaper vendor. And complete-time father and husband.

For a while, it looked as if he were going to be wiped out of the business altogether, especially the gambling part.

Many men who came into Johnson's dreamed of a successful caper there. Some of them thought there was more money in the place than at Monte Carlo or at the racetrack. Some gunslingers were challenged by this being a Capone operation; going after this joint would be like a one-on-one shoot-out with Jesse James or Billy the Kid. They studied the place carefully. How to do it? The big problem was getting a gun in. When you got inside the back door of the cigar store, there was a brick passageway to the steel-door entrance to the handbook. And there was Big Frank, armed with murderous fists and an automatic Mauser, who frisked you carefully before he'd buzz you through. Besides, it was a Capone joint. The cops could laugh at a Capone spot being knocked over, could admire the guts of the robbers, but Capone wouldn't laugh. He'd turn the town upside down. So how to do it?

Two gunslingers—Ralph Waite, who came from Kentucky moonshine country and was a two-time loser, and somebody known only as the Turk, a desperate, dark-faced, sullen, wiry man who had served time with Waite in Joliet—at last figured out a way . . . the little Jewboy.

They hung around the newsstand, bought papers, read them,

and rattled them, listened to who liked what horse in which race, watched streetcar men and cops hand slips of paper and money to Aaron, observed him going into Johnson's several times a day with the forms and scratch sheets and the bets. On one occasion the Turk slipped in with Aaron. Big Frank let Aaron pass without frisking him; the Jewboy wouldn't dare bring a gun in. But the Turk was patted down carefully before he was passed.

On a day when Jake was helping out, Aaron told him to bring the forms and scratch sheets into Johnson's. Jake was glad to do it. Big Frank, kidding around, would do a little shadowboxing with him and snort the way he used to in the ring; he'd tousle Jake's hair and say, "When you gonna take on Johnny Horse-cocker?" And Jake'd say, "One of these days." And Big Frank would say, "Wouldn't that be a kick, the little Jewboy taking on the big lug and knocking him on his ass?" And he'd laugh.

Afterward, in the back room, Tony Marcello, the manager, would snap his fingers and somebody'd take the papers from Jake. Another snap and somebody else would bring him a Coke, and he'd watch the horseplayers hit the forms as if they were the last deliveries of dope in the world. He'd watch the charts going up for the different tracks around the country, the odds being posted, the fever rising among the bettors around post time; he'd feel the intense dreams riding on the daily doubles, the parlays, the single races, and the excitement would work through him. So he'd hang around awhile, pick some horses by the sound of their names, and see how he made out.

Once, while he was there, none other than Al Capone himself came in. First a scout car drove up with five hurly-burly hoods. They roared into the joint with sawed-off shotguns, cased it, then planted themselves at all the doors. Nobody could go in or go out. Nobody was even allowed to go to the toilet. Then the Big Fella himself appeared with seven more bodyguards, carrying their weapons in violin cases; six of his soldiers were left outside to see that nobody got in. The bodyguards quickly deployed themselves around the place as Capone strolled in with the famous scar on his left cheek, a cigar in his cupid-shaped mouth, a pearl gray snap-brim fedora on his head, his heavy, bouncerlike body straining in his tight pinstripe suit. Everybody was awed. Betting stopped. The hubbub was reduced to whispers. The legend himself, as big as grand opera, was there in person.

Tony Marcello, the manager, carried away by the visit, rushed up with a bottle of private-stock Dom Pérignon.

Capone waved it away. "Chianti. A good family wine."

A bottle of chianti was produced.

"Drinks on the house," Capone ordered. "But not the kid. Who's the kid?"

Jake almost died.

"The Jewboy's kid. He delivers the forms. I'll get him outa here."

"You'll shit, too. Nobody leaves. Not till I'm gone. Give the kid a Coke."

Jake had already had one. But if it exploded in his body, he'd drink it.

Bill Johnson came out of the office to pay his respects.

"You're getting a good play here, Johnny," Capone said.

"We get a good play everywhere. You on the way to the track?"

"What else?"

It was said that Capone could drop $50,000 a day at the track and on his face it looked as if he didn't give a bibble.

"How about we turn a card, Johnny?"

"Sure." Johnson couldn't refuse.

Marcello broke open a new deck of Bicycle cards, spread them out on the bar so that the deck could be counted, scooped them up and showed the backs of the cards to prove they weren't marked, then shuffled them. He slammed the deck on the bar. Capone cut the deck.

"What is it?"

"One shot," Capone said. "Twenty grand."

"You got it."

Johnson picked an eight of hearts. Capone, flashing a rare eleven-karat blue-white diamond ring on his finger, snapped a card up, sure he could beat the eight. Five spades. Capone didn't even say, "Shit." Without a flicker he paid off from a heavy roll he pulled out of his pocket. This was a personal bet between two gamblers; it had nothing to do with the house, which Capone owned.

All that money, Jake thought.

"Better luck at the track," Johnson said.

"I need it."

Before Capone left, two of his bodyguards went out to see if it was safe. Then they came back in, and the Big Fella started out. He stopped in front of Jake and gave him a $20 bill.

"Stay away from the horses, kid."

Later Jake said to his father, "Why does he lose at the track? He could fix the races."

"Playing the horses, gambling with other gamblers is his pleasure. If he knew the outcome, it wouldn't be fun anymore. You see, Jake, when a man gambles, it's himself against the fates. That's the excitement."

But on this day, when Jake brought in the forms and scratch sheets for his father, coffee and Danish were being passed around, and Jake liked Lucky Lila in the second at Belmont because he knew somebody named Lila and Hurricane Harry in the third because any horse with a name like that had to win.

"Hey, kid, who you like?"

You never knew who had the winners.

"Lucky Lila in the second and Hurricane Harry in the third."

"That a tip?"

"I like the names."

"Hurricane Harry's a mudder. It's clear and fast at Belmont."

"He's going to run like the wind."

Kid talk, what the hell did he know?

Outside, Waite and the Turk were reading the papers, rattling them nervously, and then they made their decision. Aaron was alone at the stand after the delivery of the blue streak edition of the *Daily News*. They walked up close to him. The Turk slammed a .38 Police Special against his stomach, making Aaron gasp for air.

"Take it, you little prick."

Frightened, shaking, he took the gun.

"Put it in your pocket."

"All right, all right."

Another gun was shoved into his inside coat pocket.

"Let's go."

They marched him around the corner and headed him to Johnson's.

"You're bringing those guns inside."

"They'll kill me."

"We'll kill you if you don't."

They walked him into the cigar store. Jerry, the clerk, pressed the buzzer for Aaron, who tried to move through the door quickly. The Turk crammed into the passageway with him.

"I'm with the Jewboy," the Turk said.

Big Frank patted the Turk down while Aaron, his knees quivering, his throat hot and dry and clogged, stood there, and then Big Frank passed them both into the racebook. A few seconds later Ralph Waite was in the place. They both stood close to Aaron.

Then the Turk said, "All right, let's have them."

Aaron couldn't move.

"Let's have them, you fuck."

Jake saw his father and started for him, calling out, "Hey, Pa, I got a winner with Lucky Lila, and it's riding on Hurricane Harry."

At that moment, fearing more for Jake's life than his, Aaron was released from his trembling, speechless fear. He yelled, "Keep away, Jake. They put guns on me."

He tried to back away from the Turk and Waite, but they pounced on him and dug into his pockets for the guns. Before they could get the weapons out, four of Johnson's boys were on top of them with submachine guns. The Turk and Waite were battered senseless. Blood was all over the floor; it kept streaming from their mouths and noses as they were dragged out into the alley.

Tony, the manager, said, "Don't worry, Aaron, you'll never see them again."

Aaron, still shaking, said, "Come, Jake."

They went back to the newsstand.

"Jesus, Pa," Jake said, "you could have got killed."

"Never again. No more with the horses."

But Aaron couldn't help following the lives of his horses and jockeys, their trainers and owners. He couldn't close his ears or his mind or his heart, nor could he refuse to give an educated opinion on whom he liked in what race. The lure of gambling finally became too great. It was his spice. It made the juices of his life flow stronger. After all, he wasn't a bum; he didn't covet other women; he never lied or stole or took advantage of anybody; he had never committed an abomination; he was bringing over his mother and younger brother from Russia, which was really honoring his family. All he wanted was the fulfillment of little wire-to-wire dreams. That was not asking too much. It was no more than a little wine to redden the blood, a little schnapps to sharpen his senses.

So he began to keep his small book again. Part time only.

The night Jake decided on going to Northwestern his toes stopped itching. So did his cock. He slept the way he used to sleep.

Next morning at ten Milton B. Morgenstern, president of the Alumni "N" Men's Association, called.

"How about lunch today, Jake?"

Boy, they moved fast and hard.

"Meet me at my office. Eleven South La Salle Street at noon. And save your appetite."

Jake got into what he called his bar mitzvah suit. It was a soft Oxford gray wool which his father's cousin Chaim, the customer peddler, arranged for him to buy in the wholesale clothing district around Maxwell Street, the old ghetto pushcart neighborhood.

"*Krasahvitz,*" his mother said in Russian, chewing him up with love and admiration.

"You'll knock them dead," his sister said.

"When am I gonna get a new suit?" his brother said.

"When hair grows on my palm," his sister, the wit, said. It was a favorite expression of Aaron's. Another one was: "When the Messiah comes."

"That's never," his brother said.

"You're bright today," said Jake. "Well, I'm off."

"Be a gentleman," his mother said. "Don't scrape the plates clean." She took his scrubbed face in her hands and kissed him with a loud juicy smack. "Mmmmmmmmahhhh."

"Be a lady," Jake said. "Leave a leftover."

He bounced out of the gray-stone house and walked up to the El. Riding the Els gave him a window-smudged view of back porches and backyards and garbage-filled alleys and smokestacks polluting the air and drab factories and gasworks; a sense of depression and deprivation and desolation in a time of the jazz baby, fast car rides, a Ferris wheel ride to a star-spangled world.

But he loved the Loop, its massive size, its thick, tall buildings. Downtown meant the Illinois Athletic Club, the Chicago Athletic Association, the rich Jewish Covenant and Standard clubs, and farther up the new Lake Shore Athletic Club. It was where the rich who moved the wheels of the city relaxed, lolled around like Roman emperors in white sheets, and where he lolled around with them, playing George Gershwin and Irving Berlin records on the new orthophonic Victrola and then taking his workouts with Weissmuller and Arne Borg and Albie Karlin and Stubby Kruger and Duke Kahanamoku when he was in town. To Jake, downtown was like a huge temple where the serious work of the world was done, where you had to dress up to get in, where women were balcony observers. Neighborhoods were for sleeping, for fun, fooling around and fucking, but downtown was a man's world. Especially around City Hall, with its brass spittoons all over, and La Salle Street, where the lawyers and the big bankers and the stock-market brokers were. A hectic, driving, power-hungry world. A city always on the make. His town, Chicago. Fuck Palo Alto, California.

Twenty-five floors he rode up a fast stomach-squeezing elevator to Milton B. Morgenstern's office. And there on the glazed door: "Morgenstern & Straus . . . Attorneys-at-Law." A receptionist to announce him. Soft leather easy chairs. Paneled walls. Rich like in the movies. Rich-rich. And then Milton B. himself coming out to greet him with a welcome smile, a hearty two-handed handshake, and ushering him into his paneled office with more leather chairs and lawbooks all over.

Milton B. Morgenstern was a huge man of 250 pounds, with sparse hair, Woodrow Wilson spectacles, pudgy cheeks, heavy-shouldered and heavy-bellied. He had been the first Jew to play football at Northwestern. He had played left guard during the bone-crushing days before the forward pass and end runs were invented. His picture in his old-fashioned dark turtleneck uniform was hung proudly on the wall between his Bachelor of Arts and Law diplomas. He was the Lorenzo de' Medici of Northwestern's athletic world, spiritual father and small bankroller and patron to the pool of talented athletes there. All-American stars were as precious to him as a Cellini or a Botticelli or a Da Vinci. He beamed at you as if you were the perfect son he'd always longed for.

"You finally made up your mind," he said.

"I wasn't approached until yesterday."

Milton B. smiled benignly, lit a cigarette. He handled it as deftly as a magician. "A sneak attack. We played our game right. You won't regret it, Jake. Hungry?"

"Starved."

"What are we waiting for?"

Down the swift stomach-heaving elevator to the bustling lunch-hour street. Over to Meurice's, a Continental restaurant.

"Ah, Mr. Morgenstern." The suave maître d' in a tuxedo greeted them. "Your table is ready. This way, please."

Through the crowded place to a table with a white linen tablecloth and thick linen napkins. Seated, finally. There wasn't a woman in the place. No perfumes. No high voices and shrill giggles. No bullshit.

"You'll like Northwestern. Small. Intimate. Only thirty-five hundred students. You're an individual there. You're not mass-produced like those assembly lines at the state universities. You'll be looked after there. You'll get all the attention you want. You'll be in good hands. Anything you want, any problems, remember, I'm only a phone call away. But you'll have Albie Karlin and the athletic department to look after you. So don't worry about a thing. All you've got to worry about right now is what would you like to eat."

Jake looked at the menu. He was familiar with nothing on it. Beef Bourguignon. Escalope du Veau. Châteaubriand. Sauce Béarnaise. Tournedos. Petits Pois Françaises. Filet of Sole Sauté Belle Meunière.

"What are you going to have?" Jake said.

"How about a good steak? Let's split the châteaubriand."

He looked at the menu. Twelve bucks. Man!

"Yah, sure," he said.

A lanky crew-cut man stepped over. Christ, Jake said to himself, that's Woody Dubcek, former all-American basketball center.

"Woody, I want you to meet Jake Davidson," said Milton B. "Next intercollegiate backstroke champ."

"Glad to know you, I'm sure."

Firm handshake. The clearest, most sincere eyes Jake ever saw. A world of handshakes and sincerity. Woody set up a date to discuss a legal case he had. After he left, Milton B. said, "Fine attorney. With Huebsch, McCullough, and Hauser. Handle some of the biggest corporations in the country. You get out of school, you'll have all the contacts you need. Anything you decide to do, you'll be set up."

Oh, Jesus!

The steak was the finest, juiciest, tenderest Jake had ever eaten. The napoleon was the flakiest, most exotic pastry in the world. He couldn't do what his mother had told him; he licked every morsel, every flake.

Before the meal was over, two businessmen, influential in construction and printing, both clients of Milton B.'s, said hello, and Jake was proudly introduced as the next intercollegiate champ. And then Harrison Cantwell, former all-conference end, came by and said hello. Milton B. knew everybody.

"How's the market performing?" Milton B. said.

"Sky's the limit."

"You think I should cash in on Atwater Kent? I've got a hell of a profit there now."

"Hang on, Milton. I want you to make a real killing."

"It's been split three times already."

"Another time or two won't hurt."

"You're sure?"

"You lawyers are all so conservative. The bulls are stampeding."

"You're the boss."

"I'll call you later. I think you ought to get into RCA, too."

"Kind of high, isn't it?"

"You'll double your money."

After Cantwell left, Milton B. said, "With E. F. Hutton, the biggest. Three years out of college and he's made a fortune in commissions, not counting his positions in the market. There's your future, Jake."

Yep, everybody was making it big. And anything he wanted, it was all his. All he had to do was perform and get through school.

He'd be able to write tickets to heaven. He couldn't wait to get started.

Jake had been so sure he was going to Stanford that summer he'd missed the lifeguard tests for the city beaches and the park systems. The only way he could work as a guard was through political pull. When it came to patronage, Chicago could spot any city in the country a royal flush and still beat it. And Morrie Benjamin, the boss of the twenty-fourth ward, where Jake lived, was its Machiavelli. He made judges, senators, congressmen, mayors, governors; he was in line to make the next President of the United States. He achieved his power by being a benevolent patriarch. The Italians had their godfathers; the Poles and the Irish their saloonkeepers; the Jews had their Morrie Benjamin. Through the precinct cops and the precinct captains, he knew who was in trouble, who was involved in crimes, who his political enemies were, and who was shacked up with whom. He stopped arguments, settled disputes, ministered to the poor, arranged for bail, and put in the fix for criminal offenders. In his ward, nobody was known to starve or to pay a traffic fine. Of course, you hardly ever saw Benjamin. He was involved with the big affairs of state and the big grafts. The person you did see was Maxie Katz. He was Benjamin's sidewalk administrator.

Spring, summer, and fall, weather permitting, Maxie sat outside the brown-brick three-story building on Douglas Boulevard where he lived. He sat on a stoop or on a chair, the sun browning his bald scalp and hairy arms and tough Barbasol-shaved face, and held what was known as his court of lowly affairs. He handled any matter on the precinct level. His payment for this was writing insurance policies for the city and county auto fleets, for which he got $100,000 a year. This was the man Jake had seen two years before, when he had first wanted to work as a lifeguard. And now he had to see Maxie again. Which wasn't difficult. All he had to do was walk by Maxie's building. There he was, holding court, rocking back on his chair, listening intently, with a couple of idle precinct cronies acting as jurors and responsive audience.

A woman with a painted face and mascara tears running down her cheeks, dressed in the oldest, shabbiest clothes she could find, held forth about her heartless landlord who wanted to evict her.

"He's got something against me," she cried.

"What?" Maxie asked. He liked his pound of flesh.

"I don't know what. He's a nut."

"Is it possible your landlord gets complaints about your drinking parties? About your being a whore? They're both illegal, you know."

Maxie knew everything. He loved to sting people with his little barbs of information.

"It's talk, all talk. People making trouble for me."

"Your landlord is a big deal in the Russian *shul*. You're a disgrace to him."

"Listen, I hustle up votes for you, don't I? You don't know how hard I hustle."

"I know, I know. Without your hustling, where would we be? Go home. Pay your rent. I'll talk to your landlord. And be a little discreet when you work."

"Thanks, Maxie." She wiped her eyes. "Come by sometimes. Say hello."

Maxie nodded. He could have show girls, $50 hookers, young ambitious girls on the make; all he needed was this woman and her *nafkehs*. He looked beyond her to Jake, who was next in line.

"Hello, champ. How you doing?"

"Fine, Maxie. Fine."

To his cronies, Maxie explained, "Big swimming champ. Benjamin put in the fix to get his *bubi* and uncle in from Russia." He turned to Jake. "Your grandmother, your uncle, they come from Russia yet?"

"Another week."

"Boy, the wheels we had to grease to get them into the quota."

"We appreciate it, Maxie."

"Be appreciative with your mouth. Tell people about it. A guy like you, you're a champ, you're important people; talk from you goes a long way. So don't keep what we did for you a secret."

"Okay, Maxie, I'll do that."

"What else can I do for you?"

"Maxie, I need a letter from Benjamin again to work as a lifeguard."

"That's no small matter. That's a hundred and twenty-five dollars a month in your pocket."

"I know. I need it. I need it for college."

"Your father hasn't been very good to us."

"Why? He gave you five hundred dollars to get my grandma and uncle in. Wasn't that enough?"

"Money. What the hell is money? It isn't for us; it's for the party. What we need is loyalty, votes. We need bell ringers, mouthpieces. Christ, you're not even old enough to vote yet."

Jake hated to plead, especially in front of Maxie's cronies. Why did these guys always need an audience?

"But I'm a good guard, the best," Jake said. "People are safe in my hands. What do you want, people to drown with any ordinary *shmuck* with political clout?"

"I want Benjamin to bring in the ward one hundred percent every election. Is that asking too much, a hundred percent Jewish vote? Is it too much to ask to show the rest of the world that the Jews are together, that they got a strong voice, that you can count on them?"

Maxie looked to his cronies. Good? he seemed to ask. Am I pleading a just cause? Am I telling this punk good? His cronies nodded, impressed.

"What's all this rigamarole got to do with me?" Jake asked.

"Your father, he's still voting Socialist."

"That's only for Presidents. That's only because he couldn't vote for an anti-Semitic Irish Catholic like Smith. It'd make him sick if he did."

"So he'd be sick for a day. Big deal."

Maxie paused. A few people had gathered to ask for advice or a favor. They listened intently.

Maxie expanded, his voice reaching the larger audience. "Do you realize the *dreck* I have to swallow all day, every day for our people here? Do you realize how me and Morrie Benjamin have to push and shove and wheedle and scrounge with the Irish and the Polacks and the Huns to protect our people, to give them a little piece of the sun? You think me and Benjamin can't get sick from that?"

Two more people stopped by to listen. Christ, Jake thought. Pretty soon he'll have a *minyan,* then a whole congregation; he'll start singing like a cantor.

"You can't trust a man like your father," Maxie said. "He might go communist altogether."

"He voted Democrat for mayor," Jake said weakly.

"He splits his ticket. How can you trust a guy like that?"

Everybody nodded, muttered, "That's right," fortifying Maxie.

"We break our balls to show we're a people to reckon with, and this boy's father splits the ticket. What's he trying to prove, he's a freethinker, he's independent, he's a Talmudic big shot? Who needs guys like that?"

Nods. More "That's right." An additional "You tell him, Maxie."

"What it amounts to is—your father, Jake, is not a loyal, trustworthy man. He has no love for Morrie Benjamin. He doesn't appreciate his good work."

"But he does," Jake said. "He respects Benjamin."

"Let him show it when he votes. Tell him to vote the straight Democratic ticket. Tell him not to bother with the candidates on the whole *ferkockteh* ballot. Tell him just to put an X where it says Democrat. That'll take care of everything. Okay?"

"Okay."

"Next," Maxie said. Jake was dismissed.

But Jake wouldn't leave, not after the beating he took over his father, not after the humiliation he suffered.

"What about the letter from Benjamin?"

"What letter?"

"To get me on as a lifeguard."

"I'll talk to Benjamin. We'll see. Next."

Jake was pushed aside by a street peddler, who started right in with the hard time the cops were giving him on 12th Street for selling ties and wallets outside a haberdashery store.

"Shit," Jake said.

"I heard that, Jake," Maxie said. "You'll have to piss blue for me before I do you a favor."

At dinner that night, Jake said to his father, "Pa, you're a beaut, a real socialistic beaut."

"Now what?"

"I asked Maxie Katz to get me a letter from Benjamin so's I could make some money this summer as a guard. *Nyet.*"

"The bastard. I gave them five hundred dollars for his party."

"It was for Grandma and your kid brother."

"But the money is in their pockets."

"You don't vote right; you split tickets; you're a socialist; you make a fool out of them."

"I voted for their corrupt mayor, didn't I?"

"If there was a socialist on the ticket, you wouldn't of."

"I voted for their governor, didn't I?"

"That's because he's a Jew."

"What's wrong with that?"

"Pa, when you gonna start being a real American? Vote the straight Democratic ticket. They've done nothing but good for us. Got me a lifeguard job when I was fifteen. Got your mother and brother in on the quota. And according to them, it took the President of the United States to swing it. So why don't you forget this socialist crap and play ball like a real American?"

"Jake, you're an opportunist."

"What's that?"

"A man who plays on all sides."

"So what's wrong with that?"

"Jake, you have no integrity."

"Pop, you're really full of the *Forward* tonight. Big words. Ten dollars wholesale."

"Integrity, for your information—"

"I know what integrity is. It's a man with a mule in his head."

"It's a man who is honest, who can't be bought, who—"

"Be careful the mule doesn't kick your brains out, Pa."

"I'll talk to Maxie Katz."

"Don't, Pa. Please do me a favor. Don't."

That's all he needed, his old man to get on his integrity mule with Maxie Katz.

Later, at the JPI, after swimming a fast quarter mile, then kicking a tube for a quarter mile, then pulling the tube another quarter mile, then putting them all together for another quarter mile, he went into the showers to loosen up. Most of the guys were there. They were all set to work as guards that summer.

"Shmuck," they said, "you couldn't decide to go to North-western right away, huh?"

"What's the problem?" said Solly Landon, with his high, husky, whiny voice. He was older than the rest of the guys, a water polo nut, also a man who, with a syndicate, was buying up empty lots outside the Loop and using them as parking lots until they could be sold at a huge profit. In his business he had to have plenty of juice with the police and the political structure of the city.

"Maxie Katz, that shit," Jake said. "He won't get me a letter to the park commission for a lifeguard job."

"Why didn't you come to me, Jake?"

"I didn't think about you. Everything got all twisted up. Really screwed up, I mean."

Solly had a nose that could be used to furrow acres of land. Outside of that he was as hairy as an ape except for his thinning head of hair. He put his hairy arm around Jake under the hot shower.

"Don't worry, Jake. We'll all have a malted afterwards, and then you can go home and get a good night's sleep. Tomorrow afternoon you go to Maxie and he'll have the letter for you. I'll talk to Benjamin personally myself. Okay?"

"Okay."

The next afternoon, sure enough, when Jake stopped before Maxie Katz and his cronies, Maxie had the letter for him. But before he gave it to Jake, he said, "You see, Jake, I hold no grudges. I talked to Benjamin, and he dictated the letter right away, without a moment's hesitation."

There were always people walking up and down Douglas and Independence boulevards. They were the Champs-Élysées of the great West Side of Chicago, where the monumental stone synagogues were located, where the richer Jews lived, where the poorer Jews could enjoy their promenades under the treelined streets. It was where Maxie Katz could always attract an audience.

"Benjamin said, 'I have done nothing but good for the boy and his family. If the man chooses not to back me one hundred percent, that's his God-given right, that's what democracy is all about. The boy is a champion, a credit to his people. We have to take care of our talent, give them the best. Anything I can do for a boy like that, it's a privilege.' That's what Benjamin said. And I say, 'Hooray.'"

The cronies said, "Amen."

A bearded man smelling of horseradish butted in with a traffic ticket. "Some *farshtunkiner* cop gave me this. So I didn't see the light. So I'm a little color-blind. There was no traffic around anyway. Who did it hurt, my going through a light, the bastard?"

Maxie wrote down the man's name, then deliberately, slower than slow motion, tore up the ticket to the music of awesome sighs and wide-eyed admiration. Maxie waved the bearded man away regally. "It's taken care of." Then he turned to Jake. "So what do you say, Jake?"

"Thanks."

"That's all I wanted to hear. See that nobody drowns. Next."

Jake was assigned to Union Park. Siberia. A black neighborhood. Run-down houses. The El running behind it on Lake Street. The produce market on Ogden Avenue nearby. A bronze statue of a cop commemorating the Haymarket Riot of 1886 full of pigeon shit and dog piss. Another statue of the world's fair mayor of 1893, Carter H. Harrison, who lived on Ashland Avenue when it was a high-class neighborhood before he was killed by a lunatic.

"A famous place," his father said.

"Shvartzers," his mother said. "He'll get killed there."

"May Day originated in Chicago," said his father. "Do you know that?"

Big deal, Jake thought.

"He'll get contaminated by the black ones," said his mother.

"They fought for the eight-hour day, to abolish child labor. That's what Union Park means."

"What does that have to do with now?" said his mother.

"History is important. Men were killed and wounded. Four innocent men were hung as murderers."

"According to my history teacher, they were bomb throwers," said Jake.

"Yes, they were anarchists, but all they were guilty of was fighting for the workingman. For that they were executed."

"Why are you so concerned?" said Jake's mother. "You're a small businessman, with horses and everything. So why?"

"I'm still a workingman. I work for a living. I exploit nobody. My bones are with the working people."

"History doesn't pay the rent. Better count your nickels and pennies. Maybe we'll have time to go to a movie. You want to go, Jake?"

"No, I think I'll go to the JPI, maybe see a girl after."

"It's your America," said his father.

"Yep," said Jake. "All mine."

With the history of the working-class movement under his belt, he went to the phone and called Ida. She couldn't see him. She had to get up early for work.

"Work?" he said. "Since when?"

"Since a couple of days ago. I got a job. Secretary for a railroad union. Twenty-five dollars a week. How about that?"

"I got a job, too. Lifeguard. Thirty-two-fifty a week. Let's celebrate."

"How about over the weekend?"

"The weekend is five years away. Now."

"I can't, Jake. I've got my hair to do, some clothes to wash and iron. And I've got to get up early."

"Aw, come on, Ida."

"It's different than going to school. I've got to put in a full day. I've got to be all there all the time. And I've got to look good, too."

Christ, he wanted to be with her. "I won't keep you up late. An hour or so." He began to sing, "If I could be with you one hour tonight. . . ."

"Be a good guy, Jake. Another time."

"Okay. See you."

"When?"

"We'll see."

He hung up. Suddenly his old itch came back. He wanted to get his gun off in the worst way. He called Lila at the College Inn.

"Not tonight, sonny," she said. "I've got too many things going."

Sonny! He could kill her!

"Jake," his mother said, "we're going to the movie. Want to come along?"

"I'll see you, Mom. Have a good time."

The phone rang. It was Ida.

"Don't be mad, Jake."

"I'll be by later. Okay?"

"When later?"

"After I take a workout at the J."

This time she hung up. Shit, he could kill these cunts. He slammed out of the house. At the JPI, outside the lounge, where a hundred Jews were listening to a lecture, he called Ida.

"What do you want me to do, Ida? I don't take a workout, it'll take me a week to get back in shape again. I'll see you in an hour. Okay?"

"You come later, I won't be here."

"Where'll you be?"

"In bed."

"Great. Make it nice and warm."

"You bastard."

He laughed. He was going to have a great time tonight. He took his workout. Came out tingling. Walked on springboards to Ida's house. Felt the blood charging through his arteries like fire hydrants. He sprawled out like Lake Michigan. He zoomed under the bright-mooned sky and whispering trees like a meteor. It was his America. But that night Ida didn't think so. She wouldn't let him touch her. She wanted to talk. She talked about her job, her hopes. She said she was going to find an apartment on the Near North Side as soon as she saved enough money to buy some furniture, as soon as she knew she was becoming indispensable to her boss. She talked about her boss, an Irishman who was once a railroad engineer, with a cute potbelly and a red, cheery face and a great gift of gab. Jake couldn't care less. He listened, his mouth souring at the smells of pickles and smoked fish and herring and relishes on the kitchen table.

"How about we go out, Ida?"

"No. We're going to stay right here. No hanky-panky tonight, Jake."

"I thought we'd celebrate. Maybe go down to the Chocolate Shoppe and have a soda or malted. Maybe, if you could get the car, we could go to the lake. What a night. Sky all creamy with the Milky Way. Fat moon. We could drop into the Big Dipper and say hello."

"Another time, Jake. Tell me about you. Northwestern and all that."

"That's a long time off. Not until the fall. Meanwhile, I'll be talking to my fingers all summer, guarding a bunch of black baboons."

"No."

"Union Park. With a lecture yet from my father on the Haymarket riots."

"He's a communist, your father?"

"No. A socialist."

"What's the difference?"

"Socialists hate communists. You figure it out."

She started talking about furniture and drapes and rugs and how she'd like her apartment to be, and he put his arms around her and tried to kiss her, but she avoided him and said don't over and over, but his prick was very insistent, rubbing against her, and he kept getting hotter at the touch of her rayon dress. He tried to get his hand under her dress, but she kept pulling it away, and then she got angry and said, "That's all you think I'm good for. A little roll in the hay, that's all."

"What's wrong with wanting to kiss you, make love to you?"

"Nothing, if it means anything. Nothing, if there's love behind it. Nothing, if it's serious. But you, Jake, you're a big pig. You have no consideration. You have no interest in me, my happiness, my new job, my wanting to be fresh and on the ball at work and looking my best. All you do is want. But not tonight, Jake. You're going home now. Okay?"

"Okay."

He tried to kiss her, hold her close. She pushed him away.

"Okay," he said. "I get the message. In red neon."

He started out.

"Jake."

He turned around.

"Don't be mad."

"Who's mad?"

"Come here."

He walked over.

"You're such a little boy."

She kissed him, long, hard, deep, her mouth open, her tongue working in his mouth. She squirmed against him. He held her tight, moving against her, tighter and tighter, and he couldn't help himself. He felt himself dive over the moon. His legs caved. He had to hold on.

"Feel better?" she said.

He nodded.

"Now be a good boy and go home."

He nodded, obeyed. First he was called "sonny" by Lila. Now "such a little boy" by Ida. All of a sudden everybody but himself was a million years old.

The house suddenly became a factory of activity. Jake's father put up a mezuzah on the door. He bought candles, shined the menorah and the brass candleholders until it glistened. He ordered all the tableware to be washed and separated for dairy and meat meals. He wanted all the clothes to be hung outdoors, aired and purified.

"You're not a religious man," said Ruchel.

"I go to *shul* on holidays," said Aaron.

"You're a socialist."

"We must show my mother and my brother respect."

In less than a week they were coming from Russia.

"Who knows? They might be in New York already," said Aaron.

"Won't they let you know?"

"Who knows? The bureaucrats."

"They'll let you know," said Jake's sister, Miriam.

"This is the United States," said Jake. "Everything's open. No secrets. We got the telephone and Western Union. And the U.S. Postal Service."

Jake had never seen his father so nervous, nor his mother. You'd think the Messiah was coming.

Every day Jake was wakened early and driven out of the house.

"I don't have to start work till one o'clock," said Jake.

"Go," his father said. "Get out."

"You'll be in the way," said his mother.

His mother and sister scrubbed the bare wooden kitchen floor, the bedroom floors, vacuumed the dining- and living-room rugs until there wasn't a speck of lint or dust. The sinks, the bathtub, the kitchen stove and refrigerator were scoured. The furniture was dusted and polished until it shone. Each morning, before Jake's father left for work, he washed the walls and all the windows. Jake thought he was in a house of mirrors, everything gleamed so. Before he could get into the house, Jake had to take his shoes off. Even his socks weren't clean enough; he had to take them off, too. And the baking: challehs, strudel, sponge cakes, poppy-seed cookies, mondel bread. Jake could put on twenty pounds just smelling all of it.

Then the telegram. The *bubi* and uncle were arriving from New York on Wednesday, July 8, at 2:20 P.M. at the La Salle Street Station.

Aaron's hands shook; his face turned red. "Where is the La Salle Street Station?"

"Downtown," Jake said.

"I know downtown, but where downtown?"

"On La Salle Street."

"Jake, I'm not a fool. Where on La Salle Street?"

Jake looked through the phone book. "La Salle and Van Buren."

"That tells me everything."

"You'll go downtown with him, Jake," his mother said.

"I've got to clean the pool that day."

"You'll be sick that day. You'll go with Papa."

"You'll go, Jake," his father said, a final pronouncement.

"Sure, Pa. I'll go with you."

Then life stopped. As if waiting for an execution. Everybody counting the minutes, the hours, the days. On Wednesday Jake's father was up at five in the morning. He started going over the house like an inspector general, touching the walls, the floors, looking for dust, dirt.

"Aaron, go back to sleep," Jake's mother said. "You're making yourself a nervous wreck."

"Sleep? Who can sleep? Whoever heard of such a luxury?"

"You'll wake up the children."

"He already did," said Jake. "It'll take me a week to make up for this loss of sleep."

Jake got up and had breakfast with his father and mother and sister. For the thousandth time they went over who was going to sleep where.

"Me and Pa in one bedroom," said his mother. "The *bubi* will sleep with Miriam in the other bedroom. Uncle Nachum will sleep with little Harry on the sleeping porch. And you, Jake, on the daybed in the dining room. I don't want any arguments."

"Who's giving you an argument?" said Jake.

"So what will we have for supper tonight?" said Jake's mother.

"Gefilte fish," said Jake's father.

"All right. I have that in the Frigidaire."

"A brisket maybe."

"I'll go to the butcher shop."

"Soup maybe."

"Cabbage soup," Jake said.

"All right, I'll get soup bones and a head of cabbage. Maybe I'll make a *tsimmes.*"

Jake's mouth began to water. He had just finished breakfast, and he was getting hungry again.

"What time do you think we should go to the station, Jake?" asked his father.

It was eight o'clock in the morning, and he was ready to go.

"Be patient," Jake's mother said.

"To be patient, they say, is better than being rich, but right now I'd rather be rich."

"My Spinoza," said Jake's mother.

"I better go to work."

"Sure, Pa," Jake said. "I'll go back to sleep."

"We'll go shopping," Jake's mother said. "Come on, Miriam."

Jake's father left for his newsstand. And Jake went back to sleep. It seemed that he had just dropped off before he was immediately awakened. His mother and sister had come from the grocery store and butcher shop, and their sounds in the kitchen woke him. Just as well. He told Miriam to call his boss at Union Park and say that he wouldn't be able to work today because he had a fever and a sore throat. Then he began to *nosh* around the kitchen.

"Go out, Jake," his mother said. "Leave us alone."

"What the hell will I do out?"

"You're in the way," Miriam said.

"You women, you've always got the monopoly in the kitchen."

"What would you men do without us in the kitchen?" Miriam said.

"Discover America. Invent airplanes and radios. Build automobiles and factories. You want a few more?"

"Take a walk, Jake," his mother said. "We're busy."

He stuffed his mouth with a piece of strudel and went outside and sat on the stone stairs. The morning dragged. He walked down to Douglas Boulevard and saw Morrie Benjamin get into his black Cadillac limousine and drive off to conduct his big affairs of state. He avoided Maxie Katz, who was holding court as usual outside his building, taking care of penny-ante precinct matters.

He walked down to 12th Street, where the streetcars clanged by. The street was always dirty with discarded papers and sawdust and refuse. He passed the dairy store with the tubs of butter and thick cream cheese and sour cream and halvah . . . the sawdust-floored butcher shop with the women crowded around the kosher meat and the bloody chickens hanging from hooks . . . the fruit and vegetable store with baskets of fruit resting on the walk . . . the haberdashery shop for men like his father, who never got downtown and therefore were never really stylishly dressed . . . the Lawndale poolroom and restaurant, where they played cards and took bets on the horses in the back room and where Maxie Katz was a silent partner . . . The Chocolate Shoppe, where they served malteds so thick you couldn't use a straw . . . the Central Park Theater, where they were showing a Clara Bow movie and Al Morey's band was on the stage . . . the shoe repair shop, where you could see the shoemaker at work with his mouthful of nails and his deft hands . . . the barbershop with the guys hanging around reading the newspapers and magazines . . . the cheap five-and-dime store . . . the *shlocky* $2.98 dress shop and then the higher-priced dress shop with Spanish shawls in the window . . . the fish store with the bearded Jew grinding radishes in the window . . . the

bakery with its crisp crusty ryes and pumpernickels and challehs. . . . It was the *shtetl* marketplace on a larger scale. It was,
during the day, a woman's world. Jake felt out of place in it.

When he got home at eleven-thirty, Jake's father was already
there. He'd arranged for the morning man to take over for the
rest of the day.

"Come on, let's eat," said his father. "Then we'll go."

They had a beet borscht left over from the night before and
blintzes with sour cream. Coffee drowned in milk. And poppy-
seed cookies.

"All right, let's go," said his father.

"Pa, it's so early," said Jake. "We'll have to wait around for
hours."

"How long does it take to get there?"

"A half hour, the most."

"Till we get to the streetcar, then we'll have to wait, then who
knows what can happen with those streetcars, we don't have any
time, we better go now."

"Go, go," said Jake's mother. "You'll sit on needles here."

"We won't sit on needles there?" said Jake.

"For God's sake, Jake, go!" said Miriam.

There was no use arguing. "Let's go," said Jake.

Usually Jake's father was a calm, cool, composed man. He
could sit in the living room with his eyes closed and listen for
hours to Yossele Rosenblatt, the great Russian cantor, sing on
the Victrola. On Sunday he could spend forever reading the
Forward; he could promenade down the neighborhood streets or
boulevards as leisurely and dreamily as any *luftmensh.* But today
a demon was in him. He rushed Jake's legs off on the way to the
car line; he paced about, waiting for the streetcar. When it came,
he jumped onto the platform before the car stopped, and he sat
on the edge of the straw seat all the way downtown.

"Seventeen years," he said. "I don't know if I'll recognize my
mother. My little brother, for certain, I won't recognize. Do you
realize, Jake, I left a young man. I didn't even know how to wipe
my nose. You have no idea how ignorant I was. Sure, I spent
from early morning until night in the Talmud Torah. Sure, I
worked from daybreak until nine, ten, eleven at night, learning

to be a carpenter for a ruble or two a week. Sure, I could read and write, I could talk Russian and Polish and Yiddish and Hebrew, but I didn't know what a toilet was. Whoever heard of electricity, who knew about bathtubs and sinks and furnace heat and steam heat and automobiles and the million things we take for granted here? The distance I have traveled. The way life has changed for me. Jake, you don't know. Thank God, you'll never know."

There was a tremor in his father's voice.

"Take it easy, Pa."

"Chagall, the great Jewish artist, he makes the *shtetl* so romantic. Cows jumping over the moon. Fiddlers on rooftops. Colors so gay, so colorful. How romantic could it be, whole families living in one-room hovels and the corrosive stench of urine and human refuse right outside the wooden walls? How romantic when you see Jews with prophets' beards and rags on their emaciated bodies selling pencils and candles and brooms and old buttons and even rusty nails for a pittance? And very romantic when the Cossacks go on a rampage and you see an old Jew with his throat torn out, his face hacked in two."

Jake swallowed hard. He could only listen, the streetcar lurching him against his father, touching him, feeling him close.

"What is most remarkable is that we can tell jokes, we can rise above it all, we can have our Chagalls, our Mischa Elmans and Sholom Aleichems and Yossele Rosenblatts. The human spirit, hah, Jake?"

"Sure, Pa."

They transferred at Clark Street and rode through the deep shadows of the Loop's tall buildings. Jake's father had been downtown only once in his life, when he was sworn in as a citizen in 1921 in the county court building. He looked out on the street as if for the first time, astounded at the huge size of the city.

When they got off the streetcar, his father said, "It's twelve-thirty already."

"Plenty of time."

"How far is the station?"

"Just down the block."

"Hurry."

Noon hour. Lunchtime. It seemed as if the whole world were

out in the street. They pressed through the crowds, were shoved and jostled about. Jake thought his father was going to be hit when one brute of a man pushed him aside and eyed him with his fists clenched. Jake grabbed his father's arm. "Come on, Pa."

"Better watch out," the brute said. "I'll hand him his head."

Jake moved away quickly with his father. That's all they need now on this day, a brawl, a broken jaw.

They finally walked into the La Salle Street Station with its enormous dome ceiling and its vast waiting rooms. The large clock read: 12:35.

"Where will we meet the train?" his father asked.

"I'll find out."

At the information booth they found out that the train from New York would arrive at track ten at two-thirty.

"Where is track ten?"

"Right down there, Pa."

"Come, we'll wait there."

"Plenty of time, Pa."

"What if it arrives early?"

"They don't, Pa. The sign isn't up yet."

Somebody began to announce the arrivals and departures. Jake's father listened intently. The station became a vast hollow chamber, sounds echoing and reechoing. Articulation was lost.

"What did he say?"

"He didn't say New York," Jake said.

"You're sure?"

"Pa, one thing about trains: They don't fool around with schedules."

"All right. We'll wait."

They waited and listened to the announcements of arrivals and departures. Listened to trains steaming and clanging in, chugging and puffing out. They watched people come and go, watched people sleeping on the long wooden benches, other people huddled and waiting. Once Jake's father had to go to the men's room.

"Listen good, Jake. I'll be right back."

When his father settled down near the track again, every time a train was announced he would jump up, and Jake would say, "Not yet."

Finally, the arrival time of the New York train was posted. Jake's father leaped up, paced the floor nervously, then ran to the track opening when he heard "New York" in the garbled announcement. He and Jake peered into the dark tunnels and their endless tracks; then they saw the train, a giant beast of iron with smoking stacks and hissing wheels and one huge blinding light heaving itself in, and they ran out on the platform. People got out of the cars and were greeted by relatives or friends or went on their way alone. Jake and his father jumped from one car to the next, darting in and out of passengers.

"How will I know them? It's been so long."

They scurried about, looking, searching. Jake thought his eyeballs would fall out. He didn't even know whom he was looking for.

"Jake! Jake! They're here! Over here!"

There they were! A small, frail gray-haired old lady, with a black babushka and wrinkled cheeks and puckered mouth and no teeth and a black skirt billowed to the ground under piles of petticoats, and a short, thin-chested, narrow-shouldered black-haired man in his twenties, with a bony, emaciated face, wearing broad comic pants three inches above his ankles and a rough belted jacket and smiling with gold crowns on some of his teeth. There they were with straw hampers and one horsehide hand-made suitcase tightly strapped. There they were with pale winter on their faces and spring in their hearts, wearing garlic cloves around their necks to prevent their catching cold and influenza. There they were, finally, happy, emotional, teary, with Jake almost keeling over from the reek of garlic and stumbling backward from Uncle Nachum's kiss right on his mouth, these goddamn old country Jews always kissing right on the mouth. Uncle Nachum backed away from Jake and said with a high, giggly laugh, "Look at him, a Cossack."

Bubi kept weeping and smiling toothlessly, calling him and his father, *"Tahteh, tahteh,"* making sounds in her throat and gesturing how magnificent Jake and his father looked. She was overwhelmed and couldn't express the joy in her heart except with tears. Jake grabbed the suitcase; it weighed a ton; he couldn't understand how Uncle Nachum, a big 110 pounds maybe, with the comic suit and the high, girlish laugh, had been able to handle it. His father grabbed one of the straw hampers; it seemed to weigh a ton, too. And Jake couldn't figure how these two little people had lugged all this luggage halfway around the world.

"How'd you do it?" Jake asked.

Uncle Nachum broke into peels of shrill laughter. "With *tochis*. Lots of *tochis*."

A *quip* off his father's block.

They crowded into a Checker cab (Jake's father thought Yellow Cabs were scab vehicles because of a strike years ago). Bubi's face broadened with smiles; she was like a child, her first time in an automobile. Uncle Nachum said in English, "Sport." It sounded very funny. Then he said, "American *goniff*." Everybody laughed. Even Bubi.

"She hears," Jake said.

"No, she sees; she knows what's going on," Nachum said.

"But I heard her talk. *Tahteh*. Father. I heard her."

"That's all. It's the only word."

"How did it happen?"

"Scarlet fever. When she was sixteen. Right after she was married."

"She raised all her children like that?"

"Like that."

Jake watched her smile, in her face the wonder of the city, the childish joy of the ride, the security of being with her older son. He looked at Nachum, wriggling comfortably into the soft leather seat.

"A big city," Nachum said. "Powerful. Wonderful. America."

His father leaned back and sighed. He was an accomplished man. In bringing over his mother and younger brother he had fulfilled a promise.

When they got home, Jake's mother wanted to fill their bellies with food; they must be hungry, thirsty. But Nachum said, "Later, later." He had things for them. He opened the hampers and the suitcase. In the suitcase were cobbler's hammers, knives, lasts, needles, balls of waxed thread. "Maybe for business later."

Then he pulled out some heavy leather belts which he had made for the men and little Harry and soft leather belts for Jake's mother and Miriam. Then he proudly handed everybody a pair of soft handcrafted slippers. "For around the house," he explained.

Little Harry broke up the solemnity by yelling, "Jesus, the belt and shoes are for giants."

Then from the hampers filled with old clothes and piles of petticoats, Bubi brought out a pair of antique *Shabbes* candleholders, then an old smoothly polished samovar and some heavy copper cooking pots. Which overwhelmed Jake's mother. Suddenly Jake's father snapped his fingers and said, "I'll be right back."

"Where you going?" Jake's mother said. "You just got here."

"Show Nachum and Mama where they'll sleep. Make them at home. I'll be right back."

And he rushed out, leaving everybody openmouthed. What could you expect? He was crazy all that day.

When he came back later, he had a big bouquet of flowers. Everybody, even Jake, wound up with tears in their eyes.

Friday eve. *Shabbes.* Bubi brought out the brass candleholders she'd brought and lit the candles. She moved her lips in prayer, the babushka on her head shadowing her pale, wrinkled face; then she moved away with a big, benign smile. Jake remembered his mother doing that when he was a kid. How warm the house felt; how the chicken and challeh and cakes smelled; how clean everything was.

His father looked at Nachum as if he were looking into a mirror of himself when he had come over: so emaciated, thin-chested, consumptive-looking, with legs like a scarecrow. His mother looked at Bubi with the long skirts and the shawl always over her head and couldn't believe that long ago she looked like a healthier younger version of her mother-in-law. In a decade Jake's mother had lost thousands of years of repression and ritual behavior and was part of the revolution in America in manners and style, if not in morals, with bobbed hair, lipstick, powder, rouge, and short skirts, emancipated by the phone, the laundry, vacuum sweepers, hot and cold running water, the bathtub instead of the *mikveh.* If Bubi could talk, she'd say that Jake's mother was all painted up like a wild Indian.

Bubi talked with guttural sounds, her hands, broad facial

expressions, her gray eyes, and her heart. It was all elemental, direct, with no lies, no evasions or subtleties. She was a primitive who was still afraid of the toilet; you had to flush it for her every time she used it; the rush of water terrified her. She couldn't get used to the sinks and didn't think she'd ever learn how to use the gas stove. But the luxury of the bathtub was beyond expression; so was being able to walk on rugs and smooth wooden floors instead of on earth.

The apartment was so big and light compared to the little huts she lived in, she thought her Aaron was a baronial landowner. Nachum giggled over the wonders of America, the Victrola, the gadgets, the space of the apartment, the numerous automobiles on the streets, the pantry full of food, the refrigerator full of more food. It was all milk and honey, raisins and almonds. America, America.

Friday evening. Gefilte fish, throat-grabbing horseradish, hot soup with kreplach, crisp-skinned roast chicken, roast potatoes, peas, challeh, tea with strudel. A meal fit for kings. Then the kitchen table, where they ate, was cleared, and preparations were made to receive the *mishpocheh,* the relatives. A crisp white tablecloth was spread over the dining table under the stained glass chandelier. Decanters of wine and schnapps were placed on the table, plates of chopped liver and marinated herring, challehs, bowls of fruits and nuts and raisins and dates, cakes and strudels. The samovar brewed tea; the coffeepot perked coffee. Rogers silverware was taken out of the built-in walnut cabinet, and dishes out of the leaded glass cupboards. Walnut pillars divided the dining room from the living room, where the mohair furniture stood on an imitation Oriental rug. Off to one corner stood the pride of Jake's father: the mahogany Victrola he had made when he was a skilled carpenter. Everything was ready now for the festive occasion.

The relatives and the *landsleit* came over that night (and other nights) to welcome Nachum and Bubi, to hear what had happened in their town since they'd left it. Nachum held court. Bubi was silent, graceful, and proud.

Uncle Hymie, the rich laundry owner, with his blinking eyes and red cheeks, smashed out his cigarettes after a puff or two, with Aunt Riva, his wife, beside him in diamonds and gold. Uncle Getzel, the fruit peddler, who'd lost his trade as a harness maker because of the automobile, snatched the butts and smoked them down to his fingertips. "One thing about the rich," he said sarcastically, "they always give you a token of charity, even if it's only the remains of a cigarette." The lights of the chandelier glanced off Uncle Itzik's high forehead; he was a frustrated actor and poet, the Café Royal on 12th Street his Crimean spa, but he worked for Uncle Hymie as a laundry sorter, which gave him ulcers; he, too, smoked the leftover butts and pulled at his earlobes and hawklike nose, a regular Paul Muni. Their wives, Aunt Zipporah and Aunt Mascha, sighed and squirmed in their black dresses and tight corsets.

The cousins, who had started life in America selling brooms and rags, had a corner on the customer peddler market. Some of the *landsleit* had done well, too; some not so well. They were all members of the same *verein*, the same *shul*. The rich ones had lent Jake's father the money to bring over Nachum and Bubi: the $1,000 bonds he had to put up to the government in case they became public charges; the graft he had to pay politicians to get them into the quota; the money for living expenses and transportation, which he paid off at heavy interest rates. The rich made everything possible at a price. But the richest man in the house was Nachum; he was the center of attention, high comic pants, giggly laugh, impoverished. All of them had relatives in Russia, friends they'd left behind, remembrances. Nachum brought them up to date on everybody. Of Jake's mother's two brothers: One was a captain in the Red Army, the other a commissar. They'd been soldiers in the Czar's army, and they'd joined Budenny and fought the Whites and became heroes. Jews, heroes, yes. Nachum warmed up. Told stories of heroes and cowards and tyrants and betrayals, of the years of Civil War, the pogroms, the Jews who formed defense corps and kept their people from being demolished. He told about the mujiks who killed their cattle and horses and sheep, destroyed their crops, rather than give them up to the Bolsheviks. It was a topsy-turvy time. Starvation, disease, death by the bayonet and the gun. Twenty-five million people, they say, died in the Civil War.

No! Not even the *Forward* had a figure like that.

Yes, you could believe him, he was there, Nachum said.

Still anti-Semitism?

"You think you can wipe out anti-Semitism in a decade?" Nachum said. "The Soviets say no more anti-Semitism, it's against the law. The Cossacks, the *goyim,* the kulaks, the mujiks, they can't hear, they can't read. They still say we use their blood in matzohs, we killed their Christ, we are the cause of all the world's calamities. One day a Soviet commissar came to take the gold from the Orthodox church. The mujiks said they'd kill all the Jews if the Soviets did. It's against the law, the Soviets said. The mujiks said we'll kill them anyway. The Soviets said so go kill, we need the gold. Remember Leah, Schneiderman's daughter? Six months pregnant. Ripped open in the stomach with a bayonet. Remember Label, the hunchback, his head chopped off with a sword. Mendel, the *shamus,* was tied to a horse and dragged over the streets until he died. Naomi, the seamstress, was raped until she went insane."

"Enough, Nachum."

"And here, you have anti-Semitism here?"

"Not like there."

They *noshed* and drank, but the conversation always reverted to Narodichi. The bones, the souls, the dreams of the people in the house were still there. The *mishpocheh* and *landsleit* missed the way they used to huddle together so closely, missed their common joys and tragedies, missed the sight of rye and wheat fields, of growing vegetables and fruit trees, of the weekly gatherings at the market. They still felt like strangers here, so dispersed, even the allrightniks. They sat around Nachum and asked questions, evoking memories of the past, good and bad, seeking justification and absolution of their guilt in leaving relatives behind, wanting to be assured that they had a far better life here than if they'd stayed to suffer under the Reds.

They listened to Nachum, his tales of fear and heroism and blood. They sat and rocked and sighed heavily. That was life. Broken hearts and fear, mixed up with a few brief moments of happiness. Was this what people came into the world to endure? Was this man's fate?

Jake's father smiled wryly, then said, "Life isn't exactly a *kazatchka* and a glass of tea."
Everybody laughed.
Hoo-ha!

The summer went slowly. Nachum enrolled in summer school to learn English. He couldn't wait to get into business. One day he took a walk down 12th Street and stopped in at the shoemaker and landed a job there. Oh, happy man. Oh, wonderful America.
Bubi soon learned the wonders of the toilet, hot and cold running water, the magic of electricity and the gas stove. She divested herself of the thousands of years of ritual behavior, except for the shawl on her head and the prayers before the lit candles on Friday eve. She was always a child, no older, really, than when she had been afflicted as a young girl. Jake marveled at how she could have lived her life without hearing or speaking, absorbing the world with her eyes, sitting contentedly for hours. She was like a warm dog, happy to be around people; she was eager to be helpful; you could feel how close she held everybody in her heart.
Oh, Bubi, Bubi.
The summer dragged on. Jake couldn't wait to get to college. Neither could the guys from the JPI when he saw them. Occasionally, on his day off, he'd go out to the beach and see Albie Karlin and ask him what it was going to be like. And Albie, in his laconic way, would say, "Don't worry."
Milton B. Morgenstern called him from time to time to ask how he was doing and was he ready for the big event, the event that would shape his whole future, and he'd say he couldn't wait.
"We're depending on you, Jake. We're counting on you. Keep in touch."
He'd see Sean H. Fitzgerald at the JPI and say, "Sean, you went to college. What was it like?"
"Tough," Sean said. "Working, studying, nobody to look out for me, to pave the way, to point me in the right direction. But you've got nothing to worry about, Jake." He'd sit there in his roach-ridden office, leaning back in his swivel chair, his enor-

mous cock and balls spread over his thick thighs, and pontificate. "You've proven you're a winner; you've got guts. You've proven you've got great discipline. Once you set out to do something you succeed. That's what you've proven. That's why you're getting the cushions, the free ride, the right people to look after you. For you, college will be a breeze. And I'll be proud of you. Somebody else will take the glory, but we know who made you, and I'll be proud of you." Sean's eyes got misty, and he turned away. Jake nodded and walked out and plunged into the pool; he almost felt like crying.

At Union Park, they ran forty-five-minute swims. In fifteen minutes, eight hundred people would have to get dry, dressed, and out. Then another raging, pushing, elbowing crowd of black and white people would rush in, grabbing the thin towels and cotton trunks that were flung at them by the attendants, and they'd charge into the pool, yelling and screaming and splashing and slamming into each other. It reminded Jake of when he was a kid and had first started at the pools. He'd sit on the packed benches, waiting, sweating, suffocating from the crush of hot, sticky bodies against him; then they'd pile into the wet lockers and they'd be herded through the showers like animals, and finally, he'd be out in the open, smashing into the water as if it were going to save his life.

The cement pool, shaped in a figure eight, was eighty yards long and forty yards wide. Water was changed once a week. On the first day of fresh water everybody who hit the pool would yell, "Ice!" Toward the fourth day, when the sun had heated the water and the dirt in it hung like cobwebs, everybody would yell, "Piss!" It never varied.

There were separate days for men and women. Ninety percent of the attendance was black. You could hardly see their bodies under water. All you could see was their waxy yellow palms and the bottoms of their feet. You couldn't watch them all. You looked over the water generally and with a sixth sense knew when somebody was in trouble, and Jake, his adrenaline pumping, would smash in, grab the drowning person in a cross-chest carry, and pull him in. It was nothing to make four, five jumps a day.

It was the most boring job in the world. You stood or sat in your lifeguard suit and wooden clogs, the sun beating down on you, the screams and yells pounding in your ears, your eyes becoming glassy, your own ear tuned for the odd cry, the drowning gasp, the terrified shout. You watched the Negroes do the tap Charleston, stroll around with fuck-you insolence, do their ghetto cock-stroking, cunt-fingering cakewalks and boogie shuffles, and you'd listen to their blues and their infectious laughter. Out of sheer boredom, when everybody was out of the pool and getting dried and dressed in the wooden lockers, where four, five kids and adolescents would be crowded in, Jake and Biff Hanson and Willie O. Grubitsky, the other two guards, would get the keys from the attendants and raid the lockers. They'd find young asshole bandits shoving it into little kids, perverts sucking cocks, and a good deal of gang masturbation. They'd haul them into the towel room and pretend they were calling the cops, and the young kids and adolescents would cry and say they'd never do it again, and they'd beg to be let go, and then, when the next screaming, pounding, shoving horde was let in, Jake and the other guards would leave, and the kids who were caught would start yelling, "What do we do, what do we do?" And Jake'd say, "Beat it."

He'd have wound up in the mumbly-jumbly ward at County Hospital that summer if it weren't for that and if it weren't for Willie O., who had been the Charleston champ of the neighborhood. He had won all the contests at the Central Park Theater and the Paradise Ballroom, had traveled to other parts of the city and won the contests there. He was a big, lumbering fat young man with thick, horn-rimmed glasses, thinning hair, squinty eyes, and a heavy beak. He looked like a worried walrus. But he was light on his feet, he had a booming voice, he had rhythm; wherever he went he drew all attention to himself and he had *chutzpah*. He had been a plunging champ because of his blubber when plunging was an event. He came into his own when the Charleston was at its height. The fast, light-footed slim-jims were interchangeable in the contests. But when Willie O. came on to "Georgia Brown" or "Charleston" or "Running Wild," he was at once unique. Everybody was amazed at the way he could move. The audience would applaud as he worked into a sweat, would urge him on, "Oh, you Fat! Do it, Fat. Ha-cha-cha-cha-

cha-cha!" And then he'd lay them in the aisles when he jumped into the air and fell on his belly, his glasses flying off his face, his funny collegiate hat skimming away. The audience would scream with laughter, pee in their pants, watching him fumble for his glasses and hat and then finish his act in a frenzy, with mouth open and slobbering, arms flinging wildly, legs kicking furiously. How could you beat a performance like that?

Now the Charleston days were over, but he remembered the applause, the laughter, the attention; he wanted to be a star comic. All day long he worked on putting his act together. Funny he could look. But you had to back it up with more funny: jokes, sketches, imitations, routines. Steal from everybody until funny is part of your skin, until it's you funny, unmistakably your trademark, nobody else's. He studied everybody: Smith and Dale, Milton Berle, Jack Benny, Fred Allen, George Givot, the Marx Brothers, Joe E. Lewis, Lou Holtz, George Burns and Gracie Allen; the burlesque clowns; even the second-rate acts at the outlying theaters. He got lucky the past year. An agent in Chicago sent him out on the road. Peoria, Kenosha, Fargo, Little Rock, Waukegan, Davenport.

"All the big toilet towns," he said, "where you get up before a bunch of drunks and hicks and I-don't-get-it Americans; you perform to the walls. You hit a strip joint, and the guys jerking off under their newspapers are giving you that vacant dummy look like what the hell is that fat slob doing here, bring on the girls. You can really sharpen an act up there, huh? So I went to New York with the fox and lox crowd, the bagel benders, the *shleppers,* to hook an agent. Agent, that's a word for drop dead. Guys like you we got by the ton, they said. Punsters. So I'm back making a living, working as a lifeguard. Hoo-ha!" Then out of some insane despair he suddenly jumped out of his suit one day and yelled to all the astonished Negroes in the pool, "Hey, baby, dig this white ass! Glom this white meat!" And he did a running dive into the air, his fat, heavy body and his jong hanging there a moment, his legs already kicking the crawl kick, and then he plunged through the water and started doing a funny drowning act and rescuing himself and almost tearing his head off doing it.

"Oh, you fat bastard!"

"Oh, that funny!"

Give him a swimming pool in a theater, a bunch of black baboons without a pot to piss in, and he could give them ruptures and coronaries laughing, the bastards. "I've got to find my style," he said. "My métier, my ambience. Fancy French words I picked up on the dirty sidewalks of New York. Which means a nice big tit to suck on." With that he gave Jake his Rudolph Valentino faggot matinee idol look. He looked like a Turkish pimp. Jake broke up laughing.

"Boy, if you were only Louis B. Mayer," Willie O. said.

Each day Fat Willie O. would come to work and try his new *schticks*. He was trying to develop a machine-gun delivery, but his tongue was too thick for his mouth. He bought a small-brimmed pearl gray Borsalino, which he perched, brim up, on his head. He tried to spin it around his head, and it always fell off.

"That's funny," Jake said.

"I'm a clumsy shit, you mean."

"You go out onstage with the lifeguard suit and the hat and the wooden clogs, you'll kill them."

Willie O. said, "Why aren't you Jack Warner or Sam Goldwyn?"

One Sunday night there was an amateur talent contest at the Harding Theater on the Northwest Side.

"Jake, you've got to come with me."

"My day off, Fat. I thought I'd see a girl."

"Do me a favor. I'll pay your way in. The joint'll be full of Polacks. They could hand me my head. Be a pal, will you?"

Jake couldn't refuse. They rode up together on a streetcar with Willie O. picking his cuticles, rubbing his fleshy nose, scratching his balls, mopping the sweat off his face and glasses.

"You'll murder them, Fat."

"Polacks. Yuch. Give them a Jew and a whip, and they know what to do. But a joke—how the fuck can you tell a joke with a language full of x,y,z's?"

"They'll look at you and they'll die."

"I want you to laugh, Jake. Roll out in the aisles. Laugh till your sides split. Maybe you'll get another Polack laughing. And that'll get another."

He jumped up from his seat, the tension exploding from him.

He twirled his funny hat. People looked at him as if he were crazy.

"Ladies and germs, a tube of toothpaste!" He started squeezing his sides and blowing out his cheeks, and then spit began to dribble out of his mouth. Then: "A teakettle boiling up!" He started bouncing up and down and hissing like steam. He walked over to two men sitting together. "You two guys, enough holding hands. You think this is a fruit market?" To another man in a double-breasted suit: "You look like an exhibitionist." To everybody in the car, explaining: "Those long double-breasted jackets are for guys who like to flash their hidden jewels."

Meshugeh. The man was flipping out.

"Gevalt, Jake!" Fat yelled, grabbing Jake and pulling him to get off the car. *"Mi shlogt Yidden!* [They're beating up Jews!]" They jumped off.

"You scared the shit out of me, Fat."

Fat doubled up with laughter.

"Fat, you want to make people laugh, not scare the shit out of them."

"I'd rather see them squirm than laugh," he said when he stopped laughing. "You know something? Everybody thinks a fat man is a jolly old ho-ho-ho. Well, I'm not. I've always taken a beating. I'm fat, I'm four-eyed, I'm ugly, and I'm Jewish; the only thing I've got going for me is that I'm not black, too." He looked at Jake for a response. "That last bit, I tried to turn it into a joke."

"It's not funny, Fat."

He considered it a moment. "You're right. Sometimes I don't know serious from funny. So I'm fumbling around. I've got to find the right collage for me, another fancy French word I picked up in the ptomaine joints in New York. If I can give it to them in the *kishkes,* the guts, twist it a little bit, and make them laugh, that's me."

"You'll get it, Fat. Champion plunger, champion comic."

Like all the Balaban and Katz theaters, the Harding was dedicated to giving the masses a feeling of entering sultan's palaces, of flying on magic carpets, of being transported to the richest and most stupendous experience in the world, lavish beyond dreams. Its rococo interiors were sometimes more breathtaking, in the worst possible taste, than the extravaganzas on screen and stage. It went with the colossal Cecil B. De Mille types of productions with casts of thousands.

Jake went to the stage entrance with Fat and watched the sweat drip from his forehead as he blustered his name out, "Willie O. Jackson." That was his stage name. The sweat around his itchy pubic area must have been awful inside his jockstrap. He wore one because once, during a Charleston contest, when he jumped up and dived onto his belly he got so excited when the crowd roared with laughter that he got an erection. He kept shifting his parts around and feeling the buttons of his pants to see that they were all buttoned. Then he started shining his patent leather shoes against the backs of his pants and whirling his Borsalino and tap dancing and shuffling among the other nervous contestants, asking each one with the haughty finesse of an Oliver Hardy, "And who, pray tell, are you?" Cracking them up. He did everything but vomit.

Jake left when the contest began. He sat down amid the gum-chewing, candy-eating, lip-smacking audience. It smelled of five-and-dime perfume and powders, of sweat-dampened shirts and underwear, of old socks and hair tonics and shaving lotions, of wintergreen mints and nutty brittles and buttery popcorn and sweet chocolate. Jake got hungry. He sat through a rendition of an Italian tenor singing "Sorrento." The singer got a lot of yawns, a scattering of polite applause, a few Polack farts through the mouth, and somebody yelling, "Wait'll his *goombah* Capone hears this!" He sounded off like a machine gun.

The next act was an eight-year-old girl right out of an elocution course doing "Sleepy Time Gal" with gestures; then she finished off with a tap dance to "Me and My Shadow"— everybody was studying tap dancing and saxophone those days. Her family applauded till their hands hurt. Somebody yelled, "What, no belly dancers?"

A belly dancer didn't come out, but a Valentino did with a sultry, black-haired, hot-blooded Latin dancer in a swirling red skirt and a red flower in her hair, and they tangoed around. The hot-looking woman who wore sheer flesh-colored stockings that you could see right up to her tight whorish black panties when she was whirled about got whistles and cheers and a lot of foot stomping.

A professional juggler held the audience spellbound. Then two acrobats brought the house down. They were tough acts to follow. Fat came up next. He swaggered out in his basic black suit, black bow tie with white polka dots jiggling at his Adam's apple, a gleaming white shirt with a long, loose collar, patent-leather shoes, and the pearl gray Borsalino with the turned-up brim. He came out hoping for a laugh just at his appearance. He was stoned with silence. Sweat bubbled out of his damp face. He signaled the band behind him, which went into an introduction to the toreador song from *Carmen*. He bellowed: "El Toreadoro, don't spit on the floor-a, use the cuspidor-a . . ." then stopped.

"I give you Stanislaus Zbyszko."

He jumped into a wrestling pose, imitating the former world's wrestling champion. No laughs. Just Polack dumbfoundedness.

"It's okay, okay. I just wanted to wake you up."

Another bomb. Jake laughed. He was the only one. It embarrassed him.

Snarling bullets out of his machine-gun mouth, Fat started a routine, "This is the most exciting day for the Northwest Side since Kosciuszko was put on his bronze horse in Humboldt Park."

They stared at him. Jake started to sweat with Fat.

"Ring-a-ding-ding. I wanna tell you—a welcome like this—you can't buy it with all the savings stamps in the world."

Only Jake applauded and laughed. He felt as lonely as Fat up on the stage, sweating his bullets away. Another person clapped in the balcony. Fat leaned over, peering through his thick glasses, and blistered Jake, "You, get together with the guy up there. You make a great team. You could open up a fruit market."

Plop. Another dud.

"I want you to know out there, you're shooting great pocket pool. The greatest." Then, spreading his legs and drawing two imaginary guns out, ready for the last shoot-out, he boomed, "All right, everybody with their hands out of their pockets, hands up high so's I can see 'em."

Oh, boy! Nothing! Fat made a loose, whirling, idiotic gesture with his forefinger as if they were all whacked out from jerking off. Then he twirled his hat. It fell off his head. He tried to bend down to pick it up but pretended he couldn't. He fell to his knees and crawled over to the hat, scooped it up, got up laboriously, wiped it fastidiously with his elbow like Oliver Hardy, then perched it on his head and tried to spin it again. This time he caught it before it fell. A few laughs.

"What'd you expect, Indian clubs?" He stepped over to the bandleader. "I want a hand for the best bandleader in the world . . . who shouldn't be in the business . . . Guy Lombardo!"

Applause but no laughter.

"Turn in your piccolo. You're through."

The bandleader smiled; the guys in the orchestra laughed. They were getting him. Fat played to them. "He's sharp as a tennis ball. He's so bright, he went downtown with his mother once and thought the Wrigley Building was a Polish wedding cake and he cried, 'Ma, get it for my bar mitzvah.'"

The word "Polish" got a few laughs.

"Chi muvish po Polsku?"

Applause. Cheers.

"There were these two Poles from Chicago vacationing in Miami Beach. Partners in the butcher business. They loved it there. Stash, the brain of the partnership, the eloquent one, says, 'How about we spend the rest of our lives here?'

"'How could we do it?' says Casimir.

"' We buy a theater. We put in a hundred-piece orchestra and thirty dancing girls, naked. Then I go up there and have a party with every one of the girls.'

"'On the stage?'

"'Where else? We'll make a fortune.' "

Some women are tittering, some men are laughing, and Jake is holding his belly.

"So they sell the stockyards they own and go into show business in Miami. They spend a ton for a theater, publicity, promotion, the talent. Opening night, crowds are lined up for blocks, people are fighting to get in, the house is packed, standing room only. The orchestra starts up; the girls dance out; they throw their dreamy jewels around; then the main event.

Stash comes out, ready for action. So are the girls. He looks them over. Picks one. A superb performance. Another. Spectacular. Another. Stupendous. Still another. Fantastic. And boom! He caves in, falls flat on his face; he has to be carried out.

"The audience yells. Want their money back. The curtain goes down. The orchestra stops playing. The girls prance off to the dressing room. And Casimir, poor Casimir, everything down the drain, he faces Stash and he says, 'What happened, Stash? What happened?' And Stash says, 'I don't know. It went perfect during rehearsal this afternoon.'"

A few chuckles. A lot of I-don't-get-it. A vast bust. Jake thought he'd *plotz*. He stomped the floor; a few drops of urine dribbled into his shorts. The guy next to him said, "What's funny?"

"He laid all thirty of them in the afternoon!" It was loud enough for the whole orchestra section to hear.

Fat leaned over and said, "Thanks, buddy. Next birthday you get the Gold Coast for a present. . . . A little music, maestro."

He started shuffling around, looking like a light-footed hippo. Started a patter. "What an audience. Doing everything you can for my career. Trying to stop it before it starts. . . . I took my girl to the Drake the other night. They sell the moonlight by the yard there. You get waterlogged from the sound of the lake." He segued into the *shtick* of twirling his hat again and continued his patter. "Consider the jockstrap, if you please. Or the heart of the matter." The audience was dumbfounded. "Women call it the chastity belt; men call it the cup that doesn't brimmeth over. It's a bra for women, a tight crunch for men. Worse thing is to tighten it around your fun bone. Could make you a sad sack all your life."

He was getting nowhere. He signaled the bandleader. The band went into "Georgia Brown," and Fat stunned the audience with his fast footwork, his swinging arms, his shattering stomps. He mixed it up with some double toddles. And then his big finish, diving into the air and landing on his belly. He astonished the audience, did it again, again, going wild, and finally the applause came.

But when all the contestants came out to be judged by the audience's applause, Fat got third, $10. He twirled his hat, did a jig step, and fell on his belly to laughter and applause when he was announced, but the juggler and the acrobats beat him out.

"What can you expect from the dumb Polacks?" he said afterward as he treated Jake to a banana split at the Chocolate Shoppe. "Action, that's all they want. Indian clubs. Double somersaults. If there'd been a dog act, I'd have run out of the money."

Otherwise, the summer was a big bore. Even Fat, trying out *shticks* around the pool, got to be a drag. He expected Jake to react and laugh at every trick, every joke he stole or made up, but he didn't.

"Hey, Joe College," Fat snarled, "you getting too sophisticated for me?"

Jake didn't know how to answer him.

"Someday I'll kill 'em all.' Boff 'em, murder 'em, give 'em convulsions, lay 'em in the aisles, bury 'em."

Jake began to laugh.

"What's funny?"

"You talk like you're having a shoot-out with the audience."

"I am. Every time. Me against them. But I love 'em, the bastards . . . when they laugh."

Jake was glad to be getting out of the house. With Bubi and Nachum there it was a battle every morning to get into the bathroom. Every time he moved he bumped into somebody. There was no elbowroom at the supper table in the kitchen when he ate at home on his days off. He had no closet or chest of drawers of his own. His clothes seemed to be everywhere, mostly in the front hall closet with the mothballed winter clothes and in a small chest his father had built and installed there. Everything he wore always seemed to smell of mothballs.

"You'll go outside, it'll air out," his mother said.

He had money. He kept buying things he'd need at college. Plaid socks, loud and red, the new rage. Cordovan leather shoes. Shorts and tops, no more BVDs. Stiff yellow corduroy pants, which he kept washing to soften them up.

"What kind of style is corduroy pants?" his mother asked. "It's for bums."

"It's the big thing at college."

"You'll make them look old before you put them on."

"Ma, if they were twenty years old and worn down to nothing, they'd be worth ten thousand dollars."

"It's madness."

Nachum, the generous sport, presented his handmade horsehide suitcase to Jake. That's all he needed. Even empty, he'd get a rupture carrying it. He bought his own suitcase, elegant-looking, of golden pigskin. It was called a valise; it was a thing he wouldn't be ashamed of.

Nachum said, "You don't like my suitcase?"

"Sure I like it, Nachum. But this is for the rest of my life. You'll need yours someday."

"Yuch," his mother said. "Pigskin. It's *traif.*"

"Ma, I'm not eating it."

"He's growing up to be a *goy,*" said Nachum.

Jake was glad Bubi could say nothing. She looked on and she smiled. As long as there was talk, no angry faces, no yelling, all was well and harmonious.

"In Spain you do what the Spanish do," said his father. "In France you make adjustments to the French. In China, even, you bend to the Chinese ways. Why should a Jew in America be an exception?"

"You tell them, Pa."

Labor Day. He was through with his job. He was ready to leave. He was all packed.

Time dragged on endlessly. He found himself rummaging through the suitcase for clothes to wear. Christ, before he'd leave, everything'd be dirty again.

"When is the laundry man coming?"

"He just came," his mother said.

"I'll be out of clothes. I won't have anything to take with me."

"You worry too much, Jake."

"What else have I got to do? I'm waiting. I'm going out of my mind."

"Go to the JPI. Go see a girl. Go do something."

The JPI was his only escape. All the other guys who were going to Illinois were jumping out of their skins, too. Does anything ever happen on time?

Lala and Bo, the two fucking hoodlums, laughed at Jake and the others.

"Collegians. You guys bury yourselves in the books, we'll make the money. You want a handout, we'll be there."

Fat Willie O. came around, waggled his heavy walrus ass, pantomimed a pansy taking off for college. Lala and Bo doubled up with laughter. Lala, who was a manic-depressive, now on the manic side, pranced around with Fat. Naked, with their balls and jongs bouncing around, they looked ridiculous. They wound up smack against each other in a waltz dip and toppled into the pool. They came up *spritzing* water at the future collegians and singing, "Collegiate, collegiate, nothing intermejiate. . . ." Laughter boomed off the wet walls. The roaches scurried for cover.

Sean H. Fitzgerald, with an amused smile, said, "Pay no attention. They're only jealous."

For the next two weeks, time took a holiday. Jake had nightmares. Once he left for Northwestern in a sea of mud and drowned in it. Another time he left on the El, and it went in circles for the rest of his life. In all his dreams he never got there. He dreaded going to sleep at night; he trembled when he got up in the morning. Oh, God, I'm shaking, I'm trembling, I'm wobbling, I'll never make it.

But at last the day of departure arrived. He woke up early, exhausted from his terrible dreams, with spikes shooting through his cramped legs, his heart racing, his stomach churning. He could hardly sit still through breakfast, could hardly hold it down.

He put on his corduroy pants and his sloppy argyle socks and the plaid flannel shirt his mother had bought for him. If he could, he wanted to wave pennants, carry purple balloons, wear "Go You Northwestern" buttons. He wanted to look collegiate.

But his mother said, "Wear your suit. In the suitcase it'll get wrinkled. Look at you in the winter pants and shirt. Look at how you're sweating already."

"I won't sweat with a suit on?"

"All right, you'll sweat. But it won't get wrinkled. And you'll look like a *mensh*."

"I'm not going to a bar mitzvah, Ma, or a wedding. I'm going to college."

"In the old country you went to yeshiva in your finest clothes. Respect."

"All right, all right."

He changed into the Oxford-gray suit his father had bought him in the spring for Passover and graduation. He went through his valise to see if he'd forgotten anything, then closed it. He was ready to take off. You'd think he was Columbus going off in search of a new route to India, he was Lindbergh about to fly across the Atlantic, he was heading for the trenches in a new world war. Everybody kissing him and shaking his hand and Bubi and his mother weeping.

"I'm only going to Evanston," he said. "It's only an hour away. I'll be back next weekend."

It made no difference. Thank God it was a warm, sunny day or they'd have made him wear his rubbers and his slicker. He finally ran out of the house, hefting his valise.

It was Sunday morning, a day for outings, picnics, the beaches, the parks. The sun was hot in the sky. The empty lots were full of ragweed and sunflowers and papers and tin cans and dog shit. Jake began to drip with sweat as he lugged his valise to the El. By the time he got up on the platform his arms were numb, his clothes stuck to him, he was dying of thirst.

"Seltzer, seltzer."

For the first time in his life he was really going away from home. He would be only an hour away, a ten-cent phone call away, but the world ahead of him was going to be as new and strange as the Fijis. He didn't know how he'd make out in it. A slingshot full of nerves broke loose in him and slammed into his heart. He rode over the sunny, soot-pocked West Side, hurtling past rooftops of brick and wooden buildings; then gloom descended in the deep canyons of the Loop with only the new Union Station and the Civic Opera House like mammoth white stone cliffs among the dark old buildings. He transferred to a Rogers Park express and clattered across the river and the towering skyline at Michigan Avenue. He was out of the shadows of the Loop, skimming alongside the slummy rooftops of Wells Street blazing in the sun, then into the prosperous North Shore.

At Howard Street he transferred to an Evanston train.

He remembered Uncle Hymie coming over in his Buick touring car when he was a kid and taking the family out past Evanston for a picnic at Ravinia or Highland Park. He remembered driving along the lake, passing the iron fences, the great lawns, the huge trees, the spacious houses where the golden *goyim* lived. All that space, so cool near the lake, so peaceful under the great maples and elms and oaks, so wondrously green along the stately lawns. Uncle Hymie was going to move there someday; it was where he belonged. And Jake's father would say, "A dream a day keeps the doctor away."

There he was, Jake Davidson, in the middle of all that splendor, walking along with his brand-new pigskin valise, sweating his balls off under the brooding elms and oaks, feeling like an immigrant, his throat dry, his heart pounding, his eyes smarting from the sweat, looking very uncollegiate in his full suit, as if he didn't belong at all. If he could, he would have run into a hallway and changed his clothes. But there were no apartment buildings with hallways, not where he was, only homes. He pounded on, the valise slipping from his hands, feeling small, insignificant, a nobody in this casually dressed, tall, blond, blue-eyed, scrub-faced world. He felt like a thief sneaking into their territory. He walked on tiptoe a moment, afraid he'd blemish this pure, pristine, untrammeled neighborhood.

He stopped suddenly. There was the Phi Epsilon Pi house. The house he was going to live in. Three stories big. All white. A large porch. A swing on it. Huge trees, the leaves turning colors, a nice lawn smelling of new-cut grass. He observed the frame structure for a moment. That house, on that quiet street, under those enormous trees, I'm going to live there?

He walked up to the porch. He could hear Louis Armstrong singing "Black and Blue" on the Victrola. He knocked on the screen door. Nobody answered. He knocked again. Still no answer. He stepped into the large entrance hall with his valise. A stairway led upstairs. In the big living room near the fireplace, amid leather chairs and couches, four guys in casual dress were playing bridge. Two of them had pipes in their mouths, looking very thoughtful and collegiate. The "dummy" noticed him.

"Hi."

"Hi," said Jake.

The "dummy" walked over. He had curly hair, stooped shoulders, thick lips, and a crooked face that looked pained.

"I'm Dudley Glick, president of the house." He extended his hand.

"Jake Davidson."

"Jake!" Dudley shook his hand warmly. "Glad to know you, I'm sure. We've been expecting you. I've heard a lot about you from Albie Karlin and Milton B." He put his arm around Jake and led him to the bridge table, where he met the others, who were also glad to know him, they were sure, giving him firm, very sincere handshakes. "Let me show you around," Dudley said. And Jake was taken on a tour: the big dining room, where he'd be working for his meals; the kitchen; the library, which adjoined the dining room; then room after room upstairs which were sparsely furnished with single cots and beat-up back-to-back desks. Jake was introduced to a few young men who were unpacking their trunks and suitcases. On the third floor he was led to a room with peaked ceilings, which he'd be sharing with Albie Karlin. Hardly any light came in through the one narrow window. The place was cramped and gloomy. This was going to be his home the next four years.

"Albie'll be here later. What would you like to do now?"

"Maybe unpack, change clothes."

"Sure. Make yourself at home."

"How far is the lake?"

"A couple of blocks to campus; then just keep on walking till you hit it."

Jake unpacked, got into a silk tank suit, then into his corduroys and a blue shirt. He felt grimy and stinky. He'd take a swim and wash it away. He hung his clothes in a small closet, put his socks, shirts, underwear in a small chest. He bounced on his iron cot a few times: nice and firm, okay.

Two desks with gooseneck lamps divided the room. Albie's desk had books and notebooks piled up on it. It looked as if it had been through a lot. Jake's desk was bare but scarred. He wondered what kinds of battles he'd be going through, what kind of blood, sweat, and tears would come out of his skin. Albie had pictures on his chest of his two sisters and mother; they looked heavy-nosed, sad, and grim. Above Albie's cot was a montage of headlines and pictures of the championships he'd won. Next year, Jake thought, after Albie graduated, he'd put up his scrapbook of headlines and pictures, then add the collegiate titles, the AAU, the Olympics. He'd have his own great wall.

He went downstairs, watched the bridge game a moment. These Jews, he thought, from all over, with different accents, these Dudley Glicks he had met and Roland Baruchs and Sherwood Cohens and Delmore Belinskys, a whole new breed.

"Play?" asked Dudley.

"No."

"What's your game?" said Roland Baruch, a red-haired, hook-nosed, thin-mouthed sophomore from Kentucky.

"Poker, pinochle, *klabyesh*."

"Bridge is the game," said Nelson Krause, an oyster-eyed, bland-faced blond from Idaho.

"I'll see you guys," said Jake.

Outside again. Strolling along. Passing manors, villas, Colonial homes, Cape Cod replicas, big Victorian houses. Wanting to piss like a dog on every tree, leaving his stain, his smell. A collegian with his parents pointed out a magnificent fieldstone house with spreading trees, neat shrubs, and a putting green lawn.

"The home of Charles G. Dawes, former vice-president of the United States."

Awed, Jake thought: No shit. Then: I should have taken a leak before I left.

He could hardly contain his full bladder from dribbling out as he passed the parklike surroundings of the campus, the ivy-covered buildings, the *goyish* fraternity houses on fraternity row. He rushed down to the lake, flung his clothes onto the sand, plunged in, and felt the rush of hot urine against his body as he let go. Ah, ah, ah. That was good, so good. He drifted away into the cool lake, swam out on his back, watching the campus with its huge trees, as if they'd been growing there since the world began, recede farther and farther. Oh, how nice, the blue blue sky, the hot, bright sun making rainbows of the beads of water dripping from his sweeping arms, the lake here fresher, cleaner, bluer than any Chicago beach. This was his domain. Here he was king. Here he belonged. He jumped high out of the water,

waving his fist. "Wahooooo! Chee-wah-heeee! And fuck you!"
That was Chief Potch-in-tochis laying claim to the whole territory. He turned over onto his belly, dug into a crawl, powering
out farther. When he stopped, the campus looked small. Way
down he could see the Chicago skyline. Northward there was
nothing but trees and water. He swam back to shore and rested
in the sand against a small pier. The sun dried him and put him to
sleep. He woke up to the gentle lap of the waves. A couple of
sunny-faced girls were reading nearby; a guy was staring out at
the lake. Everything was so quiet and peaceful. Jake looked for
flat stones and skipped them out on the water. If life could be
like this for the rest of time . . . wahoo!

When he got back to the house, there were a lot more guys
around with bone-crushing, glad-to-know-you-I'm-sure handshakes, sincere looks, personable smiles, and different accents.
Most of them smoked, dangled their cigarettes with such polish
and sophistication that Jake thought he was in the center of a
John Held cartoon. Some of them, in tweeds and pipes, posed
like elder statesmen considering the fate of the world.

Most of the pledges Jake met had gone to prep schools and
military academies and had belonged to high school fraternities.
Two of his pledgemates were so rich that they could afford a
Stutz; they rented a three-bedroom house with double plumbing
and hired a full-time servant. All of them seemed to belong,
knew where they were going, what they were going to do; most
of them were going into their fathers' businesses or professions.
Only he was going to college to be an athlete, to use his talent to
shape his future. Jake felt dizzy and bewildered, meeting so
many guys.

Finally, Albie Karlin showed up. He was warm and friendly
with his handshakes, his broad white-toothed smile, though he
said little. What did he have to say? His reputation spoke for
him. All he had to do was stand there. He was a banner
headline.

Afterward, up in the room, Albie said, "How's it going?"

"Great."

"It's not so great. You're a little Jew from the West Side. All
these guys are different. But everything'll fall into place. It'll
settle down. You'll find out who you'll get along with. You'll

make your friends. The big thing is school. Getting your studies. You thought about what you want to do?"

"You said the business school was the best. That's where you are, isn't it?"

"Okay, business. First, you have to go to the liberal arts school for a couple of years; then you declare a major. If it's business, you'll concentrate on those courses the last two years. Right now we've got to figure out a curriculum for your first semester."

They decided on German because Jake's Yiddish was good. Baby algebra; you couldn't go lower. Geology, the easiest of the science courses. Beginning English. And physical education. All required courses.

"Get by your first semester," said Albie, "and Milton B. will buy you the Taj Mahal."

Everything started with a bang. Classes. Trying to find his way from building to building. Instruction and assignments pitched to him at bewildering speeds. He hardly understood his English instructor, who seemed to despise his students.

"You'd better have the dictionary tattooed on your skin," he said. "I'll shillelagh you with polysyllabic words."

"Hah?" Jake said.

He was in the Sea of Sargossa with Shakespeare and the Romantic poets.

The other instructors were dry and uninspired, the courses like racetracks, with him left at the starting post, except for German.

He was breathless the first week. Waiting on tables at lunch and dinner. Buying books. Going to the pool and working out and playing water polo against the varsity. Then two nights a week being lifeguard for a women's swim class and the Daughters of Neptune Swim Club. He couldn't concentrate on his studies at the pool, especially with those long-legged, firm-breasted, blond, blue-eyed Daughters of Neptune, who'd parade their tempting asses all over the place. In his cramped room he watched Albie work away hour after hour on his studies. He couldn't understand why it took Albie so long. He'd read a poem. Words, words. A minute, two minutes. What did they mean? Even the dictionary couldn't tell him. He'd read again. Blank. How could you do that for hours? When he had to write a theme, oh, boy. It took him all night to write several hundred words, and then he'd get an F for leaving out a subject or verb in a sentence or for too many dangling participles. Geology, forget it, it was all babble-babble. He sometimes thought that English was his second language. In a few weeks his dictionary was dog-eared. Yet when Albie asked him how he was doing, he said, "Fine."

He was not a complainer. When Pete Swanson, his new coach, whom everybody called Swanee, a tall, skinny-legged man with a potbelly, asked him how his studies were going, he said, "Okay."

"You're sure, Jake?"

"Sure."

He was sure if he said he was in trouble he'd lose his job at the pool and he'd be kicked out of practicing with the team and playing water polo.

I'm a dummy. How do I admit it? Who do I admit it to? Albie Karlin? What can he do, put a brain in my head? Milton B.? He'd throw a fit. The guys in the fraternity? He was ashamed to let them know how abysmally ignorant he was. My father? How, what? Hey, Pa, how do you do $6x - 7 = 3x + 2$? Hah? his father would say. Hey, Pa, do you know from the rocks you can tell about the Cenozoic era, the Paleozoic, the Archeozoic? You don't say, his father would say. Then he'd say, This information, Jake, what good is it going to do you? And Jake would say, I don't know. His father would nod and say in Yiddish, Do you have to go to college? His father would consider that a moment, then say, Maybe it's like an enema; it can't hurt you. All he'd get from his father was a little philosophy and a lot of sympathy.

So on weekends or over the phone, when he was asked how he was doing, he'd say, "Fine. Just fine."

And his mother would say, "Why shouldn't everything be fine? You think we raised a dummy?"

This wasn't a broken finger, a sprained ankle, a cold he was worried about. This was his brain, his comprehension, his ability to learn. If God had given him one more brain, he'd be a moron. That's how he felt.

The only place he felt comfortable was in the pool. He'd pace Tom Branch, the Big Ten backstroke champ, whom he'd beaten in the final Olympic trials the year before. Then during water polo practice he played guard against Albie Karlin, who was rough, tough, the best center forward in the country. That's where he belonged. And at the football games, which began almost as soon as he started school.

Ah, that was college, the way he'd always imagined it. Rallies before the game, the students and alumni parading in with balloons and blankets and pennants and buttons and raccoon coats, the bands playing and marching, the fans singing, the cheerleaders pepping things up, the beautiful coeds, rosy-cheeked, lip-rouged, smelling so sweet, and him selling programs, getting rid of his 200 allotment within thirty minutes and making $7, bang, just like that.

Sometimes he met Milton B. at lunch before the game, and they'd stuff themselves with hot dogs and pop under the stands, and he'd meet other important alumni, and he'd feel as if he owned the whole world, the way they treated him; then he'd go into the locker room with Milton B., who was like a god among the players and coaches. And then in the stands on the fifty-yard line, when the teams trotted onto the field and the cheers started and the bands boomed it up, tears would crop out of Milton B.'s eyes. He'd wipe them and say, "You'd think I was a little kid, huh?" Jake couldn't answer; he was all choked up, too.

Northwestern was winning games in those days. Then afterward, at the fraternity, the fraters and pledges and alumni would crowd in and talk about the game, all of them feeling like victorious heroes. Sometimes a bunch of the boys would get into cars and drive down to the South Side of Chicago, the black belt, and hit a whorehouse. Still full of the college spirit, they'd line up and hand their $2 over to the whores, and they'd be blown and fucked to the sound of rah-rahs, laughter, rowdy talk, and school songs. It was all so comradely and manly. And sometimes they'd hit the Four Deuces, Capone's whorehouse at 2222 South Wabash. It had the longest bar in town. Weekends, you could hardly breathe, it was so jammed. They'd drink bootleg beer and gin, then buy a brass check: $2 for a straight fuck; $3 for a half and half. Then you'd give the check to a whore, and she'd put it on her chain, and she'd jangle you up loaded with brass to one of the cribs upstairs with a three-quarter-size bed covered with dirty linen. There was a tiny sink; the toilet was in the hallway. She'd squeeze your cock to see if you had clap; then she'd wash it. She didn't even give you time to take off your socks. "What do you want to do, get athlete's foot?" she'd say. If you pumped her more than four times, she'd start complaining that you were trying to make a home there. That place and Capone's joint on 22nd and State were strictly fast fuck chains. Volume was what counted, and volume was what they got.

Drained and weary at last, they'd ride home worried about gonorrhea and syphilis. Except for the black whores and Capone's brass-check girls, that was the real college, the way Jake dreamed it. Not the college of worry, of study, of loneliness.

The college of sororities was not exactly what Jake dreamed of. Maybe because there was only one Jewish sorority on campus, the AE Phis. Everybody was so stiff and mannerly around the teas they had in their white-stoned Gothic house, with gray-haired housemothers and alumnae chaperones. The girls seemed way out of his class. Silks and satins and velvet, so soft, dark-eyed, sophisticated, and untouchable. Some of them owned their own cars, even their own riding horses. Jake didn't know how to talk to them, was afraid to talk to them; he felt so crude, so uncouth, so self-conscious with them.

Once some of the pledges decided to go to the Edgewater Beach Hotel, where Guy Lombardo played. They asked Jake to come along. Whom would he ask? Ida? Drag her all the way from the West Side? How? On a streetcar, the El? Lila? On a Saturday night she was all tied up at the College Inn. Who?

"Grab some pig at the AE Phi house," said one of his pledge brothers. "We're all taking one."

Who? He finally decided to ask a girl he'd met at a recent tea there: Shelley Wasserman. She was a little thick in the hips, flat in the chest, but she had a great face, with warm dark eyes, black hair, even features, and voluptuous lips. When he called, he had to tell her who he was. That killed him. "I'm about your height, blue eyes, and if I had red hair, I'd be Red Grange." That got a laugh; he wasn't doing too bad.

"Where are you from?" she asked.

"Jerusalem."

"Seriously," she said.

He gave her a little Hebrew *davening,* which he'd learned by rote as a kid.

"No, seriously."

A pledge nudged him and said, "Tell her you're a Phi Ep. All she wants to know is: Are you affiliated with the right people?"

"I'm from down the block, the Phi Ep house."

"Oh."

"Saturday night a few of us are going to the Edgewater Beach. Can you make it?"

"Well—"

He kept to the point. "Can you?"

"It's such short notice."

Always the bullshit.

"You'll be in good company. I mean, some of your sisters will be in our party."

"You tempt me."

Fuck it, he thought. "Yes or no."

A long pause. "I'd be delighted."

Which surprised him. Especially the word "delighted." Words, the way they were used, the way they came at him, were beginning to surprise him at every turn.

The car he was supposed to ride in was out of commission that night. He and Bertram Gorelik, another pledge, had to take the girls down in a cab. The whole thing was going to cost a fortune. Jake suspected that Bertram, whose father owned a cigar company, framed it that way so that he could *shnoogel* with his girl. They crowded into the back seat, Bertram's girl on his lap, with him wriggling his cheap hard-on against her.

Shelley smoked. She pulled a silver cigarette case from her purse, took out a cigarette, tapped it elaborately on the case, put it in her mouth, then gave Jake a silver lighter, and waited for him to light it for her. Bertram gave him a you-dumb-*shmuck* look as Jake fumbled with it, then took the lighter from him and lit it instantly.

"Quite a gadget," Bertram said.

"Dunhill," Shelley said.

"Dunhill!" Jake said. His rich uncle Hymie smoked Dunhill cigars. The best. The Tiffany of cigars.

"Are you familiar with Dunhill products?"

"I was brought up on Dunhill cigars," Jake said.

"Really?"

"I wanted to stunt my growth so's I could be a jockey. More

than anything in the world I wanted to be a jockey. But Dunhills didn't work for me. Maybe those cheapo five-cent cigars might have done the trick."

"Is he serious?" Shelley asked Bert.

"My friend Jake is as serious as the Spanish Inquisition."

The girls smiled. Let the boys have their fun.

Two summers before, the Fish-Fan Club, a big fishing and boozing club run by Mayor Thompson and the biggest grafters in town, had held a swimming meet at the Edgewater. Jake won the 50- and 100-yard backstroke and the 50-yard freestyle. He got a wristwatch and two swimsuits as prizes. Which was the first time he got more than a medal for a prize and which made him think that Mayor Thompson, who was hailed as a true and noble sportsman, was the greatest man in the world. So he knew the Edgewater. It was so elegant the announcer called him "Jock" Davidson. The thick carpets, the chandeliers, the rich, elegant couches in the lounge, the Edgewater was always high society in Jake's mind.

Now, in his Passover suit, he walked up the broad red-carpeted staircase, touching the curved marble bannister, with Shelley beside him in a rustling silk dress which she had bought in Paris when she had visited there with her mother during the summer. Then they came into the huge ballroom, crowded with college students and older people, with Guy Lombardo playing the "sweetest music this side of heaven." They were led to the Phi Ep table.

"So what's Paris got Chicago hasn't got?" Jake said.

"The Champs-Élysées. Light me."

She put a cigarette in her mouth and handed him her Dunhill lighter.

If she smokes, Jake thought, she fucks.

He found out differently on the dance floor. She backed away from him when he held her too close.

"Don't you toddle?" she asked.

"Not much."

"What do you do?"

"I swim."

She shrugged with her carefully trimmed eyebrows. They had little to say to each other. He found her talking to her friend Mildred about their experiences in Paris, London and Rome.

They talked like ambassadors for Cook's Tours. He found himself talking to some of the pledges about the football season and school. He was ill-at-ease with Shelley the rest of the evening, didn't know how to communicate with her. When he came up with a Yiddish expression, she didn't understand him; they were languages and worlds apart. On the way home in the cab, Bert snuggled up with his girl. Jake put his arm around Shelley, drew her close, and then kissed her. Her lips were tight and dry. She pulled out her cigarette and lighter. This time she lit the cigarette herself. She'd rather smoke than fuck, Jake thought. He didn't even bother to kiss her good-night at the sorority-house door.

He and Bert paid off the cabdriver and walked home.

"How'd you do?" Bert asked.

"You know what the Frenchman said after he'd been in this country awhile? 'By gar, they all look like whores, but by gar, I know they are not.'"

"You gotta give it time."

"Time and a bankroll and the grand tour to Europe. I'm going back to the West Side, where it's for real."

It wasn't for real anymore there either. All the next week he was horny and lonely, in that order. In a fraternity house full of guys, you couldn't monopolize the bathroom; it was hard to masturbate. He had two wet dreams. One with a curvy blonde and a Betty Boop voice, who sat next to him in English and who looked as dumb as he felt. Helpless before the barrage of polysyllabic words and complicated sentences full of "to whoms" and "of whiches" and "therefores," he kept glancing at her and wondering how she'd be and he found out in a dream. He recited, "Hail to thee, blithe spirit! Bird thou never wert" as he lifted her skirt and humped her with her stockings, her garters, and her step-ins on. The other dream, he popped while riding a motorcycle like the whirlwind. He didn't understand that one at all. He called Ida.

"I owe you two bucks."

"Jake, you're a college man now."

He persisted. "I'd like to pay my debt. I'm a man of honor. How about Friday night or Saturday? I'll be in over the weekend."

"I'm sorry, Jake, I can't."

"Both nights?"

"Why can't you give me a little advance notice?"

"How about Sunday afternoon?"

"I've got a million things to do, Jake. I'm a hard working girl. I've got to do my hair, my nails, some ironing. How about next weekend?"

"We're playing Notre Dame next Saturday."

"So?"

"Jesus, Ida, I wouldn't miss that if my life was at stake. Biggest game of the year."

"Maybe after the football season."

When he hung up, there was a deep emptiness in his stomach. He didn't belong where he was; he didn't belong on the West Side. He felt suddenly like a chicken, its head cut off, hopping about frantically trying to find it.

He came home that Friday and had supper with the family. Afterward, while sitting around the table, Nachum said, *"Noo?"*

A pall came over everybody. Nachum wanted to go into business for himself. He wanted Jake's father to lend him the money. He didn't believe that Jake's father didn't have it.

"I had to borrow money to bring you here," said Jake's father.

"So borrow some more money," Nachum said. "I'll pay it back."

"It's not so easy to borrow. People don't loan you money because you have an honest face."

"For business there's always money."

"Only if the bankers think the man behind the business will make it successful."

"I will make it a success."

"It takes time to build up a business."

"So it takes a little time."

"You just got here, Nachum. Give yourself more time. You don't even know the language."

"What's to know? I can count, add, subtract, multiply, divide. I can make change. And I'm a skilled shoemaker."

"Where would you open a store? Have you thought about that?"

"On Twelfth Street."

"There are two shoemakers there already. Very skilled. Established. You're new. You'll starve to death."

"I'll go somewhere else."

"Where?"

"Somewhere. It's a big city."

Jake said, "You better listen to your brother."

"You don't mix in, Yonkel," said Nachum.

"My father went into hock to bring you over," Jake said. "What are you making? Twenty dollars a week? It'd take you two years to pay back what Pa had to borrow to bring you and Bubi over. What would you live on? Nachum, you're not a kid. Listen to Pa."

"I don't want to live here. I want to move out. Have a place of my own. I want to have a woman, a wife, children. I want to be a *mensh*. How can I do that on twenty dollars a week?"

"Nachum, wait, please. Give yourself some time," said Jake's father.

"No. No more. I'll go to the *verein* myself. I'll talk to the *mishpocheh*, the *landsleit*. They'll give me the money."

"*Bubkes* they'll give you," Jake's father said. "Do you know how much the machinery costs for a shop?"

"No."

"Do you know exactly where your store will be, how much the rent will be, how much you'll have to spend for materials, tools?"

"Did you know everything when you bought your stand?"

"Exactly. To the penny. Figures. Pages and pages of figures. A book full. They knew exactly how much I would make. It was a good risk. They knew I would pay them back."

"Are you saying I'm not a good risk, I'm not an honorable man?"

"He's saying they're worse than a bank when it comes to lending money," said Jake. "They're more careful; they charge a lot more interest. You think they're in it for their health? They're not a bunch of boy scouts, Nachum."

"Big shot. He goes to college, he knows all the answers. I don't want you to mix in, Yonkel."

"Stay out of it, Jake," said his father, then turned to Nachum.

"If you go to the *verein,* they'll want me to make good if anything happens."

"What can happen? People wear out shoes, they get them fixed. What can go wrong?"

"Think, Nachum. You'll need several thousand dollars. If business is bad, who's going to pay the rent, who's going to pay off the debt?"

"In these times, business bad?" Nachum laughed.

"Don't listen to all the success stories."

"What should I listen to, the stories of the *shlimazels?*"

"Look at the people around here. They work hard for a living. Yet most of them are poor."

"I don't want to hear these things. You can help me."

Nachum was no longer the skinny little *nebbish* with the high, giggly laugh. He was intense, feverish looking. "I'm not a *shnorrer.* I will make good."

The women at the table kept silent. Bubi looked frightened; she didn't know what was going on. Jake watched his father study Nachum closely.

At the top of his voice Nachum yelled, "You left us to starve. You left us to the revolution, the Cossacks, the pogroms. You left me to care for Mama. All the time you had it so good, you lived so well; you didn't have to hide from the *pogromchiks,* you didn't have to starve for a piece of bread, you didn't have to suffer from disease."

"I sent you money."

"It meant nothing. It was taken from us."

"All the time I saved, I scrimped, I denied myself, I sent you money."

"It was for the Bolsheviks. Not for us. You owe me, Aaron. You owe me."

Jake's father shook his head sadly, his face streaked with pain and guilt.

"Why did I come here?" Nachum's voice broke. "Why did I spend my days and nights dreaming to come here? Better I should have rotted away there."

Jake's father sighed. The same discussion for weeks. Jake knew his father would give in.

"Don't, Pa," Jake said.

"Jake, shut up," said Nachum.

They sat silently around the table, Nachum's demands like a tyrant hovering over them. Jake's father nodded solemnly, drumming the table with his fingers. Years before he had gone heavily into debt to go into the laundry business with his brother-in-law Itzik. He had slaved so hard he almost died, then failed. He went back to work as a carpenter, took odd jobs on weekends. There was no time to relax, no time for his family. Until the opportunity of the newsstand came up. They all knew what failure meant. It moved like a ghost beside them wherever they went, wherever they slept.

Finally, Jake's father said, "The eye is a terrible thing. Whatever it sees, the heart desires."

"So you'll go to the *verein,*" said Nachum.

"I'll go, I'll go."

On Sunday, before going back to school, Jake dropped in at the JPI for a swim. Benny Gordon was there complaining about all the money being made in the stock market while he was just barely getting by as a phone man with a real estate company. A few thousand dollars, he could turn it into millions, he said. Two weeks ago he picked four stocks and made modest investments on paper. Today he'd be twenty thousand dollars richer.

"Why not a hundred thousand?" Jake asked.

"I'm being conservative."

"On paper?" said Solly Landon, the parking-lot king.

"If I'd been born five years earlier, I'd have it made now."

Lala gestured with his fist: jerk-off time.

Benny turned to him and Bo. "Listen," he said. "How about ringing me in on a hustle? A booze run from Detroit. A big heist. Some kind of swindle. Some way to get hold of a little cash so's I can get into the action in the market."

"You're not a *goniff,* Benny," said Bo.

"Once. A big score. I'll take a chance."

"Ta-ta, Benny," said Lala.

Benny turned to Solly. "Maybe you need a manager of your operations. Some parking lots. A building. I'm in real estate, you know."

"Everybody wants to be a manager. Everybody wants to start

at the top. When what I need are parking jockeys."

"Enough bullshit," said Lala. "Let's throw the ball around."

There weren't enough guys to play a game of water polo. Solly said, "The place isn't the same anymore. Everybody had to go off to college."

It really wasn't the same, Jake thought. They threw the ball around awhile, then went into the steamy showers.

"Hey, Jake," said Lala, "how's chances of getting into the Notre Dame game?"

"All sold out."

"Come on. You and Albie Karlin, you can get us in."

"I hear the scalpers are asking thirty, forty dollars a ticket."

"What's money when you got a pal out there?"

Jake knew they'd all be out for the game, badgering to be sneaked in. If he couldn't think of a way, they would.

"We'll take you back to school after we get dressed."

"You don't have to, guys." Jake didn't want to be obligated.

"We want to," said Lala, "don't we, Bo?"

Benny said he'd go along for the ride.

Lala had a Ford, which he called a short. He drove, Bo sat up front with him, and Benny sat in back with Jake. They drove down to Michigan Avenue, then up along Lake Shore Drive through Lincoln Park. The last lingering colors of fall were in the trees, and leaves were thick on the grassy meadows. The fall wind whipped in from the lake, swirling the leaves, buffeting the car, shooting up whitecaps in the water, a prelude of the hard, freezing winter ahead. Sailboats and yachts were still moored in Belmont Harbor, their masts rocking in the gusts.

"Someday," Benny said, "I'm going to have a boat out there."

"Yah, yah," Lala singsonged.

"I'll have an apartment on top of a twenty-story building. Right over my boat. I'll want to take a sail, I'll put on my captain's cap and waltz over."

"Famous dreams," Bo said.

When they got to Wilson Avenue, the car konked out.

"Fucking short," said Lala. "You guys wait here. I'll be back."

They sat and waited. Jake said, "Where'd he go?"

"Don't worry," said Bo. "We'll get you home."

Soon Lala drove up in a Cadillac.

"Get in," he said.

"Where'd you get the car?" Jake asked.

"Shut up and get in."

"What about the short?"

"Fuck it. It ain't ours."

"What about this one?"

"Will you get in, for Christ's sake?"

Bo shoved him into the Cadillac. And Lala drove off. All the way to Evanston Jake was terrified they'd be picked up by the cops. That's all he'd need. When they arrived at the Phi Ep house, Jake said, "Next time you want to do me a favor, forget it."

"That where you live?" said Lala.

"Yah."

"Let's go up and say hello to Albie."

They marched Jake up to his room. Albie, thank God, wasn't there. Jake still expected the cops to come for them any minute.

"You mean you and Albie, a world's champ like Albie, live in a crummy little room like this?" said Lala.

"Guys, I've got a lot of studying to do."

"Maybe we ought to get them a nice easy chair, maybe an Oriental rug," said Lala. "How about it, Bo?"

They'd get them, too. "Please, guys," said Jake. "I appreciate your bringing me out here, but I've got to write a theme for tomorrow, and I've got some math to do, and I'll be up all night if you guys don't beat it."

"Okay," said Bo. "Tell Albie we were here. We'll see you at the Notre Dame game."

"I'm going to stick around awhile," said Benny. "I've got a girl out here."

"You sure you don't want a ride back?" said Lala.

"No, I think I'll get laid and then take the El back."

Lala and Bo left.

"Didn't you want to go back with them?" Jake asked.

"Are you kidding?"

They heard the Cadillac take off.

"Where do I get the El from here?" Benny asked.

Jake said, "I'll walk you over."

As they walked down the street, smelling the leaves being

burned at the curbs, Benny said, "You took Ida Bravermann to the prom, didn't you?"

"Yah."

"You have a big thing for her?"

"Just a broad."

"You ever get in there?"

"Not exactly."

"You missed the boat."

Jake's heart, without reason, began to pound.

"I hear she likes strawberry jam and marmalade, not exactly on bread. She likes hot fudge and caramel syrup, not exactly on sundaes."

"What are you talking about?"

"She's an animal."

"How do you know?"

"Reliable sources. Mostly me."

He grabbed Benny, his heart pounding harder. He wanted to hit him.

"I'm sorry, Jake."

Jake let him go. "Yah," he said. He didn't know what had come over him. Except that he felt unclean, betrayed.

"Maybe you can catch up," said Benny as he walked into the El station.

Afterward Jake tried to settle down to work. He felt restless, irritated, itchy, unclean. He was waterlogged from swimming and showering at the JPI, but he took another shower. Now he felt scaly as he tried to study. He gave up. Ran downstairs and called Ida.

"What are you doing now?"

"Why?" she said.

"You doing your hair, your nails, all the goody-goody girlie things?"

"What's wrong, Jake?"

"You cunt. You dirty, miserable cunt."

He hung up, his throat tight. He went back to his room and struggled with his math assignment. Nothing checked out. Albie came in. Said hello and immediately sat down at his desk and started to study. Jake wondered if anything ever bothered Albie. He was so methodical, calculated, controlled.

He tried to work on an English theme, due the next day. Ida
kept nagging at him.

"Eleven o'clock, Jake. Let's turn in."

Jake went downstairs with his notebook so that he wouldn't
disturb Albie. He tried to write. Blank, blank, blank. He
couldn't understand what was happening to him. He didn't love
Ida. He always played catch-as-catch-can with her. So why? All
he knew was he felt bitter; the taste in his mouth was like the
bottom of Strangler Lewis's jockstrap.

Andrew Pierce, one of his pledge brothers, sat beside him,
munching a Baby Ruth. He was skinny, blond, with hazy blue
eyes.

"Want a piece?"

"Thanks."

The candy didn't help the lousy taste in his mouth.

"Andy," he said, "you get As on your themes all the time,
don't you?"

"Yes."

"I'd give my right nut for one."

"Why don't you take one of mine?"

"Great."

He forgot Ida while copying the theme. Then she came back
full force when he tried to fall asleep. That night he dreamed of
her being gang-banged by a hundred guys and she was screaming, "More! More!" Of her copping a sea of cocks and loving it.
Of being as *zoftig* as a Turkish whore in one of Capone's joints,
glowing with pride and pleasure, her neck laden with necklaces
of brass checks.

"That cunt," he said.

He turned in Andy Pierce's theme with a smile that morning.
This time he was going to get an A. He'd show that crummy
instructor of his.

When he got his theme back two days later, there was no grade
on it, just a note: "Please see me after class." He fidgeted
through the hour, wondering what was wrong, why he hadn't got
a grade. He was into a good sweat by the time the class was
dismissed. He lingered behind, waited, and finally stepped up to

his instructor, Mr. Ogilvy, a tall, slender man with a trim mustache on a half-baked face.

"Mr. Jacob Waldo Davidson."

When Mr. Ogilvie talked and lectured with his wry, superior smile, Jake always felt as if he were being cut up by a fencing master.

"Jake Davidson, sir. No Waldo. No middle name or initial."

"I could have sworn that you'd recently adopted the name of Waldo."

"No, sir."

"That paper you turned in—brilliant."

Jake wanted to smile, to feel good, but he was confused. Instead of a prick from Mr. Ogilvie's rapier he felt himself being cut in two with a cutlass.

"The fluency, the turn of the phrases, the concepts, so distinguished, luminous, keen, radiant, absolutely magnificent. . . ."

Wow! The mark of Zorro on his face. All three musketeers lunging sabers through him.

"For Ralph Waldo Emerson."

Jake was rooted to the floor. Who was that?

"Whatever possessed you to try a thing like that? Whatever made you think you could get away with it?"

Jake didn't know what to say because he didn't know what Mr. Ogilvie was talking about.

"At least, if it were an author who was not so universally known, so celebrated. What do you use for a brain, Mr. Davidson?"

"I don't know."

"Did you ever hear of plagiarism?"

Now the sword was right through his throat.

Mr. Ogilvie became a tower of scorn, his mustache bristling. "No, you wouldn't have. I'll spare you the effort of looking it up. Mr. Davidson, you have stolen, purloined, passed off as your own the ideas, the words, the writing of a great mind, a masterful essayist. You have committed a criminal outrage."

Oh, boy! Give me the F and get it over with.

"You don't understand a word I'm saying, do you?"

"I think you're trying to tell me I deserve an F."

"Great gobs of elephant turds! I could do more. Lots more. I could have you expelled!"

"No!"

"What you did is unforgivable."

"I didn't know."

"Ignorance is no excuse. What is even more incredible is that you could think you would get away with it, that I am an absolute idiot."

"No!" Tears started to Jake's eyes. With them, a torrent of words: "Once, only once, I wanted to write something good, something terrific, something that would give me an A. A fraternity brother of mine gave me his A theme, and I copied it. I thought by copying it'd help me to learn how to write. I only wanted to learn, believe me. I wanted to impress you. I wanted to make good here. You see, I'm an athlete. I'm a star swimmer. The university is depending on me. I've got to make good, see." The torrent clogged his throat. He hid his tearful face in his hands. Jesus, he thought, he's making me cry like a fucking baby.

"I don't care who you are. I wouldn't care if you were Johnny Weissmuller. You athletes, you come up here, you're wined, dined, treated like emperors, but not in my class. For me, you've got to perform academically. That's all that counts."

"I apologize, Mr. Ogilvie. Whatever I did wrong, I apologize. Just don't kick me out of school."

"What do you suggest I do?"

"Make me write 'plagiarism' five thousand times. Make me sit in a corner. Put a duncecap on my head. Anything, but don't kick me out."

"You're not a child anymore."

"I know, I know. Oh, God. Oh, shit. Oh, fuck."

"All right, all right. But I'd advise you to get out of my class if you don't start learning how to express yourself correctly, if you don't start grasping the bare rudiments of literature."

"Yes, sir."

Jake began to walk away, sniffling, wiping his tears, then stopped and turned around.

"Who is Ralph Waldo Emerson?"

"Oh, God!" Then: "That's your next assignment, Mr. Davidson. You find out who Mr. Emerson is. And I want a paper on him, at least a thousand words in length. At the end of it, write down *Webster's International Dictionary*'s definition of 'plagiarism.'"

"In addition to your regular assignments?"

"You'll be excused from nothing."

Jake waited for Andy Pierce in Andy's room till he got there. He grabbed him and said, "You sonofabitch," and slammed him against the wall. Andy slumped to his cot, blood pouring from his mouth. Jake pulled him off the cot and hurled him across the room to his roommate's cot. He grabbed Andy again and was about to smash him once more, but the look of terror in his eyes stopped him.

"You're going to help me dig into Ralph Waldo Emerson," said Jake. "You're going to help me write a paper on him."

"Sure, Jake. Anything you say."

"Come on. We're going to get started right now."

"Sure, let's go to the library."

On the way, Jake said, "Why'd you do it, Andy?"

"It never occurred to me. I do it all the time. Thoreau, Ruskin, Mark Twain, Johnathan Swift. If I'm going to do anybody, I might as well do the best."

Lila called that night.

"Jake, what are you doing Saturday night?"

"That's the day of the Notre Dame game."

"I know, *shmuck.*" She still had the dirtiest, fastest mouth in the Midwest. "After the game why don't you come down here? The College Inn is inaugurating Northwestern Night Saturday. And every Saturday thereafter. Will you make it?"

"I'll try."

"Don't try. Be here. Bring Albie Karlin with you."

"Albie'll have a million things to do. A guy like that, he doesn't sit around."

"Bullshit. Tell him he can have anything he wants on the house. Even pussy. We need some important Northwestern people."

"I'll tell him."

"Do you know Reb Beauregard?"

"The all-American fullback?"

"Get him down. Especially if Northwestern wins. Any other big athlete you can think of."

"I'll try."

"*Shtunk,* you'll get nowhere trying. Do it."

"Do I get laid, too?"

"Honey, you especially." She laughed huskily, sexily, and hung up.

Jake was surprised. Albie had nothing to do Saturday night. Neither did Reb Beauregard. Neither did Charley Brannagan, the all-conference tackle. Neither did Buzz Fazio, the captain of the basketball team. What a party they were going to have.

Jake called Lila back.

"Is it all right to bring them all?"

"The more the merrier."

"These guys'll eat you out of house and home."

"It's all peanuts, Jake."

"If they don't get laid, they'll tear the joint apart."

"Just bring them. We'll service them."

Excitement over the Notre Dame game mounted all week. Huge signs on the campus fraternities: "Sink Notre Dame" . . . "Plow Up the Green" . . . "Down the Irish" . . . "Go Northwestern" . . . "Wildcats R-R-R-R-R-RAH. . . ." At the beach, a pile of old crates, furniture, driftwood, anything that'd burn, was two stories high by Friday night. It went up into a huge flame with cheers and singing. As the fire dwindled, the crowd dispersed. Jake walked away with a glow, which diminished to ashes as he walked off campus to the Phi Ep house. He felt lonely under the vast night, the distant stars, the bare trees. It was never like in the movies. In the movies he'd be with a girl; he'd be riding wildly through the night in an open car; they'd be bundled up, their spirits soaring, up, up, up, never-ending. Or he'd be with a bunch of guys, still whooping it up. He wished he had a girl. Or he was with the guys from the JPI. These celebrations, like Thanksgiving and Christmas, were strictly for the *goyim.* In his room, with Albie working on an advertising campaign for school, clipping and pasting and writing, he said, "You don't go for this shit, do you?"

"I did when I first came up. There are more important things."

"Yah."

He buried himself under Ralph Waldo Emerson.

Only Milton B. Morgenstern and his alumni pals still carried on in the great collegiate spirit. At lunch, at Dyche Stadium, they munched hot dogs and peanuts and drank coffee, sang songs, reminisced over past glories, slapped each other's backs, and were flushed with the excitement of the coming game.

"You know, Jake," said Milton B. "You'd think, this, the game, is all there is to life. Well, I'll let you in on a little secret. That's really all there is. My profession is for bread, but you can't live on bread alone. This is the only reality." He doubled his fist. "Go, team, go. Sink the Irish. Right?"

"Right!" everybody echoed.

Jake, stuffed with hot dogs and a Milky Way, ran off to work. He picked up his quota of programs and his special pass that could take him anywhere in the stadium. The crowds started coming early, boisterous, cheerful, confident, full of rah-rah, wearing raccoon coats, mink, cashmere, heavy sweaters, carrying blankets, thermoses of coffee and flasks of bathtub gin and whiskey, buying pennants, buttons, balloons, and programs.

"Hey, Jake!" called Albie, wearing his heavy purple N sweater. "We'll have a few of those."

With him were Maxie Katz and Morrie Benjamin. Benjamin, an elegant dresser, was wearing a velvet-collared coat, an expensive Stetson, and alligator shoes. He smelled as if he'd just come out of the barbershop.

"Jake!" said Maxie. "You're really here!"

"Yep, I made it."

"What are you doing with the green yarmulke?"

"Gotta let the world know I'm a punk freshman."

Maxie turned to Benjamin. "You got Jake a lifeguard job last summer. One of our constituents. A big swimming star."

"Like Albie?" said Benjamin, shaking Jake's hand.

"Nobody's like Albie," said Jake.

Benjamin, the man who made governors, mayors, senators, smiled and said, "Anything we can do for you, Jake, you come to us." He was soft-spoken, but every word exuded power.

Maxie gave Jake a dollar, told him to keep the change, and walked on with Albie and Benjamin. Albie was really greasing up his future, Jake thought.

"Hey, boy, over here with the programs!"

There were Lala and Bo, with two known hoods from the West Side, looking like gangsters in their tight-fitting coats and their broad, snap-brim, Capone-type hats. One of the hoods with Lala and Bo was Lenny Kahn, a former preliminary fighter who had got in tight with the Capone mob after killing a few hijackers on a booze run to St. Louis and saving the life of Capone's top *capo,* Vince Danuzzio. For his bravery he was given Capone's biggest taxi dance hall in the Loop, the Pleasure Palace. He had a broken nose, and he looked dazed most of the time until he got into action; then all the cunning and craftiness of a stalking animal came into force. The other was short, squat, bullnecked Yussel Gomberg, who used to be a bust-out man in Capone's gambling joint in the Loop. You never knew how a guy with small, pudgy hands like his could put crooked dice into a game to cool off a hot pair of dice, but Yussel was invaluable that way. He was into the rackets now with his muscle and gun, the latest one being the Chicken Pluckers' Protective Association. He always carried a book with him, its pages cut out so that it could hold a gun. Now it was *The Bishop Murder Case* by S. S. Van Dine.

"What do you say, Joe College?" said Lala.

"How'd you guys get in?"

"Juice, pal."

"Up here, too?"

"Why, you think these collegians can't be muscled?"

"Look at the ducats," said Bo.

They had fifty-yard line seats.

"You look like a fuckin' idiot in that green yarmulke," said Lala. "You have to wear it?"

"I get my ass paddled if I don't."

Lenny laughed. "Better than have your ass reamed."

"Have a little respect," said Lala with mock dignity.

"Yah," said Yussel. "Reading never hurt nobody."

He opened his book. There was that little .22 in it, neat, deadly, ready.

"Who's gonna win?" said Lenny.

"Northwestern," said Jake.

"You got any money?"

"I'll have seven bucks."

"How many points you give me?"

"Points!" said Jake. "Notre Dame's the favorite by four points."

"Where's your college spirit?" said Bo.

"You gonna quibble over a few points?" said Yussel.

"An even bet," said Lenny.

"You got it," Jake said.

"You wanna come with us later?" said Lala.

"I'll be all tangled up."

"I know, with all that collegiate pussy," said Lala. "Ta-ta, Jake."

"Ta-ta."

They marched off, their coats like corsets, their hats flapping in the breeze, Yussel with a gun in his book, the others with guns in their pockets. They moved along smartly, casing everybody and everything, as if they were sizing up a caper. Maybe they were, for the future. A big holdup of the day's take. My pals, he thought.

Right after he sold his programs, Jake picked up his pay, then went into the stands. He spotted Milton B. with some of his alumni friends, all with purple N blankets which all the athletes received when they graduated. They were the prime movers behind the team, the men who helped recruit the high school stars from all over the country, promising them flags of glory, barrels of money, the moon in the shape of a lollipop. They had a championship team that year; they bragged, they showed confidence, they were full of good cheer.

"Hey, Jake!" Milton B. called. "Over here."

Jake crowded in among them. He was thumped and pawed. He felt as if he were in a cage full of woolly bears.

"Hey, Jake!"

Three rows behind them were Lala and Bo, Lenny and Yussel.

"Anybody betting on the game?" Lenny said.

"Who'd be crazy enough to bet on Notre Dame?" Milton B. said.

"Nobody," Lenny said. "But I like some action at a game. I'll take Notre Dame. Give me four points."

The bastards, running a book in the stands, Jake thought, and trying to screw my sponsors. "Notre Dame's the favorite by four points."

"What, you've got no confidence in your team?" Lala said. "Where's your team spirit?"

"You've got a bet," Milton B. said. "How much?"

"Whatever you say," said Lenny. "A C note?"

"That's a bet," said Milton B.

"Anybody else?" Lenny asked.

Lenny got $500 in bets before he was through.

"If you're for Notre Dame, why aren't you sitting on the other side?" somebody asked.

Lala answered, "We're not for anybody. Just here for a good game and some action."

All through the game the crowd jumped up and down, yelling itself hoarse, cheering its team on, letting thousands of balloons go with the first Northwestern touchdown, and Lenny was offering bets on all kinds of plays, improvising as the game went along.

"Three to one he don't make the pass. . . . Two to one they don't make the first down." He even bet against Notre Dame when they were on Northwestern's five-yard line. "Give me five to one they don't make it."

They were crazy up there, with money changing hands back and forth, and the game getting more tense with every play. When it was all over, Northwestern won by a point. Lenny and the boys made a bundle. Milton B., his friends, and other bettors didn't mind losing. The Wildcats won. They were in line for the national championship and the Rose Bowl. That's all that mattered. Milton B. had victorious tears in his eyes.

The excitement carried over to the fraternity house. The students, the alumni with their friends and wives and girlfriends, crowded in, milled around, shaking hands, pounding backs, wahooing from time to time, and hugging Milton B., as if he were the coach, the man who had called all the signals, and the man who had caught all the passes and made all the touchdowns. Jake felt as if he had been caught in a huge surf of pounding, crushing waves. He didn't catch his breath until he was on the way downtown to the College Inn with Albie in an alumnus's car that was going that way.

The College Inn was decorated with Northwestern pennants, streamers, and purple balloons. Everybody got a purple hammer when he entered so that he could pound the tables when his voice got tired. Over the orchestra floated a large banner of the score. "Wildcats 21 . . . Irish 20." The place was filling up fast.

Lila was excited, breathlessly showing Jake and Albie to a booth with leopard-covered seats.

"Anything you like," she said. "Remember, it's on the house."

They ordered filet mignon. In the middle of their dinner, a loud cheer went up. Reb Beauregard, who had pounded through the Irish for two touchdowns, and Charley Brannagan, who had torn up the Notre Dame line, had entered. Buzz Fazio followed them. They were pummeled and pounded and cheered, with Lila, even more excited, leading them to Jake's table.

Everybody ate as if they'd been starved for a week. Beauregard and Brannagan had three châteaubriands. Lila sat with them from time to time, but her eyes were everywhere, and whenever somebody important came in, she excused herself. Once, she rushed over to a smartly dressed man, looking like a movie star, with a smooth olive face and slick black hair. He was Vince Danuzzio, Capone's top *capo*, who ran the Chez Paree, the most fashionable nightclub in Chicago, which had a casino in the back. Lila led him to a table. She snapped her fingers, and one of the curviest, most beautiful girls Jake had ever seen came over from the bar and sat down with Danuzzio.

"Your friend," said Albie, "has got her eyes on the Chez Paree."

"Lila has got her eyes on everything," Jake said.

Lila came back to Jake's table and ordered a scotch and soda. She sighed and fanned her face and said, "Quite a night."

"Even Danuzzio is impressed," said Jake.

Lila smiled. "A banner night." She waved to Muggsy Spanier, the leader of the band.

Muggsy was a slender little man with a broken nose and the soulful face of a clown, who could blow a cornet so hot it could melt you down to your socks. His drummer rattled his drums and crashed his cymbals to get the crowd's attention.

"Now for the main event," he said. "We are honored tonight to have with us the boys who beat Notre Dame this afternoon— Reb Beauregard and Charley Brannagan."

The hammering on the tables, the whistling, cheering, and

yelling boomed against Jake's eardrums. A large group burst into "Go You Northwestern." Cheers and whistles again. As it quieted down, Muggsy said, "With them, the triple-crown winner of the national intercollegiate swimming championships, Albie Karlin!" Anticlimactic cheers. "And the captain of Northwestern's basketball team and all-conference forward, Buzz Fazio!" The crowd was less boisterous. "And a new Northwestern swimming star, Jake Davidson!" Jake got a few hammers and a couple of whistles.

During the bows the athletes took, Lila kept looking them over. Command decision. Reb had the neck, chest, and shoulders of a gorilla but a soft, handsome face and the gentle manners and drawl of a southerner. Charley was six-four, 230 pounds of bone and muscle with small gray eyes, blond, curly hair, and shoulders big enough to stop a Mack truck. She kept looking past Jake to Albie. Jake knew the look. She was always one look beyond you. She handed Reb and Charley keys to rooms in the hotel.

"Now for the big touchdown," she said. "When you hear a knock on the door, it'll be room service." She winked. "Have fun."

Reb and Charley left eagerly. Lila nudged Jake and gestured to a redhead working on a drink at the bar. She wore a black, clingy dress, had the creamiest skin he had ever seen, a patrician face with dark-looking eyes, and a red cap of bobbed hair.

"Is she red under the dress?"

"Why don't you find out?" She handed him a key. "Tell her Lila sent you."

"What about you?"

"Don't worry about me." She had her eyes on Albie.

Upstairs, in Room 1224, the Palmolive beacon roved past him as it probed the sky. The Wrigley Building, pure white in the glare of spotlights, towered over the river. Across the way, the Tribune Building, gothic and shadowy, brooded over Michigan Avenue. He could see the lights of the Municipal Pier glitter along the lake. Most of the city was dark, asleep, with the lamppost lights dim and gloomy under their hoods.

The redhead's name was Nellise. Her hair was red all over. She took his hand. "Come on," she said, "before we get cold."

He had gooseflesh from the chill, but he kept looking out the window.

"I've never been this high up before," he said. "I mean, at night."

"Big town."

"You a friend of Lila's?"

"We have a kind of working arrangement."

"How do you mean?"

"They let me operate around the hotel, and the cops don't bother me. We exchange favors."

Jake nodded: Oh, that Lila.

"Come on, Jake, let's warm up."

They nuzzled up in bed. She rubbed him all over with her hands. He rubbed her. Soon they were tingly and warm. Her skin glowed. Her hair was so soft and red, so strange and exotic to look at. Then she said, "What would you like? A little sucking or a little fucking?"

"Whatever it is," he said, "I don't want it little. I want it big."

"Lay back. Relax. I'll give you the grand tour."

He shivered with excitement as she worked over him.

"Tell me when you want the Eiffel Tower, the Taj Mahal, and the Vatican."

"Now!"

BOOK 2

Six months before, Herbert Hoover, a Quaker, a human-itarian, a brilliant engineer, a man of good faith and positive thinking, had taken over the presidency of the richest country in the world in its most prosperous year. His slogan was: "A chicken in every pot, two cars in every garage." America's heroes and royalty were not its millionaires, thinkers, policy makers, or generals but its movie stars, aviators, and athletes. Lindbergh's romance with Anne Morrow was still followed closely. The glamor of Hollywood was reported in the gossip columns and newsreels. Tennis and golf were considered sissy sports, played mostly by the rich, but Big Bill Tilden, who ruled the world of tennis, and Bobby Jones, the monarch of golfers, were headline heroes. Babe Ruth was still the home run king. Tunney got a Bronx cheer for hanging up his gloves and betraying the masses by going literati, which made Jack Dempsey, in defeat, more popular than ever. Johnny Weissmuller, the most famous swimmer of all time, was later going to become even more famous as Tarzan. A new era in motion pictures was under way through the "talkies". The phenomenon of radio tuned everybody in to the twenty-gun broadsides of advertising and mass entertainment. And as far as the stock market was concerned, the bulls were on a rampage. America had a fever. It was "Singin' in the Rain." It was "Runnin' Wild."

All through the years Jake's father said, "It's your America, Jake." Millions of other fathers who worked hard and became part of the country's great future sang the same litany: "It's your America, son." They felt that they were leaving a huge legacy of everlasting prosperity.

. . . Until the following week in Jake's life. The stock market suddenly, for no sensible, explainable reason, began to decline rapidly. Nobody could believe what was happening. Profit taking was the excuse. Who could blame the greedy investors? The drop was only technical, some said. Others developed the theory that the big manipulators were creating new lows for themselves so that they might buy in cheaply with their huge profits and reap more billions. Bankers radiated assurance. So did the government. But the market was too overburdened with credit, margins were exhausted, and thousands and thousands of investors were automatically sold out. "Sell" became the word. Sell. Sell. Get out from under, even if it's only ten cents on the dollar. Sell. Prices plunged deeper. The great panic was on. Black Thursday, October 24, 1929.

The big bankers tried to hold back the roaring deluge. The heads of J. P. Morgan, National City Bank, Guaranty Trust, Chase National, and Bankers Trust formed a pool to support prices. And performed a miracle. The financial world rallied behind them. Prices steadied, began to rise. But confident moves and optimistic words couldn't stop the disastrous flood of panic selling the following week. By the time Thanksgiving rolled around, $30 billion had blown away. Millionaires became paupers. Powerful board chairmen of banks were left holding worthless paper. Even lowly investors with ten-share dreams of glory were stunned. Messenger boys who worked in the financial districts were terrified to walk down Wall Street or La Salle Street for fear of being killed by a "jumper" from one of the skyscrapers.

Jake's father shrugged. Sure, a few thousand people were laid off at Western Electric, but the workers were still hopping off the streetcars and grabbing newspapers even more eagerly than before, and the cops and motormen and conductors were still placing bets with him. Nachum had opened his shoe repair shop on 16th Street. Business was slow, but that was to be expected; it took time to establish yourself. Nobody was really worried. Jake's father, until he got the newsstand, had been in and out of work all his life, good times, bad times, talk of panic and depression was nothing new to him; he was happy not having to live at the whim of a boss.

As for Jake, the beginning of the depression meant absolutely nothing. It was as if a bead of water had dripped off his body. What floored him were the grades he got at mid-semester. Out of fifteen hours, he received ten hours of flunk notices in algebra, English, and geology. Only in German did he get a passing grade. That was the Black Thursday of Jake's life.

"You dumb jumoke," Albie said. "What the hell happened to you?"

"I don't know."

"I thought you were getting along fine. That's the story you handed me."

"I thought I was."

"Jesus Christ, why didn't you tell me? We'd have done something about it."

"I didn't know. I honest to God didn't know."

"Oh, boy. You really cop the cake."

At the pool Swanee called him into his office and said, "How could you do this to us?"

As if he had flunked on purpose. "I tried, honest. I did the work, honest."

"I've got your records here. B average student in high school—"

"I got away with murder."

"IQ tests, one-forty."

"I bullcrapped my way through it. They must have made a mistake."

"I talked to Professor Boroff, head of the psychology department. No mistakes."

"I don't know what to say, Swanee."

"I don't want you to work out anymore."

"Jesus, I'll go to pot."

"I want you to save your energy for study."

"I don't swim every day I'll go crazy. That's the monkey on my back."

"I don't want you to work at the pool anymore."

"What'll I do for expenses?"

"We'll make other arrangements."

"Christ, coach."

"Go up to Biff Spalding's office. He wants to see you."

The pool, his Rolls-Royce to fame, fortune, the good life dried up on him, was bulldozed out of existence. Now he had to see Biff Spalding, the athletic director of the whole school. He was as disturbed as when he had been a kid in grammar school having to see the principal.

Biff, a former all-American guard from Wisconsin and head football coach at Indiana, was a huge, long-armed giant who wore loose tweed jackets and looked as if he were wearing football shoulder pads. He was with his administrative assistant, Heinie Drier, a red-cheeked, bright-eyed, wispy-haired dynamo who used to play basketball at Northwestern. Biff's hand was so big, Jake could hardly grasp it in a handshake.

"Jake, Jake, Jake," Biff said, pacing his office, moving among trophies and pictures of the university's hall of fame. "You of all guys. We thought we'd never have to worry about you. Bright student, big IQ, Phi Beta Kappa, we said. Didn't we, Heinie?"

"Absolutely."

"'This is a guy we'll be proud of,' we said. Star athlete. Brilliant scholar. We could brag about a guy like that. A real asset to the university. Wasn't that the way we sized Jake up, Heinie?"

"All the way."

"What are we going to do now, Jake?"

"I don't know. I'll work harder. Study my ass off."

"What seems to be the problem?" said Heinie.

"I don't know. I study, and I just don't seem to get it. Maybe you could talk to my instructors."

"No," said Heinie. "We couldn't do that. You can't talk to them. Athletes are poison to some of them. I don't know why. We pay their salaries. We put them on the map. We get them their goddamn laboratories. But some of them do everything they can to stick it into the athletes."

"Let's get him tutors for all his classes, Heinie," said Biff.

"If I flunk," said Jake hopefully, "maybe I'll be able to make it up in summer school. Some easy college, like the football players go to."

"If you flunk, you're out," said Biff. "No summer school. Nothing."

"We'll assign you some tutors," said Heinie. "Don't worry about the expense. Let's hope they can help you."

That evening Milton B. came out to see him.

"My God, Jake, why didn't you tell me? I thought we were getting along beautifully."

"I don't know what to say. I don't know what to do."

"Haven't we been treating you right?"

"You've been wonderful, like a father."

"Do you have any problems? Emotional, maybe. A girl."

"Not really."

"We could send you to a psychiatrist. He might help you."

"I'm not nuts. Dumb maybe. But not nuts."

"All right, all right. I understand you're not working at the pool anymore."

"Swanee thought it interfered with my studies."

"What were you getting there?"

"About five dollars a week."

"Okay, here's fifty dollars. That ought to take you through the rest of the semester. Anything else?"

"You could lend me your brains."

"Get in there and study, Jake. We're counting on you. Albie'll be gone. You'll take his place. We need another national championship."

Bolstered with money, primed with the backing of the athletic department, armed with tutors, the major campaign against Jake's ignorance and innocence was under way. The war was on to get him eligible.

Jake's English tutor, Arnold Bates, a kinky-haired, skinny, acned man with thick glasses, was working for his Ph.D. He never changed his sloppy corduroy pants and grease-stained green sweater. He was always in a swirl of pipe smoke, and he stank of sweat, smoke, tobacco, and musty old books.

"You fucking athletes." That was his attitude. "Diamonds as big as the Ritz in your pockets."

"What are you bitching about? You're getting three dollars an hour."

"You know what Heinie Drier said to me? He said, 'You get Jake through, and we'll give you a bonus of fifty dollars. You don't get him through, we'll take you ten miles out in the lake and throw you in.' So let's get to work."

He read Jake's themes and threw up his hands. "Three dollars an hour, I'm being grossly underpaid."

"I'll get Drier to get me somebody else."

"You'll shit, too. You got me, and you're going to get my whip. We're going to start with simple first-grade sentences. 'I have a dog. Its name is Spot.' That's how you're going to write. You're going to learn how to conceive an idea and follow it through. Simply, as elementary as can be. So that when you write your finals—and your final grade hinges on that—there'll be no automatic F errors. And you're going to learn what the Romantic poets are all about."

His algebra and geology tutors were patient and kind, leading him with logic and illustration to understanding. Unlike his instructors, who covered an enormous amount of ground, they waited for him; the more time it took, the more money in their pockets. That's what Jake needed. Time. Direction. The blank pages of his mind opened up. If he had been a religious man, he would have said, "I have seen the light." Only the light was still dim and obscure.

Weekends he brought all his books home. His folks, especially his mother, beamed at him proudly as he studied: the man of the world, of books, of profound thought, as if he were the new rabbi in town. *Nachus,* lots of *nachus* from him.

Hey, look, it's murder. I'm not making it, I'm flunking, a failure, don't expect too much from me, don't pressure me.

How could he disappoint them?

They boasted how well he was doing, their Yonkel, who could pass for a *shaigetz* with his blue eyes and light hair and his athletic talent. He's not just a nobody, they bragged. Scholarships he's got. Money he gets for just learning. He's a member of the most important Jewish fraternity in the country, where only the rich from the finest families belong. Business, he says he's going into, but he could be anything, a famous doctor, an important lawyer, a celebrated philosopher. Look at him, our Yonkel, steeped in learning, the only one in the family with a college education, look at that great mind at work.

How could he tell them how rough it was when right now, as they glowed over him, he had a hard-on? He was solving an algebra problem, and for no reason at all his pants were bursting at the crotch. His cock had a will of its own, his blood engorging it, his mind drained. He called Ida.

Her mother answered, "She's not here anymore."

"Where is she?"

"She has her own apartment."

"Where?"

She was on La Salle Street, the Near North Side. He called her. Didn't expect to find her in. The phone rang and rang. Oh, God, be in. I need some relaxation. I've got to get away from these goddamn books and this hard prick. No swimming, no action, no release, I'll go out of my mind.

"Hello."

That was Ida. Kind of husky. Kind of faraway. Kind of strange. She didn't seem glad to hear from him. Seemed moody. Seemed indifferent. But she'd see him. Yah, all right, whenever, she'd see him. He grabbed his fat anthology of Romantic poetry and rushed to the streetcar. Wherever he went, he dragged the book along. He was getting to be a goddamn fruit. He tried to concentrate on Shelley and Keats while being jiggled and jerked all the way to the Near North Side, but fantasies of fucking Ida kept intruding. It seemed as if he hadn't seen her in years.

He walked swiftly along La Salle Street after he got off the streetcar, his urgency moving him into a run. All the houses, in the dim yellow lights of the lampposts, seemed alike: three-story, stone, stairways leading up to the buildings, which had been broken up inside into small apartments. He leaped up the stairs, rang Ida's bell, and rushed in at the sound of the buzzer. Two flights up, down a faintly lit corridor, was Ida's apartment. He was breathless, buoyant.

"Hey, hey, you really made it, you've got your own pad, you're really out on your own, free, white, eighteen, fuck-you and hooray for me. Right?"

Her eyes were bloodshot, her face wan, she looked as if she'd been crying. His urgency spun away into a bleak cloud. He tried to maintain his buoyancy. He surveyed the apartment: one medium-sized room with a kitchen separated by a Japanese decorated screen. A bare oak floor, a drop-leaf table with two chairs, an easy chair, a double bed with a batik spread and a bunch of colorful pillows. Two standing lamps with tassels on the shades. A radio on the floor beside the bed.

"Hey, wow, peachy, terrific." He lifted her, crushed her to his chest, whirled her about. "The whole goddamn place is yours."

"Oh, Jake, you're wonderful." And she burst into tears.

Oh, Christ, now that, the faucets of self-pity and pain, the streams of tears that wrenched his guts and made him helpless and awkward.

"I'm sorry, Jake."

"What do you say we go out, take in a movie, get lost?"

"I couldn't. Not the way I feel."

"Come on. I'm loaded." He pulled a wallet out of his pocket and showed her ten dollars. "How about that, the kid, money?"

"I don't know if I'd enjoy it."

"Or the College Inn. Saturday night, college night. Muggsy Spanier. All that wah-wah. I've got a standing invitation from Lila. Free."

"No. Let's go to a movie."

They saw *Broadway Melody* with Bessie Love and Anita Page at the Oriental, another Balaban and Katz extravaganza in plaster and fake-gold paint, an opulent Jewish version of the *Arabian Nights*.

Afterward they had chocolate fudge sundaes at De Mets.

"So," he said, "how are all your boyfriends?"

A sad look in her eyes, a lowering of her lids. Then: "How are all your coeds?"

"There are none."

"Oh, come on, Jake. A guy like you."

"Really. But you've been pretty busy."

She nodded; her eyes got teary.

"You worried about your job?"

"Not really. Men are losing jobs, but the union goes on. The railroad union, that is."

"So what's bothering you?"

"Love."

"Oh, that thing."

"Whoever invented it, Jake?"

"I don't know. I hear King Arthur and his knights started it all. Chivalry, wearing a lady's ribbons, romancing with the lyre and all that shit."

"Do you have to talk that way?"

"Sorry, Ida. It just came out. Anyhow, Shakespeare gave it a boost, the Romantic poets a real shot in the arm."

"Maybe life was better before they came along."

"They say Shakespeare was queer, Queen Guinevere was a nymphomaniac, and Lord Byron was probably impotent."

"Now I know everything."

"All that crap, they're stuffing it down my throat, my head's dizzy from it."

"Better that than being miserably in love."

"You really got it right in the *knish,* huh?"

"With it, we go mad. Without it, it's hell."

"I thought I was the guy."

"You were, Jake. But you're too elusive. You're off on your own cloud. And things happen."

He waited for her to go on. They finished their sundaes.

"I'm a real cornball, Jake. Like the poor, ignorant, immigrant girls in the *bintel briefs,* the lonelyheart letters to the editors. Married man. Separated. Love, love, love, like you wouldn't believe."

"I heard."

"From whom?"

"Around."

"His wife followed him one night. Right to my apartment. She almost tore my eyes out. It was unbelievable. He's back with her. The kids, he says. He's got to keep the home for the kids, he says. That was two months ago."

Jake sang, "Lover, come back to me. . . ."

"You're a rat, Jake."

"What do you want me to do, Ida? Go after him like he's a movie star? Bring him to you on a pedestal?"

She shook her head; there was no answer.

"You know, Ida, I've got a geology instructor who's a little

crazy when he strays from geology, but he's fun. He says if
women were like animals, who could screw only when they're in
heat, there'd be no love, only a big gangshag; then they'd go
about their business of reproducing and foraging for food and
shelter."

"That's a big help."

"By the same token, he says, women have the most wonderful
invention in the world by being able to screw whenever they
want to. With that invention they have a powerful hold on man;
they've been able to create the home, the society as we know it
today."

"It hasn't done me any good."

He took her hand, held it. "But it will one day. You'll see."

"Boy, you're getting into all kinds of things, aren't you?"

"I don't know what good it'll do, but they're really pumping
things into me."

Now her hand was warm. He felt a spark through it.

"Let's go home, Jake."

"Let's go."

"What a nice thing to say: home. My home. My own place.
Where I can do anything I want to."

Before, when they had been together, there had always been
an urgency about Ida. She'd clutch him and shiver at his kisses
and tremble to his touch, and then she'd fumble at him, beside
herself, not knowing what to do, with fear and shame always
with her. Now, in bed, naked with him for the first time, where
he could see her full breasts and erect nipples, her sturdy legs
and strong hips, she had no fear, and there was a different
urgency, more intense. There was a deep hunger about her, a
powerful need rather than desire. In her eyes, he felt like a
thoroughbred horse, splendid and magnificent, responding to her
touch, her soft lips, her tongue, her mouth, her flesh, her hair.
She had learned to swear; she was able to abandon herself
completely. She said, "Shit. Fuck. Oh, daddy. Oh, lover. Oh, I
love to suck your cock. I love to eat your whole body. Oh, you
fuck. Slip it to me. Now. Slip it to me." She directed him, and he
plunged into her deep and hard, like diving clean and powerfully
into a wave. She overwhelmed him, possessed him, holding him
tight with her arms and her vagina, her strong muscles there

clutching him, palpitating, sucking him deeper into her womb.

Afterward he felt it had not been especially Jake she had made love to, as before; he could have been anybody. A sense of regret welled up in him. He wished he had been first. He wished she had been all his, as before, and not an instrument of her sexuality. At this moment she was like him, taking everything, giving very little, an animal. He wanted more. So did she. What would his geology instructor say about that? Desire beyond desire? Food, shelter . . . and what else? The Holy Grail?

She was in the kitchen, making coffee. She was still naked, fleshy, *zoftig,* vibrant, proud of her body and unafraid with the diaphragm in her.

"Feel better?" she said.

"Yes."

"So do I."

She didn't cling to him, as she had before, didn't submerge herself.

"Stay awhile longer, huh? The second time will be better."

Yes, she was free, white, eighteen, with a fuck-you-and-hooray-for-me look in her eyes.

Winter set in. The city, a gray, bleak, grim prison, the white snow turning to sooty drifts and dirty slush, the zero temperatures and driving winds freezing the lake and locking in the freighters and barges, the railroad trains puffing and smoking heavily over the frozen rails, the automobiles sliding and skidding on the icy streets. Jake's father getting dressed in the morning in long woolen underwear, heavy pants, woolen shirt and sweaters, a sheepskin coat which he called his *peltz,* a woolen cap with earmuffs, felt boots stuffed with newspapers, half gloves leaving his fingers free to make change. At night he'd come home, his face stiff and red, his back and shoulders aching from the weight of his *peltz,* his fingers numb. He would sit down to eat, and Jake's mother would prepare a pan of hot water for his feet to thaw out. Sometimes she'd rub liniment on his shoulders and arms to relieve the ache. And Jake could feel, in the way Bubi reacted, that a cold knife had been laid deep in her heart. Even in America everything wasn't palm trees filled with dates, hives brimming with honey, vineyards lush with grapes, days of warm golden sunshine. Especially now, with people being thrown out of work and not knowing where to look for it or what to do. Voices were shriller, more desperate. The neighborhood got shabbier and shabbier, as if the streets and buildings, too, were giving up in despair.

Jake, pounding away at his books when he came home weekends, would look up after his father had settled down for the evening, counting and wrapping his change and figuring out his winnings and losses from the horses.

"Noo, Aaron," his mother would say. Each day Jake's father left it was as if he'd gone off on a great journey and therefore he had to come back with important news of the world.

"Western Electric laid off three thousand people this week."

"Gottenyu."

"It'll be a few dollars less in our pocket."

"But it won't hurt us, hah?"

"No. But it's strange. People I have been seeing every day for years, some of them with nice smiles and a good word, suddenly I stop seeing them. Like they died. What will happen to them?"

"A sad, bitter time."

"But business is good at the coalyard. They hired a few more drivers and helpers."

"Good, good."

"Bubkes. The coalman"— Jake's father was referring to the owner of the coalyard—"is betting heavier on the horses. He hit me for two hundred dollars this week."

"Oy, Aaron, you shouldn't gamble. Times like this, it's dangerous."

"Times like this people take greater risks. Next week I'll turn the coalman over to Capone. Most of his bet anyway. Let him hit Capone for a change."

"He can afford it, that gangster. And the others?"

"The others are the others, small-time winners and losers. A dollar here, a dollar there. The senator"—Jake's father was referring to the state senator who lived in the area of the newsstand—"he's home early for Christmas. He's shaking everybody's hand. Always with a mouthful of cheer. He says the Depression is only a temporary thing. Right after the new year things will get better."

"I hope so."

"Capone never had it so good. His place is always crowded."

"How is that?"

"Maybe because it's warm in there. Maybe because he serves free coffee and doughnuts. And who knows, the horses might turn lucky and Capone will start giving money away."

"On a bitter day in a bitter year."

"Who knows? Capone says he's going to give away five-thousand turkeys for Christmas."

"A regular philanthropist."

Miriam, Jake's sister, ever since she had started menstruating, was becoming more secretive, spending more time in the bathroom, was more worried about her looks. She had a boyfriend, a star on the basketball team, and she went out of her mind, fixing her hair and face and wondering what to wear when he came over. They'd sit in the living room, which was seldom used otherwise, and they'd talk; but mostly the radio or Victrola would be on, and they'd dance and toddle.

The kid brother, Harry, wanted a bigger sled. There was ice on the street, packed down and made slick by the automobile traffic. He wanted a real coaster, one he could steer and that could go a mile. When he got a fix on something, watch out, he never let go, until Jake would yell, "Get him the sled. I'll pitch in half." Getting the sled wasn't that important; the victory in getting it was more vital.

"Such big eyes and such small pockets," his father would say.

"Kid," Jake would say, "when you grow up, you'll have to own a gold mine."

"So I'll own a gold mine. Big deal."

Nachum had moved into the back of his shop. He'd come over for dinner on Friday night, and Bubi would be delighted at the sight of him.

"*Noo,* Nachum," said Jake's father. "How's business?"

"Don't ask."

Jake's father knew how it was. "How much will you need this month?"

"Don't ask."

"Give a for-instance."

"I can't pay the rent. I can't pay the *verein.*"

Jake's father gave him the money he needed without any questions or any I-told-you-so.

"I don't understand it," Nachum said.

"What's to understand? There's a Depression."

"There's a Depression and they're singing 'Happy Days Are Here Again.'"

"That's America."

"In the newspapers, cheerful advertisements. Here. Look." He riffled through the *Daily News*. "There. A full page. 'Wall Street May Sell Stocks, But Main Street Is Still Buying Goods.' And here. Look. 'All right, Mister—Now that the headache is over, LET'S GO TO WORK!' The *momsers*."

"There's another song they sing here. 'Looking at the World Thru Rose Colored Glasses.'"

"It's a crazy country."

"What do you want people to do, tear their hair out, shoot themselves?"

"You can talk, Aaron. There's no Depression for you."

"What's my business? Two cents for a paper?"

"What about the horses? With Capone, I hear, there's no Depression."

"People are drinking more. They suffer less. They gamble more. Desperately. Like it's their last hope. I see them pool their pennies. They have ten-cent dreams. A man must dream or he gives up."

"It's not that I'm not doing good business. But people don't pay me. They bring me their shoes. They say fix them. I have to spend money for leather, heels, materials, the electricity. Then they want their shoes back without money."

"Keep their shoes."

"How can I? They come in crying. How can the children go to school? they say. They'll freeze. How can a man look for work, how can a woman go out in the streets? We'll pay you, we'll pay you as soon as times get better, they say. Soon, soon, times will get better. Hoover says so. The bankers, a *klug* on them, they say so. Even the newspapers, on the one hand bad news, on the other good. Meanwhile, everything costs money, money I haven't got."

"You're a capitalist. You're being squeezed."

"What can I do? Sell their *forkockteh* shoes? Who wants them, who can afford them? Aaron, Aaron, I came too late. It's your America."

Jake chimed in, "It's my America, Nachum. That's what everybody says. But this winter, old buddy, like Shakespeare says, it's a bitter winter of discontent."

"Hah?" said Nachum in surprise.

"Listen to the scholar," said Jake's mother. "Shakespeare yet."

It was also Jake's winter of anxiety. Work was piling up like the snow shoveled off the walks on campus, chilling him to the bone like the winds blustering in off the lake. Finals were just around the corner, when his instructors would be aiming at the jugulars of his mind. Right in the middle of it all—hell week.

It began with a bang. All the pledges were rushed upstairs and crowded into one room. Ten of them altogether.

"Everybody take your goddamn clothes off," said Randy Bernstein, who promised he was going to lead the pledges through the most grueling week of their lives. "Last two get their asses paddled." All he needed was a bunch of bloodhounds, beagles, and a bullwhip.

The pledges tore their clothes off, hopped around to get their shoes and socks off; some fell down.

"All right. You two. Assume the position."

Two of the pledges bent over, pale, hairy-legged, balls hanging, asses bared. Randy was a tall, pimply, curly-headed senior with a loose lower lip and a Mississippi drawl. He stood over the pledges with an oak paddle. And then, wham, he whacked them across the buttocks, wham, wham, the blood going out of them, leaving them white for a moment before welts of red streaked back.

"You stand there with your clothes off. Nobody sits down. I catch anybody dressed or sitting down, ten paddles."

Randy left. Naked, everybody but Jake wanted to hide; they were so exposed; they looked so vulnerable, especially the thin-chested, narrow-shouldered, and flabby ones and especially those with shriveled cocks. The windows were covered with frost. You could feel the zero cold seeping into the room. But their bodies, filled with fear, pumping their hearts, kept them warm. Soon the room began to smell from their sweat and anxiety. What next?

A few of them had been in high school fraternities, where they had dressed in outlandish costumes and done clownish things during their initiation, and it was over. A few in military academies had been hazed, had gone through some scary night routines, but in retrospect it had been fun. Paddling was an old story. They talked nervously of what they'd gone through, of what might happen here. Jake was one of the few who'd never experienced any of it. He was most alarmed, mainly because he didn't know if he could take it. Earlier in the semester Randy had paddled him for not memorizing the fraternity song. The pain had been so withering he'd jumped about and yanked the paddle away and slammed it across Randy's behind. He'd been grabbed and pulled away and calmed down. Albie had lectured him: "Kid, it's a tradition, part of the whole scam. You'll take it or you just don't belong." They had never paddled him again. He didn't know if he could really take it.

Each one was called out of the room and brought downstairs. None ever came back.

"What the hell are they doing down there?" Jake asked.

Twice they heard screams.

"Oh, Jesus!"

Jake's turn. Down the stairs, through the drafty entrance hall. Shivers going through him. Then into the living room. All the fraters there. Including Albie. All of them dressed. Him naked. Humiliatingly naked, the way they eyed him. The paddles in their hands gleamed in the harsh lights. Weapons. Murderous weapons. Every fiber of him began to tremble. Dudley Glick, the president of the house, began to talk.

"These are the sacred rites of Phi Epsilon Pi. From time immemorial young men have been put to the test. They have been cut, defiled, sent out on long, treacherous hunts, tested to the utmost, to prove their worthiness, to see if they merit belonging to the tribe. You are now about to be initiated into the exclusive ranks of the finest fraternity in America. You are now on the verge of joining a great fellowship of men. But you have not been tested yet. You have yet to prove that you belong.

Now, during this long week, you will have to earn the right of membership in our ranks."

"Assume the position," said Randy.

Jake hesitated, looked at them; they were stony-faced, studying him. His skin grew prickly. He swallowed hard. Do it, he said to himself. You've come this far. Do it. You've got to prove yourself.

The shriveling pain of the slam across his buttocks shook him. He took a deep, gasping breath, started to rise.

"Down. Stay down."

Another frater. With another paddle.

These punks have gone through it. They've taken it. You can do it. The breath rushed out of him on the next slam. He ground his teeth together. Bastard. You dirty bastards. Do it. Get it over with. Do it. Whack! Crack! Slam! Smarting tears in his eyes, his whole body trembling. His jaws locked. Oh, you bastards, you scummy bastards!

"Okay, get up."

He quivered as he stood up. Silence. He was led upstairs to another room, where the others who had gone before him were hopping about to keep warm.

"You made it, Jake."

"Yah, but I don't know how much more I can take."

"That's the worst of it. Paddling's the worst. You come out of that, you're all right."

"A whole week of it," Jake said. "You never know what's next."

"There's school, your classes. You'll be able to duck out then."

"I won't be able to sit down," said Jake.

Laughter. Nervous laughter. Even from those who'd been through it before.

"In class, we'll be like a bunch of Jews in synagogue. We'll do everything on our feet. We'll even rock back and forth."

More laughter. The pain easing. Less humiliation at being naked, so exposed. In common pain, more comfortable with each other. Is that possible? Jake thought. Pain equals comradeship. Ladies and gentlemen, a new Einsteinian formula. Bare your asses, have them beaten, and everybody becomes friendly.

At midnight, with everybody jumping around to keep from freezing, Randy came up and said, "Okay, get dressed."

He gave each of them his task for the night.

"A paddle for every one you don't complete."

Jake had to get three flies. It was five below zero now, the wind gusting off the lake, lashing you with icy whips so's you could hardly move, and he had to find flies. Where the fuck do you find flies in the wintertime? Florida? California? India? Africa?

"Do they have to be live flies?" asked one of the pledges.

"It says flies. Period."

"We can find dead ones in the science building. Especially the tsetse fly."

Jake also had to get a doorknob from the Lake Shore Athletic Club, a towel from the Racquet Club, two ticket stubs from the opera, a G-string from a burlesque dancer.

The pledges split up into two groups. They had two cars available. They bundled up, coats, galoshes, stocking caps, scarves, and rode off screaming into the freezing night, like Indians on the first test of their tribal rites.

There was hardly any traffic. Vapor came out of their mouths in the unheated car. They skidded around the icy streets. Along the breakwater on Lake Shore Drive the lake was iced in. A big white moon was out. The night was crystal clear.

Jake walked into the Lake Shore Athletic Club with a tire handle under his coat. He was met by the doorman. He said he knew Larry Conrad, who had placed second to Kojac in the Olympics. Jake had swum against Conrad a couple of times and did know him. The doorman called Conrad, woke him up. Jake talked to him, said he was in a jam, had to see him, needed his help. Conrad said come on up.

Conrad was a wide-shouldered, slim-hipped man with straight blond hair and faded blue eyes. He was in a heavy chenille robe when Jake got to him on the eighth floor.

"Sorry, Larry. Fraternity initiation. Hell week. It's my ass if I don't come up with the crap they want."

"What do you need, kid?"

"A doorknob."

"Good Christ, you can get a doorknob anywhere."

"They want it from here."

"How the hell would they know where it came from? A doorknob is a doorknob."

"You mean they don't have special doorknobs here?"

"Look."

He was right. No special markings. A doorknob is a doorknob. You could get one in any hardware store. Five smart collegiate heads couldn't figure that out.

"Sorry I bothered you, Larry."

"Good luck, kid."

Conrad went back into his room, locked the door. On the way to the elevator, Jake thought: I won't have time to buy a doorknob tomorrow. I'll have to screw up part of the morning getting flies from the science lab. All these doorknobs. He took the tire handle out, slammed down on a knob, and broke it off. He hid it in his pocket, got on the elevator, and joined the boys outside.

Getting a towel from the Racquet Club was a cinch. The doorman, who'd graduated from the University of Chicago and couldn't get a job in his field, knew about fraternity hell weeks; he went into the locker room and got Jake one. There were plenty of ticket stubs from the opera outside the auditorium. But conning a G-string from a burlesque queen was another matter. They found a bar on North Clark Street with burlesque entertainment. It was so cold even North Clark Street, a street on the make, was almost all shut in. Dixie Wanderlust was near the end of her number, down to her G-string and one last fan of feathers, with a few drunks hammering on the tables and yelling for her to take it all off. The bartender looked Jake over and said, "How old are you, kid?"

"Twenty-two."

"Drink up. It's the last show."

"I don't drink."

"What are you here for? You think this is a whorehouse?"

"I gotta see Dixie."

"You a friend?"

"Relative. Nephew."

The bartender looked at him suspiciously. Jake blew on his numb fingers and jumped from foot to foot to keep warm. Dixie finished her number with a flourish: The fan whisked away, the G-string flicked off; there was a startling glimpse of bouncing breasts and what seemed like acres of white flesh, and she was offstage, with a fanfare from the bored trio. The half dozen drunks wanted more, more. Dixie came out, demure, curtsying, then a whisk of the feathery fan, and there was all that flesh again and the breasts like white mountains, and she was off and gone.

"You'll find her in her dressing room," the bartender said.

Dixie had an old kimono on when Jake entered her room. Her platinum hair was as stiff as white shoe polish. Her mirror was ringed with pictures of herself since the days she had been a child tap dancer, and her heavily made-up face was caked with sweat. She looked as faded and tired as a weary old vamp. Costumes were strewn all over. Cigarette butts were on the floor. Dixie had a half glass of straight whiskey in her hand. There was a sour, decayed smell in the room.

"What is it, kid?"

She choked with laughter when Jake told her. Her voice was husky from cigarettes and booze.

"You're sure you don't want to lay me?"

"Just the G-string."

She stopped laughing. "That's an insult, you know."

"I didn't mean it like that. I mean, it's after three in the morning. Me and my buddies, we've still got things to do. We've got to get back to Evanston."

"You're sure?"

She let the kimono fall from her shoulders. Her face was old, but her body was magnificent. Statuesque. Firm. Curved in all the right places. With an unreal, glossy, cold-cream look about her skin. But no bush. Just the slit. That shocked him. That and the weird alabaster sheen of her skin turned him off.

"You're sure?"

"Dixie, the guys are waiting for me. It's freezing outside. There's no heat in the car."

"A quickie, huh?" There was fun and laughter in her eyes.

She started touching him. Right there. He couldn't get it up. You could lie with your mind, with your tongue, but not with your prick. Now the game was over. Grim determination grooved into her face, filled with desire to be desired.

"For the G-string. No humpie, no G-string."

He shut his eyes. Ida, he said inwardly, let me have it. Oh, Lupe, Oh, you Lupe Velez. In his mind he started whacking off. He could get a hard-on for no reason at all, but now, there it was, right there, and nothing. Come on, Lupe. Do it for me, baby. There. There. There it goes. Right in there, Aw, baby. You're doing it, baby. There. There.

"Okay, buster," she said with spikelike hardness. "You get your G-string."

As he left, she said, "Be careful with it. It's been dipped in Chanel Number Five."

In the car, one of the pledges said, "What the hell kept you so long?"

"It took a little doing."

"We froze our balls off."

"Any of you guys got any Argyrol or G-O-45?"

"You didn't!"

"I had to pay her for the article."

"You're kidding."

"Dixie Wanderlust? Guys'd give her a hundred bucks for a piece."

"That's the way it was, fellas," said Jake.

It was 6 A.M. when they got home. One of the pledges gave him a package of G-O-45. It relieved Jake's mind. He got an hour's sleep. He had an eight o'clock class. He slept through part of that class. So did most of the other guys who were going through hell week. Only nonfraternity men, most of whom lived off campus, were bright and alert. The instructor made no exceptions. He droned on and on.

Jake rushed back to the house at lunchtime to wait on tables. He slipped on a patch of ice and hurt his rump and spine. He limped through the meal and loped back to campus like a wounded animal to make a two o'clock class in German. He slept through part of that. Once, when the instructor called on him, he was poked awake. The instructor yelled, "You silly Americans with your silly games and your silly pranks. No respect for learning, no regard for the high institution you are in. Go. Go home and sleep. I will not waste my time on idiots."

Jake went to the library and slept for an hour. Exhausted, he came back to the house and worked with his math tutor for two hours. After supper he was called before the fraters. He produced the articles he had been told to get.

"Clever," said Randy, taking the rhinestone G-string, smelling it, then putting it around his neck.

"Enterprising," said Albie.

"Whose G-string?" said Dudley.

"Dixie Wanderlust," said Jake.

"Who is she?" said Randy.

"A North Clark Street bimbo," said Jake.

"I hear you put it to her," said Dudley.

"Assume the position," said Randy.

"What for?" said Jake. "I got everything."

"Nobody's perfect," said Randy.

Jake bent over, stiffened for the blow, clenched his teeth. Whack! Every nerve in his body went wild.

"Stay down."

Jake quivered, holding onto himself.

"This one is for having so much fun."

Slam! He thought the blood would rush out of all his orifices. Rigid and trembling, he straightened up. He didn't know if he could take another week of this. Randy handed him a slip of paper. Another job. The Hawthorne Inn in Cicero. Capone's suburban headquarters. An autograph on Hawthorne Inn stationery from Capone himself, two bullets from a submachine gun.

"Go on. Get going."

Sore-assed, his back stiff and aching from his fall on the ice that afternoon, feverish from lack of sleep, he hustled out of the house, taking along a geology text and a volume of Shakespeare's plays. This time he was on his own. At the El station, he tried to reach Lala and Bo. Maybe they could help him. Nobody answered. He called the JPI. Nobody there. He waited for a train, stomped about with his stiff body to keep from freezing. He thought he was shot full of novocaine by the time the train rolled in. He had to transfer at Howard Street for a Chicago El. Another foot-stomping, eternal wait. He thawed out during the everlasting ride downtown. He was too cold and sleepy to study. Before he transferred for a West Side El, he tried to reach Lala and Bo again, then Lenny Kahn and Yussel Gomberg, who were with Capone. Nobody in. Fucking muzzlers, all out on some kind of hustle. Nobody at the JPI either. Christ, another long, jolting night ride past his father's newsstand to Cicero. A northeaster was blowing off the lake, and flakes of snow had been falling for some time. By the time Jake got off the El it was past ten, and a full-grown blizzard greeted him. Down the icy, snowy streets, breathing glaciers and exhaling smoke, he trudged a mile before the Hawthorne Inn came into view. He felt like a moving igloo by the time he got there, snow in his shoes, socks all wet, drifts of snow piling up against parked cars and buildings.

The Hawthorne Inn was a dump. You'd think, with the millions and millions Capone raked in, he would live at the Drake or the Edgewater Beach Hotel. But this was the mob's castle, where they held court, had their big parties, planned their conquests of the world, their moat a dirty, snow-piled sidewalk, their means of transportation automobiles instead of horses, their colors the black hand, their weapons machine guns, bombs, and revolvers instead of swords, battleaxes, spears, and lances.

There were lots of cars outside, lots of action inside the lobby. The *capos* and soldiers, overdressed, stylish but still looking like gunsels, moved in and out of the restaurant and bar with drinks in their hands and money flowing back and forth as they played *mora* with their fingers. You could hear them yell *due, cinque, quattro*. A few were playing boccie on the lobby carpets, and others were working the slot machines. Up the red-carpeted stairway girls paraded around in slip-ons and step-ins, and the boys were coming down the stairs and going up. It was the biggest shindig Jake had ever seen.

He was afraid to go in. These ginzos, they were all suspicious, all paranoid, what would they think, how would they treat him? He froze, the wind whipping his body, the snow hardening on his mackinaw. He kicked his feet and swallowed icicles of spit. He was turning into a snowman. Suddenly something hard was shoved into his back, and a big, heavy-nosed goon with coal bags for shoulders started frisking him. He tore the books out of Jake's hands, ran through the pages as if there might be weapons or explosives between the lines. Then Jake was lifted off his feet and hurled into the lobby; one of the goons, as an afterthought, picked up the books for evidence. A heavy-shouldered, thick-lipped, round-cheeked man, looking like Capone but a little heavier and bigger, said, "Whatta we got, whatta we got?"

"I don't know, Bottles. He's clean."

His mackinaw was ripped off his back. He had only his fear to keep him warm, but it gave him the shivers.

"Who the fuck is he?"

He was frisked again. They felt his balls, his cock, his buttocks; there wasn't a centimeter of him that wasn't touched.

"He's really clean, Bottles."

"What about his mouth? You forgot his mouth."

They opened his mouth, stuck their dirty fingers in it, and poked right down to his throat. He retched, but nothing came up.

"He could be one of Bugs Moran's boys. He could be wired in his asshole, a torpedo."

"Aw, Bottles." That was the big goon who had first frisked him.

"Get it."

Jake started to run. They grabbed him. An armlock almost tore his arm off as he was pinned to the floor. His pants were pulled off.

"He's clean, Bottles."

"Do it."

Jake watched this big ginzo with his bony, calloused, yellow-stained forefinger, come down to him. He screamed with pain as he was pierced. Blood spurted out. He writhed and whimpered and felt as if his insides had been mutilated when the finger came out.

"Nothing, Bottles."

Jake got to his feet, lifted up his pants, strapped himself in. He quivered all over, could hardly stand up.

"He's FBI or Internal Revenue. They get these young punks, look like collegians, disguised with books and all that." He faced Jake, who now felt the sharp daggers in his asshole hurl up to his throat, because this was Al's brother, Ralph "Bottles" Capone. "Listen, punk, I'm going to Leavenworth tomorrow. I'm giving you G-men a year. What the hell more do you want?"

Jake couldn't find his voice.

Bottles lifted him to his toes. "Talk, you sonofabitch. Talk."

The others were ganged closely around him, the sour smells of booze, cigars, and garlic suffocating him, the dark, intent eyes burying him.

Jake swallowed a stiletto. It stuck in his voice box. Bottles shook him; his cheeks jiggled.

"Who are you, punk? What the hell do you want from me? Why do you keep hounding me? It's all set. I'm giving you a year. For Christ's sake."

The stiletto slit a jagged path down to the pit of his stomach. His throat opened. "My name is Jake Davidson. I'm a student at Northwestern University. I'm going through hell week. I'm going through a lot of shitty things I don't want to do, and what I've got to do right now is get a piece of stationery from this hotel and get Al Capone's autograph and a couple of bullets from a submachine gun. Honest to Christ, I'm no fink, no FBI, no Internal Revenue, just a college kid in a fraternity."

"That's his name, Bottles," said one of the guys who had frisked him and had Jake's wallet. "He's got a student ID card."

"Could be a phony," said Bottles.

"He looks kind of young."

"I'm seventeen, going on eighteen," said Jake.

"How do we know?" said Bottles. "What do we do, count the wrinkles in your face?"

"Just give me the autograph and a couple of bullets, and I'll be on my way."

A short, wiry man with a hooked nose, older than the rest, stepped to Bottles and said, "He's probably who he says he is and what he says he is. These screwball frats think up all kinds of wise-guy tricks. My own kid's been through it. We're clean, Bottles. Let's give him what he wants, and we'll go on with the party."

"But Al ain't here."

"You can give him the autograph, Bottles."

"I can't do that. It wouldn't be right. But I'll give him my own autograph. Hey, a piece of stationery."

Somebody brought some stationery. Bottles signed his name below the inscription "To the college punk who almost scared the shit out of us." The older man brought out his pen and wrote: "To the kid who almost broke up my brother's going-away party . . . Al Capone." Somebody took two bullets out of a submachine gun and handed them to Jake.

"Okay, kid?" said Bottles.

"Thanks."

"You wanna stick around for the party? We're having some broads over from the Frolics later."

"I gotta get back to school," Jake said. These guys, with their guns and submachine guns, getting drunker and drunker, who knew what might happen? "Thanks a lot, fellas."

It was two in the morning when he got back to the fraternity house. He got out of his wet, snowy clothes. Numb with cold, his insides feeling massacred, he shivered himself into sleep. The next day in class he could hardly sit. A couple of times his instructors told him to stop fidgeting. All day he worried about an infection. But he couldn't go to a doctor. What could he tell him, his asshole was frisked by Bottles Capone? A likely story. He almost died when he had a bowel movement. He couldn't stand up for ten minutes afterward. At night when he gave the fraters the autographs and bullets from Capone headquarters, nobody believed him.

"You probably got the autographs from the night clerk."

"But the bullets. What about the bullets?"

"You could have gone to an all-night gun shop."

"Shit."

He was paddled. The pain was so fierce he turned to Randy, the paddle master, and said, "You hit me once more, and I'll kill you."

Albie Karlin said, "That's enough, Randy."

By the end of the week he was so fatigued from lack of sleep, the pain and stiffness of his body, the cold, he could hardly keep his eyes open, he could hardly think, his reactions were all in slow motion. So that he walked like a zombie on the final night into a pack of fraters, who were grim shadows in the candlelit dining room. Dudley Glick sat at a table with a purple cloth over it and two candles at each end.

"Jacob Davidson, all week long you have been observed, you have been tested, you have been judged. It takes only one blackball to send you out of here in shame and disgrace. It takes only one person's final judgment of your character to turn you away from the ranks of Phi Epsilon Pi. . . ."

Oh, God, Jake thought, I didn't make it. After all that, I didn't make it. Some bastard is blackballing me. Like the time I tried to join the Wyandottes as a kid and two guys who didn't know me blackballed me and I was out. And now here, again, I'm not going to make it. . . ."

"Under no circumstances. . . ."

That's it. No. His mind reeled. His stiff, weary legs almost caved. For some goddamn reason, no. Some sonofabitch has blackballed me. Who? Through bleary, feverish eyes, he looked at the shadowed men standing about. All so solemn, so formidable, so powerful. Who? All he could think of was Randy. Randy, that sonofabitch, never forgetting my taking the paddle out of his hands and socking him with it. Randy, that sonofabitch. There he was. Right beside Dudley, leering, that arrogant half smile on his face. He lunged for him, grabbed him.

Immediately the whole room was in an uproar, with Randy yelling, "Get that bastard off me. Get that sonofabitch out of here. Kick his ass out of here."

Now Albie had hold of him. "Oh, Christ, you blew it, Jake. All of us wanted you here. But you blew it, blew it. Apologize to Randy. Tell him you're sorry. It's not too late. Maybe he'll find it in his heart to forget everything. Try it. Go on."

Tears were in his eyes, needles in his throat, lumps in his chest. What the hell was college without a frat? Phi Ep was the class. Now they were going to throw him out. He'd be ostracized. What would the guys on the swimming team say, the students who knew he was pledged? How would he ever be able to face anybody?

He stepped up to Randy, wanting to kill him, but said tearfully, "Randy, I'm sorry. Whatever happened, I'm sorry."

Randy dismissed him, "Oh, no, it's too late for that."

Jake grabbed him, pleaded, "I told you I'm sorry. What more do you want? Jesus Christ, you want my balls?"

Again he was torn away. Now Albie was pleading with Randy. "Look at him, Randy. All his life he's dreamed of going to college, of being a fraternity man. When I pledged him, personally pledged him, he was so happy, so grateful. Please don't destroy him. **Don't kill him.**"

"Nothing you can say will change **my mind**," Randy said.

"Please," said Jake.

Albie continued: "Whatever he did, he'll rectify it. He doesn't deserve a blackball. Think of what it'll do to his reputation. The stigma of blackball will follow him everywhere he goes. He'll never be able to face his teammates. He'll be persona non grata in the sororities. People will scorn him like a leper. Christ, Randy, how will he be able to face his mother and father, his sister? You can't do this to him. You'll force him to quit school. You'll ruin his whole future. I beg you, Randy, reconsider your blackball. There is still time." He turned to Jake. "Get down on your knees, Jake. Beg him. Beg him."

Jake dropped to his knees before Randy. "Please, Randy. All the guys want me. Give me a break. Please."

Randy stepped away from him.

"Stand up," said Dudley. "Come here."

That's it. The final word. Silence all around.

"You didn't hear what I said," said Dudley. "Listen carefully. Most carefully. Concentrate on every word. UNDER NO CIRCUMSTANCES CAN WE DENY YOU MEMBERSHIP IN PHI EPSILON PI."

He didn't get it. It still sounded as if he were rejected.

Dudley continued: "We are proud to have you in our ranks. Congratulations."

Dudley was shaking his hand. Albie was thumping his back and smiling. Randy embraced him. Jake had been a perfect target for the final ceremony. But he was in. He'd never forget the humiliation, the embarrassment, the viciousness. He who had never begged forgiveness before had been forced down to his knees, had been made to crawl; he didn't know if he would ever be able to forgive them.

"What do you say, fellows," said Randy, the bullwhipper turning into a butterball, "we go down to the South Side and get us some good old black pussy?"

Tired as they were, a few of the new fraters were eager to go.

"How about it, Jake?" said Randy. "They'll give you luck on your finals."

"No."

"Better'n rabbit's foot, black pussy," said Randy. "Better'n southern cooking and home fucking."

"No."

Fuck 'em, he thought. Fuck 'em all. He went up to bed.

Everybody shut himself into his little room with his books, drinking coffee, smoking his head off, coughing his lungs up, and worrying, worrying, worrying. No matter how smart you were, you dug in. It was final exam time.

Jake holed up with his tutors. Every conceivable question his instructors might ask was covered. He was going to get eligible if it killed him. He crammed with his tutors, made notes, memorized, tried to understand the logic of his subjects, until everything became a jumble and he felt his head was going to burst, and once he yelled, "I can't. I can't make it. Nothing makes sense anymore. I'm going out of my fuckin' mind."

Albie said, "How you doing, Jake?"

"I don't know."

"What do you mean you don't know? You've got to know. You've got it or you haven't got it."

"I'm not up against a stopwatch where I can hit it on the nose. They can throw curves I've never seen before."

"Do you realize how much time and attention have been spent on you, how much money has been invested in you?"

"That's what it all comes down to, huh? Money. Investment."

"You're not just anybody. You're worth a lot of dough to the university. You're like a piece of machinery. They'll put you to work, and you'll pay off. You're in it for medals, glory, a free ride, but they run the train, they're big business."

"All of a sudden you're such a big cynic."

"I know what makes the wheels turn. I'm going to make it pay off big."

"Well, if I can't make it here, I'll become a professional amateur. Live like Weissmuller. The AAU will give me seven dollars a day. I can get meals and a room at the IAC."

At least, in this terrible Depression, he had something to fall back on.

"You want to settle for seven dollars a day?"

"What's wrong with that? These days it's a fortune."

"What happens when you stop competing? You're an old man before you're thirty. No more seven dollars a day. Then what?"

"I'll do something."

"What? Clean streets? Haul garbage? Look at Wally Blake, who wanted you to go to Stanford. Big Olympic man, he went back to the Coast to be a lifeguard. There are guys out there and down in Florida, all big champs, now they're bucking to be the oldest lifeguards in the world. That how you want to wind up? Water on the brain?"

Oh, God, the pressure, his head bursting, his heart palpitating, his legs jelly, his nerves skittering like buckshot. And his mind blank. Absolutely blank the night before his first test in algebra. No matter what his tutor did he couldn't seem to work the simplest problem, he couldn't recall anything.

"Hysteria," his tutor said. "You've gone catatonic. You'd better sleep it off."

He had the keys to the pool from the time he worked there as a guard. He sloshed through ice and snow, opened the pool, turned on the lights, and alone, all alone, he stroked up and down the lengths, following the black line of the inside lane, turning, counting strokes, counting the beat of his kick, turning, up and down, his eyes riveted to the black line, mindless, counting, counting, feeling the rhythm, the power, 100 lengths, 200, he lost count, until he was worn out, his arms were flopping in, his legs cramped up, and he couldn't move. He dragged himself out of the pool, stepped down to the showers. He turned on the hot shower, almost scalding, and lay down on the tile floor and let it beat down on him until he was limp. He felt everything in him go down the drain.

He moved slowly into the rubbing room, sloshed himself with a combination of wintergreen and alcohol and oil; then under a blanket he stretched out on the rubbing table with the smell of the wintergreen all about and fell asleep. The following morning he went to his algebra exam, hopeless. The questions were handed to him. Suddenly everything came back. He got every one right. A hundred.

In English he wrote simple A-B-C sentences. No dangling participles, no commas, no modifying clauses. He couldn't take any chances. He pulled through with a D. He never had any trouble with German; his Yiddish helped him. B. Geology was a bullshit course. True or false. He pulled a C.

When his last grade came in, he jumped into the air. He screamed and yelled and laughed. Everything in him went screwy, and he thought that if he were in the pool now, he'd shatter all records. He ran out of his room and grabbed everyone who was around. He had made it. God damn it, the dumbsock had made it. Everybody thought he'd gone crazy. None of them knew what he had gone through. And he found that he had nobody to celebrate with. No one special person to make whoopee with. His fraternity brothers were really strangers. Even Albie Karlin. How do you make whoopee with God?

Ida was busy. The guys from the JPI who'd gone away to Illinois hadn't come in during the mid-semester holidays. There was nobody around, really. Fitzsimmons was happy for him but had known Jake could do it, never doubted it for one moment. Lala and Bo said, "So what is it, a new record or something?" Even Benny Gordon didn't appreciate his victory. "Jake, you act like you inherited a million dollars," he said.

His folks took his passing grades for granted. "*Noo,* what else?" his mother said. "You think we raised a dummy for a son? Phi Beta Kappa you'll make yet." They lived in a different world. Without Frank Merriwell and Tom Swift and Huckleberry Finn and the whole goddamn wild, wild West.

So Jake settled for Lila and the College Inn. She gave him the key to a room later and sent up Nellise again. This time the grand tour, through strands of her vivid red hair, included Shanghai, Bangkok, and Hong Kong. It was all as anticlimactic as winning any big event. He really had nobody to share his ramblin', rompin', stompin', rootin'-tootin' victory.

The athletic department received Jake's grades as soon as he did. Biff Spalding and Heinie Drier slapped Jake's back and said they'd known all along that he could do it. Swanee shook his hand warmly, gave him back his job at the pool, and added a couple of more hours to his payroll to show his confidence in him. He was welcomed back to working out with the team.

"Don't forget," he was told. "The least trouble with any course, yell, and we'll give you all the help you need."

Milton B. took him to lunch at the Drake to celebrate. The spaciousness, the thick carpets, the crystal chandeliers, the thick white tablecloths and napkins, the heavy silverware, the subdued tones of the place had him tiptoeing and speaking softly. A place fit for Lord Byron, a Shakespearean king, a Russian Czar, a Napoleon.

"I don't mind telling you," said Milton B. "You really threw a scare into us."

"I don't mind telling you I was plenty scared myself."

Nobody was worried about Jake anymore. He had won his bout against scholasticism. But there were other matters that needed attention. When the new semester began, Jake was confronted by Dudley Glick.

"Jake, we've got a problem. It's embarrassing to us. But since you started living here, we've had no room rent from you."

"I thought Milton B. was going to take care of it."

"We thought so, too. We had that understanding. But he hasn't given us a dime."

"I don't get it."

"He also said he'd foot your initiation fee. Two hundred dollars. That makes you three hundred and fifty dollars in arrears. That's a lot of money these days. We've got our expenses. Every month we've got to meet our bills. You can't expect us to foot your expenses."

"Milton B. will be good for it."

"He's been a deadbeat so far. And we've got to come to some kind of arrangement. We have to make sure that we get your room rent every month or you'll have to vacate it for somebody else. I hope you understand."

"What's to understand? Pay or get out."

"Milton B. is an honorary member of Phi Ep. We've asked him to pay up a couple of times, and he has assured us he will;

but he keeps ignoring us. I don't want to be crude about this, but we've got to know how you're going to handle this."

"I don't know. I'll talk to Milton B."

Milton B. was furious on the phone.

"I want you to come right down here, Jake. I want to talk to you."

"Lunchtime is coming up. I've got to set the tables."

"Fuck the tables. You're not working there anymore. Come down here."

Milton B. owed the fraternity $350, and *he* was mad. As soon as Jake got into Milton B.'s office, he said, "Don't they know there's been a crash, there's a Depression in this country?"

Jake didn't know what to say.

"Christ, they think we're still on a honeymoon. They don't know how much money I've lost."

"I'm sorry, Milton."

"It's not your fault, Jake. You had nothing to do with it. It's Hoover, the banks, the greedy speculators, the system, who the hell knows? But they've got a nerve, dunning you, dunning me. They should be proud to have you living there. They should pay you for being there. Albie Karlin will be gone after this term. Who the hell else have they got to brag about? You think a fraternity is any different than a university? Who the hell do they brag about, their scholars? They talk about their athletes. I go out and raise funds. You think anybody'd give a dime for some dull, bookish English professor, some chemistry teacher who stinks of formaldehyde? Who the hell knows them? But people know Reb Beauregard, they know Albie Karlin, and they'll know Jake Davidson. You talk to them, and you get money. Millions of dollars I've raised. And they dun me. Come on, let's go and eat."

Meurice's wasn't as crowded as before. The place didn't look as elegant. Jake's napkin was frayed. The drapes looked worn. The clothes the waiters wore weren't as well pressed or clean. The Continental look had turned shabby. None of the stockbrokers, the former great athletes who had been so cheerful and friendly with Milton B., were around. People there looked worried.

Milton B. was still in a rage. "I'm going to resign from that fraternity. To hell with them."

Which wouldn't take care of Jake's problem.

"What do I do, Milton? They said I've got to pay them every month. Me, personally, I've got to pay them."

"They don't trust me, huh?"

"I'm sure they do, but—"

"No, they don't. I've had their best interest at heart; I've done nothing but good for them: I've been their biggest booster. Do they know how many athletes I take care of?"

Jake could hardly eat. The meal was costing a fortune, and there was rage in every bite.

"You're not going back there, Jake. You're not going to be dependent on them anymore. No meals there, nothing. I've talked to Earl Howard, manager of the North Shore Hotel. You go see him. He'll fix you up for your meals." He took out his wallet; all transactions had to be in cash so that they couldn't be traced by any snoopy Big Ten Board of Ethics on subsidized athletes. He counted out $25. "Find yourself a room. That should take care of the first month's rent. On the first of every month, call me, I'll send you money. Imagine, that fucking fraternity house not trusting me, dunning me."

They ate silently for a while, finishing their lunch.

"What do you need for books, Jake?"

"That's all right, Milton."

"No, you're starting a new semester. You need books." He counted out $15 more. "Meals, books, room rent, you got a job, what else, Jake?"

"Nothing. Nothing, really."

"Okay." Milton B. looked as grim and bulldoggish as he might have when he had played football for good old Northwestern 100 years ago. He grabbed the check, left a $2 tip. "Fuck 'em."

Earl Howard of the North Shore Hotel was a florid-faced man with a ring of white hair around his red dome. He introduced Jake to the manager of the cafeteria. Jake was put to work wiping glasses at lunchtime for his three meals a day. He looked at the food in the trays: steak, roast beef, veal, chicken, fish, vegetables, salads, pies, ice cream, custards—he could have anything he wanted, a feast three times a day. That's going to be eating, he thought.

He found a room nearby for $5 a week: big double bed, windows, lots of light, a big desk, two lamps, an easy chair, chest of drawers, a closet, private, all his own, he'd be able to stretch out. He could even bring up a broad if he ever found one on campus. Then he moved out of the fraternity.

All he had gone through to get in, the dreams he had had of being a fraternity man, the punishment and humiliation he had suffered, all of it went like a puff of smoke right out the window. He couldn't get over how little it all meant to him now.

Jake knew how to study now. When his instructors moved too fast for him, the athletic department provided him with tutors to help him catch up. But he wasn't interested in any of his subjects. Trigonometry was a pain in the ass. In geology he was into the study of rocks and the different geological ages, which were as remote as the billions of years of the earth's history; how was that going to make him a dime? He hated German more than learning Yiddish at the Arbeiterring Shul or Hebrew in *cheder* when he was a kid; what good was it going to do him? English, well, he couldn't make up his mind about that. He was studying Victorian literature, the poets and novelists. He found Hardy's *Mayor of Casterbridge* and Emily Brontë's *Wuthering Heights* as absorbing as any movie. Poetry was still too abstract for him; he was afraid, too, that if he went for it, he'd be considered queer.

Next year, he was sure, it'd be different. He'd start preparing for business school, take courses that would have meaning, like accounting, economics, banking, but he'd still have to go on with English and German for another year. That didn't make sense. Go fight the system.

Anyhow, he found he had more time, time to see movies, time to yearn for the tall, beautiful girls on campus, time to feel lonely. He got friendly with a couple of *shiksas* in his classes: blond, rosy-cheeked, long-legged, and stunning. He asked each of them separately to go to the Edgewater Beach Hotel or the College Inn with him, but they had dates, they said; then he saw one fairly often with a Sigma Nu and the other with a Phi Psi, and he gave up. The boys at the Phi Ep house said, forget it, you'll never get a Tri Delt or a Kappa Alpha Theta to go out with a Phi Ep. Screw 'em.

So he saw Ida whenever she had time for him. And he'd go to the College Inn and go to bed with Lila or some whore she sent up to him.

Once he said to Lila, after they finished fucking, "You don't care who you sleep with, do you?"

"Sure I do. Tonight I wanted you. The point is *I* make the decisions. I don't moon around waiting for somebody to pick me out."

"You don't mind sending whores up to me?"

"Jake, I like you. It gives me pleasure to do you a favor."

"You doing me a favor now?"

"No. I'm doing myself a favor."

Jake didn't understand her. He didn't understand himself in relation to her.

It seemed now that he was marking time until the next fall. That's when he'd be eligible to compete. That's when what he was going to school for would all add up. When the term ended, he upped his English grade to C, got Cs in trig, geology, and hygiene, and a B in German. He always got an A in physical ed. Working that summer as a lifeguard without Willie O. was drearier than any he'd ever spent. It dragged on and on. He couldn't wait for school to start.

As the Depression deepened, men stopped saying, "If only I can get a job, anything." They started saying, "If only I had a racket." But anything they could think of was either taken by Capone and his boys or they were getting into it. Every morning his boys would get up and say, "Who can I muscle today for a buck? One for me and one for the Big Fella." The latest foray was into the newsstand business by no less an operator than Lenny Kahn with the assistance of Yussel Gomberg.

Jake's father came home one day and said, "A new disaster. I'm being organized or I'm being protected, I don't know which."

Jake waited for him to continue.

"Five dollars a month it's going to cost me. There are maybe a thousand stands in Chicago. Five thousand a month in these times, it's no small amount of money. Two gangsters came up to me. Jewish boys, too. Not the Mafia. They're going to organize us, they said."

"Organize you for what? Better wages, shorter hours? You're a private little businessman."

"So are the cleaners and dyers, the butchers, even Nachum and the shoemakers."

"You going to hold still for it?"

"The way they looked you couldn't give them an argument. I didn't agree fast enough, one of them grabbed me by the coat, the other showed me a gun."

"Wouldn't the newspapers have something to say about it?"

"Who are the newspapers? Their circulation managers are gangsters. They used to have bloody wars. They used to hire head breakers, killers. Where did they get them? Capone. These gangsters have City Hall in their pocket, the police on their payroll. Who you going to complain to?"

When he saw Lenny and Yussel a few days later, Jake said, "I want you guys to lay off my old man and my uncle."

"Davidson your old man, your uncle?"

"That's right."

"We didn't know. So they're off the books. Okay? We won't touch them. Okay? But remember, we're doing you a favor."

The new JPI, bankrolled by Jewish philanthropy, had been opened in 1927 to serve the Jewish community in the Douglas-Garfield Park area. Down in the basement was the poolroom, shoeshine parlor, kosher restaurant, locker rooms, showers, handball courts, health club, and swimming pool. In the summer, outdoor dances were held on the roof, a romantic place under the moon and stars and softly lit lanterns. Two full floors below the roof were devoted to clubrooms, a library, and classrooms, where you could study anything from beginning English to philosophy. On the main floor were two lounges and a large theater. One lounge was a museum of Hebraic art and culture. There sat the older Jews who looked like museum pieces themselves among the glass-encased menorahs, silver-handled Torahs, embroidered *tallis* bags, and Old Testaments. The large lounge with the couches and easy chairs and the broad library tables were where the lively ones gathered. It was a meeting place for the chess and checker players, the neighborhood intellectuals, the men and women of all ages who sought a last affair or marriage. The big event there were the forums, which were mostly political and where communists, socialists, anarchists, and even Republicans were willing to argue into the middle of the following month if they could.

During that summer Nachum started going to the JPI lounge at night. Sometimes he took Bubi along. Nachum would not get involved in the forums. *Shalom,* that's what he wanted. Why should he let the communists, who had come from Russia before the revolution, tell him here in America how it really was? Why should he listen to their *Daily Worker* propaganda, their Marxist doctrine, when he had been through the whole revolution, pogroms and everything? *Shalom.* That's why he had left. Business should only be good. That's why he had come here. *Shalom.*

In the center of it all sat Bubi, nodding, smiling, sweet and beautiful and innocent. Sometimes she asked Nachum with gestures: What, what? And Nachum would shrug, as if saying: Nothing to get excited about, people talk, let them talk, so long as blood isn't being shed. He knew what it was to live under communism, and he was beginning to know what it was like to live under the worst Depression America ever had. His eyes roved discreetly around the lounge. Who and where is the woman of my heart? He dismissed women with marriage rings, older women, women too young who might demand too much of him, women too attractive whom he was no match for. Who, where is she?

He found her finally in Esther Taibach, a timid, mousy woman with a round face, thick glasses, and old-fashioned clothes, but she was American, born here in Chicago, with a pure, flat, midwestern accent. He saw her first in the library upstairs, where he took out books to read, then would see her later in the lounge, and their eyes would meet. Finally, he worked up enough courage to talk to her. She was warm and friendly and shy: she did not mind his foreign accent; she never corrected his speech; she looked on him as a man. She worked as a bookkeeper on Market Street in the garment center. She was a high school graduate, smart, dependable, trustworthy, loyal, worth her weight in gold to any boss; she'd bring these same virtues to any man, with love. All that, and love, too, who could ask for anything more?

She brought him to the small apartment where she lived with her mother and father. Her father, a tailor, was out of work. At first he was very happy to meet Nachum. A man for his daughter, a son, a blessing. Nachum might help out. It was terrible to be dependent on your only unmarried daughter for support. He had been cursed with three daughters, two of them married to *shlimazels* who couldn't spare a kopeck. Esther had been an angel. An uncomplaining, dutiful angel. He questioned Nachum carefully about his shoemaker's business. He was a skilled tailor. He could very easily adapt himself to repairing shoes. Maybe Nachum could find a place for him. He didn't need much. He would be glad to help out. But when he learned that Nachum had just opened his shop, was struggling to stay alive, he looked on him with dread: This man might take away the bread from his table; he might exploit his dearly beloved daughter, milk her for every cent she earned, break her in two with his needs. This was no time to get serious. This was a time for waiting, looking around, seeing what happened. And what if Esther should get pregnant, God forbid? So under the circumstances she stopped bringing him home. They met at the JPI library and in the lounge. At night they would go up on the roof and listen to the music and watch the people dance. She offered to teach him the simple waltz and fox-trot, but he was clumsy; she was satisfied to sit and listen and watch. Sometimes Bubi would sit with them. Though she couldn't hear, she could watch. She'd capture the rhythm of the music as she watched the dancers, her head would sway, and in her head she was a regular Pavlova, leaping out on the floor and swirling headily to the thousand-piece orchestra in her mind. Sometimes Jake would meet them all when he went to the JPI for a workout, and he'd join them, and he'd think: This is all not for real; it's got to be like in the old country. He'd look at Bubi, a silent chaperone, lost in her own fantasies. He'd look at Nachum with his skinny, bony body and face, his high, girlish giggle, the gleaming golden crowns on some of his teeth, speaking his mixed-up Yiddish-English, and this plain, young

American woman who could hardly see without her glasses, and he'd think: A romantic couple; how do you like that, a romantic couple?

The first Jake's parents heard of this was from Jake. They, too, got worried. Now is not the time. Wait, Nachum, wait. Nachum had an answer for everything.

"Did you wait, Aaron?"

"It was different then."

"How different?" Nachum asked. "You had nothing. You left for America, left Ruchel behind, pregnant already with Yonkel. What did you have to offer? Promises?"

"That was important, the promises?"

"I'm here, where promises are supposed to be fulfilled. Already I have a lot more to offer than you."

"A Talmudist arguing with a Talmudist," said Jake's mother, who was a romantic from the word "go". "What is Nachum doing? He's showing the world he's a man; he has the normal desires of a man. A man wants, he takes. He's a polite man, he's a gentle man, he's not a wild boar, so he waits a little before he takes."

"Who's going to support his desires?"

"Aaron, I'm not asking you," said Nachum. "End of discussion."

"All right, a new discussion," said Jake's father. "How's business?"

"This month I'm not asking you for rent."

"Ah, business is picking up."

"I'm bartering a little better."

Jake's father smiled. "Nachum, I love you."

There was no wedding. Who could afford one? Nachum came home one day with Esther and said to the family, "I want you to meet my wife, Esther."

Everybody acted as if it was the greatest surprise in the world. They embraced, kissed, had some schnapps.

"No *chuppah*," said Jake's father. "But break the glass anyway."

He wrapped a wineglass in a dish towel, laid it on the floor, and Nachum smashed the glass to bits with one blow of his foot. Tradition was kept.

"Mazel tov!"

Jake's mother played a lively Yiddish dance tune on the Victrola, and they all danced to it. Then she brought out some leftover strudel and made some tea, and that was how Nachum's wedding was celebrated. For their honeymoon, Nachum took Esther to the back of his shop, where they were going to live.

"When you're in love, the whole world is beautiful," said Jake's mother with a deep romantic sigh.

"I thought it was Jewish," said Jake.

"So Jewish isn't beautiful?" said Jake's mother.

When Jake enrolled at Northwestern again in the fall, breadlines were in the streets, the stock market was lower than ever, a thousand banks had closed, every fourth factory worker was out of a job, men were selling apples on street corners for five cents. Hoover was saying with a frozen smile, "We have now passed the worst, and we shall rapidly recover." But Jake never had it so good.

He went back to the North Shore Hotel for his meals, worked at the pool, was put in charge of the vehicle delivery gate at Dyche Stadium before the football games on Saturday, for which he got $8, he was given a three-room apartment to live in, free, which he furnished with Salvation Army furniture. Then he got a job with a real estate company that was subdividing North Shore farmland for which he was paid $10 a week for one night's work. With the stock market at rock bottom, real estate began to boom. Money could burn, stocks could be wiped out, banks could fold up, but the land was always there; nobody could take it from you, nobody could steal it, the value was always there, and there was always a profit to be made. That's what they were saying. And desperate people with a few saved dollars, afraid of banks folding up and of being robbed, were beginning to believe the supersalesmen in real estate. And Jake believed them, too.

On Monday nights he'd be picked up by Roger W. Troop, sales manager of North Shore Estates, who had also given him the free apartment. He was a pal of Milton B.'s, who had played football with him, a powerful, bullnecked man with a broken nose and a winning smile. They'd go to the ballroom of the North Shore Hotel, where sandwiches and cookies and punch and coffee would be served to prospective customers. Then, before the meeting started, somebody would begin playing the piano, and everybody would sing "Happy Days Are Here Again", "Let a Smile Be Your Umbrella on a Rainy Day", "Row, Row, Row Your Boat", "Singin' in the Rain" and other happy, optimistic songs. Jake's job was to sing along with the mooches, to sound loud and cheerful. For that, he got $10. Before the sales pitches were over, however, if he'd had any money he'd have put all of it in North Shore Estates. The fortunes that had been made in land! Milton B. invested. Butch Halloran, Northwestern's football coach, bought two corner lots. The pastor of the largest congregation in Evanston became part of North Shore's happy family, thus lending the dignity of the church to the subdivisions. The largest savings and loan bank was financing the project. What possibly could go wrong? The enterprise seemed like the answer to everybody's troubles.

"I'd like to become one of your salesmen," Jake said to Roger.

"You will, Jake. Finish school first. By then business will be booming to the skies."

Jake was preparing for this world. Economics. Accounting. Principles of speech so that he'd learn to stop talking like a West Side hoodlum. And horseshit English and German. What a waste. By the time the Depression was over he'd really be ready for this world.

Everybody was expecting the swimming team to win another Big Ten and national championship. Albie Karlin was gone. To Jake's surprise he hadn't gone into business; he'd gone into law school. He had sat down with Morrie Benjamin soon after his graduation, and they took a careful look at all his options. Jobs were scarce. Nobody was breaking Albie's doors down with substantial offers. But because of his reputation as an athlete, he could go far politically. Benjamin said, "There's never a depression in politics. Bad times are murder for Hoover, a bonanza for us. So go to law school, Albie. Pass the bar. Politically you can go far. I'll make you a judge later." Albie nodded. He was a good systems man.

So Albie was gone. But they had George Wilson, who had size thirteen feet, hands that could choke basketballs, big fat balloons puffing up his chest; in practice he broke Weissmuller's 100- and 220-yard records. Pushing him in both events was Stanley Priczinski, tall, slim, quiet, a strong competitor. Jake would take Tom Branch's place in the 150-yard backstroke and on the medley relay team. Bert Denby was a sure place winner in the 440 freestyle. And Spencer Cartwright might take a place in the breaststroke. That was a hard team to beat, and they all were working into good water polo players.

Swanee didn't drive the team too hard in the fall. All the boys had been in lots of competition, had kept in good condition over the summer, and knew how to bring themselves around to top form. Swanee didn't have to worry about technique; they all were finished athletes when they came to him. His job was to keep the boys happy, to train them to their finest edges for the championships in the spring. That was a long way off. So he let the boys do as they pleased, their quarter and half miles, their pulling tubes around and kicking the boards. An hour's water polo was a great conditioner. By the time the dual meets rolled around Swanee called for some exertion; he started to put the watch on them.

Jake never performed his best in practice. He was always a couple of seconds off. He was a money competitor. But he felt as finely crafted, as powerful, as sleek, as elegant as a Lipton-race sailboat. He had little control over the world, but in the pool he was in full command. His mind, his dreams could play tricks with him, but he trusted his body; he knew it well, knew just what it could do. He knew he'd be beating his best time when competition got keener. Swanee could be up there holding a watch on him, but when he leaped from the wall and came up stroking and kicking, he could tell to the tenth of a second what he was doing each length. Because in the water he'd go deep inside himself, he'd be alone, listening to his muscles, his nerves, feeling the coordination, the rhythm, counting the strokes, turn, knees up, body slammed against the wall, wham out, way out, resting under the power of the push-off, then kick and stroke, stroke, stroke, riding even, the water surging away from him, flip, shove off, stroke, stroke, stroke, his arms like powerful oars sweeping through the water, length after length, his belly growing tighter, his body growing longer, stronger, each time asking for a little more, until it began to hurt, maintaining his rhythm, his form, riding lower to preserve his strength, now fighting against the strain, the pain more intense, working harder to go beyond the pain. Sometimes he surged over it, and he felt as if the sun had burst; then everything became like the afterglow of sunset. That was the addiction. He'd climb out of the pool swollen with power. Tingling all over. A smile on Swanee's face, warm nods from the guys, and Swanee saying, "You'll do better, Jake." Always better, that was the heart of it. Always a second, an inch, a yard, a continent, a universe beyond yourself. And the wonder of it, with your body responding. That was the only time of the day he felt good.

Otherwise, school was not very interesting. Economics was all theory. It seemed to have nothing to do with reality. Except for the stock market. Each student had to select five stocks and see how they did. Milton B., through his broker, gave him the stocks, all blue chip, all bound to do well. On paper, Jake invested $100,000. Why be a piker? In the first month he'd already lost $30,000. That was like gambling. That he understood. But the law of supply and demand, Gresham's law, surplus goods, laissez-faire, commodities, credit, division of labor, distribution of wealth, Adam Smith's theories tied his mind into knots. Accounting was a bore. Maybe he wasn't cut out for business. What was he cut out for? He could swim all his life, sure, for fun. But how was he going to make a living? If not business, what? He wished he knew where he was going.

He wished he had somebody to talk to, somebody to confide in, somebody to get him excited about something else besides swimming. Living alone now for the first time in his life, no family, no roommates, no old friends, he'd feel stones growing in his chest from loneliness. Hey, coach, I feel lonely. You got a tutor for that? You got a tutor to show me the way to my future? You got a tutor to tell me what it's all about? The boys had an answer for it. What you need is a good fuck. The solution to everything. But when he did get a good fuck, that wasn't enough. He was still left to himself, the life ahead gnawing away at him. Why can't I feel always like I feel in the pool?

At homecoming and the Notre Dame game the stadium was sold out. Tickets were going for $20, $30. For people who had money, there was no Depression. Jake was badgered; he was in charge of a gate, letting in trucks and VIP cars.

"Ten bucks, fella. Twenty? Thirty? We came all the way from New York."

And all that.

Lala and Bo came around for both games. "*Shmuck,* you can make a fortune." After he let them in, they hung around.

"Hey, here's forty bucks. Let us in."

"*Shmuck!*" Lala yelled.

"There are no seats," Jake said. "How do they get into the stands?"

"Get a pass from that guy selling programs, you dumb shit. Make a buck, it won't hurt you. Here, I'll take care of the gate."

"They find out, I'll lose my job."

Lala started shoving him toward the program seller, a basketball player Jake knew.

"You'll make more money today than you can make in a year. Do what I tell you."

When Jake got back with an extra pass, Lala and Bo had $200 in their hands and twenty men waiting to be passed into the stands.

Lala grabbed the extra pass and tore off Jake's pass from his coat. "I'll relay 'em back and forth."

At both games Jake made a total of $700. Lala and Bo wouldn't take a cut. They'd been paid off by getting into the game, they said. "A racket comes your way, grab it. It doesn't happen twice."

Then, shortly after the Notre Dame game, Jake was shocked to learn that Lala and Bo had killed a cop during a payroll robbery at the Municipal Pier. Bo had been wounded and left behind and picked up. Lala had got away. According to reports, Bo had been shot with two different bullets, one a .45 Police Special, the other a .32 Colt, the same bullet found in the cop; that meant Lala had tried to kill Bo, once he was down, to keep him from talking. Bo squealed, tried to squirm out of the murder rap, saying Lala did the shooting, but it did him no good. He was electrocuted two months later. Lala made the FBI's Most Wanted list.

For weeks, when Jake got to the JPI on weekends, that's all

everybody talked about. Fitzgerald, a highly moral Catholic, condemned Lala and Bo, then lit a candle in church and prayed for them.

"It was in the cards," he said.

"But do you believe Lala tried to kill Bo to keep him quiet?" Jake asked.

"I believe anything of Lala."

"They were pals."

"They were products of their environment."

Benny Gordon and Solly Landon and other swimmers believed otherwise.

Benny said, "The cops spread that story to mark Lala lousy."

Solly said, "According to the cops, all criminals are rats. I know cops. They're on my pad. They'd say anything, those Irish-Polack bastards, to make finks out of us Jews."

Jake, too, couldn't believe it of Lala. Bo and Lala had been closer than brothers. How could he have tried to kill Bo? Unless he had wanted to do Bo a favor, a fast bullet instead of the electric chair. But he hadn't made a clean hit. Bo had died the worst possible way. Jake shivered every time he thought of it.

But he forgot them quickly enough after the Christmas holidays. Final exams were coming up. Then the dual meets with the other universities began. He became a pinpoint of concentration in both his studies and his swimming. Training became harder. Swanee had him do things he'd never done before, more intense, more gruelling. First 20-yard sprints, a minute's rest; five of them. Then 40 yards, two minutes' rest. Then 60 yards, three minutes' rest. Then 80 yards, four minutes' rest. Then 100 yards all out. After a longer rest, he'd sprint 80 yards, swim relaxed another 80 yards, then burst out in another 80-yard sprint. Each time he worked to the peak of exhaustion. Then he'd taper off with a quarter-mile swim.

He found his stamina building up. The times of his last sprints were almost as fast as his first. Sometimes, when his muscles were knotted, as tight as high-tension wires, he'd go down to the training room, and Henry, who could manipulate you with the skill of a Cellini modeling clay, would work over him. He'd slosh the warm oil and alcohol and wintergreen over his body, then shake, palpitate, and knead the pain out of his muscles. Henry, with his pockmarked face and the touch of a genius. Under his hands Jake felt he was mainlining the drug of Narcissus.

They beat Purdue, Wisconsin, Chicago, Minnesota. Jake felt good being part of a winning team. He passed all his courses again, but he began to take that for granted. Then one day he got the strange feeling that he was being followed. He wasn't sure until that evening. While he was eating in the North Shore Hotel cafeteria, Lenny Kahn and Yussel Gomberg came up to him with trays of food.

"Jake!" They acted so surprised.

Jake sputtered. "Lenny, Yussel. What are you guys doing here?"

"We're on our way down from Milwaukee," said Lenny.

"How you doin', Jake?" said Yussel.

"All right. Fine." Jake wondered what they were really doing there.

"Mind if we join you?" said Yussel.

"No, sit down," said Jake.

Lenny and Yussel took their food off the trays, sat down with Jake, and began to eat.

"How's your old man doing?" said Lenny. "No complaints?"

"No complaints."

"Believe me, Jake, if we'd of known he was your old man, we'd never have put the muscle on him."

"That's okay."

"He got any complaints, any of my boys try to mooch him, you come to me, you hear?" said Lenny.

"Sure."

"And everything's okay with you, huh?"

"Fine."

"I see you're wiping 'em out in the dual meets," said Yussel.

What the hell did they want? Jake wondered. They weren't here just to *shmooz* with him.

"You're doing great time, too," said Yussel, the avid reader of the sports pages. "You broke the Big Ten record against Minnesota."

"Big deal."

"How's your apartment?" asked Lenny.

"How'd you guys know I have an apartment?"

"Word gets around."

Maybe I was followed, Jake thought. Maybe these guys were casing me. Why?

"How many rooms you got?" said Yussel.

"Three."

"Furnished?"

"Salvation Army."

"But comfortable, huh?" said Lenny. "Heat and all that, huh?"

"It's okay."

"What kind of heat? Steam?"

"What's it all about, guys?"

"Nothing," said Yussel, acting offended. "We're just asking; we're just being sociable." He turned to Lenny. "How do you like that? We're only interested in his welfare, and he's getting suspicious."

"What's the matter, Jake?" said Lenny. "Don't you trust us? We ever done anything wrong to you? We ever muscled you or anything? Didn't we treat your old man, once we knew who he was, the best, no trouble? I don't get you, Jake. You think because you're collegiate you gotta be suspicious?"

"Forget it, fellows."

"All we wanna know is are you getting along okay," said Lenny.

"I told you, I'm getting along fine." As if they really cared. What the hell did they really want?

"You need something, you know you could always come to us." Lenny wouldn't let go. "We respect you. We have the highest regard for you. You're a credit to the Jews. You give us a good name. Okay?"

"Okay."

"Hey, that was tough about Bo, huh?" said Yussel.

"Yah. How's Lala?"

"How the hell would we know?" said Lenny.

"They said in the papers he tried to kill Bo. At the trial Bo said it, too."

"Bullshit. The whole thing is a bum rap."

"A bum rap? They found the cop dead and Bo right near him bleeding all over."

"Who you gonna believe, us or them? I tell you it was a bum rap."

Everything, according to them, if they were caught, was a bum rap.

"You were a pal of Lala's," said Lenny. "Right?"

Jake nodded.

"How good a pal?"

"We swam together for years. We even traveled out of town to meets, slept in the same room. We were close."

"You glad Lala got away?"

"Of course I am. What do you think? How is he? Okay?"

"How the hell would we know?

"Come on, we'll take you home," said Yussel.

"That's all right, fellows. I'm not going home. I'm going to the library. I've got some studying to do there."

"We'll take you there."

"Okay," said Jake, There was no other way to get rid of them.

They dropped him off at the library. Jake didn't study. He wondered what they really wanted.

When he got to his apartment later, he knew somebody had been there. Lenny and Yussel? Nothing was missing. But the place smelled different. Sure, cigarette smoke. What were they casing him for?

He wasn't kept in suspense very long. A few days later, when he left the pool after a workout, Jake found Lala waiting for him outside the gym. At first, he didn't recognize him with the full brushy mustache, but he knew who it was as soon as he talked, as soon as he broke out in a broad smile.

"Jake, you sonofabitch. Am I glad to see you."

Jake almost dropped dead. "Lala, for Christ's sake, what are you doing here?"

"*Schweig* [quiet]," he said in Yiddish. "*Ruff mir* [call me] Mike Taylor, from Taylor Street, get it, ha-ha-ha." He laughed nervously; his father had been a tailor. "Hey, I hear you're doing great. Living alone. Nice place and all. Too bad football season is over. You could still be coining it in at the gate. Some bundle you made, huh?"

George Wilson and Bert Denby from the swimming team came out and said hello.

"Hi," Jake said. Murder, he was thinking, what the hell is going to happen now?

"This Wilson is going to knock everybody on their ass, isn't he?" said Lala. "I watched him work out. He's better'n Weissmuller."

"Not in competition."

"How do you mean?"

"There are two kinds of athletes. The kind who tighten up and fall apart, the tougher the competition, and the kind who do better when the going gets tougher."

"That's you, huh? The tougher the better."

Jake nodded, shivered from the cold, then said, "I've got to get something to eat, then come back to the pool and lifeguard."

"Come on. I'll take you." Lala moved over to a new Buick parked on the street.

"That's all right, Lala, I'll walk."

"Mike. *Ruff mir* Mike." He laughed again.

Jake started to walk away. Lala grabbed his arm. "Come on," he said. "This isn't a hot car. It's all paid for. It's legit."

"Mike, for Christ sake, what the hell do you want from me?"

"We're pals, aren't we?"

"No. We're not pals. Not anymore. Because if you're a pal of mine, you wouldn't want to get me in a jam. You'd get lost. You'd leave me alone."

Lala looked at him with the saddest eyes he'd ever seen, sadder than a basset hound's.

"Mike, I'm going to school here. I don't want any trouble. All I want to do is get by my studies and swim a little. Don't fuck me up."

Jake walked away. He felt Lala's eyes on him a long while. He had sirloin steak for dinner but didn't enjoy it. He had apple pie alamode, and he didn't like its taste. He was eating with Bang-Bang Jones, who had made all-American halfback his first season; he also worked at the hotel for his meals.

"I'm really getting a kick out of studying now," he was saying. He looked like an English bull with his crew-cut, bristly hair, low forehead, pug nose, and thick neck. "Every book I pick up, it's a big challenge. Me against it. Every fuckin' book, the enemy. I wrestle the shit out of it. That's a kick. I didn't know I could get such kicks."

Jake said, "Yah. Yah." Bang-Bang went on and on. Jake kept thinking: What the hell was Lala doing around here, what the hell did he want from him?

"You're not eating," Bang-Bang said.

"I'm not hungry."

"I'm gonna get a couple more pies."

"I'm going to work."

He looked for the Buick when he got back to the gym. It was gone. He relaxed. That sonofabitch, scaring the shit out of me. He went into the pool and opened a text on general psychology while Mrs. Wycoff, the women's swimming instructor, handled a class of adult women. Mrs. Wycoff's voice boomed off the walls, and Lala's appearance on campus nagged at him. If they ever caught him, they'd burn him. Ever since Bo had been electrocuted, Jake kept getting images of him sitting strapped to that chair and the electricity jolting him and jolting him. He began remembering Bo and Lala and him, the time they had gone to Lake Wawasee for the Indiana state outdoor championships. The first time they had ever sat in a high-powered Chris-Craft boat, how rich and important they'd felt, the thrill they'd got riding in it, then winning all their respective events, the medals they'd got, and eating their heads off after the meet. The time the team had gone up to Milwaukee for the river swim and the short events. Lala had swum the two miles for a third place. Boy, he'd been in shape then, swimming every day, staying out of trouble, manic as hell. Bo had won the 100 and 220 freestyle. A natural talent. Thin ankles, long, tapering, thoroughbred shaped legs, narrow hips, wide shoulders, a deep chest, his body had been as elegant as Weissmuller's. Except for his eyes. He could hardly see, he'd been a squinter, it had screwed up his face, it had made him uneasy, he was always looking around, as if somebody were about to leap on his back. His eyes had fucked up his life, he'd said. And oh, how they had treated Jake. Taught him how to climb up the girders to sneak up on the Els. Taught him how to walk into Thompson's, Pixley and Ehler's, grab two checks, have one punched for all the food he'd eat, then walk out handing the cashier a clean, blank check. Taught him how to sneak into the big movie houses, the McVickers, the Chicago, the Oriental. He'd even go on forays with them. "Stand outside, punk. You see anybody, holler. We'll be back in a minute."

They'd come out with pockets full of nickels. Once Lala had taken him into an empty apartment, shown him how to break open the telephone coin box. Nickels and nickels. Then they'd gamble with them, heads or tails. Oh, that Bo. That Lala. Sandpapers of guilt rubbed against his mind. Bo, all strapped up, not being able to move, kept appearing on the pages of his psychology text. A guy like Bo, smooth, sleek, long-muscled, slashing through the water like a porpoise, so free, so easy, all strapped in, not being able to move, then jolted and jolted and burned down to nothing. That fucking Lala, filling his mind with all that jazz. "Fuck you, Lala," he said to himself. "Go fuck yourself."

He got back to his apartment. He could hear the El clatter over the rails behind the building. He was tired. He started to read Defoe's *Moll Flanders*. What a cunt! There was a knock on the door. He wondered who it could be as he opened the door. It was Lala with corned beef sandwiches, pickles, mustard, coleslaw, french fries, and a half dozen Cokes.

"You hungry, pal?"

"Lala, for Christ's sake."

"This fuckin' town has got nothing. I had to go all the way into Chicago, all the way down to Lawrence Avenue to find a deli. Let's dig in." He spread the food out on the kitchen table. "Got any tea, coffee?"

"Milk."

"Milk and meat, you can't mix the two. You'll get a sin if you do." He was a killer, and he was worried about keeping a kosher house. "We'll have the Cokes, huh?" He started to wolf down a sandwich. Jake watched him. "Jake, you were always a hungry bastard. Sit down and eat." As if it were his own place, as if he were playing host to Jake. "Corn'beef, you were always queer for corn'beef. Come on, Jake."

"Lala, it's late. I've got to go to sleep soon. I've got an eight o'clock class in the morning."

"Eat first; then you'll go to sleep."

"I'm not hungry."

"You don't mind if I eat, do you?"

Jake minded. He minded very much. Was scared. Mouth-dry scared. Also curious. It was more than two months since the robbery and the killing of the cop. How had Lala got away, what had he been doing up until now?

"Nice and warm here," Lala said.

"It gets cold later. Freezing. They don't keep the heat up all night."

"Boy, this corn'beef's good. How about it, Jake?"

The spicy smell and Lala's smacking his food got to him. He hadn't enjoyed his dinner. He was hungry. He hadn't had corned beef in a long time. His mouth got all juicy. He bit into a sandwich.

"Where'd you get the Buick?" Jake asked.

"Bought it. Hard cash. I needed wheels. Safe wheels."

"Lenny and Yussel were here."

"I know. I sent them."

"They been keeping you?"

"No, but I've been in touch. I've been all over. The Drake. Imagine me, Lala Bloomberg, the Drake. The Edgewater Beach, too. And the Shoreham. Places where nobody'd think of looking for me. All the time I've been right here in town, blowing that loot from the heist. I figure, a college town, nobody'll look for me here. *Tochis,* huh?"

"Where you going to stay?"

"Here."

"You're kidding."

"I'll pay you, don't worry. More than enough."

Everything in Jake began to shake. Now he was really scared. He spit out a mouthful of food. He couldn't eat any more.

"You're kidding, aren't you, Lala?"

"Why should I kid? You're a pal of mine. You wouldn't want me to get caught, would you?"

"No."

"So what's the problem, Jake? I stay here awhile, until I figure out what to do. The longer I'm under cover, the cooler it gets."

"How long is awhile?"

"Jake, I can't give you dates. Awhile."

"What if I said no? This is my place. What if I said no?"

Lala didn't bother to answer him. He started to laugh. He took a drink of Coke and continued to laugh.

"What's funny?"

Lala laughed harder. "What's funny is, this isn't your place anymore. It's mine. Yours and mine."

"How do you figure?"

"You got two choices. You turn me in or you let me stay. You gonna turn me in?"

"Yah."

"You turn me in, I burn. You want that?"

"No."

"So what are you gonna do?"

"I'm going to turn you in."

"You turn me in, Lenny and Yussel will know. Capone will know. His button men will know."

"What are you doing? You threatening me?"

"Jake, you're my pal. All I ever wanted was the best for you. Since you were a punk kid."

Now he knew the truth about Lala. He had shot Bo. He would kill anybody who got in his way. Lala always had a laugh, a fun guy; he looked innocent and open most of the time, but he was deadly. He could laugh with you one second, kill you the next.

"You shot Bo, didn't you?"

"Who says?"

"The paper."

"Bullshit."

"Don't crap me, Lala."

Lala laughed, this time nervously. What happened to Bo didn't sit too well with him. "He was down, I didn't want him to burn. I wanted him to die clean."

"You tried to kill him to keep him from snitching, so's you'd be in the clear."

"But he snitched."

"He tried to save his hide."

"He snitched. If he'd kept his mouth shut, I'd be in the clear." He glared at Jake. "Who do you think you are, punk?"

Jake backed away. He could see a gun in a holster inside Lala's jacket, the bulge of another gun in the pocket.

"What are you, Kid Moses on the mount, throwing the Ten Commandments at me?"

"Take it easy, Lala."

"You dirty bastard. I got enough trouble. I don't need you to crawl into my head and sit there like a tin Jesus." He dug his hand into his jacket pocket, wrapping it around his gun.

"It's okay, Lala. You did what you had to do."

"You fuckin'-ay right."

"You couldn't help it."

"You fuckin'-ay."

"Where you going to sleep tonight, Lala? I've only got one bed."

"Yah."

"That's going to be a problem."

Lala took his hand out of his pocket. He smiled, relaxed. "No problem. You got a double bed. I'll pile in with you. If you're nice to me, maybe I'll bugger you." Laughter again. "How about that, Jake?"

There was nothing funny about that.

Jake couldn't sleep that night. When he did fall asleep, Lala's turning in bed woke him up. He had an extra blanket. He wrapped himself in it and lay down in the bathtub, his legs hanging over the tub. Read more Defoe, until he fell asleep. When he woke, he was stiff and tired. All that day in class, in the library, trying to study, he was afraid to go back to the apartment; he didn't know what to do. He was never more scared in his life. His stomach hurt. His whole body ached. Under his heart he'd feel sudden stabs of anxiety; he thought they were heart attacks. Christ, he could go to jail for harboring a fugitive, a killer. His career, his life could be ruined forever. He might even be held as an accessory. Maybe he'd get the same rap. Electrocution. What the hell do I do?

At the pool, he was dead through his workout. He saw Lala up in the balcony, watching the team go through its paces. Everywhere he went he saw Lala. If he turned him in, everywhere he'd go he'd see Lala. He was a prisoner of Lala's.

"You all right?" Swanee said.

"Yah, sure."

"You're way off today. Like you're dragging lead."

"I didn't get much sleep last night. Too much studying."

"You're sure you're not partying around?"

"Studying."

Christ, he thought, I'm trapped. What the hell do I do?

Lala was waiting for him outside the gym. A big smile, his hand patting Jake's back.

"What have you got in your belly, sinkers?"

"You, you bastard, I've got you in my belly."

Like he didn't hear a word. "Where we gonna eat?"

"I'm going to eat far away from you."

"Come on, Jake. The treat's on me."

"Don't do me any favors. I work for my meals. I've got my meals coming to me. So get lost."

"I'm only trying to be friendly, Jake."

"Some friend."

Lala burst into song: "Dancing with Tears in My Eyes." He covered his eyes and snake-hipped his midsection lewdly. Jake walked away from him. Walked down to the North Shore Hotel, filled his tray with roast beef, escalloped potatoes, something he'd never had at home, peas, salad Italian style, lentil soup, rolls, butter, tea, and, later, peach pie a la mode. He stuffed himself. He'd drive Lala out of his belly that way. While he was eating his pie a la mode, Lala walked in with Bang-Bang Jones, laughing and talking with him as if they were the greatest of friends.

"Hey, you know Jake Davidson?" said Lala.

"Do I know Jake," said Bang-Bang. "Asshole buddies, right, Jake? We sold programs together last year."

"Let's sit down with Jake," said Lala.

"Sure," said Bang-Bang.

Jake couldn't finish his pie fast enough. There they were, wolfing their food down, Lala talking and laughing, telling dirty jokes, with Bang-Bang getting the biggest kick in the world out of him. Bang-Bang, a virgin, was titillated by Lala.

"Did I ever tell you about the wailing wall in Berwyn?" said Lala.

"Tell me, tell me," said Bang-Bang.

"The joint's mobbed. Guys lined up three deep at the bar. Against the wall are twenty girls. Socker's paradise. You start with a dollar's worth of tickets. A real grind joint. Guys don't even bother to take off their coats. Right off, they start socking. The guys who shoot on sight get a cheap blow job. The long-winded bastards, they eat up rolls of tickets. Once I took Jake there. He thought he was building a home with the cunt he picked. Cost me twenty dollars. For that kind of money I could have got him a room at the Stevens and an all-night, three-way broad from the society pages."

Bang-Bang laughed his head off.

"Hey, Bang-Bang, you wanna get your gun off?"

"Ah." Bang-Bang didn't jump at the offer.

"Sure," Lala said. "A guy like you, all-American, with all the cunt around here, why should you go for these degenerate things like me and Jake?"

Jake could have killed him.

"Anytime you want a piece, let me know. For you, free." He started to laugh. "Hey, I just thought of a funny one—"

"I've got to go," said Jake. "Lot of work to do."

"Stick around," said Lala. "This one's really funny."

Jake left. Lala, the entertainer, the life of the party, a gun in his pocket, a laugh a minute on his face. Pretty soon, Lala'd know everybody of any importance on campus. You'd think he'd be in hiding. But he didn't care who saw him, how open he was. He couldn't figure Lala out at all.

When he got back to his apartment, Jake found a new bed in the other room, an easy chair, a chest, and a big Atwater Kent radio. His desk had been moved from there into the room he slept in. The few clothes Lala had stashed in the trunk of his car were now hanging in the closet. There was a new heavy quilt on the bed, new linen, new towels in the bathroom. Lala was here to stay.

He began pacing the rooms. The only way to get rid of him was to inform on him. He couldn't do that. Sooner or later the cops would catch up to him. If they caught him in the apartment, there'd be a shoot-out. Lala would never give himself up alive. It would be his way of committing suicide. What if Jake were in the apartment at the time? What would happen to him? Supposing he got out alive? The cops'd say he should have turned Lala over. He'd be hit with a big rap. Twenty years. Life. Maybe the chair. I've got to move out. Tomorrow I've got to move out.

He found a room the next day, but it became pointless. Lala came to the pool and watched him work out. He'd have to quit the team to avoid him. He'd really have to quit school to lose him. The following day, while Lala was out, he started to pack anyway. Lala came in.

"What are you doing, pal?"

"You can have this place. I'm moving out."

"What do you wanna do that for? Aren't we pals anymore?"

"No."

"Well, I don't care how you feel, I'm your pal."

"I'm still moving out."

"Okay, I'll help you. I got the car. I'll move you."

"Okay."

Jake went out and got a few cartons for his books and his clothes. When he came back, he continued packing. Lala helped him with his books.

"These books fall on your feet, they'll cripple you for life." Lala laughed. "What are you gonna do with all the bullshit you get out of them?" He didn't wait for an answer. He started to sing "Yes, We Have No Bananas." That's what books meant to him: senseless. Then: "Me and My Shadow" with the Ted Lewis gestures. That got Jake nervous. Why did he pop with that song? What did it mean? Suddenly it got very quiet. Lala wasn't moving around anymore. He leaned against the doorjamb and was silent as he watched Jake pack. Everywhere he went, every move he made, Lala watched him, a snarl on his lips, his forehead like a ton over his eyes. Jake moved faster. I've got to get out of here. Suddenly Lala clouted him on the nose. Blood spurted. Lala smashed into his gut. Jake doubled up, couldn't catch his breath. He fell to the floor, gasping for air.

"Who the fuck do you think you are, moving out on me?"

Jake finally gulped some air down.

"You bastard, you creep, you shithead."

Jake looked up. Lala hovered over him, a gun in his hand.

"You're not goin' anywhere, you fuck. You're stayin' right here."

Lala would kill him. Lala had tried to kill his best friend, Bo. Lala had no conscience, no loyalties, no remorse in him. That was his power. That, and the gun.

"You stayin' here?"

Jake didn't answer.

Lala kicked him in the head. "You tell me you're stayin' here."

"Okay."

"I'm the guy that's gonna leave, when I'm ready."

Jake nodded.

"You move out, you better go as far as Tokyo or Singapore. You start thinking of snitchin', I told you, Lenny and Yussel know I'm here. They know your old man; they know where to get him. We're all connected, pal. Remember that."

He extended his hand to help Jake to his feet. Jake ignored it. He walked to the bathroom, took off his bloody clothes, washed himself clean in the shower. As he dried himself and dressed, he heard the radio and Lala scat singing to Coon-Sanders from the Blackhawk Café, drumming the chest with his fingers.

"Hey, Jake," he said cheerfully when Jake was dressed, "what do you say we get laid?"

"I don't feel like it."

He put his arm around Jake. "Come on, we'll find a joint in Rogers Park. We'll get rid of all the bad blood. Right?"

"Leave me alone, Lala."

"Okay, sure. Get a good night's sleep, Jake. Tomorrow I'll buy you some new clothes. Okay?"

Jake said nothing.

At the door, on his way out, Lala said, "You're mad at me. But me, I got nothing but love for you." He started to sing "I Can't Give You Anything But Love, Baby," then laughed gaily as he left.

That night Jake didn't fall asleep for a long while. He was drained. He felt his nerves shooting wildly through his body. He had to swim against Ohio State that weekend. If this kept up, he'd be lucky if he didn't drown when he hit the water. Sleep, oh, sleep, please sleep, but he couldn't relax; he couldn't seem to lie still. He got out of bed and walked back and forth in the small apartment to tire himself until he was ready to drop. Bleary-eyed, his energy spent, he flopped into bed. Boom, the nerves started darting around again, tossing him from side to side. Somewhere, between tosses, he fell asleep. He had no sooner dozed off, it seemed, when he was awakened by the slamming of the front door, then a clanking, clinking, rattling of metal. He got up to see what was going on. There was Lala, still in his overcoat and hat, sitting on his bed, separating gold rings, necklaces, bracelets, a sterling silver service, with change clinking among them and dollars scattered about. Lala's eyes were dazzled, his hands trembling with excitement.

"There's a gold mine in this town."

Jake couldn't believe it. Lala was wanted for murder, he was on the Most Wanted list, and he was exposing himself with all-American football players, going out and getting laid, and robbing houses.

"I found a great place, Jake, on Touhy Avenue. A very clean broad. Douches herself with Lysol. Gives you a soap job with warm water before and after. You should have been with me. Afterward I'm coming home. I'm feeling good. Wide awake. I see all these big houses around here. Lots of loot here, I think. I grab some."

"While people are in there, sleeping?"

"What's wrong with that?"

"Lala, every cop in the country is looking for you."

"So?"

"With all that heat, you're not scared?"

Lala looked up at Jake, his eyes narrowing, then said, "Scared, Jake, is crawling into a corner and letting them catch you. Scared is running a hundred miles an hour till your heart drops out. Scared is living like a rat. If they catch me, I'm dead. If they don't, you live like a bird or you live like a king. Me, I'm gonna live like a king. Tell me, Jake, am I scared?"

"Yah, you're scared. All your life you've been scared. Everything you do, you're trying to prove you're not. I know. Because even right now, with all that loot, the way you're handling it, what you went through, you're shaking. You're living on the tip of your toes all the time. And you don't even know it."

Lala laughed. "I don't know what they're doing to you here, Jake. They must be putting sawdust in your brains." He picked up some tens and twenties. "Here, it's what makes the world go round. Have some."

"Keep it."

"You're my partner, pal. Half is yours."

"I don't want any part of it."

"Okay, that's your bibble."

"What are you going to do with the jewels, the silver? You going to hock them?"

"No."

"So why'd you take them?"

"They were there, *shmuck*."

"You're not going to leave them around here."

"What do you want me to do? You know I can't go to a fence."

"I don't care what you do, Get rid of them"

"Okay. I'm gonna show you what a pal I am."

The jewels and the silver service were worth thousands of dollars. He put them all in a paper bag.

"Come on, we'll get something to eat. I'm hungry. I'll dump this in some garbage can."

"You go, Lala. I want to get some sleep."

Lala grabbed the bag, jangled it. "I could probably get two grand for this."

"Not these days."

"You're right. They ain't worth shit."

He left. Jake tried to go back to sleep, but he didn't make it. He was convinced that he was holed up with a lunatic. Later, at school, he fell asleep under the droning voice of his psychology professor. By the time he got to the pool for his workout he felt as if he had been dragging an elephant around all day. He didn't know how long he could keep this up.

Each day Lala would show up in the balcony and watch swimming practice. Each day he'd offer Jake a ride to the North Shore Hotel, which was more than a mile away, and Jake would refuse.

"What's the matter, you don't like my wheels?"

"I don't want you to do me any favors."

"Why?"

"You give a guy a finger, you expect back a whole hand."

"Whatever I got is yours. I don't expect nothing."

"Why pick on me, Lala?"

"You're my pal."

"With pals like you, I don't need any enemies."

"Listen, you be careful. Lenny and Yussel aren't shaking down your old man. They're leaving him alone. You don't call that a favor?"

"That's what I mean, Lala."

"What do you mean, that's what you mean?"

"There's always the payoff. Sooner or later you stick your hand out. You're always looking for the edge, the vigorish."

"How else you gonna get along?"

"I don't want you to eat with me either."

"Screw you. I'll eat at the Orrington."

Jake walked away. My albatross. Will I have to kill him to get rid of him? Will I have to send him to the chair to be free of him? How much of him could he endure?

He had a lonely dinner. Back at the pool he watched the Daughters of Neptune swim around. Most of them looked so beautiful, so cheerful, so carefree. Long-legged, some with firm, tantalizing breasts inside their gray tank suits, others with narrow waists and curvy hips and sassy asses; sometimes their suits fitted so tight you could see the crevices of their vaginas. They didn't care how they paraded and swayed their asses around him, how they let their tits bounce as they ran up and down the walks, as if he didn't exist, as if he were a eunuch. He felt so Jewish among them. During the day he felt so Jewish among his teammates, the only one who was circumcised. Sometimes he found them staring at him, probably thinking: What a strange creature, what strange, barbaric rites the poor Jew must endure.

Now, at night, with these laughing, screaming girls, having the time of their lives, he felt like an outcast, almost as much as Lala was. He felt even more Jewish now, a victim, a tormented, persecuted man, bleeding inwardly from the barbed wire in him. Now he was tortured even more by the creases of their asses, the slits of their vaginas. He imagined them all under him, all of them twining, twisting, insinuating, pulsating, thrusting their lovely breasts, their smooth thighs, their wondrous hips against him, bursting with earthquakes of joyous sound. Then in a flash it was all over. The moment's release from Lala spun away. Time to go.

"No, Jake. Not now. A little more, Jake."

Sexuality in their shrill sounds, their laughter, their teasing, provocative voices.

"Oh, Jake, please. Hang on. Just a little bit more. More. Don't be a meanie. . . . "

As if he held the key to their pleasure. If he said, Okay, all of you, into the training room, on the table, with Henry's oils, whirlpools, warm tubs, a quick one, bang, bang . . . they'd freeze, they'd cut his heart with a look, they'd castrate his fantasies.

Outside in the cold, shivering inside his mackinaw, the snow piled up off the walks, he wished he had somewhere to go. He didn't want to go home. He might be going home to a shoot-out, though all he heard was the wind, the creaking of the dry, leafless trees. He might be going home to cops waiting for him. If not that, he'd certainly be going home to a dungeon. He called Ida.

"Jake, how are you?"

"Terrible."

"What's wrong?" Her voice worried; she still cared for him; it lightened his heart.

"Everything."

"What? What's happening?"

"I can't tell you. Not till I see you. Let me see you tonight."

"I can't tonight, Jake. I'm terribly sorry."

"Just for a little while. I need you. I need you with all my heart."

"I wish I could, Jake, but I can't."

There was a guy with her, that's why. He didn't want to know. He wouldn't ask.

"How about this weekend? Friday. Saturday."

"I can't. I'm going to Ohio. We're swimming against them. Maybe Sunday when I get back."

"Sunday I can't."

"Jesus, it used to be so easy to get together."

"That was a million years ago, Jake."

"I know."

"Some other time, huh?"

"Yes."

He walked around the quiet, frozen streets until he was chilled to the bone. He couldn't face going home. He stopped in at the Phi Ep house. On the Victrola, Wingy Manone was working on "I'm Gonna Sit Right Down and Write Myself a Letter." A couple of guys were slouched on the leather chairs, studying. Three guys were playing bridge, the "dummy" hovering over them, tapping his foot to the music. Jake wondered why he had gone in. He couldn't relate to any of them.

"How's it going, Jake?"

"Okay, okay." What else could he say? Whom could he confess to? Hey, guys, I got death in my belly. What do I do?

The "dummy," a pledge brother of Jake's said, "You know, that Wingy Manone, he must have read Maxim Gorki. You know Gorki, Jake?"

"Who is he?"

"Great Russian writer. Wrote a story about his student days. An illiterate ugly woman used to ask him to write letters to her sweetheart; then she asked him to write letters from her sweetheart to her. She had it going and coming."

"How could she lose?"

The "dummy" sang along with Wingy; then he sat down to play again. Everybody was concentrated on what he was doing. Jake felt shut out, more alone, more desperate than ever. He went home. He looked for a squad car outside his apartment, a sign of some action that would end his imprisonment. Nothing. Not a soul on the street. Nothing but the dim arcs of light from the lampposts swaying in the wind, his shadow moving along with him.

By the time he was ready to leave for Ohio State Jake had developed a cold. His eyes and nose were running; he was sneezing; his head was stuffed; he had a slight fever. Friday night, after dinner, he packed a small bag: two black silk tank suits, his woolen N sweat suit, clogs, sweat socks, shirt, underwear, and toilet things. The train for Columbus would leave after midnight. He was scheduled to board the train before 10 P.M. The team would sleep on the train and be in Columbus in the morning. Jake figured he'd get to the La Salle Street station early, go right to sleep, and kill his cold.

"Where you going?" Lala said.

"Ohio State. I told you."

Lala watched him get his things together, watched him put on his sweater and mackinaw. Then: "You're not going."

"Oh, boy."

"You're not going anywhere."

"Lala, if I'm not on that train by ten o'clock, the coach'll send somebody over here. They'll break the door down to find out what happened to me. They'll send cops if they have to. You're not fooling around with just me anymore. You're going to have the whole athletic department on your ass. They find me here, what the hell am I going to tell them?"

"You'll tell them you're sick."

"I can't be sick for every meet. It'll be my ass for not telling Swanee first."

"So it's your ass."

"What are you going to do, Lala? You going to keep me from the conference, the national intercollegiates?"

"If I have to, yah."

"Why me? Why didn't you pick on somebody else?"

"I trust you. I feel safe here."

"If you trust me, why do you give me such a hard time about leaving town?"

"Who's giving you a hard time?"

"What the hell do you think you're doing?"

"Come on. I'll drive you down to the station."

Jake doubled his fists. "Jesus Christ, Lala."

Suddenly Lala started to laugh. He slapped Jake's back. "Hey, I ever tell you the story of the turtle and the viper?"

"You don't have to."

Lala continued laughing. "So the viper wants to get across a river. He asks a turtle to take him across. The turtle says, 'If I carry you over, promise you won't sting me with your fangs.' The viper promises. So the viper gets on the turtle's back, and they start across. Right in the middle, wham, the viper lets the turtle have it. The turtle starts going down. He turns to the viper, 'Why'd you do it? Now we'll both drown.' The viper says, 'I couldn't help it; it's in my nature.'" Lala slammed Jake's back and laughed harder. "I'm your viper, Jake."

Jake blew his nose; his eyes filled with tears; his head ached. "Very funny," he said.

On the day of the meet the swimmers could do as they wished about warming up. Jake liked to hit the turns a number of times, to pick out markers he could go by. The thing a backstroker feared most was slamming into the end of the pool, hurting his hand, getting a concussion from banging his head or breaking his rhythm. Turning too soon could disqualify him. Timing had to be perfect. He liked to get the feel of the tank, then loosen up with an easy quarter mile. A hot shower; then Henry would slosh the warm oil over him and pull his muscles out, long and loose; he could fall asleep in the man's hands. This day he felt a deep chill when he dived into the water. He hit a few turns, hard, and he got out and ran into the hot showers before he froze to death. He shivered under the warm oil, the rubbing; he sat up, his muscles still tight.

"Get under a dozen blankets and go to sleep, Jake," said Henry.

At the hotel he crawled under the crisp sheets, wrapped himself in the blankets, and lay there cold, far away, a small figure on a horizon of ice, growing dimmer and dimmer, the world he knew fading away. The phone rang. Time to eat. In the dining room, steak, a small baked potato, peas, no salad, no milk, bad before a meet, tea or coffee, no dessert. Keep it light, you'll eat your head off after the meet. Some of the guys had a couple of eggs or nothing. Back up to the rooms. Quiet time. Read, but who the fuck could read? Mostly you communed with yourself, your concentration on your event building and building, nerves darting through your body. You forced yourself to take it easy, rest, while everything inside you was at full gallop. Then into cabs, over to the campus, into the lockers. Some of the guys were so highly strung they needed Henry to loosen them up with a rubdown before their event. All Jake could think of was: I'm dead, I can't breathe, I'll never finish my event, I can't get a deep breath, I'm yawning, I'm gulping, I'm straining, but I can't get any air, that's mud, not air, lumps of mud filling my lungs and my head, the pressure over my eyes, along my nose, I can't stand it, the fucking pain is killing me, it's taking all my energy away, I'll be lucky I'll go ten yards, I'll be lucky I don't drown.

"Okay, Jake, you're on."

That was Swanee. A warm, confident, give-'em-hell smile on his face, a hearty for-you-me-and-the-glory-of-Northwestern thump on the back. Daggers of icicles stabbed his body as soon as he got out of his sweat suit. Goose bumps swelled him up. He shriveled up into a snowball when he hit the water. He swam hard to the end of the pool to warm up; all his muscles tightened.

"Take it easy, Jake." Swanee again.

Jake chattered, nodded. He thought his teeth would fall out. Get it going. Oh, Christ, that starter fucking around with the gun, everybody balled up against the side of the pool ready to leap out. Go, go, go, bang! The ice melted away. A rocket of fuel thrust him ahead. He plunged into a Bessemer furnace. Wham, into the turn. Again, again. He won in the slow time of 1:49 for the 150-yard event. Later he swam his 100-yard leg of the medley in 1:05 and gave Northwestern a body-length lead for a win, then sank three goals in the water polo game afterward. He came out of the pool cramped, his head feeling as if a mountain were crushing it. Henry made him stay in the hot showers forever; then he gave him a hard rubdown.

"My head, Henry."

"You picked up a goddamn sinus bug."

"No." That was bad news, the worst.

"You've been working too hard. Look at your time."

Swanee came in. "How is he?"

"A few days out of the pool wouldn't hurt," said Henry.

"You heard the man, Jake," said Swanee.

"A few days off, and I'll have to start all over again."

"You don't take them off, there'll be nothing to start." Swanee crunched his face up confidently. "Don't worry, Jake. I'll bring you around. Just get rid of the cold. You'll do a lot better."

"A lot better? I did one-forty-five against Minnesota. Good enough to win the conference. Here I did one-forty-nine."

"You'll do better. One-forty-two or one-forty-one for the Big Ten and the nationals. You'll take them both."

Not with Lala around, he wouldn't. He'd be lucky to be alive by then.

They took an overnight train back to Chicago. In the morning his cold seemed to be drying up, but his head still ached, not sharply but heavily. His nose was stuffed; his chill was gone. A good workout was always good for a cold, he thought, like the one I had last night. He took the streetcar to the West Side to spend the day with his folks. He'd go to Evanston in the evening. Screw Lala.

All that day he lolled around the house. He couldn't let

anything happen to him. Not now. Not before all the big meets. Two years he'd been waiting for the big events, the Big Ten, the national intercollegiates, which were being held this year at the Lake Shore Athletic Club in Chicago. He had gone over his peak. Lala had pushed him over. Now he'd have to slide back and start climbing up again, until he was at the top, the very top, Mount Everest, at least; then he could coast down, oh, what a ride that would be, all the way down, if he could only reach that peak.

"You have a cold," his mother said.

"It's nothing, Ma."

"You lost weight. You look terrible. Skin and bones. You'll wear yourself down to nothing if you're not careful. Here, some tea with lemon and a little honey. It won't hurt you."

She plied him with fruit juices and tea.

"Why don't you live here? You wouldn't catch colds. You'll eat well, the best, only what's good for you, not all that *goyish dreck* in Evanston. Stay here. Do yourself a favor. Stay here. How far is Evanston, an hour away?"

"An hour and a half."

"So, an hour and a half. At least you'll be home."

How could he tell her that this wasn't his home anymore? That home was where his books were, his pool, his ambitions, his future? But his home wasn't in Evanston anymore either. It had been invaded. He belonged nowhere.

"I'm going to take a nap, Ma."

"Yes. That's the best thing for you. A nap. Rest. The best cure." She raised her voice. "Everybody quiet. Jake is taking a nap."

"Who's making any noise?" said Miriam, his sister.

"What am I doing?" said his kid brother, Harry. "I'm working on a puzzle. Do puzzles make noise?"

"Quiet, please," his mother said.

He could hear Bubi sigh as he stretched out on the living-room couch. He could hear his father rattling the Sunday *Forward* as he read it thoroughly. He could hear Miriam in the bathroom as she got ready to go out to meet a girlfriend. In the middle of one of Bubi's sighs he popped off.

He woke up with a sneeze. His nose started running again.

"That's good," his mother said. "It's not staying in your head, in your chest. You won't get pneumonia. Here, some more tea and lemon." She spooned a dollop of honey into it. "You should put on a few more pounds, Jake. A little fat won't hurt you."

"My mother, the doctor." He moved to his father. "How about a little casino, Pa?"

"Sure."

He lost four games to his father. They tried rummy. He lost most of the games, too. Klabyosh. He was hopelessly defeated. His father was the kind of guy who could remember every card, who knew just what Jake had in his hand.

"How do you do it, Pa?"

"If you can't do it, don't play cards."

"Hey, Pa, give me a for instance. Supposing a friend of yours, a real buddy-buddy, a *landsman,* killed somebody. He's a criminal."

"I wouldn't have a friend for a criminal."

"Supposing, all right? Now supposing this pal meets you, he moves in with you, he feels safe with you, he wants you to protect him."

"I wouldn't let him in. Not with my family."

"You're alone. No family. You turn him in, he dies. If he dies, you die with guilt."

"If he's a friend, he wouldn't burden you with this."

"Supposing, Pa."

"There is always the law. We have lived by the law for thousands of years. What you are supposing, there are no two possibilities."

"Everything is so simple for you."

"No, everything is very complicated. We live with corruption. It touches us all."

"Now I know everything."

"That's a peculiar problem you pose."

"A course I'm taking in morality."

After dinner he dreaded going back to Evanston. The phone rang.

"It's for you, Jake," his mother said.

It was Lala.

"You get out here fast, you bastard. Lenny and Yussel will

pick you up. Stay there. They'll be over in five minutes."

He gathered his things, got into his coat and cap, and was ready to go.

"What's your hurry?" his mother said. "Sleep over. You can go in the morning. It'll be better for your cold. Don't go out in that frost."

As if overnight it would get warm. "I've got to go, Ma. A couple of guys are coming for me."

And he rushed out at the sound of Lenny's horn. All his possibilities had run out.

In Lenny's car, on the way to Evanston, Jake said, "How about you guys picking up Lala and putting him on ice till the heat's off?"

"Who's Lala?" asked Lenny. "You ever hear of anybody named Lala, Yussel?"

"Never heard of him," said Yussel.

"Come on, you guys," said Jake. "Lala called me, told me you were picking me up. You're buddies of his. Don't crap me."

"What have you got, a fever or something?" said Lenny.

Jake appealed to Yussel. "Listen, Yussel. Ever since Lala moved in with me, I haven't been the same. I'm going to pot. My swimming time's way off. I've got a bad cold. I never had sinus trouble before. Now I've got it bad. It keeps up, there goes my whole life. I won't be worth shit. They'll throw me up for grabs."

Yussel's forehead creased. He seemed to listen hard, sympathetically, nodded as if he understood Jake's plight.

"Hey," said Lenny, "that what they teach you in college, how to cry the blues? They got a course in griping there?"

"Yussel, for God's sake," said Jake. "This is my year. I could take it all. But not with Lala around. You don't get him out of my hair I'll be finished, kaput, ge-endet, farfallen, a has-been."

"You know what he's talking about, Yussel?" said Lenny.

"Not a fuckin' thing."

They dropped him off at the North Shore Hotel with a word of warning.

"You talk, you get a dead fish in your mouth," said Lenny.

"You see what you're not supposed to see, you get an eye torn out," said Yussel.

"You hear more than is good for you, you get your eardrums broken," said Lenny.

"Be a good monkey, Jake," said Yussel.

They slammed the car door shut and drove off, leaving Jake choking from the gasoline vapors. He walked home, the cold wind driving knives against his sinuses. The moon looked down at him with an icy face; the snow on the lawns was pocked with chimney soot; he felt he was walking through a frigid wasteland. He thought his head would split open by the time he got home. Lala greeted him like a pet dog, jumping all over him. Pummeled and pawed him. All but licked him.

"How'd you do? Did you win, did you win?"

"What the hell do you care?"

Jake showed up at the pool the next afternoon to work out. Swanee took one look at his pained face and said, "See Henry. Have him rub your sinuses and arrange for you to see a doctor."

Henry had him lie down on the rubbing table. With his thumbs and fingers he kept working on the frontal sinus above the eyes and the ethmoidal sinus behind the nose. After a while the intense pressure against the upper sockets of Jake's eyes began to ease. He sighed with relief, felt that Henry was squeezing, like pus, the infection out of the cavities of his skull and face.

"Ah, Henry, you're a genius."

When he got off the table, Jake felt good again. Henry went to the phone and made a call.

"What's a good time for you to see Dr. Morell tomorrow?"

"I feel okay now, Henry."

"You better see Dr. Morell anyway. He's an eye, ear, and nose man. What time?"

"How about three in the afternoon?"

By the time the next afternoon rolled around the pressure in his sinuses was like a head of steam ready to burst his head open.

"Swimming, the worst thing in the world for it," said Dr. Morell.

"Help me, Doc."

"Bad infection you've got there."

"Get rid of it, please. I've got all kinds of meets coming up."

Dr. Morell medicated some cotton sticks and shoved them up his nose and let them stay in there forever, it seemed, to drain his sinuses. Jake felt relieved.

"Temporary," the doctor said. "We don't have a specific for

it." He gave Jake a prescription for ephedrine and told him to get an atomizer and to spray his nose from time to time. "Let's hope it helps. But you can count on its taking weeks, maybe months to heal. Pray for warmer weather. That'll help."

Some future, Jake thought, when he left. He looked up at the cold gray sky. The feeling of snow was in the air again. A deep chill went through him. Get warm. Please get warm. You up there, make the sun come out. Make it bake that bug out of me. You, do me a favor, will you? Make it warm.

Out of spite, it snowed the next day. He trudged through the snow to the pool and worked out. Henry rubbed his sinuses afterward. He went back to the doctor to have them drained. He kept spraying his nose. He didn't sleep too well, but he forced himself to stay in bed long hours. Sometimes, during the night, the pressure in his head was so fierce it woke him up. He felt as if hot irons were working through his eyes up into his forehead. He'd whimper with pain. Then he'd run into Lala's room and shake him awake.

"Get outa here. I want you to get outa here."

"You nuts or something?"

"You're driving me crazy."

"Hold out a little longer. We're working on something."

"You bastard. Everything I dreamed, everything I lived for, you're screwing it up."

"It ain't my fault."

"Who the fuck's fault is it? Ever since you moved in, I've been going out of my mind. You're not out in the morning, I tell you, you're finished."

"Don't, Jake. Don't make any wrong moves."

He shot himself full of ephedrine. The intense pain subsided, but the ache was always there. Exhaustion put him out of his misery. Every time he was on the verge of turning Lala in, he found that he couldn't. He'd see wild pictures of Lala strapped to the electric chair, bolts of lightning shooting out of his eyes, flames spurting out of his head, as he was jolted over and over and over again. He couldn't. He couldn't live with it.

He lost against Michigan in the slow time of 1:50. He was pulled out of the water polo game with cramped legs and the worst headache he had ever had, but the team won and clinched the Big Ten championship. He lost again against Iowa State. The second-string backstroker beat him and replaced him in the medley. He felt as if he had been swimming in a pool of mud. When he finished, he had to be helped out of the tank. Henry's fantastic hands took the pain out of his body, but they couldn't take the excruciating pain out of his head.

Swanee said, "I don't want you around the pool anymore. Not until your sinuses heal."

"But the conference championship is in two weeks."

"Jake, you're not doing yourself or us any good. You'll only hurt yourself. Maybe next year, when your sinuses get better."

He felt as if he wanted to die. The pain was now deeper in his chest, from inward weeping, than in his head. His freshman year wasted. Now his sophomore year was shot. Who is Jake Davidson? Whatever happened to Jake Davidson? He was going to be the greatest thing that ever happened since Kojac. He was going to explode on the horizon like a Hollywood spectacular. He was going to be a real somebody, well known on campus, a big Chicagoan, a national athletic figure, a contender for the swimming hall of fame. *What the hell ever happened to him?*

Lala, that's what happened to him. And a little bug that crawled into the cavities of his face. They both crawled into him so deep he couldn't get them out. That's the story, folks. Born March 1912. Died just before the Big Ten meet, 1931.

"Okay, Lala, you killed me. You accomplished the impossible. I'm walking around. I'm still in the flesh. But you're looking at the walking dead."

Lala stared at him, didn't say a word. For two days now, Lala hadn't said a word. Just looked at him with wasted eyes, his mustache growing wild, drooping over the sides of his mouth, giving him a sad, forlorn look.

"I don't blame you for not talking. What's there to say? You took my career and threw it away like confetti."

It got to be very creepy, talking to Lala and not getting any response. He'd look into Lala's eyes: no contact. It gave him the creeps. Jake would be studying, and he'd feel Lala hovering over him. He'd turn around quickly. No Lala. Only a ghost of his silence.

"Now you're giving me the silent treatment. You're going to kill me with that, huh?"

He didn't know what Lala was thinking. His silence was more

terrifying than his threats. He had enough pain in his head as it was. He didn't need this.

"What a character you turned out to be. Where's all the good cheer, the songs, all that bullshit? What are you trying to do?"

Lala looked at him keenly for a long while, then turned around and went to the bathroom. Silence. Jake sat down at his desk to write a theme for English. Halfway through, he felt as if he had been suddenly sucked into a vacuum. It was so quiet. Pictures started unreeling of him and Lala walking down a quiet, dusty western street for a last shoot-out. Only they weren't in western clothes. Lala was in a pinstripe suit with a broad-brimmed fedora on his head and a tommy gun on his hip. He, Jake, was in a black double-breasted suit, a G-man's star on his lapel, and a .45 Police Special in his holster. No shots were fired. In the vacuum he heard a loud thud. Somebody had fallen. Who?

He felt strange; the silence was eerie.

"Hey, Lala."

That bastard wasn't talking.

"Hey, goofball."

Silence.

He stepped into Lala's room. Empty. He knocked on the bathroom door.

"You there?"

Silence.

"Hey, that's some crap you're taking there."

Silence.

Lala had been in there more than an hour. He tried the door and opened it. There he was, the bastard, lying on the floor in a pool of blood, the color of his face drained, his eyes staring at him accusingly. Jake didn't know what to do first. He knew very little about first aid. He knew how to resuscitate a guy. He turned Lala over, straddled him, started to resuscitate him: Out goes the bad air, in comes the good. But this wasn't a drowned man.

"What the hell you doin'?"

Lala's voice seemed to burble out of the bloody floor; it shocked Jake.

"You're killing me."

The bastard was still alive, his voice weak, but he was alive.

"Hang on. I'll go for a doctor."

He clutched at Jake.

"No doctor, no hospital."

"You'll die here."

"No doctor. Cops."

He ran into his room, grabbed a couple of handkerchiefs, tied them tight around Lala's wrists. The blood filled the handkerchiefs but stopped flowing. He got more handkerchiefs, tied them over the others. That seemed to do it. He threw a blanket over him. He remembered that from his lifeguard training. Keep him warm; keep him from going into shock. He started to rub Lala's arms toward his heart to get his blood circulating. He was afraid to move him. He knelt over him, watched him carefully, began praying for him to come around. Then he stopped. What the hell am I doing that for? Let him die. Let the sonofabitch die. I'll be off the hook. Lenny and Yussel will know it was suicide. He wouldn't be blamed. He'd be free and clear. Maybe his sinus trouble would go away. He'd be able to get back in the pool, start training again, and make the championships. What the hell did I save him for? Tear the bandages off his wrists. Let him start bleeding again. Let the life go out of him. He's no fucking good. A killer. He'll kill other people. Let the bastard go. Go on. Pull the bandages off. Let the bastard go.

Lala kept looking at him and looking at him. Lala knew what he was thinking. A thin smile creased his face. As if he were saying, Go ahead, *shmuck,* do it.

The dirty bastard. Oh, the dirty bastard.

Instead, he sponged the blood off him with warm water. He cleaned him up, got him into his bed, and put an extra blanket over him.

"I'm going to get you some soup, a piece of red meat, you bastard."

He went to a nearby restaurant and brought back a container of navy bean soup and a small steak. Lala sat up in bed. He couldn't hold a spoon, knife, or fork. Jake spooned the soup into his mouth, fed him the steak. That thin, wise-guy smile was still on Lala's face.

"What the hell did you do that for?"

Lala still wasn't talking. Just ate.

"You crummy bastard."

He walked away. He should have let him go. But how do you do that? Lala could. Lala could look at him and just walk away. Lala could see his pal Bo lying on the ground and, boom, let him have it. Was it that Lala's instincts to preserve himself were stronger than Jake's? Was Lala right, fuck everybody? Was that the way to live? Or wasn't it? Because why did he try to take his life? Maybe Lala wasn't as ruthless as he thought. Maybe he did think about Bo. Maybe some kind of fury inside him made him do it. A dybbuk, maybe, working away at him. Maybe he lived with such fear he couldn't live alone. That's why he holed up with him. Maybe, maybe, maybe. A world full of maybes.

He looked in on Lala. He was asleep, his breathing regular. The color in his face was back. A guy like that doesn't die easily. Death was in his head, but he was a survivor, a regular survivor. Driven by his instincts like an animal.

Jake was trapped once again, a prisoner of his morality. A goddamn nurse, that's what he was. Nursemaid to a killer.

The next morning, Lala's voice woke him.

"*Shmuck,* how you doin'?"

Jake turned away from him. This time *he* wasn't going to talk.

Lala swayed his hips lewdly and sang "Just a Cottage Small by a Waterfall." He ripped the blanket off Jake. "What! No hard-on? Somebody take the lead out of your pencil, Jake?"

Jake got out of bed and started to dress.

"Me, every morning I get up with a big pogo stick."

He laughed and waved his bandaged wrists like red flags. Started to sing again: "Just a Little Home for the Old Folks."

He was higher than a kite.

I should never have walked into the bathroom, Jake thought. I should have let him go. Someday he'd do it again. Or if he didn't do it, the state would do it for him with a million volts of electricity. The pressure in his head started building up, crushing his eyes. I better see the doc again.

The doctor shoved the medicated sticks of cotton up his nose.

"Is there some kind of operation for this?" Jake asked.

"I wouldn't advise it."

"No chance for it to go away just like that?"

"It could go away tomorrow."

"Keep cheering me up, doc."

He went down to the pool and watched the boys work out. They were really in shape for the conference meet. He watched Wilson do :49 flat for the 100 freestyle. Nobody could touch him. Priczinski did :52.3, good enough to take the conference. One-two in the hundred. First in the 400-yard relay. Zero in the backstroke without him. Zero in the medley. With him, they could take the conference.

"Swanee, how about it? Let me get back in. Let me try."

"All right, Jake. See how it feels. Start with an easy quarter mile."

Jake slammed into the pool. Oh, it felt so good. Stroking up and down. Kicking the six beats. Smooth. As if he'd never stopped training. The water seemed to clear his head. He felt great. Wow!

But when he left the pool and hit the cold air outside, he felt as if somebody were stomping on his eyes with iron boots. He rushed home and shot himself full of ephedrine. It didn't do any good. He lay down, squirmed and writhed, and whimpered with pain. Would it never never, never end? Right in the middle of it there was a pounding on the door. Fucking Lala, he thought. Probably forgot the key. Let him knock.

The pounding was insistent.

"All right, all right."

He got up, rubbing his aching forehead.

"Okay, okay."

He opened the door to two men in black coats and gray hats. They were around thirty, red-cheeked from the cold, clear-eyed, well built, with resolute faces.

"Jake Davidson?"

"Yah."

They showed him identification cards.

"We're from the FBI."

"Hah?"

"May we come in?"

"Hah?"

"We'd like to talk to you about Lala Bloomberg."

Jake's voice cracked. "Hah?"

"Let us come in. We'll have a little talk."

"Why come to me?"

"We understand you're a friend, old swimming buddies."

They moved in, closed the door behind them. Jake stepped back. They moved in farther, their eyes missing nothing. Jake stepped farther back. He felt no pain now. Only fear.

"Who told you?"

"Sean H. Fitzgerald, your former coach, among others. We double-check."

"I don't know anything about him." Oh, shit, why'd he say that? Supposing Lala came in now? Harboring a fugitive, huh? All right, Jake, come on along. We're pulling you in.

"Mind if we look around?"

One of them edged into Lala's bedroom.

"He's not here. What do you want from me?" Why'd he say that? Compounding the felony, as they say. They'll throw the keys away. Lala, for God's sake, stay away, don't come in and screw me up, please, for Christ sake, keep the hell away from here.

"You got somebody living with you?"

"No." He was shaking all over. He was sure they could see it.

"What's the extra bed doing here?"

"Guys come over. Friends."

"You sure you've got nobody living with you?"

Terror gripped him. They knew something. Else they wouldn't be here. Some snitch had tipped them. Lala, you bastard, you dirty bastard, I'll get ten years, they'll burn me like you, stay away, stay away.

"When is the last time you saw Lala?"

"I don't know."

"You're scared of something, Jake. What is it?"

He wasn't scared. He was terrified.

"You're hiding something, Jake. Aren't you?"

"Listen, you're G-men. You're enough to scare the shit out of anybody."

"When did you see Lala last?"

How the hell do I get them out before Lala shows?

"I don't know what you guys want with me."

"You're not answering the question, Jake."

"I don't know what to tell you."

"Just tell us where Lala is, when you last saw him."

He was eased into Lala's bedroom.

"Listen, I'm a college kid. Why do you think I'd have anything to do with him?"

"Whose clothes are these?"

They nudged him toward the closet.

He gulped. "Mine."

"They're kind of jazzy. Not exactly collegiate."

"I'm not exactly a collegiate guy. I live in an apartment. I'm not a fraternity man or anything. Just a guy who goes to school here."

They looked for identification in the clothes. Nothing.

"You're on the swimming team, aren't you?"

"Yah."

"Jake, if you know anything, you'd better tell us."

"What do I know?" His voice was as tight as a cramped muscle.

"All right, Jake. If you see him or hear from him, you'd better get in touch with us."

They left. He could hardly move. Felt as if he'd been dropped from a twenty-story building. He gulped down a long drink of water. Then he looked out the window. Saw the G-men looking about. Lala's car wasn't there. Jake wondered where he was. The G-men got into a black Ford and took off. Hours later, when he looked out the window, the Ford was back, parked at the end of the block. He wondered where Lala was. The excruciating pain in his head came back. Oh, Christ, he thought, I don't care what they do. Grab me, kill me, do anything, put me out of my misery.

Lala didn't come back that night. What the hell had happened to him?

Jake moved warily out of his apartment the next day. He saw another couple of men sitting in a parked Chevy. He felt he was being followed by still another car. They'll never let go. I'm finished. Really finished.

In the evening a Studebaker with somebody in it was parked outside. Lala still hadn't come back. It felt strange being alone, not having him to worry about. Whatever had happened to him?

It turned warmer the next day. Almost springtime. He saw

some crocuses. Somebody said it was the first sure sign of spring. His head began to feel a little better. The team was leaving the next day for Michigan and the conference championships. He was definitely not on the roster. His heart turned over heavily. He still felt he was being followed. Every time he came home he expected to find Lala shot up on the street or in the apartment. It'd be all over with him, too. Then in the apartment he'd move about as if he had a hole in his belly. That fucking Lala had really crawled into his system. The pain left his head; his eyes felt clearer, his nose unstuffed. He waited for the pain to come back, as if that, too, had become a part of his system. He didn't feel right at all anymore.

Two days later a letter came. Postmark New Orleans. No return address. Inside the envelope were five $100 bills. Printed in black crayon on the top bill was the word "THANKS." He never heard from Lala again. He never knew what happened to him.

Michigan won the Big Ten championship, beating Northwestern by six points. If only Jake had been there. He'd have made the difference.

When the team resumed training for the nationals, he was at the pool, raring to start training. He hadn't had a sinus attack in four days. He felt like a huge balloon, wanted to soar like one.

"You're sure you're all right?" Swanee said.

"I'm sure."

"Now take it easy, Jake. Build it up slowly."

"There isn't any time." He wanted to start sprinting right off.

"You do what I tell you, Jake. Two quarter miles today. Easy. Half hour rest in between."

Oh, it felt so good when he hit the water. Up and down, slamming into the turns. His form, the relaxed strokes on the recovery, the pull of his arms as he dug in, the steady riding of his body, the strong kick of his legs were all there, as if he hadn't missed a day. After fifteen lengths he began to feel his breath coming hard; his shoulders tightened; his gut was strained. His rhythm broke slightly. He rode lower in the water to preserve his energy, gulped for air, trying to fill his lungs. He had started out too fast. He could hardly breathe when he finished. He felt a ton of phlegm in his lungs. It hurt to breathe.

"Take it easy, Jake," said Swanee.

Jake nodded. He couldn't talk. He swam the next quarter mile for pace. Steady, steady. Again he couldn't keep it up. After 200 yards he slowed down. He had some energy left when he finished.

That night, when the Daughters of Neptune finished, he plunged into the pool and swam thirty lengths. All alone. Himself and his body. Listening to it, feeling it, every nerve, every fiber, every muscle, with acetylene-torch concentration. His body was tuning up, hummed better, rode more easily; he could call upon it for more. Afterward his head felt fine; his nose, his cavities all clear.

That week he worked harder, picking up the pace of the quarter miles, asking for a little more each day. His chest, straining for air, still hurt when he finished, his muscles still bunched up, needed Henry to loosen them; but he didn't ache as much. He lived within the fine arc of his concentration, all nineteen years of his life now pointed to the nationals, his Himalayas. In classes, just as in high school, he kept thinking of his event: 150 yards. In the Olympics it was 100 meters. All high school backstroke events were 100 yards. The extra 50 yards made it a grueling race. It was a flat-out sprint. You had to be in top shape for it.

Jake had another week to reach his peak. He couldn't drive himself up until the very day of the meet. He'd need a couple of days to taper off, or he'd be as wound up as a cable. Tremors would shake him in class as he saw himself in the race. Quivers of arrows would shoot through his body. Once he felt an arrow hit him directly in the heart. He almost keeled out of his seat. The professors talked on and on. He hardly listened. He couldn't concentrate on his studies. Nothing made sense to him. Only the pool had meaning. Only the pool pinpointed his concentration.

He went home over the weekend. Swam at the JPI Saturday night and twice on Sunday. Fitzgerald wanted to put the clock on him.

Jake put him off. "No. I don't want to know what I'm doing yet."

"You're right, Jake. But you look good. You look awfully good, kid."

"Thanks. You know, Fitz, you should be at some big college."

"I'm working on it."

"Really?"

"Not exactly college. But high school. I'll have all my education credits this spring. In the fall I'll be at some high school."

"You'll have a winning team every year, I'm sure."

"I'll be satisfied just to develop another Albie Karlin, another Jake Davidson."

"The colleges will be looking for you."

"Thanks, Jake. You're going to win the nationals. I'm going to be there to see it."

On Monday he started sprinting. It was so grueling he thought he'd die. He realized that he was not in any condition at all. He didn't want to do the last workout of the day, the 100-yard sprint, 100 yards easy, and finish with a final 100-yard burst.

"All right, Jake," said Swanee.

He shook his arms, rolled his shoulders, kicked his legs, trying to loosen the stiffness of his muscles. He dreaded diving in.

"Let's go, Jake."

Whop, he was into the water. It was colder than usual, down to seventy. You had to swim hard to stay warm. Nobody was going to sweat in Swanee's pool. After the first 100 there were rocks in his belly, tons of iron on his shoulders, Jack Dempsey pummeling his arms, balls of jagged wire in his legs. He drifted through the next 100, stalling as long as he could before the last all-out 100. Then Swanee was yelling, "Go. Go. Let's have it." He pushed himself into gear. Felt like a rusty old truck, heaving and huffing and clanking and creaking and riding through a sea of sludge.

"Henry, make me feel like a baby," he said after dragging himself down to the training room. He groaned under Henry's strong hands, was eased into a gentle moan. "Ah, Henry, this is better than coming, better than being on clouds, you're sensational."

By the end of the week Swanee said, "Okay, Jake, let's see where we stand."

He didn't want to know, got nervous looking at the stopwatch in Swanee's hand.

"Next week, Swanee. I'm not ready yet."

"Next week is the meet. Now."

"Come on, Jake. . . . Let's go, Jake. . . . Bust it wide open."
The guys on the team urged him on.

He'd do all right for the 100, he was sure of that. But that last
grinding 50 yards. He remembered the final Olympic trials at the
Detroit Yacht Club. He had never swum a 50 meter straighta-
way. The pool had looked like an ocean. Most of the swimmers
had come back from Hawaii, where the national AAU was held
that year. They'd got used to outdoor 50-meter pools. While he
had trained indoors in a 20-yard pool. He was used to that turn,
the rest it gave him on the push-off every 20 yards. He had had
the lane next to Kojac, who had no competition whatsoever from
anybody, he was so fast. The gun had gone off, and down the
roped lane he'd sprinted. The pool had been endless. He'd swum
and twisted to see his bearings. He'd hit the cork buoys and
ropes of his lane. Where is the end? Where is that turn? Finally,
finally, zap, he had hit it, with Kojac shoving off, a body length
ahead of him. The last lap. He had given it all he had. At 75
meters he'd cracked. He remembered the time he'd seen Kojac,
an unknown high school kid from New York, swim against
Weissmuller, who was the world record holder then in the 150-
yard backstroke. Weissmuller had never been pushed that hard.
Kojac had surged ahead. Weissmuller had put everything into it,
but there was no catching up. Weissmuller had broken, his
rhythm and spirit shattered. He'd finished third. Afterward
Norman Ross, the big champion before Weissmuller had taken
over, had slapped him on the back and said, "How does it feel to
be an old man, Johnny?" Weissmuller had been only twenty-
seven then. Jake remembered the last 10 meters at the Olympic
trials, the extra 10 meters he'd never navigated before in a race.
He'd felt as if he'd been cracked wide open. His arms and legs
had gone helter-skelter, flying all over the place, moving through
the water with the effectiveness of toothpicks. He hadn't known
what he had done, how he had come out. He hadn't cared. He'd
wanted to die. Fitzgerald had dragged him out of the pool. He'd
walked on jellied legs to the showers, heaving for a breath of air,
and then dropped on the tile floor, the pain so fierce tears
flooded his eyes. Those extra 10 meters, the endlessly long length
of the pool, and himself against a killer like Kojac, who'd broken

Weissmuller in two. So he dreaded that last 50 yards.

"Anytime you're ready, Jake. I'll get you."

Jake nodded. Go. This is only practice. This isn't the main event. You don't have to kill yourself. But that watch. That relentless second hand sweeping away, eating up the time. It would tell him what kind of shape he was in. He was sure he wasn't in top form yet.

"Okay, Jake, we're waiting." Swanee patiently standing above him as he balled up for the leaping start.

Go!

He was off. He was at the turn before he knew it. Bang, he slammed into it too hard. Bang, another turn. The pool was getting awfully bouncy. Swanee hadn't raised the level to the gutters so that there'd be no waves. It was like being out in the lake in a storm. He had to ride higher so that he could gulp the air without choking on water. The 100 went well; he'd come in, he knew, in pretty good time. Now he turned on more juice. Felt the enormous strain. It was as he had expected; he was struggling, fighting to maintain the pace. The last 30 yards killed him.

He streched out long and slow afterward, easing off a few lengths, gasping for air until his chest opened like a wide barrel, making him light and buoyant. That made him feel good. His recovery was fast. Which meant that his condition wasn't that bad.

"One-forty-six," said Swanee.

"Really?"

"You'll do a lot better next week."

It wasn't bad, Jake thought, if Swanee hadn't used his "rubber" stopwatch, which was always bullshit time. But he needed at least five seconds to win. He knew he was always good for a second or two better in a meet. But where would he get the extra seconds for a possible win? Only days were left to break through that last 50. That was going to be his big mountain run. That last 50.

"Your sinuses okay?" said Swanee. "Everything okay?"

"Fine. But I could use a few more weeks of training."

"Don't worry, Jake. You're going to do just great."

Where was he going to get those five seconds to be in the

running? Sometimes at night he fell asleep to the ticking of a stopwatch. The ticking got louder and louder. Became a time bomb in his head. He woke up to the terrible explosion, his teeth aching, his heart pounding, his muscles pulled tight.

He had Fitzgerald time him at the JPI on Sunday. The last 50 yards were still murder. He looked at his face and knew that Fitzgerald was disappointed.

"I stink, don't I?" Jake said.

"One-forty-six-three. Is that bad?"

"You sure you didn't put a rubber watch on me?"

"Jake, you know I wouldn't do that."

They all did it to build your confidence, but when you accused them of it, they looked as if you were crucifying them.

"One-forty-six took the Big Ten," said Fitzgerald encouragingly.

"One-forty-one, forty-two will take the nationals. Where do I get the five seconds? I need a cushion, a little cushion, and time is running out."

"You've got a few more days. Every day you're getting stronger."

"But I did worse today than I did Friday. Maybe I'm building it up too much, I'm too nervous. My nerves are going to kill me, Fitz."

"I wouldn't worry about your nerves, Jake."

"They're not your nerves, Fitz."

"Your nerves work for you. You're lucky that way."

"Five seconds lucky? My nerves aren't going to give me five seconds. Where do I get them?"

"It's no use my saying, 'Take it easy, Jake.' But take it easy, will you?"

"Oh, Christ, that fucking sinus." Jake added to himself: That fucking Lala. He'd never told anybody about him, afraid the word would get to the FBI, and they'd come for him.

"I'm not worried about you, Jake. You'll be in there."

Boy, was he in there! Monday, Tuesday, he sprinted his heart out, but he didn't feel sharp or confident. Competition was going to be tougher. This wasn't high school anymore. He was going to be up against the best. Taking this event, if the Olympics were held this year, he'd be on the team. That's how tough it was going to be. They'd be coming from the West Coast and the East. They'd all be there at the Lake Shore Athletic Club. And he wasn't ready.

Wednesday and Thursday he tapered off at the Lake Shore Athletic Club, getting used to the pool, studying all the markers. A couple of quarter miles each day. Then a lot of turns. Keep everything loose. If you're not ready now, you never will be. You've got to save it for the preliminaries Friday. Then Saturday, the finals, if you ever make them.

All that week he walked around campus, sat in his classes, went to sleep with scalpels of worry cutting up his insides. A few seconds, that's all I want. How do I get them? If my turns are perfect, I can pick up a second and a half. One bad turn, and I need more than a few seconds. One bad turn, I could forget it. One bad turn, I could wind up with a broken hand or a concussion, ramming into the end of the pool, then I could really forget it. I can count on my adrenaline, another second or so. What about pace? There is no pace. It's an all-out sprint. What if I get a guy like Kojac next to me? He cracks me in two. He crushes my lungs. He breaks my heart. What if?

All that week he walked a tightrope. He hardly heard anybody; he hardly talked. He was so deep inside himself he turned into a zombie. In his sleep he swam the race a thousand times. Somehow he never finished. Once he was pulled down by an octopus to the bottom of the tank. Once the drain was opened, and he was sucked down by a whirlpool through a sea of muck. Once, just as he was about to finish a winner, somebody jumped in and started to drown him. Each race was more horrible than the one before. It got so he hated going to sleep. He couldn't even relax when Henry rubbed him down. Nothing was working for him. Time was against him. Where do I get those few seconds?

Thursday night. He woke up a hundred times. The night was endless. He was finally into Friday, the day of the preliminaries. He was into the day where you couldn't bullshit anybody. You made the finals or you were out. If the night was endless, the day was eternally worse. He was on a stopwatch that never seemed to move.

Suddenly Swanee was shaking him.

"You're up now, Jake." Swanee tried to look confident.

Jake detected doubt in his eyes. If I only had another week.

Swanee patted his back as Jake got out of his sweat pants. "Give 'em hell, Jake."

Jake nodded, took off his sweat shirt. He gritted his teeth. He didn't know if he was chattering from cold or nervousness.

"Who's Bruner of Stanford?" Jake asked.

"You can take him."

"What about Clyde of Yale?"

"Don't worry about them. Just win your heat. Qualify."

"In the water!" the starter said.

He didn't look at the men in his heat. He didn't want to know what they looked like. Size always intimidated him. In the water, balled up against the wall, waiting for the start, they all looked alike; he was as big as any of them.

"Swimmers ready!"

The gun sent them leaping way out over the water. As soon as Jake started to lose way, he began his kick, shooting him forward; then the strong pull of his arms moved him up like a submarine, and his arms started working like broad blades of a windmill. There were five men in his heat. At the 100 he was a body length ahead of Bruner of Stanford, a half body length ahead of Clyde of Yale. He wasn't worried about the Ohio State and the Indiana men in his heat; he had beaten them handily in the dual meets. When he shoved off on the last lap, he began to falter. Clyde started catching him. Jake dug in, the water waving over his head, kicking harder, and slammed into the end of the pool a touch ahead of Clyde.

Swanee had a big smile on his face. The guys on the team were jumping up and down. He'd taken his heat. He swam down the pool, loosening up, came back. He almost caved as he stepped up the ladder, his leg got so cramped.

"One-forty-three-four," Swanee said.

That wasn't good enough. O'Connor of Rutgers had come in with a 1:41.2 in his heat. More than two seconds better. Where the hell would he get that?

Henry loosened his shoulders, worked the cramp out of his

leg. His hand began to hurt. He must have banged it hard at the finish. He looked at it. Anything broken, any swelling?

"What's wrong?" Henry said.

"Nothing. Nothing." His arm was limp with pain.

"Let me take a look at it."

Henry felt for broken bones, made him work his fingers. "You're all right."

O'Connor from Rutgers came alone, only for the backstroke event, so Jake didn't have to go against him in the medley. But Clyde of Yale, who qualified for the finals with the second best time in any heat, swam Jake to a dead heat on their leg of the medley.

That sonofabitch is tough, Jake thought. He might murder me tomorrow night. To say nothing of what O'Connor would do with a qualifying time of 1:41. He'd be lucky to get third. What the hell good was that? He was a champion. He had never lost. Only in the final Olympic trials had he ever lost. But he'd been a kid then. And he'd been up against the best in the world, the whole world. He felt belligerent, pugnacious. I'll take 'em. Who the fuck are they? In the water I'm as big, as strong as any of them. I'll take 'em. Over and over and over again, he kept saying that. While shivers of doubt ran through his body, and he couldn't fall asleep. Sleep, please, sleep, but he turned and tossed in bed. His nerves wouldn't let him alone. I'll be a limp rag in the morning. Sleep, goddamn it, sleep. But as soon as he did fall off, he had to get up to go to the bathroom. Oh, God, give me a break, just one goddamn good break, let me pop off awhile. I'm bushed, I'm pooped, I'm going out of my mind, swimming that race in my head, don't let me leave this whole goddamn race in this bed. Oh, God, anything you want, just ask, only let me get off this Ferris wheel, let me pop off.

He curled into the lonely, tortured, exhausting, private hell of wanting victory with all his heart and feeling defeat with all his body. He was like a bullet on a target. If he didn't hit the bull's-eye, he would explode. The night went on and on with himself tightly wound into a ball of delirium. He must have fallen asleep. Suddenly the phone was ringing. Suddenly it was daylight. Suddenly it was eight-thirty. And Swanee wanted him down for breakfast.

"How you doing, Jake?" That's what everybody wanted to know. Because the team had a chance to take the title. If Jake won his event. If Jake could take his leg of the medley. They qualified both relay teams and in enough events to take it. If Jake could come through.

"Okay, okay," Jake assured Swanee and everybody. While he yawned and felt as if he didn't have the energy to pick up a pin.

He had a light breakfast at the Lake Shore Athletic Club, where the team was staying. Afterward he walked across the drive to the lake and sat down on the stone breakwater. The sun was out; there was a watermelon smell of spring in the air. He looked out at the Municipal Pier, the three-mile water crib, the sun dazzling the quiet waters. The time he had spent on this lakefront, dreaming of a day like this. Jake Davidson, intercollegiate champion. And he wasn't ready for it.

His nerves started working on him again. Darts struck him from all sides. His skin prickled. He began to walk. Oak Street Beach. All the fun he had there. The girls he fooled around with. Beyond the North Avenue breakwater he could see Lincoln Park and its skyline of trees. There was the Drake and the Potter Palmer mansion, like a medieval castle, and the McCormick palace, like a Renaissance fortress. Part of his life was sunk here, swimming and playing in the front yard of the Gold Coast, dreaming of replacing the Chicago kings of industry and one day building his own estate beside the Palmers and McCormicks. Now he didn't want kingdoms, yachts, diamonds, power, everything he was taught to strive for in school. All he wanted was a small win, which wouldn't hurt anybody. Was that asking too much?

Tonight, like at his bar mitzvah, he'd have to account for his whole life. His past was all bundled up into this night. And his future would unravel from it. It's too much. He felt choked up, a fierce cry in his throat. It's just too goddamn much.

He worked out with the team that morning. He flopped around, trying to kick and stroke the jitters out of his arms and legs and guts. He took a long hot shower afterward. Then a light lunch, toast, a couple of eggs, and milk. He went up and tried to nap. Couldn't. Felt like a knight on a long vigil, all alone in a small room, praying for victory. Then he went to a movie with some of the guys but didn't see much of it; he was too self-involved, shaken from time to time by the race he swam over and over again.

Early dinner. Nobody talked very much. You tried to kid around. A few nervous laughs, but everything fell flat. Nobody really listened; they heard only the beat of their own bodies. Afterward, in his room, Jake tried to read, tried to nap, tried to read again; it was wearing him out. His ear was tuned to the ringing of the phone. Time. The ringing shocked him. He got into his silk tank suit, sweat suit, sweat socks, clogs. He grabbed his extra suit for the medley. Anything else? What was missing? Only himself. His real self. And the championship, which seemed as far away as Mars, as elusive as stars.

Tonight, *boychik*. Tonight is the night.

Down in the rubbing room he tried to stretch out, but couldn't lie still. The light glaring off the white walls crunched his eyes. Arcs of rainbows floated about from the vapors of the showers and steam room. The tart smell of alcohol, wintergreen, and liniment made him sneeze. Fitzgerald, along with Benny Gordon and Solly Landon, came down to see him, to wish him the best.

Benny said, "Kick 'em in the balls. Show 'em who you are. You don't win, I'll break your leg."

Solly said, "I'm betting on you. Give 'em the JPI blitz."

Fitzgerald said, "Tonight you're going to prove me the best coach in the world."

Jake's voice wavered. "I'll try not to disappoint you." His eyes were bloodshot. He yawned and shuddered, stared at them. Everybody was a blur. "I've got to go."

"You're ready," Fitzgerald said. "Really ready."

It was the twentieth time since supper that he had had to urinate. Where did all the piss come from? He stood at the urinal. And stood there. A few drops finally came out, and he felt that he still had a skinful. O'Connor came up beside him. Jake looked up at the mountain of man towering over him: six feet three of rippling muscle.

"How you doing, Jake?"

"If I live through tonight, I'll live. If not, who cares?"

O'Connor laughed nervously. "I'm pissing my head off."

"Join the club."

Jake left. That sonofabitch has got good adrenaline, maybe better than mine. Oh, boy!

Milton B. and Roger W. Troop, his real estate boss, dropped by. They beamed at him proudly, as if he were their special prize.

Milton B. said, "You win, and you'll be able to write a check for a million dollars."

Roger W. said, "Give us a first, Jake, and I'll have a bonus for you at our next big sales meeting."

Milton B. pulled Jake aside. "Listen, Jake, I put up plenty for the *goyim,* but you're the guy I'm really for. Some of my best friends are *goyim,* but I want you to beat their brains out. Show them that a little Jew can kick their guts out. We'll be proud of you."

"I'll try."

"Goddamn it, last week the fucking Nazis in Munich killed my uncle. They're yelling all over the country that the Jews are responsible for the Depression. It starts all over again. Give 'em hell, Jake."

He hardly heard him. All he needed now, as quaky as he felt, was a pep talk.

Only his father and mother weren't there. That's all he'd need. Once, at a high school meet, they'd come. His mother, seeing him look so pale, so watery-eyed, so distracted, so peaked, had begun to cry and plead with him not to go into the race, he'd get TB or pneumonia or something, he looked so run-down. Even after he'd won, he didn't look any better; she'd wrapped him in a robe and flung towels around his neck and urged him to get dressed quick before he caught the flu. Never again, he said after that. Which was fine with them because they couldn't bear to see what he was going through. All that travail for a little medal, a little headline in the paper, a little glory; was it worth it?

He laid down on the rubbing table, and Henry started to loosen him up, rubbing the warm oil over him. Who was right? he wondered. His folks, who looked on all this as an American insanity, or Milton B. and the university athletic department and his own powerful need to win?

If that race doesn't start soon, I'll drop dead. He walked to the toilet again. This time he sat on the bowl, squeezing, trying to

purge himself completely before his event. He farted a few times
and dribbled out a few more drops of urine.

Suddenly he became conscious of his hand. He had hurt it
yesterday; he knew it now for sure. A sharp pain ran from his
hand up his arm and flipped a knife into his heart. He almost
caved.

"Jake! You're up next!"

He tripped on his clogs, almost fell. He flung them off and
walked as if on tiptoes into the pool. The place was packed.
Albie Karlin grabbed his hand.

"Good luck, Jake."

With him was Lila. She kissed him. "You can't lose now." As
if she'd given him her ribbons for victory.

Swanee moved up to him. "All right, Jake. Once you hit the
pool you'll be all right. Take a few deep breaths."

He had to pee again. Shit, too. I won't be able to move. Let
me go to the toilet first. I'll drown!

"Swimmers in the water!"

He wriggled out of his sweat pants and shirt, peeled off his
socks. Oh, Christ, if he could only go to the toilet once more. He
got a glimpse of O'Connor's huge back, powerful arms and legs
. . . Clyde's big chest and bulging muscles. They blurred before
his wet eyes. Fuck 'em. I'll break 'em in two. He dived in, then
swam back easily.

"On your marks!"

He coiled up, held the gutter tight with his hands, the balls of
his feet hard against the tile. Beat them at the start. Grab a few
tenths of a second. Watch that starter. Let's go, let's go.

"Swimmers ready!"

The gunshot uncoiled him like a huge wave, hurling out wildly;
then he was into the sprint, unthinking, his training, his instincts,
moving his arms, his legs, as if he himself had lost all control, his
body, his spirit taking over. Smash, into the first turn, all even.
Up from the push-off, stroking, heaving ahead, stroking, kicking, a touch behind O'Connor at the 50. Wham, swirl around,
way, way out on the shove, Clyde right beside him and
O'Connor inching ahead. Boom, into the third turn, a great one,
pushing himself ahead of O'Connor and Clyde. Now he called on
more of himself to maintain his lead. And he was straining,

breathing hard, the air not sinking as deeply, his body eating up the oxygen too fast. Zap, he hit the turn too hard at the 100, faltered, didn't curl up enough for the full power of the push-off, and he was behind O'Connor and Clyde. More, more, give it more, get in there, come on, you bastard, let's have it, more, more. Slam, a good turn, a hard push-off, hold it, save your energy, you'll need it, this is the end of it. Now, all of it, every bit, pull, you bastard, kick, you sonofabitch, dig in there, all of it, let it go, let it all out, fuck the breathing, fuck the stitch in the side, oh, Christ, before I die, hit it, finish it, smash it, go go go go. He slammed into the end of the pool, his hand striking the gutter, his head crashing into the tiles. He didn't know how he'd made out. All he'd seen was furious splashing on all sides; all he'd felt was his agony and pain as he kept fighting to finish. He struggled for air; that's all he wanted now, just a breath of air. Then he looked up. Swanee was standing over him, smiling. His forefinger was up. Number one. He'd done it. Fuck 'em all. He flung himself out over the water and swam halfway down the pool delirious with joy, all alone. This was his, all his, this moment, this victory, this Everest of his dreams, it was all his!

BOOK 3

Milton B. was as proud as a father. So was Fitzgerald. Roger W. Troop strutted like a Florentine patron. Jake was one of many children to Swanee, but that night he was the favorite. Albie Karlin had known all along that Jake had it in him. Benny Gordon and Solly Landon slapped Jake's back, pinched his cheeks, jumped on him, gave him the full JPI treatment. Jake had not only won his event, but he'd also taken his leg in the medley relay and had helped push Northwestern into the championship by one point over Michigan.

Lila invited him to the College Inn. Muggsy Spanier introduced him to the roll of the drums and the fanfare of the band. The place went wild, all the customers hammering the tables with purple wooden hammers.

After Jake had a big steak dinner and cherries jubilee for dessert, Albie said, "You think you'll be able to sleep tonight?"

"I'm so beat I could drop right here, but I know I won't be able to fall asleep. I've never been able to before. Why should tonight be any different?"

"Lila will find you some sleep," Lila said. She walked over to a platinum blonde in a white satin gown who looked like Jean

Harlow. She had Harlow's full, sensuous lips, the cleft in her chin, the sexy, sultry, slinky look. "The best sleeping tablet in the world," she said to Jake.

Up in one of the hotel rooms, Jean Harlow (that's what she called herself) said, "Did you ever have the once-over lightly?"

"No."

"Lay back. Relax."

She stroked his body with her gleaming feather white hair, her soft cheeks. She delighted him with tiny puffs of air. Her tongue and breath worked over his inner thighs up to his groin, sending tingles of ecstasy through his body; then she took his cock into her mouth, stroked it with her tongue, sucked it into her throat until he almost went out of his mind; then she sat on him and slid right down to his pubic bone and rode him like an animal with her soft hair caressing his face until he felt himself shooting everything he had right through her whole body.

But he still couldn't fall asleep afterward. He kept swimming his event over and over as if it were a race still to be swum. His nerves still kept flitting wildly about. He tossed about restlessly, his whole body painfully craving sleep.

"What's the matter, honey?"

"I can't sleep."

"Oh, honey. Baby'll take care of that."

But she didn't. Not then. Not two more times after that. He was totally drained.

"You must be a monk, honey."

"Would you believe I haven't slept for days before tonight?"

"You must be on some kind of dope."

"Yep, the biggest kick in the world."

"What else can I do for you, baby?"

He didn't know where he got the energy. This time he exhausted himself completely. His nerves finally died over her body. He fell asleep with a shudder.

At home the next day, he said, "Well, folks, you're looking at the new intercollegiate champ."

"Very nice," his father said, unimpressed.

"You look terrible," his mother said. "All dried out. Skin and bones."

"Oh, Jake." His sister, Miriam, flung her arms around him. She knew what the whole thing meant. "How wonderful!"

"What'd you get for it?" said the kid brother, Harry, the mercenary little bastard.

Jake showed them the gold medal he won.

"Hey!" little Harry said.

"That's beautiful," Miriam said.

"It's yours," Jake said.

"You'll want to give it to some girl," Miriam said.

"Right now you're the only girl I've got. Take it."

"What are you talking?" his mother said. "You have all kinds of girls."

"Nobody who means much to me."

"But you do have all kinds of girls, no?"

"Yes, Mom. All kinds."

That relieved her. Not only did she expect her son to be a brilliant scholar, a champion, a *macher,* a moving force in the world, but she also expected him to be a Casanova. Why not?

Miriam handled the medal as if it were a Tiffany diamond. "I'll take the ribbon off and wear it on my locket."

"It looks like solid gold," his father said.

"Gold-plated."

"You mean it's not worth anything?" his mother said.

He was disgusted with them. "Where the hell do you people live? This isn't the old country. This is more than bread, more than dollars and cents. It represents something. It's an achievement. It's American. All American. Look."

He grabbed the Sunday sports section of the *Tribune.* On page one a two-column headline: "Northwestern Wins Collegiate Swim Title." A box head: "Jake Davidson Clinches Victory." He showed them the paragraph that featured him: "In an electrifying 150-yard dash, Jake Davidson, a former Chicago high school record holder, touched out Tim O'Connor, the eastern collegiate champion from Rutgers, in the fast time of 1:42. He also took the lead in the medley relay to give Northwestern another victory." There was a picture of him beside the jump story on the next page.

"That's who I am. Your son, all over the newspapers. Like a racehorse, Pa. Man o' War."

His father beamed at him, then said, "You should only make a fortune like Man o' War."

"Milton B. Morgenstern said I could write a check for a million dollars if I won."

"Could you cash it?"

"Pa, you're the guy who always said money isn't everything."

His father laughed. "We say knowledge is more important. But who can learn on an empty stomach."

"Your father is worried about the Depression, the people being thrown out of work," his mother said.

But he knew later how proud they were of him. On the phone, to friends and relatives, all they could talk about was their son, the great intercollegiate champion.

When Jake got back to campus on Monday, despite the headlines in the *Daily Northwestern* and the metropolitan dailies, nothing had changed. No brass bands, no big parades, no bonfires, no triumphant marches. Very few students knew who he was. He had no N sweater as yet to make him stand out, no identification tags with his name emblazoned on them.

In class, nothing astonishing happened. The professors didn't even glance at him, just lectured on and on, were relentless in their demands. Jake felt like an insignificant smudge in the lecture rooms, on the walks beside the greening grass, under the new foliage on the trees and shrubs. He wanted to climb up a tree and shout, "I'm Jake Davidson, the new intercollegiate champ, the guy who helped Northwestern win the national title. Look at me, you bastards. Pay attention. Here I am. Jake Davidson." It was as if he'd farted in the wind.

To Ida, whom he saw the following weekend, it didn't mean much either. She'd clung to him in high school, walked in the wake of his glory. Now she didn't know what he had done until he told her.

"That's wonderful," she said flatly.

"Don't you read the newspapers? Don't you know what's going on?"

"What do you want me to do, Jake? Leap for the chandeliers? Yell yeah, team, rah-rah-rah?"

"You could show a little excitement."

"Jake, there are other things."

"Like what?"

"Look what's happening to the country. And all you can think of is winning a backstroke race."

"You don't think that's important?"

"I think that's an adolescent way of living."

He had come up wanting to lay her, but her pissing on his victory turned him off.

"Jake, you've been so spoiled, so pampered. Always taken care of. Everybody watching you, looking out for you. You're like a baby."

What a time for lectures!

"People are starving. They don't know where their next meal is coming from. Kids dig into garbage cans for a scrap of moldy food. And all you can think of is the sun rising and setting on your ass."

"What are you all of a sudden? Jane Addams? Sarah Heartburn?"

"Grow up, will you, Jake?"

"Nice seeing you, Ida."

He started to ease out.

"What would happen if you ever broke a leg, you couldn't swim anymore?"

"Thanks for wishing me the best."

She came close. "Jake, I used to love you like crazy. I always wanted the best for you. But I'm two years out of school now. And you're still there. All covered with ivy. Which is a little bit like being in the womb."

She shot him right in the balls. He opened the door.

Her eyes lit up, a teasing smile on her lips. "Haven't you forgotten something, Jake?"

"What?"

"This, you dumb dodo."

She put her arms around him and pressed herself against him. She revolved her hips, socked it in slowly. She had pissed on him just a little too long.

"I didn't forget. I'm not in the mood."

"Oh, Jake. That's a girl's excuse. What's happened to you?"

"I don't know."

He left, took a long El ride to Evanston. What the hell was happening to him? Before, he'd been able to absorb his triumphs all alone. But now it was like masturbating; he wanted something more fulfilling. He had come to Ida, not only to lay her but to share his victory with her. But she wasn't impressed. An adolescent, she called him. Spoiled. Pampered. A baby.

He was one of the best swimmers in the world, he had a rare talent, but who cared? What was really happening to him? Oh, how he wished he had someone to share his triumph! It wasn't enough to win for himself anymore, or for headlines and medals, or for Swanee or Milton B. or Northwestern. Maybe if he had won for his parents, for somebody really involved with him, he'd feel different. Maybe if he knew what he had to prove, it'd be another matter. But basically, winning was a self-centered thing. The Greeks did it for their gods. The knights and Crusaders fought to the death for their kings and their Christ and their ladies. The Jews wanted triumphs for their temples, their beliefs. Today only the self, subservient to nobody, was glorified. Life in America was a hard, driving, self-centered force. Yet he wanted somebody to share his victory with him, to fill up the hollow feeling he had. *What was really happening to him?*

He was at loose ends now. The discipline, the core of his life, had been pulled from under him. He had slid down from the peak of his own crusade so fast that it took the wind out of him. The Olympics were a year away; they seemed so far in the future. He wondered if he could ever again work himself up to the pitch of the past few months. Out of habit he went to the pool every day and swam half miles. It seemed to be without purpose. Competition was a long way off. He didn't know what else to do.

He was lonely and blue. He had never been lonelier in his life. He drove himself to study because he'd missed weeks of it. After all the glory he thought he'd attain, he was finally reduced to a bookish world, to sitting alone in a room trying to understand other minds, other worlds. Maybe Ida was right. A Weissmuller, a Babe Ruth, a Red Grange, a Jack Dempsey, could write million-dollar checks because of their unique talent. But Albie Karlin, Arne Borg, Stubby Kruger, Norman Ross, Paavo Nurmi, Joey Ray, Big Bill Tilden, and a thousand other amateur champs couldn't. Maybe sports *was* an adolescent thing. Goddamn school mixing him up, screwing up his dreams. Goddamn Ida pissing all over him. Where the hell was he going, what the hell did he really want? A deep restlessness came over him, a desire to find purpose, to concentrate him the way swimming did.

The business courses didn't absorb him. He did just enough work to get by. But he found that he was spending more and more time in English, striving harder to write better, to comprehend the works he was reading. He even went to the library and read other books that were not required.

What was going on in him?

Jake didn't know it, but like a snail, he was slowly emerging from his shell of narcissism. One phase of his life had ended, another was to begin. He was peeking about, smelling around, his antennae bristling for new signals, a different kind of hooray. It came one day in a full-page ad he saw in *College Humor*. It was offering a $5,000 prize for a novel written by an undergraduate college student. The magazine also had the right to publish any other suitable manuscript that would be submitted for a minimum advance of $1,000 against royalties and first serial rights. Wow!

"How do you write a novel?" he asked his English professor, who had excited him this past semester. He was a tweedy man in his late thirties, smelling of aromatic tobacco, who came from the South and was educated at Harvard and Oxford. His accent began in the South but got banged up at Harvard and ricocheted off Oxford, so that it wasn't easy to understand him; but he loved literature passionately, and the emotion got through to Jake.

"There are a million novels in the library. Read a few."

"I have."

"Read a few more."

"Is that the answer?"

"No. Because I've read thousands of them and I still can't write one. Why?"

"I'm going to write one."

The prof smiled. "What's the word you use for sheer nerve?"

"Chutzpah."

"Have you ever written a short story?"

"No. I'm lucky I've been able to write a theme for you."

"Mr. Davidson, you've got some *chutzpah.*"

"I've got more of a one-track mind."

He did the minimum amount of work for his classes, until final exam time, but read indiscriminately. *College Humor,* the slick magazines, Hemingway, F. Scott Fitzgerald, Zane Grey, Kathleen Norris, Ben Hecht, Dreiser, Somerset Maugham. Maugham's *The Moon and Sixpence* shook him.

"You ever read *The Moon and Sixpence?*" he asked his English prof.

"If you liked that, you ought to look at Paul Gauguin's *Noa Noa.*"

Noa Noa knocked him for a loop.

He got through the term with passing grades, had a month before the lifeguard season started. He began fattening up on novels, on books about the art and craft of fiction. He filled out more and more, began to wobble with the weight of them. He joked about it: "I'm eating for a whole new world instead of one." Everything looked different: the girls, the lake, his family, his friends, the streets, the river. Everything took on new dimensions. Life wasn't so narrow, so one-sided. He was looking for a story with an intensity he'd never experienced before, even more than his training to be a swimmer. He never thought it possible.

He called up Ida and said, "You still talking to a spoiled, pampered baby?"

"Always to the kind of baby you are."

When he got together with her, he looked at her differently: She wasn't just a lay anymore, just somebody to satisfy his animal instincts; she was somebody.

"Hey, you look altogether different," he said.

"How?"

"Different."

"Maybe it's because I'm in love."

"Again?"

"This time it's for real."

"Must be. Because you look wonderful."

"What the hell is happening to you, Jake?"

"I don't know. I feel like a pregnant woman."

"You're silly."

"Really, Ida. Ever since I decided to write a novel."

"You write a novel?"

"I know it's hard to believe. The guys'll think I'm turning fruit. But I'm going to write one."

"What about?"

"I don't know yet." He looked under her rug. "Maybe I'll find it there."

"You're crazy, Jake."

"I'm looking. On the El, in streetcars, in the pool, on the streets. Maybe I'll find it here in a teacup. They say life is in a glass of tea. Maybe I'll find my novel in it. Tell me about your new love."

"It's only the beginning. No middle, no end. No novel in that."

"He married?"

"How did you know?"

"Why should this one be different from the others?"

"You bastard."

"Ida, not too long ago you hit me right in the teeth. You called me a baby, an adolescent, told me to grow up. I'm telling you there's no percentage in married men."

"You're giving me instant Freud."

"There are reasons you fall in love only with married men. This is the third one. Why don't you find out why?"

"What if I told you it's because I can't have you?"

"Bullshit."

"You're right, Jake. Something's wrong with me."

Suddenly tears started to her eyes. He took her in his arms and held her close and felt his heart go out to her. He used to be irritated and helpless before her tears; now he was concerned. He felt himself sharing her trouble. It was a whole new experience. That was a triumph in itself.

She stopped sniveling. "But it doesn't matter, Jake. What's important is that I'm in love. It fills me up. It keeps me from being lonely. It makes me happier."

"Sure."

When he got ready to go, without making a pass at her, she said, "Jake, what are we now? Friends?"

"We're certainly not lovers."

"Until I fall out of love again. Right?" Her eyes twinkled mischievously.

"Provided I'm not in love."

"You, Jake? You in love?"

"Miracles can happen, sweetie. If you look, you'll find."

He kissed her goodnight, sweetly.

With Jake, everything he went into was an act of survival. If he failed, he thought, he would die. So he stalked the libraries, probed the fictional lives of hundreds of people. He talked to his buddies who were back from college waiting to resume their jobs as lifeguards. He wandered the streets, looking for his novel. His prize book was out there somewhere. But where? Why was it so elusive?

The West Side streets were no fit material for a novel. Who would be interested in a bunch of Jews, the way they lived? Where was a *Moon and Sixpence* in that? How could you find romance in gefilte fish and fried herring and pumpernickel bread? Imagine giving readers of *College Humor* stories about *shnorrers* and *shlimazels*, the hard-core, hard-luck characters around the JPI, about wits and wags and Talmudists spouting Spinoza and Karl Marx. Some prize he'd get.

Of the guys, the only one he confided in was Sandy Meyers; the others would massage his balls with wintergreen, make him scream with the pain of it as they laughed at him, and they'd say, "Jake, poor Jake, he went to Northwestern and wound up with water on the brain."

Sandy was a couple of years older than Jake, tall, gangly, myopic and light-haired. As soon as he finished high school, he had bummed around the western states for a year, working with construction gangs, prospecting for gold in the Colorado mountains, then came back and worked as an elevator boy before going to the University of Illinois. Now he was ready to bum out to Los Angeles to work the summer there as a lifeguard; he didn't know if he wanted to go back to school. He had read Eugene O'Neill, and he wanted to become a playwright. He thought maybe he'd go to sea for a while, like Eugene O'Neill, after he finished lifeguarding. He confessed to Jake that he'd been secretly writing while at Illinois.

"I wrote a play called *The Big Rock Candy Mountain,*" Sandy said.

"What's it about?"

"Prospecting for gold."

"Wow!"

"Two guys find it. A bonanza. And the mine caves in. They're trapped in it."

"So what happens?"

"I don't know yet. I don't know if I should make my hero dig out, but he's crazy when he gets out, or he dies in the mine."

"That's some problem."

"It's not like math, two and two is four, where it all adds up nice and neat. The trouble with writing is the fucking decisions you've got to make."

"Yah."

"I've been working on a big Americana thing called *Pie in the Sky.* About a big con man out West."

"You've got all kinds of ideas."

"Once they start rolling in you can't stop them. It's like a flood. When I get to Los Angeles, maybe I'll make some contacts on the beach, and I'll take a crack at screenwriting. Imagine, writing for the cinema."

"Man!"

"The way to crack into the movies, I read, is to write an original. After that it's the gravy train. You can forget mining for gold. El Dorado is out there."

"Some of those writers, I heard, make over a thousand dollars a week."

"Another way to bust the door open is to have a play done on Broadway or publish a novel or a good short story. It's all talkies now. They need storytellers and good dialogue writers. One thing about being a dialogue writer, nobody can tell you your English stinks. You write like people talk. People talk like English stinks. Unless they want a Noel Coward or a George Bernard Shaw or a Shakespeare, you can write stinking like people talk and get away with it. Who knows, Jake? Maybe we'll become a couple of big-time movie writers."

As kids, Jake remembered, they used to stand on street corners at night under the lampposts dreaming of being great swimmers, of how it would change their lives, and they'd stood in awe of their dreams. That's how he felt now, as if he were looking at a spectacular path to a brilliant future: writing for the movies, no less, mingling with the stars.

"It's all possible," Sandy said. "Everything is possible, as Voltaire would say."

"Who is Voltaire?"

"A great French writer. You ought to read him. *Candide* is the book. Another guy you ought to read is Anatole France. And the Russians. Chekhov, Dostoyevsky, Tolstoy. What worlds lie before us, Jake! What great revelations!"

"Yah. But where do you find a story? How do you sit down and spin it for sixty thousand words minimum? That's the requirement for the contest."

"Look into your heart, Jake. Search your soul. Turn your guts inside out. Once you find your story, sixty thousand words will go like nothing. Good luck, Jake."

The next day Sandy left for California to prospect for a new kind of gold on the beaches of Los Angeles. He said he'd be in touch. And Jake was left to wander over the city, amid the skyscrapers, the sweet, sickening smells of the stockyards, the empty lots filling up with ragweed, the contaminated oil-streaked river, the breadlines and idle men sitting on curbstones, the buildings becoming shabbier, the smokestacks standing lifeless against the sky . . . searching for a story that would win him fame, fortune, and a great new career which would eventually take him to Hollywood where Johnny Weissmuller was now cavorting with the stars, where he'd pal out with them and with Mary Astor and Richard Dix and Tom Mix and Greta Garbo—if only he could find that story and the people who would fill it up.

One day, while he was in the Public Library downtown, staring out the broad windows at the pigeons defecating on the wide sills and pecking up and down Grant Park, the novel, influenced by all the movies he'd seen, came to him. It would have a college background. It would be about a subsidized athlete who came from the back of the stockyards. He would be a star basketball player instead of a swimmer. It would be a love story. Since a story should have some conflict, he had read, then there should be some opposition. So the girl he falls in love with would be rich and beautiful, naturally, and her folks would provide the conflict.

Oh, man! He hugged himself with the excitement of it.

Now to expand the story, to fill up the pages, to make it more interesting. Bootleggers. Gangsters. His hero would need money to win his girl. He would need it fast. He couldn't wait for the long haul. So he becomes a brain guy for a gang of bootleggers, and he makes a ton of money, and his girl's father respects him at last and is glad to hand over his daughter in marriage. What a winner! Shoot-'em-up excitement! Glamour! Athletics! And a theme that a book must have: Money doesn't stink, no matter how you make it! How could he fail?

He slammed his fist into his palm and yelled, "Geronimo!"

People shushed him, thought he'd gone crazy. The librarian hurried over as he shouted, "I've got it! I've got it!" She told him he'd have to leave.

He hugged her, whirled her around. "But don't you see? It's like a vision. It struck me like a thunderbolt. The whole vision, the whole panorama."

Now people knew he was crazy. He rushed out of the library and went directly home. He could hardly contain himself as the streetcar jerked its way westward. His insides were running away from him. He held his belly to keep all he felt from pouring all over the car. Don't let it get away.

He ran three blocks from the car line to his house, keeping the thunderbolt in his body, and scurried past Bubi and his mother and Miriam into the dining room, where he grabbed a ream of paper and some sharpened pencils which he'd had ready for this moment and began to write.

"Like a madman," his mother said. "No hello. Nothing. A wild Indian."

Bubi felt his forehead to see if he had a fever.

Miriam said, "Quiet, the muse has taken his heart."

He scribbled at a fierce pace. All of it. The whole vision. Then he stopped. It was only a page long. The thunderbolt in his body fizzed out. How do I expand that one page into a couple of hundred pages? Oh, man.

He got up every morning and stared at the white sheets of paper until the world turned into a vast empty landscape of glaciers; it froze his heart. Then he grabbed the many books he'd got out of the library to see how they started. They didn't help him. How could he capture their stamp of authority? Every one of those books started out like Beethoven's Fifth Symphony. Da-da-da-rump, da-da-da-rrrrump! At the end of June, just before he began working as a lifeguard, he said, "Fuck it. Time is running out." He started to write.

He wrote every morning until noon, had a quick lunch, then went to work. Standing and sitting around the pool, watching with glazed eyes the thousands of people swimming and splashing around the huge pool, he'd think of what he had done that morning and what he was going to write in the future. He felt fatter than a Japanese wrestler with the ideas and emotions in him. Once a week he saw Ida and gave her the pages he had written and picked up the pages she had typed.

"How is it?" he would ask.

"Peachy." Sometimes she would say, "You're going to win the prize, Jake."

He swelled up with confidence. He loved her for that.

When he read the typed pages, it was as if somebody else had written them; they were so good, so stirring, so exciting. One week he wrote like Hemingway, another like Sinclair Lewis, another like Dreiser, another like Irvin S. Cobb, another like Jack London, depending on whom he was reading at the time. By the time he finished the novel he was filled with wonder over where all the words had come from, where he had found the passion, the emotion, the drama. It was a mishmash of everything he had read, flowery, romantic, sentimental, hard-boiled, full of clichés, atrociously written; but he had a full-length story, and he was certain he was going to win the prize. He sent it off to *College Humor,* and he felt as he did after winning the national intercollegiate backstroke championship: completely empty.

Now what do I do? he thought. Wait? Just wait? He began to wonder if he had another story in him. The more he wondered, the more convinced he was that he was drained. I haven't lived enough, he thought. I haven't had enough experience. If only I had a war behind me like Hemingway. Great adventures like Lawrence of Arabia or Richard Halliburton or Jack London. Big escapades like Henry Fielding's *Tom Jones*. A powerful, brooding love like *Wuthering Heights*. I don't want to live a little. I want to live a lot. I've got to get away. See the world. I'll go to California. I'll look up my pal Sandy. He said he wanted to be a seaman like Eugene O'Neill. We'll ship out. See the world. Five years. All the ports in the whole world. Then I'll write. Boy, will I write. I'll have that $5,000 from *College Humor* in the kitty. And I'll have all the time in the world to write a big blockbuster. *The Adventures of Jake Davidson*. I can see it on film already. Written by Jake Davidson. Starring John Barrymore. With a cast of thousands!

"Well, folks," he said, "you are now looking at the next Richard Halliburton, Rafael Sabatini, Jack London, and Somerset Maugham."

His mother and father looked at him wide-eyed, open-mouthed.

"Who are those people?" his mother said.

"Jack London, I know," his father said. "He's a socialist."

"They're all writers, adventurers, men who have lived, who are rich with the glories and the juices of life."

Bubi looked at him with love and adoration. She didn't understand a word, but she smiled toothlessly at his extravagant expressions.

"Right after Labor Day, right after the lifeguard season is over, I'm busting out to see the world."

"Where you going?" his mother asked, beginning to worry.

"Everywhere. All over."

"You're not going back to school?"

"Of course I am, Ma. The best school in the world. The school of experience. Tell her, Pa."

"What should I tell her, that you're going insane?"

"I've got to go. I'm going to be a writer. I've got to be on my own. I've got to live. I can't hide anymore in some ivy-covered closet. I've got to expand my horizons. Have something to write about."

"Sholom Aleichem wrote about his little *shtetl*. His bones, his blood, his heart, his flesh were in the little towns of Russia. He didn't have to go anywhere. That was enough for him to write about."

"He was a Jew. He was limited. All he had was Yiddish."

"The whole world knows him. The Jewish Mark Twain."

"But he's not Mark Twain. There was a guy. He lived. A life full of adventure."

"I won't argue with you, Jake. You're a man already. Not a man in years, but a man in size. I want you to think about your future carefully. Finish school. Get your degree. Then do what you wish."

"Listen to Papa," his mother said. "Please."

There was no use talking to them. If they could have their way, they'd tie you to them forever. His mind was made up.

He was on his way, blue-eyed, innocent, healthy, strong, a champion, with a novel about to win a $5,000 prize and every pore open for every experience life had to offer. He was at the beginning of the biggest, most fantastic, most romantic binge in the world. About to embark on the trail of the forty-niners, on the seas to Honolulu, Tahiti, all the exotic islands of the Pacific. Then China, Singapore, Hong Kong, Australia, India, the Middle East, Greece, the Peloponnesus. Maybe Russia. Then Europe. France and French fucking. Italy and Spain and hot, exotic loving. England and the world of Shakespeare, Chaucer, Wordsworth, Milton, Browning, Ruskin. Watch out, Maugham. Make way, Conrad. Look out, Halliburton. Be careful, Hemingway. Here comes Jake Davidson!

He had $20 distributed in his pockets and his shoes. He had a dressy pair of pants underneath a pair of old corduroys. Under a blue work shirt he wore two good shirts. Over that he wore an old sweater. In his pockets he had extra socks, a toothbrush, razor, bar of soap, comb, silk swimming suit, a few handkerchiefs, a wallet with ID. He looked like a shoplifter coming out of a department store.

"What are you dressed for, kid?"

"Why?"

"You're sweating your balls off."

It was hot. Indian summer weather. On the outskirts of Chicago, dust blew off the prairies. The Southern Pacific tracks gleamed in the sun, the cinders crunching under the restless feet of men on the bum. Fires in the jungle heated coffee, beans, lard, making shimmering waves. Jake needed the extra clothes, needed his hands free for grabbing trains. The man talking to him was tall and gawky with a thin, bony face, a big, curved nose, a roller coaster of an Adam's apple, and a cast in a gray eye that pinned you when he focused on you.

"Have some coffee."

The coffee in a tin can tasted like mud. Jake took one swallow and almost vomited.

"Strong enough to make your socks stand up, huh?"

"Yah."

"How about some sweet cream?" The man's voice was full of sarcasm.

"No, that's all right."

"Maybe Carnation milk will hit the spot."

Jake looked about at the men sitting near the fire—all of them dirty, needing shaves, all of them lean and hungry, in shabby clothes. They began to laugh.

"I'm not much of a coffee drinker," Jake said.

"What's your pleasure, kid? Wood alcohol? Sterno? Or Napoleon brandy?" The man rolled a cigarette from a Bull Durham sack.

Jake swallowed another mouthful of coffee. It made his hair bristle. The man laughed, put his arm around Jake.

"I was only kidding," he said. "Sit down. Relax. My name is Charley Ball." He shook Jake's hand.

"Jake Davidson."

"Jack!" Charley made a point of *Jack*. "Where you heading, Jack?"

"California. Los Angeles."

"Gonna look for work there?"

"No, just want to see the world."

"You ever been on the bum?"

"No."

"It's not exactly the best way to see the world."

"I know. But I want to be a writer. I need the experience."

Charley fell on his side from laughing. Then he said, "A word of advice, Jack. Watch your pockets. Watch out for asshole bandits. Don't let everybody know you were just born. Keep your mouth shut and look sharp. There'll be a reefer along pretty soon. Dog my steps. You'll be all right."

A train whistle from afar stirred the jungle into action.

"Right on schedule," Charley said. He was a timetable.

Then the locomotive whistled and steamed and hammered by, black and shiny and fiery and fierce as a monster on a rampage. Followed by the clattering cars: flatcars, coal cars, cattle cars, reefers, ore cars, some empty, some full.

"On my tail, Jack," Charley said.

Charley was alongside an empty boxcar, arms and legs flying, a scarecrow on the wing, hitting it and vaulting up on it.

"Come on, kid."

The cinders sprayed all over, whup; there he was, running wildly, and up, whop, right on, with Charley thumping his back, Jake had done all right. The air breezed by. Jake got his breath. He smiled. He was a bo, he was a tramp, he was on his way. Inside the car he thought he had stepped into a two-holer, it stank so. There were about twenty men there. He didn't think men could smell so bad; it was worse than the stockyards. He stayed near the open door, with Charley beside him.

Charley was a western man, a cheerful man, an IWW man, who said he was born with the badge of the working class; his purple heart in the class struggle was his eye spiked by a fink's boot during the copper wars in the Colorado Rockies. A product of Big Bill Haywood, Joe Hill, Jack London, and Eugene V. Debs, he had put in all kinds of time: railroad time and jail time, struttin' time and lonely time, whorin' time and jag-off time and lovin' time, but no time to settle down with a woman and raise a family. He was on his way to California to organize the grape pickers and pea pickers and artichoke pickers and all the other backbreakin' pickers you could name. He was a ramblin', gamblin', shufflin', organizin' man.

"You going to write about the open road, Jack?"

"About everything."

"Write about the battle of McKees Rocks, the Paterson silk strike. Write about Big Bill Haywood and the revolution. Write about the bums without a blanket; the guys who left their wives and kids to go west for a job and never located them since. Write about the stiffs who never had a job long enough in one place to qualify them to vote and about citizens representing law and order, beating up honest workers and railroading them to jail while good Christian people cheered them on. Lots to write about."

"I don't know about all that."

"You're crazy, Jack."

"Huh?"

Charley laughed. "Crazy as a coot. A crazy romantic. The world's starving. There are guys in this car who'd rather be with their families, back on their farms, than floating around looking for work. And you, like a goddamn sailor, bumming around. But don't get me wrong, Jack. The world belongs to you romantics. You dream; you dare; you're spirited; you've got mankind in your heart; you change the world. Jack London was a romantic. So were Lenin and Trotsky and the French revolutionists. And the biggest romantic of them all: Jesus Christ. The meek shall inherit the earth, huh? But not without a battle. Nobody gives up what they got without a battle."

The steady clatter of the cars, the telephone poles and wires running by, the farmlands stretching on and on, the small towns whizzing past got Jake sleepy. He began to doze in the warmth of the sun. Coming into Springfield, the train slowed down. A few more men hopped on; then two women made a run for the car. Jake woke up to the roar of the men urging the women on. They came alongside, hit the floor of the car, and several men lifted them right on. As soon as the women were in, they got right down to business.

"All right, men. Fifty cents a fuck. Jerk-off, two bits."

The women strolled into a corner of the car, their dresses dusty and spotted with dry jism, their hair stringy, their faces painted. Ten men lined up.

"I'll be goddamned," Jake said.

"You gonna have some?" Charley said.

"No."

"Of course. You're a romantic."

Charley got up and joined the line. In twenty minutes, the

women were finished, and they hopped off, running down the
cinder embankment.

"Like havin' a good sneeze," Charley said.

Men jumped off and got on.

"Thousands of them are wandering over the land, trying to
find a spot for themselves," Charley said. "A different breed of
bo now. Guys who'd lost their jobs, their homes, their land, then
their pride, their dignity, their hope. Used to be a time we all
knew each other. Meet in the vineyards, the orchards, the
camps, the trains. Now they're mostly strangers. You going to
write about them?"

Jake didn't know. He had never read about them in *Collier's*
or the *Saturday Evening Post* or *College Humor*. Who wanted to
read about derelicts, the dispossessed? People liked stories about
heroes, people making it, overcoming adversity. People wanted
to be inspired, not depressed.

"You should be riding in J. P. Morgan's private car," Charley
said. "You should be with the robber barons. That'd be
inspiration for you."

Somewhere near Joplin, in a different reefer, with a bright
half-moon riding like an engine light beside the line of freight
cars, Jake fell asleep on the wooden boards. He dreamed of
Barbara Stanwyck picking him up in a Bentley roadster and
driving him all over Hollywood, then to her palatial home up in
the hills. He dreamed of native brown Polynesian girls, soft and
voluptuous, making love to him under a coconut tree with gentle
surf caressing the shore. He woke up with a tidal wave of an
orgasm and was stunned to find a man with a stubbled beard
sucking away at his penis. Jake shoved him off, scrambled away.

"What the hell you doing?"

"Proteins. Nothing to eat in three days. Proteins." The man
slunk away, a dark shadow, whose face Jake couldn't see.

"Jesus Christ."

Charley stirred beside him. "Everything all right, Jack?"

"Did you see what happened?"

"No. What happened?"

"Shut up, will ya?"

Yes, he'd better shut up. He leaned against the wall of the car, shuddered with a sense of things crawling all over him. He thought the night would never end. The moon stared down, finally hypnotized him and put him to sleep. In the morning he woke up huddled close to Charley to keep warm. He looked about at the sleeping forms, the animal heat of their bodies warming the car. Jake no longer smelled them; he was part of the stench.

Past Tulsa and Wichita Falls the cars clattered over crossings, snarled over bridges, roared and screeched through tunnels. Idle factories rushed past, warehouses and silos and red barns and grain elevators. Through engine smoke you could see beaches of rippled dust duned up against shacks, crops drowned in the waves. On the roads, old heaps piled with possessions crawled westward.

"If they're lucky in the vineyards, they'll get five cents an hour," Charley said. "Men," he called out, "you've got to organize. You don't, you're doomed." He talked for ten minutes about one big union, everybody belonging. "The day of the exclusive craft unions, the private clubs of the AF of L, is over. The day of the big industrial union is coming for migratory workers, farmers, electricians, carpenters, office workers, everybody. Let's sing 'Solidarity Forever.'"

The men stared at Charley, faceless, bodiless, like empty carcasses hanging in freezers. Jake, as a friendly gesture, joined in the song. A few others cleared their throats and followed along.

"Let's have it," Charley shouted. "Sing it out. Make 'em hear you out there."

Most of the men watched him wearily, silently.

In and out of freight yards, past water tanks, into mountain country and great forests and arid land, past wagon trails and ghost towns where legendary gamblers and badmen and lawmen roamed, hurling by endless landscapes of creosote bushes and cacti and mesquite and Joshua trees and saguaro, across the Petrified Forest and the Painted Desert into red rock mountains and canyons . . . all bigger than he had ever imagined. It took his breath away.

That night, before they crossed the great Mojave Desert, Jake lost his shoes and all his money as he slept. His feet felt cold in the early morning; icy blasts seemed to be whirling into the car, waking him up. There were no shoes on his feet. And he had had ten dollars in them. He rubbed his feet to warm them, looking about to see who had taken his Regal cordovan shoes. It was too gray and dim to see. With the rising of the sun, light burst into the car, and there were his shoes on the feet of a guy about his size with a grizzly growth of beard. He remembered this guy, a sullen man, hopping on the afternoon before outside Gallup with another tramp, big, muscular, snarly, who was beside him right now. The nerve of the bastard, taking his shoes and wearing them right in front of him. Jake felt his pockets for the rest of his money. Nothing. All of it was gone. Taken while he was asleep. How did he do it? He watched the beard feeling his feet in the shoes, kneading the leather to break them into his shape.

"What are you lookin' at, punk?" the beard said.

"My shoes."

"Your shoes? What are you talkin' about, your shoes?"

"You stole my money, too."

Charley moved up beside Jake.

The other guy, the brute, rose up, big and powerful, and said to Charley, "Tell your friend he made a mistake. A big mistake."

Charley turned to Jake and said, "You heard the man. You made a big mistake."

"I want your friend to apologize."

"The man said he wants you to apologize," Charley said. Then, as swiftly and suddenly as an animal, Charley whirled on the big brute and kicked him hard in the balls. The brute thudded to the floor, doubled up, holding his crotch, and passed out. The tramp with Jake's shoes flung them off.

"What about my money?" Jake said.

"What money? Who's got your money? How the hell can you prove I've got your money?"

"I had ten dollars in my shoes."

"There, there it is."

The money was still in the shoes. They had more of his money, but he decided to let it go.

"You satisfied?" said a gaunt, granite-faced man in overalls with the twang of an Arkansas farmer.

"Yah, sure," Jake said. He didn't want any more trouble.

"God Almighty isn't."

A group of six strong young men, also in overalls, flocked around the gaunt man.

"We don't want these vermin around us. Before they contaminate us, we must rid ourselves of them."

The brute on the floor came to, writhing and moaning. The beard backed fearfully toward the open door.

"Times like this we need the moral support of our fellowman; we don't need scum like this." The gaunt man kicked the brute on the floor. "We'll never find the Promised Land. We'll never be delivered."

Charley intervened. "Now wait a minute, fellas. Remember what Christ said about turning the other cheek."

"'Thou shalt not steal!'" The gaunt man rose to his toes in wrath, and his sons stood firm beside him. "The Lord said, 'If you spurn my statutes, and if your soul abhors my ordinances, so that you will not do all my commandments, but break my covenant, I will do this to you: I will appoint over you sudden terror, consumption, and fever that waste the eyes and cause life to pine away.'"

He paused a moment as his sons said, "Amen."

"'I will make your heavens like iron and your earth like brass; and your strength shall be spent in vain, for your land shall not yield its increase, and the trees of the land shall not yield their fruit.'"

"Yes, yes, Lord."

The men who'd been like smudges in the shadows of the boxcar suddenly took form, hard, moral, vengeful, as though, if they prosecuted this crime and judged it and meted out punishment, they would be redeemed and the hard times would go away.

"It is men like this who have brought down the Lord's fury," the gaunt man said righteously. "Men like this have caused the Lord to make the land a desolation. You!" His bony finger pointed to Jake. "You must cast them out. An eye for an eye, a tooth for a tooth. You shall purge the evil from our midst."

Jake looked at Charley. Me?

"You, young man, deliver us!" The old man's voice shook him.

"Christ," Jake said.

"Help him," the old man shouted to his sons.

Before anybody could touch the guy with the beard, he jumped out of the car, hurtled over and over the cinder embankment into the rocky desert, then smashed up against the bony needles of a cactus plant. The big guy writhed and cried in the strong hands of the old man's sons; he bellowed with terror as he was flung out, then he was silent as he rolled over and over away from the train into clumps of creosote bushes.

"Thy will is done," the old man said. He sat down in the shadows of the car with his sons. "Let the land be revived now, Lord. Let us find our place among good people."

His sons said, "Amen."

Jake looked away, afraid their wrath might rise again. Far in the distance, as he looked back, he saw the men who were kicked out of the car shimmering in the blazing heat as they started their walk across the vast desert.

Charley said, "A different breed roaming the country these days."

Jake began the end of his journey across the Mojave, thirsty, hungry, dirty, smelling like the foul end of the Chicago River, marveling at the spiny plants surviving in the alkaline hardpan, watching swirls of dust and sand like huge ghosts below the black mountains, seeing mirages in the shimmering heat of former seas. Then the San Berdoo Mountains and the long coaster ride past groves of oranges, avocados, and walnuts, hurtling by vineyards and exotic palms and eucalyptus. A foreign world. As far away as the Casbah, the Persian Sea, the tropics.

They hopped off as the train slowed down outside the freight yards of Los Angeles. Walked the spines, crossed the tracks, out into the streets of the city.

"We made it," Jake said.

"Good luck," Charley said.

Jake hated to part from him. "I'll miss you, Charley."

"Come along with me. We'll organize."

"Not until I see the world."

"Go ahead, Jake. See your world. But remember what I told you: Watch out for asshole bandits."

Charley shook his hand. He walked away, turned around, saluted Jake with a fist, yelled, "Up the revolution!" and disappeared around a corner.

California!

Now, away from the forests and the mountains and the desert and the fruit groves, away from the sea of white and pink stucco houses with red tile roofs, Jake was in Sterno and wino country, with mission houses and "Jesus Saves" signs about, with people staggering on the walks or lying in passageways because of starvation or drink. The flophouses and fleabag hotels had elegant names like Hotel Barclay, The St. Regis, The King Edward. Sleazy bars, warehouses behind Los Angeles Street, several ten-cent movie theaters, a burlesque house, one-arm coffee joints, empty lots with alcoholics burning Sterno and dispossessed men on the hunt for jobs brewing coffee and cooking beans in tin cans—it was no different from Madison Avenue or South State Street in Chicago. Only now there were millions on the road, millions in tin Hoovervilles, in hobo jungles, in the skid rows of America.

Jake stopped in for a big fifteen-cent breakfast: eggs, potatoes, toast, jam, coffee. The place was steamy, smelled sour, but it was the first decent meal he'd had in days.

From there, Jake went to the post office. He had sent himself a check for $25 which his father had made out to him, c/o General Delivery. It was there. That'd take care of him until he shipped out. He got directions on how to get to Venice. It took almost two hours to get there. People on the buses moved away when he sat near them. He knew that his socks were ready to stand up by themselves; he itched so badly he felt ticks were crawling under his skin, but he didn't know he smelled like the bottom of a cattle pen. The sweltering heat made it worse.

"Is it always hot like this?" he asked a bus driver. "It's September. It's supposed to cool off."

"Not in LA, it doesn't. September's a bitch. 'Specially when the Santa Anas are blowing."

He couldn't get into his suit and into the water fast enough when he hit the beach. He smashed into the surf and was shocked at the coldness. The waves kept knocking him off his feet and driving him into the sand. He had never been in the ocean before, and he didn't know how to dive through the combers and get beyond the breakers. One wave crashed over him and smashed him up onshore. He felt as if he'd been shot with a thousand grains of sand and sprayed with a barrel of brine. He tingled all over when he got out.

At the lifeguard tower he asked if Sandy Meyers was around.

"He blew town."

"Where?"

"Honolulu. Got his last pay and shoved off. Said he was going to finish school there. Comb the beaches and go to school."

Shit, Jake thought. They'd exchanged a couple of letters over the summer. Maybe he'd come out there, he wrote. Nothing definite. Then he wrote saying he was really coming out, and Jake expected Sandy to be there.

"Wally Blake around?"

"He should be here later."

Jake wandered around Venice, walked along the canals. Palm and banana trees made brittle, raspy sounds. Birds-of-paradise, fuchsias, and bougainvilleas were in full bloom. Along the levees were stucco bungalows and shacks. On Windward Avenue he had a hamburger and a piece of pineapple pie and coffee. The whole area was a sun-bleached slum, but Jake thought it all very romantic. He strolled out on the beach and watched the surf roll in and looked out at Catalina and San Clemente islands humped up like giant whales against the horizon. To the north the Santa Monica Mountains curved into a huge horn out to Point Dume. You could be a beachcomber, and you could dream here, he thought.

The Santa Ana winds made the day clear, hot, and dry. He went into the water again to cool off and let the waves knock him about. He watched some people body surfing, and he imitated them. Soon he was getting the hang of it. He began to love the tangy feel of the salt, the power of the waves; he glowed all over when he came out.

When Jake got back to the lifeguard stand, Wally Blake, the former intercollegiate champ and Olympic star who had wanted Jake to go to Stanford, was there. Wally was captain of the guards in Venice. He had more freckles than ever, and he had turned to fat.

"What the hell you doing out here?"

"I'm going to bum around the world."

"After winning the intercollegiates? You must be nuts or something. Go back to school. By the time you're finished the Depression'll be over. You'll be able to write your own ticket."

Wally was a graduate engineer, a former celebrity, a man with success stamped on him; now he was a lifeguard, turned to fat, which was as close to being a beachcombing bum as you can get, but he still believed in his earlier dreams.

"You see any of Weissmuller?" Jake asked.

"He's in a different league now. Strictly Hollywood. How's Albie Karlin?"

"He's going to law school. Prepping to be a judge."

"I should have gone to law school. I could be big in politics, too."

"It's not too late."

"No."

Wally Blake depressed Jake. He used to feel so great when Wally talked to him, was so flattered when Wally wanted him to go to his alma mater, was so thrilled when he worked out and played water polo with him and Weissmuller and Albie. Now Wally was a fat man in a lifeguard tower whose big boat of dreams had sailed away without him.

Jake didn't know why, maybe it was the climate, the prevailing breezes from the ocean with the smell of the South Seas and distant ports in the air, maybe it was the restlessness and the despair he felt among the men on the bum, maybe it was his disappointment in not finding Sandy there, but he felt rootless and disconnected. He thought he'd better get a move on. He asked Wally to cash his father's $25 check. Jake needed the money to buy some seamen's papers so that he could ship out.

"Come back tomorrow," Wally said. "I'll have it for you."

"Where does a guy stay around here?"

"I'd have you stay with me, kid, but I'm shacked up with a woman and two kids, and there's no room. Try the Pacific Arms."

He watched the day turn into night along the sea. The glow, after the sun sank, was like fire for a long time; then a black hood covered the ocean, with white breakers rolling up and disappearing. It was magnetic. He got off the sands and had a tough, gristly steak, then a banana split at Ocean Park Pier. He rode the roller coaster and the Ferris wheel over the ocean, but he didn't have any fun at it. It takes two to be thrilled. Black loneliness came over him.

The Pacific Arms was a fleabag of a rooming house. He jumped about all night, bitten by bugs. When day broke, he was stiffed and tired; red welts were all over his body. Sounds of foghorns and veils of drifting fog greeted him. He got out of the room as fast as he could. He roamed the cool, damp ocean walks. The Santa Ana condition was over. He lingered over coffee and a Danish, then walked along the canals again to keep warm. At ten o'clock the sun broke through, began to warm him. He lay down on the sand and felt far away from home and far away, even, from where he was. He thought he should be somewhere else.

Wally Blake finally came on duty. He looked sleepy. After some small talk, Jake said, "You got the money for me?"

"You sure the check's okay?"

"Drown me if it isn't."

"Okay, kid." He handed Jake $25. "Why don't you stick around awhile? I'll put you to work next summer."

"No, I want to ship out."

"This is as good a beach as any. And it's easier to starve here."

"Thanks, Wally. I'll go into Hollywood and glom some movie stars; then I'll shove off."

He bummed into Hollywood and hung around Hollywood and Vine all day but didn't see any stars.

"Where are the stars?"

"Beverly Hills."

He hitched to Beverly Hills. Within thirty minutes he was picked up by the cops. They couldn't arrest him for vagrancy, because he had money, but they told him to stay out of Beverly Hills. So he wouldn't see any stars.

The following day he started out for San Pedro. By the time he got there the day was almost shot. Four ships had already left that morning. He could have been on his way. He went up to the Seamen's Union, a dusty, smoky hall, smelling of sweat, musty clothes, and brine. Men sat around, some with duffel bags near them, playing cards, checkers, cribbage, and chess. Others read newspapers, old magazines, and books. Seamen were great readers. So were lonely men. They looked a lot like the bums on the road, except that many of them were tattooed. He listened to them.

"Not much shipping these days."

"More action in Frisco, I'll bet."

"New York's the town. Think I'll hit the rods and go there."

"Used to be a time they'd shanghai you to get a crew."

Somebody began to sing: "Days I knew with you were just a memory, just a memory." Which got a few laughs.

"You mean nobody's getting out these days?" Jake asked.

"Two went out today. A hundred didn't."

"Where you from, kid?"

"Chicago," Jake said.

"You come out here to get some salt in your socks?"

"Something like that."

The man talking to him was weather-beaten, squinty, sweaty, with a stubble of beard and the tattoo of an eagle on his chest. He had an earring in his left ear. Jake watched it jiggle as he talked and moved.

"My trademark," the man said. "Girls get entranced by it. That and my eagle. Makes them curious about the real bird down below."

"Really?"

"Bought the bird, the earring, and a thirteen-year-old girl in Hong Kong for twenty-five bucks. Shacked up with her for three months and sold her for thirty when I left."

"Why don't you quit shittin' the kid, Johnny?" a cribbage player said.

"Vas you dere, Charley?" The man called Johnny laughed. Then he turned back to Jake. "Got papers?"

"No."

"You wanna buy some? Can't ship out without papers."

"How much?"

"Five dollars."

Johnny broke out an oilskin package and gave Jake some seaman's papers. He had other papers wrapped in the same skin.

"What do you do, get them by the gross?" Jake asked.

"You ship long enough, you collect lots of discharge papers."

"Under different names?"

"What's in a name?"

Jake examined the papers. "The pictures don't look much like me."

"Who looks?"

"That means I go under a phony name."

"You're very bright, kid."

"What if something happens? I mean, a ship is sunk. Nobody'll know I was on it."

"Will it make any difference? Anybody care?"

"You goddamn right."

Jake hesitated. He'd heard that this was the way to do it, but he didn't want to be conned. He stepped over to a couple of chess players. "These papers look legit to you?"

One of the chess players smoked a pipe. Chess players and pipe smokers always struck Jake as being honest. The pipe smoker said, "They'll get you on."

Jake checked with the man who'd told Johnny to quit shittin' him. "They're okay."

Jake went back to Johnny. "What does an able-bodied seaman do?"

"He stands watch; he chips rust; he paints; he ties a few knots, a few other things. Whatever you don't know you'll learn."

"Do I have to be a member of the union?"

"Get a job, you'll join."

"Under the phony name?"

"Everybody around here has got lots of names. Who cares? A seaman isn't even entitled to vote."

Jake gave him $5. He turned his new name, John Bodeen, in to the expeditor. He was all set. After three o'clock, when there were no more calls, he wandered around the town. Above the harbor and the sea, houses were built at the foot of the Palos Verdes Hills looking like pictures he'd seen of the Riviera. The wild grass on the hills was all brown, and the live oaks were gnarled and twisted from the prevailing winds of the Pacific. Walking along the hill above the port, he could see a vessel being tugged out slowly through the channel. Oil refineries were all about, but they didn't have the suffocating rotten-egg smell of

Whiting and Hammond just south of Chicago; tankers were moored near them, taking on tons of oil and gasoline for distant ports. And freighters were being loaded with lumber from the Pacific Northwest, cotton from Arizona and New Mexico, fruits and vegetables from the great valleys of California, heavy pipes and machinery brought in by the Southern Pacific and the Atchison, Topeka and Santa Fe. One channel had nothing but fishing boats rigged for sardines and mackerel and tuna with the canneries nearby. The port seemed so busy. Somewhere, Jake thought, there's got to be a job for me.

Later, at the Seamen's Institute, where he could sit in comfort and find something to read, he saw some of the same men he had seen at the union hall. It felt like family, as he nodded to familiar faces. John Bodeen, the weather-beaten salt who'd sold him the seaman's papers, asked him if he could play cribbage.

"No," Jake said.

"Checkers?"

"I stink."

"What do you play?"

"Casino. Rummy."

"Casino."

They played two-handed casino awhile, and Jake won several times.

"Want to make it interesting?" John said.

"If it's not too steep."

"Name it."

"A nickel a game."

Jake lost fifty cents to him.

"You're taking me every which way," Jake said.

"One last game for the whole fifty cents."

"You're on."

John was better than Jake's father, a card shark.

Somebody walked by and said, "Watch out he don't take your pants away."

Jake knew when he'd had enough.

"You're playing with a Mississippi gambler."

Jake got up from the table. "Got any other scam you want to make me for?"

John laughed. "I wanted to teach you a lesson. Don't gamble

with strangers. Come on, I'll buy you a drink."

"I don't drink."

"You will, son. You go to sea long enough, you will."

A man in a black suit and a benign face came over and said he was Father Lancaster. He asked Jake if he wanted to go in for evening services at the Episcopal Church, which was part of the institute. Jake said, "No. I didn't know this was a religious place."

"It's for all creeds, races, and religions."

"I'm not really religious."

"Have some coffee and cookies anyway. You're always welcome."

He had some coffee and cookies, then walked out with the book he was reading: *All Quiet on the Western Front.* The night was still and starry, the palm trees slim sentinels with shaggy heads overlooking the bay. You could see the ships' lights in the harbor and at their berths. A vessel was coming into the channel, its running lights on, looking like disembodied stars floating just above the dark waters. Weird, Jake thought. In the town, a few seamen staggered along the street, lingered outside saloons, broke and thirsty for booze. They bummed Jake for a dime, but he walked past them. He saw John Bodeen reel out of a saloon with a couple of guys he'd seen earlier; they were singing sea chanties. Tired, Jake rented a room at the White Dolphin, a white clapboard rooming house. He didn't like the idea of there being no locks on the door, but the price was right: $1 a night. He put his money and his newly bought seaman's papers inside the pillowcase of his pillow, read more of Remarque's book, and then fell asleep, as deep as he could go without dying.

He didn't get out the next day or the next or the next. Ships were coming in and going out. Very few seamen were being called. He went to the ship chandler and hung around and asked everybody connected with any ship if he needed a hand. He walked the terminals, the warehouses, the docks, talked to seamen on watch or loading. Nothing. Everybody had a berth; everybody was hanging on; even foreign seamen weren't jumping ship for the gold in America. Each day he'd see the ships go out to sea, headed for distant ports, and his heart would give out.

One afternoon he drifted out to Cabrillo Beach. Some gray

naval vessels and a few merchant ships were anchored in the
harbor. In the park, off the beach, the trees were twisted and
bent, seemed shorn off at the top, by the sea winds. A stiff
breeze came in off the ocean, hurling foamy seas over the rocky
breakwater and whipping up whitecaps beyond the crashing surf.
Graceful sea gulls and big-beaked, heavy-bodied pelicans
searched constantly for fish, swooping into the swells for their
prey; movement was incessant. A blinding sun began arcing
toward the horizon.

Jake roamed along the beach, picking up small rocks and
driftwood and throwing them out to sea. Sandstone palisades
rose sheer from the ocean at the north end of the beach. He
wondered how it'd be in Hawaii, in Bora Bora, Pago Pago,
Tahiti, his walking along the beaches of sleepy lagoons and coral
seas, riding surfboards with Duke Kahanamoku, the Kalili
brothers, being seduced by brown-skinned native girls under
swaying coconut trees, becoming part of the primitive rites of a
Balinese village, finding rich pearls in a tropical sea. Would he
ever get there? To Yokohama, Manila, Guam, the Melanesians,
Sydney, New Zealand, the Dutch East Indies? Would he ever get
to paradise? . . .

"Hey!"

Three men in jeans and overalls, their faces with several days'
growth of beard, their hair whipped by the wind, their bodies
heavy and threatening, came onto the sand toward him. One of
them threw an empty wine bottle into the ocean.

"You got any money?"

Jake tightened. The men separated as they came toward him.
He looked for a way out. One way, over the rocky breakwater,
led to the gentle bay, but it was quite a way off; the other led to
the roaring combers with the sheer cliff of sandstone at the north
end of the beach; and there was the road out to the town.

"I haven't got any," he said.

"Cough it up, you little bastard."

As they came closer, he made a dash for it, trying for an end
run around them. One of them lunged at him and tripped him,
and he fell on the sand. They jumped on him, but he managed to
kick and squirm away. As they clutched at him, trying to bring
him down again, he whirled and plunged into the ocean, his only

refuge, where he'd be stronger than all of them. The waves crashed over him and flung him up onshore. They came in to grab him as the surf receded; it sucked Jake back and drew him out to sea again. He dived through the combers until he got beyond them into the wind-capped chop of the sea. And stayed out there, watching the men onshore calling for him to come back in. Then they settled back in the sand and began to wait.

Jake's shoes and clothes got soggier and heavier. The water grew colder. The swells made him drift northward until he was facing the palisades. He had no idea how far he'd have to drift before he'd find a beach. He seemed to feel something nibble at him. It terrified him. He swam hard, his clothes making it hard to move, toward the beach and the breakwater. It exhausted him. Like patient animals, the men sat in the sand and waited. He rested awhile, then swam toward the breakwater. A wave came up and smashed him against the rocks. His breath was knocked out. He tried to grab a rock, hoist himself up. Another wave hurled him into the jagged breakwater. He thought his ribs were broken. He finally got a footing and started to climb up. There they were, waiting to grab him. He slipped on a mossy, barnacled rock. Cut and bleeding, he plunged back into the ocean. He was freezing now, his clothes like anchors. He fought hard to get away from the breakwater. The men came back down to the beach. They sat down, laughing and talking, and waited. He began to drift again. The sun was beginning to head seaward. The sky, so blue and vacant, turned pink, with his body growing numb and heavier. It would be dark soon. The terror of being lost at sea at night, of being crashed against the rocks, of being carried out on some crazy tide gripped him. He swam in, the waves like pile drivers coming down on him. He gulped. His eyes were almost blinded by the salt and the sun's glare. The men got up, came close to the shoreline. He was beached to his knees. He dug in his pocket and pulled out his last few dollars, crumpled them into a ball, and hurled it out at the men.

"Take it, you bastards!" he screamed. "Take it, you cock-suckers!"

The roar of the sea drowned his voice. One of the men rushed into the water and retrieved the money just as the pull of the sea began to suck it back.

"Keep it, you sonsabitches!"

He watched them run off the beach toward the town. He came out of the water, with seaweed in his shirt, sand in his shoes, and salt cutting his skin.

"You dirty crummy fucks!"

He was crying in the wind. He fell on the sand. The chill of his body consumed him. He shivered to his feet, began to lope up the hill. He didn't know how he did it, from time to time he had to stop because of the stitches in his side, but he made it to the White Dolphin. He rushed into the bathroom, ran the hot water in the tub, flung his clothes off, then got in and stayed there, drawing more hot water from time to time, until the warmth of his body came back. Afterward he dumped his salty clothes into the tub to clean them, then wrung them as dry as he could. He remembered the sun going down in a hot red sky and a turquoise faraway sea as he hung up his clothes to dry. Then he got under the covers, trembled some, and fell asleep.

He got up late next day. His clothes were still damp. He lay around the room naked until noon. Then he put on his damp clothes and left. When he got downstairs, the landlady was waiting for him. She was a hefty, broad-faced woman with braids like a tiara crowning her head.

"Mr. Davidson, you didn't pay me yesterday's rent."

"I was robbed."

"Mr. Davidson, I've heard all kinds of excuses, but—"

"Three men robbed me. I almost drowned."

"You mean you have no money at all."

"Not a penny. They got all of it."

"I'll call the police."

"Go on. Call 'em. The dollar means that much to you, call 'em. I don't care if I spend the rest of my life in jail. Call 'em."

He walked out.

There were no jobs at the union hall that day. He ate beef stew at the mission house; it was greasy gravy, a few peas and carrots, some strings of meat. After that he walked the docks trying to decide what to do. He had to get out. Fast. He'd stow away. That's what he'd do. But he knew nothing about a ship. Where do you hide? He wandered about, studying tankers and freighters, the covered lifeboats, masts, booms, ventilators, funnels, coiled ropes, the midship and afterhousings, the holds. Where do you hide? Then he got to the SS *Columbus,* a passenger liner leaving for Honolulu at 4 P.M. It was enormous, a city block long, as tall as a skyscraper, the decks crowded with passengers and friends. A big crowd, he could get lost there. Honolulu!

He couldn't pretend he was a passenger, not the way he looked. He could be a relative of somebody sailing. That was it.

He walked up the gangway. Two pursers with clipboards were at the head of it.

"Name?"

"Jake Davidson."

"Your boarding ticket?"

"I'm here to say good-bye to my uncle and aunt."

"Their names?"

Fuck it. He walked back down to the dock. Looked up. The happy people. The rich, lucky bastards. The ship's whistle blew.

"All ashore who's going ashore."

People started coming off. Passengers were leaning over the rails, waving good-bye. A dreamy Hawaiian song came over the loud speaker. The hawsers were flung away from the moorings. Ship's bells. Gradually the *Columbus* eased away from its berth. Honolulu bound. Jake had tears in his eyes.

Another plate of slop at the mission house, then over to the Seamen's Institute for coffee with lots of milk and cookies. He picked up a copy of Dos Passos's *42nd Parallel* and forgot about having lost paradise that afternoon. The book was a kick in the head, a sock in the stomach; it blasted his heart. When he had to leave, he hid the book in his sweater and walked out. They had no room for him at the mission when he got back there.

"Usually we're all filled up right after evening services," he was told.

"You mean I've got to pray with you first and then I get a bed?"

"You just have to get here earlier these days."

He slept on a park bench and froze. His clothes got damp from the night precipitation. About 3 A.M. a cop rapped his thighs with his nightstick.

"You can't sleep here."

"What do I do?" Jake asked.

"I told you you can't sleep here. I catch you here again, I'll pull you in for vagrancy."

"What does that mean?"

"Thirty days in jail."

He started to walk away. The cop caught up with him.

"You can't walk around all night either."

"What do I do?"

"Leave town."

Jake started to walk again.

"You're walking the wrong way," the cop said. "That way is out of town."

He walked down to the harbor. Looked back. The cop was still watching him. He knew he was out of sight when he got to the tuna boats. He wedged down between two piles of nets which were damp from the dew. He was too cold to fall asleep. He couldn't move about; the cops might spot him again. He sat up on the nets, rubbing his arms and legs. A drippy, chilling fog began to creep in, shrouding the boats and the humps of nets on the dock; lamppost and harbor lights looked bleary-eyed at him. Jake's teeth began to chatter. He thought he'd spiral out into space, he was so cold. Then he began to hear cars rumble up on the docks, voices, activity on the boats. The albacore fishermen were getting ready to go out. Jake jumped out from the nets, began to run in place.

"Hey, kid, whatcha doin'?"

"Getting warm," Jake said.

"I make coffee. You get warm."

The man sounded like the Slavs and Poles around Chicago. Other men sounded the same. They were mostly Yugoslavs who had fished with their fathers in the old country. Over coffee, Jake told them he was trying to ship out.

"Hard times. Three years ago any ship, you go there, they give you job."

"You need a hand on your boats?" Jake asked.

"Place only for sons, cousins."

He was born too late. Guys like Maugham, Conrad, Dos Passos had all the breaks, were at the right places at the right time. He told them about the cops.

"They don't do nothing for vagrancy. They go by law, millions people in jail. Who's got room?" They laughed. "You go home, boy. Maybe later you get ship. Better times, hah?"

Before dawn a half dozen fishing boats eased into the foggy channel, blasting their horns, disappeared into the mist. With daylight, Jake felt better. He went over to the union hall and learned that two boats were leaving that day: the *Coral Sea* for Honolulu, the *Eastern Light* for Papeete. They both had full crews. He decided to stow away on the *Coral Sea*.

The ship was loaded, hatches battened, and the decks were piled with lumber, wired firm to chocks and cleats. Nobody seemed to be around. He cased the vessel carefully, then hopped on at the after end, bent so low that he couldn't be seen from midships. Halfway down there was an opening between two loads of lumber. He squeezed in between, sure he was hidden from sight, and began to wait stiffly for the ship to leave. The smell of the redwood and pine made him heady. They make alcohol out of wood, he thought. The kind that could blind and kill you. He took short, shallow breaths. Will you get going already?

He shifted his weight from foot to foot. One of his legs fell asleep. He shook it to stop its tingling. In his mind, to pass the time, he tried to write of his experiences of the night before. His mind went numb. How long would it be before they got going? He prayed that nobody'd find him before the ship left. Then he heard the crew on board. The mate was checking the cargo. He heard bells ring, the engine begin to hum. He heard somebody say she was getting up steam. The skipper said hello to a man who came aboard who was referred to as the pilot. The thud of the tugboat shook the ship. Any minute now. They were about to shove off. His heart leaped. He was going to make it. Then after the ship was at sea, twelve miles out, beyond territorial waters, beyond his being put off on any tug, he'd step out and ask to see the skipper, and he'd say, "I'm a stowaway." What could the skipper do to him? Throw him overboard, put him in chains, starve him on bread and water? He'd never heard of such a thing.

So all right, already, let's get going. "All I want to do is get to Honolulu," he'd say. "Then you can put me off. You don't have to pay me for the work you make me do. Okay, captain?" What could the captain do, feed him to the sharks? No way. So let's get going. He heard the crew walk on deck. More bells. The ship was so solid with its load Jake thought he was on land. Maybe he made a mistake. Maybe he *was* on land. He peeked out. No, he was sure he'd jumped onto the vessel; he was sure he was on board; he could hear the engines, could feel their throb. The ship's whistle shocked him, vibrated right through him. Now. Now she's ready. Let's go. Will you get going, please? Come on, before I become a mummy. Before the smell of the redwood and pine makes me pass out, let's go. Suddenly he became conscious of a presence, of breathing. He shut his eyes tight. If you don't see it, it won't see you. Go away, whoever, whatever, it is. Go.

"All right, kid."

Two seamen in front of him.

"Don't say anything. Please."

"The old man knows you're on. He wants you off."

He couldn't move out. As if he were stuck to the gummy sap of the wood. As if it had a tight hold of him and wouldn't let go.

"Come on, kid. We're not fooling around."

"I can't move."

One of the men grabbed him. Jake was so stiff he fell into him.

"Cut it out," the seaman said.

"I can't move."

They carried him off the ship and dumped him on the dock. Gradually his stiffness left; he got to his feet. He saw the hawsers running up the chocks. Then the ship eased away from the dock and was tugged out into the channel. You bastards. Hours you let me stand stiff as the boards. You glued me to the goddamn ship. The last minute you kick me off. I wish you luck. I wish you reach a million ports and you're found dead in all of them. I'll get a better ship, you'll see.

By the time he got to the *Eastern Light,* bound for Papeete, it was gone. He got to the mission house early, sang and prayed with the other homeless seamen and bums for his supper and bed. Slept that night on an iron cot in a bullpen with twenty-five others, not feeling good about the praying, the religious singing, feeling he had betrayed himself, his family, friends, his ancestors all the way back to Abraham. The slop he had eaten kept backfiring on him. The sour odor of the men, the sickening smell of disinfectant, the raucous and sullen farts, and the snoring about him kept him from falling asleep. He tossed from side to side. He tried to bury his head under the covers, but the disinfectant choked him. He finally fell into a deep sleep. He got up to a gray morning.

He tried the *Mitsui Maru,* bound for Manila. The Japanese were more merciful. Two minutes after he got on he was kicked off after they found him climbing the davits to get into a lifeboat. He was stopped at the gates of the Richfield Oil Company. Without a pass he couldn't get near its docks. Esso was forbidden. On a tanker, with its open decks, it was too hard to find a place to hide anyhow. He lasted two hours on the *Southern Star,* which was going to Auckland. By the end of the second week, broke, scroungy, five pounds lighter, hungry, he felt as if he'd been in a two-week marathon and the finish line were a million miles away.

He gave up.

BOOK 4

He had hitched a ride from Los Angeles to Fort Worth with an old Texan who had gone to visit his daughter only to learn that she had separated from her husband and had become a $2 whore. Out of Fort Worth he got a ride with a Hollywood fan magazine writer, who tried to bugger him when he invited him to stay in his room at night, but Jake put him off and slept in his car instead. In Tulsa he flagged down a guy who'd picked up three deadbeats, hoping they had money to buy gasoline; when Jake turned up with empty pockets, they siphoned gas from parked cars, enough to get to St. Louis. The last ride Jake hitched was an express from St. Louis. Seventy miles an hour with a salesman who was a nervous chain smoker with a heart-stopping way of careering around curves on two wheels and passing while oncoming cars flew at them full tilt. He was dropped off alive at 22nd and Crawford.

Home.

There at the newsstand was his father in a sweater and cap, face weather-beaten, the money changer strapped around his waist, selling papers and talking to horseplayers.

"Pa."

Surprise. His father looked at him as if he'd never expected to
see him again.

"Jake. You're home."

His father embraced him.

"Oh, Pa."

"You look fine. A little skinny but fine."

"How is every little thing?"

"Good, good. Go home. Mama will be so happy to see you."

He started to walk home.

"Where you going?"

"Home."

"Here. Be a sport. Take the streetcar." He gave Jake a dollar.

"Thanks."

His mother shrieked with joy. Bubi patted his cheeks with
tears in her eyes. Miriam was glad to see him, too; she pecked his
cheek. Only little Harry was brusque.

"What'd they do, Jake? Kick you in the teeth out there?"

Harry was picking up the language of the streets.

"Go," his mother said. "Take a shower. You stink. I'll give
you a meal tonight fit for a prince."

At supper, over brisket and *tsimmes,* she said, "You're skinny
as a needle. Didn't anybody feed you? Didn't you have any
money for food? How could the world let you look like that?"

You'd think he was down to the bare bone.

"Out there nobody looks after you," she continued. "Out
there it's cruel. Out there, with all the trouble, nobody cares
about anybody but their own greedy skins. Oh, Jake, it's so good
to see you."

"So, Jake," said his father, the practical man, "what are your
plans?"

"I don't know."

"Go back to school."

"I'll think about it."

Miriam brought a large fat envelope to him. "I didn't want to
show you this till you settled down."

College Humor had returned his manuscript with a form
rejection slip. Something dropped in Jake.

"They had a lot of contestants," Miriam said.

"Their loss."

"There are lots of publishers."

"Yep."

"It's your first one," his father said. "Did you win the first race you ever swam in?"

"Yah, Pa. Eighth grade in grammar school. I won the twenty-yard dash for kids under eighty-five pounds."

"The body matures fast, but for the mind and heart it takes time. Writers grow with the years. Look at Tolstoy. He was an elderly man when he wrote *Anna Karenina*."

"Look at Somerset Maugham. He had his first novel published when he was twenty-three."

"You're not even twenty yet."

"I'll read my book over again. I'll see how I feel about it."

"You had so many phone calls," his mother said. "Albie Karlin, Milton B. Morgenstern, your coach from Northwestern, Mr. Swanson. What happened? they wanted to know. Why did you run away? How can they get in touch with you? I was so embarrassed. I said you were in California. For all I knew you might have been in China or Japan. Will you call them?"

"Sure, Ma."

"So," she said, "what happened out there?"

Somehow he couldn't tell them.

"It wasn't a picnic, hah?" she said.

He had come home, but he felt, somehow, that he should be somewhere else. He was still restless, incomplete, unfinished. When would this rootless feeling leave him?

"But tell us, how was it out there?" his mother insisted.

You don't come from faraway places and sit about the round kitchen table without some word of what they were like.

"It was very beautiful, Ma. The desert, the mountains, the beaches, the ocean."

"More beautiful than Lake Michigan?"

"Different."

"But you were in Hollywood. Did you see any movie stars?"

He couldn't disappoint her.

"Greta Garbo," he lied.

"No!"

"Yes."

"*Oy*, yonkel."

"Nazimova, too." Why not lay it on?

"*Oy, oy.*" She clutched her hands.

"John Gilbert." Her romantic idol.

"*Oy,* Jake."

For his father he had Charlie Chaplin.

His mother went to the phone and called everybody. Her Jake was home. Greta Garbo he had seen, in person. Nazimova. John Gilbert. *Oy.*

Later Miriam said, "Did you really see them?"

"Why not?"

That fall a momentous event took place in Chicago. Two Goliaths of the world met under extraordinary circumstances. Colonel Robert R. McCormick, the bull-headed, oligarchical publisher of the *Tribune,* was having labor trouble with his chauffeurs and drivers. He called Max Annenberg, his circulation manager, up to his eagle's nest in his Gothic tower and said, "They're not going to get what they want, and they're not going to strike on me. I want you to do everything necessary to beat them."

"I'll get Capone."

"Is that the only way?"

"He's the only man who can handle the situation."

"All right, talk to him."

"You may have to meet with him."

"Never. It's a matter of pride."

Annenberg, a Bismarck in the circulation wars of Chicago, who had worked with Capone before, called him that morning at the Hawthorne Inn in Cicero, then at his Chicago headquarters in the Metropole Hotel on 2300 South Michigan Avenue, which he had opened after he put Mayor William Hale Thompson in office. Capone was in the middle of listening to Enrico Caruso singing "Vesti la giubba" from *Pagliacci* when the call came. He didn't like being interrupted.

"What does the man want?" he asked.

"The man says it's important," said Machine Gun Jack McGurn, one of Capone's top *capos.* "A matter with the *Tribune.*"

"Those fuckin' muzzlers are always giving me a hard time."

All this while Caruso was singing his heart out on Capone's new orthophonic Victrola with the big sound.

"The man says they need you."

Capone picked up the phone, listened to what the matter was about, then said, "I can take care of that little thing for you."

"Great," said Annenberg. "When can we meet?"

"But I don't want to meet with you. I want to meet with the Colonel."

"He's a busy man."

"I'm a busier man."

"I'll see what I can do."

Later that morning Capone had an appointment with Mayor Big Bill Thompson, whom he had put in office with money for his campaign, buying votes at $3 a head, stuffing ballot boxes, and having flying squads of the thousand soldiers on his payroll at the polls intimidating the voters to vote for Thompson. At the top of McCormick's drop-dead list were Al Capone and Big Bill Thompson.

At City Hall that morning, with the brass spittoons everywhere, Capone wanted some ordinances changed so that he could increase his booze and slot machine operations in the city; then he told Thompson he knew that the old cowboy had to put up a front of fighting crime, but he didn't want him to be so noisy and sincere about it, and he didn't want him ever to use his name again.

He thrust his face forward, giving Thompson the full Mussolini pugnacity, and said, "Give the kids free tickets to Riverview. That's a good racket. I'll pop for them. Talk about your old water polo and football-playing days. But lay off the crime angle. Okay?"

"Okay."

Then Capone said, "Who do you think wants to waltz around with me?"

"Who?"

"Colonel McCormick."

"That bastard. I'm going to sue him. Me and the city."

Thompson had been brought up in the rough-and-tumble world of Chicago politics under the tutelage of Hinky Dink Kenna and Bathhouse John Coughlin, monarchs of the lurid First and Second Wards, the Levee district, where the streets were as wide open as the wild, wild West. They ran the whorehouses, the gambling, the burglar rings, the politics of the town. Even the Everleigh Sisters, who operated the most elegant, most exclusive, brothel in the country, had to kick in. They groomed Big Jim Colosimo, former railroad water boy, to run the cribs, then the beer, then the gambling. When Big Jim got too busy with his fine restaurant at Wabash and 22nd Street and his love for the opera, he let his nephew Johnny Torrio move in. Torrio imported Capone from Brooklyn to help him take the town over. Soon afterward they arranged to have Big Jim killed, and they inherited Big Bill Thompson, who was in office then. But the big double-chinned, heavy-bellied mayor was beginning to believe, in his third term, that he was good for the city, so he slipped occasionally and knocked the criminal element of the town, which always pointed to Capone. And he, considering himself a public benefactor, was sensitive to being called a gangster, a criminal. He had a villa in Florida, a family, millions of dollars, thousands of people depending on him for a living, he gave to charity; what else did he need to prove that he was a respectable man? Which is why he wanted to meet with the Colonel in person. That was aristrocracy from way back. The Colonel was a man connected to the McCormicks of the farm machinery empire, to the Medills and the Pattersons of the newspaper empires in the East. A meet with the Colonel would put the stamp of respectability on Capone. At least he could tell him where to head in.

Capone hit a bull's-eye in the spittoon with his cigar and his parting word was: "Go ahead and sue the big bird Colonel. 'Be a Booster! Don't be a Knocker!' like you used to say. And lay off me."

When Capone got back to the Metropole, where he and his entourage occupied fifty rooms, Annenberg had already called. Capone sat down at his big table in his office, which was set up like conference rooms he had seen in movies and at City Hall, and he glanced up at blowups of three great Americans, in his estimation: George Washington, Abraham Lincoln, and William Hale Thompson. Then he said, "Get me that Jewboy."

When he was reached, Annenberg said, "You sure you have to meet with the Colonel?"

"No meet, no favor."

"Okay. Two o'clock. The *Tribune* Tower. Come alone."

Capone never traveled alone. He walked past his sentinels in the corridors, followed by his elite eighteen-man private guard.

He got into his bulletproof car; even the doors had special combination locks so that they couldn't be jimmied in case anyone wanted to plant a bomb. In front of him rode his reconnaissance car. Following close behind were two touring cars, packed with men and machine guns. Heaven help anyone who tried to get between the scout car and the rear guard. When his car passed the Michigan Avenue bridge and pulled up in front of the *Tribune* building, his men ran out onto the sidewalk and formed a cordon. Nobody could move past until the Big Fella was safely inside the skyscraper. From there on McCormick's own private army of police took over.

"It's okay, men. I'll be safe here."

Reluctantly, his men let four private cops lead Capone into the tower elevator.

Annenberg met Capone on the tower floor, shook his hand with the greatest dignity. A nod, and a uniformed guard frisked Capone crisply and efficiently, shredding his dignity with each pat.

"What the hell is this?" Capone said. "You know I wouldn't pack any heat."

"Sorry," Annenberg said, then led him past several secretaries and uniformed guards to a panel without a knob or hinges. A buzzer went off. Another buzzer clicked the panel open. Capone hesitated. Annenberg nodded for him to enter.

"Alone?" Capone said.

"That's the way the Colonel wants it."

Capone, the emperor, who ruled by the gun and the bludgeon, who inspired terror wherever he went, who wanted to meet his arch enemy face to face, was rooted to the floor.

"It's all yours," Annenberg said.

"He alone?"

"Of course."

"No funny shit now. My boys'll blast this joint wide open if I'm not down in fifteen minutes."

"You're safe here."

Capone squared his beefy, bouncerlike shoulders, stuck his chin out, and walked in. As soon as he entered the Gothic tower from which thunderbolts were rumored to be hurled, the panel behind him closed. He looked about frantically. There wasn't a door or hinge in the room. He stepped back to where he thought he'd come in. No door. Nothing. He was locked in. Claustrophobia gripped him. In terror, he faced the tall, bristly-mustached, austere-looking aristocrat in English clothes, who sat in his thronelike chair like a horseman.

"Who do you think you're fuckin' around with?" he said.

McCormick measured him quizzically. It was rumored that he had axes at hand in case he was attacked; that with a buzz, doors would spring open and fierce Dobermans trained to go for the jugulars would leap out; that this tower was a last redoubt should the Colonel's world topple. But all he had, as he sat behind a large polished slab of stone, which was his desk, was a German shepherd lying in a corner and a lazy English pit bulldog at his feet. Behind him were souvenirs from World War I, documents from his secret-agent days, pictures of his hunting, polo-playing, man-about-the-world period. There was also a portrait of Lincoln holding the Emancipation Proclamation and a large picture of the Baha'i Temple, a great white-domed glassy nine-sided building on the North Shore of Chicago.

Then the gloomy man spoke in his sepulchral room: "I see you're taken with the Baha'i Temple. It's superior to the Taj Mahal, don't you think?"

"I don't know. I never saw either of them. But I see you're a fan of Abe Lincoln's."

"A great man. He believed in America first."

"I'm a fan, too."

Now, with the small talk over, McCormick got down to business. "You know I despise everything you stand for, Mr. Capone."

"You know you don't keep it exactly a secret. But let me tell you something. You hate whores, too, but when you need them, you call on them. And where do you think you get the scotch you drink?"

"Not from you."

"From somebody like me. Listen, if people didn't want booze, a fella would be crazy trying to sell it. Nobody points a gun at a man to gamble. People want booze, gambling, and women. Like a public utility, I supply them. Why don't you print that? If you want, I'll get Ernest Hemingway to write an editorial for you. How about that?"

"Sit down, Mr. Capone."

"No."

"I've got problems."

"I know what your problems are. They're not exactly diarrhea or a little case of the clap."

"Can you handle them?"

"There's a cure for your problems. But I need a little curing, too. You've got to lay off me."

"You know, you're famous, like Babe Ruth. We can't help printing things about you."

Capone leaned in close. "You want a strike? You want your paper crippled? You want this tower to fall into the river? Then you keep putting me in the headlines."

"I'll see what I can do."

"That's a deal. You see what you can do, and I'll see what I can do."

That was the end of the meeting of the two big monarchs of Chicago. All week not a word was printed about Capone. The following week the strike threat was called off. McCormick always wondered if Capone had rigged the whole thing just to humble him.

On a lesser scale, but just as momentous in Jake's world, Sean H. Fitzgerald was appointed to the physical education department of Lane Tech in charge of swimming. He also married one of the older swimmers from the JPI, a petite Jewish girl with curly, bobbed hair and a flashy smile. All the guys had been afraid he'd break her in two with his gladiatorlike body and colossal equipment. It was like matching a great Dane with a toy poodle. But her smile was flashier than ever; she positively glowed. "Looks like she likes his tools," the guys said.

Moish Bender, the 1928 Olympic water polo man, who had married the year before and now had a baby girl, took over. "A graveyard," he said. "With nothing left for me but athlete's foot. What a destiny."

That weekend at the JPI, with Solly Landon and Benny Gordon around, Moish growled, "Well, *shmuck.*"

"Well," Jake said.

"So who'd you fuck in Hollywood?"

Jake shrugged: noncommittal.

"Clara Bow? Jean Harlow?" Benny asked.

"What do you think?" Jake said.

"You're a bullshitter," said Moish.

"So why do you ask?"

Everybody who had ever gone to Hollywood had screwed them, they said. They did it for their religion, their people, their God, their country. Why should Jake be unpatriotic?

"Why should Jake be an exception?" Solly said. "Ezra Malinovitz, the rabbi's son, when he was at Northwestern and went out there to swim against USC, he went to parties left and right, and he got the clap from Clara Bow. And what about Albie Karlin when he went to the intercollegiates at UCLA? Didn't he slip it to Jean Harlow, before she became a big star?"

"What about it, Jake?" Benny asked. "Did you get the clap?"

"Nope. I got the herpes progenitalis."

Moish punched Jake's arm. "You bastard."

"Did you or didn't you?" Benny asked. He wanted to believe that Jake had laid the stars.

"Geronimo!" which was the West Side war cry of victory.

"Go to Hollywood," Solly said. "Sleep with the stars."

"Well, why not?" Moish said. "When I was in Paris after the 1928 Olympics, didn't I boff Josephine Baker, the star of the *Folies?*" He looked out dreamily over the pool, beyond the wet walls, the constant din. He even believed it himself.

Albie Karlin came in for a workout. He was gunning for the 1932 Olympics. Being an Olympic man wouldn't hurt him in his law and political career.

"Jake, you bastard. What the hell did you run off like that for? Why didn't you tell anybody? You better call Swanee and Milton B. Jesus, what a thing to do."

"Hey, Albie," Benny said. "Shake hands with your brother-in-law, Jake. He socked it into Jean Harlow."

"Why not?" Albie said. He couldn't call Jake a liar. "She's there, and he was there. Possible, isn't it?" He changed the subject. "Did you see Weissmuller?"

"No," Jake said. "Wally Blake said he's gone Hollywood."

"Not Johnny," Moish said. "He's too rattlebrained to go Hollywood. With all that pussy there, who'd have time to fool around with palookas like Wally Blake?"

"Clear a lane for me, Moish," Albie said. "I've got to get back to the lawbooks."

Albie swam ten 20- and 40-yard sprints with one- and two-minute rests. Then a fast-paced quarter mile. He was in great shape.

"He's going to take the Olympics next year," Moish said. "I'll see to that."

"With Morrie Benjamin goosing him, he'll have to," said Solly. "I'll bet he took Albie out to dinner and said, 'Albie, you don't win the Olympics for me, for the Twenty-fourth Ward, and the *Rushishe shul,* no judgeship."

"He's got everything going for him, the lucky bastard," Benny said.

"What about you, Jake?" Moish said. "You going to take the Olympics, too?"

"I don't know," Jake said. A year ago he'd have said, "You goddamn right." Now he didn't know; he didn't know about anything.

"Get in there, you bastard," Moish said. "Start working out."

"Didn't we treat you right?" Milton B. asked.

"Sure you did," Jake said.

They were having lunch at Meurice's, which was even shabbier and less crowded than before. Who could afford Continental lunches anymore?

"But the past is past. We've got to think of the future. There's still time next semester for the conference and national championships. And this is the Olympic year. You're going to represent us on the American team."

"What if I don't go back to school?"

Milton B. was aghast. "I don't believe it."

"I've got big decisions to make. I'm a writer now."

"Oh, Jesus."

"You don't believe it? How do you like this for a line about subsidized athletes? 'Lots of benevolence and very little bread.'"

"You're not going to pull that crap on us."

"Worthy of a George Bernard Shaw."

"Quit kidding around, Jake."

"I'm serious."

"What kind of a writer?"

"A novelist."

"Can you get a job as a novelist? What are your qualifications?"

"You reduce everything to the weekly paycheck, huh?"

"I reduce everything to: How do you make a living, *boychik?*"

He was right. A novelist can't even start as a trainee, except on his own time, at his own expense. You can train a guy to work a drill, to punch out buttons, to measure a piece of cloth, but how do you train the heart to respond, the eye to see, the senses to be engaged, the brain to conceive? How do you go into training to look at the world with a special, unique, original sensibility? Who's going to pay you to train to be an oddball?

"What do I do, Jake? Do I get an apartment for you again? Fix you up for your meals? Tell Swanee to give you a couple of more hours at the pool? To quote you, if you don't go back to school, you'll get *no* benevolence *or* bread out there."

"Milton, you've got yourself a student and an athlete again."

Milton gave him that go-you-Northwestern smile and handshake. "You won't regret it. Start getting in shape."

So instead of being on a ship bound for all the exotic ports of the world, instead of living it up in Hong Kong and Singapore and Madagascar and Rio, he went back to school. Same apartment, cruddier Salvation Army furniture, same job at the North Shore Hotel for his meals, a few more hours at the pool with no cut in pay. So what was missing?

It would have helped if he could have qualified for the special comprehensive English survey course, for which only a few brilliant, selected students were chosen; that might have been a good training ground for his future. Instead, by default, he went into the School of Journalism. If he were in the middle of a big love affair, maybe that would have filled up all the empty spaces within him, but nobody around took his heart. Swimming had been so easy; everything had come together so fast for him. But writing—when does it all gel? Yet swimming was still there for him. Every afternoon, working out and playing water polo with the team, he lost himself in the pool; it engaged him completely.

But a strange thing began to happen. He found that he had stopped trying to go beyond himself, that he wasn't nervous before the dual meets, that his adrenaline wasn't pumping him into a frenzy, that his time was off. It began to worry him. He was losing the two ingredients that had driven him to the top: the trust in his body and his intense concentration. Without them he had nothing. What was happening? Was his mind turning his body to pulp?

Everybody tried to cheer him up. "You'll be in there. When it counts, you'll be in there."

But the drive was missing. He knew it. Deep down in his gut he knew it. Burned out at twenty, when I should be at my peak? Burned out the Olympic year?

He stopped reading as much as he did. Read only for his classes. Relaxed in movie houses, away from Dostoyevsky, Flaubert, Maupassant, Zola, Freud, Sherwood Anderson, who were enough to sink a whale. Worked out at the JPI with Albie Karlin, who was getting stronger every day he was getting older, a cinch to take the 100 meters.

"How are your bowel movements lately?" Moish Bender asked.

"Why?"

"You swim like you've got sludge in your belly."

"I can't figure it out."

"You're getting heavy in the head, that's the trouble."

"I stopped reading."

"Stop thinking for a change."

"Is it possible a guy gets burned out in the head?"

"What every athlete should do before he starts training is go to a good surgeon and get his brains cut out. Then he's got no problems, nothing to interfere with his body."

"Give me more cheerful earfuls, Moish."

"Shut up and swim a good fast quarter mile."

He went to see Sean H. Fitzgerald, the coach who had made him.

"Drive, drive, drive, Jake. This is your year."

"I don't seem to have that extra ounce."

"Lay off a few days. Tell Swanee you're not feeling well. Lay off until that monkey on your back forces you to go back in, until you feel you have to break through walls to get back into the pool. Then you'll be right there."

He laid off. The monkey never pounced onto his back. He didn't get the drive to break walls down.

"Feel better?" Swanee asked when Jake got back to training.

"Yah."

"Let's go."

A has-been at twenty?

He won against Wisconsin, Purdue, Indiana, Iowa. Lost to Murdoch of Michigan, a sophomore. Lost by a half body length. That last 50 yards, instead of driving ahead, pushing himself beyond his limits, he dropped back. He finished more exhausted than if he'd won. Henry had really to work over him to take the kinks out of his muscles, to get him ready for the medley relay, which he also lost to Murdoch on his 100-yard lap. That trip hadn't done him any good, Jake heard somebody say.

Swanee, cheerful, always confident, said, "One-forty-three. You've done better. You'll take him in the conference."

He'd have to win the conference to qualify for the final Olympic trials or get at least second in the nationals. Swanee worked him harder. He broke 1:43 against Minnesota. Got down to 1:42 against Ohio State.

He was studying philosophy, abnormal psychology, modern life and letters, contemporary thought, newspaper reporting and writing, copyreading and headline writing, cramming it all in as if he were racing against a stopwatch. He went over his peak, got a slight cold. He was terrified his sinus condition would come back. Waited for it to split his head apart, to destroy him completely. Heady, sluggish, afraid the fates were working against him, he worked the cold out.

He was in top form when the conference championships came up at the beginning of spring. But somehow he wasn't dreaming about the meet at night and thinking about it during the day. He wasn't getting the quivers, the sudden shakes; he wasn't all wrapped up in the event. He left for Ohio State with the team at night and slept through the night whistles and the clattering of the train without dreaming once about the meet. He went through the day without yawning too much, without watery eyes, without having to urinate countless times. Was this the real Jake Davidson? Was this the same Jake Davidson who used to work himself into a nervous frenzy before his event? He looked at himself in a full-length mirror. An impostor, a phony. Whatever had happened to the real Jake Davidson?

He won his heat in 1:44.6, qualifying for the finals. Murdoch of Michigan, tall, loose, broad-shouldered, glazy-eyed, came in with a 1:45, but he wasn't pressed.

"Murdoch's not there," the guys on the team said. "You're a shoo-in. In the finals, you'll break his heart."

That night something like the real Jake Davidson came to life. He began to think about the event. I don't win this, I can kiss the Olympics good-bye. O'Connor of Rutgers had come in that year with a time of 1:40. A new guy, Borovich of Stanford, had hit 1:39. How would he ever get down to that in the next few weeks at the nationals? I've got to take Murdoch. That'll get me into the Olympic trials. In June, at 100 meters, it'll be a different story. I'll have a chance. I can be one of the four to go. His nerves began to shoot through him. He tossed about in bed. Felt his body grow feverish. I'll go all-out, right from the start. I'll never let up. I'll do the last 50 as fast at my first. Faster. My heart will pump me through. I won't let up. Not a second. His teeth began to hurt from his grinding them. Oh, Christ, I'm really worked up. Oh, let me sleep. Please, just a little sleep. Take me off, way, way off, only a little sleep.

Finally, he made it. Instead of dreaming, as before, of drowning, of never finishing the race, of swimming through mud, he dreamed that he was in bed with the redhead at the College Inn, and he was blown to the biggest wet dream of his life. He thought he was going to drown in it. Oh, Jesus, there it goes, the last ounce of my life. He was totally exhausted when he woke up.

All that day he drooped about, his legs lifeless. He had four eggs for breakfast. He had heard that oysters, too, brought back the jism. He ordered a dozen for lunch. After the first one he rushed off to the toilet to vomit. He slept restlessly that afternoon. Felt even droopier afterward. How the hell was he ever going to win this one? His gut felt like a washing machine, sloshing away.

He had a small steak and a baked potato at four-thirty. The steak made him feel alive again. He left the table hungry. Went to his room to keep his lonely vigil with all his nerves and all the gods he could call up to help him. He paced about the room for a while, then lay down and started to read The Great Gatsby. It was hard to get into it; then suddenly he was right in there, with all those people, moving about in their lives; then bang, he was shot out of there by the ringing of the phone: it was time to go. A nerve exploded in his heart.

The real Jake Davidson, quivering all over, got ready to go.

But the real Jake Davidson didn't swim that race. In the end he couldn't get up that extra tenth of a second to win. He was touched out: 1:42.1. A tenth of a second off the time that had won him the nationals the year before, a touch off winning a shot at the final Olympic trials. Two whole seconds off the time the real Jake Davidson should be doing. Whatever had happened to him? Was that extra umph squeezed out by his romantic binge to the West Coast? By *Crime and Punishment, The Interpretation of Dreams, Pygmalion, Madame Bovary,* Immanuel Kant, *The Great Gatsby?* Could he unload all that from his mind before the nationals? Could he get back into the real skin of Jake Davidson?

Hey, up there! Turn the clock back. The Olympics are coming up. I've put twenty years into it. Give me a shot at it, will you? Will you?

The team was happy. They'd won the conference championship. Jake had done his part, had certainly earned his keep. But on the way home, his eyes misty, his heart heavy, he thought: I've got to go through the whole godamn thing again. At the nationals I'll need three seconds. Where'll I get them? Hey, Jake Davidson, come on back, will you? Just for a few weeks. Huh?

There were moments during practice, while walking around campus in his purple N sweater, while studying, when he felt spurts of his old self, when his concentration on his sport was absolute. He was going to qualify for the Olympics and win, become champion of the world. But in the final showdown at Yale, Jake, the defending intercollegiate backstroke champion from the year before, came in third. Borovich of Stanford took the event in the fast time of 1:38.4. O'Connor was a close second. Jake broke 1:40, by far his fastest time. For a moment he thought he'd won. It was touch, touch, touch, all of them finishing within a second of each other. He felt as if his guts had been pulled out when he learned that he'd lost.

That night, alone in his room, he wept a little. Some part of him had died, and he mourned over it. On the way home, looking out over an Appalachian spring, the new green leaves in old trees, the tilling of the black soil in Ohio and Indiana, he seemed to be speeding past an era of his life and heading for a fresh one. His heart began to grow lighter. He would now stop dreaming of being an Olympic champion, and he would now start concentrating on the work that would take him through the rest of his life. Okay, baby, I'm going to knock you off now. There he went, thinking like an athlete again, taking on the whole world of literature. Easy, man. Don't be so pugnacious. There are giants out there.

A nervous spasm, just as if he were about to enter a meet, went through him. Oh, man, guts and adrenaline and training till it hurts, is that what I'm going to need for my new career? Or will I just need the hide of a walrus and a head of granite for the battering I may take?

A whole new quiver of arrows found a new target in the pit of his stomach.

That summer, Fasso Sardell, whose real name was Chaim Sardowsky, came home from the University of Illinois, where he was studying art, and worked with Jake at McKinley Park as a lifeguard. The park was on 39th Street, right in front of the stockyards, where you could choke from the smell of slaughtered animals. The pool was so big that a rowboat was needed to help guard the swimmers. Fasso used to be a jolly kid around the JPI, rolling his belly, bursting into song from time to time with his nice tenor voice, and laughing over every little thing with his wide mouth and nigger lips. Now he was more serious.

"What's happening, Fasso? Everybody's getting so goddamn serious."

"The world's going to the dogs, that's what's happening."

"We used to be so punchy, have such good times. Where are the laughs?"

"Ask the Okies who are being tractored off their land. Ask the workers in the breadlines, twelve million of them out of work now. Ask the poor *shmucks* who were wiped out when the banks closed. You want laughs, there are a hundred million of them out there."

Jake knew where Fasso was getting all this propaganda. His brother, Boris Sardowsky, the artist, had come back to Chicago from Mexico where he'd been friends with Rivera, Orozco, and Siqueiros. He'd come home a communist to work for the revolution in America. He was known as a *farbrenter,* a fiery one, a passionate one. Half the guys at the JPI had posed for him at his art classes when they were kids. Now he lived at the Hull House, which was in a far worse slum than when Jane Addams founded it. For his room and the use of the studio, he taught a couple of art classes. Among other people who there lived was Walter S. Pemberton, professor of English at the University of Chicago and contributing editor of the *New Republic,* a man with a kind heart and a distinguished reputation. He conducted a writing class on Wednesday nights at Hull House.

At the time, *Scribner's Magazine* had announced a $10,000 prize novelette contest. So that summer Jake edited and rewrote the novel he had submitted to the *College Humor* contest. It seemed that he was always competing for first place. He also started to play the role of the writer. He bought a Harris tweed jacket and a couple of cheap pipes and tobacco. He endured racking coughing spells while he learned to smoke. If he didn't really look like a writer, at least he looked collegiate.

"So you want to be a writer?" Fasso said.

"Yah. Why shouldn't I be?"

You'd think they were about to square off for a fight, they sounded that belligerent. Jake was in the rowboat, Fasso on the concrete walk, with a thousand people splashing about.

"You want to write, you've got to have something to say," Fasso said. "What have you got to say?"

That was one of Jake's big problems. He wasn't passionate about anything. He had no cause. He didn't know yet what he wanted to say about the world.

"You going to write about that old bourgeois horseshit?" Fasso said. "Romance, Horatio Alger, everybody can become President, all that capitalistic *dreck?*"

"What are you painting about?"

"I'm painting the working class."

"They're not the only people alive, you know."

"I'll paint the other people from the point of view of the working class."

"Got an answer for everything, huh?"

"Dialectical materialism."

"What the hell is that?"

"The theory of the working class."

"You're sure it's not diarrhetical materialism?"

"Laugh, Jake. Go ahead, laugh."

"You used to be a lot of fun, Fasso."

"I'm still fun. Only I'm more concerned now."

"Okay, Florence Nightingale. There's a kid drowning. Save him."

Fasso jumped into the water and dragged a kid to safety. Jake laughed, giving him mock applause, then a big raspberry.

Afterward Fasso said, "Jake, how about coming to Pemberton's class? Maybe he can help you."

It was a hot night the first time Jake went with Fasso to Hull House. It was ninety-two, as if the broiling sun were still out. The people of the whole Near West Side seemed to be outside, promenading about, standing under lamppost lights, sitting on wooden crates and stoops, leaning against hot brick buildings and fanning themselves; it was suffocating. The Greek and Italian coffeehouses set tables and chairs out on the baked sidewalks, and the cardplayers sipped muddy coffee and played their games. Kids never minded the heat; they played and yelled as if there were icebergs on the streets. The brew of garbage and garlic steamed out of the run-down buildings.

"Descartes was right," Jake said. "I stink, therefore I am."

They walked through the stuffy, dusty halls of Hull House.

"Through these portals," said Jake, "walk the hungry, the poor, the oppressed, the deprived, the great impoverished proletariat. What have they got to lose? Their chains?"

"That's not funny," Fasso said.

"Workers of the world, unite. After the revolution, air conditioning for everybody."

Jake was talking out of nervousness. He had part of his manuscript with him. He was going to read it aloud. There were going to be faces, reactions. People would listen . . . or wouldn't listen. They'd like what he read . . . or be indifferent . . . or wouldn't like it. It wasn't going to be like sending a manuscript to an editor, his reading it alone, then sending it back without comment, with a printed rejection slip. This was live, your voice, your words, your gut wide open.

"Who wants strawberries and cream?" Jake's voice cracked. He cleared his throat. "A seventy-degree world, that's what we want."

"Take it easy, will you, Jake?"

Fasso opened the door to Professor Pemberton's apartment. Hot, stale air. Shabby gentility in the dusty old couches and chairs and tables. Books all over the place, a moldy, library smell. A half dozen people were already there, including Fasso's brother, Boris, a short man with a potbelly, a pudgy face, almost bald, and a benign look. A Mexican woman was reading a sketch about a Mexican woman at a milk station who didn't have three cents for a paper cup of milk and crackers for her little girl. Professor Pemberton nodded, emphasizing the woman's punctuation as she read. He was a tall, slender man seated in a frayed easy chair. His sparse hair was white, his face pale, a sweet hello in his large blue eyes. Sweat poured out of everybody's face.

When the woman finished, there was a moment's silence; then Boris said, "That's beautiful. That's real proletarian writing. I would send it to the *New Masses.*"

Professor Pemberton filled his pipe and nodded. Jake filled his pipe and nodded, too. He felt like Watson to the Sherlock Holmes of this group.

The Mexican woman said, "I sent it to the *New Masses.* It was rejected."

"Impossible," Boris said.

She showed Boris the rejection slip.

"It's too good for them," somebody said. "The *New Republic* should publish it."

Everybody focused on Professor Pemberton.

"I'm not the editor," he said. "But I will send it to them."

The woman was overwhelmed. "You liked it, professor. You liked it."

"It has merit." There wasn't an unkind bone in Professor Pemberton's body. "It's worthy of consideration."

Boris read the beginning of a pamphlet he was writing: *The Artist's Struggle.* It was crude, badly written, with lots of slogans and exclamation points. Everybody was very kind.

"You tell them, Boris," somebody said.

"Yes," Fasso said. "The artist must side with the working class or he won't survive. It's the working class who will butter his bread."

Another woman, who was wearing a gold cross, said timidly,

"What about the de' Medicis, Renaissance art, the church?"

"That was a great period," Professor Pemberton said.

"History," Boris said. "We are talking about today. Even Picasso is a communist."

"You have a point there," Professor Pemberton said.

Jake was asked if he had something. Suddenly he didn't want to read what he'd brought. His sweat turned cold and clammy; his skin grew prickly. His throat clogged up, and he went into a coughing fit.

"Would you want me to read it?" Professor Pemberton asked.

Jake nodded. Perhaps if the piece he brought was read by Professor Pemberton, it wouldn't be attacked; it would be treated with respect.

His story was still about a subsidized basketball player who was out to make a lot of money so that he could win the rich girl he had fallen in love with. The theme was still money doesn't stink, no matter how you make it. Professor Pemberton read a romantic scene in which Jake's hero tells his girl that he's going to prove to her father that he isn't just a dumb stinking athlete from the stockyards, that he's got a brain; then he meets up with a big bootlegger, formerly a boyhood pal of his, and goes to work for him.

As Professor Pemberton read, dryly, haltingly, Jake watched the faces about him. Fasso, Boris, the Mexican woman. Boy, did that story stink. His sweat was no longer cold and clammy; it steamed out of him. He wanted to stop the professor. Enough. Please stop.

Boris put the final period on it: "Bourgeois tripe."

"Horatio Alger wins the girl and the bottle of Napoleon brandy," said Fasso. "So what?"

"I wouldn't dismiss the story like that," Professor Pemberton said. "There's some flowery language, yes. Perhaps the idea is a little trite. But there is a marked vitality in the writing at times. If Jake could reconceive the thrust of the story, get down to the changing values of today, he might come up with something."

That's all Jake had to hear. To hell with the rest of them. Professor Pemberton was encouraging. He thought he had it. He ought to know. Big English professor. Editor of the *New Republic.* He was an expert. He felt his heart thumping wildly.

So he reconceived the story. Instead of becoming a bootlegger, his hero goes into the laundry business of his girl's father. He doesn't like the life there, the way the workers are exploited, the arrogance of his future father-in-law. He rebels against the job and her father. He forces the girl to make a choice between her father and him. The girl chooses her father, and he goes on the bum in search of the meaning of his life. That would be better, he thought. That was dealing with the changing values of today.

That summer, as he worked on the novelette, he began to go deeper into himself. Hey, you longhair in the crew cut, who are you? Where do you stand? Everybody seemed to be asking that: the bohemians at the Dill Pickle Club on the Near North Side; the anarchists, socialists, communists, atheists, technocrats, Trotskyites, paranoids, hell-and-damnation religious freaks, snake-oil medicine men and enema healers, at Bughouse Square on North Clark Street; the communists and fellow travelers at the John Reed Club on South State Street; Professor Pemberton's literary group at the Hull House; the Jews in the big lounge at the JPI.

Who are you? Where do you stand? Society is hurting, bleeding, dying; what are you going to do about it? You can't be a dumb, punch-drunk athlete all your life. One of these days life will stop being all wine and roses. Then what'll you do, where'll you stand? You got a headache, boy? Look at the guy on the breadline, the women with children whoring for a piece of bread, the families crowding into hovels of cardboard and tin.

Jake listened and hardly talked. He had nothing to say, nothing to argue about. But he envied those who had firm opinions, who knew where they stood. After the talks he eyed the girls. Most of them, he understood, believed in free love. Just make a pass and you'll get. Bullshit. To most of them he was just a college kid, too young to bother with. They talked too fast for him; they were too smart.

Once he overheard a woman say, referring to him, "Him, it'd be like going out with my kid brother. A lot of rah-rah, that's all I'd get."

He felt like a kid in a world of grown-ups who were ready to turn the world upside down. Make way, kid. No time to fool around. We're on the move.

But he didn't need the radical girls. A couple of girls around the pool were handing it out. Sometimes he saw Ida when she wasn't busy. Lila had a new job handling publicity and entertainment for the Chez Paree, the class nightclub and gambling casino in Chicago, run by the Capone mob. Sometimes, after wandering around the Near North Side, he'd stop in to see Lila at the Chez. She was really hot stuff, in control of all the talent there.

"You like the show girls, Jake?"

"Yum-yum."

"Pick one."

"Yummie-yummie, momma."

Lila laughed, hugged him. She was a pal. There hadn't been any sexual involvement in a long time.

"What next, Lila?"

"Hollywood. Once I control all this talent, I'll have Hollywood by the well-known cannons."

"How do you do it?"

"Lila's secret. I know what tickles the fancy of men."

"Send on the girls."

She still had access to the rooms at the Sherman Hotel, also controlled by the mob. Which made everything so cushy.

He tried to read Karl Marx that summer. That was heavy going. Friedrich Engels was easier. So were Alexander Berkman and Emma Goldman. Lenin and Trotsky were heavy, too. Fasso brought to the pool the *New Masses, International Literature,* published by the Russians, and communist pamphlets; he lent them to Jake.

"What do you think?" Fasso said.

"I'm getting a headache."

One night, toward the end of summer, while he was listening to a symposium on art and politics at the John Reed Club, Jake's mind started to wander. His eye roved over the dark paintings on the wall with symbolic hammers and sickles, red flags, heroic workers, oppressed people, tenement scenes, hardworking sharecroppers and their dilapidated shacks; most of them heavy-handed, all of them with messages. And then his eye settled on a girl sitting on a bench in a corner of the badly lit, hot, stuffy hall, leaning against the drab wall, looking as if she were huddled within herself. She had silky chestnut hair, large, dark, haunting eyes, a pale face with high cheekbones, a long, slender body. She looked a little like Greta Garbo. He couldn't keep his eyes from her.

Afterward, at the table where they served coffee, cookies, and a cheap punch, he moved in close to her. She was with a younger girl, a very healthy, hefty 4-H Club version of her. Up close, the girl Jake was attracted to looked as if she'd seen everything, even death, and had come back. She was a year or two older than Jake, but in her face, it seemed, there was a lifetime of living. After getting a paper cup of coffee and a couple of cookies, he purposely bumped into her as he turned from the table.

"As I live and breathe," he said. "Greta Garbo."

She was astonished.

"May I have your autograph?" He pulled out a small pad and a pencil.

"I don't believe this," she said. Her voice was like music.

"I'm wrong. You're Emma Goldman."

She laughed. He was ravished by it.

"Who are you anyway?" she asked.

"Rosa Luxemburg's son."

She laughed harder.

"Here." She took his pad and pencil and autographed the names of Greta Garbo and Emma Goldman.

"I'll put it in my scrapbook. I'll cherish it for life."

She turned to a bushy-haired, skinny little man with thick glasses. "Do you know this man?"

The skinny little man shrugged. Fasso poked in. "That's Jake Davidson, national intercollegiate swimming champ."

"What's he doing here?" she asked.

"I'm a refugee from hot showers and chlorinated pools," Jake said, trying to be bright.

"Better go back to the showers," she said. "You'll only get dirty here."

The liveliness of her laugh and smile suddenly went dead. She turned to her sister. "Let's go."

He held her a moment. "Hey, we just met."

She started to move out with her sister.

"Can I see you again?"

She moved faster, as if she would die if she were there another minute.

"How about it?" he said.

"Yes. Okay. Why not?"

And she was racing down the stairs with him shouting, "Where? How?"

Back in the hall, Fasso said, "That's Natasha Lubin."

"Sounds like somebody out of a novel by Dostoyevsky."

"Her old man was in the 1905 revolution in Russia."

"What does that make him, an American commissar?"

"Natasha popped out of her mother's womb yelling, 'All power to the Soviets.' She waved a May Day flag when she was one year old. That's how long she's been in the movement."

"What else do I have to know?"

"You like her?"

"What's to like? She's dying on the vine."

"Stay away, Jake. She's a neurotic broad."

"I hear they're the best lays. Lots of imagination, lots of fantasy."

"Lots of heartache. She had a bad love affair at Illinois and suffered a nervous breakdown."

"Did you know her there?"

"Of course. She organized the Student Union and then fell *plotz* in love with her French professor, a ballsy boulevardier with powerful bedroom manners. People called him the French Lick."

"What'd he do, screw the revolution out of her?"

"Something like that."

Jake finished the novelette and sent it off to *Scribner's Magazine,* sure he was going to win first prize. He went back to school.

Les Fishel, sports editor of the Chicago *Evening American,* was looking for a sports correspondent at the university, and Art Balzerini, publicity director of the sports department, recommended Jake. He spent a good deal of time with the football team that fall, writing gossip pieces, color stories, and interviews, then wiring them into the *American,* for which he got space rates. Sometimes Les Fishel himself put his by-line over a story Jake had written, which filled him with pride. He even covered a couple of football games for the football writer who got too drunk to write the copy. Milton B. loved him. Athletes sought his favor, hoping he'd do a story about them. Jake was a big potato on campus, not only as an athlete but as a newspaper correspondent. He loved the word "correspondent." Much better than "reporter." It made him kind of special.

When he could make it, he'd go down to the John Reed Club on Friday or Saturday nights. Maybe he'd see Natasha again. He couldn't seem to get her out of his mind. He wrote to Fasso, who was back at Illinois, and asked how to get in touch with her.

Just before the end of the football season he called her.

"Hello," he said. "How are you? This is the son of Rosa Luxemburg."

"Jake!" she said.

"You remember my name."

"That's one of my big troubles. Too much memory."

"How are you feeling?"

"Better. Much better." As if he knew she'd been ill.

"Still looking like Garbo?"

"More like Claudette Colbert."

"I'll take that combo. I haven't seen you around the John Reed Club."

"I haven't been up to it. I've been looking for work."

"At what?"

"Teaching. French. Romance languages."

"Any luck?"

"It's freezing out there."

"Hey, the School of Speech here is doing *Anna Christie.* Would you like to see it?"

"Love to. When?"

"Friday night. Let's have dinner together; then we'll see the play."

"Where'll I meet you? I couldn't ask you to come out here to pick me up."

"Where are you coming from?"

"Albany Park."

"Oh, God." That was like being at the end of the world.

"Just tell me where to meet you."

He told her to meet him at the North Shore Hotel and gave

her directions. She seemed awfully anxious. He wondered why. An attractive girl like her, with a brain, could have all kinds of guys. Maybe the brain put them off. The way he remembered her, she looked as if she'd experienced everything exotic and decadent in the world. Is that what he couldn't get out of his mind?

By the time Friday evening rolled around he was nervous with expectation. But everything in him dropped when he saw her enter the hotel. She came in wearing a black sealskin coat, looking frail under the bright lights. As she searched about for him, she suddenly turned frightened and hurt, and his heart caved.

"Natasha!"

Her face lit up, like that of a child patted on the head.

"You look elegant." He referred to her fur coat.

"Blame it on my father. He's a furrier."

"Hungry?"

"Starved."

He took her into the cafeteria. "Anything you want, take."

"Gallantry will get you everywhere." She laughed brightly.

After dinner she said, "Ever have French coffee?"

"No."

She showed him how to pour the cream over a spoon so that it stayed on top. His lips hit the cool cream; then the hot coffee strained through.

"Delicious," he said. "What's with the French, everything French?"

"They're so civilized, so cultivated. And the language is the language of love."

"I thought you were a revolutionary."

"Precisely. It's love that makes us want to change the world."

"How romantic."

"Didn't you know that the most romantic people in the world are revolutionaries? They're dreamers, idealists."

"With blood on their hands?"

"To make the many happy instead of the few. But the revolution has been far from my mind of late. My heart's been a little too heavy for it."

"I'll bet you read *War and Peace* at eight."

She smiled. "At twelve. *The Brothers Karamazov* at thirteen."

"Ah, vodka. If I had a few serfs and a whip and a Russian bear to dance with, I'd be happy."

"I'm glad you called, Jake."

"Why?"

"When I met you, it was the first time I'd been out since last spring."

"A little too early to hibernate, isn't it?"

"That's why I came out tonight."

"Well, let's take a look at *Anna Christie.*"

Afterward they walked out under the bare trees and the fallen leaves on campus, silent, the mood of the play a brooding cloak over them.

"O'Neill, an Irishman with a Russian soul," Jake said.

She nodded.

They walked down the quiet streets to the El. When they passed his apartment, he said, "Will you come up for a bit?"

"Yes."

Upstairs they sat on his bed and talked; then he reached over and kissed her. They made love silently with the brooding spirit of the night over them. Afterward he felt tears on her face. She didn't tell him why.

"Everything all right?" he asked.

"Yes."

"I'll take you home."

"No."

"It'll be a long ride. The El. The streetcar."

"I'd rather go alone."

There was no kiss good-bye as she left. When he looked out the window, she looked lost under the dim lamppost lights, a shadow in a sealskin coat among other shadows; then she disappeared.

I'll never see her again, he thought. This broad could tear your heart apart. She was a lousy lay. She didn't even move. Wouldn't even take her clothes off. She just lay there, submitting herself to a greater wound than she felt. This woman, whom he'd awaited with nervous anticipation, with the aura of the French way about her, turned out to be the lousiest lay he'd ever had. But he worried about her getting home safely. He called the next day.

She said she'd made it home fine, thanks. He was glad, he said. He didn't want to see her again, so he hung up. But there was something unfinished between them. He had to see it through. His heart was lost to her.

Two weeks later he called her again.

"How are the brothers Karamazov?" he asked.

"Neatly buried in my memory."

"Can I drag you downtown tonight?"

"What's up?"

"The Chez Paree."

"The Chez Paree?"

"Ever been there?"

"No. But it's so extravagant, so decadent. You don't have to impress me that way, you know."

"We'll live a little."

"Where'll I meet you?"

"I'll pick you up."

"That'd be too much trouble. I'll meet you. Where?"

There she went again. Independent to the core. They agreed to meet outside the Chez Paree at nine-thirty.

"Save your appetite. We'll eat there."

"It's too expensive."

"Nothing's expensive. As long as there's a pencil and I can sign the tab."

The Chez Paree in the 1920s and 1930s was a bootlegger's dream: a fashionable nightclub with fine food, superb entertainment, and an elegant, carpeted, heavily draped gambling room in the back. The most important people in town, including the lawmakers of the city and state, went there with their wives and friends and were given the red-carpet treatment. Often their tabs were picked up, and they could gamble without fear of scandal. To them and to all important businessmen, the mob was very liberal with credit. The outfit considered markers, or IOUs, the surest way of putting important people in your pocket. The Chez Paree was the slick, sleek, sophisticated glitter of the Capone empire. It was the kind of place in which Lila Shulman flourished. She had a remarkable memory for faces and names, could make anybody whom she thought important feel as if he owned the place; she was a good judge of entertainment values, and she knew how to hand out favors. If you wanted to hit the big time, the eye to catch was Lila's. From the Chez Paree you could go anywhere.

The maître d' no longer needed a nod from Lila for the grand welcome when Jake entered; he already knew Jake.

"This way, Mr. Davidson."

Jake felt like a Nero, a Pharaoh, a Czar, a King David, as he and Natasha were led past the richly clothed, fashionable, bejeweled, perfumed people to a black leather booth, the table covered with thick white linen, the lights mellow, with Ben Bernie playing gentle dance music.

"My God," Natasha said after they were seated and handed the big red elegant menus.

Jake smiled shyly. This was the life Jake had always admired: the easy life, the mark of success. He had moved within it at the rich clubs but was never really a part of it. He was seduced by it every time he entered.

"Who are you, Jake?"

"The caviar and champagne kid. Would you like some?"

"It'd make me sick."

"Nothing too good for the working class, you know."

"Is that what you want, all this?"

"It's what I thought I wanted."

"And now?"

"It's like a stick of candy. I like to suck on it."

"You're full of contradictions, aren't you?"

"Why should I be an exception?"

She looked at the menu. "Oh, my God, the prices. I couldn't eat here. Let's go."

"Don't worry, Natasha. Enjoy. It's all on the cuff."

"Who are you, Jake? Really."

"Let's say I'm a pet poodle."

The waiter stepped up and asked them what they'd like to drink.

"Vodka and orange juice," Jake said.

"I'll try the same," Natasha said.

"Lenin's drink. Stalin's."

"Without orange juice."

"Touché. The drink of the revolution."

She laughed. "You're awfully good for me."

"After the revolution we'll turn this into a museum. We'll show the world how easy it was to get booze during Prohibition, how decadent we were while half the world was starving. Chez Paree and the last days of Pompeii."

She drank to that. Later Jake had filet mignon and Natasha ordered chicken Kiev. Then coffee and crêpes suzettes with the brandy and the flames and everything.

"It's so easy to be corrupted," he said.

"Touché again."

Sophie Tucker came on. Breasty, fat, sequined, all *shmaltz,* all *Yiddishe Mama.* The audience loved her. Even the Italian mobsters.

"You like?" he asked.

"Chicken soup," Natasha said. "How can it hurt?"

He excused himself and went over to Lila to arrange for a room at the Sherman Hotel.

"Who's the pig?" Lila said.

"Jealous?"

Lila laughed. "I'm not on men anymore."

"You're kidding."

"What's a man got a woman hasn't got?"

"You don't need me to tell you."

"I can get a dildo for a buck. It can last all night."

"Does skin come with it?"

"Go," Lila said. "Fuck her. I'll provide the bed. That's how jealous I am."

But Natasha didn't want to go to the Sherman; it was too demeaning.

"What do I have to hide?" she said.

"Nothing."

"What's wrong with your place?"

"I didn't think you wanted to travel that far. The Sherman is right around the corner."

"If it's what I want, I'd travel to the ends of the earth."

"Let's get going then."

"Patience, Jake. A woman needs lots of patience. Tenderness. A little love."

"Okay, we'll take a cab."

"That'll be too expensive."

"What are you, my accountant? You adding up my pennies?"

"Patience, Jake. There's lots of time."

After all that glitter, all that elegance, he was reduced to a long, dreary ride to Evanston, only to get into his shabbily furnished, dirty, cobwebby apartment. He lost his appetite for her. He was still so bourgeois.

"What's wrong, Jake?"

"It reminds me of a story. Moe and Izzy are walking down Fifth Avenue in New York. Moe says, 'Izzy, I've got to go something terrible.' Izzy, the quick-witted one, says, 'So go. There's Tiffany's. They must have a toilet there.' Moe comes out awhile later, and they proceed to promenade down the avenue, and Moe stops Izzy and says, 'Izzy, I've got to go so bad I'll do it right in my pants.' Moe says, 'You went into Tiffany's. What happened?' Moe says, 'I'll tell you what happened. I step in. It's sparkling with jewels and crystal chandeliers. The music is soft. The salesmen are in tailcoats with flowers in their lapels. I'm ashamed, but I ask the salesman where the men's room is, and he tells me where to go. It was magnificent. A Solomon's palace. Fragrance everywhere. The floors terrazzo. The urinals Carrara marble. The music from *Scheherazade*. I open my pants. I take it out. It looked so shabby . . . I couldn't.'"

Natasha doubled up with laughter. It brought them very close. This time they undressed, took their time. Jake thought he'd melt away.

What did it matter that Natasha had flabby breasts, a light soft down on her face, a slender, vulnerable, submissive body that gave him love without too much passion; that she looked nothing like the tall, cheerful, well-scrubbed, open-faced all-American coeds on campus? What did it matter that Lila thought she was a pig? Lila couldn't recognize radical beauty in a thousand years. What did it matter that a number of YCLers, black and white, had gone to bed with her since she was fourteen because she had had to prove she was free from bourgeois morality? She was an Anna Karenina who had abandoned herself to one love affair after another and was finally crushed on the romantic rocks of her French professor, who talked to her in the language of love and violated her with the brutality of rejection. She was Raskolnikov's Sonya, the prostitute, so clean in spirit that she could purify your soul, even though it was damned. She was Isadora Duncan, a soaring giant of a woman, as free as the wind when she danced, but anchored by the forces around her. She was all the star-crossed women of books and life, an emotional loser, with a mind grounded in dialectical materialism and a heart enslaved to the notion of love. All of it made no difference. She discussed his stories with a sensitivity and intelligence he had never experienced. She opened the symphony and the opera to him. He'd been stung by her. She pumped through his bloodstream and filled him to the brim with life. When *Scribner's* rejected his novelette and gave the prize to James Gould Cozzens, he wasn't alone for the first time; she supported him, he dared to hope, he had already won a new world.

She was open and honest with him about everything but where she lived, with whom. She never let him come to her house, always met him at his place or downtown.

"How come you never let me take you home or pick you up?" he asked.

"It preserves my independence."

"What are you hiding? Your father a bootlegger? You living in a whorehouse? You a kept woman or something?"

She always smiled.

"Come on, Natasha. What's the secret?"

She evaded him with a kiss.

One day he called. Her mother answered. Natasha was ill. Natasha didn't want him to come over, didn't want him to catch her cold. He insisted. She protested. He came over. And learned what she was hiding. She had a ten-year old brother who was a mongoloid. Everybody called him Shatzie.

Natasha's mother looked like a peasant, strong-faced, heavy-legged, broad-hipped. She walked around the house in her bare feet. She believed in yogurt, wheat germ, blackstrap molasses, dried fruits, periodic enemas, and the class struggle, probably in that order. When the boy hung on her, she lifted him to her hip and carried him about, a burden which she had to suffer. Natasha's father was a stern, rawboned, hardworking furrier who owned his own shop, owned the three-bedroom brick house they lived in, and contributed heavily to the Communist party. There was a sense of shame and guilt over the boy, they tried to keep him in his bedroom; but he kept coming out, to drool, nuzzle in Jake's lap or hold his leg tightly when he stood up. It was embarrassing. But as the evening wore on, everybody ignored Shatzie; they treated him like a pet.

Deep down, Jake knew, the family had been hurt by this boy. He had left a scar, had already conditioned their lives. It brought Jake closer to Natasha, filled him with a greater emotion about her. He was young, he was healthy, he was immortal; he'd inject Natasha with his strength and his vigor; nothing could ever possibly happen to them.

Jake was busier, happier, and more involved that winter and spring than ever before in his life. He was taking courses in the modern novel, creative writing, newspaper work, and contemporary thought. He was covering sports for the *American*. He was playing water polo and swimming with the team. Though he wasn't a champion any longer, he was good enough to make the all-conference water polo team and the all-American swimming team. And he was in love.

"They ought to charge me amusement tax for being alive, for having so much fun," he said.

"It's the grimmest winter in the history of America," Natasha said, "and you act like you're floating on inner tubes in seas of sugar and spice. Somebody will kill you if you're not careful."

"Be happy," he said.

But she couldn't. She had tried everything to get work as a teacher and failed. For a time she worked as a waitress but was stiffed too often, rushed too much, and made to feel worse than a slave. Sometimes she made less than $1 a day. She worked with people who were evicted from homes, who needed relief, talking to them, passing out leaflets, but most of them didn't want ideas, dreams, hammer-and-sickle futures; they wanted bread. Now. She felt herself sinking in a world of despair.

"I don't know if you're good for me or bad for me," she said.

"I'm good for you."

"You look like nobody I'd ever fall in love with. Your hair is too short. You're too clean. You take too many showers. You look like you don't have a brain in your head. You're an athlete.

If anybody had ever told me I'd go out with an athlete, I'd have laughed myself silly. Do you know, there are two writers at the John Reed Club who are doing stories about you? You're something exotic, an incongruity."

"In short, an oddball."

"No. You're right with the world, Jake. You look right, like an American Legionnaire, a Rotarian, a man most likely to succeed. What are you doing among us bomb throwers?"

He laughed. "Imagine, in left-wing circles I'm a character when all of you look like characters to me."

"Sometimes I think you're crazy."

"So do I."

"Anybody who wants a better world to live in has to be a little mad."

"We're in such good company."

"I love you, Jake."

"So do I."

Jake's sister, Miriam, was happy, too. She got married to Bob Stein, the basketball player, who'd gone into his father's used auto parts business after graduating high school. He was twenty-one now, handsome, blond, blue-eyed, a good responsible worker who would make a decent living. Jake's parents gave them a wedding in the back room of the Café Royal on 12th Street, where more than a hundred relatives and friends drank and ate and danced. Miriam looked so beautiful in white, so pure. They were married under a *chupah*. Afterward the relatives said, *"Noo,* Jake, how about you?"

He had brought Natasha to the affair and had introduced her to his mother and father and said, "This is the girl I'm going to marry."

"Oy, Jake." His mother, overwhelmed with the idea of her older son getting married, no matter who the girl was, kissed him. "I hope so, I hope so."

They danced *sherralahs* and *kazatchkas*. Even Bubi got carried away and danced. Tears cropped to Natasha's eyes.

"What's wrong?" he asked.

"Nothing," she said. "Everybody cries at weddings and funerals."

"I didn't think you were that sentimental."

"That's the trouble. You're brought up on Marxist logic, there's no room for sentiment. But my heart is touched."

He held her close and kissed her, then said, "Why don't we do it?"

She didn't seem to hear him at first.

"How about it?" he said.

"What?"

"Get married."

"Married?"

She looked stunned.

"Sure," he said. "Why not?"

"Oh, Jake, you're just carried away; you can't be serious."

"Come on. We'll grab the rabbi. He's still here. We'll make it official."

Her pale face blanched. There was a look of terror in her great dark eyes. She turned away.

"How about it?"

She tightened her fists, steadied herself.

"You're so young, Jake. You haven't finished school yet."

"I just turned twenty-one. I'll finish school next winter, for whatever good that'll do me."

"Where'll we live?"

"My place."

"How long will you have it? You can't be supported as an athlete all your life."

"I'll get a job."

"Doing what?"

"Reporting. Writing. I've got a job now."

"But it's connected to the university. Once you're out of school, then what?"

"I'll take care of us, don't worry."

"Jake, you live in the clouds. Nothing ever really touches you. You don't know what it's like out there."

"What's with all the life-is-earnest, life-is-real all of a sudden?"

"Because I need reality. I need it more than anything in the world. Because I've got to control my fantasies, to keep them from running away."

"Is love a fantasy?"

"It's all fantasy, an illusion. You see rainbows where there aren't any. You can whip the world even if you're a cripple."

"I don't understand all this bullshit. Do you want to be with me or don't you?"

"Everything is so simple for you."

"Why do you have to complicate everything?"

"You don't understand."

"What do I have to understand? I want you. I like being with you. I respect you. You're good for me. I feel you alive inside me. I worry about you. I think about you all the time when you're away from me. What more do you want?"

"I think," she said slowly, "we'd better stop seeing each other."

"You don't want to make a commitment, is that it?"

"I don't want to hurt you, Jake."

"How will you hurt me?"

"You're so persistent. You're such a boy."

"Now you're hurting me."

"Good-bye, Jake. I won't see you anymore."

She burst into tears and ran out of the place. He stood rooted there for a moment, then ran out after her. She wasn't on the street. She had disappeared. He ran to the corner. Where the hell had she gone? He finally went back to the wedding celebration.

"Where's your girl?" his mother asked.

"I don't know."

"What happened?"

"I wish I knew."

"You said you were going to marry her."

"Maybe later, Ma."

"You have plenty of time." She left to join her sisters.

Uncle Nachum came by. "You're not dancing? You're not enjoying?"

Jake shrugged.

"You had a pretty girl with you. What happened to her?"

"She left." He looked at Nachum, still with the buck teeth and the gold crowns, Americanized only in his clothes. "How's your marriage?"

"Without my wife, I'd be another mouth to feed in your house. No shoe store anymore, no job, I read the papers and I walk the streets. God forbid my wife should lose her job."

"You had to come to America?"

"I wonder."

Later he called Natasha. She was asleep, her father said.

"Ask her to call me tomorrow."

Natasha didn't call. He phoned again. She wasn't in. He rode out to her house. She wasn't home. Shatzie greeted him at the door with his runny nose and red-rimmed eyes and dumb, flat face. Natasha's mother said, "She moved in with a friend from college, busy with party work."

"Where?"

"I don't know where."

"Ask her to call me."

"Yes."

As he was about to leave, she said, "What happened?"

"I don't know. All I did was ask her to marry me."

Her mother nodded sadly, offered no explanations, and he took a long gloomy ride back to Evanston. He wished he knew what made Natasha's wheels go around.

She was alive inside him, gnawing away at him. He walked around lonely, empty. Went to the John Reed Club affairs, looking for her. Asked whoever knew her where she might be. Books he read broke him up, made him feel sadder than ever. Music he listened to made him moody. His swimming career was over. He didn't even have that to get lost in.

It was an exciting, crackling, hopeful time. America had a new President. Hoover, who had become a villain in everybody's eyes, was out; Roosevelt was in. His crisp, resonant, aristocratic voice, his cocky way of raising his chin upward, his broad smile, his exuberant, dynamic look set a tone of confidence in the nation. For the 15,000,000 out of work the promise of a crumb was better than nothing. That man in the White House was a daring, courageous man. He was like a gunslinger who'd come to town to clean it up. He closed the banks, then reopened them. He repealed Prohibition. Who cared if Capone made more money than ever? Beer was flowing again; things were opening up. The eggheads, the brain trusters, were coming in with all kinds of new ideas: They devalued the dollar, brought in crop control and lifted farm prices, got the CCC going for young men, got Congress to pass a bill for public works, aided the unemployed with federal relief, and then there was the NRA, which gave working people the right to organize and bargain collectively. Those first 100 days of Roosevelt's term were dynamite. There was hope in the land. All promises, the communists said, a New Deal to save the capitalist system; but it was only a finger in the dike, with the torrents of disaster ready to pour through. The specter of communism was haunting not only Europe but America, too.

Jake read about all this, listened to all the different opinions, but couldn't get much involved. Most of his thoughts were about Natasha. She was his private specter. He went to the Chez Paree, where Lila said, "It's all legal now, all but the gambling in the back room. The boys never had it so good." Then she said, "What happened to that pig you brought here?"

"I don't know."

"She find a better pen?"

"I guess."

"I've got the perfect remedy."

She fixed him up with a girl on whom the back room had markers. She said, "Comes from a fine North Shore family. Very sophisticated pussy, a degenerate gambler."

He saw Ida one night.

"I got it right in the gut this time," he said.

After they had made love and she had a cigarette, she said, "Feel better?"

"Yes. But no."

"I know what you mean."

"She was a lousy lay, but it didn't make any difference. You're the best there is. But it's more than just fucking."

"You're telling me."

"But don't let us knock fucking. Okay?"

"I know what you mean."

He had an erection again.

"I really know what you mean."

Toward the end of the semester, just when he was beginning to think that the affair was all over and the feeling about her was becoming more and more of a memory, he saw Natasha on campus at a symposium on the NRA. Everything in him leaped toward her, but the hall was packed, the aisles were blocked, he couldn't get to her. On the stage was a banker from Chicago, the head of the political science department, and Clark Hanover, one of the first organizers of the Communist party in the United States and a member of the central committee. He was a tall, bald, dry-faced man, with wrinkles like cracked earth; his hands were factory-hard and callused. Natasha seemed riveted to him. Hanover was forceful, dynamic, irrefutable, in command of his statistics and logic. His theme was that Roosevelt was a demagogue, long on promises, short on delivery. There was still one-third of a nation starving or in need, still corruption in government, still farms being taken over by the banks, still hungry speculators in the stock market, still big profits being made by industry. The banker and professor were shooting blank guns against Hanover's big cannons.

Natasha sat breathless before him, as if he were an icon come to life.

He finished with, "Chicago has opened its world's fair, chronicling A Century of Progress. And who steals the show? None other than Sally Rand, the fan dancer. A dancer in small-time cabarets, she never made any money until she took her pants off. That's progress. Some progress."

The crowd roared. Natasha jumped to her feet, screaming, laughing, applauding. And so did half the audience. The communist even had humor.

Afterward Jake pushed his way to the stage, where Natasha was.

"Hi," he said.

"Oh, Jake, wasn't he wonderful?"

"Yes. Terrific."

"I want you to meet him."

"Sure."

She took his hand, pulled him up to the stage. Her excitement electrified him. When she got to Hanover's side, where he was talking to a few faculty members, she waited patiently until he noticed her. Her hand trembled when he finally turned to her and said, "Natasha, I'm so glad you came." His voice was warmer, not as crisp and sharp as before; his face, which looked earth-hard onstage, broke open with a smile. He kissed her softly on the lips. As she held his hand, he could feel her melt.

"You were magnificent, Clark."

"I like young people. I like to talk to them." He glanced toward Jake.

"This is Jake Davidson."

Hanover shook his hand firmly.

"Jake is a big athlete on campus. A writer."

"How nice," Hanover said. "What has he written?"

"Nothing yet. But he will."

Long on promises, Jake thought, short on delivery.

Hanover turned from him and said to Natasha, "Stay awhile, dear. We'll have dinner later. I want to talk to you."

She stepped back as Hanover said his good-byes to the banker and faculty men on stage.

"Where've you been?" Jake asked.

"Staying with friends from school, the Berkovers. You know Billy. He's a member of the John Reed Club."

Jake nodded.

"How's school?" she asked.

"One more semester to go."

"Then what?"

"Maybe we'll have our revolution by then. Clark Hanover might make me commissar of athletics."

"You sound bitter, Jake. Please don't be bitter. I'm so sorry about the way I behaved at your sister's wedding."

"I hoped we could spend some time together tonight."

"Another night, Jake. Tonight Clark needs me."

Suddenly he was jealous. He had never minded all the screwing around she had done before; it had never been a threat to him. But now he felt hurt.

And threatened.

"You had an affair with him before?"

"Oh, Jake."

"What do you mean he needs you?"

"He's away from home. Alone. He's got to be with somebody friendly, warm. He's got to unwind."

"And you're the key. The crowds wind him up, and you unwind him."

"Don't be angry, Jake."

"Your folks know him?"

"Of course."

"What'd they do, hand you to him, the vestal virgin? The prize for all tired communist leaders away from home?"

Tears suddenly stung his eyes as she slapped him. Then she walked to Hanover's side. He smiled at her, took her arm, and they strolled away.

Jake stood there, his chest hard, his fists tight. She's a cunt, he told himself. All that sensitivity, that intellect, that emancipation of women bullshit, that left-wing idealism, she's nothing but a hero-worshiping cunt. What do I have to be for her, a Lenin, a Stalin? He moved around that day feeling as if nails were being hammered into his heart.

And leaped to the phone when it rang the next afternoon.

"I'm sorry I slapped you yesterday," she said.

"I'm sorry about what I said."

There was a pause; then she said, "It happened to be the truth."

The truth gave him no satisfaction, no sense of victory. Fourteen, and handed over to the big important revolutionary mogul. Everybody had his hero.

"When can I see you?" he asked.

"Now. I'll be right over."

She arrived with extra-bright touches of lipstick, rouge, and mascara, smiling cheerfully, her teeth glittering. She flung her arms around him, kissed him extravagantly, talked manically about the days and days she'd spent with the Berkovers, handing out leaflets and talking to unemployed steelworkers in South Chicago and Gary, trying to get them to organize an industrial union, to do something about their plight. "You'd think," she said, "they'd grasp anything, but they were like stunned animals, most of them, waiting for some kind of miracle without knowing that the only miracle left in the world rested in their own hands, their own power."

Suddenly she began to cry. "He left for St. Louis this morning."

He took her in his arms, held her close.

"Don't say anything, Jake. Just hold me, be good to me."

"I want to be good to you."

"I loved him at one time when he lived in Chicago."

"Do you still love him?"

"No. I don't think so. Yet when I know he's coming to town, when I see him, I tremble all over. Like I'm a child."

His throat tightened.

"You're the one I love. I know it's you I love. But let's not talk about marriage. I'm not ready for it yet. Neither are you. I know you're not. Someday you'll thank me for making you wait. Just believe that I love you."

He believed her. She loved him, but not 100 percent. She loved him short of marriage. Maybe that should be enough for a while. He was wrong in having pushed it so soon. Maybe he'd have regretted it later if she had agreed. Maybe that's what she was afraid of, any future regrets.

"So where do we go from here?" he asked.

"Just make love to me."

She went to the bathroom, washed her tearstained painted face, and came back naked. This time she was a good lay, moaning, clutching him passionately, thrashing about under him, and finally throbbing and trembling with orgasm.

Was that what he needed, he thought afterward, a Clark Hanover to prepare her for him, to make her so desperate for a love Hanover couldn't give her that she'd run to Jake for it? She moved close to him, held him tight. Hey, Freud, he said inwardly, what have you got to say about this?

After dinner that night, while they were walking to Jake's place from the North Shore Hotel under the leafy trees, Natasha said, "I'd better go home."

"I thought you'd stay the night."

"I haven't been home in a while."

"So you'll get home a day later."

"No. I feel I should go home tonight."

He felt a restlessness in her. He said, "Fuck 'em and leave 'em, huh?"

"Oh, Jake."

"I thought that's what men did. Women usually hang on."

"I'm not all women, Jake."

"You fuckin'-ay you're not."

"All right, let's go back to your place."

"No, forget it."

"I want to. Really, Jake."

As soon as they entered his apartment, she moved up close against him, kissing him long and hard. It was almost like an attack.

"Come on, Jake. Love me."

She got out of her clothes quickly and wanted him to mount her as soon as he was undressed. No preliminaries. Bang. Get it in, get it over with. She was dry. She squirmed beneath him as he tried to penetrate her. Held him tight, moved up high and hard. A kind of self-rape. Gradually she became lubricated; he got through, sank deep within her. She gasped; he didn't know if it was pleasure or pain. Then she began to move to his rhythm. It seemed studied, calculated, designed to give him pleasure. Then, as he came, she said, "Oh, Jake. Oh, dearest, Oh, love." And she began to cry.

Then she pushed him away, got out from under him, and went into the bathroom, taking her clothes along. A communist in her head, he thought, a bourgeois bitch in her cunt. A victim, she would say, of capitalist contradictions. She had an answer for everything.

When she came out, she was dressed, her face made up.

"I'd better go now," she said.

"Okay."

"You're mad."

"Me mad?" He laughed falsely. "I'm a big juicy stud. Studs don't get mad. They do what they have to do. Up, down, in, out, that's their life."

"When will I see you?"

"Why?"

"Because you're important to me now."

"When do you want to see me?"

"Don't you have any final exams?"

"All writing courses. No finals. All my work is in."

"How about the Rachmaninoff concert Saturday night?"

"You've got a deal."

When they met at the auditorium, she already had the tickets.

"What is this?" he said.

"My treat."

"I don't understand you, Natasha. You want me to be gallant, and you take it away from me. You want me to be bold, decisive, a man, and you're wearing the balls all of a sudden."

"I feel less guilty."

"Where'd you get the money?"

"My father. I'll let you pay for the coffee afterward."

"You're gallant; you're bold; you're ballsy. What can I say?"

"Let's enjoy the concert."

They had front-row seats. Rachmaninoff was an old man with a tragic face, as strong, stern and somber as his Prelude in C Sharp Minor. He had the authority of an emperor onstage. His fingers were like hammers, the throbbing veins of his temples like rivers ready to burst open. He played Chopin and Liszt. And when he played his own compositions, the whole auditorium was electrified. The audience was brought to its feet: "Bravo! Encore!"

On the way out Natasha was speechless; her face was flushed and beautiful with excitement. This was her world, where she could soar into her wildest fantasies.

Jake said, "Exhausting."

She took a deep breath. "Thrilling."

On top of an open-air bus they rode through the cool spring night along the lake; they felt the fresh wind against their faces through Lincoln Park, up Sheridan Road, where Jake always wanted to live so that he could walk to the beach in his robe and a pair of clogs. They got off the bus at Howard Street to take an El to Jake's place.

"That was like Paris," she said. "Oh, how I would love to live there."

"Someday we will."

"Will we, Jake? Tell me, truly, will we?"

"And Rome and Athens and London and Tahiti and Hong Kong."

"All the wonderful places in our minds."

"What about Moscow?"

"Ah, Moscow. Chekhov's people, full of ennui, always going to Moscow." She sounded like Garbo.

"And Sorrento."

She hummed "Sorrento." He loved her so deeply it hurt. He loved her so tenderly in bed every nerve quivered, and it hurt even more. She was moody; she was changeable; she was unpredictable; she filled all the empty spaces of his life. She was impossible, a bad trip, a nowhere girl, with a sleazy history, but he felt better with her than without her. Was that love: the choice of better or worse?

In the morning, with the glaring sun and the clatter of the El outside, with Chopin and Liszt and Rachmaninoff's magic gone with the night, Natasha said, "All those places Jake, how would we ever get there?"

"I'll be a writer. Famous and rich, but proletarian. We might even get an invitation from Stalin to visit the Kremlin."

"'Where the telescope ends, the microscope begins. Which of the two has the grander view?'"

"Hah?"

"Victor Hugo. *Les Misérables*. It was lovely, last night, Jake. I wish it could last forever."

"Why couldn't it? Why don't you move in with me?"

"I couldn't."

"We don't have to get married. We'll just live together."

"What would I contribute?"

"You. We'd be together."

"That wouldn't be enough."

"What would make it work?"

"My independence."

"You'd always have that."

"No, I wouldn't, Jake. I'd be taking from you, giving nothing in return. Without a job, there'd be no meaning to my life."

"You mean to say you must have a job before you'd have any meaning to your life? My mother never worked. Millions of women never had jobs. Their lives are full of meaning."

"They're different. Psychologically, emotionally, intellectually. I can't be free to love until I'm independent. Engels said, only when women are free from economic want, from being an appendage to a man, only then can they truly be released to love. From the world of necessity to the kingdom of love. That's what he said."

"You'll have to wait until after the revolution."

"Until I get a job teaching."

"But you will. Things will get better."

She kissed him. "Let's wait a bit longer, Jake."

He had to settle for that.

Natasha's folks had a small cottage off the lake near South Haven, Michigan. Right after Jake's semester ended, she went up there with her sister and little brother. He could have killed her. He didn't know how he'd endure the long, hot, windy summer in Chicago working as a lifeguard without her. Before his job started, he bummed up there. He hardly recognized her. She had a deep tan; the sun had bleached her hair; she'd put on ten pounds; she almost looked *zoftig*. He fell in love with her all over again.

"What the hell did you turn into, a Stakhanovite?" he said.

"Nuts and berries." She laughed, her eyes dancing, her face shining, her teeth gleaming. "Long walks along the beach."

"You don't need a revolution. All you need is the country."

"And minks to make it all possible. I'm so glad you came, Jake."

"I'd have gone crazy if I hadn't."

He walked the woods and the beaches with her, swam long distances in the lake, ate nuts and berries and wheat germ but didn't take any enemas, which her mother strongly recommended. In the woods they found a bed of soft, downy pine needles surrounded by bushes, and they made love there every afternoon. In the evening they watched the magnificent sunsets over the lake, listened to symphonies and the opera on the Victrola. At night he slept on a cot under the eaves. She crawled in with him when everybody was asleep, and they whispered like children, then made love like grown-ups. Afterward she'd go back to her bed, and he'd listen to the night rhythm of the land and the dewdrops falling from the eaves before he'd fall asleep. He was no longer tuned in wholly to himself. He was full of antennas, listening to her more than to himself. Occasionally, during the day, when she was wiping Shatzie's nose or combing his thick hair from his low forehead, that sad, haunted look would fill her great eyes as if she were peering into pools of her future with her own children. Then she'd shake her head and laugh cheerfully and call Shatzie beautiful, lovely, her dreamboat. Jake was hopelessly lost to her. He didn't want to go back to Chicago.

"I'll come and see you during the summer," she said.

"If you don't, I'll come up here."

"That's not a threat, you know."

She walked out to the highway and waited until he hitched a ride. All the way back to Chicago she flowed through him.

The summer was relentlessly long. Hot, burning days, with more and more dust blowing in from the dry, rainless prairies. More and more farmers were forced to give up their land. More workers, despite the New Deal, were sweating it out on the pavements, growing thinner and hungrier. It was humid, sticky, stifling, the asphalt melting, the cement walks and brick buildings blazing, and the smell of the stockyards was a puff of wind away from Jake's nose. A summer to end all summers.

Jake's mother walked about in her bare feet, griping. Bubi fanned herself silently. His father danced in the summertime, a regular Fred Astaire, without the heavy clothing of winter. Even the horses, on dry, fast tracks, were running well for him. Somehow there was more betting than ever, desperate betting. People pooled dimes and quarters, making collective bets, usually on long shots, praying for a win. Even women were putting on the line what little grocery money they had and whoring afterward for as little as half a dollar a head to get back what they lost. Jake's father had seen bad times, but never like this.

"Ruchel, I'm sending you to Union Pier," he said. "You and Bubi and Harry. Pack up. Go."

"What will you do?"

"I'll start running around with the *nafkehs* on the West Side."

"Where'll you eat?"

"Ruchel, there are restaurants in this town."

"You'll get skinnier than ever. And Jake, what will he do?"

"Ma, I've been living away from home for years," Jake said. "Suddenly I can't take care of myself?"

"All right. All right. I'll go." As if she were being exiled, she began to cry.

"Your rich sister is there," said Jake's father. "You'll have company."

She stopped crying, became defiant. "I said I'll go."

"Weekends I'll come up and see you."

"Don't do me any favors."

"All right, I won't. With all the beautiful *nafkehs* around, I'll stay, I'll enjoy." Jake's father smiled, his eyes twinkled.

"I'll fix him up with the broads at the Chez Paree," Jake said, laughing.

"Now I can go. Because with them he'll be safe."

His mother felt proud about going. Her husband could afford it. She was now an allrightnik.

Jake had the mornings to himself. From time to time he wondered what had happened to Lala. He tried to write about him but couldn't make Lala come alive, couldn't meld him into a story. Once he met Lennie Kahn and Yussel Gomberg at the Chez Paree. They were big in the syndicate now. There was talk that they were going to be sent to the West Coast to take over there: the unions, the movies, the gambling, even the racing wire.

"You ever heard from Lala?" Jake said.

"Lala?" Lennie said. "You know somebody named Lala, Yussel?"

"How would I know anybody with a *klutzy* name like that?"

They were playing the same old game. "So what else is new?" Jake said.

"I hear you're turning fruit," Lennie said. "A fuckin' poet. What a character."

Jake shrugged. Go talk with wise guys like that.

"So who do you know here? Lila?" Lennie asked.

"Who else?"

"Hey, you get out to California, we'll give you Jean Harlow on a platter."

What a world. Everybody had Jean Harlow to give away on a platter.

"Next time you're in touch with Lala, tell him I'd like to do a story on him. Ask him to give me a middle and finish, will you? I'd appreciate it."

They didn't look as if it were funny. He parted from them to spend some time with Lila.

But most of the time he lived for the occasional weekends when Natasha came to town. Her father would go up to South Haven, and she'd have the whole house in Albany Park to herself. She looked better each time he saw her. She seemed happier, as if she'd reached some inner peace. They went to the concerts in Grant Park, lay on the grass, and looked at the moon and the stars as the Chicago Symphony Orchestra with all its string and wind instruments played background music to their love. They went to the Art Institute and roamed the galleries, living in the beauty, elegance, grandeur, and romance of the past. Who cared how hot it was? What did it matter how they sweated, how they stuck to each other when they made love? Jake couldn't wait for those weekends. He couldn't wait for the summer to end. It was as if something big and important would happen after Labor Day. As if a date had been set. From here on I start a new life. But all that faced him was Evanston, a last semester of school. His swimming career was over. However, Natasha would be back. That would make a difference. He would be able to see her more often. That would make all the difference.

He didn't know why he continued with school; he didn't need the degree to be a journalist or a writer. But he was compelled to finish what he'd started, and he always had a buck in his pocket there. Inwardly he was reluctant to face the real world, the world that forced Albie Karlin to go to law school, that turned Wally Blake into a lifeguard, that made Moish Bender a candidate for permanent athlete's foot at the JPI, the world of thousands of great athletes and millions of capable men sitting idly in the parks, standing on breadlines, fighting over remnants of garbage, filling out endless forms for relief.

He wondered once again if he should ask Natasha to marry him or live with him, but he was afraid she'd turn him down. Her tan had worn off. She was looking pale and slender again, her cheeks hollow like a movie star. The summer was definitely over, and she wasn't talking about whatever was eating away at her. She seemed to drift away and come back like the tides, a creature of the moon. Let things ride, he thought. What am I, some bourgeois jerk? I don't need her full time. I don't have to own her. I'm not jealous. I trust her. She's faithful to me. What more could I ask for? I'll finish school. I'll get a job. I'll get a nice apartment, buy some decent furniture. I'll show her I can provide for her. I'll show her I'm no fly-by-night. Maybe she'll have a job by then. And pop, we'll be together full time. So let it happen naturally. In due time, due time.

But right after Thanksgiving he stood in shock before her when she said, "I'm going to New York."

"New York!"

"I've made up my mind, Jake. I'm going."

A chill came over him.

"There's nothing here for me."

"Nothing? What about me?"

"I've sent forty letters to different school systems. No. No. No. From every one. Total rejection."

"What did New York say?"

"I haven't tried the East. I'll go there in person."

"Stay here, Natasha. We'll get married. I'll take care of you."

"That isn't the answer. I don't want to be taken care of. I want to take care of myself. I want to be able to take care of you if you need me. All my life I've been taken care of. I've got to know that I can care for myself, that I'm not a cripple."

"But it's not your fault."

"For years I've been dreaming of being with high school students, of teaching them. I'd be good, Jake. I know I'd be good. I've got to find out how good I'd be. I've got to find out my worth, my value, if I'm any good at all to society."

"You're going to find out in New York?"

"It's a big city. They use a lot more teachers. I'm going to try."

He knew that he couldn't talk her out of it. "When are you leaving?"

"In a few days."

"We're not through, are we?"

"Jake, you know I love you."

"What happens when I finish school?"

"Maybe I'll be back here. Maybe you'll come to New York. Let's see what happens, Jake."

"No promises, huh?"

"Jake, I can't live with you. Not until I find myself."

When she left, a vital part of him went off to New York with her. He stood in limbo, the courses he was taking before graduating hardly distracting him from the aching emptiness he felt. A letter from her drenched him with showers of love:

New York is cold, but it's vibrant, a city in ferment, a passionate city, where everybody seems to be your comrade, where you can find a sustaining force even in your despair. Operas, plays, concerts, museums, lectures, foreign films, pages and pages to choose from in the *New York Times* and the *Daily Worker*. It's the center of the world. It's where everything is happening. You must come here. Triumphant bands will welcome you. You'll unfurl the banners of your talent. It'll be your city, your world.

Later her letters were less exciting; there was no work for her there either, but she was involved in the movement. Then no letters at all. He wrote to her at her aunt's house in Brooklyn, where she was staying. No answer. Worried, he called her mother in Albany Park. Natasha was fine, she said. Still staying with her aunt. Still hoping to get a job but very busy with party work.

He had hoped she would be back over the Christmas holidays. All he got from her was a card wishing him the best for the new year with the word "Love" above her signature. He wrote to her, asking her to come back. No answer. Day by day he felt as if he were looking at tattered remnants of their relationship, struck stiff by the cold winds sweeping in from the lake. He wrote again. Why was she so determined to find her own way? Why was she so stubborn about it? He would have to find his way, too. Why couldn't they do it together on familiar ground, where they had friends and relatives, where you had a feeling of home everywhere you went? She wrote back saying she still loved New York.

Fuck her, he said to himself. I'll get a job right here in Chicago. I'll make it big. She'll come back. Broken. I'll take her in. I'll say, Quit crapping around. Comes the revolution, I'll be commissar of sports, you'll be commissar of getting jobs for unemployed schoolteachers. But until then, let's live a little. That's what I'll do. I'll get set here, go to New York, give it to her gently: Natasha, quit fooling around; you're coming back with me; no backtalk. Gentle enough?

He didn't want to go to New York. It was too huge. All the big guns were there. They could crush him. The only person he knew was Joe Ruddy, coach at the New York Athletic Club. Boy, did he know him. Hello, how are you, Joe. Good-bye. That's how well he knew him. Outside of him and Natasha, nobody. So he'd have a pool he could swim in. So what? No, he wasn't going to New York. Not if he could help it.

Jake tried to line up a job during his last month at school. Here he was, a sports celebrity around Chicago; a correspondent for the *American;* a member of Purple Key, the most exclusive honor society in the university; a man with three purple N sweaters and a purple blanket in recognition of his services as a star athlete; a likable, personable, presentable, clear-eyed, scrub-faced, crew-cut, honest-looking, healthy young man; a very likely candidate to succeed; a man of fine moral fiber, brought up under the laws of the Talmud and the go-gettem philosophy of American schools . . . would you give this young man a job?

Confident, head cocked high, with that toothy Franklin D. Roosevelt smile, Jake first went to see Les Fishel, sports editor of the *American.*

"Les, I'm graduating in a month. I'll need a job. How about putting me on full time?"

Les had bushy, wiry hair, thick glasses, and a kind face.

"Jake, I wish I could."

"I'm covering basketball for you, did a couple of football games, even some interviews you put your by-line on."

"Jake, you're covering basketball because I had to let two guys go this year. We're in a bind. Everybody's doubling up."

"I was kind of counting on going full time here."

"You're good. You're capable. It breaks my heart to say no, Jake."

He meant it; he really meant it; there was a tear in his eye.

"Another time, Les."

"I'd put you on in a second if times were normal."

Jake started out.

"Wait a minute."

Les phoned the city editor, told him about Jake. Les reacted as if he'd been hit in the head and hung up.

"The sonofabitch yelled at me."

"Thanks, Les."

Jake knew all the other sports editors in town. They wished they could do something for him, but there were men they'd laid off who had first priority when times got better.

He saw Milton B.

"What a year you picked to graduate, Jake!"

"Would it have been any better last year, the year before?"

"Maybe next year."

"You know everybody, Milton. Nothing? Nothing at all?"

"Jake, I'm digging deep into my pocket these days to keep the boys going. There isn't a goddamn thing around."

"Jesus, Milton, when I first came to school, the whole goddamn world was in my pocket. 'You're going to write your own ticket, Jake.' That's what everybody said."

"How did I know the world was going to turn upside down."

"I'm not blaming you."

"Why don't you go to law school like Albie did?"

"I'm not fit for it."

"These days you do anything you have to do."

He saw Albie Karlin in the city attorney's office. Morrie Benjamin was keeping his promises, having put him in there right after he'd passed the bar. A judgeship next, and who knew what after that?

"Did you cover all the papers?" Albie asked. He was an important man now behind that desk piled high with papers.

"Yep."

"How about Hugh Kerdoon, managing editor of the *News*?"

"What about him?"

"I did him a favor." Albie telephoned Kerdoon, told him about Jake, listened, then hung up. "Sorry, Jake. From what he says, if you were the publisher's son you'd have a tough time. Why don't you keep on going to school? Get a master's in journalism."

"Albie, degrees are shit in newspaper work. As a matter of fact, they're handicaps."

"Go to law school or medical school."

"You mean go through the motions, mark time, until things break loose?"

"I went to law school. It didn't hurt me."

"You had Benjamin behind you."

"Push doorbells, talk the Democratic party, be a ward heeler; Benjamin'll put you to work tomorrow."

"Oh, shit."

"You too proud?"

"I'd rather play the horses."

"You'll lose your ass."

"It's my ass."

"What are you getting mad about? I didn't screw up the world."

"I don't know." Suddenly Jake felt like crying. "It's just that everything is so fucked up."

"I know. When I got out of school, I thought I had the world by the balls, too. So I rolled with the punches."

"Thanks, Albie. You hear of anything, let me know."

The instructors in the school of journalism were too removed from their newspaper pasts to do any good but hand out advice and sympathy. The placement office did little more. It suggested he go to some of the small towns around the country; some paper might have a need for him.

When Jake got his B.S. in Journalism (the B.S. standing for Bullshit that year) he had nothing but a wild, crazy notion that he wanted to write stories, a desperate need for Natasha, and the promise of a lifeguard job in the summertime, a sure $250 for the year. Which wasn't bad for two months' work, considering that the average yearly earnings for steel and textile workers was slightly over $400, a public schoolteacher $1,200, a doctor $3,000, a dentist $2,300, a secretary $1,000. No wonder most graduates with money went abroad to play around or stayed on at school for master's and Ph.D. degrees.

He went home and sat around the house and wondered what to do with himself. All these years he had had a place to go to, he had belonged somewhere: school, the JPI, working as a life-guard. Now he was unhinged, didn't know where to turn, what to do. All of him yearned to go to Natasha. But if he couldn't get set here, what chance would he have there, the big town, the big time? The faith, the optimism he had in himself slowly eroded. The America he had always believed in had betrayed him. His heart was heavy, his spirit crushed; even a swim at the JPI couldn't cheer him up.

Bubi shook her head worrying about him. His mother and father whispered. They loved him deeply, but what could they do about his bafflement, his wounds, his pining for Natasha, his restlessness?

One night his father came home half frozen, his fingers numb, his back broken from the weight of his sheepskin coat and sweaters, his legs bone-weary, but with a broad smile on his stiff, cold red face.

"I picked a daily double today, a long shot, it paid two hundred dollars for a two-dollar bet," he said, shedding his clothes. "Everybody thought I was insane. But I smelled this hunch. This combination was good. Hoo-ha. On top of that I held back fifty dollars in bets I didn't turn in to Capone. Today was a day, hah?"

"I should have black caviar for you," Jake's mother said. "Raisins and almonds and beauty steaks. Why didn't you tell me?"

"Whatever you have I'll enjoy." He washed up and sat down to eat. Then he said, "This money I won today, I said I'm betting 't for Jake. I'm going to let Jake do whatever he wants with it. He can even go to New York if he wants to." He put $200 down on the table. "Take it, Jake. It's yours."

"It's too much."

"You'll go to New York; you'll see your girl; you'll see what goes on. To be immobile is to be in chains. It's not good you should be like that. So take. Go."

All of him wanted to go. It was all he thought of. But he was afraid. He, who had hardly known any fear before, who had felt that he could have anything he wanted, he was that sure of himself, he was afraid of what he'd find in New York, of what had happened to Natasha. He was afraid most of all that he'd fail there, too, fail right in front of her.

"So take," his father said.

"It won't hurt you, Jake," his mother said. "Take."

He took $100. "All right," he said.

Four days later, after a long twenty-four-hour bus ride through snow in Ohio and parts of Pennsylvania, then sleet and freezing rain out of the Appalachians, with the bus sliding and skidding and almost crashing into other cars, he finally arrived in New York.

New York, New York!

As soon as the bus had come out of the Holland Tunnel, Jake was overwhelmed. The whole city was vertical. It was all like downtown Chicago, miles and miles of skyscrapers, packed together, dark, powerful, grim, towering over the narrow streets. You could get a permanent crick of the neck from looking up.

It was nine at night when the bus pulled in on 42nd Street, across from Grand Central Station. The walks were slushy from a recent snowstorm, and it was freezing. He had called Natasha before he departed from Chicago, but she wasn't in. He had left word that he was coming. Now he called again.

"Jake!"

She sounded so excited, so happy to hear from him. It was so good to hear her voice.

"I'm here at Grand Central Station. How do I get to your place?"

She gave him directions. "Hurry, hurry."

Down through subterranean tunnels and over the Brooklyn Bridge the Sea Beach express roared and screeched; then it hurtled through miles and miles of dense houses with a sameness and monotony and wintry ugliness that was worse than Chicago. No passageways, no alleys, no empty lots, no sense of neighborhoods, no parks, nothing to relieve the eye, nothing but buildings jammed against buildings, a tightly packed city crisscrossed with fire escapes, vast and forbidding in the night. Out of the train, Jake hefted his pigskin valise and portable typewriter, moved along the tall brick apartment buildings, then into a side street of brownstones.

She saw him through the window when he arrived at her aunt's brownstone, rushed to the door to greet him. He slid on the slippery stone stairs running up to her, sprawled all over, his heavy valise flying out onto the sidewalk, but he held onto his typewriter. She came swiftly after him and helped him into her arms. She was so genuinely glad to see him that all his earlier fears about coming to New York flew away.

He met her aunt, who was as strong, sturdy, and peasant-looking as Natasha's mother, but she seemed more sophisticated. Natasha's uncle, who ran a dry goods store with her aunt in Flatbush, was a neat, slender man with a Ronald Colman mustache. They were polite, hospitable, told Jake to make himself at home, then went to sleep. Natasha fixed him a toasted cheese sandwich and poured him a glass of milk. He couldn't keep his hands off her.

"I'm starved in more ways than one."

"We'll have to be careful. My aunt and uncle are apolitical, small business people with Babbitt minds."

"Sure, sure."

"You'll sleep on the living-room couch."

"Where will you sleep?"

"I have a bedroom. It used to belong to their daughter before she got married and moved off to Cleveland. Oh, Jake, I'm so happy you came. This is going to be your town. I'm going to show you everything."

"Right now, just show me your bedroom."

"We can't, Jake. God, I want to, but we can't. It isn't my place."

"We'll be quiet."

"Please, Jake, I wouldn't feel right."

He kissed her, held her tight, moved against her, tried to arouse her.

"You're acting like a demure bourgeois virgin."

"I'm sorry, Jake. Let's wait until you get settled. But right now we ought to go to sleep. Tomorrow we'll start doing the town."

It took him a long while to fall asleep. In a few minutes, it seemed, he woke up with an erection so big and tight it hurt. It wouldn't go down. To hell with it. In the dark he found his way to her bedroom, opened and closed the door softly, and crawled into bed with her. Her body was afire as he stretched out beside her.

"Oh, Jake," she whispered.

"Shhhhh."

"Oh, God, Jake."

"Shhhhh."

"It's so hard and powerful."

He kissed her passionately.

"We shouldn't."

He penetrated her.

"Jesus, Jake."

She lay still as he moved against her.

"Quick, Jake. Before we wake somebody."

He hated taking her this way. Felt like a brute. Especially when her body quivered afterward. He didn't know whether it was pleasure or pain or both.

"You really needed that."

"Yes."

"You'd better go now, Jake."

He kissed her gently, then moved away from her. Back on the mohair couch, smelling faintly of mothballs, he felt himself shrinking: a stranger in a strange town; even the girl he loved felt like a stranger. He drifted off to sleep finally.

At dawn he heard Natasha's aunt and uncle having breakfast in the kitchen, then using the bathroom, and at last banging the door shut as they left for their store. He went to the bathroom with a big piss hard-on. It went down for a moment after he urinated; then the thought of being alone now in the house with Natasha brought it right up again. Oh, it'll be nice now, he thought as he stepped to her bedroom. It'll be dreamy. But she was reading in bed, all dressed, and she jumped up brightly.

"I'm so glad you're up. Come, I'll fix you some breakfast."

"But I thought—"

"Come on, Jake. Don't be a noony." She took his hand and led him out of the bedroom. "Get dressed while I hustle up some food."

A half grapefruit was ready for him when he came into the

kitchen; then she served him two sunny-side-up eggs, toast, and coffee.

"We'll need all this to keep ourselves going this morning."

"Boy, you'd think I was in training for the Boston Marathon."

"You are. You're going to make it here. You're going to get a job and make it."

"What about a place to live in first?"

"We'll take care of that, too."

"All of a sudden you're like my mother."

She kissed him softly and smiled sweetly.

Forever it took, just like Chicago, to get into midtown. The skyline from the Brooklyn Bridge was breathtaking. Then bang, underground, whirling through the bowels of the city, and up, and there was Times Square, people like confetti from the whole world whirling at him, crowding, pushing, jostling.

"Where the hell are they going?"

"What difference does it make? They're going. It gets in your blood."

He felt like a hick. The kid from Chicago, that big, blustery, heavy-shouldered, smoke-filled, heaving, puffing, toddlin' town, a gawking hick.

She didn't show him the Empire State Building, the Statue of Liberty, Macy's, the Music Hall, but they wandered up Broadway with all the movie houses and all the theaters: Eugene O'Neill's *Ah, Wilderness,* Sinclair Lewis's *Dodsworth,* Erskine Caldwell's *Tobacco Road,* Gertrude Stein's *Four Saints in Three Acts,* the Ballet Russe at the Winter Garden, at Carnegie Hall not only the New York Philharmonic but also the Philadelphia Orchestra with Iturbi. Then blintzes and baklava at the Russian Tea Room with Jake staring at people who looked like opera stars, composers, musicians, ballet dancers, artists, and writers. Then strolling through the elegance of the Plaza and Fifth Avenue, a quick look at the Modern Museum, then along Rockefeller Center and the Public Library.

"This is where you finish your education, Jake. Everything will come together for you here. If you thank me for nothing else, it'll be for bringing you to New York. After that, Paris, Rome, and London, and you will have had it all."

"Hey." He grabbed her, held her tight a moment. "What's all

the anxiety for? You act like you want me to love this city more than you. To hell with this town. I'd love you anywhere. So relax."

"There's more." She was breathless. "Much more."

Then the *pièce de résistance:* Union Square and the crowds of unemployed in the park, the radicals and the nuts talking and haranguing, while in the second-floor window at Klein's *shlocky* department store, models paraded in cheap fur coats and dresses.

"At least in Chicago's Bughouse Square we give them dignity—the background of an important library," Jake said.

"But wait."

Down 13th Street next, Communist party headquarters, the Workers' Bookstore on the main floor crowded with people, jammed with left-wing books, pamphlets, periodicals, everybody calling each other comrade, you'd think the revolution had been won.

"You don't have to be scared here," Natasha said. "You can feel like you really belong."

Then dinner in the Village on 8th Street with the literati, the artists, the bohemians.

"You feel it, Jake? The creative spirit? The music in the air? The smell of canvas and paint? The poetry, the novels being discussed?"

Jake didn't know what he felt. Wherever he appeared in her world, in the world he believed in, he felt out of place with his thick, muscular neck, crew cut, and athletic look. How do you get that dissipated, man-of-experience appearance, that passionate aspect of saving the world, that gesture of radical sophistication, of intellectual know-it-all? Even if he grew his hair long and read everything from the Bible to Karl Marx, he could never get rid of that clean, scrubbed look of the swimmer.

"It's your world, Jake."

She was saying it the way his father and mother said, "It's your America, Jake." But this was a different America. New York, with its sights and sounds, especially its smells, was a foreign city, like nothing he'd ever expected.

Maxwell Bodenheim staggered into the restaurant. He looked as if he'd been rolling in the gutter for years, his face drawn, his deepset eyes gripping you with accusation, his gaunt body moving from table to table. He read poetry from soiled, wrinkled sheets of paper, his new work, and from tattered dog-eared books, his old work, slobbering over his audience, and snatching the nickels and dimes handed to him. Jake squirmed at the sight of him.

"He's supposed to be a communist now," Jake said.

"He's a derelict."

"Wasn't he a pal of Ben Hecht's?"

"Another decadent derelict who made it big in Hollywood. Instead of booze he drinks money. Old bohemians."

"I hear that when they lived in Chicago, they used to make bets on Michigan Avenue on who could throw the most convincing fit of DTs. They used to scare the shit out of everybody."

"I'm sure they didn't have to fake it."

"They were like the Dadaists in Paris. Louis Aragon, who is one of the big French communist writers today, used to go to the opera in a big purple cape and come out pissing on the street right in front of the carriage trade."

"Postwar reaction. Defiance of the bourgeoisie. And so futile."

Bodenheim stumbled to the door, turned around, waved a limp fist, and shouted, "Comrades, thanks for your monumental generosity. Up your buffalo-nickeled asses." Then left.

"A good actor," Jake said. "Exits on a great, memorable line."

She laughed. Then said: "I've got to go now."

"Where?"

"Party work."

"What about me?"

"I've given you the grand tour, Jake. Now you're on your own. Explore the Village. I'll see you at my aunt's later."

"I'll go with you."

"I'm sorry, Jake. You're not a party member."

"I'll join."

"I'll see you later, Jake."

It was too cold to do much exploring. He bought some stationery and took a long, thundering train ride to Brooklyn.

"You alone?" Natasha's aunt asked when he came into the house.

"Yes."

"Where's Natasha?"

"Out."

"Night after night she's always out. You'd think with a friend here she'd come home with him."

"She had something important to do."

"Always something important." Natasha's uncle looked up from the *New York Times* he was reading. "Always ready to save the world. Just like her father and mother."

"I have some things to do anyhow. Some typing." He felt bad about having been left alone but defended her. "Do you mind?"

"No."

He spread some newspapers on the dining-room table, set his portable on it, and began writing letters to the sports editors of all the papers in town, telling them who he was and asking for a job. In a few days he'd find out where he stood. If he didn't land something, then what? He needed a room; then it'd be easier to stay with Natasha; she might even move in with him. Then what, if he didn't connect with a job? He had $75 left from the $100 he'd taken from his father. He could live on $1 a day if he held his appetite down, but a room would cost him almost that much. Then there was Natasha, an occasional movie, maybe a play, a book he'd like to buy. A month, and he'd be finished. Then what? Failure? Right in front of her? What could he say: We'll live on air, the best things in life are free? Somehow he didn't feel confident his letters would hit the jackpot. Everything used to be so easy. Wherever he went he had felt like a conquering hero. Whatever had happened to the old confidence, Jake? Come on, Jake, get out those big gunboats. Let 'em have it.

He picked up the *New York Times* want-ad section. Nothing. Not a thing for him. Now that didn't take long, did it, Jake? So what else is new? Carnera, the big palooka, with an eighty-six-pound advantage, is going to take on Tommy Loughran. Hoo-ha! Big thing going on at Madison Square Garden. J'Accuse: The Case of Civilization Against Hitler. One year in office: Roosevelt against the Depression, tie score— a few hits, no runs, no errors, still trying to prevent the further advance of hard times. Russian trade unions state that only revolution can liquidate the Depression. Confidence, baby, read the *New York Times*.

Midnight. So quiet. He tried to fall asleep, but the smell of the mothballs got him coughing. He took a drink of water. Where the hell is she? He picked up a copy of *Cosmopolitan* and read a few stories. Where is she? Tired, his eyes bleary, he doused the light. Still no sleep. Boy, she's really out. Cut it out now, Jake. She's not married to you. She's free, completely liberated. Don't let your imagination go wild. Sleep. Will you, for Christ's sake, fall asleep?

He heard the front door open quietly. Close. Footsteps on the rug.

"Natasha?"

"Shhhhh."

He turned the light on. "How are things?" he whispered.

She tiptoed to him, whispered, "Too late to talk."

It was one-thirty. She looked flushed, excited.

"That must have been some meeting."

She put her finger over his lips.

"You could have come up with a big five-year plan to solve the Depression in all that time."

"We'll talk tomorrow."

He pulled her onto the couch.

"I'm so tired, Jake."

Kissing her, aroused, he forgot his earlier anxieties of failure, his lack of confidence. He needed her to be close. He felt he could knock over a bank with her.

"You have such a one-track mind, Jake."

She lay back passively.

"You all right now?" she whispered.

He nodded.

"I'm so tired. I must get some sleep."

He let her go. He turned out the light after she got to her bedroom. He felt as lonely as an orphaned kid.

The next morning she was bright and cheerful at breakfast.

"We had a wonderful day yesterday, didn't we, Jake?"

"Like they say in the cigarette ads: fully packed."

"It'll be better today."

"How about we lounge around a little, take it easy?"

"Jake, this is New York. There's so much to see, so much to do. Come on. Let's go. Time's awasting."

Down to the Metropolitan Museum, lunch at the zoo with the seals performing in the bright sunshine, a quick glance at the Frick Collection, a whirlwind subterranean ride to the Village and the Whitney. More nervous and frenetic than the day before.

"Natasha, what's with all the art, what's with all the shagging around?"

"All you had in Chicago was the Art Institute. But look at all this. And you haven't seen Fifty-seventh Street yet."

"Natasha, I like art. I like to see things through your eyes. But my main interest isn't exactly art."

"Tell me. If you went to Paris, would you miss the Louvre?"

"No."

"Would you miss the Tuileries, the Left Bank?"

"Natasha, I don't have to see everything in one day. I'm not going to die tomorrow."

"But don't you see, Jake, each day you have to live like you're going to die tomorrow."

"What next, generalissimo?"

A brisk walk up University to the Workers' Bookstore. Naturally.

"Home plate," Jake said.

She smiled, nodded, then looked away and said, "I have to leave you now."

"Where you going?"

"I have to meet some comrades. We're going to the Ballet Russe. We made the date before I knew you were coming."

"I'll go along. I want to see it, too."

"They're all sold out. We had to get tickets over a month ago."

"Doesn't everybody know there's a Depression on? There's no money for such frills?"

She laughed. "Sometimes, for a piece of culture, you starve."

"So I'll wind up with the *New York Times* again."

"Lots of people here, Jake. Browse around. You might find some good companionship."

"I don't want good companionship. I want to be with you."

"You're sweet." She kissed him lightly and left.

He browsed around. Picked up a copy of the *New Masses* and the *Daily Worker*. He browsed over the people in the place. They were better dressed than in Chicago, in hats, in suits and stylish tweedy overcoats, more businesslike, more middle-class. Many of the people knew each other, talked to one another. There was a sense of comradeship, but he didn't feel part of it. He resented her palming him off here. What the hell was she trying to do? What the hell was going on?

He had a couple of hamburgers and a piece of pie for supper. Then he went up to 42nd Street and walked into a movie house to see *The Grand Illusion*. He forgot Natasha, everything. All of a sudden he felt a hand on his jock. He jumped up, "Hey, what the hell's going on?"

The guy next to him had a silly grin on his face.

"Sit down, creep."

He moved out into the aisle, shuddering. He found another seat in the back of the house, all alone, but he couldn't get back into the film again. Shit. He got up and read the *Daily Worker* all the way back to Brooklyn; the communist box score on Roosevelt's year in office was displayed in a cartoon of Roosevelt, the big smile exuding confidence, wrapping himself in the flag of the swastika.

This time he fell asleep before Natasha came in. He didn't get up until nine the next morning. She had breakfast ready for him. Her face was flushed and excited again.

"I found a room for you, Jake."

"Great. Where?" Now he was excited.

"East of the Village. Second Avenue near Sixth Street. Right near where all the action is."

"How much?"

"Ten dollars a month."

"Wow!"

"It's in the flat of an important Yiddish poet and critic. He's a contributing editor of the *Freiheit*."

"Terrific. Let's go."

Second Avenue was a lot like Halsted or 12th streets in Chicago. It had a Cafe Royal, which catered to the tea-drinking Jewish artists and theater people who mostly read the socialist

Forward. It had Jewish restaurants and grocery stores. There was a Yiddish theater and a movie house that showed double features and eight acts of vaudeville for a dime. It smelled of 100 years of cooking, of sweat, of living and dying. Every tenement had a fire escape, the unique feature Chicago didn't have. Just down a ways were the Bowery and Chinatown. It was all one closely packed slum.

They stepped into a dirty-tiled entrance, then up three flights of scuffed stairs to Mordecai Ginsberg's flat. Natasha rang the bell, and Mordecai Ginsberg answered. He looked like a red-faced Indian with black hair that rose high in the center and was cropped close at the sides. His dark eyes were alive; he had a captivating smile; his greeting was friendly. He was a neat, graceful, light-footed man; there was something of the dandy about him. He offered them tea and conversation, then showed the flat. Jake's heart dropped when he saw the room he was going to rent. It was a small crypt. No window. There was an iron cot with a faded red spread on it, a small chest, a narrow table and chair, a shelf and a flowered drape that would serve as a closet; the wooden floor bulged in various places.

"How do you like it?" Natasha said.

"It's not exactly Evanston or Albany Park."

"You're a comrade," Mordecai said. "The whole house is yours."

"That'd be wonderful," Natasha said, "wouldn't it?"

"Yah. I guess so."

"Come on. We'll get your things, and you'll move in."

Outside, Jake said, "You really want me to move in there?"

"Until you get set, Jake. You'll never find a place as cheap. Besides, you'll be helping Mordecai out."

"Me, a philanthropist. How do you like that?"

They spent the whole morning, it seemed, on subways. After he unpacked in the little room, Natasha said, "You'll get used to it. You'll like it. There's so much going on around here. You'll spend little time in this room anyway."

"Sure."

"Hungry?"

"Starved."

They went into a dairy restaurant on Second Avenue, where

they had hamburgers made of nuts and lentils, peas and mashed potatoes. Afterward she said, "What would you like to do now?"

"I'd like to make love to you."

"Oh, Jake."

"Listen. Since I've come here, you've been running me from one place to another. It's been wonderful. It really has. But I haven't spent any time with you. I mean, alone."

"I thought we've been together a lot."

"Always with a lot of people around us. Somehow I haven't felt any intimacy. Like you've been pushing me off."

"How can you say that?"

"Maybe I'm wrong. Or I'm tired. Or I don't know what."

She looked at him a long while, studying him, then said, "All right. Let's go up to your room."

Nobody was in the apartment. It was cold. Barely any heat came up during the day. The room was hardly a place to do any entertaining. They got undressed and jumped into the cold cot and rubbed each other to warm up. When he turned out the light, it was pitch-dark. They felt as if they were in a cave. Then they settled down to making love. Suddenly, soon after he had penetrated her, she began to tremble and weep.

"What's wrong?"

She wept harder. He slipped away from her.

"What'd I do?"

"Nothing, dear, nothing." She clutched him, held him close. Her tears were hot. "Oh, God, God."

He tried to comfort her.

"You mean so much to me, I don't want to hurt you. I love you so."

He brushed her tears away, kissed her eyes.

"I'm so miserable. I don't know how to tell you. I don't want you to be angry. But while you were in Chicago, I don't know how it happened, maybe I was lonely, I don't know, but I fell in love with somebody else."

He pulled back from her, but she moved with him, held him close.

"I didn't want to, Jake. But I couldn't help it."

He sat up and turned on the light. He couldn't believe what he was hearing. He had to look at her.

She hid her face. "Please turn it off. Please."

"What do you mean you fell in love, you couldn't help it?"

"There was something about him, something happened to me. I just lost control."

"Why'd you let me come out here?"

"I didn't write. I thought maybe that would put you off. I didn't realize how much you loved me."

"You should have told me."

"Jake, I'm so sorry. Please turn that light off."

"This guy, who is he? Litvinov? Another Clark Hanover? Some big shot in the party?"

"I didn't want to hurt you. Believe me."

"Not much, you didn't."

She crawled out of bed, shivered, began to dress. Goose bumps appeared on her skin. "I still love you, Jake. I want to be your friend."

"Boy, what a runaround I've been getting. Love New York. Love the Met. Love this. Love that. But don't love me anymore. What'd you think, I'd fall in love with a statue, a painting, a street, a building? I'd have slugged it out in Chicago if it weren't for you."

"Please don't be angry."

He wasn't angry. Not much. He was seething, beside himself, choked with things he wanted to say but couldn't express.

"Don't hate me, Jake."

Black silence in him.

"I want to be your friend."

He glared at her.

"You'll remember what we had together. You'll forgive me. We'll be comrades again. I want to do something for you. Something to relieve the hurt."

"Don't. Please don't do anything more for me."

"Will you go back to Chicago now?"

"I don't know."

"I'm sorry, Jake."

She walked out. He felt as if he'd been left in a roaring wilderness. He got out of bed. Dressed. Paced the crypt. Two steps here, two steps there. Like an animal in a cage. He broke out of the room, ran outside, started walking up Second Avenue, his nerves bombarding his body.

What do I do now, go back to Chicago? Hey, Jake, you back

so soon? What'd New York do, kick you in the balls?

Hey, Jake, what's the good word, what are you doing?

Looking for work.

You, too? A guy like you? You have to go to college, be a big shot, only to wind up roaming the streets?

There was nothing for him in Chicago. He couldn't crawl back. Not yet.

He had jumping beans in his arteries, buckshot shooting from his spine, moving him, moving him, all the way into the fifties, then crosstown. There was the New York Athletic Club. God damn it, that's what he needed, a good long swim. The uniformed doorman announced him to Joe Ruddy, the coach. Okay. He was ushered in. Like the IAC. Chandeliers. Deep carpets. Rich smells. Expensive furnishings. Masculine. Quiet, dignified, unlike the tumult of the JPI, the shabby crowds of the streets. Depression? Here? You must be kidding.

"How are you, Jake?" Joe Ruddy greeted him, pink-faced, big-shouldered, big-chested, with a handshake that crushed bones. "How's the IAC? How's old Bachrach?"

"Still wearing his buckskin shoes."

"Still trying to see over his belly when he pisses?"

"He'll never make it."

Joe Ruddy laughed. "What's he doing without Weissmuller?"

"He's building a water polo team."

"How's Swanee?"

"Great." Jake wanted to hit the water.

"Moish Bender?"

"He's at the JPI."

"The way of all flesh. Why don't you come around at five, play water polo with us?"

Jake said he'd think about working out with Ruddy's team. Right now he wanted to hit the water and get lost.

He swam a mile at a good pace and forgot the world. He meant to exhaust himself so that his nerves would quiet down, so that his weariness would overcome his pain. He climbed out of the pool tingling, heaving for air, with tight bands around his chest and steel clips in the muscles of his legs. He got into a shower stall that was almost as big as his room. He turned on the hot water and let the dozen shower heads hit him from every angle. Gradually, as he loosened up, his mind came alive again, Natasha began to gnaw at his heart, and his nerves got edgy again. He took another long swim, then a steam bath, hoping he could sweat her out of his system, then another hot, needly shower, praying for that good old vigorous feeling he used to have after a workout. But it never came back. Too many things had happened.

Back in the pool area, dressed, he thanked Ruddy.

"How long do you plan to stay?" Ruddy asked.

"I don't know. I'm looking for a job."

"Doing what?"

"Newspaper. I used to work for the *American* in Chicago. Sports. Got any connections, Joe?"

"I thought I did. I tried to line up my nephew. I got shot down everywhere."

"Anything else around?"

"A good salesman, I hear, can always make a buck."

"Everywhere I go, good news."

"Come back anytime, Jake. If you get a chance, work out with the team."

He walked over to the Plaza, sat in Central Park for a while, until he got chilled; then he walked until nightfall. He had something to eat in a cafeteria, lingered, felt numb for a while, then he watched a derelict going from table to table stuffing leftovers in his mouth. His nerves started to work on him again. He got up and walked to Times Square, where he drifted about in a sea of people. He went in to see a Cagney movie, but it didn't grab him; it seemed senseless to him. He walked out, pounded through the dead, quiet streets of the garment center with the ghosts of love still haunting him. He wandered into the Village. It was getting colder and colder. He began to shiver. He finally crossed the grim, empty night streets around Wanamaker's, then climbed the three flights to his room. He felt as if he had moved into a tomb.

Tired as he was, sleep didn't come quickly. He turned and tossed about restlessly. Suddenly there was a thud against the iron bars along the bottom of his cot. Another thud. Then scratching, scuttering sounds on the wooden floor. More of them. More thuds. The whole room came alive with scurrying, thudding, pattering feet. Mice, he thought. Rats. Coming out of the walls. Hundreds of them. Running a derby. High hurdles, low hurdles, jumping, vaulting. It went on and on. He turned the light on. The room stood still. The silence overwhelmed him. He fell asleep finally, staring at the light.

The following morning he heard the doorbell ring. Then there was a knock on his door. He was naked.

"Just a minute."

He stepped into his shorts.

Natasha was with another girl when he opened the door. She looked as if she hadn't slept all night.

"How are you, Jake?"

"All right."

"I want you to meet Amy Panetta."

He said hello without looking at her.

"I hope you're still not angry. I hope you're feeling better."

"Come on, Natasha. Let's cut the crap. We're finished, all right? So let's be finished."

"I didn't want to hurt you. I want you to be my friend. I couldn't sleep thinking about you."

"Listen, you don't have to feel guilty about me. You fell in love. All right. It happens. I'm glad it happened now. Not later."

"Oh, Jake, I'm the worst thing that could have ever happened to you. I'm no good for you. I'm too neurotic, too sick for you. All I could do is drag you down. Once you get some perspective, once you see the truth, you'll realize it."

"Okay, I'm getting the message. So long."

"I wanted you to meet Amy. She's quite beautiful. You'll like her."

He still didn't look at Amy. "Listen, Natasha. I don't want any consolation prizes. I'm a champ, a winner. I never settle for less than first prize. Please go."

"Anytime you want me, anything I can do for you, please let me know."

He eased them both out. He found he was trembling, holding back tears. Jesus Christ!

That morning and that afternoon he went to every newspaper

he'd sent letters to, even out to the Brooklyn *Eagle*. Nothing. Some of the sports editors wouldn't even see him. He came back to his room feeling as if everything within him had been eviscerated. He threw himself like a lump on the cot and stared at the ceiling. Now what?

For days he wandered the streets. Passed the breadlines in the Bowery, the crowds outside employment agencies. In the evening he knocked himself out playing water polo at the New York AC. He asked the guys if they knew of anything. He was put in touch with an advertising agency, a public relations firm, a book publishing company. They all were sympathetic and polite; they took his name and address for future reference. When they heard the Second Avenue address, a cloud would come over their faces. From now on he'd say he lived at the New York AC.

Sometimes, after his wanderings about town, he'd drift over to the Workers' Bookstore. Subconsciously he wanted to see Natasha, even if it was painful. One day he thought: I'll try the *Daily Worker*. They used to have a sports column. Maybe they could use another one. I'll try.

He stepped into the rickety, beat-up elevator, crowded with functionaries of the Communist party.

"The *Daily Worker*," he said.

Eyes turned to him. He felt like a misfit. It wasn't that he wasn't dressed as well as the other passengers, with an overcoat, a suit of clothes, but he didn't wear a hat, didn't have that New York Union Square look, that sense of revolutionary fervor. He still looked like a college athlete. He'd have to let his hair grow, get rings under his eyes from a lot more reading, appear engrossed with weighty Marxist thoughts. He was let out on the sixth floor.

The offices were guarded by a bruiser who looked like a bouncer: smashed nose, puffy lips, killer eyes.

"What do you want?"

"I want to see the editor."

"Who? Hathaway? He's not here."

"Paul Logan. Used to run the sports column."

"He's the city editor now."

"I'd like to see him."

334 • Windy City

The bruiser studied Jake carefully. Then he picked up the phone and dialed.

"Who wants to see him?"

"Jake Davidson. Tell him I want to do the sports column for him."

The bruiser talked into the phone, then turned to Jake and said, "He's not interested."

"Tell him I used to be the national intercollegiate backstroke champ, I worked for the *American* in Chicago, I'm a member of the John Reed Club. Tell him."

The bruiser hesitated.

"Go on. Tell him."

The bruiser told him.

"Okay," he said to Jake. He pressed a buzzer. "Go on in."

Paul Logan sat alone at a large, scarred desk which was piled with newspapers, newsprint, proofsheets, copy from reporters, columnists, and the United Press. He was in a flannel shirt, his sleeves rolled up, a nice Jewish kinky-haired man with a long nose and a loose mouth. The placed looked nothing like a newspaper office. No slot. No copy desk. Just a number of plywood cubicles, typewriters rattling away in them. Logan talked out the side of his mouth. "So you're Jake Davidson."

"In person."

"Member of the party?"

"No. I just got out of college."

"Fellow traveler?"

"You could say that."

"What'd you do for the *American?*"

"Football, basketball, wrestling, track, you name it. I can write about all of them."

"School of Journalism?"

"Guilty."

"You know you won't get rich here."

"I figure."

"You won't even get famous. Maybe more like infamous."

"I'd like to do a column for you."

"We can't really pay you."

"I've got to live."

"Can you get along on ten dollars a week?"

He felt his stomach squeezed tight. "I'll try."

"Okay, Jake. You've got your column. I don't know how long it'll last. We're all battling for space. Come in tomorrow. Do it."

"Thanks."

Logan wrote out a pay requisition. "Go to the cashier and pick up some money. Good luck."

He danced out of the place. It wasn't the *Times,* the *Daily News,* or the Hearst papers, but he had a job, he was going to do a column. Hey, Westbrook Pegler, Red Smith, Paul Gallico, John Kieran, watch out. The dialectical materialism of sports, how do you like that? I was a subsidized athlete for the Workers' School: my first column.

In the crowded elevator, then among the browsers in the bookstore, he wanted to tell everybody: "Hey, I'm right in there now, a functionary, on the staff of the *Daily Worker,* chief commissar of sports. Hey-hey."

Jesus Christ, there wasn't anybody to talk to, not a soul. He couldn't go to the New York AC and say, "Hey, crack a bottle of champagne with me; I'm on the *Daily Worker.*" But he had to tell somebody. He called Natasha in Brooklyn. Told her the news.

"Hey, I'm not mad anymore."

"I'm so glad for you, Jake."

"Celebrate with me."

"You'll be so wonderful at the job. So good for the party. You're a pro, Jake. A real pro."

"Come on down. We'll have dinner."

"I can't. I wish I could. Really, I wish I could."

Everything in him went flat and hollow.

"Yah," he said. "Yah. Okay. I understand."

"Don't be angry, Jake. I'll see you from time to time."

"I'll be kind of busy after tomorrow."

"Good luck, Jake. All the best."

He hung up and said, "Shit."

He buried himself in his room and wrote a biting satirical piece on "Stadiums and Colleges: Who Supports Who?" He rewrote it in his plywood cubicle at the office the next day. Logan liked it.

He was in. He reeled out of the office to Stillman's gym, where Carnera was working out. Carnera was heavy, slow, a Goliath. Jake tried to talk to him. His handlers swarmed all over him.

"Hey, kid, what do you want, who are you?"

"I'm the sports editor of the *Daily Worker*."

"Get the fuck outa here, you fuckin' commie."

From now on, Jake thought, I'll tell them I'm from the *Daily News* or the *Times*. He did a piece on Carnera: "Goliath Comes to Town: a Barnum & Bailey Circus." When he saw his by-line, he thought he'd burst.

Once the pressure and excitement of doing his daily column eased, he found plenty of time on his hands, time to feel lonely, to think of Natasha. At night he'd listen to the rats in his dark room. They were holding regular Olympic Games now. In and out of the walls, they were running all over the place. And Natasha would begin to gnaw at him. He got more and more objective about her, took some good long looks at her.

Natasha had a mind grounded in Marx and Engels and a heart stirred by Tchaikovsky and Sibelius. While a Young Pioneer she had studied Lenin and Marx, but she dreamed of being swept up by Arabian princes and made love to on magic Persian carpets. She fantasized pirates conquering mystic islands for her and loving her with brute force; always she was overwhelmed, swept away, made love to extravagantly by men with minds like Bukharin and looks like Spencer Tracy. She wanted to act upon the world like an Isadora Duncan, but she was really a Madame Bovary, a born loser emotionally, living on codeine crutches.

So how could he possibly fulfill her? How could anybody? What did she see in him to begin with? He could only fail her. Is that what she looked for, somebody to fortify her own failure? Well, he wasn't going to give her that: neither his failures nor his triumphs. If he was to come out of this, his first big affair, intact, he had to forget her, go out on his own lonely journeys until he found somebody else. God knew, he too had to find himself, he too had to know his worth, his place in the world. So onward, comrade, he said to himself, while the rats were now running steeplechases, on to the quest for your own holy grail.

Jake felt no compulsion to join the Communist party. Nobody

urged him. He said, "I'll do sports, you throw in the class struggle." But everybody assumed he was a member of the party, a part of the central committee, a young man who helped form policy. He was never invited to editorial meetings. Clarence Hathaway and Paul Logan were the liaisons from the ninth floor, where the national committee was located. The William Z. Fosters and Earl Browders never came down to the sixth floor. But Jake felt himself a vital part of the inroads the communists were making among the depressed people in the country. Its cultural arm, the John Reed Club, was a flourishing organization, attracting more and more intellectuals, artists, writers, composers, musicians, theatrical and motion-picture people. Their talents, he felt, were rubbing off on him.

As he got acquainted with the staff, he started to go to parties and left-wing affairs. He met more people. Though he received very little money from the *Daily Worker,* he found that he got a lot of fringe benefits. You'd think he owned Cadillacs, had access to Café Society, was an international playboy, the girls were that impressed when he met them. When they asked him what he thought of a particular political problem, he'd smile evasively and say, "I'll tell you tomorrow, after I've read the *Daily Worker.*" Laughter. "Very cute."

He met important literary people who were great sports fans and who offered to write columns for him for free, and he obliged them. He'd sit at their feet, hardly being able to talk, and just admire them. The *New Masses* had announced a prize contest for the best proletarian novel. He began working on one during his free time. It was the same old story about a college athlete who falls in love with a rich girl whose father takes him into his laundry business. Now he gave it a proletarian slant. Depression time. Workers exploited. The athlete's values change; he organizes the workers, leads them in a strike. The girl now forces him to choose between her father's values and his new way of life. He decides to remain with the workers, continue with the strike. That, he thought, should be a winner.

Then Eddie Lopkin, the editor of *The Pioneer,* a magazine for kids, called and asked him to do a sports story for his magazine. "We don't get enough sports stories," he said. "We're heavy in the *Weltschmerz* and politics departments; but kids like sports, and we're lightweights there."

"No class struggle?"

"Just a good sports story."

But when he turned in a story, Lopkin wanted a little struggle in it. Lopkin was a tall, skinny man with thin blond hair, a pudgy nose, and a mustache. He could whistle whole operas. Sometimes, to help him think, he'd whistle arias. He came up with a little class-consciousness idea. Jake rewrote the story. It appeared the following month with illustrations. It impressed the shit out of Jake. It also impressed Natasha. She called.

"My God, Jake, that story was wonderful."

He had almost forgotten her, he'd been so busy.

"I told you you'd make it. I'm so happy for you. What about everything else? How are you doing?"

"You mean how's my love life? I go to affairs, give them that Maxim Gorki look; they think I'm shaking hands with Earl Browder; what more do I need?"

She laughed. "A little more money?"

"Or a schoolteacher for a wife."

"Then you wouldn't be free to Gorki around."

"Are you kidding? Behind nearly every twenty-dollar-a-week functionary is a good, honest, hardworking wife who keeps the home fires burning while he fiddles in other homes."

"Cynic."

"The top political brain here, his wife does publicity at Doubleday, when I want to know where the best pickup spot is, I follow him. And how are you doing?"

"Fine, Jake. Fine."

"Working?"

"Not yet."

"Still in love?"

"More than ever."

"Terrific."

"I just called to tell you how proud I am of you, that I think of you often."

"A little more money, and I'd be happier. It's rough when I can't blow somebody to a dinner, not even a cup of coffee and a bran muffin after an affair. On ten dollars a week, there's nothing left for gallantry. I'm a bourgeois at heart."

"You can always say, 'How about a nightcap, your place?'"

"Only Clark Gable or Cary Grant could get away with it."

She laughed, then said, "Still love me?"

"No more, Natasha. I've finally worked you out of my system."

"Are you my friend?"

"Yes. I can be your friend now."

"A warm friend?"

"A friend friend. One of the boys. Not an intimate friend."

"Too many accommodating girls over the dam, huh?"

"If you want to put it that way," he said.

"I'm glad it's all working out for you, Jake."

He thought he detected a tear in her voice.

"May I call you again?"

"Anytime, Natasha."

"I'm glad you're happy, Jake."

This time, before she hung up, her voice cracked. He wondered what that call was about. But he didn't have time to dwell on it. Logan called him and asked him to write some heads; then he went to work on his novel; then Eddie Lopkin phoned and asked if he'd like to go to a party with him.

"Sure," Jake said.

"Should we have dinner together?"

"Why not?"

It was springtime. The weather was clear, crisp, turning warmer. People on the streets didn't look as grim as before. If they weren't eating well, at least they had more color in their faces. Jake met Eddie at the Kavkaz, a Russian restaurant on 14th Street near Second Avenue. Jake budgeted his expenses as carefully as he could. Fifteen cents for breakfast, twenty-five or thirty cents for lunch, thirty-five cents for dinner. Another twenty cents for tips, but when he ran short, he had to stiff the waiters. Rent $2.50 a week. That left him with a huge $1 for laundry, subway fares, an occasional movie, a big time on the town. Clothes, forget it. If he got sick, Bellevue. He had lost four pounds, but he felt good.

He splurged at the Kavkaz: beef stroganoff and coffee.

"No baklava?" Eddie said.

"You have some. I'll take a piece of yours."

Eddie made $20 a week; he could afford the finer things in life, like Baklava.

"Where you staying, Jake?"

"Some rat-infested tenement."

"I saw a railroad apartment on Seventeenth Street, a pretty good deal."

"How much?"

"Thirty a month."

"I'd have to give up the Stork Club and Twenty-One."

"What are you paying now?"

"Ten a month, but even that's too much. Some days I feel my belly button touching my spine."

"Let's take the place. You kick in with the ten, and I'll handle the rest."

"What about gas, electricity?"

"A few dollars."

"If we only had that Moscow gold everybody says we get."

They moved in the next day. Jake scrounged a table, chairs, a mattress from the Salvation Army. Eddie had linens, towels, and some furniture from his last place. The flat looked huge to Jake. He listened that night for the sound of rats. Silence. Cockroaches were all over, but they made no noise. The air in the freshly painted apartment felt cleaner. If worse came to worst, he could live on that.

People were losing faith in Roosevelt despite his cocky smile, his confident speeches, his populist appeal. The farmers wanted higher prices; labor found the government ineffective in enforcing its right to organize; business feared, mistrusted, and rebelled against him; the millions of unemployed, their savings used up or lost in bank failures, were more desperate than ever. More and more people began to look to the left. On May Day a quarter million people marched down the streets of New York and gathered in Union Square; another half million watched the parade and cheered. Jake thought the revolution, not necessarily a bloody one, would take place the next day. The left now was his religion, his family, his hope. It concentrated him, made him feel alive, gave his writing direction. Still, he didn't join the party. There was an inner core in him that held him back. Maybe he was too much like his father: a socialist, a good Jew, but a member of neither the Socialist party nor a synagogue, a believer but not a joiner. Maybe it was fear, or an inability to surrender himself to the party's disciplines and doctrines, or the years of dreaming of making it big in a democracy or of depending solely on his own guts and talent from the lone spirit of his swimming days. His individuality, he felt, was a sacred jewel; nobody must rob him of it.

Eddie said, "Why don't you join up?"

Jake had no logical excuse to offer.

"You're for us, aren't you?"

"A hundred percent. You're the Cubs and the Sox for my money."

"You're on the *Daily Worker*. Everybody thinks you're a member. You might as well be one in fact."

"I'm not a joiner."

"What about the teams you were on?"

"I was still a loner."

Eddie didn't push it. Neither did anybody else. Not even Natasha when he was close to her. He was grateful for that.

From time to time, through his sister, Miriam, Jake heard from home. Everybody was getting along fine. His father had arranged a loan for Nachum to buy a newsstand on the Northwest Side; his wife was pregnant and would have to quit her job soon. Miriam was also pregnant. His brother, Harry, was getting to be a real goldarnit. Thirteen years old, just bar mitzvah, and he was yelling for a car, and he'd already made it with the girl next door, who was a junior in high school; it was a scandal. His mother, the original romantic, went to the movies a couple of times a week; at ten cents you couldn't afford not to go; she kept asking when he, Jake, was going to write a movie, a big romantic one for Garbo or Joan Crawford or Claudette

Colbert with Clark Gable or Fredric March or Ronald Cole-
man.

Then a sad letter. Bubi had died. His sister wrote:

"To the last, she was cheerful, satisfied, glad to be alive, happy
when people were around her. Never complained. If she had any
pains, nobody knew it. Maybe because she couldn't communicate. Like a baby in an old body. No words. Silence. Always
silence. Only eyes she had. She went to sleep one night last week
and died. It was her heart. The doctor said it was painless. She
may have had an attack or two, but we didn't know. She is now
resting in peace."

Jake was choked up. Ever since she'd come to Chicago, when
he had met her at the La Salle Street Station, he wondered what
her life had been like all those silent years in Russia, bringing
sons into the world, caring for them until they grew up, this
innocent, speechless, unhearing person, then coming here to
America. What were her hopes, dreams, frustrations, anxieties,
desires? Was it like living in a cave at the bottom of the sea?
Imagine her bewilderment and terror in not being able to hear or
speak when she came out of her scarlet fever. Imagine bringing
up her sons, never hearing their cries or their joyful laughter,
never really knowing what they felt. How closely she had to
watch people to feel what they were thinking or saying. What
love she must have needed to survive, to keep from becoming a
bitter, resentful, angry woman. How quick she was to respond to
everybody's needs, to give everybody her love. Was that her
secret of preventing people from hurting her? That, and her
patience, and her acceptance of her fate?

Oh, Bubi, Bubi.

Summer rolled in, hot, humid, sticky, every street like a set
from Elmer Rice's *Street Scene.* At night the sheets got wet from
sweat. Jake's clothes got threadbare. He cut down on his meals
so that he could buy a few shirts, socks, a pair of pants. He
wasn't starving, but he was always hungry. He lost a few more
pounds. He was looking gaunt. He'd joke about it: "I'm down to
my fighting weight. . . . It's that Chinese food; instant hunger

afterward." He stopped going to the New York AC. He thought he was beginning to look seedy. He asked Logan for a raise.

"We don't have it, Jake. Maybe you ought to do what other guys have done. Marry a girl with a good job. It'll solve all your problems."

"Other guys are getting at least twenty a week."

"They're full time. Necessary."

"Sports is dispensable, frills and thrills, huh?"

"Let's face it, Jake. Our readers aren't really interested."

"The masses go for sports. Most workingmen, the first thing they turn to are the sports pages."

"We don't have the masses. If we did, we'd have enough money to pay you." Logan gave him a couple of dollars out of petty cash. "Expenses."

Jake left. *Mene, mene, tekel.* He could see the handwriting on the wall. He sweated over his novel. It had to be good; he could see the perspiration staining the pages. He wrote some short stories, hoping for a big quick buck, and sent them to *Liberty* and *Cosmopolitan* and the *Saturday Evening Post.* They all were rejected. He occasionally played the horses in a poolroom on 14th Street, but he picked losers. Hey, Pa, give me a horse, a long shot. Better yet, give me a daily double or a three-horse parlay.

Summer heat and hunger wore him out. He began to lose interest in his column. So he fought for the Negroes to get into baseball. So he wrote about the great surge in sports in the Soviet Union, about fighters with fantasies of glory, about the exploitation of professional athletes. So what? All of it seemed so unimportant. As the boys said: "First you gotta eat; then you can fuck." When it got too hot, ten-cent movies in air-conditioned theaters cooled him off.

Right in the middle of the summer, Natasha came back to him. She seemed to whirl out of the Workers' Bookstore as he got out of the elevator from the sixth floor.

"Jake!"

She looked something like when he had first met her: her eyes dark and haunting, her face pale and pained, with that Garbo look.

"Natasha."

"I'm so glad to see you."

"How you doing?"

"I read your column every day. It's the first thing I turn to. It's bright; it's crisp; it's wonderful."

"Write a letter to my boss. Maybe it'll get me a raise."

"Where are you living now?"

"Over on Seventeenth Street."

"Can we go there? Talk?"

"Sure."

The hardwood floors were dusty; there were cobwebs about; newspapers were piled up in a corner of the living room. A mattress with a batik spread on the floor was the couch; there were a few chairs around it. In the bedrooms the beds were unmade, the linens soiled. It was hot and stuffy. But she said, when she entered, "How nice." She was on the verge of tears.

"Hardly the Taj Mahal."

"It's your own place."

He'd made a mistake in bringing her; he was suddenly very uncomfortable with her. "It's too hot in here. Let's get something to eat."

"Later."

"No, now. Let's go." He took her hand and led her out.

In the restaurant she talked compulsively about how wonderful New York was, even in the summertime. There was always so much going on. She'd gone to Camp Unity for a couple of weeks and had a grand time there: lectures, concerts, plays, dancing, hiking, swimming, always something going on, a summer retreat, a cultural haven, with comrades about that you could trust.

The frayed edges of her life, which she was trying to hang onto, slowly slipped away. Tears came to her eyes. She fought hard to keep from sobbing. "Oh, Jake, what a mess I've made of my life. What a mess."

He took her hand, held it, hoping the touch would comfort her; he didn't know what to say. People were looking their way. He felt embarrassed.

"We better go, Natasha."

"Yes, yes. Let's go."

Outside, walking to his place, she cried out, "Why did I ever come here?"

"You wanted to find a job, find yourself."

"Jake, I lie to myself, I lie to myself all the time. Even the man I fell in love with, a lie, something in my imagination. Oh, God, what I do to myself. How I destroy myself."

"You'll get over it."

"All the time it was you I loved. What a mistake I made."

He found himself retreating from her.

"I've been such a fool," she said.

Eddie was in the apartment when they got there. Jake was glad. Maybe she'd control herself. But after the introductions she acted as if she were alone with Jake. She flung her arms around him and cried bitterly. Eddie retreated to his bedroom.

"Let's go home, Jake."

"What do you mean, home? I am home."

"I mean Chicago, where we belong."

Icebergs formed in his belly.

"We were so happy before we came here. They're all strangers here. Nobody cares. Back home we have friends, people who love us, a different climate. We can be happy again there. I'll make you so happy, Jake."

Over the months he had built up a wall of armor. He didn't ever want to be hurt again. The icebergs in his freezing belly jammed tight.

"I've got a job here, Natasha, things to do."

"They're exploiting you. They don't care about you. You'll do better in Chicago. You can get something there. You'll be a far more important person."

"Natasha, what we had between us, it's over. We can't pick up where we left off."

She wasn't listening. "Together we can make it. I'll find work there. We'll get married. You wanted to marry me, didn't you?"

He nodded. "But not anymore, Natasha."

She heard only her own anguished heart. "We'll find a place of our own. The Near North Side. It'll be so wonderful to live there. Right near the lake, near Michigan Avenue, where everything is happening. We'll have a nice place, good friends.

All my opera records, symphonies. People will want to visit us. Oh, Jake, it'll be so nice."

She held him tight, kissed him. Icicles hung from his heart. He moved away from her.

"What's wrong, Jake?"

"I don't love you anymore."

"You will again. I'm the same person you loved before."

"But I'm not. I've changed. So have you. You just can't turn it off and on like that."

She couldn't seem to believe it. She looked small, abandoned, fear piercing her eyes.

"Oh, God, I'll kill myself."

"Come on, Natasha. You left me when I came here. You'd fallen in love with somebody else. There'll be others."

She threw herself on the living-room mattress and gave herself over to her sobbing. Eddie came out of his bedroom.

"What's going on?"

Jake gestured; he was helpless.

"Can I do anything?" Eddie asked.

Jake stood limply by. Eddie stooped down to Natasha.

"Can I do anything? Get you a drink or something?"

She shook her head. She got up, wiped her eyes, blew her nose. "Will I see you again, Jake?"

"We better not."

"You're sure? You don't want to try?"

"I'm sorry, Natasha."

She looked forlorn. His heart turned over. He put his hands deep in his pockets, rooted himself to the floor.

"Good-bye, Jake." She started for the door, beginning to cry again.

Eddie stepped to Jake. "You can't let her go home alone like that."

"That's all right, Eddie," Natasha said.

"You going to let her go home alone like that?" Eddie said.

Jake held himself firm, didn't move.

"Come on." Eddie took Natasha's arm. At the door, before he left with her, he said, "You bastard."

Jake went out later and walked the hot streets. Sweat poured out of him. All over, people were standing and sitting outside their buildings, looking as moist and drained as he felt. Some people were bedding down on fire escapes. Over and over again, Jake said to himself, "I'm not a yo-yo. I'm not going to hang myself on her emotional flip-flops. If I go back to her, she'll destroy me; I can't do it, no matter what."

"What'd you say, mister?"

"Nothing," Jake said. He was talking to himself, had the mumblies. So many people in New York had the mumblies. Especially on a hot, breezeless, humid, frenzied, sleepless night. Back in his apartment he took a cool shower, then worked on his novel awhile. It was his escape hatch. He looked up when Eddie came back from taking Natasha home.

He knew at once that Eddie was in love with her. Eddie, who could whistle whole operas, he *would* be a sucker for her. Oh, boy!

"I don't understand you, Jake."

"What's to understand? I'm out, and you're in."

But that wasn't true. She kept coming around, to see not Eddie but him. He was always busy, always had a sports event to cover, something to do. When he came to the *Daily Worker* and left, he began to use the 12th Street exit because many times she'd meet him outside the Workers' Bookstore on 13th Street. He stayed away from the apartment as much as he could.

Earlier, at a left-wing affair, Jake had met a girl who was a social worker. She had a good steady job, shared an apartment in Chelsea with another social worker who was shacked up with a left-wing, soccer-playing, unemployed Hungarian with few principles and a lot of charm. This girl, Elaine, had a Rubenesque body with voluptuous breasts, thick hips, and large buttocks. She was a robust, anything-goes lay, who took him to the theater, sometimes cooked gourmet meals for him, and was more generous with all her possessions, including her body, than anybody he'd ever known. She had given him the key to her apartment, a symbol of total commitment to him. She was the kind of girl a guy like Jake, who wanted to write, should have moved in with. But she excited him only in bed; he kept looking for other girls. Sometimes, late at night, when he was lonely and horny, he'd come to her, and she would love him without question.

Now, to stay away from Natasha, he virtually moved in with Elaine. He brought some of his clothes over. She took it as a sign that he had moved in with her. But he hadn't. He had his dinners alone or with a friend or two from the *Worker,* and he'd spend time with some of the literary people he had met, and he'd go to the movies; then he'd go over to Elaine's. He always felt like a thief, letting himself in with her key, stealing into her room, crawling in beside her, taking what he needed, then sneaking off into his deep sleep and finding her gone when he woke up. She demanded nothing of him, and all it did was fill him with guilt. But during this time, to protect himself from Natasha, he needed Elaine. A weak moment, and he might crumble.

Jake hoped that Eddie's having fallen in love with Natasha might make her forget him. But Eddie was too easy, too soft, never up to any of her fantastic dreams. He loved her platonically. He listened to her talk about her sad love affairs and her love for Jake. And he fell deeper in love with her.

"You don't mind if I go out with her," he said.

"Not at all," Jake said.

"Why don't you love her anymore?"

"I just don't. Explaining it is impossible."

"She's so beautiful, so sensitive, so cultivated. She's got everything."

"I hope you'll be happy with her."

"But it's you she wants."

Eddie kept seeing Natasha, then told Jake how much she still loved him. He was a messenger, falling deeper in love as he pleaded her case, while Jake escaped nightly to the fervent, *zoftig* arms of Elaine, who gave him comfort and guilt. It was all like something out of a Chekhovian nightmare.

The only way out was to find a place of his own or to quit his job and leave town. He knew that he was the most unnecessary man on the staff of the *Worker.* Maybe he was asking to be fired, but he asked Logan again for a raise.

"I can't make it on that money." he said.

"What'll make you happy?"

"Twenty a week. I'll become a general reporter and rewrite man, too."

"Hathaway is out of town now. I'll take it up with him and the board when he gets back."

It was a feverish time. Europe was in turmoil. Hitler was becoming more powerful every day, threatening Austria today, tomorrow the world. Stories of his extermination of Jews, political opponents, and Catholics, were becoming more prominent. Russia was growing stronger and stronger, making deeper inroads in the minds and hearts of people everywhere. Strikes were breaking out all over: general strikes led by the teamsters in Minneapolis, by the longshoremen in San Francisco. John L. Lewis with his powerful mine workers was threatening to leave the AFL to form a big industrial union, terrifying the craft unions and the establishment; it was Wobbly talk. The sharecroppers were organizing; so were the teachers, the poor on relief, the vets. Big news stories were breaking every day. America was at the brink of a revolution, and Roosevelt was working hard with his brain trust to save the country from communism and disaster, to bring about a quiet, peaceful revolution of his own.

With all that going on, Jake's column was cut out from time to time. The battle for space in the few pages of the *Daily Worker* was so strong that one week his column was dropped four days in a row. Jake fought for his column, his job, for more money, but knew it was a lost cause.

Early in the fall Natasha got a job substitute teaching in Harlem. She called Jake at the office, breathless with excitement.

"I'm so thrilled. It's so wonderful. Let me take you to dinner tonight."

"I'm sorry, but I have a date."

"Tomorrow night."

"I'll be busy."

"Jake, I want you to share my happiness."

He had enough icebergs in him to sink the *Titanic* and hated himself for it. "I'm all tied up. Meetings, sports events to cover, trying to finish my novel. But I'm so happy for you, Natasha.

We'll run into each other, okay?"

"Okay." Her voice sounded as if he had kicked her guts out.

That night he was impotent with Elaine.

"What's wrong, honey?"

"I'm not a nice person."

"What happened?"

"Sometimes I feel like my heart's been torn out of me. Like ice is running through my arteries. Like I've been shot full of novocaine."

"Oh, honey."

She worked at him and worked at him. Nothing. He fell asleep. He woke up later feeling as if he'd fallen into a Bessemer furnace. It was her body.

"Oh, honey," she said. "You're all there. You're really all there."

"Yes," he said. "Burn me up."

The following day Logan called him over to his desk.

"Well, Jake."

One look at Logan's face, with his twisted mouth in a sour droop, his dark eyes full of sympathy, told him what he expected. "You don't have to tell me, Paul."

"Sports is very superfluous at this point."

"I know. Who cares who made the touchdown when the money is on the revolution?"

"Something like that. The boys said it's a luxury. Whipped cream on a picket line."

"Well, Paul, it's been fun." He'd expected the ax all along, but it didn't lessen the hurt.

"What'll you do?"

"I'll take all my clips from the *Worker* and send them to Hearst. I'm sure he'll give me a job."

They both smiled bitterly.

"After the revolution we'll give you three pages of coverage, a car, a dacha in Miami, an honorary place in the May Day parades."

"I can't wait."

Logan shook his hand. "Good luck. What else can I tell you?"

When he got outside, he felt as if he'd been cut adrift. There was no reason for him to be here any longer. He walked to his apartment and packed. Tomorrow he'd go back to Chicago.

There was a knock on the door. It was Natasha. She had a date to meet Eddie. She saw the suitcase in the living room filled with his clothes.

"Where are you going, Jake?"

"Home."

"Chicago?"

"Yes."

"What happened to your job?"

"It got sandbagged by the revolution."

"Don't go, Jake."

"There's nothing here for me."

"I'm here."

Eddie came in at that moment. He said hello, but she disregarded the greeting.

"I don't want you to go, Jake," she said. "You haven't finished your novel. You haven't done a lot of things."

"Don't, Natasha."

"I've got a job now. Not full time but enough to take care of us. I don't want you to worry about anything. I know I've hurt you, but I'll make up for it. I want you to stay."

He shook his head. He knew that after a while, once she had him, she'd fall in love with somebody else. Her illusions, her desires were too big. Who could fill her great romantic heart? Sibelius could send her off in search of some noble Finn. Dumas could whirl her into the arms of some lusty swashbuckling Frenchman. Schnitzler could send her into sweeping waltzes along the Danube. Who could compete against such fantasies?

"Say good-bye, Natasha."

"You'll regret it."

"Let's say I'll never forget you."

She smiled wanly, dry-eyed: a small consolation. She turned to Eddie. "Where are we going?"

"We'll have dinner first."

After they left, Jake had a lonely dinner. He walked up to 42nd Street and saw a Russian movie. Then he walked to Elaine's to say good-bye.

"Will you come back?" she asked, hurt but undemanding.

"Someday."

"I won't be here for you."

"I know."

"Love me."

When he got back to his apartment the following morning to collect his valise and typewriter for his trip back home, he found Natasha in bed with Eddie. She had finally given herself to him, and he could stop being her Cyrano. Jake hoped they would be good for each other . . . at least for a while. Oh, love, oh, careless love.

BOOK 5

The bus trip was long and tedious, rainy and gray. The fields were wet and harvested, the trees bare, the flat landscape monotonous; an autumn chill worked through his bones. Everything, even the people in the small towns standing idly about, seemed lifeless. In Gary, Hammond, East Chicago, South Chicago, most of the Bessemer fires were banked, most of the smokestacks stood stark and useless against the sky; the refineries were working at less than half capacity; the Calumet River was sluggish with empty boats on its banks. The great industrial belt of Chicago drooped at half-mast. The best you could say of hard times was that the air was cleaner, the laundry bills were smaller.

Once the bus tooled down the Outer Drive and Jake saw the vast expanse of the lake and the beauty of the Chicago skyline, his heart began to beat harder. That was the city he knew. That was where he'd had his great triumphs. That was where he didn't have to explain himself. That was where he belonged. He didn't have to ask anybody any questions about where to go or how to get there. He knew this town, every mile of its transit system, its seasons, its violence, its hard, bustling, driving ways, every ugly blemish, but also its grandeur, its poetry, its heartbeat. It was home.

Back on the West Side, it didn't matter that the neighborhood looked slummier, that people were losing their pride, giving up under the stress of the times, looking more hopeless; the houses still looked familiar, and so did the people. They nodded, said hello, smiled; he wasn't among strangers.

"Hey, Jake, how was New York?"

"Fine, fine."

"You back for good?"

"Who knows?"

"Glad to be back?"

"Oh, boy!"

His mother was alone when he came in. Surprise, surprise. She almost fainted. Later his brother, Harry, greeted him with: "How's the big shot?"

"Still shooting at elephants."

Harry had really grown, was almost Jake's size, broader, heavier in the beam, dark-eyed, black-haired, handsome. His mother called him her little Valentino.

"Already a regular lover," she said. "A sheik, no?"

Jake tousled his hair. It embarrassed Harry.

"Boy," Jake said to his father when he got home from the newsstand, "I could have used you as a handicapper in New York."

"You mean you would have turned the *Daily Worker* into a race sheet?"

"Hey, I'd have been indispensable. A winner every day for the working class."

"So, Jake?" Which meant: What are your plans?

"Pop, you think the *Jewish Daily Forward* could use a good sports reporter?"

"As much as they could use a good bookie. . . . So?"

"I've got a novel to finish."

"Good." Which meant: Whatever Jake wanted to do, it was okay with his father.

His mother said, "He takes after your father, the *sofer*, the scribe."

"An honorable profession."

"My son, the novelist."

They didn't ask him what had happened in New York, why he hadn't taken the town by storm, why he'd come back. They saw that he was thinner, his clothes were threadbare, he hadn't fared too well. He was alive and well; that's all that mattered. They accepted him for what he was. He was home.

The house seemed quiet. Harry at school. His father at work. Miriam married. Bubi, though she had always been silent, gone. Nachum, away now for years. Only his mother in the kitchen or shopping. Everything was so clean and orderly. It was almost unbearable. He could hardly write in the immaculate silence.

It was nothing new for men to be out of work on the West Side. Now it was an accepted fact. But the unemployed men stayed indoors discreetly; they were ashamed to be seen. Daytime belonged to the women. Jake could hear them.

"Mrs. Davidson, your son is home?"

"Yes, thanks God."

"What's he doing?"

"He's a writer. A novelist."

"Oho!"

Sometimes, when he left the house, he could hear them.

"Don't worry, Mrs. Davidson, your son will be all right."

"I'm not worried."

"All he needs is time."

They were full of mock pity and relief that even he, Jake Davidson, a college graduate, a celebrated athlete in a country where athletes were like gods, even he was walking the streets.

Where was he going? The JPI, where he could take a swim and crap around with the guys. Joey Gans was in medical school. Fasso Sardell and a couple of other guys were substitute teaching while waiting for teachers to die or retire so that they could get a regular appointment. A little clout from Morrie Benjamin and Maxie Katz went a long way, but they had a lot of unemployed teachers to take care of, so they had to spread the wealth. Sooner or later, the boys said, everybody dies. Sandy Meyers was back from Hawaii, writing plays and working for his brother the button manufacturer and organizing the workers into a union. Benny Gordon was hustling wax products for floors; he called himself a safety engineer, which was a high-class title for handling janitor supplies. A couple of nights a week Jake played water polo with the JPI team. Other nights he went to left-wing affairs and to John Reed Club meetings.

Where else was he going? He dropped in on Les Fishel at the *American.*

"Jake, what have you been up to?"

"Writing." How could he tell him he'd been with the *Daily Worker?*

"Where? What?"

"The *Midweek Pictorial* in New York," he lied. "It went out of business."

"Hey, that's something. What else?"

"I'm working on a novel."

"No kidding. That's great. Hit it with a novel, and you've got it made."

Les got busy working on a headline. Jake stood there.

"Still swimming?"

"A little."

Silence. Jake looked down at Les's knotted hair, his pencil crossing out a word, inserting another to make the head fit. Jake shuffled about, hated the half-truths, lies, evasions of his present life. Les was in a sweat, burying himself in the headline.

"Anything doing, Les?" He hated how hoarse his voice got. "Anything around?"

Les didn't look up. "Not a thing, Jake. Sorry." The final truth.

He dropped in on Milton B., who was in conference with a client. Milton B. had been out or in conference every time he called him.

"Tell him I stopped by," Jake said to Milton B.'s secretary. "I'd appreciate it if he called me."

He was right near City Hall, so he might as well drop in on Albie Karlin. Albie couldn't duck him; he'd have to face him sooner or later at the IAC or the JPI. So he greeted Jake heartily.

"Jake! How are you?"

"Fine, fine."

"I hear you've been to New York."

"Word gets around."

"I hear you've turned commie."

"Not quite."

"After the revolution you're not going to put me against the wall and shoot me, are you?" Albie laughed.

Jake gave him a small smile.

"Well, we're not too far apart. Day by day Roosevelt's going more and more socialistic."

"That'll be the day."

Albie started glancing at a brief. Jake wondered what he was doing there. His feet began shuffling about; lately they were getting into that habit, as if they couldn't get comfortable.

"Big fraud case," Albie explained.

"Sure."

"You come up to see me for anything?"

"Just to say hello, Albie."

"If I can do anything, let me know." A regular politician.

"How's Milton B.?"

"Fine, fine. Great."

"The sonofabitch is out to me all the time."

"Everybody's on his ass, Jake. You've got to understand."

"Sure, sure."

"Come around to the club. We'll work out together."

"Thanks, Albie."

What else did he do, this idle man, clear-eyed, still in his prime, still looking like an all-American? He dropped in on more editors, rode out to local neighborhood papers, introduced himself, chatted, rode back home with sample copies of the papers and no promises, ate a well-prepared dinner that his mother made with love, then went off to the JPI, his little island, his little Tahiti, his never-never land of exhaustion and forgetfulness. Sometimes on Douglas Boulevard he'd pass Maxie Katz still holding court outside his building with the people in the neighborhood needing one favor or another, with more urgency now than ever before.

"Hey, Jake."

"Hi, Maxie."

"How are things going?"

"So-so."

Maxie winked to his cronies. Watch him, he was saying.

"I hear you took New York by storm." That was the needle.

Jake shrugged.

"You gave them the old Chicago treatment. Siss-boom-bah!"

The people around laughed slightly.

"Your pal Albie Karlin." Maxie explained who Albie was. "The Olympic champ. A nice Jewish boy, a credit to his people. From the West Side, too." Back to Jake. "He's doing great."

Jake didn't know why he didn't buzz off, why his feet weren't shuffling him away. Why all the palaver, the big show? What did he have in mind?

"A Roosevelt man," Maxie said. "You for Roosevelt, Jake?"

"Kind of."

"What's kind of? You're for him or against him."

"Well, there are still fifteen million unemployed."

"Seven."

"I won't argue the numbers."

"Where do you get your numbers, Jake? The *Daily Worker?*"

"The *Tribune.*"

"The *Daily Worker* of the right. Same difference. I hear you were really partying around with the commies in New York."

"Where did you hear that?"

Maxie turned to his cronies. "Did you know we've got a famous guy with us here? A former intercollegiate swimming champ, a man who could write his ticket to the moon, where do you think his mug winds up?"

"Where?"

"Police headquarters. A big item with the Red Squad."

Jake was stunned. "You're kidding."

"Boy." Maxie beamed at his cronies. "He looks beautiful. Right there with all the big shot Bolsheviks." Back to Jake. "I'll bet you were coming around to see me about a job, huh?"

"Forget it, Maxie." Jake started to walk away.

Maxie jumped out at him. "Wait a minute. I want to talk to you. I've got a job for you. Don't run away."

"You're a fuckin' fascist, Maxie."

"Ho-ho, names he's calling me." For the benefit of the cronies. "I've got a job for him, and next, he'll be calling me a Nazi." He pulled Jake away, then quietly, tightly: "You think I'm kidding about the Red Squad?"

"I know you're not."

"I can get you off the hook."

"I didn't do anything, Maxie. I'm not in trouble."

"It's not what you do, jerk. It's what you think, who you associate with."

"Why all the concern?"

"You can do us a favor. You can work for us."

"Jesus Christ!"

"You're in, Jake. A *Daily Worker* man. They trust you. I'll put you in touch with the right people. All you've got to do is keep them informed."

"You bastard."

"Fifty a week."

"Shove it."

"I can get people to kill for that kind of money."

He grabbed Maxie, wanted to hit him. Terror suddenly gripped him. He began to run. As if he were being pursued. He ran until he was breathless, then sat down on a stoop and buried his head in his hands. He found his body trembling, his hands shaking. He couldn't believe what he'd heard.

For days afterward he stayed in the house. His mother thought he was sick. She worried and fussed over him. He kept looking outside, feeling he was being watched. Who am I? What do they want from me? I'm not even a member of the party. But why shouldn't they approach him? No job, enough humiliation and demoralization, a weakened condition; maybe he could be had. What did they have to lose by approaching him? It was the age of humiliation and demoralization. Every morning you woke up swallowing a mouthful of them. You took them with your cocktails and dinner afterward. So maybe he was fed up now and he could be had.

Gradually the sense of paranoia left him. He rationalized that he was one among thousands; the Red Squad couldn't keep tabs on all of them. He started going out again. But he felt strange when he went to John Reed Club meetings. What if somebody there knew he'd been approached? Every left-wing organization, he knew, had its informants. Who were the snitches in the Reed Club? Would any of them know he'd been approached?

For a while, when he attended general meetings of the Reed Club, the literary faction meetings, the lectures and affairs, he studied everybody as a possible stool pigeon; then he said to hell with it, he'd wind up at the state hospital in Elgin if he suspected everybody. His own conscience was clear. He'd forget the whole thing, go back to trusting everybody as he always had. After all, he was not a member of the party; he had never got any Moscow gold; if you killed him and opened him up, there wouldn't be a secret in his body.

So he gave himself over to his novel, finished it, sent it off to the *New Masses,* and waited anxiously for the prize. When he got it back a month later with a polite rejection slip, he felt as bleak as the winter days that had come over the city. What does it take? he wondered. When do you connect? How do you make it all gel? What's the secret? But at least he wasn't alone. Other writers commiserated with him. Rejection slips, they had tons of them. They were the bricks that built a writer. Someday they'd be traded in for all the good things in life. All they needed were the hide of a walrus, the guts of a bank robber, the stamina of a marathon runner. Jake was well fortified with all of them. . . . Or was he?

Maybe he had been stunted for a literary career. He had once asked a professor of his, "How do you become a writer?"

The professor said, "Do you *have* to be one?"

"I don't know."

"If you don't know, you won't be a writer. You've got to be driven by it. Tenacious, bullnecked, and insanely driven. You can't just yearn for it. You can't just say, 'Hey, that's a pretty cushy life, no clocks to punch, live as the spirit moves you, money in the bank, people lionizing you, Hollywood stars chasing you, travel the globe, not a bad life, huh?' But that's the dreamy part, after you've won the sweepstakes. First comes the hard part, the works, the defeats, the crazy drive that overcomes everything."

"What else do I need?"

"Read. And read. And read. Until it comes out of your pores."

"What about experience?"

"Emily Brontë never left the moors. Marcel Proust lived in a cork room. Stephen Crane never saw a war, but he wrote about the Civil War as if he'd invented it."

"What else?"

"Feel. Get into a stone, a piece of wood, a boat, a steel track, most of all a person. Feel. See. Then make us feel and see."

"What about brains?"

"Everybody doesn't have to be a cerebral writer like George

Bernard Shaw, Thomas Mann, Voltaire. You can be a blood writer, like Hemingway, Faulkner, Dreiser, Dostoyevsky. You don't need a brain, but boy, you've got to have heart."

So maybe he had been shortchanged. A big brain he knew he didn't have. He didn't know how well he could see because when he tried to recall what he had seen, he found it hard to come by. As for heart, compared to a Dostoyevsky, a Dreiser, a Faulkner, he was like a chunk of granite. Look at what had happened with Natasha: icebergs, glaciers. Experience? Even if some geniuses didn't have any to speak of, most writers had lots of it: great love affairs, big wars like those Dos Passos and Hemingway and Tolstoy had, journeys to distant places, where they lived among different people. What did he have: school, the West Side of Chicago, a little bumming trip out west, a nothing love affair, a starvation job in New York? Boy, had he been shortchanged. But he couldn't give up. Was that the crazy drive the professor had been talking about? What is it with you, Jake, you get into something you won't give up? You keep nagging and nagging away at it. What is it you've got to prove?

Whatever it was, there wasn't much else to do. He had given up trying to get a job. He read and read. The more he read, the less he wrote; reading was so much easier. But he was always looking for ideas, stories, looking and looking and jotting down notes. He tried to write about Lala again, but it didn't come. It was like going out to sea without a compass and losing all sense of direction. So he settled for smaller things: sketches of people he knew; incidents he'd experienced or heard about, some of which he sent to magazines only to get them back promptly.

His rich uncle Hymie, the laundry owner, would come over with his wife and say, *"Noo,* Jake, you still writing?"

"Yep."

"I'll give you a job in the laundry. You'll learn the business."

"Nope."

Hymie would turn to Jake's father and say, "A rich father he's got."

Jake's father would say, "A rich father he hasn't got; but he needs some time, and I'll give it to him."

"So what's for something to eat?" Hymie would say, dismissing Jake. "Herring and potatoes?"

"For you, what else?" Jake's mother would say.

Jake didn't need Uncle Hymie to fill him with guilt about not working, to remind him that he was sponging off his father. So when a job was offered to him by Solly Landon, the parking lot king, he grabbed it, even though there were conditions. The water polo team at the JPI was in the middle of the midwestern championship games and had a good chance of winning the title. Jake was erratic about showing up for practice. So Solly, who would rather win a game than a million dollars, said, "You gotta show up for practice on time, every time."

"Okay," Jake said.

"The days we play you get the day off."

"Do I get paid for it?"

"Yes, you muzzler."

"How much?"

"Twenty a week."

"Twenty-five."

"Okay, twenty-five, you bastard."

"I'll get rich, you know."

"Who cares? As long as we win the championship." Solly turned to Moish Bender, the growling coach. "Okay, Moish, he don't show up, he gets docked. You're a witness."

That was the coldest winter of Jake's life. Now he knew how his father felt at his newsstand. Jake wore winter underwear, two sweaters, a mackinaw, a scarf, two pair of sweat socks, a stocking cap pulled down over his ears; he stuffed newspapers inside his clothes; he moved around stiff-faced, numb-footed, hand-frozen, like a robot; he built bonfires in metal drums to keep warm. The fires attracted bums who warmed their hands, their threadbare, thin-clothed bodies: former engineers, shopkeepers, foundry workers, evicted farmers, carpenters, laborers. From all over the country, they came and went, while Jake collected quarters for parking on Landon's lot near a railroad freight yard outside the Loop. Near the end of the day Solly would come around to collect the coins.

"I don't like the fires around here."

"I'll freeze."

"They bring the bums. They might hold you up."

"You're insured, aren't you?"

"Sure, I'm insured. But they might hurt you. Then you won't be able to play."

"Don't worry."

"You coming to practice tonight?"

"If I ever thaw out."

"A good steam, a hot shower, it'll be like a summer day."

Sometimes when the snow was falling and Jake looked more like a snowman than a human being, Solly would come around, collect his money, look at him, and say in Yiddish, "Do you have to go to college?"

Sometimes Solly would say, "You know, Jake, I never read a book in my life."

"Is that the secret of your success?"

"Instinct. Making the right moves at the right time."

"Like an animal in the jungle."

"Don't make fun of it. The survival of the fittest."

"Where'd you read that?"

"I didn't. I've got good ears." He'd part with the litany: "You have to go to college?"

It was not only the coldest winter but the most boring. He had gone from the dignified days of being a subsidized athlete at Northwestern University to the humiliating days of being a subsidized water polo player at the JPI. A pro without a pot to piss in. How much lower could you sink?

So they won the water polo title. Which made Solly Landon and coach Moish Bender and all the guys happy. Which earned the JPI another trophy to put in a glass case among other tarnished loving cups, and which got the guys another gold medal they never noticed afterward. Solly took them all to Chinatown and blew them to a big dinner, anything they wanted, à la carte. So what?

Right after that, when Solly paid him, he said, "From now on it'll be twenty a week."

"How do you like that?" Jake said. "And I was just going to ask for a raise."

"Why?"

"We won the title, didn't we? Don't I deserve something more than a gold medal?"

"I didn't know you were such a greedy guy, Jake. Also, I didn't know you were so dumb."

"Why am I so dumb?"

"Because your timing stinks. Times like this, I can get guys on this lot for fifteen a week, ten a week. I pay guys twenty because I don't want to exploit them; I want them to be happy."

"I won't be happy at twenty, Solly."

"I paid you twenty-five because you were playing on the team. I knew it'd make you happier. I was being very charitable."

"You'll want me to play next year, won't you?"

"I'll raise you to twenty-five again."

Jake couldn't help himself; he began to laugh.

"What's funny?"

"Five dollars a week for playing on the team. That's all I'm worth, Solly, five big dollars a week?"

"What do you want? It's an amateur game."

"Thanks a lot, pal."

"Jake, I'm not a philanthropist. The job is only worth twenty dollars. I've got to live by my principles."

"So long, Solly."

"You're going away mad now."

"Not mad, Solly. Humiliated."

On Monday he didn't show up for work. Solly called.

"What are you doing to me?"

"I'll work as a lifeguard this summer. Thirty-two-fifty a week."

"That's a dirty trick, leaving me like this."

"They'll give me a uniform and dignity. To the kids I'll be a hero."

"Okay, be a fuckin' hero. Don't come to me for a job again."

"What about next year, Solly, when the water polo season starts up again?"

"You gonna be around?"

"Only if you read a couple of books by then."

"You bastard."

"And as long as I play on the team, you'll read a book a week. That's my pound of flesh."

Jake laughed and laughed as Solly slammed the receiver onto the hook.

The lifeguard job that summer lasted four days. He thought his eardrums would burst from the roar of the mob rushing into the pool every hour on the hour eight times a day. The days seemed endless as he stared vacantly at the splashing, thrashing, diving, jumping bodies. He talked to himself, sang all the songs he knew. He got jumpy, edgy; the clock never seemed to move. Relentless boredom, worse than at the parking lot job, set in. He came home one day and said to his father, "Pop, how good a handicapper are you?"

His father smiled. "On good days I'm the best."

"How about we go into the handicap business? We'll get out a tip sheet."

"You?"

"Why not?"

"What will your communist friends say about that?"

"They'll say it's corrupt, depraved, and counterrevolutionary, but another day as a guard and I'll go out of my mind. How many tips do you sell a day?"

"Fifteen, twenty. They go for half a dollar. I get half."

"That's five dollars a day for you. If I could do that well at the track and I'd keep all the money, I'll do pretty good."

"The sheets are pretty well known. They have a following."

"I'll undersell them. Thirty-five cents. You're as good as any of them. Better. You'll get a reputation. They'll swear by your handicapping. What'll we call the sheet?"

"Jake, this isn't like you. Bums sell tips. Touts."

"Come on, Pop. Give me a name."

"If you play favorites, you win thirty-three percent of the time. Nobody wants favorites; they want action, excitement, five to one or better, a killing. If you hit ten percent, you're lucky."

"Pop, I'm talking business and you're giving me numbers. If people were realistic, horse racing would drop dead. With all your statistics, you still play them, don't you?"

"It's my recreation. I'm a fool."

"So give me a name."

"Clocker's Special."

"Pa, you've been holding back on me, you've been thinking about it for years."

His father smiled sheepishly; he wouldn't deny it.

"A honey of a name. Like we've been there at dawn, clocking them, then flash, a bulletin, here they are, the best firsthand tips from the horses' mouths. I'll give you a piece of the action."

"Don't. I'll give you a present."

Next day he ordered a thousand envelopes and reams of colored paper with "Clocker's Special" printed in bold black type. He bought a dime-store printing set. Each morning, after the scratch sheet came out, his father gave him his selections. Jake stamped them out on the paper, folded them, stuffed them in the envelopes, then went out to Hawthorne, where the horses were running. The first day he sold five. Before the last race he stamped out several winners and what they paid, whether his father had picked them or not, then slipped them into parked cars and tacked them onto fences and posts. He operated just like the other touts. By the end of the week he was selling ten to fifteen a day. The following week, twenty.

Toward the end of the Hawthorne meeting a couple of stocky, dark-faced, solidly built puncheros from Little Italy came up to Jake. They looked very sharp, very sporty, with checked suits, binoculars, white Borsalinos, and Jake could see their guns bulging inside their tight jackets. They bought a *Clocker's Special* and looked at the selections.

"How you doin', fella?"

"Okay," Jake said.

"Looks like you got some hot ones here."

Jake knew they weren't just buying a tip.

"Never saw you around here before."

"I've been around."

"You'll have to kick in, fella."

"Who you guys with?"

The talker laughed, said to his pal, "Who we with, the fella wants to know. As if we have to be with somebody." Then, with a heavy smell of cologne and garlic, he leaned in close to Jake. "Do we have to be with somebody?"

"I'm a friend of Lenny Kahn's and Yussel Gomberg. I know Bill Johnson, too. He runs the books for Capone."

"Oh, you're really well connected. Usually the tab is five dollars, but because you know the right people we'll give you a special rate. Six dollars."

"Come on, guys."

"We'll collect now. Somebody'll be around every week."

That night he called Lenny Kahn at his taxi dance joint.

"Tough tiddy," Lenny said. "I've got no control over there. Pay the men."

Six bucks less a week. It was still a living. They followed him to

Lincoln Fields and Arlington. He sold more *Clocker's Specials.*
They squeezed more dollars out of him. He wasn't starving. He
had thought earlier about going to Florida, spending a warm
winter at the tracks, and making an easy buck. But he dismissed
it. He heard the gunsels were in Florida, too.

That year he felt utterly depraved. He made a few feeble
attempts to find work, then gave up. He slept late, read a lot,
wrote a little, and waited endlessly for the mail every time he
sent a story out, only to be crushed by a printed rejection slip.
He saved himself with afternoon swims at the JPI, wasted himself
at matinee movies, and stalled restlessly for night to fall. He
went to Lenny Kahn's taxi dance hall on Wabash Avenue near
Madison, and while the Els clattered by the windows, he socked
away at the girls. Sometimes he took them home at three in the
morning and made love in their small furnished one-room
apartments with in-a-door beds. He frequented dance mar-
athons, which had become known as poor men's nightclubs, and
watched the contestants brutalize themselves during the whistle-
shrieking, face-slapping, passing-out grinds, while clowns did
pratfalls and made funny faces, all for free meals and a cot a few
minutes a day for as long as they lasted. Jake sometimes felt he
was watching freaks and geeks at a carnival and despised himself
for being there. In the taverns on North Clark Street he drank
thirty-six-ounce steins of beer for a dime with free pretzels and
talked into the morning hours with other struggling writers and
artists. He went to left-wing affairs and took girls home afterward. In the morning they were total strangers to each other;
sometimes they had forgotten each other's names or hadn't even
known them to begin with. He thought he was a character in a
book: *A Thousand One-Night Stands.* Subtitle: *No Love for the
Wicked and Heartless.*

Out of it all he wrote one story that was accepted by an
English anthology of modern writing. He appeared with André
Malraux, Christopher Isherwood, W. H. Auden, Stephen
Spender, Ignazio Silone, E. M. Forster, and Mikhail Sholokhov.
He walked on springboards for a week. Little pay, lots of
prestige, but nobody was breaking his door down for more
stories; he was rejected as often as before. He went back to
passing the time away, feeling like a degenerate. Oh, to be as

totally involved as he had been in his youth. His goals had been so simple then; his desires were so complicated now. God, the way he'd been able to throw himself into everything he did before, the way he could use himself up, the pride he'd had in what he'd done, the confidence he'd had in every venture. Take me, love me, burn me up, use me completely all over again. Give me back my confidence, my pride. . . . He found that he had passed from the tender lap of care and love to the frigid realms of rejection.

One night he saw Ida.

"Surprise, surprise," she said. "I'm in love, madly, insanely, and he isn't married. I'm playing with fire. If he leaves me, I'll be utterly destroyed."

"I wish I had your capacity to love."

"Loving is easy if you're willing to give. You've got to be a masochist to love. How about it, Jake? Surrender. Take your kick in the teeth."

"I've already had it."

"You?"

"I found out my heart wasn't all muscle."

"I never thought it'd happen to you. You were always so cocky. Like you owned the world. Impervious. Steel walls around you."

"That was me."

"Spoiled rotten."

"You make me feel like a million."

"Now you know how poor slobs like me feel."

"You don't always have to get kicked in the teeth."

"You do if you're vulnerable."

They were sitting on her couch in her small living room, working on a bourbon and water. He put his arm around her, a tentative pass. He took it for granted that he'd go to bed with her; she never said no.

"And, boy," she said, leaning her head against him, "was I vulnerable with you. Just being near you got me goosey. Thinking about you got me trembly all over. Anything you wanted, it was yours. When you made love to me I thought I had all of you, your manhood, your strength, your confidence. I was pregnant with your power. You could have put me in your pocket, and I would have stayed there as quiet as a mouse."

He drew her closer. Kissed her. She withdrew from him.

"You're still an adolescent, Jake."

Everything in him shriveled up.

"When will you stop thinking that the world revolves around you? When will you grow up?"

He felt her spiked shoes pierce his belly. He got up.

"Thanks for the drink," he said. "Thanks for bringing me up to date with myself." He started out.

She took his arm and turned him about. "Come here, you shit." She kissed him with her mouth open, her lips trembly. "You're in a state, aren't you?"

"I hang around you, I'll turn into a slob, too. So long, Ida. Good luck with the new one."

He went from there to the Chez Paree. Maybe Lila would give him a lift. But that depressed him even more. It reminded him of a time when he'd thought he had the world in his pocket, and that world no longer glittered for him. Lila was dressed in the latest Paris fashions, made up in the best that Helena Rubinstein could provide. Her voice was brassy, her laugh assured. One minute she greeted you as if you were the most important person in the world; the following minute she was looking over your shoulder to welcome the next most important person in the world. Just like the way she'd made love in high school: doing one thing and calculating the next move.

"What can I do for you, Jake?"

"You can make me your star attraction in your next show."

She laughed. "Still writing?"

Jake nodded.

"Write that book. I'll get it to Hollywood for you." As if that were the only reason for writing. "Better yet, write a play. That's where the real money is. I'll cast it for you. I'll promote it. Then Hollywood. Jack Warner, Louis B. Mayer, Harry Cohn, Sam Goldwyn, I know them all."

A half smile on Jake's face. "I'd just like to write a good book."

"Bullshit on a good book. It'll sell four copies. A great book, fifteen copies. *Anthony Adverse* is what they want. *Grand Hotel. Abie's Irish Rose. Shmaltz.* Swashbucklers. Big tits. A role for Garbo. Then you can write your good books."

How about a job? he wanted to say. But that would be like going to the racetrack with a millionaire friend and sneaking up to place a $2 bet while he was plunging at the $100 window.

"How's the back room?"

"For a high roller like you, always open." She laughed huskily.

He went to the dice table in the back room and got lucky. He put $2 on the pass line and cashed it in later for $350. That was better than an advance in royalties that most publishers gave to first novelists.

As he pocketed the money, a voice like a soft, mellow chime rang in his ear.

"You're my lucky charm."

She was royal-looking in a soft black velvet evening gown, a string of luminous pearls around her swanlike neck, an emerald bracelet on her wrist. She was sunny blond with green eyes, ivory skin, smelling of a fancy French perfume. She had deep dimples in her cheeks when she smiled and the classical features of an Egyptian queen. He had seen her at the other end of the dice table and had had a momentary fantasy of being carried away with her on billows of dreamy clouds, but had torn himself away to concentrate on the play. He had seen her before at the tracks when he was touting *Clocker's Specials.* From time to time, after driving up in a white Cord roadster, she had bought his tip sheet with $1, $5, sometimes $10 and never waited for change. She was jockey club pussy all the way, a dream beyond all dreams.

"You held the dice like you owned them," she said.

"If I'd owned them a little longer, I'd have broken the bank."

"You did beautifully."

She had a rack of $100 chips which she was ready to cash in. Probably twenty grand there, Jake thought. Which was the difference between the $2 and $500 bettor. She handed him ten $100 chips.

"I owe you."

"No, please."

"I was down ten thousand when you started to roll."

"I got my little bundle, thanks." He also had his pride.

"How about a late supper, then a drink?"

"Fine. Great."

He waited as the cashier paid her off in $1,000 bills, watched her cram them into her black Mark Cross purse. When they stepped into the dining room, Lila noticed them.

"Hello, Mrs. T."

Who was this woman? Jake wondered.

"I see you did pretty good, Jake."

"I just got an advance to write my next book."

Lila winked slyly and said, "You could say you did better than that."

"You write?" Mrs. T. said.

"In a way," Jake said.

"Good. I like to be around writers."

They had a couple of Chivas Regals on the rocks to calm down. Then filet mignon. Then Courvoisier for sniffing and sipping.

One thing about gambling, Jake thought. Around the tables, if you've got the stake of a $1 minimum bet, you can stand right next to the millionaire $500 bettor. Around the tables you find the truest democracy.

But his luck carried farther, away from the tables, into the dining room with the big red menus and the big-name entertainment. With more luck maybe he'd get into the big-name bedroom of Mrs. T., whoever she was.

He tried to find out who she was, but she eluded him with a mysterious smile at every question, every insinuation. All he knew now was that she smelled like money, her dress rustled like money, she had "big shot" and "royalty" written all over her.

"You alone?" he asked, wondering about the "Mrs." tag.

"In a way," she said.

"In what way?"

"In a way to say, 'Why don't you come home with me?'"

"No husband, nothing?"

"Nothing to worry about."

On the way out, Lila was very impressed. She said, "Come back again."

"With my kind of luck, why not?" Jake said.

Her home was a penthouse on East Chestnut Street overlooking the lake. Jake stepped out of an elevator into a foyer with a Rodin and a Brancusi on each side of a Moorish archway that led into a sunken living room with a beamed cathedral ceiling and a large fieldstone fireplace. He stepped down to a Persian rug in a vast room with rich tapestries on one wall and Picassos, Miros, Vlamincks, a Monet, a Gauguin, and two Van Goghs on the other walls. On marble tables there were antique inlaid mother-of-pearl music and cigarette boxes and crystal ashtrays. The furniture was Sheraton and Chippendale. What, Jake wondered, did the Art Institute and the Metropolitan Museum have that she didn't have?

"Make yourself comfortable," she said.

"Here?"

She laughed.

"What would you like to drink?"

"Whatever."

He followed her into the kitchen. A twelve-burner stove, no less, with three ovens. A butcher's table scrubbed clean. Cupboards and cupboards of dishes and glasses.

"After midnight we fend for ourselves," she said.

She brought out a bottle of Martell Cordon Argent and a couple of tall heavy crystal glasses. Then she opened a door and walked into a refrigerator with cases of Coke, soft drinks, and soda, boxes and crates of oranges and tomatoes and lettuce and apples, sides of beef and ham and bacon, frozen chickens and turkeys and cold cuts to *nosh*.

"You could hole up here forever," he said.

"Hungry?" She filled a silver ice bucket and handed it to him.

"We just ate."

"Maybe later."

She picked up a bottle of Canada Dry and fixed two drinks in the kitchen, then led him into the living room. When he took a drink, the bouquet alone made him drunk; he thought he was right in the middle of all the vineyards in France. He looked out of the broad open windowed doors onto the large roof garden and watched the Palmolive beacon range through the sky. What was she, he wondered, the Queen of Sheba in a Chicago castle in the sky, a high-class call girl, a madam with the nicest girls from the most exclusive finishing schools, a kept woman, or just filthy rich? Tell me, tell me!

"Nice night," he said.

"Lovely."

She had moved out onto the roof, flowing along like Ginger Rogers, and he followed. It was early fall, an Indian-summer night, with the lingering smell of burning leaves in the air. He could see the beads of light from the Municipal Pier out on the lake, the lights of buoys and distant boats, the lingering lights of a sleeping city. Small trees in large plant boxes cast shadows on the roof. It was the season for chrysanthemums, and they grew profusely in boxed areas. On the far corner of the roof was a platform of bonzai trees with rippled sand like the bottom of a peaceful river meandering around it. The two-story house looked like a mansion.

"From up here you can really see the working-class struggle," he said.

Her smile was pure Gioconda. Jake was calling her Connie now. He didn't care who she was, he was suddenly and overwhelmingly in love with her. He didn't know if it was the excitement of winning money, the rich drinks, the exotic wealth of her surroundings, the smell of her French perfume, or her beauty, but he was in love with all of it. He hated himself for being so easily seduced, but he didn't care.

"I love you," he said.

Again, the sweet, faraway, mysterious smile; then she kissed him; it was as if he were being touched by rose petals.

"It's the liquor," she said.

"It's everything, but it doesn't change how I feel."

He kissed her long and deep, her lips and tongue like rare candies. Why me? he thought. Why me?

"It's getting chilly," she said. "Shall we go in?"

She led him into a room with a sunken marble tub like a small Roman pool; it had sculptured handles of full-breasted nymphs and satyrs with hard marble cocks. She sprinkled some powder into the steaming hot water, stirred it with her bare foot, and magic suds of pink and blue and turquoise, smelling of jasmine and gardenias, bubbled up. There was a breathtaking flash of voluptuous breasts and slim ivory thighs and curved hips, and she was in the pool. Quickly he got out of his clothes and jumped in. The bubbles popped, blew up, floated away in myriad colors as she came close. He eased down beside her, sliding and slithering against her hot, wet skin, the bubbles bursting all over, and then she began to soap him. He melted away.

"Did I tell you I love you?"

"Yes."

She touched his penis, stroked it tenderly. He fell into a mist of hot colored bubbles. He kissed her. She opened her mouth and sucked his tongue and kept on stroking him. She was as slippery and soft as whipped cream as he held her.

"Not now, dear."

"When?"

"Later."

She moved out of the pool, trails of colored bubbles dripping from her, into a sauna. She rubbed perfumed oil over herself and over him. Smoothly they glossed it over their bodies. Would the guys at the JPI ever believe him?

All the time he had a feeling of being watched, mostly by her, but he didn't care.

"'Behold, thou art fair, my love. . . . Until the day break, and the shadows flee away, I will get me to the mountain of myrrh, and to the hill of frankincense.'"

"That's beautiful," she said.

"From the Song of Solomon. Makes everything kosher."

She took his hand and led him into a large bedroom with a king-size bed and mirrors all about. Even the ceiling.

"My fucking chamber," she said. "Do you mind?"

"Not at all. Not at all, not at all."

The rug was softer than fur, the sheets silk as he got into the bed, her body like satin, her lips like tender clouds. He felt like an Oriental potentate.

"Now," she said.

"Oh, God, yes."

For a while they both watched each other intently. The

complete five-cornered voyeurs. It was so exciting he could hardly contain himself, but he wanted to go on and on. Then he stopped looking, went inward, felt his passion mounting . . . when all at once he felt a presence, like somebody at his back, and he knew then that he had been watched all the while, for there in the mirrors, from all directions, he saw naked men with bald heads, potbellies, and scrawny legs, their hands pumping away on enormous, swollen, red, purplish cocks.

"Don't stop!" The voices bellowed from every wall. "Jesus Christ, don't stop!"

Connie wrapped her legs around Jake and clutched him tightly. "Oh, love, do it, do it, please don't stop!"

"What the hell's going on?" Jake yelled.

"Fuck, honey, fuck," Connie said desperately.

He went limp and rolled away.

"Get him, Connie. Don't let him get away. I'm almost there."

The many mirrored men turned into one man, still pumping away, working himself into a frenzy, as Connie threw herself at Jake and went down to his penis and took it in her mouth and began moaning deliriously as she sucked at it.

"Oh, there!" the man groaned. "Oh, you cocksucker, you lovely, hot cocksucker. All of it. Take all of it. There! There!" And he began to spurt all over the rich Persian rug.

Jake was now hypnotized. It was as if he were above it all, and through all the varied mirrors, like peepholes, he were viewing this three-ring circus, with himself growing hard in Connie's mouth and the man, now in bed with them, holding Connie tight with his penis growing bigger and bigger against her buttocks, and then he reared up like an animal and thrust it deep into her anus.

"Oh, you lovely asshole! Oh, you lovely cunt! Suck it! Suck it!"

That wasn't him. It couldn't be him, filled with horror and excitement, both, all of him pulling away and all of him at the same time moving in her mouth, and then he burst out of his skin, it seemed, but she held on and held on.

"Yes!" the man moaned. "Now! There! Don't let go! Don't! Oh, Christ! Oh, Jesus! Oh, love!"

They fell away from each other and lay like three wounded warriors on the big silky bed.

"I don't believe it," he said after a while, getting out of bed.

"What?" She rose to her elbow. She looked so beautiful, so innocent, so untouched.

"This."

"Oh, that," she said.

"What the hell went on?"

"You ever read Havelock Ellis?" the man said.

"Krafft-Ebing, too," Jake said.

"So?" Connie said.

"Isn't everybody on their own kick?" the man said.

"Not on the West Side," Jake said.

"Why don't you get back into bed?" Connie said.

"Please," the man said. His penis was hard again, and Connie was stroking it gently.

Jake went into the bathroom, found his clothes strewn about the Roman pool, and started to get dressed. They were in chenille robes when they came in.

"Why don't you have something to eat with us?" Connie said.

"No."

"How are you going to get home?" the man said.

"By streetcar."

"At this hour? It'll take hours."

"I'll wait."

"Take my car," Connie said.

"The Cord?"

"Why not?"

The way they tempted you.

"No," he said.

"Stay," the man said. "You can have the run of the house, money in your pocket, the use of the car. What more could you want?"

"My pride, my dignity."

"These days?"

"Stay, Jake," said Connie. "We can be good to you."

"What you need is a bull. Not me."

*　　*　　*

He went back to the Chez the following night and found out from Lila who Mr. and Mrs. T. were. He was the heir to one of the large meat-packing fortunes; Connie was from a prominent family from Highland Park. Somehow he knew Connie would be there. He didn't look at her, nor did she seem to recognize him. They played silently amid the noise of the dice table, losing steadily. When Jake dropped half his winnings from the night before, he stepped to the cashier's window to cash in. She was beside him.

"Looks like we both lost," she said.

"Cold dice."

"But warm hearts. Can I make it up for you?"

"No."

"My husband and I like you. You're young, clean, vigorous, intelligent. Come home with me. Please."

Looking at her patrician bearing, he couldn't believe she'd willingly be a part of the act.

"What do you get out of it?"

"Everything."

It was a play, a peep show, a spectacle, and he'd only seen the curtain open. I'm fucking everything on two feet. I'm eating my guts out. I'm depraved. Why not?

But there wasn't as much horror or excitement that night or the following. He had been seduced; he was now a willing victim; they had used him up. So that on the fourth night at the Chez he played the game silently, as if they were strangers, but when he went over to cash in his chips, she was no longer beside him. She was smiling sweetly at a tall, broad-shouldered blond man next to her, the new victim. But he had to play the game out to the very end. He walked up beside her and said, "We finished?"

"In a way."

He decided to give the play a dirty turn. "I'll sue you."

"For what?"

"How about alienation of affection?" That was a big trick in those days for girls who were jilted by wealthy men.

"In a *ménage à trois?*"

"Why not?"

She laughed, knowing he wasn't serious, and handed him a

$100 chip. A token of the rich. He cashed it in. At least he'd got the price of a very high-class call girl. As he walked out on the street, he felt as if he'd hit the bottom of a sewer.

He stopped going to the Chez for a time. He dropped what winnings he had left playing cards at Johnson's joint. Then he began to dip into the money he made as a tout. The house took 10 percent of every pot. Everybody in the games was a shark; they figured the odds at every flick of the cards. Everything he did, he was taken.

Jake needed to lose for punishment. The Civil War was raging in Spain. The Germans and Italians were trying out their arms and military know-how against the Russian supplies and generals. The Spanish people were caught in between. Friends of his had joined the International Brigade. Some of their wives took him to bed and urged him to go while they spent their passions with him.

He got a brief letter from Eddie Lopkin:

Natasha is teaching full time now. She finally got to Europe last summer and had a disastrous affair in Paris. Hates France but still loves the language. She says the only way to say "I love you" is in French. If you're not doing anything pressing, why don't you come to Spain with me? We'll knock off a few fascists. You with me?

A week after Eddie got there he was killed.

In his head Jake wanted to go. *There* was a war, baby. Hemingway was in Spain. Malraux. Dos Passos. Orwell. Vincent Sheean. Ring Lardner's son. *There* was an experience for him. There was a book in it, if he ever got back alive. Go man, go. But in his guts he didn't feel it was really his war. Always sitting on the fence. Waiting for feeling to catch up with him. A zombie, that's what he was. Couldn't even fall in love. The one-night-stand man. At some time in his life his nerve ends had been cut. His heart was an iron plate. Who the hell ever told you you'd be a writer? You don't want to be a writer. You want to be a fuck-off. The easy life. Like swimming. Be a tout. Pay the gangsters. You're maggoty with corruption. So who are you trying to kid?

Fortunately he didn't have to kick himself around too long. Spain, even with Russian help, was lost. The Nazis, who put Franco in, demonstrated their military supremacy in their first testing ground and were ready to move into larger conquests. And Jake lived in a limbo of mindlessness. Marking time. For what? The revolution, which he probably didn't have the guts to fight for? All right, the revolution, and he'd put his heart into it. So what was it going to do? Was it going to make him gel as a writer, make him go clickety-click, give him everything he wanted? Was it going to give him the fulfillment and completeness he yearned for? Where does a guy find it in himself? I tried out for human being, and I didn't make it. What a way to go.

The Federal Writers' Project renewed his hope, his optimism, his vitality. He got on relief, qualified as a writer, and was hired at $94 a month. After doing some work on the *Illinois Guide,* he was assigned to excerpting columns and columns of events from crumbly old newspapers in dusty libraries until he thought he'd wind up with silicosis. Then the director of the project gave him permission to do a novel on the steel strike of 1919; all the project wanted in return was his research. He never got the novel published, but he did sell a few more short stories and articles. After that he got involved in the radio division of the project, writing dramatic documentaries that were produced over the local stations. Each week Jake met with a half dozen other writers, got their assignments, discussed their stories, then had their work produced. There was a golden sense of comradeship in the group. It was an exciting time.

Conditions were a little better, but most people were still struggling for survival. Labor was on the move with the great sit-down strikes. The CIO was growing bigger and more powerful. The John Reed Clubs had been dissolved and replaced by the League of American Writers, designed to attract all writers of radical inclination to accelerate the destruction of capitalism and the establishment of a workers' government. Communism was winning a greater respectability.

Jake finally joined the Communist party and met weekly with the writers' branch. But meetings became dull. Jake tried to get active. He helped unions write leaflets, worked mimeograph machines, distributed *Daily Workers* and pamphlets outside factories, walked in local picket lines, participated in antifascist demonstrations, went to popular front mass meetings, but he was never emotionally involved. Eventually he always came back to his own self. He always felt like an outsider, like a man who understood how machines worked but never touched them, never got hurt or cut up or maimed by them, never got into their oil and grime. He liked the coffee klatsches after the meetings, the beer and gin at places like the Three Deuces on North Wabash, and listening to good Chicago jazz and staying until all hours of the morning at jam sessions when hot jazz musicians from all over town would drop in. But he'd begun a new novel, and he wanted to spend more time with it, so he attended fewer branch meetings until he virtually dropped out. He felt guilty about it, more of an outsider, more of an emotional zombie.

Passion was what he needed. Love. The belief of a zealot. He didn't find it in sex or in listening to jazz or in drinking coffee while discussing writing and the impossible market. He stalked the Chicago streets, looking at times as if he were searching for his soul. He went to left-wing dances with a pint of Old Overholt in his back pocket, drank it straight, got drunk, offered it to women he met, who got high and sometimes went to bed with him. But as belief in himself eroded, the harder it was to find his own soul.

A great pickup place in those days was the Artists' Union and the fund-raising affairs they ran. There was always good conversation, wine, punch, nibbles, and walls crowded with works of art. At one of these affairs Jake met Rhoda Haven. She was slender, well proportioned, with thick dark hair, large, expressive gray-green eyes, and a cameo like face.

"Hello," he said, wide-eyed, attracted, slightly drunk, nursing a paper cup of punch at the punch bowl.

She smiled warmly and said, "Hello yourself."

"Where have you been all this time?"

"Here and there."

"I'll bet if I kissed you, you'd taste like mint."

"That cool?"

"That refreshing."

He moved her away from the crowded punch table, pulled out his pint of Old Overholt from his back pocket, offered her a swig.

"Like that? Straight?"

"It'll make your nipples stand up."

"Do I want that?"

"It'll give you a nice massage inside. It'll warm you all over."

She took a drink. She choked. Tears came to her eyes. He took one after her, grimaced.

"A little pain," he said, "to feel no pain."

"Geronimo," she said huskily, wiping her eyes.

He laughed. She laughed with him.

"I'm Jake Davidson. I'm a writer. I'm on the Writers' Project. I write radio scripts that are produced at WBBM and WGN. I just finished doing a script on Seurat, the pointillist, 'Sunday on the Island of Grande Jatte,' for the Great Artists series."

"I'm Rhoda Haven, an artist. I'm on the art project, and I'm not in that class."

"I'm not in that class either. I write short stories, most of which are rejected. And I write novels that just can't find a publisher."

"I don't make all the shows I submit to either."

He offered her another drink. This time it went down more easily.

After a strong pull at the bottle, Jake said, "You know what Somerset Maugham said?"

"No. What did Somerset Maugham say?"

"He said, after considering the multitude of failed published books, that the writer—and this should include the artist as well—'should seek his own reward in the pleasure of his work and in release from the burden of his thought; and, indifferent to aught else, care nothing for praise or censure, failure or success.'"

"Now that's what I call walking around your own eggshells."

Somebody started a Benny Goodman record on the Victrola.

"Dance?" he said.

"I'm terrible. Clumsy."

"I won't tell you what my left foot is doing if you don't tell me about yours."

As long as she clung to him and they didn't move much, she danced well. When he tried to jitterbug, she was hopelessly lost. He liked it better holding her close anyhow. Her body felt awfully good.

"No more talk?" she said.

"What's to talk about? This is the only real, honest thing there is."

"Dancing?"

"Whatever."

When the music stopped, she said she had to leave, had things to do, people to see.

"When will I see you? Where?"

"Around. Later, maybe, at the punch table."

He was hot, flushed, horny, heady with rye whiskey. "You can't leave me like this."

She smiled, not teasingly, coquettishly, but with a sense of loss, then walked away. He looked for her later, but she was nowhere to be found. He wound up with a sculptress with a Maillol-like body. She lived in a huge loft on La Salle Street. The double bed looked lost in the place. As he made love to her, he had a peculiar feeling of being stared at by the statues of reclining women, athletic men, horses, dogs and sheep that she had created. He dreamed afterward that he had fucked one of the statues.

Two weeks later he saw Rhoda again at the Artists' Union open house, which was held every Saturday afternoon. It was right after a story of his had appeared in the *New Masses*.

"I loved that story," she said.

"For that, I'll buy you the Palmolive Building."

"I couldn't believe it was written by the guy I met a couple of weeks ago."

"If you have some dinner with me, I'll bring the guy who wrote the story out of the closet."

"I'm sorry. I can't."

The reason why she couldn't walked over. He was tall, with a sallow face, a long nose, and sleepy eyes.

"This is my husband, Jake. Sandor Haven."

He had read the story, too, but he wasn't as impressed or at least as complimentary as Rhoda. Jake walked away, looked around for other talent while glancing at Rhoda from time to time, then gave up and left. He called her early in the week.

"I'd like to see you."

"You met my husband, Jake."

"It doesn't scare me. My father can fight his father."

"I don't want to get involved."

"You putting me on your drop-dead list?"

"Oh, Jake, I'd like to see you, talk to you, but I want to be honest with you."

That's the way it was with so many of these left-wing broads: no wiles, no intrigue, no coquetry, no bullshit. If she were going to go to bed with you, she wouldn't fool around, she'd do it.

He knocked on her door one afternoon. She was living in a converted loft on Dearborn near Grand. The one large room contained their bedroom and living room, her studio in one corner, a pullman kitchen and a bathroom off to one side. A folded Ping-Pong table was in the center of the place. They played Ping-Pong and had coffee afterward.

"That your technique to keep the guys off? Tire them out on the Ping-Pong table?"

"The pleasure is more lasting, and the posture isn't as ridiculous."

"Except that I'm a well-trained athlete."

"How about another game?"

"I'd rather take a swim."

So they played Ping-Pong and swam. He liked her paintings. They were in the proletarian genre with touches of cubism, as moody as Picasso's Blue Period, as sad as Modigliani, sometimes as harsh and terrifying as Soutine. Some of them had hung in prestigious shows at the Art Institute, the Carnegie, the Pennsylvania Museum, the Palace of the Legion of Honor, the Whitney. She was even in the Art Institute's permanent collection.

"You're really something, aren't you?" he said.

She smiled bashfully.

"All that gorgeous talent."

She laughed. "What about yours?"

"Oh, me? Forget it. I'm a habitual reject."

Their admiration was mutual. It extended to swimming. They swam to the breakwater off the Lake Shore Athletic Club, which was a quarter mile out. She had never swum so far out or with anybody like him, never felt so secure in water even though she was an excellent swimmer. They walked along the breakwater, then sunned themselves on the great bleached rocks while listening to the lapping waves. Sweating and overheated, they dived into the water and swam again. Then she had to go back. Sandor worked for his father's law firm. He spent most of his time and made most of his money playing bridge and pinochle in the offices around him. He took on labor cases, cause cases for communists and minorities, which didn't bring him a penny. Though he was a communist, he was also the oldest son of a traditional Jewish family, and he expected his wife to adhere to all the bourgeois amenities. Always she had to go back: to prepare a meal; to run an errand; to get ready for Friday-night dinner at his parents, which gave her migraines.

"You ever hear of the palace revolution?"

"Yes."

But she always had to go back. He couldn't believe it, but he was carrying on a platonic affair. He was screwing his head off with other women, but loving her; he didn't know why. Then suddenly he wasn't able to reach her. He called during the day. She didn't answer. Nobody was at home in the evening either. One Saturday afternoon he met Sandor at the Artists' Union.

"How's Rhoda?" Jake asked.

"Fine, fine."

"Don't see her around anymore."

"Oh, didn't you know? She's in New York. Studying. Making all the museums and galleries. It'll do her a lot of good."

He resented her for going off without telling him. He wondered why she had gone off so swiftly and suddenly and secretly. He wondered even more when Sandor, the next time he saw him at the Artists' Union, asked him to share an apartment.

"What about Rhoda?"

"She's too involved in New York, studying at the Art Students

League, painting, making contacts for a gallery to handle her
work. She won't be back for a while."

"She's a pro. Why is she studying?"

"She has always felt she never had enough formal training.
How about it, Jake. The apartment."

"No, thanks, Sandor. You'd make a lousy fuck."

In time Jake got heavily involved in other affairs and in his
work. He adapted a short story of his for an NBC radio show
called *Author's Playhouse,* sold it, and was beside himself with
happiness. It brought him face to face with Peter Mason, the
production head of NBC. It was like meeting God. He was
ushered into Mason's office by Bill Clancy, the bald, pudgy story
editor. Mason had a great mane of wiry, silver gray hair, a pale,
bony face with a prominent nose and the deepest-set blazing blue
eyes Jake had ever seen. He sat at a shiny neat desk in a highly
polished leather chair in his Hickey-Freeman suit and Sulka
necktie, as lean and hungry-looking as Cassius. His office was
large, with leather couches and easy chairs and heavy carpeting.
His voice was deep and resonant. The man talked as if he were
on top of a mountain. He's got to be God, Jake thought. But
Mason's talk was good; it was about how great Jake's story was,
about how he, personally, was going to cast it with the best talent
in Chicago, and that was good. Then Mason went out of
character.

"We've got to find a kid with balls. What twelve-year-old kid
has got balls around town?" he asked Clancy.

"We'll send out a call for one. Better yet, why don't we try one
of our juvenile stars? He could sound like a kid, and he'd have
balls."

"No. It wouldn't be honest. We need a kid with a husky voice,
as if he's been yelling all day long on the streets. A kid with a lot
of heart."

"That's a tough order," Clancy said.

"Turn over the town, Bill. I want Jake to get a better
production than that Hemingway story we did."

"He'll get it."

"We need a different ending, Bill."

Jake was right on top of that mountain with Mason, even

though he talked as if Jake weren't in the room, but he slid down into the pits with the suggestion of a different ending. The story was of a poor boy whose aunt, with whom he was living while his father was away, was on relief and couldn't afford to buy him a pair of shoes. The boy didn't know his father had spent a year in jail. When his father came home and saw his son running around in his bare feet, he went out and stole a pair of cowboy shoes. The police came, arrested him, and took him to jail again. A real, no-hope, Depression story.

"We'll find one," Bill said.

Now Mason drew Jake into the fold. "Listen, Jake." His voice quivered, it was so emotional. "The man just got out of jail. He comes home to this deprived boy, whom he loves so much. He hasn't been a good father. He feels guilty. And God, how he loves that boy. We can't have him go back to jail again. We've got millions of people out there listening. We·can't give them a complete tragedy. Their hearts will be broken enough as it is. Let's give them something more than a tear. Let's keep the man and the boy together. With a statement of hope: that somehow things will work out for the better. And we can make another statement: that a man who steals out of desperation is not really a thief, that this man is essentially a good man. How about that?"

How could Jake reject it? He was thrilled by Mason's quivering, dramatic rendition. To hear Mason talk about his script, you'd think it was the greatest story ever told.

"Oh, oh, I've got it. *Broadway.* Lee Tracy was the star. Remember *Broadway?* Oh, that's it. We're at the end. The detective is about to take Tracy off to jail for murder. Suddenly he looks at Tracy, shakes his head, walks away, looks back, and says, 'What the hell would we do with you there?' Or words to that effect. And curtain. Boy, that's it. And you come out of that with a wonderful feeling, a sense of completion, because the murder was justified and you wanted Tracy to get away with it. But in your story, Jake, we've got an extra ingredient. A man and his son, their love for each other. We could end it with the kid saying, 'Who was that man, Pop?' And his father answering, 'A very good friend.' I like that."

"Sounds terrific," Clancy said.

A moment's silence. Now Mason pondered over what he had said; he looked like a gray eagle, hunched in his chair. Then his bony hand crashed down on the table. "I like that very much. There won't be a dry eye in the house. That was sensational, Jake. Write us another one."

On the night of the broadcast he heard the play with his mother and father, his sister, her husband, who had the equipment to record the show, his kid brother. The theme of the show was from Rachmaninoff's Second Symphony. When the musical theme came up, his mother started to cry.

"Mom, the show hasn't started yet."

"I know, I know."

When his name was announced as the author of both the great short story and the radio play, his mother clutched Jake's arm. *"Oy, oy, oy."* He thought she was going through a coronary.

"Mom, let's enjoy the show."

Then bang into the production. You could hear the show from every apartment; his mother had spread the word. The sound ricocheted from every window. His mother gasped. The drama was unbearable. Even the kid brother was hooked. And then it was over. Everybody stirred and fulfilled. His mother's handkerchief wet with tears.

"Better than a Garbo picture," she said.

Immediately the telephone rang. Relatives and friends telling his mother how great the show was. She was so proud. It wasn't Jake's night; it was hers.

"You'll win the Nobel Prize for that."

"Mom, it's only a radio show."

"Millions of people out there heard it. Written by Jake Davidson. They'll remember the name." Then: "You think they heard it in Hollywood?"

"Everywhere."

"You'll go to Hollywood. You'll see. You'll get offers. *Oy,* Jake, you should only go to Hollywood."

Hollywood. Shangri-la.

The next one Jake wrote was an adaptation of Ring Lardner's "A Frame-Up." The star of the show cracked up, he thought it was so funny. The whole cast got hysterical during rehearsal. The director, a slick-looking, dark-haired man with a deadpan face, had difficulty mounting the show.

"If the cast thinks it's funny, you're dead," he told Jake.

"Lardner is a wry, bitter, alcoholic writer, but he comes out funny."

At air time the cast stopped laughing long enough to do the show straight. It came out sweet and funny and lovable, and the star of the show went to Hollywood soon afterward to become a big movie star. Jake became known as the maker of stars. Hoo-ha!

The director of the show called him and said, "Listen, I'll show you wry, bitter, but really funny. Come on over." He handed Jake a collection of James Thurber short stories which included "The Greatest Man in the World." "There's funny."

It was a takeoff on the Lindbergh flight, except that the world created a hero out of a monster, then didn't know what to do with him. "We'll do it like it's happening. Announcers, reporters, from all over the world. We've got the best announcers in the country right here. I'll get an okay from Mason. I want you to do that for me."

Mason wouldn't let him do it like a news event. It would create too much havoc, he said. The show was done with the regular Rachmaninoff theme, the opening format of the show. The director hated it. "As an event, it would have been sensational. But as pure satire, bloop. Who wants Voltaire or George Bernard Shaw in your living room with a can of beer in one hand and a bunch of pretzels in the other?"

Jake was so involved that the Nazi-Russian nonaggression pact and the subsequent start of World War II stunned him only temporarily. He fluttered around like everybody else, going to meetings, reading the *Daily Worker* and the *New Masses,* listening, questioning: What's going on, how could it have happened? The communists had a simple explanation: Russia was surrounded by enemies; it was not prepared for war; by this strategic and masterful move it had averted a German attack; it was buying time to build up its war machine.

Was it still anti-Nazi, anti-fascist? Yes, the communists said; it was humanitarian, for the people of the world, for the classless society, against war. It was all so cynical, so incredible. After all the years of reading about Nazi atrocities, after being geared to fight facism on every front, even agitated to go to Spain to give his life, Jake found the doctrine of the end justifying the means hard to grasp. But he couldn't cut himself adrift from friends and comrades who were accepting the new turnabout and calling for the United States to stay out of the war—he was enough of a loner. Disillusioned intellectuals were dropping out of the Communist party and its fringes by the thousands. A few of them grabbed Jake.

"How can you justify that pact?"

"I don't know," Jake said. "I don't know."

The *Daily News* published a cartoon of a big Russian bear with a Stalinlike face dancing happily with a devil looking like Hitler, both with weapons of war in their hands.

Gradually the talk subsided. The war stalled; it became known as the great "bore" war. Everybody seemed neutralized. The Depression began to recede. People stopped talking about it. Wise guys were saying, "Hitler has ended the Depression. He's bailing us out." He was, in a sense. But at what a price.

Jake continued his bread-and-butter radio work for the project and got lost in as much sex as he could find. *Author's Playhouse* went off the air. He tried to do scripts for *First Nighter* and *Grand Central Station,* tried to create a soap opera, but failed. So he started swimming again to fill in the time. It always made him feel alive. In any pool, on any beach, he felt that he belonged.

One night at a fund-raising affair thrown by the Chicago Repertory Group, a left-wing theater organization, Jake's heart suddenly went wild. He saw Rhoda Haven dancing with a man. He asked a girl to dance with him. He fox-trotted directly to her.

"Hello," he said.

"Jake!"

"I'll meet you at the bar right after this dance. Okay?"

"Okay."

"Thanks a lot," said the girl he was dancing with.

"My sister," Jake said.

"Sister, hell. She looks more like unfinished business."

"Would you believe we're platonic?"

"If you're platonic, I'm Helen of Troy."

At the bar later, he spiked the drinks he bought with Old Overholt.

"I see you still carry your own antidote for weak drinks," she said.

"It gives me a better view of life. Where's Sandor?"

"Home, I guess."

"You guess?"

"I wouldn't know."

"You mean you're no longer married?"

"We're separated."

"Then, when you went to New York, you left him."

"Yes."

"What was all that bullshit he was handing me that you were only studying there, you were coming back?"

"He hoped I'd come back. He couldn't believe I was serious."

"We got friendly after you left. He wanted me to share an apartment with him. I turned him down. Said he'd make a lousy fuck. But I wouldn't have turned you down."

He took a long drink, looked at her steadily for a while, then said, "I'm not going to hold hands with you anymore. No more Ping-Ponging around or going for long cold swims. Like the Russian commissar said to the lovely lady beside him on the train, after a few remarks about the weather: 'Enough lovemaking. Let's fuck.'"

"I hear you, Jake. Loud and clear."

"Your place or my place?"

"You are a persistent bastard, aren't you?"

"The kid on the pogo stick. Say no and I'll fall off."

"I'm not ready for you yet, Jake."

"I'll warm you up, get you massaged, bathe you in myrrh and aloes and cassia, with Louis Armstrong and Duke Ellington making music for us."

"I couldn't. Not now. Not yet."

"I'm in the phone book. Rush Street. In case you change your mind."

A few weeks later he saw her at the Artists' Union open house. She was with Sandor. Later, over some bad punch, he said, "He was right. You went back."

"No. We just had lunch, then came here."

"You getting a divorce?"

"I don't know. Everything is so difficult."

"Why?"

"You live with a man for nine years, it isn't easy to break it up. Especially if he's a good guy and you haven't really had any fights or bad scenes."

She looked worn-out, emotionally spent.

"Where you staying?"

"I've got a small place near the University of Chicago."

"So what's going to happen?" Jake said.

"I don't know. I can't seem to make up my mind about anything. I get up early in the morning and shag way out to a frame factory on the West Side and paint pictures to go with their frames. They sell the whole package. Then I come home dead. Only to have Sandor nagging me. Then there were other things."

"What other things?"

"It's all so complicated."

"Why don't you quit your job and get back on the project? Maybe that'd make things simpler."

"I understand the project isn't going to last long."

"Ask Sandor to support you."

"I couldn't. I just wish I was back in New York."

"Why'd you leave?"

"It's a long story."

Sandor came over. "I see you two know each other." He was trying to be cheerful, but that was always a rough go for a man with a long nose and a doleful face.

"Yes," Jake said. "We met here some time ago. I met you then, too."

"Oh, yes." Sandor's voice exploded. "Sure. You just had a story published in the *Masses*. Great story."

Nobody was comfortable.

"I'm going home, Sandor," Rhoda said.

Sandor looked at Jake suspiciously for a second; then: "I'll take you."

"No, I can go alone. It'll be too big a trip for you."

"No trip at all. It'll be my pleasure."

"I don't want you to bother, Sandor. We'll talk again. Goodbye." She left.

Sandor watched her walk out, his face darkening; then he turned to Jake. "What'd you talk about?"

"This and that."

"She's confused."

"That's putting it mildly."

"She'll come back."

"I wouldn't bet on it, Sandor."

His face hardened. "She'll come back."

That night Jake asked information for Rhoda's phone number and called her.

"What are you doing?" he said.

"Nothing."

"Why don't we do it together?"

"I'm so glad you called."

"I'll be right over."

If anything was designed to dampen the romantic spirit it was Chicago's geography and transportation system when your girl didn't live right in the neighborhood. You nearly always felt as if you were in a waiting marathon for a bus, streetcar, or El. Then the rides were so jerky, dismal, and long that your anticipation got lost on some far-flung street. There was nearly always a few blocks' walk to your destination. And by the time you got there you were hard pressed for her toilet facilities. You needed the endurance of a lion in heat to overcome all that.

Jake fortified himself with a book of short stories by Erskine Caldwell and a bottle of Seagram's, which he didn't drink. Three streetcars, a half-mile walk, and an hour and fifteen minutes later he arrived at 53rd and Dorchester to a one-bedroom apartment. A double bed with a Mexican blanket and a bunch of colorful pillows was the couch. The floor was bare. There were a few chairs, a table, and a bookcase full of art books and pamphlets. The place was clean and orderly. Jake came in puffing.

"Seltzer, seltzer."

Rhoda smiled.

"You think the Jews had it bad when they left Egypt? You think the Red Sea was so tough? They'd have needed more than Moses if Chicago had been the scene. Where are the facilities?"

She laughed, directing him. He plunked the bottle of Seagram's on the dining-room table.

"Maybe you can fix us a drink."

When he came back from the bathroom, she had two drinks ready, some crackers and cheese.

"The gold at the end of the trail," he said. "To the liberation of Rhoda Haven."

They drank to that.

"Have you had dinner?"

"Yes."

"Well, we've both had dinner. I've seen all the good movies in town. Any good affairs around that wouldn't take all night to get to?"

"I wouldn't be interested."

"It's springtime. It's beautiful. Let's go out."

"You're sure you want to do that?"

"I want to take you in my arms and hold you and make love to you. That's what I really want to do."

"Let's go out."

They walked to the lake, then along a rocky promontory, and sat down facing the lighted skyline of the Loop and watched the Palmolive beacon wash the sky with its blue light. He felt the water. It was cold.

"New York hasn't got a lake," he said.

"It's got an ocean."

"It hasn't got a promontory, parks, neighborhoods."

"It's got everything else. And the subways."

"That I'll buy. So why did you leave?"

She was silent for a time, then said, "I didn't like myself there."

"Do you like yourself better here?"

"Not much."

"Where would you like yourself better?"

"Rome, maybe. Paris. Or an island in Greece."

"Wouldn't we all?"

"But there's a war on."

"What if there weren't a war?"

"Greece would still be too far away."

"What about Sandor?"

"There'd be strings. He'd expect me back."

"You lefties and your fierce independence."

He lifted her to her feet, and they walked off the promontory. He hailed a cab.

"We can walk home," she said.

"We're not going home. Do you like boogie-woogie?"

"I don't know."

"You're too much of an egghead. I'm going to introduce you to the lower things in life."

"But you don't have to be extravagant."

"That's another thing about you lefties. You're always worrying about other people's money, always afraid of being corrupted."

They rode into the heart of Chicago's black belt and stopped off at the Aces, a saloon with a bar, a dozen tables and chairs, a small dance floor, and at the piano Albert Ammons, who played more boogie-woogie than anybody in the world. The beat, as they walked in, was hard, rollicking, rocking, and filled with joy. A few couples were jitterbugging in the small space. Others were jerking their heads and rolling their shoulders to the beat.

"Fantastic," she said.

"That's real saloon music, rent party music, street music."

They had a drink and couldn't sit still. They got up, rolled, boogied, stomped, ground against each other.

"That's more like belly music," she said.

"That piano's got more beat than the whole Chicago Symphony."

Jake threw a dollar into the cigar box on top of the upright piano. Ammons nodded, laughed, kept rolling the music out. By the time Ammons got through Jake and Rhoda were laughing and sweating and holding each other tight. They had another drink, easing out from the beat of the music but still feeling the thump of their bodies.

"Prelude music," he said.

"Prelude for what?"

"The chamber."

"Do you use such primitive means with all your women?"

"Only when they're special."

"I like you, Jake."

"Meaning?"

"You're obvious, no bullshit about you, and let's go."

"Another thing about you lefties, nobody can ever seduce you."

By the time they got to her apartment the beat and the playfulness had gone out of them. He took her in his arms and kissed her after they entered, but it was an awkward gesture. He laughed.

"You know," he said, "preludes to the chamber are like big workouts, big athletic events. You take a rest, and you've got to warm up all over again."

She smiled. "I'll fix you a drink."

He went into the kitchen with her, took the drink she handed him. Then she cut up some ham and cheese.

"Hungry?"

"I'm hungry for something else."

"Fuck first, then eat. Right?"

"That's another thing about you lefties, you express yourselves so well."

She walked out of the kitchen and took the Mexican blanket off the bed in the living room, then got undressed. She was lovely in the soft light that came from the kitchen: her legs long and shapely, her hips curving into a slender waist, her breasts small, firm, with protruding nipples, her back arched like a Degas ballerina. The spring-cool night got warmer and warmer as they explored each other.

"We're like little dogs," Jake said, "smelling, poking, nudging, licking, kissing, touching. You think we'll know each other the next time we meet?"

"If we leave our scent with each other."

But they finally came at each other like grown animals: fierce, clutching, breathtaking, pounding, explosive, and overwhelming.

"Would you like to eat now?"
"Yes," he said.
He was a goner.

After that they saw each other nearly every weekend. Sometimes during the week. They went to movies, the Art Institute, concerts, plays, left-wing affairs. Late in the spring and during the summer they swam a lot off the promontory and sunbathed on the hot slabs of rock. On weekday mornings, when the alarm went off at six, he felt guilty lying in bed as she hustled about to get to work. He'd fall asleep again after she left, wake up later, have a leisurely breakfast, then go off to his furnished room on Rush Street, where he'd loaf through the day, reading, trying to write, doing some project work, going to the lake, browsing in bookstores, strolling down Michigan Avenue, looking in on galleries, feeling at times as if he were on the Left Bank in Paris. He no longer appeared desolate and hungry or as if he were looking for his soul. But he worried about a lot of things. The phony war was over. The way the Nazis had overwhelmed France and were pounding Britain displayed a terrifying power. Maybe Hitler's boast of "tomorrow the world" wasn't just the talk of a braggart.

The first peacetime draft was enacted, and Jake was subject to call. Roosevelt developed the policy of lend-lease and was supplying England with planes and arms, gasoline and oil. American merchant ships were being sunk by U-boats. The war was getting closer and closer.

He worried mostly about himself, his inactivity; that so very little was happening with his writing; that it was being rejected so often; that, outside of Rhoda, he wasn't taken up by something as consuming and imminent as his athletic days. He worried, too, about the project. It was being curtailed. Any day it might come to an end. Then what? Try to get a job in a war industry, overeducated, without any skills? Maybe newspaper work. Maybe. Things were picking up. If he lost his job on the project, what would he do about Rhoda? He wasn't a kid anymore. He couldn't go running to his old man to bail him out. He wasn't as brash, as confident, as in the last days of college, when he had thought, even during those hard times, that everything would come easily. The years had made him more careful. A sign of old age? At twenty-eight?

So he never discussed any kind of permanent arrangement with Rhoda, marriage or otherwise, though he wanted it. He let things ride. Except when she became mysteriously busy and couldn't see him. He couldn't ask her what she was doing, why she couldn't see him. He was afraid she wouldn't tell him if he pried, or she might deceive him. Jealousy ate through his guts during those times. She wasn't like Elaine in New York, who had given him the key to her apartment and thus committed herself to him. He had to make dates with Rhoda. There was never any indication of any sharing on her part. He was kidding when he had called her fiercely independent, but she wasn't.

"You're a secretive person, aren't you?" he said once.

"I don't always like to walk around naked."

"I thought you did." He tried to be light about it.

"Jake, even if we were married, I'd respect your privacy."

"Okay, you keep your skeletons in your closet, and I'll keep mine."

Once he said to her, "You don't mind living alone?"

"You don't know what a luxury it is," she said. "Do you realize that I was one of four children? And one bathroom. Never a moment alone. Never a bedroom of my own. I used to say jokingly that I got married to get out of the house. Maybe it wasn't a joke. So I went from a large family to a single person with his habits and his life to adjust to. My brothers, I could tell them to bug off, get away, scream and yell at them, but how do you tell your husband you want to be alone, you don't want him looking on while you're making up, you don't want him in the way while you're preparing a meal? Sure, I feel lonely at times. I'm eaten up by it. But oh, what a luxury not having to listen to somebody when you don't want to, not to hear sounds that offend or annoy you, to make your own uninhibited noises, to listen to your own music, even your own silence, and especially not to have to listen to the ball games."

"I get the message."

"Jake, for the first time I'm alone. I'm making my own decisions. I'm not responsible to anybody. I can make my own mistakes. I can fail big or small or succeed. I don't have to pussyfoot around anybody's emotions because he just happens to be there. I've got a freedom I've never experienced before. Don't step on my new world, Jake."

He hated going to left-wing affairs with her because once the men knew she was unattached they dismissed him and flocked around her. He felt at times as if he were bringing a prize whore everybody wanted. He'd be shoved into the background, and he'd hardly see her all evening. She would be plied with drinks, and she glowed in the flattery and attention paid to her. He would observe it all in a jealous rage.

After one of those affairs he said, "Thanks for letting me take you home."

"Don't be angry, Jake."

"I can't believe I'm alone with you at last. You left the crowd for me. I'm so flattered."

"Don't be bitter."

"What is it, some secret smell you've got that attracts them all? Is it the whale's ambergris about you? The smell of rare orchids? Gardenias out of season? Whatever it is, you've got them flocking all over you."

"You don't possess me, Jake. I'm not some chattel, some piece of property."

"Oh, now I get my lesson in Engels and Marx. Women's rights, equality, and all that jazz."

"Oh, shit."

"You express yourself so beautifully."

"Go home, Jake. Get lost."

"That's another luxury you can enjoy. You can tell me to fuck off."

"Right."

"So long, baby."

He pounded down the stairs of her building. When he got outside, she was leaning out of the window.

"Come back, Jake."

He looked up, hesitated. She looked so beautiful to him.

"Don't be a child, Jake."

Somebody yelled, "Shut up!"

Suddenly the whole scene looked so ridiculous. Romeo at the bottom of a beat-up, smoky old building with an arrow of jealousy in his heart; Juliet, married, about to get divorced, far from starry innocence, with male animals from everywhere ready to bay at her window. He burst out laughing. And came back up.

"What's so funny?"

"The human condition."

"That's funny?"

"Stand it on its head, it's ridiculous."

In bed later she surrendered herself to him completely. What more could he want?

Sandor showed up once at the Artists' Union open house. He talked to Rhoda awhile. She seemed very tense and uncomfortable with him. Then he stepped up to Jake.

"You're a shit," he said.

Jake decided not to get angry. "That doesn't leave much room for discussion, does it?"

"You pretended to be my friend, and all the while you were her lover."

"I was never your friend. You asked me to share an apartment with you. Asking doesn't make me your friend. And I was never her lover before she went to New York."

"You're still a shit."

"You really like to lock me into the toilet, don't you?"

He blustered. Made fists and loosened them.

"You want to hit me, go ahead," Jake said. "It won't solve your problems."

"It'll make me feel better."

"I doubt if anything but forgetting Rhoda would make you feel better. You want to go outside?"

Sandor hesitated.

"No point in upsetting all the people here," Jake said. "Let's go."

Jake walked outside. Sandor followed him.

"All right, Sandor, get it out of your system."

Sandor glared at him. Spit dribbled out of the corners of his mouth. Jake braced himself to block the first blow, calculated how he would strike back.

"You bastard," Sandor said, and walked off.

Rhoda came out, looking worried. Jake had never asked her

what her difficulties were with Sandor, why they were incompatible, why she'd left him. He didn't want to know. It could have been as mundane as he snored too loud, ate apples with his mouth open, made funny faces while he picked his nose, was a lecher or pervert or a premature ejaculator. He didn't want to hear about their intimacies.

"What did Sandor want?"

"He wanted me to stop being a shit. He wants me to give you back to him."

"I'll talk to him."

"Will that stop him from thinking the worst of me?"

"I'll tell him the truth."

"What is the truth, Rhoda?"

"Nobody took me from him. I had to take myself away, or I'd have gone crazy."

"Was life that impossible with him?"

"It was more impossible with myself."

Soon afterward he met the man who had helped her leave Sandor.

They had come out of a movie when this man approached them.

"Rhoda!"

Rhoda tightened.

"I'm Dan Stein," the man said, offering his hand to Jake.

"Jake Davidson," Jake said, shaking his hand, observing him, watching Rhoda swallow hard.

The man was almost twenty years older than Rhoda. Bald, heavy eyebrows, dark, penetrating eyes, vital-looking, medium-sized, with a little potbelly.

"How are you, Rhoda? How are you? Did you like the movie? It was wonderful, wasn't it? It was a hel of a movie." He talked nervously, in vast discomfort. "Everything all right? Are you getting along all right?"

"Yes," Rhoda said.

Jake said nothing.

"Imagine meeting you like this. All the way from New York, I go to a movie and meet you. It couldn't happen again in a million years. But why shouldn't it happen? You're a moviegoer, I'm a moviegoer; it could happen, it could happen."

Jake stood there awkwardly with Rhoda beside him as Dan Stein talked on and on. Then he said, "I won't keep you. It was really nice meeting you." He shook Jake's hand, then turned to Rhoda. "I'll see you. Take care." And he walked swiftly away.

"Small world," Jake said.

"Yes."

They started to walk to her apartment.

"Should we stop off for some coffee?" he asked.

"No. Let's have it at home."

"Good."

Silence.

"Old friend?" he asked.

"Yes."

Silence.

"New York?"

"Yes."

"Just like out of a Noel Coward play."

"Only not as bright and faggy."

"We could play twenty questions."

"Let's not."

"Did you like the movie?"

"Not any more."

Silence. Down cold streets. Under bare trees. They walked faster to keep warm.

"Gonna be a long cold winter," he said.

"Aren't they all?"

In her apartment a trickle of heat came from the radiator. She prepared some coffee and toasted a bagel. A treat. It cheered them up somewhat. Then they went to bed. They stroked each other to get warm, held each other close, moved against each other. Soon their hearts were beating hard, their blood was pumping faster, their bodies became moist, and the whole world was forgotten. Only they existed. Only sensation. Rippling, roaring in. Right in the middle of it, a knock on the door.

"Rhoda."

They weren't sure. A harder knocking.

"Rhoda."

"No," Rhoda said.

Knocking turned to pounding.

"I know you're in there. Open the door."

"Oh, God."

"We better let him in," Jake said.

"He's insane."

"Let him in, Rhoda."

Jake got into his pants and shirt. Rhoda threw on a robe. She opened the door. Dan came charging in, breathing hard. His eyes were burning. He looked wild, glancing from Jake to Rhoda to the rumpled bed, back and forth.

"I knew you were in here."

"Why shouldn't you know?" Jake said. "You followed us here. You've been following us all night."

"No. I swear."

"Bullshit."

"What do you want, Dan? What is it you want?" Rhoda said.

"I wanted to meet him."

"All right, you met him outside the movie. What more do you want?"

"I wanted to talk."

"There's nothing more to say, Dan. I told you in New York. I told you here, too."

"No, I've got more to say. I left my wife."

"Dan, you've seldom been around your wife. You've had your own apartment. You did whatever you wanted. You never were really married."

"I'm going to divorce her. This time I've made up my mind."

"It doesn't make any difference. I never wanted to marry you. I never asked you to. I don't want to marry you now. We had an affair. I needed it. How do I make you understand it was just an affair?"

"You lived with me. It was more than an affair."

"Please, Dan. It's late. I'm tired."

"Nobody has ever left me before."

"For God's sake, Dan. You've had a thousand affairs."

"Yours was the big one. The only one."

Jake stood on the sidelines. It was as if he weren't there.

"What the hell has he got to give you?" Dan pointed at Jake. "A writer. WPA. Hasn't got a pot to piss in. He'll never have a pot."

"Right now he's got everything I want."

It was her first real declaration of love for him.

"Pretty soon he'll be drafted. We'll be in the war. He'll get his ass blown off."

"I don't want you to talk like that."

"I can offer you a life, a good life, comfortable."

"But I don't want it. We've been through all this before. I told you and I told you."

The energy and intensity suddenly seemed to go out of him. He sagged down on a chair and began to cry, "I'm sorry, so sorry." He looked up at Jake. "All those things I said, I didn't mean it. Forgive me." Then to Rhoda: "I just want you to be happy. I don't want you to make any mistakes. I think only of you."

"You'd better go now, Dan."

"Yes, yes." But he didn't move. Then: "Where'll I go?"

"Wherever you're staying."

"Yes."

He buttoned his coat and got up. Now he looked like an old man as he shuffled to the door.

"I won't see you anymore?"

"Please, Dan. There are other women out there. Lots of them."

He shook his head, sniffled. "I'm sorry, Jake. Forgive me. I'm an old fool, Rhoda. Why do I feel so desperate?"

She patted his back, opened the door. "Take care, Dan."

He left, the fury, the sap gone.

Rhoda stood there, shuddering. Jake put his arm around her, led her to the bed, and pulled the covers over her. He took his clothes off, turned out the lights, crawled in beside her, and held her tight. Then her body began to shake with sobbing.

Jake held her closer. Understood what she'd been going through. Her husband after her. Then her lover. Understood why she had left New York, why she hadn't liked herself there, why she wasn't ready for a lasting affair or a commitment. She fell asleep in his arms.

In the morning, over breakfast, she said, "I'm sorry you've got to be a part of this whole thing."

"You love me, don't you?"

"Yes."

"What is it they say: 'for better or worse'? It's been better."

"I guess you have it all now."

"Would you have left Sandor if Dan hadn't come along?"

"Eventually. Dan made it easier. Jake, I committed one dishonest act in my life. I married Sandor without really loving him. I was pushed into it. His father was a lawyer. He was starting out as a lawyer. Had a bright future. Good family. My mother kept agitating me. I said, yes, okay, yes. In bed he was a disaster. We were just terrible together. I threw myself into keeping busy. Studied art, spent as much time as I could working at it, quivered with wanting to be an artist. Then I got involved in the party. When I met Dan, I was prey to any man. He prided himself on being a Don Juan. And he was. He opened up the whole world of sex. Then deception crept into my life. The lies I had to tell and live with. The guilt. So when Dan asked me to go to New York with him, I did. But I couldn't hurt Sandor. More lies. I lived with Dan for a while. But that got kind of messy. He was fooling around with other women, wanted me to fool around with other men, like I was some possession he was passing around. I got a job and moved out. He kept after me to move back. Sandor came to New York, begged me to come back. It was a nightmare. Everywhere I went, Dan followed me. I finally came back here.

"What else is new?"

"You."

"You going to get a divorce from Sandor?"

"Now I will. No more dishonesty, no more deception."

"You love me."

She kissed him. "That's an honest, no-bullshit kiss."

Early that spring the McCormick and Tractor Works of the International Harvester Company had gone on strike. Jake was bogged down in a new novel he was trying to write. He decided to get away from it and help the strikers if they needed him. He went over to El Rancho Grande, a tavern in the industrial belt on the Southwest Side of Chicago. Headquarters for Local 108 of the Industrial Farm Workers Union (IFWU) was in the back. The place was crowded with picket signs, workers, and their wives.

"Who do I see to help out?" Jake asked a man in a lumber jacket. "I'm a writer."

He was directed to a cubbyhole of an office, where a man was working on a leaflet, his partially bald head a few inches from the paper. Jake recognized him immediately when he looked up. He was Charley Ball, the Wobbly organizer he'd met when he bummed to California, the sight of his one eye worse, his Adam's apple bonier, his body as thin and long as it always was. He embraced Jake.

"I knew sooner or later the romance would be kicked out of you and you'd see the light. Did you ever make your grand tour?"

"No."

"You should have stuck with me. Oh, what a time I'd have shown you."

Jake didn't know how Charley had fared in the West, but he'd become a hero and a legend during the great sit-down strikes in Flint and Detroit. He had started the first sit-down strike in Flint. But in the struggle for power afterward Charley had lost. He was kicked out of the union as a Red and blacklisted in the industry. Under an assumed name he had come down to Chicago, got a job in the foundry at the McCormick Works, and organized the whole plant. When the company wouldn't agree to a National Labor Relations Board election, Charley had pulled his men out. Local 101, the Tractor Works, followed.

"I thought you never stayed put," Jake said. "I thought you were always a ramblin', gamblin', rootin'-tootin', organizin' man."

"I was. Until I got to Detroit to help organize auto. I got balled there, then chained. Next thing I knew I had a kid."

"You mean you lived long enough in one place to vote?"

"I finally got to exercise my rights as a citizen. Now, what are you doing here?"

"I want to help. Use me."

"Finish this leaflet."

After Jake finished the leaflet, Charley read it over and made some suggestions.

"Always the rewrite," Jake said.

"Nobody's perfect."

When Jake turned in the rewrite, Charley said, "You working?"

"I'm on WPA."

"I've got a better job for you. A real job."

"Doing what?"

"Publicity."

"But I've got a job."

"Jake, I'm going to get you so involved you won't see straight. I'm going to put you smack in the middle of something you'll really be able to write about."

Charley grabbed his arm and started leading him out. Jake felt helpless before Charley's insistence.

"I want to have you with me on this one," Charley said. "I need a guy I can trust."

He took Jake over to IFWU headquarters nearby. It was a big hall with several offices, also crowded with people and connected with another tavern. There he was introduced to Larry Ashburn, a skinny, light-haired, blue-eyed man with an iron jaw and teeth parted in the middle; he was in charge of publicity.

"We can use him," Charley said. "Writer. Newspaperman." He showed Larry the leaflet Jake had written.

"I'll have to take it up with the treasurer."

"You don't have to do anything. I'll hire him for my local."

"Don't go off half-cocked, Charley. We're not the teamsters. We're not auto. We're begging for money."

"We need him," Charley said.

Larry turned to Jake. "You're not going to ride on cushions here."

"I came down to help out for nothing," Jake said. "I've got a job. I don't need this one."

"Don't listen to him, Larry. He needs this job. More than he thinks."

Jake felt a tension between Charley and Larry. He was to learn later that Larry was a powerhouse in the union, its mouthpiece, with the officers depending on him and Charley for leadership. Larry made a quick decision.

"Will you take forty a week?"

"Whatever you say," Jake said. It was a fortune compared to what he was making on WPA.

"You'll work with me," Larry said, trying to gain control.

"Bullshit," Charley said. "He works with me."

"Okay," Larry said. He pulled out a thick file covering the history of the union, the demands and grievances, the struggles with the company and the government in terms of who represented the workers, what had happened since the strike began a week ago, and the background of the Harvester works from the time Cyrus Hall McCormick had begun manufacturing the reaper in 1847 through the Haymarket riots until the present. "Read it all. Tomorrow I want you to write a radio speech for Powers Hapgood, who'll be coming in from Washington. He's John L. Lewis's man. Big brass from the miners' union."

"It's not going to be easy, Jake," said Charley.

"When I was born, nobody guaranteed me the easy life."

Jake read all afternoon and made notes for Hapgood's radio talk. He took some of the material and went down to the Writers' Project offices on Chicago Avenue near the lake and told his director he was taking a leave to work for the strike.

"If we're still in business afterward, come back."

"Thanks," Jake said. "This may turn my whole life."

"Good luck."

From there he walked to his cramped furnished room in what had once been a carriage house on the Near North Side before it and the main house facing the street had been broken up into small rooms and apartments. But he liked the neighborhood, the nightclubs on Rush Street, the medieval Water Tower on Michigan Avenue, the Palmolive Building and the beaches nearby, the short walk across the Wacker Drive bridge to Kroch's bookstore, where he could browse and meet other writers. He submerged himself further in the union file, had a quiet dinner at Thompson's Cafeteria, then took a streetcar to the South Side, where he had a date to see Rhoda.

When he told her about the new job, she said, "You're always shifting gears, aren't you?"

"I'm accident-prone."

"What about your novel?"

"Nobody's breaking my door down for it. I'll get to it later."

"Careful. You might get so caught up you'll never get back to it. Action can be a drug."

Rhoda was right. The action was fierce, completely absorbing, a real drug. There were ads to write, the union paper to set up, radio time to be arranged, speeches to be written for local presidents and visiting union officials, meetings to attend into the night, news releases to the press, telegrams to word to the NLRB, the secretary of labor, even to President Roosevelt. Everybody was on him for words and more words.

Sometimes he didn't have time to go home. He'd stay at Charley's place, a small two-bedroom apartment on 28th and South Kedzie Avenue, in the heart of Bohunk town, a heavily industrialized district with factories, breweries, utility plants, railway lines, and the Chicago Drainage Canal running through it. The area was called Ceske Kalifornie; the streets were lined with buildings and bungalows fashioned after German and Czechoslovakian houses.

There was a gypsy feeling about Charley's place. Nothing ever seemed to be in place. The bathroom was always hung with damp drying clothes. His wife, Meg, a big, heavy, cheerful woman who was ready to giggle and laugh at nearly everything that was said and done, was a former waitress who had come from hillbilly, moonshine country in Tennessee. There was a three-year-old boy underfoot. Meg giggled and laughed out of nervousness and fear.

"What do you think of me?" Charley said. "Right smack in the middle of Bohunk country."

"One thing about Charley," Meg said, giggling. "He's got one foot planted right in the middle of a labor battle and the other aching to run to wherever else there's trouble."

"He's a man with seven-league boots and a Paul Bunyan heart," Jake said.

"That's me," Charley said. "Like horseshit, I'm everywhere."

Meg screamed with laughter. "He was brought up on the go. I honestly believe he was born in a covered wagon. With giddy-yap in his soul. If we didn't have the little boy, Lord, Lord."

"Lordy, Lordy," Charley said, slapping his knee.

Then he'd pick up a knicked guitar, beat time on the scrubbed floor with his feet as he played and sang his ramblin', gamblin' songs of rascals and tramps and railroad workers and riverboat men and road builders. He had a twangy voice, his raw Adam's apple would bob up and down, but when he closed his eyes and that one dead eye of his didn't fix on you, there'd be a long softness to his face, and you could see that he didn't belong being married, that his body yearned to be roving where the songs led him. As he sang, Meg held the boy tightly and rocked to the rhythm, but her face grew sadder and sadder; sometimes a slight twitch of fear would cross her face.

Charley was in a very complicated situation. It wasn't just a big corporation he was in conflict with; it was three other unions: a company union; the AFL Amalgamated Farm Workers (AFW); and the powerful Industrial Auto Workers Union (IAWU). Each claimed the majority of employees and the right to represent them. The company would recognize only the company union. It spread rumors that the IFWU was communist-led, that Charley Ball had been kicked out of auto because he was a Red. The men at the plants didn't care what Charley's politics were. They liked Charley, trusted him. He stood for higher wages, seniority, and better working conditions. He had the guts of a gorilla. If that was Red, they'd go to bed with him, they said. Charley called for a strike. It was the only way to prove who had the majority of workers, to force a Labor Board election.

But it took money to run a strike, and the IFWU hadn't had a chance to build up a war chest. Auto offered $100,000, good jobs, and better pay for all the organizers, the power of its 1,300,000 members, if the IFWU came in with them. Charley didn't trust auto. He wanted his union to be independent, free of big union politics; he was strong enough to vote auto down. So the IFWU began to hurt for money. Other CIO unions contributed small amounts, which were eaten up immediately. Even John L. Lewis didn't go all out for the IFWU; he was afraid of Charley Ball's Red taint; he felt the IFWU would be better off in auto. The company was well aware of the interunion strife. It would let both the AFL and CIO's auto break the strike. But the men at Tractor and McCormick kept the plants shut.

Jake was confused by the conflicts among the unions. Watching them in action began to erode some of his idealism. He was so busy he hardly had time to see Rhoda, but once, when he did see her, he said, "It's bad enough battling a company. But when you're also fighting the AFL and another big union who wants to take over, it's murder."

"Why?"

"Power. Once you taste it, you can't seem to get enough of it. I look at the officers in the union. They're all former working stiffs, insecure guys with a life of layoffs, poor pay, fear of being fired, a struggle just to exist. The union gives them a whole new life. They're good social animals; they talk shop; they're good drinking buddies in the saloons. Men listen to them. Men follow them. That's the first taste of power. Then they're elected to office. No more clocks, no more foremen on their backs, no more sweat in the shops. They've got money in their pocket, expense accounts, bigger cars. They've earned respect, not only from their fellow workers but also from their bosses. They even feel a kind of fear in their bosses. Now that's power. Real power. They won't give it up. Nobody's going to kick them out, take over. They'll kill, if they have to, to keep that power. Even Charley Ball, a gypsy at heart, suddenly got a taste of big power, of having thousands of men at his command; even he's been corrupted by it."

"What about you?"

"Me? I just work for them."

"In their most dangerous period. Why couldn't you have worked for them in a peaceful situation?"

"Let's talk about something else. Like how's your divorce coming along?"

"Sandor's taking care of it."

"In his own sweet time, huh?"

"What's the hurry?"

"You might change your mind."

"I love you, Jake. What more do you want?"

"That's all I wanted to hear."

"I just hope you don't get your head broken."

The leadership of the IFWU was in conflict about going into auto. Each day the workers on strike suffered greater hardship. They needed rent money, food and clothing for their kids, more contributions for their soup kitchens. Pressure was put on them by the company, which sent out letters telling them they'd be without jobs if they didn't come back to work. Auto gave them handouts and promised their war chest if the IFWU came in with them. Some of the leaders saw themselves in the saddles of more power if they affiliated with auto; others saw themselves back in the shop. Charley Ball held them together through their fear of losing what they had.

Most of the leaders already felt the exhilaration of power. They could call up John Steelman, the federal mediator, and Labor Secretary Frances Perkins and talk to them. Through them they were involved with the President of the United States. Harvester was a defense plant, and Roosevelt, with his policy of aid to Britain, didn't want anything to interfere with military production. His pressure to settle the strike was felt everywhere.

Here were men who had hardly ever gone out of their neighborhoods, some of whom had never finished grammar school, and they were now meeting with Mayor Edward J. Kelly and Governor Henry Horner, traveling to Washington and staying at the finest hotels and dining in the best restaurants and meeting with the secretary of labor and the secretary of the army and federal mediators and congressmen and senators, then running down to the Tri-Cities on the Mississippi and Peoria and Fort Wayne and Richmond, Indiana, wherever farm machinery was made, and organizing those plants. Here were men who had led dull, uneventful lives. Going to the ball game or fishing or to a picnic or downtown to a movie was a big event in their lives. Payday, when they were working, you would find them in their favorite saloon outside the plant and in their neighborhood, having a good time. Many of their wives would come to meet them at the factory to take most of the pay or they'd have nothing to eat all week. Here they were now, listened to, respected, in control, with more money than they ever had, with a dizzy sense of power. Most of them were still idealists, believed fervently in the destiny of the workingman, but they were spoiled for going back into the plants, spoiled for the deadening, robot, routine lives they had led. They'd rather die than go back. They talked to Charley about affiliating with auto. Maybe that was the only way to go. Charley said no, never, don't sell out.

One day, late at night, in a cold, early-spring rain, as Jake was going home with Charley, two cars jolted to a halt, and five men with blackjacks and ax handles ran out and attacked them. Jake was slammed across the face with a blackjack. He thought he'd run into an iron fence. Another blow across the side of his head made jelly out of his knees, and he fell into a rain puddle. He wasn't totally out, but he was numb, he couldn't move for a time, and he watched Charley being beaten mercilessly about his head and body. Jake staggered to his feet and blindly tried to wade in, but he was slugged again. The beatings were swift and silent. As Jake came to, one of the men said to him, "Tell that one-eyed bastard to get lost. Next time he'll get a pine box." Then he heard somebody say to Charley, "Beat it, Charley. Get out of town. Or you're dead." Then they drove off.

Stiff, hurting all over, Jake got up and helped Charley off the wet ground, the rain pelting them.

"You all right, Jake?"

"I'm alive. How about you?"

"I thought my other eye was gone when they hit me."

"Who were those guys?"

"My pals from auto."

"Why, Charley?"

"They want to gobble us up. They want to be sure they'll take over after we bust our ass to win the strike."

"The dirty bastards."

"But I won't let them take over."

Meg, Charley's wife, woke up when they got in. She was horrified when she saw the swelling around Charley's good eye, the blood smeared over his face and clothes.

"Oh, God, God, God."

She ran into the bathroom, came out with a wet towel, and washed the blood off his face. Then she brought some ice out, wrapped it in two towels, and gave them to Charley and Jake for their swollen faces.

"He gave an eye already," she cried. "Next, it'll be his life."

"Meg, please."

"Jake, talk to him," Meg said. "They call up. They warn him. He won't listen to me. Talk to him."

"Meg, you don't talk to mules," Jake said. "You just hit them in the head. Over and over."

"How do I tell him he's done enough?" Meg said. "He's got me, a kid; what more does he want?"

"A world that belongs to the workingman," Charley said.

"They'll kill you first."

"Meg," Charley said, "don't play God."

"I'm not God. I'm your wife. I don't want you dead."

"I don't believe in God," Charley said. "But if I did, even God lets people die once in a while. Every day he lets them go, thousands, millions, all over the world. So who the hell am I?"

"A guy who might get a bullet in his heart," Jake said.

"Look who's talking," Charley said. "Forty bucks a week. No future. Not even a stake in the strike. He gets his head beaten."

"You're both crazy," Meg said.

Charley pulled a bottle of Old Crow from the kitchen pantry, took a pull at it, and offered it to Jake.

"The cure for everything," Charley said.

They killed the bottle. Woozy, weak-kneed, Charley went to bed with Meg, and Jake flopped on the couch, his head whirling. Maybe I'm wrong, he thought. Maybe Charley is the only incorruptible man in the world. A guy like that, a guy you can't buy off, he can scare the shit out of you.

The rain pounded on the next morning. Jake's head wanted to burst, it felt so swollen and achy from the beating and the booze. Meg fixed them some breakfast. Her big breasts flopped about inside her robe as she hustled about. There wasn't a giggle or laugh left in her.

"Why'd I ever marry you?" she said to Charley.

"If you hadn't, I'd still be roving the country."

"Maybe you'd have been better off. You'd still be around the grape pickers and the lumberjacks. You wouldn't be mixed up with these gangsters."

"It was in the air, Meg. The big powerful unions and you."

"You regret me, don't you?"

"How could I regret having a beautiful kid and the best humping in the world?"

"But you'd rather die for the working class than enjoy humping with me."

Charley fixed his one eye on Jake. It was bloodshot, shaken up from his beating. "She's always trying to make me choose sides.

When I'm always telling her I wouldn't enjoy humping without a cause." He laughed.

"I want to be the only cause," she said. "Me and our kid."

"You're a selfish woman, Meg."

"There's no talking to him, Jake," she said. "Take care of him, will you?"

When they got to union headquarters, they were stunned to find full-page ads in the daily newspapers: The company, claiming that a majority of workers affiliated with the AFL and the company union wanted to go back to work, announced that the McCormick plant would open the next day. The AFL organizer stated in a front-page story that AFL men would return. The strategy was to crack the McCormick plant, then open the Tractor Works.

All that day Jake and Charley and other union officials threw themselves into mobilizing all the workers from Harvester and all the local CIO unions to meet outside union headquarters the following morning to prevent strikebreakers from entering the plant. Jake tried to buy radio time and put Charley on the air to talk to the public, but there wasn't a radio station in town that had any time available. He tried to place a full-page ad in the night edition of the *Tribune,* but the paper wouldn't accept it. He and Charley sent a flying squad of 100 men and women to the McCormick mansion on Lake Shore Drive. He talked to Charley about going out to Waldheim Cemetery and praying at the graves of the Haymarket martyrs.

"I don't pray," Charley said.

"Don't pray, you dumb bastard. Just stand there. We don't want another Haymarket. I'll inform the press. We can't buy ads or radio time, but we can make a stink in the press."

"Maybe."

"We've got to try."

"Okay."

Two hundred people got into cars and rode out to the Far West Side to Waldheim Cemetery and stood in the rain over the graves of the Haymarket martyrs, stood in silent and prayerful vigil. The press covered it. Even the *Tribune.* They even covered the pickets at the McCormick mansion with their signs bobbing in the rain.

Inside the gray-stone palace the McCormicks, who had dominated Chicago industry and society in a regal manner for years, were terribly upset by the turn of events. Some of them, fearful of another Haymarket, wanted to settle with the union, to give them their election. But the company was no longer wholly in their hands. They walked on rugs once owned by the Shah of Persia. Amid Byzantine tapestries and Buddhas from Chinese temples and priceless Renaissance paintings, they sat on royal Napoleonic chairs and ornate Louis XIV couches. They ate from Napoleon's golden service, which consisted of 1,000 pieces and contained more than 11,000 ounces of precious metals. They would rather have dwelt in the memories of the opera they'd brought to Chicago, of the flamboyant days of Mary Garden, of the great days of Enrico Caruso and Galli-Curci and Tetrazzini. But another Haymarket faced them again while they listened to the fierce winds blowing in off the lake and to the chant of the pickets outside in the rain.

Two bodyguards were assigned to Jake and Charley. They tagged along wherever they went. That night, weary to the bone, Jake decided to spend the night with Rhoda.

"I'll see you," he said to his bodyguards.

They were big, intimidating men, who had worked in the foundry. One of them had the mashed nose, swollen lips, and cauliflowered ears of a boxer. He had had to quit fighting when he'd broken one of his hands. "My punch was too strong for my hands. If my hands were stronger, I'd have killed bulls."

"What do you use now?"

"This." He pulled an iron bar out of his pocket. He probably had a gun, too.

As Jake started to leave the hall, they followed.

"Where you going?" Jake said.

"We'll take you."

"Listen, I'm going to my girl's. I'm staying the night."

"We'll take you."

"Hey, Charley. Get these goons off me."

"They're your ball and chain, Jake."

They led him to one of their beat-up cars. One of them lifted the hood; the other examined the insides for any explosives.

"Get in."

Jake couldn't shake them. He got in and told them where he wanted to go. When they reached Rhoda's apartment building, Jake said, "Thanks, fellas. So long."

They got out with him.

"Hey, wait a minute. Next thing, you guys'll want to get into bed with me and my girl."

"She good looking?" the ex-pug said.

"Maybe you got an idea there," the other guy said, laughing.

"Get lost, will you, guys?"

They followed him to the door. When Rhoda opened it, they moved in swiftly and cased the place.

"What's going on?" Rhoda asked.

"My pals," Jake said. "They won't even let me wipe my nose."

"Okay," the ex-pug said. "Stay put till we pick you up at six."

After they left, Rhoda said, "They're playing for real, aren't they?"

Jake nodded. Then she noticed his swollen face.

"What happened to you?"

"I walked into a door."

"Oh, God." She clutched him and held him close. He felt her tremble. "I read the papers today."

"Then you know the whole story. Tomorrow's Armageddon."

"I'm so glad you came, Jake."

Jake looked out the window. The heap was still outside, the motor running to keep it warm, the rain down to a drizzle, the streets shiny under the lampposts.

The next morning, at 6 A.M., the boys knocked on the door. It was still dark out. They came in cold and damp. Rhoda made hot coffee and a quick breakfast.

She began to shake. "Christ, I feel like I'm fattening you up for the kill."

"Take it easy, baby." Jake held her close.

The ex-pug said, "We gotta go."

"So go," she said. She clenched her fists as they left.

Daylight was creeping into the city as they rode off to union headquarters. The streets were still wet, the sky murky and gray, threatening more rain; the air was bone-chilling. Crowds of people were already in the street when they got to the union building. The soup kitchen was in full operation. The hall was mobbed. Picket signs were being hastily put together. World War I vets wore their souvenir helmets and Legionnaire caps. A light drizzle began to fall.

The march to the McCormick gates began with Charley and Jake and other union officials leading it. Hundreds of signs bobbed in the air. Jake estimated 8,000 men and women were in the line of march. As he walked along, he thought of Republic Steel in South Chicago on another spring day in 1937, when ten men had been killed. He thought of Haymarket in 1886 on still another early-spring day, when a general strike for the eight-hour day had been called for May 1. Three months earlier 1,500 employees of the McCormick Reaper Works, striking for higher wages and the eight-hour day, had been locked out and replaced with strikebreakers. At a mass meeting near the plant, several hundred men had broken away to demonstrate at the gates as the strikebreakers were leaving for home. A large detachment of police had appeared and fired into the demonstrators, killing six and wounding many others. A rally at Haymarket Square had been called to denounce the atrocious act. It had been a peaceful rally on a drizzly day. A day like this, Jake thought. Even Mayor Carter Harrison, who attended the meeting, had been satisfied that nothing would happen. But Inspector John Bonfield of the Desplaines Street Police Station had sent 200 police and ordered the gathering to disperse. At that moment a bomb had exploded, killing 8 policemen and wounding 65 others. In the gunfire that followed, many more civilians had been killed and wounded. Seven of the labor leaders had been sentenced to death; four of them had been hung, one had exploded a fuse cap in his mouth before going to the gallows, and two had been pardoned years later. Haymarket, Jake thought, as the crowd, exhilarated, sang songs and chanted slogans and locked arms in solidarity.

Eighteen hundred cops were waiting for them with their clubs and billies and helmets and .45 Police Specials and shotguns and tear-gas guns. Three fire companies were on hand with their high-pressure hoses attached to fire hydrants. The ten men who were allowed to picket legally were like tiny specks in the blue sea of armed police at the gates. Sergeant Barnes and his Red Squad were there; so were his photographers and cameramen among the newspaper and newsreel men. But the union men and sympathizers marched on. When they were less than fifty yards apart, Charley called a halt.

They stood facing each other for minutes, but it seemed like hours to Jake, the cops grim, at the ready, the strikers singing and shouting slogans. His clothes were damp; his face was wet from the drizzle. He felt naked. The huge force and power of the men and women behind seemed to be pushing him forward. I'm right up in front, Jake thought. If the shooting starts, there's nobody between me and the cops. Hammers tripped off in his heart, pounded in his head. Keep it peaceful. Don't let there be another Haymarket.

At 8 A.M. the gates opened. Police Captain John Prendergast proclaimed that the rally was unlawful, ordered the crowd to disperse. The workers edged closer, shoving Jake forward. Then from a side street, 200 professional strikebreakers and 100 bona fide Harvester workers started to march to the gates. With terrifying, angry shouts, the workers broke for them to keep them out. Immediately streams of water from the powerful hoses knocked people down, and the police broke ranks, came in wielding their clubs, and started shooting volleys of tear gas. Jake thought his eyes had caught fire when a shot of tear gas exploded near him. He was knocked to the ground by a club, was trampled as he tried to scurry away. Blinded and choking and coughing, his face and his insides burning, he was shoved about and knocked down again and again; then he scampered to his feet and ran as two flaming cars hurtled past him and slammed against the fence and stopped in front of the gates. His eyes still afire, he swooped down to a pool of water the fire hoses made, doused his eyes, and drank some of the water to clear his throat.

The workers were soon dispersed, and the strikebreakers were herded into the plant. Ambulances came in with their loud sirens. Twenty men and women were hospitalized. A rally was held outside union headquarters. Later 500 men marched on City Hall to protest the police violence. The union leaders met with Mayor Kelly and Governor Horner. They agreed to confer with the NLRB and the company on an election. The Defense

Mediation Board stepped in and forced an election to be held.

Charley was happy now. He was sure of victory.

"We're going to take it," he said. "Then we'll take the rest of the farm machinery plants. All of them all over the country. And it'll be us in the saddle. Independent. Clean. All for the workers."

He asked Jake to have dinner with him. He had bought a bottle of California Cabernet Sauvignon. On the way home, he said, "Meg'll be happy. No more roaming around. This union'll keep me put."

As they stepped from the car, a shot rang out. Then another. Charley stopped suddenly as if he'd slammed into a wall. He bulled forward a couple of steps, stunned; then a flower of red blood burst from his shattered face, and he toppled to the walk. Jake ran to him as two men piled into a car and streaked off. They looked like two of the men who had beaten them up. At a scream, Jake looked up. Meg was at the open window, clutching her little boy in her arms, her eyes wide and full of grief.

Jake rushed back to union headquarters. He accused auto of killing Charley.

"I saw the guys," he said.

"Can you identify them?" Larry Ashburn, the publicity director, said.

"I don't know. I'm not sure. But they're the same two guys that beat us up."

Later Larry took Jake aside and said, "You want to get yourself killed, too?"

"No."

"Then lay off."

"He made that union. He made this one."

"Grow up, Jake. What the fuck do you think unions are, a private crusade, a theory of Karl Marx's? They're big business. They elect Presidents. They make wars. Who the fuck is a Charley Ball, a Jake Davidson?"

The next day Jake was fired.

The union accused the company of killing Charley Ball. Hammered away at it. Rallied the workers behind his memory. Made a martyr of him.

Later that spring, behind the slogan "A Vote for IFWU Is a

Vote for Charley Ball," the IFWU beat the AFL and the company union in a Labor Board election. Right after that, auto came in with $100,000 to help organize the other farm equipment plants. They offered its organizational might and promised to keep the officers of the IFWU at their jobs at higher salaries and bigger expense accounts if they'd come in with auto. There was no Charley Ball to keep the union independent. Jake felt as if a hole had been torn open in his gut when the IFWU affiliated with auto.

The Writers' Project was still in existence. He went back to it and the novel he had started months before.

Right after Rhoda's divorce Jake took her to the Three Deuces to celebrate. They listened to Jimmy McPartland and his Chicago-style band, which had been inspired by Bix Beiderbecke, and then, during one of the intermissions, he said, "Listen, I like to sleep with the windows open, even in winter. We both like to sleep naked. We seem to react to hot and cold the same way. We're crazy about swimming. I like the way you cook, and you like the way I react to your cooking. You're a compulsive reader, and so am I. I think you're talented, and you think I am. We fuck like there's no tomorrow. Sooner or later the draft's going to get me. If you don't marry me, it'll be sooner. I'm a devout coward. So save me from the army. Save me from being killed. Save me from my loneliness. Marry me, marry me."

"Oh, Jake."

"I can't give you diamonds, a cottage small, a honeymoon to Niagara. My only collateral is a lot of rejection slips, a couple of unpublished novels. All I can give you are promissory notes and all of me. How about it?"

"I'll marry you, marry you."

They passed their Wassermann tests.

"Our certificates of virginity," Jake said.

They got married in City Hall: fee $2.

"The price of a good lay, stamped, approved, and sanctioned by the powers of the state and God, amen," said Jake.

On Sunday he brought her to his mother and father.

"Folks," he said, "this is Rhoda. Her name used to be

Hirshman." He said nothing about her former marriage. "Now it's Davidson. She is now a member of the tribe."

"What is he talking about?" his mother said to his father.

"I think he's trying to tell us they're married."

"Jake, true?" She clutched her hands.

"True."

"*Oy.*" She grabbed Rhoda, tears bursting from her eyes, and kissed her.

His father shook Rhoda's hand. "Welcome."

Rhoda kissed his cheek. He was touched.

"Aaron, a glass wine," his mother said. "I'll get some sponge cake, make coffee. I'll do something."

His mother and father, very nervous, became overbusy.

"Jake," she called from the kitchen, "help me."

She didn't need any help. Only information.

"Who is she?"

Jake said, "She's beautiful, isn't she?"

"Of course she's beautiful. She's young, I hope she's healthy. Why shouldn't she be beautiful? But who is she? Where does she come from? Who are her parents?"

First, he told her the most important thing she wanted to know: "She's Jewish."

"Thanks to God."

"A West Side girl. A graduate of Marshall High School. An artist."

"No wedding? Her parents couldn't give her a wedding? You got married just like that without a rabbi, no *chupah? Who are her parents?*"

She found out soon enough. A cousin of Rhoda's father's lived in the next building. Who were the Hirshmans, the snooty, hoity-toity, hotsy-totsy Hirshmans? He had been a manufacturer. A capitalist. Hot Springs in the winter. Lake Geneva in the summer. Automobiles when nobody had automobiles. The good life. The father, a Talmudic man, well educated. The mother, high-toned, like a cameo she looked, with the snobby manners and speech of English royalty. But the business had failed. Then they had got into high-fashion dress shops. One failure after another. Then *shlock*, $2.98 dresses, with fancy Spanish shawls in the window to give them oomph. Until they had become nobody: he, a tailor, she, a seamstress, in a little flat on the North Side, right back where they had started. But the mother, even with heart attacks, still held her nose high, her pride poured in cement.

Jake's mother knew who they were. She had bought a couple of dresses when they had had their store on 12th Street right next to Davey Miller's restaurant, where the gangsters and politicians and the fight crowd hung out. She remembered when they had gone out of business. Some thieves had broken in, taken everything. A week later their eldest son, Richard, who was operating a chain of *shlock* stores, had been contacted and offered the so-called better dresses from his father's store at a third of wholesale. The son was going to buy the lot and give them back to his father. But the store was a lost cause by then. It had been losing money. It was better to collect the insurance, declare bankruptcy, and keep a few dollars. That was the high-class Hirshmans.

They kept their marriage a secret from her mother and father. At the time her mother was in the hospital recovering from a heart attack. Jake was introduced at first as "my good friend."

"It sounds like I'm a member of the Roosevelt clan," he said with a smile.

Jake could see where Rhoda got her good looks. There was still a cameo beauty about her mother. He could see where she got the reputation of being snooty. Her head was always high; there was a delicacy about her; she was elaborately correct with her manners, unlike Jews who acted first and apologized later; her English was impeccable. She called Rhoda "baby," the last in a string of four children.

Rhoda's father was a small gray-faced man, pudgy, round-cheeked; what little hair he had was also gray. He had tried vainly with his wife's help to keep his hair in the once-fashionable pompadour style, but now, with her sick, his hair strayed every which way, causing his wife to say, "Eli, brush your pompadour." Which he did with his fingers and palms.

Rhoda was very attentive to them, and they were grateful she could come. They were really two destitute people, alone, with very few friends. What delighted them most—and they looked like two children who'd just been handed ice-cream cones—was when their eldest son, Richard, came to visit. He was a dandy, dressed in tailor-made suits, tall, slender, slick, with larceny in his heart and utter contempt for everybody. He always came with a bottle of booze and consumed half of it before he left. He now operated a successful women's apparel store in Gary, Indiana. He'd get up after an hour's visit and say, "Gotta get home to the little woman." That was his wife, who was gentile and never visited. But Rhoda was sure he was going to finish the night playing cards and whoring around. Her other brothers were concerned, hardworking men. One worked for a large plumbing supply house and always announced himself as the toilet man; the other was a social worker who was married to another social worker, a Russian émigré from Odessa who seemed to have come right out of Chekhov's *Cherry Orchard.*

After Rhoda's mother was well, Jake's mother insisted on a get-together.

"We're a family now," she said. "We should meet."

"Only the family," Jake said.

"All right, only the family."

Jake's mother got busy cooking and baking and cleaning the apartment. On Rhoda's side she invited her brothers and the neighbors who were cousins to Rhoda's father. On her own side, only her sisters and their husbands, Jake's sister and her husband, his brother, Harry, who expected to be drafted into the army any day, and Nachum and his wife. It was a full house even without Richard and his wife, who didn't show up.

"I thought only family," Jake said. "I promised Rhoda only family."

"This isn't family?"

"It's the whole *mishpocheh.*"

"The whole *mishpocheh,* we would have to rent the grand ballroom of the Stevens Hotel."

Everybody got acquainted. Both families took a full measure of each other. Both families were so proud of their offspring. Rhoda felt like a manikin in a store window. Jake felt like some prize bull. At one point he wanted to say, "What am I bid?"

The affair didn't last long. A couple of hours after dinner, Rhoda's mother complained of still feeling frail and begged to be forgiven for having to leave so early, but they had a long ride home. Mike, the plumbing-supply son, and his wife, a slender, kind-looking, jolly woman, were obliged to take them home. Burton, the social worker, and his wife, who looked something like a burnished samovar, had a long ride ahead of them on a streetcar and a hard day's work facing them the next day.

Jake's mother didn't urge them to stay. No "you just got here." No "the evening is young." Just "It's a pleasure to know you. Let's hope our children will be happy and blessed." There were no postmortems at their departure because Rhoda was still there. But there were plenty afterward.

On the way home later Rhoda said, "Do you feel your ears ringing?"

"My mother took me aside and said, 'Very fine, high-class people, Rhoda's family. A little standoffish, a little high-toned maybe, but refined.' My father said your father is a very educated man."

"My brother Burton said, 'You sure Jake's a writer? He talks like a gangster.'"

They laughed. Then, seriously, she said, "Let's make a deal, Jake."

"Right. No family obligations. I'll handle mine; you handle yours."

"Not that I don't want to see yours from time to time. Not that I don't want to be concerned about them. But no regular Friday-night things, no rigid schedules."

"We're not like that. We don't even celebrate birthdays. My mother and father don't know when they were born. Neither do I for that matter."

"But that's terrible. You'll never know what sign you were born under. You'll never be able to have an astrological chart made."

"As long as I'm healthy."

They laughed.

"I'm glad it's all over," she said.

"So am I. Now we're officially married. You know what my rich uncle made me do? He took me into the bedroom with a wineglass and a napkin. He made me stomp on it and break it. 'Now,' he said, 'you're really married.'"

Another laugh.

She swelled up in him. Even when she wasn't around, she was something inside that grew bigger and bigger; she was something wonderful and palpable in him. Gradually he moved away from the world of the loner.

Shortly afterward Jake was laid off the project. Right in the middle of a radio play, right in the middle of a new novel.

"Don't worry about it," Rhoda said. "We'll get along. Finish your novel."

"If I don't get this one published, I'll quit."

"Famous last words."

But even as he worked on the novel, he felt guilty lying in bed when Rhoda got up at six and froze as she hurried about in the ice-cold morning, getting ready to go to work. After she left, the steam started to crackle through the radiators, and he slept on until the apartment got warm; then he loafed through breakfast, reading the morning *Tribune,* which he hated. Jokingly he'd say, "I read it only to test my sense of rage." Then he'd get to work and finish around noon, when he'd fix himself some lunch. He'd wonder what to do with himself. He'd go down to the Near North Side and bowl with other guys from the project who'd been laid off or he'd sneak off to a movie. Sometimes he'd go to Lyon and Healy and listen to the latest Benny Goodman or Artie Shaw or Louis Armstrong records and buy one, or he'd make all the bookstores from Kroch's to Marshall Field's to Carson's to Bill Targ's to Brentano's to Max Siegel's to Paul Romaine's, passing the time like a *luftmensh.* By the time she got home and started to prepare supper he felt guiltier than ever. When he'd tell her about it, she'd say, "You and your Jewish bourgeois upbringing. Bring home the bacon, smoke Bull Durham, ride wild mustangs, and all that Billy the Kid stuff. One of these days you'll be telling me you're going to join the RAF. Rah-rah, the big adventure. Forget it, Jake. Do what you want to do while you have the chance. You can be sure you'll be the breadwinner most of our lives."

He started to sing "Just a Gigolo."

"You'll get your book published. It'll be a hit. Even if it isn't, you'll go to Hollywood."

"Dreamland."

"Isn't that what always happens? You publish a book and the Hollywood moguls bring you out there?"

"That's the fantasy. A thousand dollars a week. You do nothing. They forget you're there. You get paid every week. After thirteen weeks they renew your option for thirteen more weeks. You try to write your own things, but you worry more about your option being picked up. By now you've got a villa, cars, a swimming pool, kids, maids, more responsibilities than you can handle. You worry like a Midas that they'll take it all away. Utter boredom and lots of money. Until out of sheer guilt and fear you shoot yourself."

"Everybody should have such worries, such fears."

He tried to do some radio plays, but nothing he did sold. So he went back to his novel. It was like working in a vacuum. He wondered if he was a bum at heart, if being a sun-stoned lifeguard and a spoiled athlete hadn't made a lazy lotus-eater out of him. Is that why he'd become a writer, so that he wouldn't have to conform, to face the nine-to-five routine and demanding bosses? So that he might achieve instant fame and fortune, everlasting blue skies and sunlight, a beach outside his door, a lounge beside a swimming pool? Or was he just being a clown, a runaway kid at heart, wearing a mask through life?

Maybe he ought to go into the army or navy or merchant marine. See some action. Live through a real blood-and-guts story, an adventure that'd make the world sit up and take notice. But it still wasn't his war. Roosevelt was bringing America closer to the brink. The way he spoke, Great Britain was America's last fortress; it had to be armed to the hilt. Supply ships were being torpedoed right off the Atlantic coast. That man in the White House, people were saying, was going to get us into that war. Jake's kid brother, Harry, was drafted. Only twenty, so young, so handsome with his black hair and dark eyes, so vulnerable. The war got very close.

Right then he got a call from Moish Bender at the JPI.

"What are you doing, Jake?"

"Writing."

"Nothing else? Nothing more pressing?"

"No."

"Get over here pronto, you bastard."

While working as swimming director of the JPI, Moish had been selling medals and trophies on the side. He had been so good at it that he had been making more money than his regular job. He had been offered the midwestern managership of his trophy company at four times his JPI salary plus commission.

When Jake got there, Moish said, "You want this job?"

"All my life that's all I've been dreaming of. I went to college to prepare myself for this. I hoped you'd die so that I could take your place. Who cared if all I'd face for the rest of my life was a world full of cocks, naked asses, athlete's foot, and water on the brain? All I ever asked for was a chance to dedicate my life to the JPI."

"The job is yours. I talked to Kaplan." Abe Kaplan was the athletic director. "He said okay. A hundred fifty a month."

"Shit, that pays two cents more than a lifeguard's job."

"But you get a glorified title here: swimming director. You want it or don't you? There are five thousand guys waiting for this job."

"I'll have to call my wife."

He picked up the phone and called her at work and told her about the offer.

"Do you want it?" she said.

"It's a job."

"You didn't finish your novel yet."

"I'll have all the time in the world on this job. Every morning. A couple of afternoons. All day Saturday, the *Shabbes*. It's totally mindless. It'll make us rich."

She laughed.

"I won't have to sponge off of you."

"Take it, Jake."

He hung up. "Okay, Moish."

So he had come full circle from a thirteen-year-old kid who yearned with all his might to become a member of the JPI swimming team to swimming director. What more was there to life? What other worlds could he conquer?

His hours were as complicated as a railroad schedule. Tues-

days and Thursdays from noon to two, from seven to ten.
Monday and Wednesday from one to seven. Friday from noon to
five. Saturday from seven to ten. Sunday from ten to twelve,
then from two to five. Seven days a week. Time off for the
Jewish holidays. A month's vacation.

He thought he'd have his mornings to write, but it took him
more than an hour to get to work. He had breakfast. By the time
he figured out what he was going to put down on paper he had to
leave for the JPI. Sometimes it was nearly midnight when he got
home, and Rhoda was asleep. What destroyed him was the time
between shifts. He went to matinees, to the library, visited his
mother, but mostly he went out of his mind killing time. On the
days of the split shift, it was like working ten hours a day; with
travel, thirteen hours. They were certainly mindless days, but as
far as writing was concerned, with this perfect job for it, he felt
immobilized.

Toward the end of March one of Chicago's freak blizzards
blew in. When he left work after ten that night, the snow, with
gale-force winds, almost hurled him off the streets. He got down
to the car line to go home, waited and waited for a streetcar.
After a half hour, frozen, he gave up. Half blind, covered with
snow, he ducked into the howling wind and walked through the
drifts to where his parents lived. He was half dead when he got
there.

He woke Rhoda up when he called her.

"I was worried about you," she said.

"It didn't stop you from falling asleep, did it?"

"I was so tired, Jake."

"I won't be home tonight. I'll be staying at my folks."

"That's a good idea. Will I see you tomorrow?"

"I don't know. With anymore snow I'll need some huskies and
a sled."

"You sound angry."

"I am."

"I didn't make the blizzard. I was battered by it, too."

"It's all that fucking shagging around. All that wasting time.
All that not having a home to go to between shifts. Shit."

His mother, listening, said, "Jake, you shouldn't talk like
that."

"Fuck."

"I'll see you tomorrow," Rhoda said.

He didn't see her until two days later, after the snow plows had cleared the streets.

"We're going to move," he said.

"Just like that, we're going to move, I don't have anything to say about it?"

"Christ, we spend half our lives traveling to and from work. What's so wonderful about the South Side, about this crummy little apartment?"

"I hate the West Side."

"Why?"

"I just hate it."

"Give me one good reason."

"I didn't like my childhood there. It wasn't a happy one."

"You mean you were an anti-Semite then. You still are. The snooty Hirshmans."

"All right, I'm an anti-Semite."

"Your folks had the money when you were a kid. Maids, autos, all that shit. Why didn't they move to the South Shore, Belmont Harbor, Evanston?"

"I don't know why."

"Because they were living it up. Because they were all show. Phonies. Nothing real to back them up."

"Okay, Freud, you've got all the answers."

"I thought you were a straight, honest, no-craperoo person. What's all this pretentious shit the West Side isn't good enough?"

"You think I haven't thought of moving there, even before we were married? You think I haven't thought of how much easier it'd be to get to my job, not freezing on street corners waiting for streetcars, not being crushed by the after-work crowds?" She began to cry. "You bastard, accusing me of anti-Semitism. All right, I was an anti-Semite. I still am. I hate Jews. I hope Hitler kills them all. You feel better?"

He took another tack. "All the wandering around I do. Can't write. Can't concentrate. Can't even read. We hardly see each other. Hello, good-bye, that's us. Pretty soon the draft'll catch up with me. Boom, they'll take me away. Maybe forever."

"Go on. Make me feel guiltier."

"I don't feel like I've got a home."

"What do you call this?"

"I come home so late. You're asleep. I wake you up."

"All you think of is your fucking before you go to sleep."

"What about you? Isn't that your sure cure for insomnia?"

She wiped her tears. "All right. Enough. We'll move."

Guilt struck him. Maybe he had been laying it on; maybe he was being too selfish. Maybe life would be so miserable for her after the move he'd regret it.

"No," he said. "You're not going to make the big sacrifice. We won't move."

"Yes, we will. Life here has become intolerable."

"We'll stay right here."

One Sunday, while he was at work, she found a two-bedroom apartment with a Colonial porch off Independence Boulevard, a few blocks from the JPI. A month later they moved.

Rhoda set up her easel, taboret, and drawing table in one of the bedrooms and made a studio out of it. Jake's father built a rack to store her paintings. Jake worked at a small desk in the dining room. She was only a couple of miles from her job; he was only a few minutes' walk from his. A perfect place for a newly married couple. Except that Rhoda hated the West Side more than ever. The Depression had taken its toll. The neighborhood looked blighted. The stench was greater, the streets dirtier, the buildings filthier, the noise of children and parents louder than ever.

"Everybody lives at the top of their voices," Rhoda said.

It was hard for her to bury the unhappy memories of her childhood: of her fears when she had gone to school; of living with all her brothers in a crowded apartment; of having to run errands for her mother in horrible-smelling butcher shops and grocery stores; of watching her mother and father fail in one dress business after another, with creditors pursuing them, threatening to wipe them out and kick them out on the streets; of preparing meals while her parents attended their *shlocky* affairs; of nobody paying any attention to her drawings when all her heart since she was four went into them. The West Side wasn't exactly dreamland for her.

And Jake, with more time on his hands, began to play four-wall handball, then drown himself in long swims. He wrote every morning, but it seemed so unimportant with the war hovering over their lives.

The second day of summer Russia was attacked by Germany. The war took a new turn. Everybody Jake and Rhoda knew pushed hard for the United States to plunge in and save the world from the Nazis. The German blitzkrieg roared through Russia, conquered one city after another, crushed its defenses from Leningrad to the Ukraine, and knocked out its air force. Huge American convoys to Britain and Russia were too little, too late. The American communists could again defend the nonaggression pact: Hitler's attack proved that the Soviets had only wanted to borrow time against the invasion, but now it had run out. By winter, despite American aid and the scorched-earth policy of the Russians, the Nazis were in the suburbs of Moscow. It looked as if the world were coming to an end.

That winter, on a quiet Sunday, while Jake was having lunch with Rhoda and listening to a concert on the radio, he said, "I hate to go back to the pool this afternoon."

Rhoda said nothing. She'd heard the same complaint countless times. Suddenly the concert was interrupted. Japan had attacked Pearl Harbor.

"What was that?" Jake said.

"I don't know. Something about bombs, warships, planes destroyed."

"Listen."

They listened all that day. To the radio. To everybody reacting. Eight battleships, five cruisers, twenty-six destroyers, half the aircraft of the Pacific base were destroyed. The next day America was at war, and recruiting offices were jammed with volunteers. Hitler was jubilant that American naval power had been crippled. The war immediately began to go badly in the Pacific, and the draft boards started calling up more and more eligible men. The only good news came when the Russians held firm in Moscow, then counterattacked and drove the Germans back.

There was no way Jake could stay out. He had no dependents.

He was certainly not in any essential war industry. The draft board was getting closer and closer to his number. He had finished his novel, had sent it to an agent in New York, only to get negative reactions from a number of publishers. He was a most expendable man.

His kid brother was in California in the Signal Corps. Every day more and more young men from the JPI and the neighborhood enlisted or were drafted. He spent the mornings loafing around, reading, staring into space. At the pool he talked about the war and felt guilty not being in it. The noise of the pool got more deafening. Monotony set in. He was drained of spirit and vitality. A vast restlessness came over him.

"It's like I'm under a hot shower all day," he said to Rhoda. "I come out wilted, no good for anything, totally useless."

"You think you'll be more useful crippled or dead? You men, you're all like kids. War is a game, the big adventure."

"It's our war. The war against fascism, against tyranny, against extermination."

"I know all the slogans."

"This isn't World War One, the bullshit save the world for democracy."

"What do you want to do, enlist?"

"Sooner or later they're going to call me. There isn't a thing wrong with me. I'll be in."

"Your job's a deadly bore. You're restless. You're a romantic. You want a change of scenery."

"All my life I feel like I've been an outsider."

"Even when you were a swimming champ?"

"No. I felt I belonged then. But only then."

"All right, Jake. Change the scene; join the gang; become a star, a hero again; belong."

"You don't want me to go."

"I don't want you to get killed."

"You think I've fallen out of love with you."

"Haven't you, Jake?"

"I've fallen out of love with myself."

"So? You can't love anybody if you can't love yourself. Right?"

"Rhoda, what am I saving myself for? What am I, some hothouse flower? I didn't have the guts to go to Spain. I never really had the guts to put my body where my mouth was. Ideas, abstractions, slogans, all crap if you can't put yourself on the line."

"Jake, I'm not standing in your way. I know you're going to be called. I know you're going to be in. Whatever you do, I'm with you, I love you."

"I think I'd like to get into the merchant marine."

"Oh, Christ, Jake."

The news was full of torpedoings, airplane attacks, the sinking of ships.

"You really want to get into it, don't you?"

"All the way."

She was cool when he made love to her that night.

"You're mad," he said.

"You could wait until they call you. You might get into an easy branch of the service. You're a college graduate with a high IQ. You might never be sent overseas."

"I know."

"The merchant marine. Every time you go out you're in the thick of it. What are you going to prove?"

"Maybe that I'm—not a devout coward."

"Or that you're a zealot, a throwback from Masada."

"Rhoda, I love you. I'll love you more once I get my feet wet, once it's all over."

"I'm sorry, Jake. I'm just scared."

She flung her arms around him, clutched him tightly, and loved him as if she wanted to move her whole heart into him.

The next day he gave the JPI notice that he was joining up. They treated him with handshaking, backslapping patriotic fervor. A month later, in the summer of '42, he shipped out to the merchant marine training camp on an island in the New York Narrows called the Rock. Rhoda stayed in Chicago a short while, selling some of the furniture, then moved to New York. She found a one-room apartment on 15th Street off Fifth Avenue and got a drafting job at Sperry Rand. After his first month of basic training, Jake came home on liberty every weekend. He was outfitted in a pair of tight-fitting bell-bottom pants and a loose blouse, and he wore his white sailor hat jauntily. He always felt boyish and foolish in the uniform. Rhoda could never get used to it; she was embarrassed by it.

"Imagine, me with a sailor," she said, laughing.

"Imagine, me with a girl in every port."

"Next thing, you're going to get tattooed."

"Strictly with your colors and your design."

"The last guy I thought I'd ever be seen with was a sailor."

"Bums, my mother called them. No goods. But I had a sailor suit when I was a little kid."

"Didn't we all?"

They got free passes to the theater, rowed boats in Central Park, went to movies, saw friends they'd known from the past, went to the Met and the Whitney and the Museum of Modern Art and all the galleries on 57th Street with Jake looking at the world through Rhoda's sensitive eyes, her knowledge, her critiques, her excitement. It was an emotional time for them, kind of sad because soon he'd be leaving for the war zones, carrying dangerous cargoes, with his future always in doubt, and kind of exciting since they saw each other afresh each weekend and plunged into everything with abandonment they had never known before. There was an elegance about everything they did, even the restaurants they went to and the food they cooked; they lived a civilized, cultured life they never had in Chicago. It didn't matter that neither of them wrote or painted; they felt needed and purposeful and, most important, childish. Nobody cared much who you were or what you were before. The men were reduced to the anonymity of a uniform, and they all were united in a common cause. Nothing more was expected of them than to serve their country and to win the war. It was a time of heartbreak and hardship, dislocation and loss, but the resilience, fortitude, and fellow feeling that sustained people through the Depression were forged tighter in this greater battle for survival.

On the Rock Jake learned seamanship, all about ropes, knots, splicing, the handling of lifeboats, even sailing them with romantic red sails. The Rock was the size of two battlewagons. From it you could see Coney Island, the roller coasters, the parachute jump, the Statue of Liberty, and the heavy necklace of submarine nets wriggling in the Narrows. In the evening he sat on the walk and watched the sea go by. He was another guy in a blue shirt; he didn't have to explain himself or apologize for his failures. A big bunch of guys and himself, starting from scratch. Maybe Rhoda was right. He'd joined the gang. Back to childhood.

From the Rock he could see the convoys come in and go out, and he'd wonder where they were going, what battles they had come from. He watched them steam in and out of the Narrows, water curling against the ships' bows like foamy lace collars. Once he saw a freighter move in with a hole in her side big enough for a tank to crawl through. Another time a destroyer came in with a stack blown off. While he watched the ships go by, he sailed to every sea and every port the convoys headed for, saw himself in every battle from the North Atlantic to the South Pacific, then come back exhausted and alive and safe; he was immortal.

After the IQ tests, the captain in charge offered him a job on the base as a yeoman at $125 a month, food, and board.

"We need guys like you to do the paperwork. You can sit the whole war out here. Safe."

"I don't know."

"Out there you'll get your ass shot off. Once you're outside the Narrows, you're shark bait."

Boy, they made it tough for him. He really wanted to go out, but he wasn't a hero.

"Out there you don't just get your knees skinned or a bloody nose. You can get the deep six."

"I wanted to see some action."

"You fucking romantic writers."

"Maybe I'm just a romantic Jew."

"They're the worst." The captain laughed. "Okay, Jewboy. You can do anything you want to, become a mate or an engineer or a purser-pharmacist."

"I think I'll go for purser."

"If you change your mind, let me know. We can use you here. Talk it over with your wife."

That weekend he held back telling Rhoda about the offer. He'd made up his mind he was going to ship out. He didn't want to sit on the Rock for the duration.

She sensed something was up. "All right, Jake. What is it?"

"I was offered a job as yeoman on the Rock. Pretty good pay, and I could sit the war out there."

"But that'd be a bloody bore, wouldn't it?"

He nodded.

"You're afraid your kids will look down on you when they ask you what you did during the war."

He smiled, biting on her irony.

"Imagine, your kids going out, bragging about you: 'You know what my daddy did in the war? He was a paper pusher. Yah, a paper pusher.'"

"You want me to take the job, don't you?"

"Don't ask me. I don't want you to die. I don't want to worry my head off when you go out there. But it's your war, Jake."

"It's your war, too."

"Jake, you're not just some guy I kiss and send off to war. You're the guy I want to spend the rest of my life with. And to be corny about it, I'm the girl who is going to be left behind."

"You're not the only one."

"But you have a choice. Wow, wouldn't most of the guys who are slugging it out like to be in you spot!"

"I don't feel I really have a choice."

"No, I guess you don't. You're a goddamn voyeur. You've got to see what it's like."

"Don't be angry, Rhoda."

"What I am is mixed up. I think you're a stinker, but I'm so damned proud of you."

She kissed him so hard he thought she'd go down his throat and wriggle through his body and lie there for the rest of his life.

Eight hours a day he went to Pharmacy School, learning anatomy, first aid, pharmacology, the diagnosis and treatment of disease. He was expected to be the ship's doctor for a merchant crew of fifty and a naval gunnery crew of twenty-four. Every Friday examinations, then weekend liberty. After six concentrated weeks of lectures and study and four more weeks of practical work as a male nurse at the naval hospital in Sheepshead Bay, he was classified as a first-class chancre mechanic. Then four weeks in Purser School, learning ship's business from signing on a crew to making out the payroll. Commissioned as a purser-pharmacist mate, he was outfitted with a one-stripe ensign's uniform at Brooks Brothers.

That winter he was put into a pool at the Chelsea Hotel in Manhattan. He was on twenty-four hours standby to ship out. Since the Chelsea was only a few blocks from where he lived, Jake managed to get home every night. It was a tense time for him and Rhoda. Any minute he'd be leaving for ports unknown. Then he got his first assignment. An Esso tanker carrying high-octane gasoline.

They made love as if it were the last time they'd be together. In candlelight they had squab for dinner, a French wine from before the war. They listened to Rachmaninoff's Second Symphony and remembered his radio plays for *Author's Playhouse*. They talked brightly, heroically. They made love a couple of more times during the night, tenderly, not as desperately. Early the next morning he was off.

Where?

He didn't know.

For how long?

He knew nothing. His whole life from now on was going to be a mystery; it was in sealed papers, a blinkered message in mid-Atlantic.

His first ship, the SS *Rockport,* was new, trim, sleek, battleship gray, with only one voyage behind her, a shakedown trip. Tons and tons of gasoline were being pumped into her from the dock. A cargo of fighter planes was lashed to her decks. She was low in the water, almost full up to her Plimsoll line. This was no ship he was casing to stow away on. This was his ship. It was cold out, but he stood there with his canvas seabag beside him, his mouth hanging loose, trembling with excitement.

A guy in a sheepskin coat and a black woolen watchcap called out, "Hey. Who you?"

"The purser."

"Get on."

He was the chief mate, studying the trim of the vessel.

"You took your fucking time getting here."

"I was just assigned."

"The skipper's at the convoy conference. There's some stores at the slop chest. Put them away before the crew grabs them."

"Where's the slop chest?"

"You one of the ninety-day wonders?"

Jake smiled. "Frankly, I don't know my ass from a hole in the ground."

The mate was a toothy man with a reddish blond stubble of beard, blue eyes, hard-faced, well trimmed, with a lot of authority. He laughed, then called out to somebody walking across the catwalk.

"Hey, stew. Show Wonder-boy around."

Stew, who was the steward, backtracked midships. Jake heaved his seabag onto his shoulders and joined him. The steward showed him his quarters: a bunk, steel desk, typewriter, and adding machine on it, filing cabinets, a closet for his clothes, his own bathroom and shower, another closet full of medicine and first-aid equipment. Home.

Down the passageway were a few cartons of cigarettes, candies, clothes. The slop chest was opened. Shelves were piled with cigarettes, tobacco, candy bars, toilet articles, a miniature department store for the crew.

"Everything here but Chanel Number Five," the steward said. "You're boss over it. You'll have to break it open tonight. The crew brings shit aboard. What they want mostly are those two-for-a-nickel candy bars and those sixty-cent cartons of cigarettes."

As they stowed the cartons into the slop chest, a shaggy-headed, heavy-shouldered bruiser of a man stopped by. He was the second mate. He shook Jake's hand warmly.

"From you," he said to Jake, "I'd like some sulfa pills. I fucked broad last night I think had the clap."

"Bragging again," the steward said.

"From you," the second mate said to the steward, "I want filet mignon, crepes suzettes, and a good wine every night but Sunday. On Sunday I want pheasant and champagne."

"You'll get shit, too," the steward said.

"You hear that, Jake? The SS *Starvation,* that's what we're on. A Polack steward and a Nazi cook, what can you expect?"

"For you, second," the steward said, "a special treat. Strychnine in your soup, tacks in your hamburgers, ground glass in your pies, piss in your coffee."

The second laughed, slammed the steward's back. "Come on, stew, let's get some of your homemade piss."

In the saloon later, Jake met the radio operators and a couple of engineers. They all wondered where they were going. Nobody knew, but they guessed Scotland, England, maybe Murmansk, maybe Africa.

"What kind of provisions we got, stew?"

"Enough to last six months."

"You're kidding."

"We going to be gone that long?" Jake asked.

"We could be gone forever if we're hit. We're on a torch, Jake. A floating torch."

"Bullshit," the chief radio operator said. "I had my astrological chart read two days ago. Clear sailing. A cruise."

The chief engineer, toothless, mashing his gums, pounced on the radio operator. "You sure? That what your swami said?"

"Would I kid about a thing like that? Would I go fucking around with the stars, the signs up there?"

"No. No, for Christ sake."

The chief mate poked his head in. "We got steam up, chief?"

"You know we got steam up. We had it up since yesterday."

"The skipper's just come aboard."

"Sailing time," the steward said.

There was a change of attitude. Everybody tightened.

"I thought we were still loading," the chief said. Jake could see a tremor in his right hand.

"All trim," the mate said. "Ready to go."

Everybody but the steward left.

"Everybody have to go on watch now?" Jake asked.

"No. But everybody suddenly gets torpedo fever."

"What do I have to do?"

"Say hello to the skipper. Let him know you're here. After that, nothing. You and me, the gunnery officer, and the army security officer are the supercargo. We have no watches."

"You mean I don't do a fucking thing?"

"Just take care of the slop chest and anybody in the crew who gets sick. When we hit port, you'll advance the crew part of their pay if they want it. You have no manifest, nothing. You're a glorified passenger, Jake."

Jake found Captain Adam Guidry in the chart room studying a navigational chart and introduced himself.

"Ever sailed before, mister?"

"No, sir," Jake said.

"Have some coffee."

The captain picked up an electric percolator and poured Jake a cup of coffee. He had a weather-beaten face, wrinkled and crunched by the sun and the wind, but there was something soft and gentle about his blue eyes and upturned nose and sandy hair that was thinning in the center. His hands looked soft, too, but there was a cat's lightness about his body.

"You'll be handling the ship's business, whatever there is of it."

"Yes, sir."

"The crew is all signed on. You'll have to sign the articles yourself."

The captain handed him the ship's articles. He signed on.

"That's about it, mister. Set a time to open the slop chest. Right after supper will be fine. I've got morphine, if you should need it, locked up in the safe. I'll let you know what has to be done as we go along."

"Thanks."

The captain went back to the chart and began to plot the course to the rendezvous position of the convoy. The mate and second mate came in.

"How's the weather going to be, mate?" the captain said.

"With me aboard, fair all the way."

The mate had sailed with the skipper before; they trusted and liked each other.

The skipper smiled. "We ready to shove off?"

"Whenever you say."

"Noon."

They hovered over the chart. Jake went below to his cabin and changed into khakis. He wandered about, not knowing what to do with himself. He looked out of the porthole at the dock. He tried the typewriter. It worked fine. Tried the adding machine. Great. Unpacked his clothes and put them in drawers. Looked in the medicine closet. Shelves and shelves of pills and ointments and bandages, enough to supply a hospital ship. He lay down on his bunk. Silence. Everything waiting. Hollow sounds from the engine room. His stomach hollow. He got up and went to the slop chest, opened cartons of cigarettes and clothes, arranged them on shelves, priced them. Hunger came over him. He crossed the catwalk to the saloon. Had halibut, mashed potatoes, and peas. Bells rang. The hum of the engine rose. They were shoving off. He went out on the afterdeck, watched the ship move out into the stream. The cold wind sent shivers through him. He went to his cabin and put on his pea jacket and climbed up to the bridge. The ship was so big and so solid he didn't know it was moving. It felt like an island. In the Narrows the nets were pulled away. Past Staten Island, out into the open ocean. They were on their way. Now Jake could feel the vessel in the waves as it gathered speed. Now excitement worked through him.

He was finally out at sea. Soon there was no sight of land. Only endless horizons. At last the romantic binge he'd hoped for when he'd bummed to the West Coast was beginning, in a different direction, in a different way, not as a stowaway in aimless pursuit of experience and adventure but with a greater purpose and with danger all the way.

Four hours later, in the cloudy afternoon light, the ocean gray and ominous and choppy, the convoy formed up. Sixty-five merchant vessels, a small British aircraft carrier with a cargo of planes, a destroyer at the head, which was going to be the escort commodore, and six destroyer escorts, which would flank the fleet. Two planes hovered overhead and followed the ships until darkness.

A moonless, starless night enveloped the convoy. The

Rockport was near the rear, among the dangerous ships carrying high explosives and high octane. It was quiet on the bridge: the mate on watch, the old, stoop-shouldered AB at the wheel, his face yellow in the light of the binnacle, the young ordinary seaman on lookout, the captain in his cabin, and Jake watching the sea run ceaselessly against the ship. When it was time to eat, he fought the icy blasts whipping across the catwalk, hanging onto the rails as the ship lurched and swayed. At seven o'clock he opened the slop chest. Everybody who wasn't on watch crowded in on him, buying the things they needed and the things they would need onshore to get the girls.

"Hey, purser, why don't you store up with silk stockings? Them's the real cunt grabbers."

"What's wrong with a bar of chocolate and a pack of cigarettes?"

"We're just starting out, and everybody's got channel fever."

They had all the time in the world, but their demands were fierce and insistent. Nearly everything was bought on credit. They were afraid he'd run out of merchandise. There was a lot of buying, but two hours later, when the slop chest was closed, there was plenty left over. The ship was well supplied. You never knew how long you'd be gone.

Later the moon and stars came out. You could see the ships like stationary hulks silhouetted in the night. You could hear the hum of the diesels, the creaking of the structures, see the white banners of spray shoot off the ship's side and occasional blobs of phosphorus. Jake finally went down to his cabin and got into bed. He lay there feeling the ship plunge down and rear up, swerve from side to side, shiver and hurl herself into the troughs between waves. He felt more alone than ever before in his life. The night, with its strange sounds and sensations, seemed endless.

In the morning, when he got up and wrapped himself warmly to face the winter North Atlantic, he was dazzled by the sun, the glitter and calm of the sea, the balmy air. The convoy was in full view, stretched out for miles and miles. His eyes hurt from the glare. The catwalk was a breeze to navigate.

In the saloon the steward greeted him. "How do you like the yacht we're on? You couldn't do better on J. P. Morgan's

Corsair. Later you'll be able to go out on the sun deck and get burned."

The first assistant engineer, Arne, a slender Swede with black hair and a well-trimmed mustache, who had just come off watch, said, "How about some shuffleboard, purser?"

"Nice," Jake said.

"How about a deck chair?" the steward said. "Tea and crumpets at eleven."

"How about some breakfast first?" Jake said.

The steward stood at attention and took his order with elaborate gestures. "Kippered herring. Eggs over easy. An orange, fresh, for the passenger. Coffee coming right up. No steak?"

"No steak," Jake said.

They had their laugh.

"Where are we?" Jake asked.

"The Gulf Stream."

All that day it was lovely out there. The men off watch sunned themselves. Everybody but the men who had been under attack and torpedoed was lulled into safety. A couple of men complained of headaches, and Jake dispensed aspirin. The security officer was seasick, and Jake gave him dramamine, but it didn't help. An oiler cut his hand. Jake cleaned it, sprinkled sulfa powder on it, bandaged it.

The swells lifted and rolled the ship. Nothing seemed to change in the convoy. The sun began to ease down in the huge sky. Sometimes a cloud floated across and spotlights flooded the sea. As the sun sank, the colors of clouds changed; then they became like rumpled patches of purple tissue paper, the edges frayed and burning from the heat of the sun. The ocean grew darker, and the surf shooting from the bow got milkier and brighter. Then the sun became a hot liquid mass melting into the sea. After it sank, its orange glow stayed in the sky a long while. Then night came with a half-moon and clusters of stars. The rushing wind and soughing sea lifted Jake beyond any world he ever knew. He began to lose himself in the dazzling beds of phosphorus bursting from the *Rockford*'s hull. A spell was cast over him.

*　　*　　*

They were on a course along a parallel above the Azores: destination unknown, to be named later by code over wireless. Thus, the convoy could be split up or go on as a whole to England, Ireland, North Africa, India, or even Murmansk from the United Kingdom. For five days the trip seemed like a cruise: sunny, warm, no winter gales, uneventful. On the fifth night, while Jake was in his cabin writing up notes of the trip, the naval escorts, through their sonic devices, picked up definite underwater contacts. First, Jake heard a heavy sledgehammer blow against the hull; then the deep tanks rumbled from the underwater concussion of the depth charges. He rushed topside to the bridge. Up ahead he saw a geyser of white foam shoot up from the dark sea; then phosphorus sprayed out like a bouquet of Christmas lights as more depth charges exploded.

"What's up?" Jake asked.

"Submarine contact," said Captain Guidry.

It was quiet for a time after that.

"Maybe they're blowing up whales," the mate said.

"Maybe," the captain said.

A naval gunner on watch, who was cued into the TBY, the convoy's intercommunication mechanism, yelled, "Contacts again."

The dull thud of distant depth charges was felt in the ship.

"Sounds like a pack," the mate said.

No comment from the captain.

"Should I sound the alarm?" the mate asked.

"No," the captain said. "We'll wait. Let the men sleep if they're sleeping. There'll be plenty of sleepless nights later if we've run into a pack."

Jake, like everybody else who was up, watched and waited. At midnight the navy gunners were released from general quarters, the watches were changed, the TBY was quiet, and Jake turned in.

The sky was overcast the following morning. Everybody worked and walked about with an uneasy feeling of danger, his life jacket on or nearby. There were very few peacetime seamen on board. Most of them were men from the farms and the cities and the small towns of America who had decided to try the merchant marine instead of the army or navy. They'd never bargained for this kind of experience.

At noon flags were hoisted on the commodore vessel to indicate the rendezvous position for the following day, so that if a ship broke down or straggled, she'd know where to meet the convoy. Then a new set of flags was flown, reading: "Submarines in vicinity. Keep closed up." A mist began to envelop the fleet.

"That's all we need," Captain Guidry said. "Dirty weather and submarines."

Jake dug his hands into the pockets of his pea jacket. The cruise was over. This was action in the North Atlantic. He couldn't keep off the bridge. That's where all the information was. He felt it necessary to be in on every briefing, as if he could do something about it. He felt totally helpless.

The sky, with shreds of mist hanging from it, looked exhausted. A damp smoke seemed to rise from the sea. The *Rockford* was the sixth ship in the sixth column, its code number six-six. On the port side one ship after another was chopped from view by the shortening horizon. On the starboard an escort was closing in with the horizon. From there a geyser of mist and foam heaved out of the sea; then came the booming report of the underwater explosion. Jake peered ahead as Captain Guidry looked through his binoculars.

"Black flags flying," he said.

Jake stepped into the wheelhouse, where a naval gunner was on the TBY.

"What have we got?" Jake asked.

"Suspicious contact. They're hunting."

The fog got thicker. The ship ahead was carrying a full cargo of high explosives; the freighter behind had 7,000 tons of high octane in drums. A shudder ran through Jake. By the time the chief mate came on watch the stack was veiled, no other vessel was visible, and the white-rimmed sun, like a floating porthole, rode high above the mist.

"Fog buoy rigged up, mate?" Captain Guidry asked the chief mate.

"Yes, sir."

"Can't see the buoy ahead, huh?"

"No, sir."

"Stern lights on? All running lights?"

"Yes, sir."

"I don't hear any whistles yet."

Captain Guidry groped for something else to do. He paced the deck as if the activity would lift the blind mist.

"Lieutenant," he called to the gunnery officer, "we were told at the conference to open up the TBY in case of fog. Will you see if Flags can contact the ship ahead and find out if her fog buoy is out? Also, get her speed."

Flags, the gunner on the TBY, cleared his throat, then spoke into the microphone: "Six-five, this is six-six. Can you hear me? Over."

No answer. Flags continued calling. No answer. Then a voice came through from the ship behind.

"Six-six, this is six-seven. Is your fog buoy out? We can't see it. Over."

"Six-seven, this is six-six," said Flags. "Our fog buoy is out."

"What is your speed, six-six? Over."

"Nine knots."

Six-seven went dead. Flags couldn't contact the ship ahead. Captain Guidry told him to keep trying at intervals. He stalked by the wheel and looked at the compass. The ship had rolled off course. "Keep her on ninety-eight," he said to Paddy, the AB on the wheel.

"Ninety-eight, sir," said Paddy, who strained hard to see the compass.

"What's wrong?" the captain asked.

"Nothing, sir. Got a fly in my eye, sir. Something."

"In winter?"

"It's a condition, sir. Not a fly, exactly."

"Mate!"

"Yes, sir," the mate said.

"Do something."

The mate called the ordinary seaman on watch. "Take the wheel, Kellogg."

The young ordinary jumped to the wheel, but Paddy, the old AB, wouldn't let go.

"Let go, Paddy," said the mate.

"I can't."

"What do you mean you can't?"

"I can't."

It took both the mate and the captain to pull him off the wheel.

"Purser," said the captain, "see what's wrong with him?"

As Jake took Paddy's arm to lead him down below, he heard the ordinary seaman say, "What do I do?"

"Keep her on ninety-eight."

"Wow."

"You feel that ship under you?" the mate said.

"Wow."

In his cabin Jake found that Paddy could hardly see.

"Where are your glasses?"

"I broke them."

"You never had any."

"I can see fine. Things just get a little blurry in the fog."

They heard a ship's whistle from far off. Another whistle signaled. Another. Then another. At intervals. Then the *Rockford*'s whistle blew: one long blast and four short screeches, pause, then one long and four short repeated. She sounded like a wounded, agonized giantess stumbling through vast swirls of unknown space.

"What are you gonna tell the skipper?" Paddy asked.

"You're no good on the wheel anymore but all right for chipping rust and painting."

"It's no life for a man."

Jake looked at Paddy's gnarled hands, bent knees, stooped back, and wondered why he had kept shipping all these years.

"Why don't you quit, Paddy?"

"I don't know. I quit lots of times. But that sea is like a trap. I can't shake it. I guess I'll die with the salt in my socks."

"When we hit shore, maybe we can get you fitted for some glasses."

"Sure. But glasses just don't look right on a sailing man."

When Jake got up on the bridge, the whistles were still blowing, and everybody on watch, including a man at the bow, peered through the blind fog. Then Flags called out, "Captain, Commodore just called. Says we're three hundred yards out of position."

"Forward, stern, starboard, or port?"

"Commodore didn't say. Just said we were out of position and to pull in before we collide."

"Get him and see how they've got us charted on the screen."

Flags talked into the TBY, listened, then said, "Commodore says we're three hundred yards to port and pulling our stern ship with us. She's been warned, too."

"Get a bearing."

"Bear one-two-five," said Flags after talking to the commodore.

"One-two-five easy," Captain Guidry told the ordinary seaman, who repeated the order. "Mate, get her up four revolutions."

The mate called down to the engine room to speed up.

"Ask the commodore to let us know when we're in position," Captain Guidry said to Flags. He walked onto the wing of the bridge and tried to see through the murky walls about him. Jake felt the captain's tension. A whistle sounded, terrifying him; none had been that close before.

Suddenly the bow of a freighter loomed out of the fog, heading directly for the *Rockford*. The captain saw it at the same time, rushed to the whistle, blew a series of short blasts, and yelled to the helmsman, "Hard left!"

Time became endless as Jake felt his whole body pulling the *Rockford* to the left. She veered ponderously, straining and quivering through the long swells. Jake held his breath, watching the sea cuff of the freighter's bow as she steamed onward, fully under way. Then the freighter swayed, lurched toward the *Rockford,* and dipped to the left. The breath was knocked out of Jake and he grasped the rail as the beam of the freighter crashed into the *Rockford*'s after end. Gasoline sizzled and gushed through the tanks, surging hard against the plates. The *Rockford* stood jarred for a second, rolled far to the left with the blow, then leaped to the crest of a wave and shook like a dazed animal as she weaved back against the freighter; then, with angry sparks glinting from her steel side, she crunched onward.

"Hard right!" Captain Guidry yelled.

The vessels jiggled together, crackling amid the spine-hot tremor of the whistles, broke loose, and foamed through the great swirls of agitated seas. More sparks flew, and any minute Jake expected an ignition that would explode both vessels. As the freighter eased away, finally, two lifeboats from the after boat deck crashed into the sea, and the mangled davits toppled over the side. The rails were broken and the upper plates caved, and smeared over the side, like blood from a deep wound, were huge streaks of rust and red lead.

"Easy to one-fifteen," Captain Guidry said.

"All clear, captain," said the mate.

"That was the ship behind us, wasn't it, mister?"

"Yes, sir, the one with the high octane."

"Drop speed to eight revolutions."

"We might lose the convoy."

"To hell with the convoy. We want to get cleared and secured. Then go aft and determine the damage."

The freighter was slowly eaten up by the soft gray gums of the fog until it was swallowed like the lump that thumped down Jake's throat. The *Rockford* shuddered as she slowed down, then quivered and sighed through the long swells.

"The TBY is out of whack, captain," Flags reported.

"Why didn't the commodore warn us sooner?"

"I don't know."

"Think you can fix it?"

"I'll try."

"Get Sparks to help you, if you need him."

"Yes, sir."

The mate came back with a report of the damage. "Lifeboats three and five are gone. The starboard rails are broken, and the plates caved."

"No cracks in the plates?"

"No, sir. We were hit pretty high up."

"How would we do in a heavy sea?"

"I don't know."

"Anything else?"

"A few portholes were smashed, and some of the cabins messed up."

"Anybody hurt?"

"No, sir. A few men in the fo'c'sle were jarred, but most of the men were on deck when the whistles blew."

"How about the engine room?"

"The first said everything is in order."

"Very well, mate. Thanks."

"We could use a little breeze," Jake said.

"What happened to your fair weather, mate?" the captain asked.

"They're saving it up there."

"We should be out of convoy now. Run her half speed for thirty minutes; then bring her up. Keep the whistle going."

With the coming of night, the *Rockford* slipped into a black seabag. Jake had never experienced being so darkly enclosed before. The vibrating of the engines, the dull thud of the stern squatting into the sea, the boom of the evaporator system, the steam crackling through the pipes, the static from the radio shack, the warning whistle of the ship were pulses in his arteries, quickening him to his blind state. He listened hard for the sound of other ships that might have dropped out of the convoy. For all Jake knew they all could be wandering about blindly, dead reckoning their courses. Alone now, the vessel was a prey to any submarine. Altogether it was a beautiful voyage.

"Hey, Flags," the mate said, "how you doing on the TBY?"

"I'm getting there."

"You been laid lately?"

"Not in over a week."

"Did you pay the whore?"

"I don't go to whores. I get it for nothing."

"You navy guys never pay the whores. That brings on the bad weather."

"What's the whores got to to with it?"

"They're mad at us. You navy guys never pay them off. They put the heebie-jeebies on us."

Flags tested the TBY. Nothing. "I better bring it down to Sparks," he said.

The chief engineer stepped up to Jake. "I don't feel good, doc. What have you got for me?"

"What's wrong?"

"Everything. I don't feel good."

The chief looked worn out. He hardly slept. Catnapped during the day and wandered through the night, seeing that the crew and officers observed the blackout. He hadn't been down below since the voyage started.

"It's torpedo fever," the mate said.

The chief turned on him. "Don't give me that torpedo shit. You been in an open boat? Don't talk if you haven't been in an open boat. Not once. Twice. I don't have to take that shit from you. I'm the chief engineer. I can shut the goddamn plant down."

"Take it easy, chief," Jake said. "I've got something for you." He'd given him placebos before because there was nothing wrong with the chief but fear. He'd give him some phenobarbital, get him to sleep. The man was totally exhausted.

The chief ran up to the captain, who had just blown the whistle.

"You have to do that?"

"Yes."

"You're telling them where we are. Them goddamn subs can hear. You're giving us away with that goddamn whistle."

"We don't want anybody to ram us."

"You want a tin fish, that's what you want. I'm gonna cut the steam off that whistle. I'll give you a whistle, right up your ass."

"Get off the bridge, chief."

"You're dying to get us all killed." The chief's voice broke with fear.

"Get off the bridge, chief."

"Come on, chief," Jake said, taking his arm.

The chief yanked away from Jake. "I'll break you, captain. Once we get ashore, I'll have your license. I'll break you in two." He began to whimper like a child.

Jake grasped the chief's arm firmly. "I got something good for you. Let's go."

He led him down to his cabin. He took his temperature, his pulse reading, looked down his throat with a flashlight. He did everything deliberately and thoroughly, as if he were a doctor.

"You think it's just I'm scared, doc?" The chief trembled.

"No. Your temperature's up a little; so's your pulse." He lied. "There's a little spot in your throat."

"I knew it was something. That's why I don't feel good. What is it, doc?"

"Locomotor aphasia." Jake made it up.

"It's that fucking engine room. It's being down in that goddamn engine room all these years."

"I'm going to tell the skipper you don't have to go down there any more. You're allergic to it."

"You fucking-ay."

"I've got just the thing for you."

He gave him three phenobarbital pills. That should knock him out for the night. Maybe in the morning he'd feel better. Running scared for a solid week, how long can a man last?

"I want you to go to your cabin and lie down. Just for a few minutes. You'll feel better, you'll see."

"The fucking mate, telling me I got torpedo fever. The fucking skipper ordering me off the bridge. I'll have their asses."

"Sure you will, chief. Just lie down for a few minutes and give the pills a chance to work."

"Okay, doc."

Jake was exhausted himself by the time the chief left. He said, "To hell with it." He took a couple of phenobarbital pills and konked out for the night.

The ship was still shrouded in fog when he crossed the catwalk for breakfast. The whistle sent shudders through him. He had a leisurely meal. The chief engineer came in.

"How you feeling, chief?" Jake asked.

"Better. What the hell did you give me?"

"A Mickey Finn."

"You bastard."

"You're none the worse for it, are you?"

"What if we'd been hit or rammed?"

"Think positive, chief."

The chief looked rested but he seemed to be standing on his toes, ready to take off. Every time the whistle blew he jumped up, walked about, then sat down. Since the last time he was on a torpedoed oil tanker he'd been beached to shore relief jobs. That had been six months before. They needed a chief for the *Rockford;* there was nobody available; he had been forced to go or he'd lose his rank and seniority, even his retirement pay.

"A guy's gotta be crazy to go to sea." The chief got up and left.

Jake followed him out, walked through the soupy weather amidship, but there was a different feel to the air. It was as if somebody from far away had puffed on his cheek, made it tingle. He went up to the wing of the bridge and watched the mate rub his fingers as if he were feeling precious silk.

"Feel it?" the mate said.

"Yah."

The breeze started from the starboard bow, came in stronger. The ship seemed to be plowing harder into the fog, gathering speed, forcing her way through. Jake could feel himself pushing the sky upward. He could see the bow now, beckoning like a coy whore as the ship rolled. Then a patch of the sea, the foam rushing against the bow.

"So who's the fair-weather mate?" the mate said.

"You are, old buddy."

All at once, the fog was behind them, the sky blue and clear, the ship pounding through the swells with nothing in view but limitless horizons. The captain came out and took a sight. The mate looked through his binoculars.

"See anything of the convoy?" the captain asked. "Any stray ships?"

"Not a sign."

The captain left to chart the *Rockford*'s position. When he came back, he said, "We should be on our rendezvous position by noon. Open her up, mate. The sooner we join the convoy, the better."

The ship gathered speed.

"Hit the sack, skipper," the mate said.

"I think I will." The captain looked strained and spent. "Wake me if you see the convoy."

The watches were changed; the morning got warmer. The steward came up on the top deck, where Jake was sunning himself. Naval gunners were also lying about in the sun. But Jake felt as if he were in the center of the whole universe.

"We're on a cruise again," the steward said.

"Yes," said Jake.

"This is the way it was in peacetime. All alone. Nothing to worry about. Fog, you've always got to worry about, no matter where you are, but in peacetime you don't have a whole sea full of ships going back and forth." He looked about at the gunners. "A fucking bunch of passengers. That's the life."

Segments of the convoy were sighted before noon. Later more and more ships joined it until it was all formed up again. The tension had eased. Many of the men said the fog had been a blessing; they might have lost the submarines. Anyway, they felt safer within the arc of the escorts.

It was the eighth day out, and the convoy was traveling a few points south of east. They weren't far from the Azores. They seemed to be headed for Gibraltar. Sea gulls skimmed over the swells now and then, hovered over the ship. Which meant they weren't too far from land. The men relaxed. They were curious about where they were going. They grabbed Jake. He was the purser; he was supposed to know everything. Wasn't he the captain's paper man? Didn't he have to make up the cargo manifests?

The boot, an AB who'd made three trips and now considered himself an old salt, was going to find out where they were going. Not by asking directly. Oh, no. You'd never get an answer. He'd get Jake by the well-known bazookas.

"Hey, purser. How'd you like me to fix you up with the hottest broad in Glasgow?"

"What if we don't go to Glasgow?"

"I know a nurse in England. Liverpool. Oh, man."

"Forget Liverpool." Jake, amused, played the game.

"I know a belly dancer in North Africa. Terrific jelly in her rolls. You interested, you interested?"

"I'll tell you after I know where we're going."

"You mean you really don't know."

"That's the truth."

"Then what the hell am I being so generous for?"

All that afternoon that's the way it went. In the gunners'

quarters they were dancing and singing to records by Benny Goodman and Glenn Miller and Louis Armstrong, with some of the off-watch crew joining them. Others were reading or sleeping in the foc's'le and midship or shooting the breeze on the poop deck and in the messroom. The fog and the danger of submarines seemed far behind them.

The night came on clearly and crisply with a three-quarter moon. You could see the convoy silhouetted against the night. A deceptive night. Jake went up on the bridge after closing the slop chest, breathed deeply. He observed the third mate on watch massaging his thinning head of hair.

"Good for the scalp," the third mate said. "I'm massaging it with female hormones."

"You losing your hair?" Jake asked, as if he didn't know.

"Tons of it. If I'd had me some steady humping instead of being caught up by this war, I'd still have all of it. 'Curly' they used to call me."

Jake laughed, watching him. "When you get to the brain, stop, before you scramble them."

"Boy, the way the girls used to stroke and fondle this head of hair."

Jake had to turn away, he wanted to laugh so hard.

"Only twenty-three years old, and look at me. Another few years I'll have to wear a rug."

Suddenly the ship rocked, and the sledgehammer blows of depth charges reverberated through the tanks. Jake ran out on the wing of the bridge. All he could see were the ships framed against the vast mountains of night. Another blow against the hull left him vibrating from the shock. Then a spout of water shot up from the starboard bow, and it geysered out like a million lighted matches. The undersea explosion coursed through the *Rockford* as if a huge chain had been flung through her insides.

"Close," the captain said. He was nearby.

Flags came out. "Sounds like a whole pack."

"Keep a sharp lookout," the captain said.

Everybody scanned the sea and the ships. Jake's eyes grew hot from the strain.

"They start dropping those charges in the middle of the convoy, they can crack our plates open," the captain said.

Close by, Jake picked out an escort sliding into a swell and churning it up into surf as it swung about and rode high-breasted and low-rumped between the *Rockford* and the freighter astern. The escorts were hunting and tracking their prey in the midst of the convoy, crashing down the open lanes.

Another depth charge, close, slamming against the ship.

"What the hell do they think they're doing?" the captain yelled. "They'll bust us wide open."

Flags ran out of the wheelhouse. "Captain, prepare for emergency turns. Follow zigzag pattern twelve."

"Keep your eyes open, mister," said the captain to the third mate, then left.

"If the fuckin' subs don't get us, our own goddamn escorts will," said the third mate as another depth charge pounded against the hull of the *Rockford*.

Jake felt useless; he had no function in the running of a ship. He also felt totally helpless. If the ship were hit, she'd just blow, that was it. He was rendered even more helpless as he watched the men on duty go about their tasks. *They had something to do.*

The captain came into the wheelhouse and clamped a slip of paper with the zigzag pattern beside the amber light of the binnacle. He set the zigzag clock and said to the helmsman, "Can you read this?"

"Yes, captain."

"The clock will buzz every ten minutes. Every time it does, start on the indicated course."

The helmsman nodded.

"I'll be close by during the maneuvers." He turned to the third mate. "First turn will be to the starboard."

"Yes, sir."

"Ten minutes later we'll swing to the port. Every ten minutes a turn."

"All through the night?"

"That's about it."

A whistle moaned. The shrill siren of an escort wailed above it.

"There it is, captain," said the third mate.

"Not yet, mister. There'll be another whistle from the column leaders for execution."

Jake stared into the night, waiting. As if he were condemned. I could have sat this whole thing out, he thought. But I had to be a hero, had to get involved. Heroes did things. What the hell was he doing? He was just there, waiting, looking. He shuddered when a whistle mourned heavily in the night. Another whistle, another, punctuated with sharp crescendos of the escorts' sirens. The clock in the wheelhouse buzzed.

"All right," the captain said to the helmsman. "Easy to the right to one-twenty."

"One-twenty, sir."

"Better get her up two, mister," the captain said to the third mate.

Jake watched the convoy make its maneuvers. He saw a ship loom through the dark with a crest of green-white foam surging against her. She looked angry in her heaving turn, as if she'd been roused from a deep sleep.

"One-twenty," the helmsman reported.

"Steady as she goes," the captain said.

Jake felt the ship bite into her course as the deep power of the screw propelled her forward. He saw the vessels ahead and alongside lunge forward to new positions. All was well so far.

The whistles went off, and the clock buzzed again. But before the captain could order the new course, the torpedo detector went off. It banged through the wheelhouse with the sound of a sheet of tin being unfurled.

"You hear anything?" the captain asked Jake.

"Only the detector."

"No depth charges?"

"No."

"There's a torpedo loose," the third mate said.

"Where?" the captain said.

"It's gotta be," the third mate said.

"Easy to the left to fifty," the captain said to the helmsman.

The third mate grunted as though he'd been slugged in the belly. The helmsman squeaked the order out. Jake swallowed hard.

"We're heading for the torpedo track," the third mate said.

"We're proceeding according to plan," the captain said.

"Murder."

"We don't maneuver we'll get rammed."

The torpedo detector went off again. Jake thought he saw a couple of ships on the horizon shake mightily, then sway and dip, as if they'd been hit.

"See anything, mister?" said the captain.

"Not a fuckin'," said the third mate.

Jake kept his mouth shut. He wasn't sure what he was seeing. Not even the gray line of steam fizzing into the night, then popping and dazzling out in a fiery whiteness. A second rocket made everything look more unreal.

"That's where the torpedo track is," the third mate yelled. "We're right in the beam."

More flares rocketed up and exploded. The captain rang the general alarm.

"Hard over to fifty," he said to the helmsman.

Jake was riveted to the deck. There was nowhere to run, nowhere to hide, not a thing he could do except strain with the ship away from the torpedo track as she made her turn. He leaned to the left, began to ache from the exertions. Slowly, slowly, he felt the ship turn, heaving into the wake of the vessel ahead, while he searched for sight of the torpedo.

"Fifty, sir," said the helmsman finally.

"Steady on fifty," the captain said.

Then Jake winced and yelled. He didn't know which came first, the sound or the sight, for the explosion and the great burst of flame on the horizon to the left came simultaneously. The torpedo detector sounded as if a whole tin mill had clattered to the deck, its indicator jiggling from left to right. Jake grabbed the rail as he felt the *Rockford* rear upward, then heave and tremble downward.

"Jesus!" the third mate cried.

Flags appeared with the second explosion and burst of flame, his face grimy red in the blaze.

"Speed convoy to thirteen knots," he reported.

"What else?" the captain asked.

"That fuckin' pack is bustin' through all over."

"What are you standing there for, mister?" the captain yelled at the third mate. "Thirteen knots. Get her up there. Get her up before we're plowed astern."

The third mate rushed to the telegraph and bawled, "Up to thirteen knots."

Somebody yelled, "Submarine off the port bow!"

There it was, the submarine periscope, like the grim but curious head of a huge turtle, cutting through the dark swells down the lanes between ships. It hypnotized Jake. He waited for the naval guns to beat the sub off, but firing was withheld because other ships were in the line of fire. Then Jake saw it, the rush of wild phosphorus surging from the ejected torpedo as it hurled toward the ship opposite the *Rockford* several hundred yards to starboard.

"Fire!"

Blobs of purple and red spit from the heavy guns, and the night became streaked with the red and blue dashes of tracer bullets from the automatic weapons. The *Rockford* recoiled from the barrage, then lunged ahead, as the submarine slunk under the pelted water and glided down beyond the stern. Then, in the ship's downward plunge, the horizon came up sharp, breaking into a million fragments of orange and red and purple and blue as the vessel alongside blew.

Jake saw the men running, making small, jerky, strange motions in the great torchlight of flame; then they were obliterated when another explosion followed. All that was left was the reflection of death in the orange glow of the captain's face, the third mate's, and the helmsman's.

His attention was jolted up ahead. Another ship had blown. This time Jake saw bodies hurtling out into the fiery night. More explosions, as the convoy ran and ran. The steady flames sank lower and lower on the horizon, until the ring of fire disappeared. Then it became quiet, as if the rushing sound of the wind and the waves had sent the *Rockford* into the hush of a strange and peaceful world.

Jake expected more to happen; he strained for it. Come on, you bastards, get it over with it, come and get it. The glow of the fires remained in the frayed night for a long while. Then it was dark again.

"Anything on the TBY?" the captain asked Flags.

"Quiet."

"They say how many they got?"

"Last count was twenty."

"Mister," the captain said to the third mate, "Ring the dismissal signal on the general alarm."

It was approaching midnight. The watches were changed. The third mate couldn't move. Neither could Jake. This night, he thought, would never end for him.

At dawn the following morning a small task force joined the convoy: an aircraft carrier, a cruiser, and four destroyers. Planes flew overhead all that morning, tracking and searching over great distances, then came back to the carrier. Flags were hoisted. The convoy was split, one part going to North Africa, the other to the United Kingdom. The *Rockford* maneuvered into the convoy going to the United Kingdom. They were into the most dangerous part of the voyage, but it was all anticlimactic now. They had faced death and had come out of it. The greatest threat to them was death. What more could they face, except their own fears?

The task force stayed with them. Somehow Jake felt invulnerable now. Not because of the task force's power but because he had survived his first crucible of fire. He felt a kind of victory in it.

Jake made nine voyages across the North Atlantic on the *Rockford* with the same skipper, but the rest of the crew changed often. During that time he wrote a good many pieces about his experiences. He gave them to an agent he had met during one of his shore leaves, but none of them found a market. The agent, Eric Weiss, a slender, ruddy-faced, bald Austrian man, who had a number of important European and American authors on his list, urged Jake to find a way of incorporating the pieces he wrote into a novel.

"What you have are mainly sketches," Eric said with a slight German accent. He was a cosmopolitan and sophisticated man. A ladies' man. A man who hobnobbed with some of the greatest living writers. "What you must do is find a story to put them in."

That's all. Find a story. A guy rides a tanker carrying high-octane gasoline across the Atlantic trip after trip. Every trip he's under attack. Wolf packs come in. Near the European coast

Stukas bombard the ships; dogfights ensue in the air. They go through fog, rammings. Sail through minefields in thick fog, anchor, and find mines all about when the fog lifts. He meets hundreds of men who react in different ways to the war. And he can't find a story, can't find one thread that will hold all the little threads of his experiences together.

Call that a writer? . . . Some writer.

In the summer of '44 he had a month's leave accumulated. With Rhoda's urging he decided to take it and get off the *Rockford*.

"You've been living under a terrific strain, Jake," she said.

"Really? How's that?"

"Before you went away, you used to sleep right through the night. Nothing ever bothered you. Now any little off-key sound and you're up. A police siren, the crashing of a bottle on the street, any little thump, and you're up, and you're wandering around."

"And I thought I was on a luxury cruise all the time. And being paid very well for it. Hundred percent bonus in the war zone."

"You're restless as hell when you're in port. Do this, do that, you want to be busy all the time, like every minute is the last one. You can kid yourself, Jake, but not me. Let's forget the war. A whole month. You might even find the story you're looking for."

"You know exactly how to seduce me, don't you?"

"Maybe afterward you might find a safe ship to sail. Is there such a thing?"

"Sure. Anything without gasoline or explosives. Food, for instance. Lumber. Medical supplies. Steel. War isn't all airplanes and ammunition, you know."

"Let's not worry about that now."

They went up to the Adirondacks, rented a canoe and a tent, and staked out an island for themselves on Lake George. They canoed into Bolton Landing for their groceries, built fires for their meals, played cards at night by candlelight, went to bed early, got up with the birds, and lived in the water and on the water for three weeks. It was the most primitive life they'd ever

464 · WINDY CITY

led; they got closer to themselves than ever before.

"This is the acid test," she said. "If we can put up with each other like this, I think we'll be able to make it forever."

"That's because of all the gourmet cooking."

"What about all the gourmet fucking?"

"Now you're bragging."

"To say nothing of being the star paddler on the canoe team."

The water was soft and cool and mountain fresh. They swam themselves into splendid condition. They looked so goddamned tan and healthy they felt they wouldn't be fit for New York ever again. When it was time to go back, it took all day to pack up their few belongings, to return the tent and canoe; they felt as if they were giving up the best part of their lives. But during the dreamy days when they lay around silently, pleasantly tired, with the waves softly lapping on the pine-tall shore, Jake would go deep inside himself, and the voyages across the Atlantic would come back. One story kept popping up at him over and over again—the story of an oil tanker which had come out of a submarine attack with its stack smoking, thus endangering the whole convoy. The engine couldn't be fixed. The ship had to drop out of convoy to blow its tubes, and she could never catch it again. The tanker was ordered, through her black smoke, to decoy the submarine pack away from the main convoy, to sacrifice herself for the other ships. That was the story.

Gradually he began to fit in the various characters he had written sketches about. He had the thread of a story; he could weave his smaller stories in and out until the explosive finish. Rhoda thought it was brilliant.

"I'll go to the bank and cash your encouragement and excitement into a ten-thousand-dollar advance from a publisher and a one-hundred-thousand-dollar movie sale," he said. "Okay?"

"Get a safe ship, Jake, and write that book."

Back in New York he signed on a Liberty ship. It was carrying structural steel for bridge work and a cargo of planes on deck.

"What could be safer?" he said to Rhoda when he said good-bye.

"At least if you're hit you've got a chance."

"I'll see you in six to eight weeks."

That was in September, 1944. He went to Philadelphia, where the SS *Hawkins* was docked and was ready to set sail, but orders were held up a couple of days; then the vessel moved to another part of the port. In each hold, Jake watched high-explosive detonators being loaded. They were carrying matériel to build bridges and to blow them up. A floating vessel of dynamite. What could be safer?

The day before the convoy left, the skipper, Andrew Walker, called Jake into his quarters and said, "How's your slop chest?"

"Pretty good."

"I want to be sure we've got enough of everything. I don't want to run short. I want to be ready for every emergency."

"The purser before me ordered his head off. I can hardly move in the storeroom."

"You know where I just came from, mister? Casablanca. Shuttling back and forth to the United Kingdom. Eleven months. We ran out of everything. I don't want that to happen again."

"I'll order some more supplies."

"If we don't use them up this trip, they'll be there for the next."

"Yes, sir."

The skipper looked a bit like Wallace Beery. Same sprawly, wrinkled face, loose mouth, and a drinking man's nose, except that he didn't drink.

"I want you to charge a little extra for everything. In case you come up short. Remember, I'm responsible for everything aboard; it's my money you're handling. I'm not going to shell anything out of my own pocket. That clear, mister?"

"But that would be making a profit from the crew?"

"Fuck the crew. They'll screw you every time they can. So you make a dime on them. What the hell is a dime?"

"All right, captain."

Jake had learned early in this career: Never argue with God, because that's what the skipper was on his ship.

"Another thing. You're a man who has no watches, no specific duties while on the voyage. I don't want you lounging around on deck; I don't want you looking like a glorified passenger; I don't want you drifting about. I want you to look alert, look like you're about some kind of business. You think you can manage that?"

Jake didn't know how he could, but he said, "I'll try."

"We got our usual run of draft dodgers in the crew?"

"A number of first trippers, yes, sir."

"Wartime seamen, shit. You just about have to sail the goddamn vessel yourself. Had a second mate last trip, mister, the navigating officer. Would you believe, first day out, he takes a sight, and charts us five hundred miles off course? That was a beauty of a trip. Had to do all the navigating, had to practically stand the second mate's watch myself. I'm not a young man anymore, mister."

Jake didn't know what to say. "Yes, sir," and he'd be agreeing that the skipper, who was about fifty, was an old man, over the hill. "No, sir," and he'd be countering his statement. So he said, "You've still got a lot of good years left in you, captain."

"You fuckin'-ay right I have. Eleven months in Casablanca, bombarded nearly every day, pulling out in those big African tides to get away, then docking again, then shuttling up to England, and those fuckin' planes and subs at us all the time. You fuckin'-ay right I've got a lot of years left."

This man, Jake thought, was shell-shocked. He should have been beached. Boy, this was going to be one honey of a trip. A safe ship. Just what he bargained for. With a thousand tons of detonators in every hold. And a battered hulk of a shell-shocked captain. Oh, it was going to be a great trip.

It started right off great. The afternoon of the second day out the convoy ran into the tail end of a hurricane. Jake had always before been on tankers which rode low in the water and weren't as vulnerable to the buffeting of gales and storms. But when the hurricane hit the *Hawkins,* he thought he was on a wild bronco. All day he was bucked, jounced, pitched, and flung from side to side. At night he couldn't sleep; he could hardly stay in his bunk. There were times when the screw was lifted so far out of the sea as the bow plunged down that he thought it would drill right through the vessel; then, when it sank and bit into the water, he thought it would tear the ship apart she shook so hard. There were times when the ship got into a thirty-degree roll, then rolled more to the other side, and he felt that on the next roll she would topple over. The wind howled; the rain pelted down; you couldn't walk across the roped deck to the saloon for supper, and who wanted to eat anyway? The jumbo block broke loose and began smashing up parts of the ship. The skipper ordered the block to be lashed down, but nobody would go out on deck. He got hysterical, fired everybody in the crew. He ran down to Jake with the log.

"I want you to log everybody. I want it all down on record. From the chief mate down to the fuckin' ordinary seamen. They're all logged. I'll have their asses."

"Yes, sir."

Then suddenly he got sick. He ran into Jake's head to vomit. He was green when he came out, looking as if he were going to die.

"They told me to take a month. I had the fuckin' month coming. God damn it, why didn't I listen to them? What have you got for me, mister? Please, mister, give me something, will you?"

Jake gave him some dramamine, then helped him up to his quarters, where he passed out.

"Poor fuckin' skipper," the chief mate, Tim Connors, a gruff, burly Irishman, said. "Imagine going to sea all your life and you get sick in storms."

"This isn't a storm, man; it's a hurricane," Jake said. "You think we'll make it?"

"If the plates hold out. These fuckin' Liberties, they've been known to crack in two."

"Everywhere I go, good news."

The convoy had broken up long ago. All hundred ships were being tossed about, with the rain driving hard and the wind whistling and rasping through the stays. Nobody could go out in that weather. You gave yourself up to the sea and hoped for the best.

In the morning, when the *Hawkins* had passed out of the squalls into fair weather with the sea whitecapped to the horizons, it was found that one of the life rafts and the number three lifeboat had been torn from their davits and that the main winch had been broken up by the jumbo block. The skipper, not feeling too good, was back in command, entering the damage in the logbook. Later, after the ship joined convoy and the sea grew calmer, the captain came down to Jake's quarters and said, "Mister, did you log everybody like I told you?"

"Not yet, sir. Weather was too rough. But I'll do it."

"Forget it. I changed my mind."

The next morning Jake was awakened by the ordinary seaman on watch. It was seven-forty-five.

"What's up?"

"Captain wants you to be at breakfast with him."

"Fuck."

Jake burrowed under the covers, tried to go back to sleep. The ordinary seaman stood there.

"Captain said I had to bring you back."

Jake was tired, felt he hadn't slept for days, but he got out of bed, dressed, walked to the saloon, where the captain sat at his own little table.

"Good morning, mister. Nice morning. Bright, beautiful."

"Captain, I didn't get any sleep."

"You think any of us did? The men had to stand watches. They put toothpicks in their eyes to keep them open. You think anybody got any sleep?"

Jake shrugged. Go argue with God.

"I want you to have breakfast with me every morning, mister."

"Are you lonely, captain?"

"Let's say I like you."

That's all he needed. Wallace Beery to like him. Next thing he'll be like a big hound slobbering all over him.

"Bad for the morale, you sleeping in the morning. I like the crew to know that you're up."

"Yes, sir."

"Enjoy your breakfast." The captain, who had already finished his, left.

Every morning after that he was awakened by the ordinary seaman on watch and he had breakfast with the captain. When he found out that Jake was a writer, he read sentimental doggerel that he wrote for his daughters, one eleven and the other fourteen.

"I knew you'd appreciate things like this, mister."

Suddenly they were soulmates.

One morning Jake complained of the coffee's being too cold, and he sent the messman back to heat it. The messman came back, filled Jake's cup, then the captain's. Jake tasted his and said, "Just right, thanks." The skipper took a long swig of his and sputtered it out in pain.

"You burned the fuckin' coffee."

"He just heated it up," Jake said.

"The coffee was burned, goddamn it. I'm the skipper here, and I don't want burned coffee anymore."

The coffee was always lukewarm from then on. Jake couldn't even enjoy a hot cup of coffee in the morning. Really a great trip.

Then they came under attack. Day after day after day, the black flags flying, the escorts running up and down the convoy, the depth charges being dropped, hammering against the hulls of the ship, with the skipper nervously pacing the deck, running around at night to see that the blackout was in force, worrying about the power plant, afraid of having to drop out of the convoy and going it alone on a slow Liberty, calling the gunnery officer up and questioning him about the readiness and battle capability of his crew. Then he developed a terrible itch.

"Purser, what have you got for me?"

Jake gave him a bottle of calomine lotion.

"Think that'll do it?"

Only a rocking chair on some beach will do it, Jake thought.

"Let's hope for the best, captain."

"Most skippers, I can't tell you how many skippers I sailed under, the minute they stepped on board, they hit the bottle and they didn't stop until the trip was over. They let the mate run the ship. Not me. Nobody you can trust anymore. Millions of dollars involved. Lots of lives. The skipper is responsible. The whole shebang is on his back. How the hell can a guy go inside a bottle? Tell me how, mister."

"I don't know."

"Would you like me to join the bottle gang?"

"No, sir."

"Fuckin'-ay. Who'd run the ship? The mate? The mate's okay. Not enough experience, though. A slow thinker. A slow-witted man. You'd be at the bottom of the sea in an emergency. The second mate? He still needs help with his navigation. The third mate? He's got too much to learn. So what have we got, mister?"

"You, captain."

"You can thank God for that. Here, let me read you a poem I wrote to my daughters this afternoon:

In this autumn of sunny light
I hope this finds your spirits bright.
But should you need a bit of cheer
Remember the skipper is always near.

How's that?" There was a tear in his eye.

"Terrific, captain. I'm sure your girls will appreciate it."

"Soon's we get to port I'll airmail it to them."

With a straight face, Jake said, "They'll be delighted when they get it."

"I'm glad you're aboard, mister. You're the only guy I can talk to. You don't know how lonely a skipper can get." He jumped, startled, at the sledgehammer slam of a depth charge. "Fuckin' war." He ran up to the bridge.

Before the day was over, two submarines had been hit. Jake and the captain sighted the oil gurgling up, then flowing into a huge black slick over the water; then debris from the sub floated up. But the black flags still flew.

Later the sun sank quickly, suddenly splashed into the sea and spattered the dusk above it with blood. The coral glow turned to copper; then stars broke through, and a reddish moon came up. The world seemed to hang suspended and hushed for all time. The captain walked about the ship, enforcing the blackout. He looked as if a huge beast were on his back. He kept scratching at it. He looked like hell with the calomine lotion on his face.

"I'm in great shape," he said.

The following day the black flags were down.

"Maybe they did get those subs," the captain said. He began to relax. All the way into the Thames estuary he relaxed. He went in to London for the convoy conference, came back, and said, "We're stuck here until further orders."

He stopped relaxing when the buzz bombs and rockets flew overhead.

"What the hell we waiting for?"

Nobody really knew. The battle of the Scheldt River in Belgium was raging, with thousands and thousands of men being killed. But nobody connected that battle with this convoy, part of which had broken for Liverpool and Glasgow. Jake gave the captain another bottle of calomine for his itch.

During the day Jake wrote his novel; it seemed to be going well. He read a lot from the ship's library. At night he sat around the saloon drinking cups and cups of coffee; then he roamed the decks looking at London in the distance and recalled the English novels and plays and poems he'd read in college. Then he had more coffee and kept going to the head all night to get rid of it. It was deadly out there, and boring. Then the skipper was called in to another conference. The ship had steam up. He came back aboard. Everybody was eager to get going, no matter where.

"We're going to the Firth of Forth," the skipper said. "Edinburgh."

"Great," Jake said. They'd unload and then go back home.

When they got to the firth, another conference. The skipper came back and said, "We anchor here until further orders. No shore leave. We're on hourly notice."

The crew was nearly crazy. There was land. Nobody could go ashore. Day after day the men loafed around, developing headaches, itches, backaches, toothaches. Toothaches were the answer; they were something Jake couldn't treat. An AB and a wiper were the first, one with a swollen jaw.

"Skipper," Jake said, "they've got to see a dentist ashore. One of them has an abscess for sure; the other will get one."

"All right. They're to be back by six o'clock."

A lighter came and took the AB and wiper to shore. They didn't come back. Two days later the captain said, "They jumped ship, the bastards. I want you to go in and sign on two more men. I want a full complement on this ship."

Jake didn't argue; he was glad to be going ashore. It was one of the few sunny days he'd seen in Scotland. It was October, and everything looked greener than green in the hills rising from the firth. There was still color in the leaves that hadn't fallen. Edinburgh, just like Glasgow, looked like one vast slum to him: crowded old tenements, narrow windows, no passageways, the smoke and soot and dirt of centuries eroding them. Only the area around the castle had the grandeur he'd imagined in his readings. That was on a sunny day. But usually, with the ever-prevalent low-lying fog, it looked like a weather-beaten ruin.

Jake saw the American consul, an elderly man who hated the paperwork entailed in men jumping ship and getting new men to sign on.

"What if the men come back?" the consul said.

"I don't know. The captain wants a full complement."

"Why the hell is he in such a hurry? Why can't he wait?"

"We've got steam up, ready to leave on orders."

"All right, come back tomorrow. I'll have a couple of men for you."

Jake roamed the city that day. In the afternoon, fog began to creep in, it got damp and misty, and the city depressed him. He got a room at the officers' club, had dinner there. Later he went into a pub, where he was rationed to two drinks. He had his two drinks, watched the men in and out of uniform work on their rations, then went out into the dark, damp night to the club, where he read awhile, then went to sleep. The following day was gray and dreary. He signed on the two men with the consul, witnessing the articles, then brought them to the *Hawkins*. When he got aboard, he found the AB and the wiper had come back.

"Take the new men back," the captain said.

"The consul will kill me."

"Sign them off. That's his job."

"Yes, sir."

"What the hell can I do, mister? The men are on the articles. I'm responsible for them."

"What about the new men on the articles?"

"It was a mistake. But I want you to log the AB and the wiper. Three days, no pay."

Jake took the new men back. Jake thought the consul would bust his jugulars.

"My skipper is by the book," Jake said.

"Your skipper is crazy."

Jake went to Leith on the firth and rented a room in a small hotel. In the evening, after dinner, he wandered along the firth, all black and damp, listening to the foghorns. Nothing in the world was more mournful. Chilled, he went into a pub and ordered his two drinks. Two rather attractive women sat at the table next to his. His shipmates had said, when he'd first gone over, that if they had teeth, they were good-looking. These two women had magnificent teeth. He got into a silly conversation with them about toothpastes and methods of brushing teeth. They thought everything he said was hilarious. What an audience. He said if they laughed once more, he'd charge them amusement tax. They almost spilled their last drink they laughed so hard. He knew he couldn't have been that funny. They were just lonely women, one whose husband had been killed in North Africa, the other whose husband had been away for years. With their rations gone, Jake said, "Where do we go from here?"

"Another pub, right?"

"Right," he said.

They had two drinks apiece at two more pubs; then it was curfew time.

"Where do we go from here?" Jake said.

"Home," they said.

"What about me?"

"We'll steer you home."

When they got to his hotel, it was all blacked out, and the doors were locked. He rang the bell, knocked on the door, forget it.

"They locked me out, the bastards," Jake said.

"They can't do that to you."

The women called out, "Open up. The man belongs here. He's a Yank. Where is your Scottish hospitality?" They kicked at the door.

Then one of them said, "We can't let you freeze all night."

The other said, "You take him home, Liz. I don't think my mother-in-law would understand."

"Now you promise you'll be a good boy, Jake," Liz said.

"If you'll promise to be a good girl," Jake said.

They howled.

Liz had a crowded, musty one-bedroom flat. There was a sense of deprivation about the place. "Shhhh," she said. Two kids were asleep in the bedroom.

"No baby-sitter?" Jake said.

She tittered. "This isn't America, Yank. The kids take care of each other."

She fixed some tea. Afterward Jake said, "Where do I sleep? On the floor?"

"Here," she said.

She took a batik spread and some pillows off a bed which doubled as a couch.

"Remember," he said. "You've got to promise to be a good girl."

She smiled. "Just don't get into the bed naked, please."

She went into the bathroom and got into a cotton nightgown, then got into bed.

"Now go to sleep," she said turning her back to him.

His erection was so hard it pained him. The heat of her body seemed to move thickly over him, like lava. He kicked his legs free of the quilt. He thought he'd suffocate. Then:

"You married, Yank?"

"Yes."

"How long has it been?"

"Over a month."

"Your wife good to you?"

"Yes."

"What would she say?"

"She'd understand."

"My husband's been gone three years. Only one leave. I don't know what he looks like anymore."

"Rough."

"I think he'd understand, too."

She sat up and took off her gown, and Jake got out of his

shorts and undershirt. She came up close, kissing him hard, squirming against him, pushing her breasts against his chest. "Oh, Jesus," she said. "You ready? I'm burning up."

He came almost as soon as he penetrated her. She whimpered a little, held him close, throbbing against him, as he grew limp within her.

"Don't worry about it, Yank. It feels so good."

Later the lavalike heat of her body overwhelmed him again. He was better this time, in a fierce sweat before they were through.

"Always better the second time around," he said.

"What about the third?"

"You're a glutton."

"We'll save that for the morning before the kids get up. Harry, my husband, he always liked one in the morning. A going-away present. The dirty bastard, being away that long."

"What about the kids in the morning?"

"You're a friend of the family. They're too young to know about the facts of life. Now go to sleep, Jake."

The night after Jake got back to the *Hawkins,* Julio Sixto, a messman from Argentina, jumped overboard. Jake was lying in his bunk, reading, when he heard the chilling cry "Man overboard!" Then the general alarm went off. Life preservers were thrown over the side; the ship's lights went on, flooding the waters and picking up Sixto struggling in the icy sea. The mate directed the lowering of a lifeboat. Nobody knew what to do, with the mate and captain shouting orders. The boat tipped, and the crew almost fell overboard, and the boat had to be brought up again to be righted. Jake reacted automatically with the years of training he'd had as a lifeguard; he threw off his sweater and jumped over the side. The shock almost stopped his heart. He grabbed a preserver and pulled it to Sixto and grabbed him and held onto him and started to yell, "Get me out of here before I freeze to death!" A line was thrown to him. He looped it around Sixto, and the crew hauled him up.

"Get me out of here!" he screamed.

The line was lowered again. He looped it around his chest, and he was pulled up. He felt icicles forming on his clothes as he was hoisted. He rushed into his cabin, flung his clothes off, ran into the shower, and let the hot water run and run and run. Finally, finally, he stopped shivering. He got into a pair of warm winter underwear, climbed into bed, and lay there for an hour until he got good and warm. Then he got dressed to find out what happened to Sixto. The captain had given Sixto a shot of morphine and put him in the sick bay, a cabin amidship that had six bunks in it.

"What happened?" Jake asked.

"He went out of his head," the captain said. "He picked up a knife in the galley and tried to attack a couple of messmen; then he went overboard."

"No argument, nothing?"

"He thought the Argentine navy was after him."

"I don't get it."

"One of the messmen speaks Spanish. Says Sixto met a Puerto Rican girl in New York and jumped an Argentine ship to be with her, then joined our merchant marine. He thought it'd make him a citizen."

The next day Sixto didn't know where he was or who anybody was. He stared directly ahead and said nothing. He looked catatonic.

"You'd better take him ashore," the captain said.

"Where?"

"The nuthouse, I guess. Call the consul and ask him. Then sign on a new messman."

In a fog thicker than Jake had ever seen, he rode with Sixto in a cab to a naval hospital on the outskirts of Edinburgh. For a while Sixto's eyes darted about; he looked excited, and Jake thought he might make a break for it. Maybe he had faked the whole suicide attempt to get ashore. But then he went inward again, slumped back until they reached the hospital. Jake checked him in, then left. Jake couldn't figure the whole thing out. Sixto had jumped a peacetime navy to join a merchant fleet that was at war. It didn't make sense. So many things didn't make sense. He came back later to Leith and saw Liz after she got home from work. They had their rations of Scotch at several pubs, but the best rations were Liz herself in bed.

"The second time is always better," she said.

"What about the third time?"

"You better go home, Yank. You'll get to be a habit I won't be able to shake."

"Captain," Jake said, "you don't give the men shore leave, they'll all jump overboard."

"Maybe you're right. Okay. One officer and two seamen a day, that's all."

Shore leave was granted after three o'clock, long after any convoy conference would be called. The men were ordered to be back by noon the next day. Anything, the men promised. Anything for one night on the town, even if it was all blacked out, even if it was foggy-damp and miserable. Even if the rations were only two drinks, a drinking man will always find his way to more, and a skin man will always find his way to pussy.

Every day the crew would listen to the radio to see how the battle of the Scheldt was going. One day they learned that the Allies had finally taken the river, that minesweepers were now clearing it. The next day the skipper was ordered to a convoy conference. At noon he came back aboard and said, "We're shoving off." The *Hawkins* steamed back to the Thames estuary and anchored.

"Now what?" Jake asked the captain.

"I await further orders. The fuckin' war can drive you crazy."

The following morning the skipper went ashore again. When he came back, he was shaken.

"I'm not going," he said.

"What do you mean you're not going?" Jake asked. "Where we going?"

"Antwerp. It's still mined. They're bombing the shit out of it. Buzz bombs, rockets. I don't know how to get there. I've never been there. I don't know those waters. I won't go without a pilot."

"Can you refuse?"

"I'm the captain, mister. I command this ship. I'm responsible for it. These Germans, they've got these fast torpedo boats. Hit and run. They come in, smash, and run."

"You're the captain."

He was shaking. "Yesterday, a convoy of three ships with two escorts tried to get through. All three got it. So did one of the escorts. I'm not going to risk my ship or the lives of my crew. No, sir. Fuck 'em."

The crew waited, wondering what all the shuttling around was about; they were ready to take off. But the captain didn't make a move. He locked himself in his cabin, became incommunicado. The chief mate tried to reach him. The chief engineer wanted to know whether to keep the steam up. No word.

"We're not moving," Jake said. "Captain won't go to Antwerp."

"Can he do that?" the chief said.

"I don't know," Jake said. "I'm not a seagoing lawyer. I don't know who the final authority is."

"The captain is," the mate said.

"Maybe he wants a personal visit from FDR," Jake said.

"They'll take the fuckin' ship away from him," the chief said. "This is wartime. Nobody's indispensable. Nobody plays God anymore."

But the ship didn't move. And nobody knew what to do. At eleven o'clock a tugboat headed for the *Hawkins.*

"Here comes the word," the mate said.

The "word" was a huge man with a bristling red mustache, who climbed up the ladder in a commodore's uniform. When he stood up on deck, he overwhelmed everybody.

"You must be John Wayne," Jake said.

The commodore smiled. "I'm Martin Frisby. We're going to be the commodore vessel. Where's the skipper?"

Jake ran to the captain's cabin. "Skipper, the commodore's aboard. We're going to be the commodore ship. He's taking over the whole bit."

The captain opened his door. "What'd you say?"

Jake repeated the news. The captain sank into his chair with a sigh of relief. "Tell the commodore I welcome him aboard. I'll see him on the bridge shortly."

The captain was relieved of command. The ship was in good hands. The commodore had sailed the route in peacetime for Cunard. There were six ships and four British escorts. They started the run across the North Sea on a gray, murky day, alert for attack from the air and from the fast hit-and-run torpedo boats. As they came into the Scheldt estuary, Jake saw the broken merchant vessels of the earlier convoy that had been hit. Minesweepers were still clearing the channel. The *Hawkins* had to thread her way carefully through a safe lane. Then the buzz bombs started flying overhead. You could see the flames coming out of them, and they sounded like old tin lizzies rattling in the air. Antiaircraft went after them and destroyed some of them in midair. But you couldn't see or hear the rockets, not until they struck; then you'd hear the devastating explosion, and you'd see houses shattered with debris flying for hundreds of yards. Once inside the mouth of the Scheldt, the convoy moved slowly. It took hours to go through the locks. Each time everybody aboard felt he was trapped in the small locks as the buzz bombs flew overhead and the rockets exploded all around. The ship was finally piloted to her berth and tied up.

An army captain came aboard and begged Jake for some smokes and candy for his men, who'd been battling for their lives for weeks with no supplies. Jake had begun to ration his slop chest supplies a month before; he didn't know if he'd have enough for his own crew, but he let the captain have a pound of Prince Albert tobacco.

"I don't have any paper," Jake said.

"We'll find a way to smoke it, don't worry."

That was the first of many officers who'd come aboard begging for supplies for their men. The following day the skipper went ashore to find out when he'd unload.

"Shit," he said when he came back. "I should have taken this trip off. I should have taken a rest. Eleven months in Casablanca, shuttling back and forth. Now this. Oh, shit."

"What's up, captain?"

"We're liable to be here for the duration. You know what they're doing? Unloading only front-line supplies. Guns, tanks, ammo."

"What about our detonators?"

"They blew up all the bridges they want to blow."

"They'll need our steel for the bridgework."

"What we've got they'll probably never use. This is our home, mister. Figure on the duration."

"On this fucking powder keg, with those goddamn rockets and buzz bombs flying all over?"

"That's it, mister. What a home away from home, huh?"

What a beautiful safe cargo I wound up with, Jake thought.

"What about shore leave, captain?"

"Give the crew their advances and let them go."

The port of Antwerp became the supply depot for the Allied forces in their final drive into Germany. It also became the last-ditch battleground of the German army to beat back the Allied forces. Near Antwerp, the Wehrmacht mounted its last big offensive. It became known as the Battle of the Bulge. The big front at times was only twenty miles away. But another front was at the port and in the city of Antwerp itself because a special crack unit of English-speaking Germans in American uniforms were spreading panic and confusion, committing acts of sabotage and murder, right in the middle of American-held positions. Paranoia spread; troops began to distrust each other; everybody was trigger-happy. The buzz bombs and rockets didn't help any.

The first night Jake spent in town, a rocket went off while he was asleep. Everything on the walls dropped down; the windows were shattered; his bed fell apart. When he went out the next morning, all of the next block was devastated. You weren't safe anywhere. Dense fog day after day made matters worse. Now you couldn't see the buzz bombs, you could only hear them, and you screamed inside as you waited for them to land. Planes couldn't go up to attack them. It became much easier for the American-dressed Germans to infiltrate. One night, as Jake was coming back to his ship, a military guard stopped him, his M1 thrust out.

"Halt. Who are you?"

"I'm the purser on the SS *Hawkins*."

"Dock number?"

"Ninety-six."

The soldier cocked his rifle.

"Who's Joe DiMaggio?"

Oh, shit, Jake thought, but scared, because the soldier's finger was twitching on the trigger. "Left fielder for the Yankees."

"Dizzy Dean."

"Pitcher for the Cards. Won over thirty games."

"Ever heard of the Four Horsemen?"

"The Notre Dame backfield."

"Okay, you sonofabitch."

"What's all this shit about?"

"Last night a fuckin' Nazi got through. Cut the throats of two guards, then spread enough grenades around to blow up the whole fuckin' dock. Buddy of mine caught him. Boom, boom."

You wanted it, Jake thought. Action. The whole *shmeer*. You could have stayed home. A shore job. A desk jockey. Not a thing to worry about. With Rhoda around, nice and cozy, cushy and rosy. But you had to worry about why you didn't put up for Spain, the books you wanted to write, what you'd tell the kids you don't have. *Shmuck,* every step you take might be your last one. You could well wind up with nothing to tell, nothing to write.

Antwerp was bombed ruthlessly. Every day blocks and blocks crumbled under the rocket attacks. The people, who had first welcomed Jake when he came ashore, now looked at him with hatred.

"Go home. Look what you have brought."

"Would you rather have the Germans?" Jake asked.

"The Germans were good. They were orderly. They were disciplined."

"You don't care who you live with, do you?"

"We will live with anybody. We want peace. When it's all over, what difference does it make who's in power? We will have our shops, our families, what's left of them, maybe a little love. What else is there?"

The American dream, Jake wanted to say. Every person can be a millionaire, have his own power, be President. But he knew that the class structure in Europe was almost as rigid as the caste system in India; hardly anybody moved out of his class. Their dreams were anchored.

The people were listening to both German and Allied broadcasts. It looked as if the Germans were going to overrun Antwerp again. The Allies were in trouble; that's what everybody heard. The 101st Airborne Division was trapped at Bastogne. The Wehrmacht had blitzed to the Meuse, seized the Allied main supply center at Liège, and was ready to mount a drive to Antwerp. If they could control the port again, they could chop the Allied armies in the vicinity and to the south. With the Allied air command grounded because of the deep fog, the Germans continued to advance.

The only safe place was Brussels, which had been declared an open city. One weekend Jake went into Antwerp to see a movie, but instead decided to go to Brussels; it was only forty miles away. He rode in a train over the devastated, deep-cratered, foggy countryside. Halfway there, because the tracks had been bombed out, he had to walk a mile over muddy fields to get on another train which took him to Brussels. He rented a room in a hotel that had a bidet and a toilet, but he didn't know what the bidet was for. Then he roamed around the Grand' Place with its Gothic and gilded Baroque buildings, looked into the shopwindows and the cafés, and was amused at the "Mannekin-Pis." This was Europe, altogether different from Glasgow and Edinburgh. Toward the end of the day he stepped into a gallery and looked at the work of a modern artist which he didn't like. It must have shown on his face.

"You not like?" a woman said to him. She was in a mink coat and an elegant feathered hat. She had a round face, black hair, and stunning eyes. And her body, through the open coat, looked sturdy and well proportioned. Last, he noticed a small dictionary in her hand.

"No," he said. "I don't like."

"Oh." She fumbled through her dictionary. "Terrible. *Parlez-vous Français?*"

"No. English. *Deutsch.*"

"You go *Grand Musée? Palais?*"

"No."

"Come. I take."

She became Jake's guide. It took her ten minutes, through the dictionary, to tell him it would be awful for him to leave with a bad impression of Brussels. "It is little Paris," she said. She took him to the Ancient Museum, but Jake had seen similar work of old masters in Chicago and New York. He wondered what the living artists were doing; that's why he had stopped in at the gallery.

"Ah, *oui.* Yes, yes. I take. Premier artist Belgium. Paint King and Queen."

He wondered what this stylish, elegant, attractive woman was doing leading him around like a schoolteacher.

"We eat. Then I take."

First, she took him to her fur shop in the center of the city, where there were displays of mink and sable in the windows. He reached for her dictionary, and, after riffling through it, said, "Women still buy furs?"

"*Oui, oui.*" She took the dictionary from him, then said, "Not too much now. Little, little."

He nodded. He was becoming a master at charades. She made several phone calls, then said, "Hungry?"

"*Oui.*"

"*Bien.* We *mange.*"

She led him across the dark plaza to the La Maison du Cygne, a warm, intimate restaurant. Jake felt as if he were in a Charles Boyer movie. Everything was so Continental: the half bow from the maître d', being led grandly to a white-clothed table, the singsong French, then the waiter in a white jacket standing by discreetly and patiently. She suggested duck à l'orange. Jake said, "Fine, fine." But first they had an aperitif; then she suggested a white wine.

"We buy one thousand bottles a year," she said after a lot of probing through the dictionary.

"My God," Jake said. "You must have a warehouse to support your habit."

"*Quoi?*"

"*Rien.* Nothing."

It was all impossible, but it was fun, and who cared? Suddenly he realized that he didn't even know her name.

"My name," he said, "is Jake Davidson."

"Oh. My name is Jeanne Marais."

He proposed a toast to their acquaintance. Then he realized that she had said "we" about buying wine.

"Who is we?" he said. "You and who else?"

"My husband. He is not here." With much difficulty he learned that he had collaborated with the Germans, then disappeared. She didn't seem much concerned about him. "He was not a good man. He was not a man." With some embarrassment she said, "He was too much with other men."

Which translated into homosexual for Jake.

"But we lived together."

"Bad for you?"

"Sometimes yes, sometimes no."

"*Amour, amour.*"

"Sometimes yes, many times no." She laughed.

After the food and the wine, Jake was feeling mellow, relaxed, safe, as far away from the war as he could be. He glowed in it silently for a while. The woman with him looked serene, didn't feel it necessary to fight the battle of the dictionary for a while; she let him dwell in his silence. Then she said, "Come. We must go."

He called the waiter and asked for the check, *l'addition.*

"It is not necessary," the waiter said.

"What do you mean it's not necessary?"

"It is taken care of."

"How? Who?"

"Come, Jake," Jeanne said.

"You?"

"It is nothing. I will pay later."

"No, please," Jake said. "This is above and beyond. I mean it's ridiculous."

He was wasting his breath. She didn't understand a word. He turned to the water. "Give me the check."

The waiter looked at her, at Jake, then shrugged and handed him the check. Jake pulled his wallet out and said, "Me gallant. Me no gigolo. Me pay."

"I took you here," she said.

"Only because you know the place better. It'll be my pleasure. *Comprende?*"

She nodded, smiled. "*Oui.*"

The artist Jeanne brought him to lived on the third floor of an old building. The living room was huge, half of it his studio, with a skylight for a ceiling. The artist, André Froissart, was a white-haired man in his seventies, with strong, gnarled hands and a slender, vigorous body. With him was a younger woman, very chic, very attractive, who spoke with an English accent. She was Angela Delacroix, a good friend, who was going to be the translator of the evening. Froissart was an excellent portrait painter, who could render perfect likenesses. He could create a romantic aura around women. He gave men dignity, stature, a sense of being somebody important in the world. He was a society artist. His landscapes had a romantic, pastel quality about them. Jake didn't care for any of the work, though he admired the man's technique, but he said, "Excellent. Wonderful. Handsome." If Rhoda were here, he thought, she'd dismiss the work with a sardonic twist of her mouth.

They had tea and some delicious petits fours, and they talked about the war, Mark Twain, Hemingway, Faulkner, about the artists in America, whom Froissart was interested in. Occasionally the sound of a buzz bomb could be heard, and then through the skylight they could see its flames as it traveled. Conversation would stop, they'd listen, they'd watch; then, after it passed out of sight, they'd continue.

"How can a man work with all that going overhead?" Jake asked.

Froissart laughed. "You work. As long as you hear it, you're all right."

"But you can't hear the rockets."

Froissart was also a philosopher. "As long as a man is alive, he is immortal."

Imagine, Jake thought, a rocket, a misdirected buzz bomb coming through that skylight.

Everything was said twice that evening, translated and re-translated. Angela did a superb job. To Jake, anybody with an English accent sounded ultrasophisticated and cultivated. With Angela's French translations, then the English, he felt as if he were in the midst of all Oxford and the Sorbonne. Angela stayed on after Jake and Jeanne left. So she was going to be more than a good friend to Froissart tonight.

Outside they found a taxi.

"My place?" he said.

"Okay, yes."

And they spent the night together. Her perfume excited Jake. Her creamy white skin and ample breasts, her probing kisses, the close movement of her body excited him even more. There was no need for any dictionary; their bodies were far more eloquent. A little lovemaking, Jake thought afterward, and it pushes into the background all the monotony, the dullness, the fears, the horrors of war. When all that is forgotten, this will be remembered. Which is what makes war so romantic.

They had dinner the following night, then went to the opera, and wound up in his room again. The war receded farther and farther. The next day he bought a lace tablecloth and some crystal glasses and a bottle of Revillon perfume for Rhoda, then started back for Antwerp, a wiser man; he knew the secret of the bidet. When he got to the docks and headed for his ship, Jake saw his captain coming toward him.

"Captain," Jake said.

The captain looked at him in surprise, then: "Jake!" He'd forgotten to call him mister. He ran to him and embraced him.

"Jesus, Jake."

"What's wrong, captain?"

"I was just going in to report you missing."

"Why?"

"That movie house—the gunnery officer said you were going there—a rocket hit it, and a thousand men were killed. I couldn't figure what happened to you. I figured you had to be in there."

"I just got lost for a couple of days, captain."

"I'm just glad you're back, mister. Glad you're back."

Wallace Beery, Jake thought. Gruff, tough, by the book, but a sentimental slob at heart.

Nothing had been unloaded from the *Hawkins* except the planes she carried. Nothing in her cargo was needed. The crew watched wistfully as other ships that had come in weeks after the *Hawkins* were emptied, took on ballast, and sailed for home, while they kept sitting on a block-long keg of dynamite. It was as if the *Hawkins* and her cargo had been forgotten.

Antwerp was razed still further by bombs. A third of the city had been reduced to rubble since the *Hawkins* had arrived. It got harder to go into town. There wasn't much there anyhow but thousands of GIs, rubble, a population that resented the Americans, and earthshaking concussions from the rockets and buzz bombs. Jake couldn't get to Brussels anymore. More tracks had been destroyed, and the trains had stopped running. Home was the ship; somehow it felt safer there. He escaped from it all through his novel. He kept working hard at it. He was near the finish, and he wanted to get it off before anything happened. At least *that* might be the one thing left of him if he were hit.

As he worked, Field Marshal Montgomery's forces, General Bradley's armies, and General Patton's divisions threw all their power against the Nazis, but the Germans continued to advance, splitting the Allies farther apart. Suddenly, around Christmastime, the suffocating fog lifted. The air became filled with the sight and sound of thousands of Allied planes. The crew of the *Hawkins* ran out on deck, jumped up and down, cheered.

"Get the bastards! Tear 'em apart!"

What a sight!

"Kill the bastards!" Jake yelled. "Kill the fucking Jew killers!" His eyes got misty, filled with tears.

"End it up there!" he continued to yell. "Let's go home, for Christ sake. Bring us home up there!"

Another sunny day. And another. Thousands of sorties were flown, paralyzing the enemy, knocking out the Luftwaffe. Germany's last-ditch stand was broken. Bastogne was saved. There were heavy casualties on both sides, with the Germans suffering more, but the march into Germany had begun.

"We got 'em by the balls," Jake said. The taste of victory was deep in his throat. And he thought: "Let's go home. Unload us, please. Take what we've got, and send us home before anything happens. The rockets and buzz bombs slammed into Antwerp relentlessly, increasing in intensity as the Germans retreated.

Jake airmailed his manuscript to Rhoda, asking her to read it, then to send it to his agent. Get there safe, he prayed. Please, let it get there safe. He felt as if a good part of his life had gone off in that carefully packaged manuscript.

Then one cold, snowy day in March the cranes moved up to the *Hawkins* and started to unload her. First the explosives. Everybody aboard shouted with relief. Then the structural steel began to go. Five days later the ship proceeded out of the locks into the Scheldt and formed a convoy with eight other ships and three destroyer escorts. On the way out, Jake saw more ships sunk by bombs. He felt he had lived a charmed life. Let it stay with me, he prayed. Let me get back home.

They made it safe across the North Sea into the Thames estuary. Laid over several more days. Then a convoy of fifty vessels started back across the English Channel. Outside the Scilly Islands, a dozen more ships joined them from Bristol and Liverpool. Then they were on their way across.

They ran into a violent storm in the middle of the North

Atlantic. The *Hawkins,* with a light ballast of sand, was tossed and rolled about, shaken and battered for two days. All you could eat were sandwiches, if you could eat. You could hardly drink any coffee. The convoy was broken up, then re-formed, then broken up again when it ran into dense fog off the Grand Banks.

"We're getting the full treatment, mister," the captain said to Jake.

"The fates up there, they just won't let us alone."

"Somebody on this ship is a whistler, or somebody killed an albatross, or somebody didn't pay the whores. Because somebody's got it in for us, goddamn it."

They ran blindly, dead reckoning for a day and a half, with the whistle blowing and driving everybody crazy. Finally they sailed clear of the fog.

"We going to join the convoy?" the mate asked the captain.

"Impossible. We'll make it alone."

The skipper stood firmly on deck, proud, on his own, in full command. Probably feeling like Columbus, Jake thought. Admiral of the ocean.

"I'll get us in," the captain said. "Don't worry. They haven't got our number yet. We're going to make it one more time."

Soon they were past Coney Island, into the Narrows, with land on both sides, and then into the Hudson, up the West Side of Manhattan. Everybody had shore fever. Everybody was going to go home with a heavy load of cash. Everybody was just about jumping out of their skins. They were all packed. All ready to go.

As soon as the *Hawkins* docked at the 23rd Street Pier, the company paymasters came aboard and helped Jake pay off the crew. Six months pay, most of it in the 100 percent bonus zone. The voyage was finished.

"Mister," said the Captain to Jake, "sign on for the next trip. I just got word we'll have ten days here to load up. A safe load. And we're going to the South Pacific."

"For how long?"

"Can't be too long. The war's almost over."

Jake calculated: It'd take maybe three weeks to get where they're going, another week to unload, three weeks back, if they turned around quickly, that was two months already. With a nervous, shell-shocked skipper having me up every morning to have cool coffee with him and being a captive to his lousy doggerel, forget it.

"There'll be a lot of time out there. All the time in the world to write."

And Jake thought: All your life you wanted to go to the South Pacific. Palm trees, balmy breezes, lovely bronze-skinned native girls, coral beaches. But there'd still be that cold coffee and dreadful doggerel. He shook the temptation away.

"Thanks, skipper, I'll take a raincheck. I've got a month coming. I'm going to take it all."

Maybe by then the war will be over, Jake thought. I'll see the South Pacific at my own expense. With Rhoda. It'll be more fun, a greater experience. He couldn't wait to get home to her.

BOOK 6

When he got home, Rhoda wasn't there. Of course, she'd be at work. He felt so strange in the apartment, an intruder. Everything so neat, so tidy, everything smelling of her, even the oils of a freshly painted canvas on her easel of a boy sitting forlornly on the edge of a pier, the mood blue. He roamed about the place, touching everything, listening to the powerful sounds of the city instead of the ship and the sea. Once a friend had joked to Rhoda about his coming home: "You'll have to rig up a hammock and slosh buckets of water against the wall to make him feel at home." It wasn't such a joke after all. The sounds, the rhythm, the feeling of city life were really different.

He could hardly believe he was back. All afternoon his throat was constricted with emotion. A powerful restlessness came over him. He went out and bought some filet mignons, a rich chocolate whipped cream pie, a bottle of California Pinot wine, a dozen jumbo shrimp for an appetizer with the makings for a good sauce. Tonight they'd have a grand feast. Back home, he cooked the shrimp and peeled them, then put them in the refrigerator to get cold. He put a couple of Idaho potatoes in the oven. All of it made him feel more at home. What else? he thought restlessly. Wait. Patience. He called his agent, Eric Weiss.

"Jake! I was just about to call you." Eric hadn't changed a bit. He was a man who never called, but every time you phoned you got the same response.

"I just got in."

"Where were you?"

"Antwerp. Brussels."

"Ah, wonderful Antwerp. Beautiful Brussels." The Continental man talking, with nostalgic memories.

"Not the way I saw it."

"Oh, yes. I know. The Battle of the Bulge."

"Eric, did you read my book? What did you think?"

"I liked it. It's with Harper's. Let's have lunch."

"When?"

"Tomorrow. Noon. Maybe I'll have a good word for you."

Eric's reaction thrilled him. He was feeling more at home by the minute. He couldn't wait for Rhoda to get home. He made a salad. Prepared the coffee. Fixed the horseradish sauce for the shrimp. Set the table, with two candles, the new Belgian lace tablecloth and the crystal glasses and the bottle of perfume. Then, not being able to settle down and read, he paced about, waiting for her.

He was tired by the time she arrived. And rejuvenated at once at the sight of her. He grabbed her, lifted her, kissed her, felt her joyous tears fall on his face.

"I thought you'd never make it," she said.

"I did, baby."

She was overwhelmed by the gifts but more overwhelmed by his being there. They had a stiff drink, then went to bed. That was their first big hunger to satisfy. Then by candlelight, relaxed, they had their dinner, and talked, and caught up with each other. She no longer worked at Sperry Rand. She'd got a new job illustrating fashions and advertising art for a small agency called Carl Rosen Associates. She was quite happy there. Full and mellow, they dawdled over the wine.

"I loved your book, Jake. Now I know what it was like out there.

"Eric liked it, too. It's at Harper's."

"Well, you've had your war and you've got your book. What else is left?"

"A little relaxation. The easy life."

"Won't you have to go out again?"

On the way back from Antwerp, and all that day, he had thought: Each time he had gone out, there was a strong possibility he'd never come back. Each time he did come back he felt as if he'd won a reprieve. He didn't want to chance it again. The war was almost at an end. He'd braved the worst part of it; he'd done enough. Maybe if he went out again, it'd be one time too many. Let them catch up with me, he thought. It'll all be over by then.

"I'm not going out again," he said.

"You're sure in a month you won't get restless, you won't feel guilty, you won't feel you'll have to go?"

"I don't know. But right now I don't feel strained, I'm not scared, I feel safe, and that's the way I want to feel. Like my father would say, I'm entitled."

Later they went to bed again. They were more relaxed with each other. They enjoyed each other more.

"Nothing like home fucking," Jake said.

She laughed and held him tight.

Rhoda took a few days off. They loafed around, walked the peaceful streets, roamed through Central Park, blew themselves to a fancy dinner at the Plaza, took a boat ride up the Hudson, saw their friends.

She went back to work, and Jake flew to Chicago to see his folks. The city always excited him. No matter how far he had gone and what he had experienced, the big, sprawling, monotonous, smoky, ugly prairie town had a terrific pull for him, as if the lake and the river were tidal bodies of water. So it didn't have the medieval history, the pure Gothic architecture, the beauty and neatness of a Brussels, the grandeur of Loch Lomond, the Scottish lore of Edinburgh, the great seaport of what was once Antwerp, the vertical, intellectual, and cultural power of New York. But it had the factories, the slaughterhouses, the brawn, the know-how, the morale to help win the war. What was more important, Jake's bones were there. And his memories. No matter how far he drifted, the pull was always there. It was home.

His kid brother, Harry, was still in the Signal Corps near San Francisco; he'd never gone overseas. His mother showed him pictures of Harry, handsome, dark, jaunty in uniform, in convertibles with beautiful, sunny California girls.

"Harry," Jake said. "Wherever he goes, he's making out."

"Go start up with Harry," his mother said proudly.

His sister, Miriam, had three kids already, the oldest eight.

"So, Ma," Jake said, "you're a grandma."

"I'm too young to be one. Nobody believes it."

"It cramps your style, huh?" Miriam said.

"I don't even have gray hair yet, and I'm a grandma. But I would sacrifice my youth to be a grandma for your children, Jake."

"You're the prince," Miriam said without being offended.

"What's the matter you don't have a baby?" his mother said. "You get married, you have babies."

"The war, Ma. We've got time."

"A beautiful woman like Rhoda, a handsome man like you, with brains like both of you have, oh, what babies you could make. You should start a factory."

"You've got grandchildren, Ma."

"Not from my oldest son."

He turned to his father, changing the subject.

"So, Pa," Jake said, "how are the horses?"

"They're still running."

"Who's going to win the Derby?"

"Hoop Junior."

"No matter what, the races go on, huh?"

"That's the beauty of America. Baseball, football, prizefights, all the sports, war or no war, they still go on. Better to watch them fight than a bunch of people with guns and cannons."

The West Side was still the same. Douglas and Independence boulevards, with their big synagogues and the JPI, were still the showplace avenues. But the side streets had never got over the Depression. They looked shabbier, more uncared for, more run-down. Maxie Katz was still holding court on the boulevard with his cronies, arbitrating disputes and passing on favors. His boss,

Morrie Benjamin, was more powerful than ever. He had kept his promise to Albie Karlin, the greatest Jewish swimmer who ever lived, who was now the youngest judge in the superior court.

"You could have written your own ticket, too, Jake," Albie said when they had lunch one day. "But you had to go left on us."

"The fates, Albie. You're the lawyer. I'm trying to be a writer."

"Any luck?"

"So far, very little. The war took a few years out of my life."

"Didn't it for nearly everybody?"

"Not for the guys who stayed home."

"You sound bitter."

"I'm not, Albie. Believe me. I could have stayed home, but I wanted to get into it. Not that I was a hero. I just had to. Maybe it was opportunism for me. I don't know."

"I hope you get what you want, Jake."

His uncle Nachum had a couple of girls now. And he was doing fairly well at his newsstand on the Northwest Side.

"I am an American *goniff* now," he said. It didn't take much to make him happy.

Sean H. Fitzgerald was still a great coach, producing championship teams at Lane Tech. Benny Gordon had moved to California, the West Coast representative of a floor wax corporation. Ida Braverman, he'd heard, was married with a couple of kids. Lila Shulman had left the Chez Paree and was now a big talent agent in Hollywood. A number of friends he had known since boyhood had been killed in action. Those were the big changes. But the city felt the same, strong, vital, and he was comfortable in it. The pull back to New York was Rhoda, along with a desire to make good there.

It was spring in New York, a lovely, lively, growing time, the parks and the trees in the squares turning green, but Jake didn't feel right there, didn't feel he belonged. He'd always felt like a stranger. Very, very small and insignificant and overpowered.

At dinner with Rhoda one night, soon after he got back from Chicago, he said, "My mother talked about children when I was there. Said we should open up a factory."

Rhoda didn't answer.

"My mother, she loves the state of pregnancy," Jake said lightly. "On other people."

"She's right, you know. We're not getting any younger."

"Then you've been thinking about it, too."

"Jake, a woman always thinks about it. It's built into her. Especially if she's been married a good number of years. I didn't want one with my first husband. I didn't love him. But you're the guy I love. All the time you've been away, how wonderful, I thought, if I'd had your kid. No matter what happened, I'd have had that."

"We talked about it." Suddenly he was feeling sullen. "We said we'd wait."

"I know, I know. But I couldn't stop myself from thinking about it." She leaned forward. "The war is over now, Jake."

"Not for me it isn't. I'm still liable to the draft. I don't have a job. I don't know where I am."

"Jake, we've been married four years. The longer you postpone, the harder it is to make a decision."

"Do you want a baby?"

"Yes. Before I grow too old to have one—yes."

"You're only thirty-three."

"That's getting on."

Tightly, his voice rising, he said, "Do you want one? Now?"

"Don't push me, Jake. I'm not going to make the decision for you."

"It isn't time."

"You brought it up, Jake. It must have been on your mind."

"We've got to get set first."

"What will you call set?"

"When we each have a little taste of success. When we have a little fulfillment."

"Will you know when it comes?"

"Yes." He pounded the table. "By God, yes."

"Then forget it."

"All right, we'll forget it!"

He glowered through the rest of dinner. How could they think of having a child with him feeling so incomplete, so disconnected, so rootless? It would be so unfair . . . to them as well as to the child.

In bed that night, he said, "I'd love a baby with you, Rhoda."

"Don't think about it. I know you're in limbo."

"All the time I was overseas I thought about it, too."

"I know, Jake. Later maybe, we'll try to open up the factory. Right?"

"Right."

Rhoda worked all day and was so glad he was home when she arrived from her kind of war that it helped him forget the long, restless days. Though many men were in civilian clothes, he continued to wear his uniform on the streets; it was his badge of honor, his not having to explain himself to anybody, his way of telling the world that he was in transit. During the day he walked the streets and lounged around the apartment, waiting. Waiting for the war to end. Waiting for word from his agent. Each time Jake called him, Eric said, "I was just about to call you." Arousing his hopes. But the word wasn't good. The word was rejection.

"Publishers like the book," Eric said. "But the timing is wrong. They don't think it will sell."

"What the hell does it take to sell a book?"

"Write another one. Not a war book. I'll keep working with this one."

"Jesus Christ!" It was like howling in a hurricane.

Write another book. Go on, go ahead. Write another one. What? What other book? How many books does a guy have in him?

"You'll write another one," Rhoda said.

"That's all I need," he snapped at her. "The word from you. Bang, there's another one."

"You've written other books."

"All bombs. Worth three dollars in paper and a typewriter ribbon, not counting the cost of pencils. For my sweat, a penny's worth of salt. No more books."

"All right, Jake, no more books. Now what?"

"Oh, you're a honey, you're really a beaut. You talk like they grow on trees."

"If you're a writer, you'll find another idea, and you'll work it out. If you're not. . . . Jake, what are we talking about? You think I've got it any easier with my art? You think anybody wants my work? I do it because I have to. It's a disease. We're both sick with it. Let's go to a movie."

So they escaped for a couple of hours in a movie. And they escaped in bed through sex. At least they had that. But then, alone, he came smack up against himself again. What do I do with myself?

His month was almost up. Any day he expected a notice from his draft board that his 2B deferment had run out, and he'd have to sign on another ship to stay out of the draft. He tried to relax, to forget it, but it hung over his head, kept him immobilized.

One day, while Jake was at a Yankee-White Sox game, an announcement came over the loudspeaker that Germany had surrendered. The whole Stadium jumped and cheered, everybody hugging and laughing and crying, and somebody sang "God Bless America," and everybody joined in. Jake started to leave. He was all choked up. He wanted to be with somebody close. He wanted to be home. Thousands of fans began to leave, too. For once in their lifetime they couldn't care less who won; the game was insignificant. The subways were full of happy, cheering, talking, victorious people. Everybody was friendly. The drinkers were already getting drunk. It seemed that the whole world was heading for Times Square. Jake, in uniform, was crushed, kissed, his hand shaken until it was limp, his back broken from the pounding. He couldn't get home fast enough. But first he stopped for a bottle of champagne.

Rhoda was there when he arrived. She flung her arms around him. They both wept.

"You heard," he said.

"My boss let me off. Nobody could work anymore. We all had a drink, then rushed off to be with somebody we loved."

"I'd have gone nuts if you hadn't been here."

"Me too."

"I can't believe the war is over."

He popped open the bottle of champagne. It fizzed all over them. They laughed hysterically. Poured drinks. Guzzled them down.

"You're supposed to sip it," she said.

"Not the way I feel, you don't."

He peeled off his clothes, and she followed. Drunk, they reeled onto the bed and fucked forever, it seemed, until they were exhausted. Then they rolled away from each other. Rhoda curled up. Jake stared silently at the ceiling. And they fell asleep. When they woke up, subdued, they turned and looked at each other. Smiles formed on their faces. They felt like naughty kids.

"We can relax now," he said. "We've got a whole lifetime ahead of us."

The next day he put on his civilian clothes. They were old, dusty, and musty. He went up to Rogers Peet and bought himself a new wardrobe. He felt released, sprung from his indecision and restlessness. Now he was going to get a job, get busy. If he had to write he would do it in his spare time.

He wrote to Peter Mason, who was now in charge of production nationally at NBC in New York: Would he have anything for him? He sent a number of résumés to newspaper and radio news editors. While he waited, he wrote a radio show for *Grand Central Station* and for *First Nighter*.

Peter Mason answered quickly, asking him to come in to see him. He enclosed a rave recommendation he'd sent to NBC's story editor to put him on staff.

The gray eagle, when Jake entered Mason's executive office, was grayer, more stern-looking, almost forbidding, as he spoke on the phone about some production problem. His desk was littered with memos, which he kept shoving around as if they were parts of a puzzle. Then he hung up, sighed, and greeted Jake with warm eyes and a warm smile and handshake. They talked a bit about the war; Mason wanted to do all he could for the talented boys who'd been overseas. He was interrupted twice by must-answer calls, then said to his secretary, "No more calls. I don't care if it's David Sarnoff. I'm not in."

Which made Jake swell with importance.

"Get me Ed Stark." He turned to Jake. "That's our story editor." Then into the phone: "Ed, I've got Jake Davidson here, the writer from Chicago I wrote you about. Can you see him now?"

He nodded, hung up, and faced Jake, his deepset eyes burning in his head. "I've sent him a memo, and I've talked to him about you. If he has any regard for talent, he should put you on staff. I told him I'd approve. But I can't order him to hire you, even though I'm his boss. Organization policy. It drives me crazy sometimes. Drop by after you've seen him. I want to know what happened. Good luck."

He picked up the phone, dismissing Jake. "All right, Bess. Let the headaches start coming in."

As Jake started out, Mason looked withered, as if the beleaguered gray eagle's strength had ebbed.

Ed Stark was a shaggy-browed, stocky man with a hard-lined jaw and hair growing out of his ears and nose. He shook hands with Jake, then sat behind his script-laden desk and talked as if he had a pencil in his mouth.

"Mason thinks a lot of you," Stark said, rocking in his swivel chair. "Tell me about yourself. What have you done?"

That desk was like an ocean between them. Jake fidgeted. What had he done? What were his accomplishments?

"Well," he paused.

"You worked for Mason in Chicago. Correct?"

"I did a few *Author's Playhouse* for him. One of them an adaptation of my own published story."

"Pretty good show. Prestigious, not very commercial. What else?" Stark wasn't impressed. Now he actually put a copy pencil in his mouth and started to chew it.

Jake cleared his throat. "Did some shows for WBBM and WGN in Chicago. *Great Artists. Museum of Science and Industry.*"

"Documentaries. Any dramas, comedies, soaps?"

Jake lied, squeezed out, *"Grand Central Station."* He couldn't say *First Nighter.* It was an NBC show; Stark'd know. *"The Human Adventure,"* he exploded. That wasn't NBC.

"Fine documentary. Anything besides documentaries?"

"The war caught up with me. Almost three years."

"Overseas?"

"Yes."

"Action?"

"Plenty."

Silence. Stark gnawing at his pencil, looking away from him, rocking in his chair. Jake squirmed. The squeak of the chair and the pencil rattling in Stark's mouth were unbearable.

"Anything you can do," Jake blurted. "I'll start anywhere. As an apprentice writer, if you have such an animal. I just want a chance."

Stark's sharp eyes fixed on him a few seconds. Jake suddenly felt he'd sounded like the most desperate man in the world. Well, he was desperate. He had to get connected. Somewhere. Sometime. Stark leaned back in his chair, the protective pencil in his mouth, the desk an uncrossable moat.

"Jake, I've got men here with hundreds of scripts behind them. They're the best in the business." He took the pencil out of his mouth. "Everything has to be done last month. There is no room for apprentices here. We tried it once, and everything got snarled up, everything had to be done over again. We just can't take any chances. Too much pressure. We can't disappoint the millions of people listening. Top drama they want. Top comedies. Top soap. . . ."

Jake stopped listening. No, Stark was saying, loud and clear, no more pencil in his mouth.

"I might become one of your top men," Jake finally said when Stark paused a moment.

"Sorry, Jake."

Back in Mason's office, when Jake told him what happened, Mason sprang from his desk. "That cocksucker." It was shocking, coming from the godlike eagle. "That stuffy, conservative prick. He couldn't recognize talent if he was hit with a George S. Kaufman, an Elmer Rice, and a Robert Sherwood, that bastard. He's scared, that's the trouble, scared to take a chance, scared he may have to work a little harder, scared of his big play-safe ass. Christ, back in Chicago we took chances; we really developed radio; we had a hell of a lot of fun. Sure, we bombed, but we made money too. Lots of it. Here it's all the big time. The best, the best, the best. We're New York, the big apple. The turkeys I could show you of the best. I'm sorry, Jake. Sorry as hell."

"I'm grateful, Peter."

"I'll keep my eyes open. One of these days you'll show them."

The buzzer on his desk had been working constantly. His secretary stepped in. "It's Mr. Sarnoff."

"Shit."

He grabbed the phone. As he listened, his shoulders sagged. He waved to Jake and covered the phone. "Keep in touch."

The following week one of his radio scripts was accepted by *Grand Central Station*. The producer asked for another. He soared to the clouds. Then, in answer to his letters for a job, he was called in for an interview at WQXR, the *New York Times* station. He was hired as a radio news writer.

"Oh, baby." He lifted Rhoda off her feet. "We're really swinging."

"Isn't it wonderful?"

"New York, I love you."

He had made a dent in the big town. He was beginning to feel that he belonged.

After a week of working with the regular staff in the afternoon under the supervision of the editor, he was transferred to the shift he'd been hired for. He was there at 6:30 A.M., looked at the A wire of the Associated Press, tore off the latest five-minute news summary, edited it. He glanced quickly at the morning papers to see if there was an important story the A wire hadn't carried. If he had time, he'd bang it out and add it to the summary, then hand it to the announcer. The station opened with the news broadcast at 7 A.M. If anything else broke in the next fifteen minutes, he'd add it to the 7:30 newscast and edit out other material. Then he had to write a full five-minute summary of his own for the eight o'clock news, which was supposed to be fresh and different. Every hour a new summary and a fifteen-minute roundup for the noon broadcast, which was supposed to have color, verve, personality, a match for the networks. Then he was finished for the day.

That summer was exciting for Jake. Up at five-thirty. A fast breakfast, toast, juice, coffee. A run to the subway. An empty train uptown to 56th Street. A brisk walk in the fresh morning, Fifth Avenue empty, the streets quiet, Tiffany's across the way, the whole city waiting to get started with the morning news. It felt so good alone, the wire service clicking away, the long-haired music playing, the news starting to come in from Washington around ten-thirty, news of the war from overseas, the bells ringing out bulletins, him typing the summaries with variations as the stories broke, and then, at noon, out into the crowded streets, everybody in a rush, jamming into the Continental restaurants on the side streets, then relaxing and strolling around the Plaza, down Fifth Avenue, coming home early, and having the whole afternoon to himself. Then Rhoda would come home, and they'd have dinner and go to a movie or play or visit with friends. It was a happy time for them. Especially when Jake finally got a fix on the Lala Bloomberg story and began working on it afternoons.

He decided that after Lala's payroll robbery, when he killed a cop, he had met a plain, innocent girl while on the run and used her for his getaway. He would develop this into a love story as well as a story of terror, in which the victim and the captor fall in love. He bulged with the idea, bulged with his new feeling about New York, bulged with his new freedom. Then the first atomic bomb fell on Hiroshima. That morning the bulletin bells rang out of control. He kept ripping the stories off the wire, editing them as fast as he could, rushing them to the announcers, who interrupted the regular broadcasts. The news of the bomb's devastating power was overwhelming. It ended the war.

"Now what'll we have to worry about?" Jake asked.

"Just plain ordinary living," Rhoda said.

"Just think, Rhoda. As long as we've known each other, we've been worried about survival. The Depression, then the war. The two big emotional bangs in our lives. We'll be lost without them."

"We can find another one."

"What?"

"A child."

"As soon as I finish my book."

"Promise?"

"Promise."

Life became filled to the brim. Jake got deeper into his new novel. Rhoda, in her free time, got involved with her painting.

"It's a wonder we find time to make love," Rhoda said.

"Always time for that. That's the go button in our lives. Confucius said, 'Make love and you won't fight; it's the secret of happiness.'"

"Love that Confucius."

That winter he finished a draft of his new novel. He put it away for a few weeks, then started to rewrite it. One day he stopped in at his agent's.

"What's with the merchant marine book?" he asked.

"I've shown it to every publisher who might be interested. Sorry, Jake. Maybe we'd better put it away for a year or two, then show it again. It seems to be the wrong time for it."

"Who has seen it?"

Eric gave him a list of nine publishers.

"What else have you got?" Eric asked.

"I'm about a third finished with a new one."

"Let me have it. Maybe I can make a deal on what you have."

The next day, Jake brought him a hundred pages of his new work. Eric read the first page.

"I like it, I like it."

"Can I cash it in at the bank?"

"This time you will."

Jake took his merchant marine manuscript and left Eric's office. Across the street was Thurston and Levy, a reputable publishing firm. Jake looked at his list. They hadn't seen the novel. What the hell, he thought. It won't cost me a penny. He walked over and left the script with the receptionist. No return postage. Nothing. Just his name, address, and phone number.

"If it's rejected, call me. I'll pick it up."

The receptionist made a note of it.

He promptly forgot about it. Several days a week he played handball and swam quarter miles at the 92nd Street YMHA. Sometimes on the way home he brought mouth-watering napoleons and whipped cream pies.

"Just to remind us that the war is over and we're living the good life," he'd say.

One day, as he and Rhoda were about to sit down to dinner, the phone rang. Rhoda answered it.

"A man named Robert Thurston," she said.

"Who's he?"

"I don't know."

Jake shrugged, answered. In a few seconds his heart ran away from him. It was the publisher himself, hesitant, with a high, refined voice, fumbling for words, excited.

"You don't know how rare it is for an acceptable manuscript to come in over the transom. One in a million gets up to me. You were there, weren't you? You were really there."

"Yes," Jake said in a small, squeaky voice.

"It has authority. It smells of the sea. I can see the barnacles on that old rust bucket. Simon Lèvy and I would like to meet you. When? When can you come down?"

"Tomorrow. The day after. Whenever you say."

"Tomorrow afternoon. Three o'clock. How's that?"

"I'll be there."

"What? What?" Rhoda said when he hung up.

"It's him. Robert Thurston, the publisher, the great editor, that was him."

"What did he want, what did he want?"

"I don't know. He liked my book. He wants to meet me. Him and Simon Levy. I'm meeting them tomorrow afternoon."

"I don't believe it."

"Believe it, believe it."

They squeezed their breaths out hugging each other.

Fantasies, fantasies. They talked and talked. Dreamed and dreamed. They couldn't fall asleep, even after they'd made love. They got up and read. Who could concentrate?

"Let's work the *Times* crossword puzzle."

"Fine."

Then they played casino. Then they talked some more. Then they had napoleon and coffee.

"Jake, you've got to be up at five-thirty and go to work."

"What can I do?"

"You'll be all worn out by the time you see them."

"It's like the night before a big swimming meet. I never could fall asleep. I'll trust my adrenaline."

"Let's make love again. Maybe that'll calm us down."

"Big tranquilizer."

They did fall asleep afterward. A minute later, it seemed, the alarm went off. And he was rushing off to work in his best gray flannel suit. He got there late. He tore off the latest summary, edited it quickly, handed it to the announcer for the first newscast.

The day was hectic. He couldn't concentrate on what was coming in. He edited badly. Sometimes he wrote unwieldy sentences. The announcers came in to say, "You must be kidding."

"What's the matter?"

"It's like throwing a peck of potatoes in my mouth. Come on, Marcel Proust, cut 'em down. Make it crisp."

What could he tell them? Listen, I'm meeting a publisher today. I'm going to be an author. I might be famous. Listen!

Who cared? Everybody worried about his own skin.

How would he ever get through the day?

Noon. His boss came in. He wanted to tell him his news. But he didn't have a definite deal; nothing was sure; he didn't want to spook it. How would he ever get through the day?

He hardly tasted his lunch. It lumped up in him. He dawdled restlessly, then walked out. He strolled around the Plaza. Down Fifth Avenue. Watched the ice skating at Rockefeller Center. He got his shoes shined. Went into a newsreel theater. Window shopped. He'd go into Abercrombie & Fitch, outfit himself like Ernest Hemingway, go on a safari or something. He'd ride a horse and buggy through Central Park and go to wild chi-chi parties like F. Scott Fitzgerald. The phone would start ringing. Sam Goldwyn wanted him. So did Louis B. Mayer. John Ford wanted to direct his novel; Humphrey Bogart wanted to star in it. Oh, God, it's three o'clock. He rushed up to Thurston and Levy.

"I'm Jake Davidson. I have an appointment with Mr. Thurston and Mr. Levy."

"Yes, Mr. Davidson," the receptionist said. She already knew who he was. "They'll be with you in a minute."

He glanced at some books in a showcase of authors he admired. Someday he'd be in there among them.

"Mr. Davidson?"

He faced a florid, reddish blond, slight man with glasses, dressed in a brown worsted business suit.

"I'm Bob Thurston." He shook Jake's hand firmly. "Come in. Come in. I'm so glad to meet you."

"Likewise." Oh, God, just like Jewish kid from the West Side who had never gone to college or written a book that a publisher was interested in.

He was led into a conference room. A large table, a dozen chairs, a broad bank of windows, rich walnut-paneled walls, and he was shaking hands with Si Levy, a black-haired, easygoing young man with a winning smile who was connected to one of the richest families in America. And then he was introduced to Lester Krantz, a shy stutterer who looked as if he'd just got out of college, an assistant editor who had first read Jake's book and passed it on.

"You might say that Lester discovered you," Thurston said. "He sent the script over to me without comment. I loved it. I was enthralled by it. It's not only a war novel but a terrific sea novel. As I read it, there were times when I thought I was looking at a Turner painting. Then Si read it. He agreed with me. How did you happen to bring it to us?"

Jake was in a sweat. He pulled his damp collar away from his neck, loosened his tie, cleared his throat. "A funny thing happened to me on the way down Fifth Avenue one day."

Laughter. Si Levy leaned back in his chair; he was a leaner into chairs, a sprawler over tables, his face alive with fifty million things in his mind.

"We like it," Levy said. "We want to publish it. We want to be a part of your career. What else have you got?"

"I've got a third of a new book."

"What's it about?" Thurston said.

"I call it my minor *Crime and Punishment.*"

"We'll buy it sight unseen. Where is it?" Levy said.

"My agent has it."

"Has he shown it to anybody?"

"I don't know. I gave it to him a month ago."

"Who's your agent?" Levy said. He was the one who made the deals.

"Eric Weiss."

"Tell your agent we want you," Levy said. "We'd like to have both your novels. We hope you like us enough to say yes."

"What's not to like?" Jake said. "You guys love me. I'm a pushover."

He left the publishers and walked directly across the street to Eric Weiss's office. As soon as he entered, Eric said, "I know, I know. They've been on the phone with me."

"What do you think?"

"I just talked to Reynal and Hitchcock. They want your unfinished novel."

"They turned down my merchant marine book."

"Now they say they want that, too. Why don't we go for the most money?"

"No. Thurston and Levy wanted the sea novel first. They're buying my new book sight unseen. They're buying me, my talent. Let's do business with them."

Three days later Thurston was on the phone.

"Jake, that new book, it's a cliff-hanger. I can't tell you how exciting it is. Have you got a title?"

"*The Dark Invader.* Do you like it?"

"Love it. When will you have it finished?"

"Tomorrow."

Thurston laughed.

Later that day Eric Weiss called.

"I got you one thousand for the sea novel, fifteen hundred for *Dark Invader.*"

"Don't tell me any more. I can't breathe."

"They'd like to come out with *Invader* first."

"Why?"

"They think it'll do better, will establish an audience for you. Then the sea novel."

"Whatever they say."

"They'd like to schedule it, announce it. When do you think you'll have it done?"

"Last week."

The next day he quit his job. By the end of the week he was replaced. And suddenly, when he sat down to work, he found that he couldn't write. He had all the time in the world now, and he couldn't write. Sentences didn't make sense. The meaning of words escaped him; he was looking everything up in the dictionary. He reread what he'd done. It seemed terrible, lifeless, badly done, crude. He was never more scared in his life. Each morning he shook as he approached his desk. He had to walk away, get physically involved: handball, swimming, walking. Only there could he trust his reactions.

"They want you," Rhoda said. "They love you. They're paying you good hard money. They wouldn't be tossing it around if you didn't have it."

"I know, I know. I keep telling myself that. But this is it. This is the big time. I'm against all those guys out there."

"This isn't a meet, Jake. There is no competition out there. Everybody has his own special quality, his own unique way of seeing the world. It may appeal to a lot of people or only a few; but it's still something unique, and that's all you have to think about—you, only you, not Henry James or Hemingway or Tolstoy or Balzac or even Margaret Mitchell."

"What if I fail?"

"How can you fail? You're being published. Victory number one."

"They're liable to tear me apart."

"You know everybody isn't going to love you. They crucified Fitzgerald's *Tender Is the Night,* Hemingway's *To Have and Have Not.* Look at Cézanne, Van Gogh. Nobody gave two cents for their work while they were alive."

"Oh, great. Jake Davidson, unheralded genius, acclaimed after death."

"But you're not going to be unheralded. You're going to be published. They're going to take a good look at you."

"That's the trouble. A good look. Warts and all. Why couldn't I have had the book finished before it all happened?"

"You know what you've got, Jake? The prenatal jitters."

They went down to Nick's and listened to Eddie Condon's gang. A married couple they knew came in and passed a joint around. They gave a stick to the clarinet player. Jake got high that night, forgot everything.

The next day he was still bound up. Thurston called and asked him to lunch. He took Jake to the Yale Club.

"How you doing, Jake?"

"So-so."

"What's wrong?"

"I'm muscle-bound all of a sudden from the eyes up."

Thurston smiled wisely, knew the symptoms well.

"Do you know a good masseur who could take the kinks out of my head?"

"Don't press it, Jake."

"How about Ex-Lax? Will that unbind me?"

"Don't worry about it. You've got time. One thing about writing novels, Jake. There are no deadlines."

"I'd do better if I swam the rest of the book."

Thurston smiled, then looked at him awhile. "I'll tell you what, Jake. We'll do the merchant marine book first. There's just some slight editing to do there, and I'll get my notes to you in the next month or two, as soon as I've cleared away another project."

"You'll really do that?"

"Of course. That's the novel we were interested in first. If you hadn't had the other, we'd have gone with it anyhow. So forget the *Invader* for a while. Just relax."

But Jake couldn't forget it, couldn't relax. The book was under his skin, and it had to come out. Soon, without the pressure of bringing it out first, he hit his stride again, and he was working well. After all, he had a draft done. It was all there. It was just a matter of losing his fear of spoiling it, of forgetting every writer who had ever lived, of gaining the optimism he usually lived with.

Thurston really knew how to handle writers. When he talked to Jake on the phone or took him to lunch, he talked only about the sea novel, never mentioned the *Invader*. There was no pressure from him whatsoever. In the spring Jake finished *The Dark Invader*.

"Bob," Jake said to Thurston, "I've got a surprise for you."

"Bring it over, Jake. Or should I have a messenger pick it up?"

A few days later Thurston was on the phone, excited and enthusiastic. Several days after that, Levy said he liked the book enormously. *The Dark Invader* was scheduled to be brought out first.

"When?" Jake asked.

"Too late for fall," said Levy. "We're thinking of January, the first of the spring list. Very few books coming out. We want to give the book every chance for reviews. We think it'll get a good reception."

He couldn't wait. He thought he'd burst out of his skin. The days lasted forever.

"Rhoda, let's move."

"Boy, you're restless."

"I feel all cramped up here."

"You can't wait to blow your money."

"What money? We can't live in one room all our lives."

"All right, we're going for expansion, what about a baby?"

"Okay. That, too. You want a baby, we'll have a baby."

"It's not me, Jake. You've got to want it, too."

"Okay, the whole *shmeer*. A book, a larger apartment, a baby, the works."

"I take it all back. You're not restless; you're manic."

He combed the ads, prowled the streets for weeks. Finally he found a one-bedroom apartment on 72nd Street off Central Park West in a high rise with a doorman and a uniformed man running the elevator. The apartment was on the ninth floor. Rhoda loved it. The light was magnificent. You could look out and see the city. The kitchen was small and compact, separated from the living room by two French doors. His study would be in a corner of the living room. Rhoda said they could divide the bedroom with a large bookcase. Her studio would be near the windows. After the baby came, it would be the baby's room.

For a moment she turned sad. "The way we talk. We don't even have a baby yet."

"We're working on it, aren't we?"

"You think because I've been using a diaphragm all these years it's become impossible?"

"How can that be?"

"I don't know. Maybe I've built up some kind of resistance. Psychological or something."

"We don't connect this month, we'll go to a doctor."

"Some women, you look at them and they're pregnant."

"Let's cut out the horseshit, Rhoda. The baby will come."

Packing, moving, working on the baby took care of some of Jake's restlessness. Then he was tossed up on a big rock candy mountain. Eric Weiss called and said the story head of RKO had phoned and asked what Jake wanted for *The Dark Invader.*

"I said one hundred thousand dollars," Eric said. "All right?"

"All right! That's sensational! Hemingway only got fifty grand for *The Bell Tolls.* That's all Margaret Mitchell got for *Gone with the Wind.* What'd they say?"

"They said I was out of my mind and hung up."

"So what happens now?"

"We wait."

Rhoda had her period again the following month.

"Maybe it's tension," she said. "Maybe we're trying too hard."

"Maybe it's me. I haven't got what it takes."

"No, it can't be you. It has to be me. I'll go to a doctor."

"Okay. Fine. If he wants to see me, I'm willing."

She came home with a chart and a thermometer.

"The doctor says I'm fine, in good shape to bear children. You don't have to screw every day, fifteen times a day, to conceive. You have to do it the right days, the right time, when my temperature is up. It would even be better to skip a day or two so that your ejaculation will have more force."

"You mean we've got to ration our fucking?"

"I thought it was so simple, but it's becoming so complicated."

"I bet if I raped you, you'd have been pregnant the next day. There's something to be said about rape, I think."

Jake and Rhoda watched her temperature every day. He called his agent every other day. But there was nothing new. Silence. Only pieces of publicity appearing in the press and in the trades, which was getting the book talked about and which brought queries from the studios.

"It's too early," Eric said. "Galleys aren't ready yet. Only two copies of the script are circulating. Patience, patience."

"That's all right to say to some stargazer, some sheepherder. But you're talking to a man who's trying to get his wife pregnant, who's going to have a family, who's going to have big responsibilities."

"I thought all you wanted was fame."

"A little fortune won't hurt me either."

It came along shortly after that. Peter Mason called.

"What are you doing, Jake?"

"I'm sitting on a dime, waiting for my new novel to come out."

"How would you like to come to work for me?"

"Tell me more."

Mason had left NBC to set up his own production company. He had a deal with the Mutual Network to do a half hour weekly detective series, with a minimum commitment of thirteen weeks over the summer if he came up with the right script. Would Jake come down to his farm in Bucks County over the weekend? Sure, Jake said.

"Perfect," Rhoda said when she heard the news. "I hope you get so busy you won't be able to think straight."

"What about the temperatures?"

"What can I tell you, Jake? We've missed five years. What's another month?"

"Why don't you come along?"

"I'm not going to sit around a farmhouse over a weekend while you're up to your ass in a story conference. What if you're held over and I have to come back alone?"

"But we've been working so hard on the temperatures."

"I'm sure I'd run a temperature there for all the wrong reasons. Imagine, conceiving a baby in Bucks County." She began to laugh. "I'd rather he was manufactured in New York. It'll be more Jewish."

He was caught up in her laughter. "Oh, how you like your home fucking."

Mason's brother-in-law, Allen Nightwood, picked Jake up in Trenton on Saturday morning and drove him over the gently rolling farmlands to Mason's ninety-acre farm. Allen was a well-built, rangy, sunny-faced man who'd been a tournament tennis player when he was younger, competing against men like Big Bill Tilden.

"Peter finally left the company," Allen said.

Jake didn't ask why.

"Every Monday morning he'd leave for New York with a

terrible migraine. On Friday, when he left the city, the headache disappeared. It went on for years."

"Hmmmm," Jake said.

"Ever since he's been on his own, no more headaches. I hope you come up with a show for him. It'll solve a lot of problems."

"We'll give it a good shot."

"I'm supposed to talk to you about money. I'm with the company. Business manager, producer, whatever."

"All right, tell me."

"Two hundred a week until we get sponsored. Top buck for the budget."

"Okay. I do all the scripts huh?"

"Peter likes it best when he works with one writer. You get a piece of the action if you want it."

That meant they wanted to hook him into the show, make it virtually impossible to walk away from it. At this point the one thing he wanted was freedom to do anything he wanted.

"That's very generous of you. But I'll pass on that. Later on I'll take more money instead." He smiled. "When I become indispensable."

"You'll be worth it." Allen was very serious. "All we've got to do is create now."

A great Dane, panting and quivering, greeted them when they drove up to the thick-stoned early-Dutch farmhouse. It was hot out, but inside the house it was cool. Mrs. Mason had lunch ready. She was a light-haired, gentle-faced woman. They had no children, but Mason called her Mom. She looked tired.

When they sat down to eat, Mason said, "Now don't fuss, Mom. You had a rough night. We'll eat, then get to work. We'll take care of the dishes later." He looked healthier, tanned, more like the gentleman farmer than the big New York executive. He explained to Jake: "We've got two sick cows. Mom stayed up all night with them. And yesterday she had to shag all over the countryside for our Dane. He chased a bitch in heat twenty miles, broke down a screen door to get to her. He's still all shook up from it. Come on, let's eat. Then we'll see how brilliant we can get."

They began in the homey living room with Allen sitting quietly beside the big stone fireplace and the great Dane sprawled out on the hooked rug, huffing and slobbering.

"We're looking for a crime show," Mason said. "Private eye, detective, policeman, any law enforcer, but something that isn't on the air."

"Private eyes, they've got," Jake said. "Detectives, too. And you can't beat *Mr. DA*. A cop on the beat, his field is too limited. What about two cops in a squad car? I like the title: *Squad Car*."

"I like that, too."

"Is that too narrow?"

Mason closed his eyes, listened.

"Two guys in a squad car, a team." Jake spitballed. "They've got each other to talk to. That's a plus. It doesn't have to be all street stuff. A murder on Fifth Avenue, if we use New York, they're the first guys there. A caper of a whole apartment building. They're right on scene, right in the thick of it."

"I like it, I like it. I like it better all the time. I really like the title. And the sound effects, which will be our opening. A siren. The announcer: 'Squad Car.' Siren again. The kids will pick that up. That's half the battle."

"But their authority is limited." Jake, still freewheeling, started to piss on the idea. "Homicide comes in if it's murder, and our guys in the squad car are out. We need somebody big, somebody with size, somebody who can hustle people around, somebody who can take over when everything gets fouled up."

"A police commissioner. They don't have a police commissioner on the air."

"He's too big. He's the mayor's man. Nobody identifies with a guy like that. I've got it. A police captain. That's power. He can ride herd over everybody. He can get into things. We can identify with him."

"Go on."

"His name is Hackett. A good strong, authoritative name. That's the name of the show. *Captain Hackett*."

"What kind of introduction do we get, what kind of sounds?"

"What kind of sounds do you get with *Mr. DA?* The announcer comes in with 'Mr. District Attorney.' Then an echo-chamber voice with the oath of office."

"I like sounds. There's something about a sound that captures an audience."

"Let's worry about that later. Are we agreed it's a police

captain? He can go anywhere; he can do anything. I can see him. He weighs over two hundred pounds. He's got a big, deep voice. He's dedicated. He's got a heart, too. We'll give him a wife for that."

"We can do a sympathetic show, his relationship to a kid, like the one you did for *Author's Playhouse*. He can have a heart as big as a mountain. I've got the actor for him. He'd be sensational. And I know just the woman for his wife. She was in *Oklahoma!*, that big, zesty, folksy woman, Mary Deardon."

"Let's figure out a story. The captain will grow as we get him into action. You got any good stories, Peter?"

Mason kicked around some *Mr. DA*s he'd heard. Allen came up with some detective and private-eye stories he'd heard. Jake listened hard, looking for a springboard, something different.

"Arson," he said finally. "A big crime. Maybe twenty people killed. Big apartment-house owner. Gangsters involved who supply the torch. Hackett, our captain, really gets emotionally involved. This isn't just a bank robber, a Dillinger, or a Mafia character shaking somebody down. This is big-business crime. Cynical as hell. Who cares how many people get killed? Arson. I read the other day billions of dollars go up in fire every year, most of it arson. We can get the statistics. Make it sound god-awful true. How about that?"

Mason leaned his head back, closed his eyes. Allen stared at the Dane silently. Jake got up and paced the floor. Then, with his eyes still closed, Mason said, "Arson. I like that. I like that very much. Lots of action, terrific sound. Strong, powerful adversaries. An emotional story. Great identity. It'll have a lot of sock. Nobody will turn the dials on that one. Oh, I like arson. I like it very much." He opened his eyes. "All right, Jake, what's the story?"

"Let's kick it around."

All afternoon they kicked it around. Later, they sat in the shade of an apple tree. They walked about. The Dane sniffed something in the air and ran off again. Jake got heady from the smell of the fields and the drive for the story. He took notes. He walked away from them to be alone, to think alone, to get his own picture of the police captain and the criminals. By the end of the day they had a story worked out to everybody's satisfaction.

Then dinner. Fresh chicken. Fresh corn. Fresh tomatoes and lettuce.

"I'll give you some to take home to your wife," Mrs. Mason said.

"She'd appreciate that. She's a glutton for anything fresh."

That night they worked out the format for the show. The title was changed to *Lockup*. Sounds of iron doors in a big prison being slammed shut. A voice: "All prisoners present and accounted for." Dead air pause. Then: *"Lockup!* Police Captain Hackett's Fight Against Crime!" A siren dwindling into silence . . . into the show.

The following day Jake started on the script. Everybody went to church, and he worked. He finished a draft in the afternoon. Mason studied it carefully. Read it out loud to himself. He was going to direct it. He suggested some changes. On Monday Jake did a final draft. Mason loved it.

"It's a little long," Mason said. "But we'll tighten it. That'll give it greater intensity."

The Dane came back, foaming, trembling all over; he'd had his rendezvous with his bitch. Mrs. Mason fed him a dozen eggs and a half pound of meat. The dog slopped some food up, then lay down panting hard, quivering all over before he crawled into a corner to recuperate.

After dinner, Mrs. Mason gave Jake two bags of fresh vegetables and corn. Mason and Allen drove him to the railroad station.

"We'll be in first thing in the morning," Mason said.

"Good luck," Jake said.

When Jake got home, Rhoda was asleep. He woke her up.

"How'd it go?" she asked.

"Great. I think we've got a show."

"When do we celebrate?"

"They'll let me know."

Later, as he crawled into bed, she said, "I was in heat while you were gone."

"It figures. If I were a dog, I'd have known it and rushed over." He told her about the Dane.

"Well, shall we do it for fun?"

"If you please."

"That's one thing we've got over the dogs, huh?"

Mason called on Wednesday.

"We're in. We go on Friday night."

"You're kidding."

"I've cast our Captain Hackett and his wife. Want to come down to meet them?"

He didn't want to get involved in the production.

"I'd rather be surprised."

"Think about another script for next week."

"You don't give a guy time to breathe."

"That's radio."

When Rhoda came home, he said, "Don't prepare dinner tonight."

"Why? We've got all those things from the farm."

"We're going to Café Society."

"You made it!"

"First show Friday night."

The following day Mason called again.

"They love the script here at Mutual. But Loomis, the story editor, wants some changes in one of the scenes."

"What are they?"

Mason told him. The script was too long, and the editor wanted him to enlarge the scene. If there were cutting to be done, that was the one scene that could go out; it was a character bit.

"Will you come in and fix it?"

"No," Jake said. He decided right then he was not going to rewrite for the editor of the network. Right now was the time to determine who had final authority over the show, his producer or the editor, or he'd be running down to make changes all week.

"We go into rehearsal tomorrow, Jake. We want to get everything right."

"Peter, I want you to cut that scene. You're going to be long, and you'll have to cut. That scene can go, and nobody'll miss it."

"But he likes that scene. He wants it in, with his changes."

"He's not going to get it. Right now, Peter, we've got to establish who's boss over the show. I'm working for you, not Loomis. We've gone over the story and the script very carefully.

We're satisfied. You're the producer; you're the boss. You make a stand. You take it up with the production chief. Let's make it our show, not Loomis's. Now do what you have to do, but I'm not coming in."

"You're not leaving the show, are you?"

"You establish the authority, Peter."

Jake didn't know why he'd taken such a strong position. Maybe it was a sudden surge of power he felt as a writer that made him do it. Maybe, in this act, he was kicking in the teeth every editor who had ever rejected him. But when he hung up, he was shaking. He thought: What's come over me?

When he told Rhoda about it, she said, "Wow! Jimmy Cagney in action. Next thing you know you'll be washing their faces with grapefruit. So now what happens?"

"I don't know. I haven't heard anything further."

"You know what I think? You don't care. Nobody pushes anybody around if they don't care."

But he did care. They listened to the show on Friday. The scene they'd hassled over had been cut.

"You won, you won," Rhoda said.

Later Mason called. "How'd you like the show?"

"Great," Jake said.

"I took the whole matter up with the chief. We're in control. From now on Loomis reads the script only for censoring. When do we get together?"

"First thing Monday morning."

"Got a story?"

"We'll have one."

"Jake, I'm glad you pushed me. I feel terrific."

He turned to Rhoda when he hung up. "Imagine, a little *shnook* like me, I make a guy like Mason stand up for himself. Me, what have I got to lose? This little sixty-seven-fifty apartment, a few scraps of furniture, the couple of dollars we've got in the bank, the insecurity we've always felt? I can tell them where to get off. I haven't been corrupted by big cars, fancy houses, the executive front, the good life. But it took a lot of guts for Mason, with his gentleman's farm, his sick cows, his brother-in-law to support, his cars."

"More than you think, Jake. Remember, you've got a new big

ace in the hole: your forthcoming book. Mason doesn't have that. You've got another career, more important to you. Mason doesn't have that. Maybe you're not such a little *shnook* after all."

After that every Monday morning Jake got together with Mason and spent the day working on a story. Usually he came in without an idea in his head, and he'd start the day with: "What have you heard lately?"

Mason would recount some shows he'd listened to. Allen would be called in, and he'd relate some stories, and then Jake would start foaming in his head. By the end of the day they'd have a story. Jake would write it the next day, turn it in, do whatever rewrites that had to be done on the following day. Mason would begin casting on Tuesday from the story outline. The show ran smoothly.

Jake had finished his revisions on *The Dark Invader,* and the script had gone off to the printers. There was nothing to do now but wait. One day, Eric Weiss, his agent called, and said, "Ludwig Von Reinstein would like to meet you for breakfast tomorrow. He liked your book and wants to talk to you."

"Why me? Why doesn't he talk to you?"

"He's a peculiar man. He likes to meet the author first."

"How did he get a copy?"

"He walked into my office several days ago. A copy, just returned from MGM, was on my desk. He took it. I couldn't refuse. We're to meet in the St. Regis dining room at nine-thirty. All right?"

"All right."

Ludwig Von Reinstein was an important German producer before he came to Hollywood as a refugee. He had made several good films which Jake had admired, one of them directed by Fritz Lang. A film by Von Reinstein was always treated with respect and was always considered a quality picture. His interest was exciting to Jake.

Jake arrived at the St. Regis in his best gray flannel suit. Eric and Von Reinstein were already in the large, elegant, linen-clothed dining room eating grapefruit. Von Reinstein was shaved bald, had baggy eyes, flabby cheeks, a prominent nose, sensual lips, and a relaxed, regal manner, as if the world were in attendance ready to shine his boots. He had a big, beaming smile, a thick accent, and a grand European manner. Eric Weiss had known Von Reinstein in Europe during his impresario days and was awed in his presence.

"Ah, Jake, Jake, Jake," Von Reinstein said. "So we meet finally. Sit down please." He snapped his fingers. "Waiter. Please." To Jake: "Anything you want, please. A man with your talent, nothing is too good."

"Sunny-side-up eggs, crisp bacon, rye toast, coffee," Jake said to the waiter.

"That's all? You're sure that's all?"

"That'll be plenty."

Von Reinstein waved the waiter away, then to Jake: "I stole your book from Eric. I came to my suite here. Manuscripts, I see all kinds. I look at them, fondle them. I dream, I hope. In which script am I going to find my new world, my new love, my new life, my diamond? Oh, the promise in those pages. You read one page, two pages, three pages, yech, pfui, you are destroyed with disappointment. But you, Jake." His voice filled with emotion; his eyes got watery. How that man commanded the stage, Jake thought. "I went beyond the third page. I was drowned in your story. I couldn't escape. I couldn't put it down. Two important appointments I missed. Who cared? Eric, where did you find him?"

Eric smiled, flattered.

"Oh, you have a way of discovering talent." Von Reinstein reached out to everybody. "I knew, when I was in your office, I would find my gem. I smelled it. He writes like the European man, doesn't he, Eric?"

Eric nodded.

"How they will love his book in Europe. Hah, Eric?"

"No question about it," Eric said.

"The European, he is so sympathetic to the criminal. I don't know why, but he is. Maybe because the criminal, the killer, wants to take the world in his own hands, wants to shape it his own way but he is flawed; that makes him vulnerable, a tragic figure; it touches all of us; that makes him heartbreaking. Right from the beginning, your hero is doomed. The European understands that, the doomed man, the man trying to break out of his trap."

Jake thought: Have I got all that in my book?

"You have such a dramatic sense, Jake. You write like a screenwriter. We don't even need a screenplay." Von Reinstein considered that a moment, cocked his head as though he were listening to echoes of himself. He liked what he heard. "How would you like to do the screenplay?"

"I haven't thought about it," Jake said.

"Oh, ho-ho!" Von Reinstein's eyes bulged; he looked and sounded a little like Cuddles Sakall. "He hasn't thought about it." He poked Eric. "A natural dramatic writer like that, he hasn't thought about it."

Breakfast arrived and was spread out in front of them.

"He has written for radio," Eric said. "At present he is doing a weekly crime show for the Mutual Network."

"I knew it. I knew he was a dramatic writer. You didn't have to tell me. I knew it all along. Right from the first page of the book. But he has a pictorial feeling. And mood. How he creates the heat of the day, the sweat on a man's body, the fever in his soul. Fifteen years ago I would have had Peter Lorre in it. It would have been his masterpiece."

Is that me the man is talking about? Jake wondered as he ate.

"Anybody can write fade in and fade out, long shot, dolly shot, dissolve, all mechanical. That's not a screenwriter. It's the interior that is important, what happens inside a man's heart, his belly, that is what is important. *Nein, Eric?*"

"Absolutely."

"Eat, eat, Jake, eat." Now he was a Jewish mother. "It's only the beginning. Anything you'll want, you'll have it. Go ahead, Jake, eat, enjoy." Von Reinstein slurped down some of his eggs, wrangled with his toast, breathing heavily. He sloshed it all down with some coffee.

"Now to the essence of our meeting," he said, turning to Jake, pinning him down with his bulging, baggy eyes. "How would you like Fritz Lang to direct the film of your book?"

Jake gulped. "That would be sensational."

"I have talked to him already. He can't wait to do it."

Fritz Lang. God, what he would do with it.

"We'll get Bogart to star. I have talked to Jack Warner. I can get him. But I am also considering Spencer Tracy. Which one would you like, Jake?"

"Either one. They'd both be great."

"Fritz worked so well with Tracy in *Fury*. Maybe we'll let him decide. After all, he will be making the picture. *Nein?*"

"Yes," Jake said breathlessly.

"Who's the girl? Who's the girl? Lilli Palmer? You know, I have made pictures with her. No, no, no, too European. No accents. It's an American picture with a European heart. I know, I know. Dorothy McGuire."

"She'd be wonderful," Jake said.

"All right, it's settled then."

Jake looked quickly to Eric. What, what's settled? What's the deal? Tell me before I *plotz*.

"We had a little talk before you came," said Eric. "What Von Reinstein wants is this: He will give you fifteen thousand dollars for the film rights."

"Excuse me," Von Reinstein said. "I must make a phone call. You talk it over." He left.

"Only fifteen thousand?" Jake said.

"A dollar for every copy you sell up to one hundred thousand dollars. Plus ten percent of the profits."

"I understand nobody ever sees a dime of profits."

"If a picture makes a lot of money, the distributor can't hide it all. Somebody has to share."

"What about the screenplay?"

"A thousand dollars a week for ten weeks. You will work with the director he hires."

"That's twenty-five grand up front. Right?"

"Plus a lot of promises."

"What do you think, Eric?"

"Nobody else has made an offer yet."

"What about RKO? They ever get back to you?"

"No."

"Nobody's knocking themselves out for the book, are they?"

"I'm sorry, Jake."

"You're saying take it."

"It's your decision, Jake."

"Can he get Fritz Lang, Bogart, Tracy?"

"He's a big filmmaker."

"Yah, yah, yah, I know."

"He wants a decision now. He's going back to California this afternoon."

"Shit."

"There's a hitch."

"Ah, always the hitch."

"He wants a handshake on the deal for thirty days. He has to go to California to get the front money."

"You mean, this big shot, he hasn't even got fifteen grand to make the deal?"

"He's an independent, Jake. He has to make his deals. Only the studios or a Sam Goldwyn can lay out that kind of cash, and if you can get more than five thousand from a Goldwyn, you're getting a lot."

"You mean that's Hollywood, the real Hollywood?"

"That's the real Hollywood. The Hollywood we all hear about is the dream factory."

"Oh, boy."

"He's coming back now. What do you say, Jake?"

"Only thirty days? We take the book off the market only for thirty days?"

"That's it."

Von Reinstein came back with a big smile. "I talked to Fritz Lang again. He said he has already talked to Spencer Tracy. Tracy said he liked the idea of the story, of working with Lang again. He is excited about the prospect."

How do you say no to a guy like that? Jake thought.

"So what have you boys decided? Are you going to make me a happy man? Are you going to give me a big love affair with the world all over again?"

"I've spelled it all out to Jake," Eric said. "It's up to him."

"So, Jake, I am in your hands."

The man suddenly looked like a tavernkeeper, with his hands

outspread, the waiting smile, the body ready to serve, the imperial bravado gone, all of him full of *Weltschmerz* and totally vulnerable. The sonofabitch, Jake thought. How can I kick him in the balls?

"We've got a deal," Jake said. "Thirty days."

Von Reinstein shook his hand. "You won't regret it. In thirty days you will have the money and be ready to come out to California to start working. Your future is assured."

Rhoda screamed with delight when he came home.

"A man like Von Reinstein. Boy! That's the big leagues."

"You want to go to Hollywood?"

"I don't know. I'm scared."

"You think I'm not?"

Thurston was happy for Jake when he sat down with him and Levy and spelled out the deal. Levy didn't like it; he thought Jake could have done a lot better.

"You know," Jake said, "for a while in the dim past I was a compulsive gambler. But it was for nickels and dimes. These are big stakes. Suddenly I'm scared to gamble."

"I think Jake made the right decision," Thurston said.

"We'll just have to sell a lot of copies and get Jake the money he really deserves," Levy said.

Walking up Fifth Avenue after he left Thurston and Levy, Jake started to get depressed. Up until recently all he had thought about was doing a novel, a good one, and getting it published. He had never thought about the market and sales. He had hoped the book would receive some attention and a good-sized ad in the *New York Times*. Maybe it would get him a $200- or $300-a-week contract in Hollywood, where he could earn enough money to write another book. Now that the manuscript was finished it was seldom referred to as a novel; it had become a property; he had been tossed into a different world of finance, tricky deals, and decisions. He started to bite his fingernails.

Two weeks went by. Nothing from Von Reinstein.

"Did you call him, ask him how he's doing?" Jake asked Eric.

"He says he's close, close."

"What happens if he wants an extension?"

"Don't think about it. Keep writing your radio show."

On Monday mornings, when he got together with Mason, his mind was emptier than ever. It was taking him longer and longer to spark. Sometimes they'd go out to lunch without a glimmer of an idea. Sometimes they'd have to stare at each other, breathing heavily, all the way into the next day. Then Mason would get nervous about casting, not being able to get the people he wanted, and Jake would get jittery about working right up to broadcast time, and the network would begin pressing for the script so that it could go over it for policy.

Rhoda blew her temperature charts by missing a couple of days when Thurston asked if she'd do the cover for Jake's book. She got so involved in the project that she just forgot. *The New Yorker* had taken a couple of her scratchboard drawings, and she decided to go that way with Jake's book jacket. She came up with a black-and-white work of the dark shadow of a man on the run through a trapped, dead-end street of tenements and skyscrapers. Thurston and Levy both praised it.

"It's a work of art," Thurston said. "It'll make all the book pages."

"Next month, God willing, back to the thermometer," Rhoda said.

"August, a very good month," Jake said. "A vintage month."

Then one afternoon, a call came in from Hollywood. It was Lila Shulman, from her offices at MCA.

"Jake, darling. What's this I hear about you and Von Reinstein?"

"What do you hear?"

"That he's bought your book."

"Well, he didn't exactly buy it yet." Jake told her what the deal was.

"*Shmuck.* Von Reinstein is a deadbeat. His last two pictures were flops. One film he made was so bad it was never released. He can't even get himself arrested."

"Von Reinstein?"

"Von Reinstein. He's announced your book in the trades. He's hawking it all over. He'll kill it. Who handled the deal?"

"Eric Weiss."

"Another Prussian. I'm not knocking him for books. But he

doesn't know his ass from a hole in the ground about movie deals."

"What do I do?"

"Don't let him shake your hand again, no matter how much he begs, no matter how close he says he is to making a deal. When his time runs out, turn it over to me."

"What about Eric?"

"Tell him he'll get his five percent and not to worry. Ah, you little naîve, innocent *shmuck* from Chicago, you should have called me in from the beginning. Now you tell Eric I'm interested in you."

He told Eric what he'd heard.

"Don't believe everything she says," Eric said. "These big agents, they will lie, they will cheat, they will do anything to gobble up the talent of the world."

"She's not just one of the big agents out there. She happens to be a friend of mine."

"She's loyal only to the dollar bill."

Whom was he to believe?

Just before the thirty days were up, Eric called and said, "Von Reinstein wants more time."

"No."

"He says he has Fritz Lang signed. Within a month he will have a commitment from Spencer Tracy."

"Do you believe him?"

"I don't know. He's interested. He's still working on it."

"Your advice is to give him more time."

"Yes."

"Okay. He can have more time if he can show me something in writing that he has Fritz Lang, that Tracy is interested."

"I'll tell him."

An hour later the phone rang again. Von Reinstein.

"Jake, I don't blame you. I understand exactly how you feel. You don't know how it pains me to ask for an extension, to deal with a talent like you in this manner. But you must understand the picture business. I have commitments from Fritz Lang and Spencer Tracy. Only verbal. Nothing in writing. You must understand that I cannot have anything in writing until I have the two million to make the picture. I am budgeting it big. Very big. The best cast, best cinematographers, the finest set designers and composers. All Academy Award artists."

The longer Von Reinstein talked, the less Jake believed him. He finally said, "I'll let you know."

He got back to Eric.

"I'm not going to give him an extension."

"You'll break his heart."

"It's his heart or mine."

"All right, I will tell him."

"He's probably killed the property already. But I want Hollywood representation on the book, Eric. Preferably Lila Shulman."

"All right, I will have Hollywood representation, but not Lila Shulman or even William Morris. You will get lost there."

"Who will you deal with?"

"Sam Jaffe or Famous Artists. Or somebody smaller. When the galleys are ready, I will send it to them."

"I don't want to hear from Von Reinstein again."

"I'll see that he doesn't bother you."

When he hung up, he felt sick to his stomach.

But he missed not hearing from Von Reinstein, not hearing about what was happening, not listening to flattery. Attention had been a drug. He had been hooked on it ever since he was a swimming champ. There were a lot of lean, no-attention years. Once hit by it again, he was in agony from withdrawal symptoms. Even Thurston had nothing to say to him. It was as if the book had gone underground and he had been buried with it.

The galleys came. The first sign of the novel at last, the black type so clean, so readable. He and Rhoda admired it, looked at it from various angles, compared it to the type of other books. This type had power, delineation; you could read it without strain. Finally, he sat down to read it. And he began rewriting. He grew unhappier and unhappier as he read on, to a point where he didn't know what was on the page. He gave up in despair.

"It's so awful," he said.

"Don't, Jake. Don't destroy yourself."

"I hate it."

The production editor called asking for the galleys.

"I can't read them."

"Jake, we've got a schedule. Send them back. We'll read them for you."

"No. I want to postpone publication. I want to rewrite the book."

"You can't. It'll cost a fortune."

"It's my book."

Thurston took him to lunch. He said, "The one person I thought we'd have no trouble with was you."

"The book doesn't make sense to me."

"Jake, it's a good book. Take my word for it. There's a spontaneity about it I don't want you to lose. Sure, you can refine it, but you can also take the life out of it. Leave it alone, Jake. Go on to another book."

"This one's dried me out."

"What have you got in your drawer?"

"A couple of old rejects."

"Take one out. See how you feel about it. Maybe one of them might inspire you. Forget *Dark Invader*. That's behind you. That's up to the gods now. Get into something else."

"Okay, Knute Rockne. One for the old Gipper, huh?"

Thurston laughed. "Throw away the galleys you have. Wait for the finished books."

"That's the trouble, the waiting."

"That's the business, waiting."

It was the hottest day of the year. When he got into his stuffy apartment, he grimly picked up the galleys of his novel and threw them into the incinerator. He looked out at the waves of heat shimmering over the city and thought he saw the ashes of his book scattering over the rooftops. Then he took a long, cool shower. When Rhoda got home, she couldn't get into the shower quickly enough. Afterward he said, "Let's go to an air-conditioned restaurant for dinner."

It didn't cool off in the evening. They sat in the park awhile, then came up to their stifling apartment. She took her temperature dutifully, then said, "Now, Jake."

"You're kidding."

"I'm in heat. Just like an animal."

"If we connect this time, the baby isn't going to be born out of pleasure."

"He'll be born out of all the other pleasures."

"What do I do, flex my muscles, spit on my hands?"

"Just tell your semen to plunge in and swim the best goddamn race he ever swam right to the target."

"Okay, love. Swimmers ready. . . Go!"

It was probably that hot when the world was created. Nobody could say they didn't throw themselves into a furnace for this one. Despite all the sweat, it was exciting and pleasurable, When he came, he said, "Swim, you bastard. Go on, whip that tail. Don't stop, you bastard, don't stop till you hit those eggs. Crack 'em wide open."

"Go, go, go," she said.

In the morning she took her temperature again. It was still up there.

"How about another one for good measure?" she said.

"What every woman needs, a man pole-vaulting on the bed every morning, all fresh for the rigors of making babies." Then like Humphrey Bogart: "Here's looking at you, sweetheart."

Afterward, before she left for work, Rhoda said, "Try to get a nap this afternoon. I should still be in heat tonight."

"I'll have eggs for lunch, oysters and shrimp for dinner."

"Keep the home-fires burning."

He tried to think of a radio story that morning but drew a blank. It seemed that he couldn't get going without Mason. He started to think about *The Dark Invader,* of Hollywood, of not hearing from Lila again, of Eric's silence. He called up Eric.

"I was just about to call you," Eric said, as usual.

"Anything new?"

"Nothing. Not a thing."

"You get any galleys from the publishers?"

"I just ordered a half dozen copies."

"We should get some action soon, huh?"

"You'll be the first to know."

He took a nap and had the first of many recurrent dreams. He had written a brilliant comedy. Opening night. The actors were coming forth with the funniest dialogue in years. The audience was doubled up with laughter. He was in the back, listening, cool; everybody was reacting as he had expected. The play was sensational. He thought he should be feeling good when he woke up, but instead, he felt peculiar. He was a serious novelist. Why was he writing brilliant comedy in his dreams? What did it mean? What would Freud say about that?

He dug into his desk drawer, pulled out a couple of rejected manuscripts. Began to read one and didn't like it anymore. Started the other and was taken up by it. He saw the flaws, was still interested in the characters. He started to take notes as he read; his juices were flowing. That was his next project; it'd help him keep his sanity.

A month later he showed Thurston and Levy sixty pages of the new novel. They offered him an advance of $1,750. That buoyed him up. Three days a week he worked on the radio show, four days on the novel. *The Dark Invader* and Hollywood drifted into some distant past. Right after that, Rhoda said, "Guess what?"

"Don't tell me."

"I'm a week late."

He became as corny as every character in every movie he had ever seen.

In the fall the radio show was canceled. Jake didn't mind. He had been split between the new novel and the show, and he felt as if he were constantly under the gun. Now he could work more leisurely on the book. The more he could concentrate, the better he felt. But *The Dark Invader* lay in the back of his mind and in the front of his hopes. Occasionally he'd be jolted with nervous spasms, as in the days before a swimming meet. The more silence surrounding the book, the greater the spasms. He felt at times that the novel was the world's most carefully kept secret.

His recurrent dream came more often. The comedy in it got funnier and funnier. Audiences left exhausted with laughter. He was more delighted with every dream. Once, at lunch with Thurston, he said, "I must be a frustrated playwright. In comedy." He told him about his recurrent dream.

"No, you're not, Jake. You're a novelist, a true novelist, and you're going through prepublication jitters. You want an opening night. You want the curtain to go up. Immediate reviews.

Instant acclaim. Like the athlete you were, you want to know if you won or lost. But with a novel, Jake, the curtain never goes up. You have a publication date and that's all. It'll appear in the *New York Times* in the tiniest print, along with all the other books published that day. Nobody may ever know it came out except for the ads we're going to run. The book may not be reviewed for months, if at all. Curtains just don't go up on novels. That's my interpretation."

"I think I'll go to Timbuktu. You know of any interesting safaris?"

"Sit tight, Jake. Hang on. This may still be the most exciting year of your life."

He sat. He played handball. He swam. He worked on his new book. He watched Rhoda begin to bulge in the middle. She looked serene, beautiful, taken up more and more with what was growing inside her and still finding room to love him more. But remnants of *The Dark Invader,* which *he'd* given birth to, were still in his belly, stabbing him at times with fear and pain. It was an unseen child, with no voice yet, surrounded by silence.

They both loved the proof of the jacket. Rhoda's black-and-white design of the stark running silhouette of a man trapped by his crime and the dense enormity of the big city evoked the contents of the book. His picture on the back of the jacket looked good.

"I'd like to read a book by a man who looks like that," Rhoda said.

"You're prejudiced."

"No. He looks like he's got something to say. He looks like he could write a good book."

"How many copies do you think that picture will sell?"

"A million."

"That's not Clark Gable on that jacket."

"Who's Clark Gable?"

"Okay, I can count on a big active sale to my closest relatives. What about the jacket copy?"

"I couldn't put it down."

"Pretty impressive and important, huh?"

"Don't interrupt me. I can't stop reading it over again."

Middle of November, finished books. The whole package.

Silence, silence, silence. Snow in December. The book crawled into a cave and hibernated. Echoes and echoes of silence.

He was on the phone with his agent. "What's happening?"

"The book is out. It's being read."

"Who's reading it?"

"Everybody."

"And no word from anybody?"

"Not yet."

"Von Reinstein killed it. He hawked it around. Nobody wants it now."

"Somebody will want it. You'll see."

"I never thought of Hollywood when I wrote it. But RKO calling and asking what we wanted, then Von Reinstein, they put a bug in me, the bastards. They gave me a disease. As if it isn't bad enough being diseased with the writing bug."

"Try to relax, Jake."

"I kill myself in the handball courts. I'm swimming miles. I'm trying to exhaust myself so that I can't think. But that goddamn bug keeps crawling through my veins."

Thurston and Levy had sent the book to some famous authors they knew. Advance reactions, which they could use in publicity and in blurbs, started to come through. They were full of praise, calling Jake an exciting, genuine new talent. The first blow came with the first trade review: Virginia Kirkus didn't care for the novel.

"Who the hell is she?" Jake asked Thurston.

"Unfortunately the booksellers read her."

But *Publishers Weekly* and *Library Journal,* in their advance reviews, heralded the book.

"They'll help offset Kirkus," Thurston said.

He struggled with his new novel, but he fought a losing battle. One ear was tuned to the phone; the other listened for the mail. Most of his mind was on what was happening out there in that vast world where the booksellers, the reading public, the exploiters of books lived. He walked into bookstores, took one look at the thousands of titles and walked out. How does anybody ever select a book? . . . He was happy only in his recurrent dream. There, several times a week, he was acclaimed.

No book clubs selected *The Dark Invader.* No big cocktail or autograph parties were planned. There was a first printing of 5,000 copies. The book wasn't expected to storm the literary world. Sales were modest. The Chicago newspapers were loyal to him, using publicity puffs that were sent to them. Kup, who had known Jake in high school, used a few pieces on him in his column, selling him more as a swimmer than a writer.

Through Christmas and New Year's, Jake was down. The only thing that lifted him was the miracle of the baby stirring in Rhoda's body. A few times, while having intercourse, he felt the baby kick him.

"Sonofabitch is trying to kick me away. That's where the Oedipus complex begins."

"He'll love you."

"You know what I wanted for him this new year? A big Hollywood sale, a big best seller. What a way to start out in life!"

"You could have asked for a few ocean liners, some airplanes, and a couple of railroads while you were at it."

"Dreams, dreams. But what I wished for was within the realms of possibility."

"Let's wish for a good healthy boy. Or a girl."

"I'll settle for that."

Excitement whirled in with a big snowstorm right after the new year. Paramount was interested in *The Dark Invader* for Alan Ladd. A. C. Spectorsky, who ran a literary column for the *Sun-Times* in Chicago and was associate editor in New York for Twentieth Century-Fox, interviewed Jake at the Ritz, showed him a big recommend stamp on the outline they'd done on his book, and a wire from Zanuck instructing the eastern story department to get Eric Weiss to hold up any bidding until he got to New York.

"What does that mean?" Jake asked.

"It means he wants time to read the book."

The Ritz became Jake's hangout for a while; next to the Algonquin it was *the* literary spot. Thurston brought Harvey Breit of the *New York Times* down to interview him. That was a good sign. Sterling North, literary editor of the Chicago *Daily News,* talked to him for a column. Right in the middle of it, **Carl** Sandburg, who was with Bill Targ, editor of World Publishing, stepped over and berated North for not reviewing his latest

1,000-page novel. North was embarrassed and said he'd get to it soon. Famous authors were not afraid of stepping on critics.

Then bells rang, bugles blew, drums rolled, roman candles flared, banners streaked across the skies, and rockets exploded all about them. Eric Weiss called.

"I just got fifty thousand dollars for your book from George Stevens."

"Huh?" He was stunned.

Eric repeated what he said.

"Rhoda!" he yelled. "Did you hear?"

"What? What?"

"Fifty thousand."

"What? What are you talking about?"

"The book. George Stevens bought it."

"Who's George Stevens?"

"One of the greatest directors in the world. Big Academy Award winner."

He grabbed her, whirled her around.

"Jake, you'll crush the baby. Stop."

He stopped, patted her belly. "I didn't hurt you."

"Jake, you're still on the phone."

He picked up the phone. "Eric, Eric, you still there?" The phone was dead.

"Tell me," Rhoda said. "What's the deal?"

"I don't know, I don't know. I heard fifty thousand dollars. I heard George Stevens. A firecracker went off in my head."

He dialed his agent. Busy. Dialed again. Busy, the bastard.

"Do you know who George Stevens is?"

"Tell me. Who?"

"Don't you ever read the credits?"

"Don't get mad at me, Jake. I just forget them."

"George Stevens produced and directed Theodore Dreiser's *American Tragedy*."

"With Elizabeth Taylor?"

"He made *Penny Serenade* with Cary Grant, and *Woman of the Year* with Spencer Tracy and Katharine Hepburn."

"That's who bought your book?"

"That's what I just heard. But I've got to find out for sure."

He dialed Eric again. Still busy. Oh, boy. Dialed again.

"Maybe he's trying to reach you," Rhoda said.

"Maybe."

He stopped dialing. Waited and waited.

"That bastard never calls me."

He dialed again. Dialed and dialed. Finally got through.

"I was just about to call you again," Eric said. "What happened to your phone? You disappeared."

"Tell me again what you told me before."

"I, personally, sold your book to George Stevens of Liberty Films for fifty thousand dollars."

"Is that firm?"

"You'll be able to walk to the bank with it."

"Any percentages?"

"It's a flat deal. That's a lot of money. A big price."

"What happened to RKO?"

"Liberty Films releases through RKO."

"Who is Liberty Films?"

"Frank Capra, William Wyler, George Stevens. Three of the biggest picture makers in Hollywood."

"Did you hear that, Rhoda? Frank Capra and William Wyler are involved, too."

"No."

"Yes." Back to Eric. "Tell me more."

"What else can I tell you? The contracts will be coming soon. You'll sign them. You'll go to the bank a rich man."

He called Thurston, told him the news. Thurston was delighted. His mother screamed with joy when he called Chicago.

"Hollywood, Hollywood." That was about all she could say.

A week later the *New York Times* carried Jake's name in a headline on the entertainment pages. In the subhead was the title of his book and the price he had got: $100,000.

"That's Hollywood," Jake said.

Several Broadway producers called immediately afterward, asking him to invest in plays. Two automobile agencies and a number of real estate brokers phoned. United Jewish Appeal was on the phone; so was a friend connected with a Jewish synagogue.

"It's tax-deductible," they said. As if it weren't going to cost him a penny.

A member of the central committee of the Communist party called. A drive was on to save the *Daily Worker.*

"That's not deductible, is it?" Jake asked.

"No, but it's a worthy cause."

His insurance man touted a $20,000 policy. "Not for yourself," he said. "But you're going to be a father. You've got to protect your family."

A stockbroker friend came over. "Jake, how much are you really getting?"

"Fifty thousand."

"Don't invest in the market."

"You are really a friend."

"You'll have to lay away a good fifteen thousand for taxes. Who's got pieces of you?"

"My agent, ten percent. My publishers, ten percent."

"Okay, Jake, your fifty thousand is now reduced to twenty-five."

"You're kidding."

"If you want to buy a house here, a gray-stone or brownstone, you've got to ask yourself: Do I want to be a landlord?"

"No."

"Now ask yourself: What does money mean to you? For every person it has a different meaning."

"It means time. It buys me time. All I want is time. And freedom."

"Put your money in the bank. Draw interest. Let it buy you another novel or two. That's your capital investment. But no matter what happens, keep fifteen thousand apart for taxes."

"Thanks."

In college he had taken economics, money and banking, and accounting. He didn't know the first goddamn thing about money.

"Everybody dreams of having money," the stockbroker said. "But when they get it, they go on spending sprees, they go wild, they become suckers for the con artist. So take it easy, Jake. You need any advice, come to me. If anybody presses you, say you have no control over your money, it's in the hands of your accountant. Okay?"

Jake nodded, grateful for the advice.

Other friends talked to him as if he'd won the sweepstakes. Some of his jealous friends said, "I suppose you'll go to Hollywood now." As if he'd already sold his soul to the devil.

"All of a sudden," he said to Rhoda, "it's like I've become a heavy. They're gladhanding me with one hand and slapping me down with the other."

"Not with our good friends, Jake."

"Even Thurston is afraid I'll go to Hollywood. 'I hope you'll finish your new book,' he said to me. 'You're a novelist, remember that,' he said."

"He's worried about you, Jake. He doesn't want you to make any mistakes, any big changes."

"Who's making changes? I'm still the same guy, the same *shnook* from the West Side of Chicago."

"No, you're not. You've outpaced yourself. You've gone a long way."

But Lila Shulman still thought he was a dumb, innocent *shnook* from Chicago. She was in town and took him to the Rose Room at the Algonquin, arranged a banquette across from Harold Ross of *The New Yorker,* with publishers and authors and agents spread through the middle of the room. She was dressed in a Balenciaga original, and she was turned out by Max Factor. She enjoyed being looked at, and she nodded to anybody who was of any importance.

Over a drink, she said, "If only you had come to me, I'd have got you a hundred Gs for that book. A piece of the action, too. We'd have packaged the whole thing."

"Weiss sold it himself."

"You mean he sold you out himself. All he wanted was the whole ten percent. How the hell did you ever get him anyway?"

"He tried to sell my work long before you showed up. I had to let him run with it."

"Loyalty. You'll wind up with copper instead of gold. Jake, agents have got hundreds of clients. If one doesn't make it, the other does. We just spray the field with shotguns. But you, Jake, you've got one bullet. If you don't make the kill with it, throw the gun away, you don't get another chance."

"What could I do, Lila? I've got to live with myself."

"Do you have a contract with him?"

"Just a handshake."

"What about Hollywood?"

"I hadn't thought much about it."

"*Boychik,* this is Lila Shulman. I copped your cherry. Who you kidding?"

"The truth is, I used to dream of Hollywood. You didn't have to be a writer or an actor to dream of it. All of us were raised on the movies; it was our escape hatch, our never-never land. But right now I'm in the middle of a new book. You know me, Lila, one track at a time."

"All right, all right. When you get ready to come out, let me know. So who you screwing these days?"

"My wife."

"You told me she's pregnant."

"She's still a lot of fun."

"Jake, you carry loyalty a little too far."

Thurston sent him a wire a few days later: "Ordering second printing. Small, but encouraging. Congratulations." That was more important to him than the Hollywood sale. Then Weiss reported that publishers in France, Italy, and England had bought the book. Then George Stevens came to town with Anthony Vellier, the screenwriter, who was affiliated with Liberty Films. Thurston called him and said George Stevens and Vellier wanted to have lunch with him the following day. Would the New York Yacht Club be all right?

Cool, cool, he said, "Fine. I'll be there."

But not so cool, he called Rhoda at work. "Well, it looks like Hollywood is coming to me."

"How do you mean?"

"George Stevens and Anthony Vellier want to have lunch with me. You know where? A new rendezvous. Special, not the run-of-the-mill literary klatsches or the show-biz dives, but the exclusive New York Yacht Club. That's Levy's department with his multibillion-dollar connections."

"Your mother should see you now."

"Hoo-ha."

"Jake, get yourself a new suit. You're wearing out the gray flannel."

Dutifully, he went down to Saks and bought a sporty tweed jacket and a pair of black slacks.

"Now you look like a writer," Rhoda said. "Knock 'em dead."

At lunch next day in the staid, masculine dining room of the New York Yacht Club, most of the talk was about *the Dark Invader.*

Thurston said, "I hope you don't make a slam-bang picture out of the *Invader.* I hope you'll be able to capture the philosophical overtones."

Stevens, broad-shouldered, light-skinned, with dazzling blue eyes, was warm, self-effacing, and low-keyed. He said, "We love the book. We'll try our best." He turned to Jake. "Who do you see in it?"

"Bogart?" Jake said tentatively.

"Cagney would be great, too," Vellier said. He was debonair, dark-haired, and soft-spoken.

"So would John Garfield," Stevens said.

"What would you think of Charles Boyer?" Vellier said.

"A Frenchman?" Levy asked.

Jake was stunned.

"Think about it," Vellier said. "Your hero doesn't necessarily have to be American. He could be anybody. We could go the obvious way with Cagney or Bogart. But Boyer would be offbeat, the unexpected. Remember, we've got a great love story here, a doomed love story. Boyer could tear our hearts out. Don't forget how great he was as Pepe le Moko in *Algiers.*"

The way these guys think, they're sensational, Jake thought.

"There's a young actor we saw in *Truckline Cafe,*" Stevens said. "He's crazy, unpredictable, and he's fresh. His name is Marlon Brando. He's never been seen before on screen. He sent shivers through me. I think that's the kind of actor we need, if he reads right."

"Anyhow," Vellier said, "there's plenty of time. We have to prepare a treatment, then a screenplay. It's all at least a year away."

After lunch, Thurston and Levy left. A photographer began to take pictures of Stevens and Jake for publicity purposes. After the pictures they took a cab to the Sherry Netherlands, where Stevens and Vellier were staying. In the suite, overlooking Central Park and the Plaza, there were at least a dozen copies of *The Dark Invader.* The full Hollywood treatment, Jake thought. Then Stevens asked questions about the geography of Chicago, and Jake drew maps of the locations in the novel.

"This picture is not going to have a studio look," Stevens said. "Chicago is fresh. We'll do the whole film, except for the interiors, on location."

All Jake could say was: "Terrific."

Then Vellier said, "We'd like you to come to Hollywood to work for us."

Jake's heart almost leaped out. "On *Dark Invader?*"

"No. Something else. Either an original or on any property we have that you might like. You'd work either with George or Capra or Wyler."

That was as big as you could go.

"We could talk to your agent about money. It won't be less than a thousand a week, we can assure you."

"Are you going to adapt *Dark Invader?*" he asked Vellier. "You'd do one hell of a job."

"I hope I will. But we haven't decided. We just bought a new novel by John Steinbeck. You might be interested in that."

"I don't know."

"Think about it."

"I'd better not. It'd drive me crazy. I'm in the middle of a new book."

"You can finish it later."

"If I leave this town now, I don't know if I ever will."

"Think about it, Jake," Stevens said. "We'd love to have you."

Suddenly terror gripped him.

"No." It blurted right out of him. It was too much, all too much. His hands were trembling.

Vellier and Stevens stared at him a moment.

"All right, Jake," Vellier said. "We understand. Later maybe. After you finish your new novel. If you change your mind, let us know."

He went down to the bar and had two straight shots of I. W. Harper. Then, squinting through the glare of the sun on the snow in Central Park, he walked home. He had a couple of more drinks.

"What happened to you?" Rhoda said when she got home.

"You're looking at a guy who just threw away a whole new world. Nine out of ten writers would have given their balls for the deal I was just offered. A thousand dollars a week. More.

Working with George Stevens, Frank Capra, William Wyler. I said no."

"Just like that, you said no?"

"No, I said. In spades. No. Without a second's hesitation."

"Why, Jake?"

"I was terrified. All of a sudden I began to shake. It was like a big wave had overwhelmed me."

"I don't understand. You used to dream of going to Hollywood."

"Dreams, dreams. All of a sudden it was all so real, it scared the shit out of me."

She wasn't sympathetic. She looked hurt.

"Why did you have to be so definite? Why couldn't you have said I'll think about it?"

"You think I made the wrong decision?"

"No. For you it was the right one."

"Then what's the problem?"

"The fact that you made the decision alone, all by yourself, without consulting me or thinking of me."

"I thought I had the right to make that decision."

"Not any more, Jake. You're not a kid in high school or college anymore, a loner, a cowboy. I'm involved now. So is our baby, our common future. You can't act alone anymore."

"I'm scared, Rhoda."

"So am I."

"All that success, I don't know if I can handle it."

"Neither do I. I don't know what it's going to do with our lives."

"You talk like you want to go to Hollywood."

"It's the last place I want to go. You know that."

"Then what's this all about?"

"It's about your growing up, about your accepting the responsibility for me and our baby. It's about not thinking with your gut first, about not acting alone anymore."

"You talk like we're penniless. I've got fifty thousand dollars coming. Money for foreign rights. My merchant marine book is in the wings. And I've got an advance on another one."

"I'm not worried, Jake. We're in great shape financially. But you could have said, 'Maybe, I'll think about it, I'll let you know.' The point is, Jake, I'm not just a roll in the hay, good for a few laughs and a little sympathy. I'm wholly involved with you, and I want you to be that way with me."

"What do you want me to do, go back to them, say, 'I changed my mind, take me'? The door is still open."

"No. You've made your decision. And it's probably the right one for both of us. It's all so academic now, isn't it?"

"Yah."

"I'm kind of shaken up inside, too. How about mixing me a drink?"

Trying to be light, he said, "I don't want my kid to become an alcoholic."

"He needs it more than me. He's been kicking hell out of me the last few minutes."

The Dark Invader was well received critically, but it didn't do well in the bookstores. Nobody seemed to know how to sell it. Some stores carried it in their mystery and crime department, others in their fiction racks. Was that the handwriting on the wall for him as a novelist? Was he going to be dependent on subsidiary sales to make it? Well, there was still time. Thurston wasn't worried. Jake was an author, not a single book writer; he'd come along; Thurston was sure of it.

Jake settled down and worked harder on the new novel, demanding more of himself, because that's what he was, a novelist.

Lila called one day. "What are you doing, Jake?"

"Working on my new book."

"Oh, you dumb dodo, working on an iffy book, when you could be out here making millions of dollars. Swimming pools, mountains, warm, sunny days, Jaguars and Cadillacs to ride around in. You could have it all."

"What can I do, Lila? I like the North Pole and living with the monks."

"I mentioned your name at Metro. They'll give you twelve-fifty a week to come out here, a twenty-six-week guarantee with options for seven years."

"Generous."

"I bumped into George Stevens the other day. He's still

interested in you. Wants you to come out here."

"Who are you, Lila? Faust? Salome? You want my head?"

"*Shmuck.*" The old Lila. "They want you out here."

This time he didn't say no. "I'll let you know."

He discussed it with Rhoda.

"What are you going to do?" Rhoda said.

"Oh, that's great. First you tell me not to be a cowboy; then you say, go ahead, decide. You really are a honey."

"How's your book going?"

"It goes. But who knows? All it might make is my advance."

"They're throwing halvah and whipped cream at you, and you're acting like you hate it. They're sadists. How can they be so cruel?"

"So what do I do?"

"What if you went for twenty-six weeks?"

"Would you want our kid to be born in Hollywood?"

"You've got a point there."

"So what if I did go?"

"Life would never be the same."

But Lila pressed him. She called a few days later.

"Why haven't I heard from you?"

"I haven't decided yet, Lila."

"Oh, God. Metro called this morning. They're up to fifteen hundred a week."

"You bitch. You Sodom and Gonorrhea."

"It's Gomorrah, *shmuck.*"

"Lila, I'll let you know."

"Don't stall too much. Out here, you're hot today and gone tomorrow. Your book isn't exactly a best seller. If they don't make a picture of your *Invader* in the next year, you'll be forgotten. That's Hollywood, baby."

"I'll still let you know, Lila."

Then none of it mattered. His sister, Miriam, called one night and said, "Pa is dying."

He felt something very sharp plunge into his heart.

"What's wrong?" Rhoda, who was nearby, asked.

"My father's dying."

"Jake," Miriam said, "are you still there?"

"Yes, Miriam."

"Are you all right?"

"Yes. What's he dying of?"

"Cancer."

"Oh, Jesus. How long has it been going on?"

"Quite awhile."

"Why didn't you let me know?"

"You know Pa. Jake's got enough troubles of his own, he said."

"I'll be there tomorrow or the day after. As soon as I can get a plane. I'll let you know. Tell Pa to hang on. I've got to see him."

"Yes, Jake."

He was able to get out the following morning. Rhoda said she wanted to go along. He was grateful for that. Most of the way to Chicago, he was silent. They served a lunch, but he didn't have much appetite for it.

Rhoda apologized. "I've got to eat for two, Jake."

"I know."

More silence. Then: "I had fantasies of going back to Chicago a literary lion. Big autographing and cocktail parties. Interviews in all the papers, on all the radio shows. My town, Chicago. We'd have had one big ball."

"Don't think about it, Jake."

"They didn't let me know. What am I, something marked fragile?"

"What's important is they thought of you. They always thought of you."

"I know, I know."

His kid brother, Harry, dressed in *Esquire*'s latest fashions, met them at the airport in a station wagon. He was becoming known as the surplus king of Chicago. Right after he'd got out of the army he went to his father and said, "Pa, give me two thousand dollars. I'm going to buy a load of surplus merchandise and turn it into five or six thousand."

"You're sure?"

"Don't ask questions, Pa. Just give it to me. I'll pay you back in ten days with interest."

"I'll tell you what, Harry. I'm not going to worry about the money. I'll give it to you as a present. Your coming home present from the army. Good luck."

The following weekend Harry rented a vacant store, advertised big, and sold out everything he had. In a year he had six surplus stores going. Turn Harry loose in any buying situation, and he was like a kid in a toy shop. "I'll take that thousand pair of shoes. Give me those five hundred pair of khaki pants, and those three hundred GI field jackets." Oh, the power he felt.

They embraced each other when they met. Harry kissed Rhoda.

"Pretty soon, huh?"

"A couple of months away," Rhoda said.

"A spring baby. Better than a winter one."

"How's Pa?" Jake asked.

"Not so good."

"What happened?"

"About six months ago, he keeled over one night in the bathroom. Scared the shit out of Ma. He said, 'It's nothing, nothing.' You know Pa. Never sick a day in his life. Christ, he may have been sick as hell, but nobody'd know it. Not from him, they wouldn't."

"Then what?"

"He passed out at the stand one day. They brought him home, a couple of his horse racing pals. He wouldn't go to the doctor. A stubborn man."

"Like his father in Russia. Did you know that in the dead of winter, below zero, everything frozen, he chopped through the ice and plunged in to purify himself before he'd go to work on the mezuzahs and the Torahs? He died that way."

"You're a lot like him, Jake. A *stubborner*. So am I. Maybe it runs in the family."

Jake looked at him. His kid brother, Harry, was a man now. Not somebody who had taken up room around the house, a kind of nuisance, a disturber of the house's tranquillity with his "Buy me, buy me." Suddenly he was no longer a little kid, no longer a stranger. Jake put his arm around him as he drove along the cold, windy Chicago streets.

"So Mom called Dr. Kaplan to come over," Harry said. "He looked him over and said, 'Aaron, I'm taking you to the office. I have to run a couple of tests.' I think Pa was scared. 'What is it with the tests and everything? I'm a healthy man.'

"'That's what I want to find out,' Dr. Kaplan said. 'I want to find out how healthy you are. Do you realize, as long as I've known you and taken care of your family, I have never treated you for anything, I have never had you in my office?'

"'Because I have never been sick,' Pa said.

"So with Mom's pushing and Dr. Kaplan's wheedling, they got him to the office. Turns out Pa's got cancer of the prostate. He tells Mom first. She goes to pieces, then says, 'Don't tell him. He mustn't know. It will destroy him.'

"'What do I tell him?' Dr. Kaplan says.

"'Tell him nothing. Just tell him if he feels any worse, you want to see him again.'

"'But he's in pain. The man is in pain. It will get worse. He will need drugs.'

"'Don't tell him, please,' Mom says."

"A stoic, that's what Pa was," Jake said. "Never wanted to be a bother to anybody, never wanted to make waves. I remember one of his drivers beat him up. I wanted to go after him. 'No,' Pa said. 'It's not your problem. It's mine.'"

"How did he settle it?" Harry asked.

"I don't know. But the driver never touched him again."

"He loved people," Harry said. "Loved his family."

"For his family he'd go through fire," Jake said. "Always protective of Mom. Never wanted to worry her or us. A *shtarker*. Always wanted us to see him as the strong man, a man we could depend on, a man who would be around forever. My old man."

Harry continued: "When the pain got worse, Pa began to ask Mom, 'What did the doctor say? What did he say was wrong?' Mom put him off. 'He didn't know what he was talking about,' she said.

"'What did he say?' Pa wanted to know.

"'We'll go to the Mayo Clinic,' Mom said. 'We'll find out.'

"It took a lot of doing to get him up there, but he went. They operated. Too late. He was shot through with it. After that the pain must have been terrific. He went to Dr. Kaplan for drugs. He didn't have to be told anything. He knew."

"Let's go to the hospital first, Harry."

Jake's father was sleeping when they stepped into his room. The shock of the way he looked took Jake's breath away. His father had always been thin and bony, but he'd been tan in the summer, ruddy in the winter; his eyes had danced; he had glowed with health. Now his cheeks were sunk, his skin bloodless parchment drawn tight over the bones, his whole face and body ravaged by the consuming disease. When he woke up, his eyes seemed to burn inside his head.

"Look who's here, Pa," Harry said.

"Jake."

Jake rushed to his father's weak, outstretched hand, held it tight.

"Rhoda."

Rhoda bent down and kissed his cheek.

His father's eyes stopped burning for a moment, took on life. "Look at you, Rhoda."

"Seven months," she said.

A tear sparkled in his father's eye.

"Life," he said. "Life." He wiped his eyes with his hard knuckles. He sat up, let his skinny legs dangle over the bed. "Imagine, Jake. Me in a hospital. Did you ever see me like this?"

"People get sick."

"People get well, too."

"So you'll get well, Pa."

His father smiled. Always that touch of irony around his mouth. "I like the games people play. Nobody will ever admit a person is dying. So I'm dying." He looked about defiantly. "Is it the first time it's happened to a human being? What is so rare and remarkable about that?"

"It's not exactly wonderful either," Jake said, his chest hard. "Especially when a man isn't old. Especially when people love that man."

"There aren't other people to love?"

"Not a guy who can handicap horses like you."

"Jake, I've had plenty of losers."

"But look at all the fun you had."

"That's the point, Jake. I did have fun. When I was a boy, I never thought I would have any fun. Life was so serious, so grim. If you laughed, you felt guilty. Even our jokes had the thrust of a knife in them. I'm a lucky man. I raised a family. I found my fun."

Still the hero, Jake thought, the *shtarker*. In the face of those he loved, he showed no pain, no fear: Don't worry, don't trouble yourself over me.

"Now there." His father pointed to Rhoda. "There is a picture of a woman. How do you feel, Rhoda?"

Rhoda smiled. "Tired. My little one is getting restless."

"Sure. He wants to come out, screaming, yelling, take notice, like he's the first one ever to be born. *Ay,* Rhoda, I'm so glad you came." A spasm of pain streaked across his face. He grabbed the headboard of the bed, the blood draining out of his hand. Then he smiled weakly. "A man gets up from a nap, he has to go, huh?" He stepped down from the bed and started feebly to the bathroom.

Jake made a move to help him. Harry shook his head; leave him alone. Jake watched him go into the bathroom and stand over the toilet; he didn't have the energy to close the door. His father stood there, gripping a handrail, for minutes and minutes. There was no sound. He watched his father's hand grow tighter and tighter on the rail; then his neck and body began to quiver, and a whimper of pain came out of his throat as the first drops of urine dripped into the bowl. Harry left the room. The dripping lasted a long while, stopping and starting. His father's face was in a sweat; he looked completely drained as he stepped out of the bathroom back to his bed. Jake wet a washcloth and wiped his father's face.

His father smiled weakly. "When you were a little boy, I used to wipe your face."

"Sure."

"I'm tired, Jake."

"Sure. I'll come back later."

Harry came back with a nurse.

"You all right, Mr. Davidson?" the nurse said.

"Yes. Fine."

"How about a little shot, huh?"

"See you, Pa."

"I'm so glad you came, Jake."

On the way out they met Dr. Kaplan, who was making his rounds. He had a strong face and a full head of bristly white hair. Some patients called him Dr. Professor; he'd studied in Germany. He'd been the family doctor since Jake was a kid. He felt nobody understood him, so he was gruff, abrasive, a shouter: "You'll take the medicine every four hours. Drink lots of water. You'll do what I tell you. *Verstehen sie?*" A Jew talking like a Prussian. "You don't take the tonsils out, don't call me again. I'll have nothing to do with you." Who could defy a man like that? He made a pariah out of you if you didn't obey. But he was really a good man, a kind man, with a black satchel full of medicines he dispensed, and you could count on him around the clock. His bark, they said, could make you well.

"So, Jake, under these circumstances you come to Chicago."

"I wish it were better."

"I hear they want you in Hollywood."

"Yes." Having a book out wasn't very impressive, Jake thought. Hollywood hit them where they lived.

"I read your book," Dr. Kaplan said. "I was proud of you. It will make a great movie. Could it be, that little boy with his chicken pox and his measles and his strep throats and his delirium, that little boy I sent to the Y — 'let him swim,' I yelled, 'even in the winter, even below zero'— could it be that same boy wrote that book?"

"He isn't the same boy anymore," Rhoda said.

"Ah, the woman is right. Because that boy I'm talking about wasn't capable of making a woman pregnant." He paused. "All right, Jake, I won't keep you in suspense any longer. I don't know what keeps your father alive."

"No hope at all?"

"Miracles don't grow on trees."

"Couldn't you have done anything?"

"Sure, if he'd come to me years ago with his first pain. What is pain? It's a warning. Like fever, another warning. Infection, it's saying. But fever fights back. Pain doesn't. The mind can subdue it. I don't know how your father stood it."

"Then it'd be an act of mercy if he died?"

"I'm afraid so, Jake."

At home, Jake's mother was preparing dinner. Gefilte fish, *knaidlach* soup, roast chicken, *tsimmis,* everything Jake liked. The house she kept now for herself and Harry and for the day her husband would come home was immaculate. She was still hopeful. Miriam was there, too.

"Why the feast, Ma?" Jake said.

"You're here with Rhoda. It's a celebration. Pa will get better. You'll see. We'll have a big celebration. We'll sing and dance then."

"Sure, Mom."

Alone with Miriam a moment, Jake said, "Does she really believe that?"

"No. But what else has she got to believe in?"

"What'll she do when Pa goes?"

"We'll cross that bridge when we come to it. But Mom is stronger than you think. She really is."

"That's a comfort."

After dinner Jake said, "I'm going back to the hospital."

"Do you want me to come along?" Rhoda asked.

"If you have to ask, don't."

"What does that mean?"

"It means you don't really want to go."

"I do, Jake. But it breaks me up to see him like that."

"What do you think it does to me? Anybody else coming?"

"Jake, we've been going every day," Miriam said. "At night he's so drugged he doesn't know you're there."

"Let me have your car, Harry."

"I'll come with you," Rhoda said.

"Don't come out of guilt," Jake said.

"You're the one who's going out of guilt."

"Now you've got me on the couch. Instant analysis."

"Don't, Jake," Miriam said. "You're upset. Don't take it out on Rhoda."

"How about the car, Harry?"

Harry threw him the keys.

"Wait just a minute," Rhoda said. "I'll go with you."

Jake's heart pounded as he watched her waddle to her coat.

"No, you stay here," he said. "I didn't mean to sound off. You're in no shape. I've got to go. I won't feel right if I don't."

He left before another word was said.

At the hospital he sat silently beside his drugged, sleeping father, hurting all over. Then he got up angrily and began to pace the floor, yelling inwardly: "Pa, why didn't you do something? You felt pain. It was a warning. Why didn't you go to Dr. Kaplan? Why didn't you reach out for help? You were always quick enough to call the doctor for everybody else. But you, not by you, Charley. What were you, immune, immortal? What were you afraid of? He'd find out something was wrong; you'd be laid up, have an operation maybe; you'd lose a few days at the stand? What were you afraid of? The horses would stop running; the world would collapse? Christ, Pa, there were warning signs. You might have been saved."

A nurse came in. "Can I get you anything? Some juice, ice cream?"

"Nothing, thanks."

"I'm sorry."

He nodded, then sat down beside his father again. His mind flooded with memories: the smell of his father's sweat mingled with sawdust after a day's work when he'd been a carpenter; his coming home from building barracks during World War I with presents and presents; boat rowing in Douglas Park and Jake's watching his father's wiry muscles leap along his biceps; drinking the rotten, egg-smelling mineral water in the park because it was supposed to be healthy; going to the Russian steambath and suffocating on the higher benches, then being shocked in the cold plunge, then eating herring and potatoes, then putting on the clean underwear his mother made them take along.

Oh, Pa, you counter of pennies, you $2 dreamer, you listener, you unstinting giver, you protector, you honest, simple unpretentious, trustworthy man . . . you who fled poverty, oppression, persecution, you who came to a strange and alien world full of hope and new dreams . . . how could you have deceived yourself in the end? How could you have said to yourself, it'll go away, and suffered so with pain? Oh, Pa, how we all deceive ourselves from time to time, until at the end there is no more time. . . .

His father's eyes half opened.

"Pa?"

His father's mouth twisted into an ironic smile.

"Pa. How you doing, old buddy?"

"Jake?"

"It's me, Pa. Hey, remember we used to tell jokes? A millionaire wants to learn what the secret of life is. He travels all over the world, sees the most famous philosophers."

His father was nodding back to sleep. Jake finished fast: "The most famous said, 'Life is a cup of tea. . . .'"

His father's eyes closed completely, the twisted smile still on his face.

The nurse came back in. "Visiting hours are over."

He got up early the following morning and left the apartment before anyone awoke. It was clear and crisp out. He walked down the dusty, dirty streets, past the garbage-laden alleys to Douglas Boulevard, moved along past the big synagogues and the large brick apartment buildings. He walked past the JPI, everybody's haven, from the starry-eyed athlete to the immigrant learning English to the next infamous killer. He felt his bones on the streets, on each corner a memory, in the air familiar smells. People come and go, memories remain, he thought. But crowding everything out were memories of his father. These were the streets he had walked. This was where he belonged. Soon he would be nothing but memory.

It was too early to go to the hospital. He had breakfast on Roosevelt Road, which had been 12th Street before the war, then took a streetcar downtown. The Loop was fairly quiet; its pulse hadn't started to beat yet. He had never been in the Loop that early before. It seemed abandoned, so strange. He walked up Michigan Avenue past the Art Institute; where he had fallen in love among the masters with Natasha and then Rhoda; the IAC, where he'd won his first high school swimming meet; the Public Library, where he had borrowed tons and tons of books, it seemed, and hadn't made a dent in its stacks. Then he went over to Lake Shore Drive and walked along the breakwater. He paused before the Lake Shore AC, where he'd won the national intercollegiate backstroke championship; he'd thought then that was it, the peak of his life, only the Olympics were left, but how all his values had changed in so short a time.

Home, he thought, wasn't a physical thing; it was where your memories were. Even his father, when he got together with his relatives, his *landsleit,* talked about the little village he came from in Russia as his home. So did all of them. They loved America, but they always felt like strangers; their memories were in Russia. Jake's coming back this time would be a memory he'd never forget.

"Enough," he said.

He hopped onto a bus and rode to the hospital. His father was freshly shaved, his skin taut over his bones. He looked a little better. Maybe it was the brightness of the morning, or Jake wasn't as shocked at the sight of him.

"Hi, Pa."

"You here alone, Jake? So early?"

"I wanted to be alone with you. I'm selfish." Jake noticed yesterday's racing form in the wastebasket.

"An old habit," his father said. "Maybe you'll get me one later."

"Sure."

"You look like you have a lot on your mind, Jake."

"I have."

"I hope it's not about me."

"A lot of it is."

"Jake, you know there are always two possibilities. If I don't die, I've got little to worry about but when I will die. If I do die, I'll be buried in a Jewish cemetery. What could be bad about that? But there will still be two possibilities." He gritted his teeth as a spasm of pain contorted his face.

"Seriously, Pa."

"Seriously, I worry about Mama. She was a child when I married her. She knows nothing. I took care of everything. Who will take care of her?"

"There's Miriam. She's close to Mom. Harry's living with her. He's not married yet."

"He will be soon. He has a girl. You can't expect a son to care for his mother. In Europe, yes, it was expected, whole families lived together. Not in America."

A neat man, tidy, orderly all his life, he wants it to finish that way, all the loose ends tied, Jake thought, but death is never neat or tidy.

The nurse came in to give his father a shot.

"No. Not now. I must talk with my son."

"But, Mr. Davidson— "

"Not now. Later." He got out of bed, slipped into a robe, sat in a chair. "All right, Jake, enough of that. What about you?"

"They want me to go to Hollywood."

"Do you want to go?"

"I don't know. They're offering a lot of money."

"Is money important to you?"

"It makes life easier. Gives me a sense of freedom."

"Will you feel like that there?"

"I don't know. I'll be working on things they want me to do. I can get fifteen hundred dollars a week."

"That's a lot of money. What do you give up for it?"

"I'm in the middle of a new book. I could get back to it later, I guess. If I do good there, I mean if it turns out I can write screenplays, I can make a fortune."

"And the books?"

"I might never get back to them"

"Jake, I have been listening to you carefully. I know most people are brought up to admire money, to think only about money. To live that way is grotesque. You're talking fifteen hundred dollars a week. Maybe more later. Then more. That's the way we are. The money becomes more important than what we're doing. Once you're way up there, the fear of failure must be terrifying. I would be frightened to death."

He turned away from Jake to hide the tremor of pain that crossed his face. He clenched his hands for a time; then the agony was buried, and he spread his hands out. He took a deep breath and continued: "You have written a book. It has been published. That is your success. The money isn't that important. The fact that you got a lot of money for it helps. It gives you time to do other things. What is important is your accomplishment. Now this should be your guide. Will it be an accomplishment to work on what they order, or will the only accomplishment be the big money you earn? A long time ago I told you, Jake, you don't measure success with money and possessions. You measure it with your heart, with what you set out to do. If you've dreamed of going to Hollywood—go. If not—write more books."

"Thanks, Pa."

"You know what I regret, Jake?"

"What?"

"Not seeing your little one. How I wish I could see his world."

The pain shook him, and he fell off his chair. Jake grabbed him, shouting, "Nurse, nurse!" He lifted him. This man, who used to lift him as if he were a feather pillow, felt so frail, so delicate, as he quivered like a bird in his arms. He laid him down gently on his bed.

"Nurse!"

She came running in with a hypodermic. "You should have had it earlier, Mr. Davidson. You wouldn't listen."

She injected the needle. His father breathed hard, sweat breaking out all over. He bit his lips. Jake felt helpless. Just stood there with his hands out. Gradually the drug took effect. His father calmed down. His quivering stopped. Then he looked up at Jake.

"I didn't want you to see me like this, Jake."

"What can I do, Pa?"

"What can anybody do?"

Three days later Jake's father was buried in the Jewish cemetery on the West Side of Chicago. Jake sat *shiva* in his socks for seven days with Rhoda, his mother, Harry, Miriam, and Uncle Nachum. The whole family was together except his father. Twice a day he went to *shul* with Nachum and Harry and said Kaddish. All the time they held Jake's father close to their hearts.

It was sad to part from them, but he finally did. Rhoda was very uncomfortable, getting closer to her time.

"Go, go," his mother said. "Don't worry about me."

She was getting to be like his father. Through the months of his illness she had found her own strength.

On the way home Rhoda said, "Your father left you with a lot, Jake."

"Yes." He looked at her a moment, then said, "I'm not going to Hollywood, Rhoda."

"I didn't think you would."

"You don't feel bad about it?"

"Feel it, Jake."

He put his hand on her belly. He felt the life stirring in there, bigger than ever.

"*Shalom,*" he said.

Ross   c.1
   Windy city.